UNDERWORLD

Don DeLillo is the acclaimed author of fifteen novels and three plays. He has won the National Book Award, the Jerusalem Prize, the *Irish Times* International Fiction Prize, the PEN/Saul Bellow Award for lifetime achievement in American literature and, most recently, the Library of Congress Prize for American Fiction.

D1513821

UNDERWORLD

DON DELILLO

With an introduction by Rachel Kushner

PICADOR CLASSIC

First published 1997 by Scribner, an imprint of Simon & Schuster Inc., New York

First published in the UK 1998 by Picador

First published in paperback 1998 by Picador

This Picador Classic edition first published 2015 by Picador
an imprint of Pan Macmillan
20 New Wharf Road, London N1 9RR
Associated companies throughout the world
www.panmacmillan.com

ISBN 978-1-4472-8939-5

1 3 5 7 9 8 6 4 2

A CIP catalogue record for this book is available from the British Library.

Printed and bound by CPI Group (UK) Ltd, Croydon, CR0 4YY

INTRODUCTION

These are things I don't forget:

A secretary in a Mondrian dress. A sixties sexy secretary. And advertising. And Mondrian.

A man who grabs an oil drum with a fire burning inside it, drags the drum toward baseball fans, fathers and sons lined up on a cold night to buy world series tickets. This scene is in the early fifties and the man is black, the fans white. He aims to please them, but by a complex operation in which skin color is acknowledged and then set aside in the name of a fair transaction, the sale of what he's got in his pocket. The hot metal sears his hand when he drags the oil drum. He pretends it does not. His burned hand scars the reader's memory, her emotions pressed on by this subtle scene.

A Jesuit priest who asks his student Nick Shay to name the parts of a shoe, and Nick Shay cannot, and neither can you.

Nick Shay's youthful fantasy, his hopeful treatise, that George the Waiter keeps a room in the basement in the Bronx in order to have paid sex with a woman. When in fact George the Waiter's business in the basement is a solitary and existential matter, in the room where he quashes Nick's idea that this selfsame room is for sex with unknown women.

The nun who frets that if the children forget to wear their dog tags, they won't be saved from nuclear annihilation.

Om and Bomb, which do not rhyme, and only look that way.

These are elemental bits of *Underworld*—scene, language, detail—that have shaped who I am as a person, as a writer, and yet which also reflect what I care about in a way that precedes their formalization into language, into art.

Underworld is a novel, quite simply, about what was experienced in the United States in the second half of the twentieth century. An era shaped by the advent and then cancellation of the Bretton Woods agreement. Nuclear proliferation. The withering away and relocation of American manufacturing, and the rise of global capitalism. Jazz. The Cuban missile crisis (through the voice, as DeLillo has it, of Lenny Bruce). Civil Rights. The CIA. Bombs on university campuses. Artists on New York rooftops, and around them, the old industrial framework of bygone city life, something aesthetic and exotic, either marveled at or ignored. This is a novel that restores luminous pockets of lost life, most strikingly in the Bronx—the ravaged South Bronx where one elusive character, Esmeralda, is sacrificed, and the mid-century street scenes of Arthur Avenue, which DeLillo himself would have known, the children's games that "take a pockmarked world and turn a delicate inversion," and the "screechsong" of old laundry lines drawn through rusted pulleys, a realm produced, one senses strongly, from DeLillo's own memories, made vivid in the act of writing the book. The book is itself an act of memory. And while big structures of history shape the characters (as they do us), this novel is also filled with glimpses of people alone and together with their private faiths, their unspeakable thoughts, artfully converted to language, into naked epiphany, subtle and precise.

Underworld starts in 1951, the night that Bobby Thomson hit the homer that won the Giants the pennant. The novel then jumps forward to the early 1990s, and from there moves more or less directly backward to the night of the home run, which, as one character puts it, "was maybe the last time people spontaneously went out of their houses for something. Some wonder. Some amazement." Because then people fracture and retreat. Their shared experiences are media spectacles they merely observe, the Kennedy assassination, Watergate, fear of a nuclear first strike, or a second one. Plots whose constructedness makes its impact on people separately and simultaneously, one person in a darkened room to the next.

As a child of the twentieth century, I suppose this book speaks to me. It precipitates into meaning movies I've seen, books I've read, quotes I know by heart, like a line from Robert Oppenheimer's letter to a friend his freshman year at Harvard: "My two great loves are physics and desert country. It's a pity they can't be combined." Om and Bomb do not rhyme, but they interlinked on a mesa called Los Alamos, and in the desert expanse of God's felt absence, atomic fires were lit, leading some to consider the "spiritual repercussions of the atom bomb," such as the French philosopher and Jesuit priest Teilhard de Chardin. I remember Watergate as the single time the adults in my house watched television, angling a bent coat hanger for reception. I remember Lenny Bruce, never mind that he died two years before I was born—his ghost rose, there was a feature film, he was a household name. Another ghost in every home was the specter of nuclear war, which kids thought about, talked about, dreamed about, all through the 1970s and 80s. "Om"—a resonance or divine energy, a common soul, maybe, was a popular concept imported from Hinduism, and scientific horror had invaded that soul. At fifteen I worked at a science museum founded by Oppenheimer's younger brother Frank, a particle physicist who emanated a tone—not "om"— a vibratory constant awareness of doom or so I was convinced.

What I don't know directly of the history in *Underworld* I know through inheritance, my parents' lives. My father, two years younger than DeLillo, went to Ebbets Field though and not the Polo Grounds, and he was educated by communists, not Jesuits, and is Jewish, not Italian. But what does my personal experience, the lowly intimate grit of the reader, have to do with this epic novel? Nothing and everything. It is a book for a person like me, formed and cross-hatched by the history the novel's pages traverse, and it will also be for new generations, like the ones that Walt Whitman imagined, whom he addressed, in the poem "Crossing Brooklyn Ferry": the people of the future.

Some authors go for sweep and others sentences and yet *Underworld* is both. Sentence by sentence it may have the highest density of great sentences of all DeLillo's novels, at two or three times as long as the rest. How did he sustain it? I have no idea, and the how is not for me to wonder. The book exists. It raises the bar on what can be done. Its 827 pages are filled with hell-bent ambition and yet also a deep reserve of uncommon, even egoless humility: DeLillo never insists, never veers into showy knowledge or egregious or paranoid plot. He merely goes to the horizon-line of his furthest understanding, and plumbs his love of, and respect for, the great mysteries inside us, between us, among us. The book is filled with echoes, and yet the story lines, the set pieces, are not over-connected into false or forced verisimilitude. Instead, rhymes of various sorts layer to produce meaning. Take Moonman 157, a Bronx graffiti artist, and the Texas Highway Killer (whose name is plenty descriptive): what do they have in common? One wields spray cans, the other a .38 with a gloved left hand. Moonman paints subway cars, and the Texas Highway Killer shoots random lone drivers. They both create languages that rise up, become visible, in the fog of collective life: each language is expressed by one individual who remains anonymous. As a natural consequence of this, they each have imitators.

Then there's Moonman 157 and Klara Sax, a feminist ideal of Land Art (ambition, work crews, the endless real estate of the West). What do *they* have in common? Genealogy. The graffiti is first; Klara's more culturally legitimated art comes after. To graffiti is to bomb. He bombs train cars, she bombs bombers, defunct B-52s. Moonman announces himself to the commuters who see his work flash by, the people on the 5:10 to Dreamland. Klara Sax talks into the twin vacuums of historical time and the desert. She's going larger-scale, and for a more abstract audience.

A few more echoes:

What do a baseball and the radioactive core of a nuclear reactor have in common? They are both the size of a baseball. (Especially the baseball.)

Sister Edgar and J. Edgar Hoover? Aside from their shared name, they are people haunted by their own convictions. People who know too much.

What do Jayne Mansfield's breasts remind adolescent Eric of? The bumper bullets on a Cadillac. Eric whose explosion of pubescent desire does not take place in a void (nothing does), but in his own epoch, the 1950s. His family resembles a full-color product brochure with a bomb-shaped shadow darkening its pages. His mother is entranced by Jell-O. Meanwhile Eric masturbates into a condom that reminds him, with its metallic sheen, of a surface-to-surface missile with a 40-kiloton warhead. Eric engages in his secret activity behind closed fiberglass curtains while his father, with nothing to hide, "simonizes" the family car in the breezeway. What connects boy and man, one acting in secret, the other openly? They are both engaged in the physical act of *polishing*. Both actions are borne along by dreams.

Some connections are more direct, but also more subtle, hidden in the deeper structure of the book. Like the woman who shows up, seemingly out of nowhere, on page 521, a Freedom Rider in Jackson, Mississippi. She's a logical descendant of the backward chronological march into tumult, but she is also another character's daughter. And there is Eric Deming, Matt Shay's colleague in weapons work: same Eric who as a boy compared his condom to a warhead and ate Hydrox cookies "because the name sounded like rocket fuel." These links are not what Matt Shay calls the clammy hand of coincidence. They are the cunning hand of history: inevitability, but in the form of drift.

My favorite passage connects to nothing else, really. Instead, it thickens the tone of the novel, producing harmonies. A man and woman travel across America in a lowered 1950 Mercury—hers. They argue and make love and go to drive-in movies. It is a brief few pages, "the scene of a whole long brutal marriage compressed into weeks." They stop in Bisbee, Arizona and Bakersfield, California, and the prose, both grave and ironic, evokes the reckless intensity of the passions of the young. The male character seems to be Nick Shay, in a passage of his life that did not last, and its temporary nature is inlaid into the scene itself, in its status as a one-off: some of what defines us, permanently, is not lasting. Maybe even much of what defines us is not lasting.

Which is why the eternal fate of Sister Edgar becomes the major miracle of the novel. Sister Edgar whose excitement, whose (foreign word alert) *jouissance* was destruction, gets subsumed into the multitude, into ecstasy, a human ecstasy and also a religious one. If the human swell in which Sister Edgar loses and finds herself is a bit more Fellini-esque than the thousands pouring through the turnstiles of the Polo Grounds, it is no less affecting. Collective streams are real, a crowd has a personality.

"He speaks in your voice, American," so the opening of *Underworld* goes, introducing one boy whose yearnings echo those of the masses converging on the stadium. This is Whitman territory and tone. The "you" is a Whitman you, and the entire symphonic sequence of the baseball game can be seen through the lens of Whitman, of crowds of passengers on Brooklyn Ferry, of the certainty of others, of fires from foundry chimneys, of all sights "to me the same as they are to you."

DeLillo has written of crowds before, in *Mao II*, and he has cited, from Cheever's journals (where Cheever's greatest writing took place), the following passage, on a night spent in Shea Stadium: "Who do these people think they are? They are who they are. Fathers with sons. Some good-looking women." Cheever calls the spectacle of the ballpark "apocalyptic," and says, famously, "the task of the American writer is not to describe the misgivings of a woman taken in adultery as she looks out of the window at the rain but to describe four hundred people under the lights reaching for a foul ball." DeLillo took up Cheever's challenge, but then he put the adulterous woman in, too—in fact more than one of them, although they don't quite seem to suffer from the primly middle-class "misgivings" to which Cheever refers. Cheever's self-lacerating reference to the woman, his own less exalted artistic terrain, need not be expelled from literature of course. But it is the crowd that links *Underworld* to a certain poetic tradition, from Emerson to Whitman to Thoreau to Crane, then Stevens: the American sublime, which, as Harold Bloom has said, "is always also an American irony." Jayne Mansfield. Bumper bullets. Dog tags as protection from nuclear war.

The final two lines of Whitman's "Crossing Brooklyn Ferry" are these:

You furnish your parts toward eternity.

Great or small, you furnish your parts toward the soul.

This is what Esmeralda does, a martyr of the South Bronx and of the nuns who try to save her. The martyr of this novel.

It is what Sister Edgar does, first willfully, in devoting herself to God, and then miraculously, by ascending into cyberspace, "the lunar milk of the data stream," a collectivity of brain or soul (what Teilhard de Chardin called the "noosphere"), which seems to forecast both the death of the printed book, and the eternal life of some new universal mind, or in Whitman's terms, "soul."

Great or small, you furnish your parts toward the soul.

Finally, it is what Don DeLillo has done, in writing this magnificent book, which is filled with grace, furnished of experience, of wisdom, of sacrifice, of insights that continue for hundreds of pages, all different, perfect, and true. It is a book that will have its place in the lunar milk, the collective soul, a work of art delivered over to the crowds to come.

Rachel Kushner

UNDERWORLD

TO THE MEMORY OF

MY MOTHER AND FATHER

THE TRIUMPH OF DEATH

He speaks in your voice, American, and there's a shine in his eye that's halfway hopeful.

It's a school day, sure, but he's nowhere near the classroom. He wants to be here instead, standing in the shadow of this old rust-hulk of a structure, and it's hard to blame him—this metropolis of steel and concrete and flaky paint and cropped grass and enormous Chesterfield packs aslant on the scoreboards, a couple of cigarettes jutting from each.

Longing on a large scale is what makes history. This is just a kid with a local yearning but he is part of an assembling crowd, anonymous thousands off the buses and trains, people in narrow columns tramping over the swing bridge above the river, and even if they are not a migration or a revolution, some vast shaking of the soul, they bring with them the body heat of a great city and their own small reveries and desperations, the unseen something that haunts the day—men in fedoras and sailors on shore leave, the stray tumble of their thoughts, going to a game.

The sky is low and gray, the roily gray of sliding surf.

He stands at the curbstone with the others. He is the youngest, at fourteen, and you know he's flat broke by the edgy leaning look he hangs on his body. He has never done this before and he doesn't know any of the others and only two or three of them seem to know each other but they can't do this thing singly or in pairs so they have found one another by means of slidy looks that detect the fellow foolhard and here they stand, black kids and white kids up from the subways or off the local Harlem streets, lean shadows, bandidos, fifteen in all, and according to topical legend maybe four will get through for every one that's caught.

They are waiting nervously for the ticket holders to clear the turnstiles, the last loose cluster of fans, the stragglers and loiterers. They watch the late-arriving taxis from downtown and the brilliantined men stepping dapper to the windows, policy bankers and supper club swells and Broadway hotshots, high aura'd, picking lint off their mohair sleeves. They stand at the curb and watch without seeming to look, wearing the sourish air of corner hangabouts. All the hubbub has died down, the pregame babble and swirl, vendors working the jammed sidewalks waving scorecards and pennants and calling out in ancient singsong, scraggy men hustling buttons and caps, all dispersed now, gone to their roomlets in the beaten streets.

They are at the curbstone, waiting. Their eyes are going grim, sending out less light. Somebody takes his hands out of his pockets. They are waiting and then they go, one of them goes, a mick who shouts *Geronimo*.

There are four turnstiles just beyond the pair of ticket booths. The youngest boy is also the scrawniest, Cotter Martin by name, scrawny tall in a polo shirt and dungarees and trying not to feel doom-struck—he's located near the tail of the rush, running and shouting with the others. You shout because it makes you brave or you want to announce your recklessness. They have made their faces into scream masks, tight-eyed, with stretchable mouths, and they are running hard, trying to funnel themselves through the lanes between the booths, and they bump hips and elbows and keep the shout going. The faces of the ticket sellers hang behind the windows like onions on strings.

Cotter sees the first jumpers go over the bars. Two of them jostle in the air and come down twisted and asprawl. A ticket taker puts a headlock on one of them and his cap comes loose and skims down his back and he reaches for it with a blind swipe and at the same time—everything's at the same time—he eyes the other hurdlers to keep from getting stepped on. They are running and hurdling. It's a witless form of flight with bodies packed in close and the gate-crashing becoming real. They are jumping too soon or too late and hitting the posts and radial bars, doing cartoon climbs up each other's back, and what kind of stupes must they look like to people at the hot dog stand on the other side of the turnstiles, what kind of awful screwups—a line of mostly men beginning to glance this way, jaws working at the sweaty meat and grease bubbles flurrying on their tongues, the gent at the far end going dead-still except for a hand that produces automatic movement, swabbing on mustard with a brush.

The shout of the motley boys comes banging off the deep concrete.

Cotter thinks he sees a path to the turnstile on the right. He drains himself of everything he does not need to make the jump. Some are still jumping, some are thinking about it, some need a haircut, some have girlfriends in woolly sweaters and the rest have landed in the ruck and are trying to get up and scatter. A couple of stadium cops are rumbling down the ramp. Cotter sheds these elements as they appear, sheds a thousand waves of information hitting on his skin. His gaze is trained on the iron bars projected from the post. He picks up speed and seems to lose his gangliness, the slouchy funk of hormones and unbelonging and all the stammering things that seal his adolescence. He is just a running boy, a half-seen figure from the streets, but the way running reveals some clue to being, the way a runner bares himself to consciousness, this is how the dark-skinned kid seems to open to the world, how the bloodrush of a dozen strides brings him into eloquence.

Then he leaves his feet and is in the air, feeling sleek and unmussed and sort of businesslike, flying in from Kansas City with a briefcase full of bank drafts. His head is tucked, his left leg is clearing the bars. And in one prolonged and aloof and discontinuous instant he sees precisely where he'll land and which way he'll run and even though he knows they will be after him the second he touches ground, even though he'll be in danger for the next several hours—watching left and right—there is less fear in him now.

He comes down lightly and goes easy-gaiting past the ticket taker groping for his fallen cap and he knows absolutely—knows it all the way, deep as knowing goes, he feels the knowledge start to hammer in his runner's heart—that he is uncatchable.

Here comes a cop in municipal bulk with a gun and cuffs and a flashlight and a billy club all jigging on his belt and a summons pad wadded in his pocket. Cotter gives him a juke step that sends him nearly to his knees and the hot dog eaters bend from the waist to watch the kid veer away in soft acceleration, showing the cop a little finger-wag bye-bye.

He surprises himself this way every so often, doing some gaudy thing that whistles up out of unsuspected whim.

He runs up a shadowed ramp and into a crossweave of girders and pillars and spilling light. He hears the crescendoing last chords of the national anthem and sees the great open horseshoe of the grandstand and that unfolding vision of the grass that always seems to mean he has stepped outside his life—the rubbed shine that sweeps and bends from the raked dirt of the infield out to the high green fences. It is the excitement of a revealed thing. He runs at quarter speed craning to see the rows of seats, looking for an inconspicuous wedge behind a pillar. He cuts into an aisle in section 35 and walks down into the heat and smell of the massed fans, he walks into the smoke that hangs from the underside of the second deck, he hears the talk, he enters the deep buzz, he hears the warm-up pitches crack into the catcher's mitt, a series of reports that carry a comet's tail of secondary sound.

Then you lose him in the crowd.

In the radio booth they're talking about the crowd. Looks like thirty-five thousand and how do you figure it. When you think about the textured histories of the teams and the faith and passion of the fans and the way these forces are entwined citywide, and when you think about the game itself, live-or-die, the third game in a three-game play-off, and you say the names Giants and Dodgers, and you calculate the way the players hate each other openly, and you recall the kind of year this has turned out to be, the pennant race that has brought the city to a strangulated rapture, an end-shudder requiring a German loanword to put across the mingling of pleasure and dread and suspense, and when you think about the blood loyalty, this is what they're saying in the booth—the love-of-team that runs across the boroughs and through the snuggled suburbs and out into the apple counties and the raw north, then how do you explain twenty thousand empty seats?

The engineer says, "All day it looks like rain. It affects the mood. People say the hell with it."

The producer is hanging a blanket across the booth to separate the crew from the guys who've just arrived from KMOX in St. Louis. Have to double up since there's nowhere else to put them.

He says to the engineer, "Don't forget. There wasn't any advance sale."

And the engineer says, "Plus the Giants lost big yesterday and this is a serious thing because a crushing defeat puts a gloom on the neighborhoods. Believe me, I know this where I live. It's demoralizing for people. It's like they're dying in the tens of thousands."

Russ Hodges, who broadcasts the games for WMCA, he is the voice of the Giants—Russ has an overworked larynx and the makings of a major cold and he shouldn't be lighting up a cigarette but here he goes, saying, "That's all well and good but I'm not sure there really is a logical explanation. When you deal with crowds, nothing's predictable."

Russ is going jowly now but there are elements of the uncomplicated boy in his eyes and smile and in the hair that looks bowl-cut and the shapeless suit that might belong to almost anyone. Can you do games, can you do play-by-play almost every day through a deep summer and not be located in some version of the past?

He looks out at the field with its cramped corners and the overcompensating spaces of the deep alleys and dead center. The big square Longines clock that juts up from the clubhouse. Strokes of color all around, a frescoing of hats and faces and the green grandstand and tawny base paths. Russ feels lucky to be here. Day of days and he's doing the game and it's happening at the Polo Grounds—a name he loves, a precious echo of things and times before the century went to war. He thinks everybody who's here ought to feel lucky because something big's in the works, something's building. Okay, maybe just his temperature. But he finds himself thinking of the time his father took him to see Dempsey fight Willard in Toledo and what a thing that was, what a measure of the awesome, the Fourth of July and a hundred and ten degrees and a crowd of shirtsleeved men in straw hats, many wearing handkerchiefs spread beneath their hats and down to their shoulders, making them look like play-Arabs, and the greatness of the beating big Jess took in that white hot ring, the way the sweat and blood came misting off his face every time Dempsey hit him.

When you see a thing like that, a thing that becomes a newsreel, you begin to feel you are a carrier of some solemn scrap of history.

In the second inning Thomson hits a slider on a line over third.

Lockman swings into an arc as he races toward second, looking out at left field.

Pafko moves to the wall to play the carom.

People stand in both decks in left, leaning out from the rows up front, and some of them are tossing paper over the edge, torn-up scorecards and bits of matchbook covers, there are crushed paper cups, little waxy napkins they got with their hot dogs, there are germ-bearing tissues many days old that were matted at the bottoms of deep pockets, all coming down around Pafko.

Thomson is loping along, he is striding nicely around first, leaning into his run.

Pafko throws smartly to Cox.

Thomson moves head-down toward second, coasting in, and then sees Lockman standing on the bag looking at him semi-spellbound, the trace of a query hanging on his lips.

Days of iron skies and all the mike time of the past week, the sore throat, the coughing, Russ is feverish and bedraggled—train trips and nerves and no sleep and he describes the play in his familiar homey ramble, the grits-and-tater voice that's a little scratchy today.

Cox peers out from under his cap and snaps the ball sidearm to Robinson.

Look at Mays meanwhile strolling to the plate dragging the barrel of his bat on the ground.

Robinson takes the throw and makes a spin move toward Thomson, who is standing shyly maybe five feet from second.

People like to see the paper fall at Pafko's feet, maybe drift across his shoulder or cling to his cap. The wall is nearly seventeen feet high so he is well out of range of the longest leaning touch and they have to be content to bathe him in their paper.

Look at Durocher on the dugout steps, manager of the Giants, hard-rock Leo, the gashouse scrapper, a face straight from the Gallic Wars, and he says into his fist, "Holy fuggin shit almighty."

Near the Giants' dugout four men are watching from Leo's own choice box when Robinson slaps the tag on Thomson. They are three-quarters show biz, Frank Sinatra, Jackie Gleason and Toots Shor, drinking buddies from way back, and they're accompanied by a well-dressed man with a bulldog mug, one J. Edgar Hoover. What's the nation's number one G-man doing with these crumbums? Well, Edgar is sitting in the aisle seat and he seems to be doing just fine, smiling at the rude banter that rolls nonstop from crooner to jokesmith to saloonkeeper and back. He would rather be at the racetrack but is cheerful enough in this kind of company whatever the venue. He likes to be around movie idols and celebrity athletes, around gossip-meisters such as Walter Winchell, who is also at the game today, sitting with the Dodger brass. Fame and secrecy are the high and low ends of the same fascination, the static crackle of some libidinous thing in the world, and Edgar responds to people who have access to this energy. He wants to be their dearly devoted friend provided their hidden lives are in his private files, all the rumors collected and indexed, the shadow facts made real.

Gleason says, "I told you chumps, it's all Dodgers today. I feel it in my Brooklyn bones."

"What bones?" says Frank. "They're rotted out by booze."

Thomson's whole body sags, it loses vigor and resistance, and Robinson calls time and walks the ball to the mound in the pigeon-toed gait that makes his path seem crooked.

"The Giants'll have to hire that midget if they want to win, what's-his-name, because their only hope is some freak of nature," Gleason says. "An earthquake or a midget. And since this ain't California, you better pray for an elf in flannels."

Frank says, "Fun-nee."

The subject makes Edgar nervous. He is sensitive about his height even though he is safely in the middle range. He has added weight in recent years and when he sees himself in the mirror getting dressed, thick-bodied and Buddha-headed, it is a short round man that looks back at him. And this is something the yammerheads in the press have reported to be true, as if a man can wish his phantom torment into public print. And today it's a fact that taller-than-average agents are not likely to be assigned to headquarters. And it's a further fact that the midget his pal Gleason is talking about, the three-foot seven-inch *sportif* who came to bat one time for the St. Louis Browns some six weeks ago in a stunt that was also an act, Edgar believes, of political subversion—this fellow is called Eddie Gaedel and if Gleason recalls the name he will flash-pair Eddie with Edgar and then the short-man jokes will begin to fly like the storied shit that hits the fan. Gleason got his start doing insult comedy and never really stopped—does it for free, does it for fun and leaves shattered lives behind.

Toots Shor says, "Don't be a shlump all your life, Gleason. It's only one-zip. The Giants didn't come from thirteen and a half games back just to blow it on the last day. This is the miracle year. Nobody has a vocabulary for what happened this year."

The slab face and meatcutter's hands. You look at Toots and see a speakeasy vet, dense of body, with slicked-back hair and a set of chinky eyes that summon up a warning in a hurry. This is an ex-bouncer who throws innocent people out of his club when he is drinking.

He says, "Mays is the man."

And Frank says, "This is Willie's day. He's due to bust loose. Leo told me on the phone."

Gleason does a passable clipped Britisher saying, "You're not actually telling me that this fellow stepping up to the wicket is going to do something extraordinary."

Edgar, who hates the English, falls forward laughing even as Jackie takes a breathless bite of his hot dog and begins to cough and choke, sending quidbits of meat and bread in many directions, pellets and smithereens, spitball flybys.

But it is the unseeable life-forms that dismay Edgar most and he faces away from Gleason and holds his breath. He wants to hurry to a lavatory, a zinc-lined room with a bar of untouched oval soap, a torrent of hot water and a swansdown towel that has never been used by anyone else. But of course there is nothing of the kind nearby. Just more germs, an all-pervading medium of pathogens, microbes, floating colonies of spirochetes that fuse and separate and elongate and spiral and engulf, whole trainloads of matter that people cough forth, rudimentary and deadly.

The crowd, the constant noise, the breath and hum, a basso rumble building now and then, the genderness of what they share in their experience of the game, how a man will scratch his wrist or shape a line of swearwords. And the lapping of applause that dies down quickly and is never enough. They are waiting to be carried on the sound of rally chant and rhythmic handclap, the set forms and repetitions. This is the power they keep in reserve for the right time. It is the thing that will make something happen, change the structure of the game and get them leaping to their feet, flying up together in a free thunder that shakes the place crazy.

Sinatra saying, "Jack, I thought I told you to stay in the car until you're all done eating."

Mays takes a mellow cut but gets under the ball, sending a routine fly into the low October day. The sound of the ash bat making contact with the ball reaches Cotter Martin in the left-field stands, where he sits in a bony-shouldered hunch. He is watching Willie instead of the ball, seeing him sort of shrug-run around first and then scoop his glove off the turf and jog out to his position.

The arc lights come on, catching Cotter by surprise, causing a shift in the way he feels, in the freshness of his escapade, the airy flash of doing it and not getting caught. The day is different now, grave and threatened, rain-hurried, and he watches Mays standing in center field looking banty in all that space, completely kid-size, and he wonders how the guy can make those throws he makes, whirl and sling, with power. He likes looking at the field under lights even if he has to worry about rain and even if it's only afternoon and the full effect is not the same as in a night game when the field and the players seem completely separate from the night around them. He has been to one night game in his life, coming down from the bluff with his oldest brother and walking into a bowl of painted light. He thought there was an unknown energy flaring down out of the light towers, some intenser working of the earth, and it isolated the players and the grass and the chalk-rolled lines from anything he'd ever seen or imagined. They had the glow of first-time things.

The way the runner skid-brakes when he makes the turn at first.

The empty seats were Cotter's first surprise, well before the lights. On his prowl through the stands he kept seeing blank seats, too many to be explained by people buying a beer or taking a leak, and he found a spot between a couple of guys in suits and it's all he can do to accept his good luck, the ease of an actual seat, without worrying why there's so many.

The man to his left says, "How about some peanuts hey?"

Peanut vendor's coming through again, a coin-catching wiz about eighteen, black and rangy. People know him from games past and innings gone and they quicken up and dig for change. They're calling out for peanuts, *hey, here, bag,* and tossing coins with thumb flicks and discus arcs and the vendor's hands seem to inhale the flying metal. He is magnet-skinned, circus-catching dimes on the wing and then sailing peanut bags into people's chests. It's a thrill-a-minute show but Cotter feels an obscure danger here. The guy is making him visible, shaming him in his prowler's den. Isn't it strange how their common color jumps the space between them? Nobody saw Cotter until the vendor appeared, black rays phasing from his hands. One popular Negro and crowd pleaser. One shifty kid trying not to be noticed.

The man says, "What do you say?"

Cotter raises a hand no.

"Care for a bag? Come on."

Cotter leans away, the hand going to his midsection to mean he's already eaten or peanuts give him cramps or his mother told him not to fill up on trashy food that will ruin his dinner.

The man says, "Who's your team then?"

"Giants."

"What a year hey?"

"This weather, I don't know, it's bad to be trailing."

The man looks at the sky. He's about forty, close-shaved and Brylcreemed but with a casual quality, a free-and-easy manner that Cotter links to small-town life in the movies.

"Only down a run. They'll come back. The kind of year it's been, it can't end with a little weather. How about a soda?"

20

Men passing in and out of the toilets, men zipping their flies as they turn from the trough and other men approaching the long receptacle, thinking where they want to stand and next to whom and not next to whom, and the old ballpark's reek and mold are consolidated here, generational tides of beer and shit and cigarettes and peanut shells and disinfectants and pisses in the untold millions, and they are thinking in the ordinary way that helps a person glide through a life, thinking thoughts unconnected to events, the dusty hum of who you are, men shouldering through the traffic in the men's room as the game goes on, the coming and going, the lifting out of dicks and the meditative pissing.

Man to his left shifts in the seat and speaks to Cotter from off his shoulder, using a crafty whisper. "What about school? Having a private holiday?" Letting a grin slide across his face.

Cotter says, "Same as you," and gets a gunshot laugh.

"I'd a broken out of prison to see this game. Matter of fact they're broadcasting to prisoners. They put radios in cell blocks in the city jails."

"I was here early," Cotter says. "I could have gone to school in the morning and then cut out. But I wanted to see everything."

"A real fan. Music to my ears."

"See the people showing up. The players going in the players' entrance."

"My name's Bill Waterson by the way. And I'd a gladly gone AWOL from the office but I didn't actually have to. Got my own little business. Construction firm."

Cotter tries to think of something to say.

"We're the people that build the houses that are fun to live in."

Peanut vendor's on his way up the aisle and headed over to the next section when he spots Cotter and drops a knowing smile. The kid thinks here comes trouble. This gatemouth is out to expose him in some withering way. Their glances briefly meet as the vendor moves up the stairs. In full stride and double-quick he dips his hand for a bag of peanuts and zings it nonchalant to Cotter, who makes the grab in a one-hand blur that matches the hazy outline of the toss. And it is one sweetheart of a moment, making Cotter crack the smile of the week and sending a wave of goodwill through the area.

"Guess you got one after all," says Bill Waterson.

21

Cotter unrolls the pleated top of the brown bag and extends it to Bill. They sit there shelling the peanuts and rubbing off the tissuey brown skin with a rolling motion of thumb and index finger and eating the oily salty flesh and dropping the husks on the ground without ever taking their eyes off the game.

Bill says, "Next time you hear someone say they're in seventh heaven, think of this."

"All we need is some runs."

He pushes the bag at Bill once more.

"They'll score. It's coming. Don't worry. We'll make you happy you skipped school."

Look at Robinson at the edge of the outfield grass watching the hitter step in and thinking idly, Another one of Leo's country-boy krauts.

"Now there's a law of manly conduct," Bill says. "And it states that since you're sharing your peanuts with me, I'm duty-bound to buy us both some soda pop."

"That sounds fair enough."

"Good. It's settled then." Turning in his seat and flinging up an arm. "A couple of sportsmen taking their ease."

Stanky the pug sitting in the dugout.

Mays trying to get a jingle out of his head, his bluesy face slightly puffed, some catchy tune he's been hearing on the radio lately.

The batboy comes down the steps a little daydreamy, sliding Dark's black bat into the rack.

The game turns inward in the middle innings. They fall into waiting, into some unshaped anxiety that stiffens the shoulder muscles and sends them to the watercooler to drink and spit.

Across the field Branca is up in the Dodger bullpen, a large man with pointy elfin ears, tight-armed and throwing easily, just getting loose.

Mays thinking helplessly, Push-pull click-click, change blades that quick.

In the stands Special Agent Rafferty is walking down the stairs to the box-seat area behind the home team dugout. He is a thickset man with a mass of reddish hair—a shock of red hair, people like to say—and he is moving with the straight-ahead look of someone who doesn't want to be distracted. He is moving briskly but not urgently, headed toward the box occupied by the Director.

Gleason has two sudsy cups planted at his feet and there's a hot dog he has forgotten about that's bulging out at each end of his squeezed fist. He is talking to six people at once and they are laughing and asking questions, season box holders, old-line fans with their spindly wives. They see he is half swacked and they admire the clarity of his wit, the fine edge of insult and derision. They want to be offended and Jackie's happy to do it, bypassing his own boozy state to do a detailed imitation of a drunk. He goes heavy-lidded and growly, making sport of one man's ragmop toupee, ridiculing a second for the elbow patches on his tweed jacket. The women enjoy it enormously and they want more. They watch Gleason, they look at Sinatra for his reaction to Gleason, they watch the game, they listen to Jackie do running lines from his TV show, they watch the mustard slide down his thumb and feel too shy to tell him.

When Rafferty reaches Mr. Hoover's aisle seat he does not stand over the Director and lean down to address him. He makes it a point to crouch in the aisle. His hand is set casually near his mouth so that no one else can make out what he is saying. Hoover listens for a moment. He says something to his companions. Then he and Rafferty walk up the stairs and find an isolated spot midway down a long ramp, where the special agent recites the details of his message.

It seems the Soviet Union has conducted an atomic test at a secret location somewhere inside its own borders. They have exploded a bomb in plain unpretending language. And our detection devices indicate this is clearly what it is—it is a bomb, a weapon, it is an instrument of conflict, it produces heat and blast and shock. It is not some peaceful use of atomic energy with home-heating applications. It is a red bomb that spouts a great white cloud like some thunder god of ancient Eurasia.

Edgar fixes today's date in his mind. October 3, 1951. He registers the date. He stamps the date.

He knows this is not completely unexpected. It is their second atomic explosion. But the news is hard, it works into him, makes him think of the spies who passed the secrets, the prospect of warheads being sent to communist forces in Korea. He feels them moving ever closer, catching up, overtaking. It works into him, changes him physically as he stands there, drawing the skin tighter across his face, sealing his gaze.

Rafferty is standing on the part of the ramp that is downhill from Mr. Hoover.

Yes, Edgar fixes the date. He thinks of Pearl Harbor, just under ten years ago, he was in New York that day as well, and the news seemed to shimmer in the air, everything in photoflash, plain objects hot and charged.

The crowd noise breaks above them, a chambered voice rolling through the hollows in the underbody of the stadium.

Now this, he thinks. The sun's own heat that swallows cities.

Gleason isn't even supposed to be here. There's a rehearsal going on right now at a midtown studio and that's where he's supposed to be, preparing a skit called "The Honeymooners," to be shown for the first time in exactly two days. This is material that's close to Jackie's heart, involving a bus driver named Ralph Kramden who lives with his wife Alice in a shabby Brooklyn flat. Gleason sees nothing strange about missing a rehearsal to entertain fans in the stands. But it's making Sinatra uneasy, all these people lapping at their seat backs. He is used to ritual distances. He wants to encounter people in circumstances laid out beforehand. Frank doesn't have his dago secret service with him today. And even with Jackie on one flank and Toots on the other—a couple of porkos who function as natural barriers—people keep pressing in, showing a sense of mission. He sees them decide one by one that they must speak to him. The rigid grins floating near. And the way they use him as a reference for everything that happens. Somebody makes a nice play, they look at Frank to see how he reacts. The beer vendor trips on a step, they look at Frank to see if he has noticed.

He leans over and says, "Jack, it's a great boot being here but you think you can put a towel over your face so these people can go back to watching the game?"

People want Gleason to do familiar lines of dialogue from the show. They're calling out the lines they want him to do.

Then Frank says, "Where the hell is Hoover by the way? We need him to keep these women off our beautiful bodies."

The catcher works up out of his squat, dirt impacted in the creases that run across the back of his ruddled neck. He lifts his mask so he can spit. He is padded and bumpered, lips rough and scored and sunflaked. This is the freest thing he does, spitting in public. His saliva bunches and wobbles when it hits the dirt, going sandy brown.

Russ Hodges is over on the TV side for the middle innings, talking less, guided by the action on the monitor. Between innings the statistician offers him part of a chicken sandwich he has brought along for lunch.

He says to Russ, "What's the wistful look today?"

"I didn't know I had a look. Any look. I don't feel capable of a look. Maybe hollow-eyed."

"Pensive," says the statman.

And it's true and he knows it, Russ is wistful and drifting and this is so damn odd, the mood he's been in all day, a tilting back, an old creaky easing back, as of a gray-haired man in a rocker.

"This is chicken with what?"

"I'm guessing mayonnaise."

"It's funny, you know," Russ says, "but I think it was Charlotte put the look in my face."

"The lady or the city?"

"Definitely the city. I spent years in a studio doing re-creations of big league games. The telegraph bug clacking in the background and blabbermouth Hodges inventing ninety-nine percent of the action. And I'll tell you something scout's honor. I know this sounds farfetched but I used to sit there and dream of doing real baseball from a booth in the Polo Grounds in New York."

"Real baseball."

"The thing that happens in the sun."

Somebody hands you a piece of paper filled with letters and numbers and you have to make a ball game out of it. You create the weather, flesh out the players, you make them sweat and grouse and hitch up their pants, and it is remarkable, thinks Russ, how much earthly disturbance, how much summer and dust the mind can manage to order up from a single Latin letter lying flat.

"That's not a bush curve Maglie's throwing," he says into the mike.

When he was doing ghost games he liked to take the action into the stands, inventing a kid chasing a foul ball, a carrot-topped boy with a cowlick (shameless, ain't I) who retrieves the ball and holds it aloft, this five-ounce sphere of cork, rubber, yarn, horsehide and spiral stitching, a souvenir baseball, a priceless thing somehow, a thing that seems to recapitulate the whole history of the game every time it is thrown or hit or touched.

He puts the last bite of sandwich in his mouth and licks his thumb and remembers where he is, far from the windowless room with the telegraph operator and the Morse-coded messages.

Over on the radio side the producer's saying, "See that thing in the paper last week about Einstein?"

Engineer says, "What Einstein?"

"Albert, with the hair. Some reporter asked him to figure out the mathematics of the pennant race. You know, one team wins so many of their remaining games, the other teams wins this number or that number. What are the myriad possibilities? Who's got the edge?"

"The hell does he know?"

"Apparently not much. He picked the Dodgers to eliminate the Giants last Friday."

The engineer talks through the blanket to his counterpart from KMOX. The novelty of the blanket has these men talking to each other in prison slang. When they switch to black dialect the producer gets them to stop but after a while they're at it again, doing a couple of reefer Negroes in the fumy murmurs of some cellar room. Not loud enough to be picked up on mike of course. An ambient noise like random dugout buzz—a patter, a texture, an extension of the game.

Down in the field boxes they want Gleason to say, "You're a dan-dan-dandy crowd."

Russ makes his way back to the radio side after the Giants go down in their half of the sixth still trailing by a run. He's glad he doesn't have a thermometer because he might be tempted to use it and that would be demoralizing. It's a mild day, glory be, and the rain's holding off.

Producer says, "Going to the wire, Russ."

"I hope I don't close down. My larynx feels like it's in a vise."

"This is radio, buddy. Can't close down. Think of what's out there. They are hugging their little portables."

"You're not making me feel any better."

"They are goddamn crouched over the wireless. You're like Murrow from London."

"Thank you, Al."

"Save the voice."

"I am trying mightily."

"This game is everywhere. Dow Jones tickers are rapping out the score with the stock averages. Every bar in town, I guarantee. They're smuggling radios into boardrooms. At Schrafft's I hear they're breaking into the Muzak to give the score."

"All those nice ladies with their matched sweater sets and genteel sandwiches."

"Save the voice," Al says.

"Do they have tea with honey on the menu?"

"They're eating and drinking baseball. The track announcer at Belmont's doing updates between races. They got it in taxicabs and barbershops and doctors' offices."

They're all waiting on the pitcher, he's a faceful of boding, upper body drawn forward, glove hand dangled at the knee. He's reading and reading the sign. He's reading the sign. Hitter fidgeting in the box. This son of a buck can bring it.

The shortstop moves his feet to break the trance of waiting.

It's the rule of confrontation, faithfully maintained, written across the face of every slackwit pitcher since there were teams named the Superbas and the Bridegrooms. The difference comes when the ball is hit. Then nothing is the same. The men are moving, coming out of their crouches, and everything submits to the pebble-skip of the ball, to rotations and backspins and airstreams. There are drag coefficients. There are trailing vortices. There are things that apply unrepeatably, muscle memory and pumping blood and jots of dust, the narrative that lives in the spaces of the official play-by-play.

And the crowd is also in this lost space, the crowd made over in that one-thousandth of a second when the bat and the baseball are in contact. A rustle of murmurs and curses, people breathing soft moans, their faces changing as the play unrolls across the grassy scan. John Edgar Hoover stands among them. He is watching from the wide aisle at the head of the ramp. He has told Rafferty he will remain at the game. No purpose served by his leaving. The White House will make the announcement in less than an hour. Edgar hates Harry Truman, he would like to see him writhing on a parquet floor, felled by chest pains, but he can hardly fault the President's timing. By announcing first, we prevent the Soviets from putting their own sweet spin on the event. And we ease public anxiety to some degree. People will understand that we've maintained control of the news if not of the bomb. This is no small subject of concern. Edgar looks at the faces around him, open and hopeful. He wants to feel a compatriot's nearness and affinity. All these people formed by language and climate and popular songs and breakfast foods and the jokes they tell and the cars they drive have never had anything in common so much as this, that they are sitting in the furrow of destruction. He tries to feel a belonging, an opening of his old stopcocked soul. But there is some bitter condition he has never been able to name and when he encounters a threat from outside, from the moral wane that is everywhere in effect, he finds it is a balance to this state, a restoring force. His ulcer kicks up of course. But there is that side of him, that part of him that depends on the strength of the enemy.

Look at the man in the bleachers who's pacing the aisles, a neighborhood crazy, he waves his arms and mumbles, short, chunky, bushy-haired—could be one of the Ritz Brothers or a lost member of the Three Stooges, the Fourth Stooge, called Flippo or Dummy or Shaky or Jakey, and he's distracting the people nearby, they're yelling at him to siddown, goway, meshuggener, and he paces and worries, he shakes his head and moans as if he knows something's coming, or came, or went—he's receptive to things that escape the shrewdest fan.

It is a stone-faced Director who returns to his seat for the seventh-inning stretch. He says nothing of course. Gleason is shouting down a vendor, trying to order beers. People on their feet, shaking off the tension and fret. A man slowly wiping his glasses. A staring man. A man flexing the stiffness out of his limbs.

"Get me a brandy and soda," Toots says.

Jackie tells him, "Don't be a clamhead all your life."

28

"Treat the man nice," Frank says. "He's come a long way for a Jew who drinks. He's best buddies with world leaders you never even heard of. They all roll into his joint sooner or later and knock back a brandy with Toots. Except maybe Mahatma Gandhi. And *him* they shot."

Gleason flares his brows and goggles his eyes and shoots out his arms in a nitwit gesture of revelation.

"That's the name I couldn't think of. The midget that pinch-hits."

People around them, hearing part of this and reacting mainly to inflection and gesture—they've seen Jackie physically building the remark and they knock together laughing even before he has finished the line.

Edgar is also laughing despite the return of the midget business. He admires the rough assurance of these men. It seems to flush from their pores. They have a size to them, a natural stamina that mocks his own bible-school indoctrination even as it draws him to the noise. He's a self-perfected American who must respect the saga of the knockabout boy emerging from a tenement culture, from backstreets slant with danger. It makes for gusty egos, it makes for appetites. The pussy bandits Jackie and Frank have a showy sort of ease around women. And it's true about Toots, he knows everybody worth knowing and can drink even Gleason into the carpeting. And when he clamps a sympathetic paw on your shoulder you feel he is some provident force come to guide you out of old despond.

Frank says, "This is our inning."

And Toots says, "Better be. Because these shit-heel Dodgers are making me nervous."

Jackie is passing beers along the row.

Frank says, "Seems to me we've all made our true loyalties known. Shown our hearts' desire. We got a couple of old-timey Giant fans. And this porpoise with a haircut from Brooklyn. But what about our friend the G-man. Is it G for Giants? Fess up, Jedgar. Who's your team?"

J. Edgar. Frank calls him Jedgar sometimes and the Director likes the name although he never lets on—it is medieval and princely and wily-dark.

A faint smile creeps across Hoover's face.

"I don't have a rooting interest. Whoever wins," he says softly. "That's my team."

He is thinking of something else entirely. The way our allies one by one will receive the news of the Soviet bomb. The thought is grimly cheering. Over the years he has found it necessary to form joint ventures with the intelligence heads of a number of countries and he wants them all to die a little.

Look at the four of them. Each with a hanky neatly tucked in his breast pocket. Each holding his beer away from his body, leaning forward to tease the high scud from the rim of the cup. Gleason with a flower in his lapel, a damp aster snatched from a vase at Toots' place. People are still after him to do lines from the show.

They want him to say, "Harty har-har."

The plate umpire stands mask in hand, nearly blimpish in his outfitting. He is keeping the numbers, counting the pitcher's warm-up tosses. This is the small dogged conscience of the game. Even in repose he shows a history thick with embranglement, dust-stomping men turning figures in the steep sun. You can see it in his face, chin thrust out, a glower working under his brow. When the number reaches eight he aims a spurt from his chaw and prepares to take his whiskbroom to the rubber slab.

In the stands Bill Waterson takes off his jacket and dangles it lengthwise by the collar. It is rippled and mauled and seems to strike him as a living body he might want to lecture sternly. After a pause he folds it over twice and drops it on his seat. Cotter is sitting again, surrounded by mostly vertical people. Bill looms above him, a sizable guy, a one-time athlete by the look of him, getting thick in the middle, his shirt wet under the arms. Lucky seventh. Cotter needs a measly run to keep him from despairing—the cheapest eked-out unearned run ever pushed across. Or he's ready to give up. You know that thing that happens when you give up before the end and then your team comes back to perform acts of valor and you feel a queasy shame stealing over you like pond slick.

Bill says down to him, "I take my seventh-inning stretch seriously. I not only stand. I damn well make it a point to stretch."

"I've been noticing," says Cotter.

"Because it's a custom that's been handed down. It's part of something. It's our own little traditional thing. You stand, you stretch—it's a privilege in a way."

Bill has some fun doing various stylized stretches, the bodybuilder, the pet cat, and he tries to get Cotter to do a drowsy kid in a classroom.

"Did you ever tell me your name?"

"Cotter."

"That's the thing about baseball, Cotter. You do what they did before you. That's the connection you make. There's a whole long line. A man takes his kid to a game and thirty years later this is what they talk about when the poor old mutt's wasting away in the hospital."

Bill scoops his jacket off the seat and puts it on his lap when he sits down. Seconds later he is standing again, he and Cotter watching Pafko chase down a double. A soft roar goes up, bushy and dense, and the fans send more paper sailing to the base of the wall. Old shopping lists and ticket stubs and wads of fisted newsprint come falling around Pafko in the faded afternoon. Farther out in left field they are dropping paper on the Dodger bullpen, on the working figure of Labine and the working figure of Branca and the two men who are catching them and the men sitting under the canted roof that juts from the wall, the gum-chewing men with nothing to say.

Branca wears the number thirteen blazoned on his back.

"Told you," Bill says. "What did I tell you? I told you. We're coming back."

"We still have to score the run," Cotter says.

They take their seats and watch the hitter steer a look right up the line at Durocher dummying through the signs from the coach's box at third. Then Bill is on his feet again, rolling up his sleeves and shouting encouragement to the players, common words of spark and heart.

Cotter likes this man's singleness of purpose, his insistence on faith and trust. It's the only force available against the power of doubt. He figures he's in the middle of getting himself befriended. It's a feeling that comes from Bill's easy voice and his sociable sweaty gymnasium bulk and the way he listens when Cotter speaks and the way he can make Cotter believe this is a long and close association they share—boon companions goes the saying. He feels a little strange, it's an unfamiliar thing, talking to Bill, but there's a sense of something protective and enclosing that will help him absorb the loss if it should come to that.

Lockman squares around to bunt.

31

There's a man in the upper deck leafing through a copy of the current issue of Life. There's a man on 12th Street in Brooklyn who has attached a tape machine to his radio so he can record the voice of Russ Hodges broadcasting the game. The man doesn't know why he's doing this. It is just an impulse, a fancy, it is like hearing the game twice, it is like being young and being old, and this will turn out to be the only known recording of Russ' famous account of the final moments of the game. The game and its extensions. The woman cooking cabbage. The man who wishes he could be done with drink. They are the game's remoter soul. Connected by the pulsing voice on the radio, joined to the word-of-mouth that passes the score along the street and to the fans who call the special phone number and the crowd at the ballpark that becomes the picture on television, people the size of minute rice, and the game as rumor and conjecture and inner history. There's a sixteen-year-old in the Bronx who takes his radio up to the roof of his building so he can listen alone, a Dodger fan slouched in the gloaming, and he hears the account of the misplayed bunt and the fly ball that scores the tying run and he looks out over the rooftops, the tar beaches with their clotheslines and pigeon coops and splatted condoms, and he gets the cold creeps. The game doesn't change the way you sleep or wash your face or chew your food. It changes nothing but your life.

The producer says, "At last, at least, a run."

Russ is frazzled, brother, he is raw and rumpled and uncombed. When the teams go to the top of the eighth he reports that they have played one hundred and fifty-four regular season games and two play-off games and seven full innings of the third play-off game and here they are tied in a knot, absolutely deadlocked, they are stalemated, folks, so light up a Chesterfield and stay right here.

The next half inning seems to take a week. Cotter sees the Dodgers put men on first and third. He watches Maglie bounce a curve in the dirt. He sees Cox bang a shot past third. A hollow clamor begins to rise from the crowd, men calling from the deep reaches, an animal awe and desolation.

In the booth Russ sees the crowd begin to lose its coherence, people sitting scattered on the hard steps, a priest with a passel of boys filing up the aisle, paper rolling and skittering in the wind. He hears the announcer from St. Louis on the other side of the blanket, it is Harry Caray and he sounds like his usual chipper self and Russ thinks of the Japanese term for ritual disembowelment and figures he and Harry ought to switch names about now.

Light washing from the sky, Dodgers scoring runs, a man dancing down the aisle, a goateed black in a Bing Crosby shirt. Everything is changing shape, becoming something else.

Cotter can barely get out the words.

"What good does it do to tie the score if you're going to turn around and let them walk all over you?"

Bill says, "They're going into that dugout and I guarantee you they're not giving up. There's no quit in this team. Don't pull a long face on me, Cotter. We're buddies in bad times—gotta stick together."

Cotter feels a mood coming on, a complicated self-pity, the strength going out of his arms and a voice commencing in his head that reproaches him for caring. And the awful part is that he wallows in it. He knows how to find the twisty compensation in this business of losing, being a loser, drawing it out, expanding it, making it sickly sweet, being someone carefully chosen for the role.

The score is 4–1.

It should have rained in the third or fourth inning. Great rain drenching down. It should have thundered and lightning'd.

Bill says, "I'm still a believer. What about you?"

The pitcher takes off his cap and rubs his forearm across his hairline. Big Newk. Then he blows in the cap. Then he shakes the cap and puts it back on.

Shor looks at Gleason.

"Still making with the mouth. Leave the people alone already. They came here to see a game."

"What game? It's a lambasting. We ought to go home."

"We're not going home," Toots says.

Jackie says, "We can beat the crowd, clamhead."

Frank says, "Let's take a vote."

Toots says, "You're tubercular in the face. Sit back and watch the game. Because nobody goes until I go and I ain't going."

Jackie waves down a vendor and orders beer all around. Nothing happens in the home half of the eighth. People are moving toward the exit ramps. It is Erskine and Branca in the bullpen now with the odd paper shaving dropped from the upper deck. Dodgers go down in the top of the ninth and this is when you sense a helpless scattering, it is tastable in the air, audible in the lone-wolf calls from high in the stands. Nothing you've put into this is recoverable and you don't know whether you want to leave at once or stay forever, living under a blanket in the wind.

Engineer says, "Nice season, boys. Let's do it again sometime."

The closeness in the booth, all this crammed maleness is making Russ a little edgy. He lights another cigarette and for the first time all day he does not reproach himself for it. He hears the solitary wailing, he hears his statistician reciting numbers in fake French. It is all part of the same thing, the feeling of some collapsible fact that's folded up and put away, and the school gloom that traces back for decades—the last laden day of summer vacation when the range of play tapers to a screwturn. This is the day he has never shaken off, the final Sunday before the first Monday of school. It carried some queer deep shadow out to the western edge of the afternoon.

He wants to go home and watch his daughter ride her bike down a leafy street.

Dark reaches for a pitch and hits a seeing-eye bouncer that ticks off the end of the first baseman's glove.

A head pops up over the blanket, it's the engineer from KMOX and he starts telling a joke about the fastest lover in Mexico—*een May-heeko*. An amazing chap named Speedy Gonzalez.

Russ is thinking base hit all the way but glances routinely at the clubhouse sign in straightaway center to see if the first E in CHESTERFIELD lights up, indicating error.

Robinson retrieves the ball in short right.

"So this guy's on his honeymoon in Acapulco and he's heard all the stories about the incredible cunning of Speedy Gonzalez and he's frankly worried, he's a highly nervous type and so on the first night,

34

the night of nights, he's in bed with his wife and he's got his middle finger plugged up her snatch to keep Speedy Gonzalez from sneaking in there when he's not looking."

Mueller stands in, taking the first pitch low.

In the Dodger dugout a coach picks up the phone and calls the bullpen for the eighteenth time to find out who's throwing good and who ain't.

Mueller sees a fastball belt-high and pokes a single to right.

"So then he's dying for a smoke and he reaches over for a second to get his cigarettes and matches."

Russ describes Dark going into third standing up. He sees Thomson standing in the dugout with his arms raised and his hands held backwards gripping the edge of the roof. He describes people standing in the aisles and others moving down toward the field.

Irvin dropping the weighted bat.

"So then he lights up quick and reaches back to the bed finger-first."

Maglie's already in the clubhouse sitting in his skivvies in that postgame state of disrepair and pit stink that might pass for some shambles of the inner man, slugging beer from the bottle.

Irvin stands in.

Russ describes Newcombe taking a deep breath and stretching his arms over his head. He describes Newcombe looking in for the sign.

"And Speedy Gonzalez says, Sen-yor-or, you got your finger up my a-ass."

Russ hears most of this and wishes he hadn't. He does a small joke of his own, half standing to drape the mike with his suit coat as if to keep the smallest syllable of raunchy talk from reaching his audience. Decent people out there.

Fastball high and away.

The crowd noise is uncertain. They don't know if this is a rally in the works or just another drag-tail finish that draws out the pain. It's a high rackety noise that makes Russ think of restive waiting in a train station.

Irvin tries to pull it, overeager, and Russ hears the soul of the crowd repeat the sorry arc of the baseball, a moaned vowel falling softly to earth. First baseman puts it away.

Decent people out there. Russ wants to believe they are still assembled in some recognizable manner, the kindred unit at the radio, old lines and ties and propinquities.

Lockman stands in, the towhead from Caroline.

How his family used to gather around the gramophone and listen to grand opera, the trilled r's of old Europe. These thoughts fade and return. They are not distractions. He is alert to every movement on the field.

A couple of swabbies move down to the rail near third base.

How the records were blank on one side and so brittle they would crack if you looked at them cross-eyed. That was the going joke.

He is hunched over the mike. The field seems to open outward into nouns and verbs. All he has to do is talk.

Saying, "Carl Erskine and fireballer Ralph Branca still throwing in the bullpen."

Pitch.

Lockman fouls it back into the netting.

Now the rhythmic applause starts, tentative at first, then spreading densely through the stands. This is how the crowd enters the game. The repeated three-beat has the force of some abject faith, a desperate kind of will toward magic and accident.

Lockman stands in once more, wagging the yellow bat.

How his mother used to make him gargle with warm water and salt when he complained of a sore throat.

Lockman hits the second pitch on a low line over third. Russ hears Harry Caray shouting into the mike on the other side of the blanket. Then they are both shouting and the ball is slicing toward the line and landing fair and sending up a spew of dirt and forcing Pafko into the corner once again.

Men running, the sprint from first to third, the man who scores coming in backwards so he can check the action on the base paths. All the Giants up at the front of the dugout. The crowd is up, heads weaving for better views. Men running through a slide of noise that comes heaving down on them.

The pitch was off the plate and he wrong-wayed it and Harry started shouting.

The hit obliterates the beat of the crowd's rhythmic clapping. They're coming into open roar, making a noise that keeps enlarging itself in breadth and range. This is the crowd made over, the crowd renewed.

Harry started shouting and then Pafko went into the corner and Russ started shouting and the paper began to fall.

One out, one in, two runs down, men on second and third. Russ thinks every word may be his last. He feels the redness in his throat, the pinpoint constriction. Mueller still on the ground at third, injured sliding or not sliding, stopping short and catching his spikes on the bag, a man in pain, the flare of pulled tendons.

Paper is falling again, crushed traffic tickets and field-stripped cigarettes and work from the office and scorecards in the shape of airplanes, windblown and mostly white, and Pafko walks back to his position and alters stride to kick a soda cup lightly and the gesture functions as a form of recognition, a hint of some concordant force between players and fans, the way he nudges the white cup, it's a little onside boot, completely unbegrudging—a sign of respect for the sly contrivances of the game, the patterns that are undivinable.

The trainer comes out and they put Mueller on a stretcher and take him toward the clubhouse. Mueller's pain, the pain the game exacts—a man on a stretcher makes sense here.

The halt in play has allowed the crowd to rebuild its noise. Russ keeps pausing at the mike to let the sound collect. This is a rumble of a magnitude he has never heard before. You can't call it cheering or rooting. It's a territorial roar, the claim of the ego that separates the crowd from other entities, from political rallies or prison riots—everything outside the walls.

Russ nuzzles up to the mike and tries to be calm although he is very close to speaking in a shout because this is the only way to be heard.

Men clustered on the mound and the manager waving to the bullpen and the pitcher walking in and the pitcher leaving and the runner for Mueller doing kneebends at third.

They are banging on the roof of the booth.

Russ says, "So don't go way. Light up that Chesterfield. We're gonna stay right here and see how big Ralph Branca will fare."

Yes. It is Branca coming through the dampish glow. Branca who is tall and stalwart but seems to carry his own hill and dale, he has the aura of a man encumbered. The drooping lids, leaden feet, the thick ridge across the brow. His face is set behind a somber nose, broad-bridged and looming.

The stadium police are taking up posts.

Look at the man in the upper deck. He is tearing pages out of his copy of Life and dropping them uncrumpled over the rail, letting them fall in a seesaw drift on the bawling fans below. He is moved to do this by the paper falling elsewhere, the contagion of paper—it is giddy and unformulated fun. He begins to ignore the game so he can waft pages over the rail. It brings him into contact with the other paper throwers and with the fans in the lower deck who reach for his pages and catch them—they are all a second force that runs parallel to the game.

Not far away another man feels something pulling at his chest, arms going numb. He wants to sit down but doesn't know if he can reach an arm back to lower himself to the seat. Heart, my heart, my god.

Branca who is twenty-five but makes you think he exemplifies ancient toil. By the time he reaches the mound the stretcher bearers have managed to get Mueller up the steps and into the clubhouse. The crowd forgets him. They would forget him if he were dead. The noise expands once more. Branca takes the ball and the men around the mound recede to the fringes.

Shor looks at Gleason.

He says, "Tell me you want to go home. What happened to let's go home? If we leave now, we can beat the crowd."

He says, "I can't visualize it enough, both you crumbums, you deserve every misery in the book."

Jackie looks miserable all right. He loosens his necktie and undoes the top button of his shirt. He's the only member of the quartet not on his feet but it isn't the shift in the game that has caused his discomfort. It's the daylong booze and the greasy food.

Shor says, "Tell me you want to go home so I can run ahead and hold the car door open and like *usher* you inside."

Paper is coming down around the group, big slick pages from a magazine, completely unremarkable in the uproar of the moment. Frank snatches a full-page ad for something called pasteurized process cheese food, a Borden's product, that's the company with the cow, and there's a color picture of yellowish pressed pulp melting horribly on a hot dog.

Frank deadpans the page to Gleason.

"Here. This will help you digest."

Jackie sits there like an air traveler in a downdraft. The pages keep falling. Baby food, instant coffee, encyclopedias and cars, waffle irons and shampoos and blended whiskeys. Piping times, an optimistic bounty that carries into the news pages where the nation's farmers record a bumper crop. And the resplendent products, how the dazzle of a Packard car is repeated in the feature story about the art treasures of the Prado. It is all part of the same thing. Rubens and Titian and Playtex and Motorola. And here's a picture of Sinatra himself sitting in a nightclub in Nevada with Ava Gardner and would you check that cleavage. Frank didn't know he was in this week's Life until the page fell out of the sky. He has people who are supposed to tell him these things. He keeps the page and reaches for another to stuff in Gleason's face. Here's a Budweiser ad, pal. In a country that's in a hurry to make the future, the names attached to the products are an enduring reassurance. Johnson & Johnson and Quaker State and RCA Victor and Burlington Mills and Bristol-Myers and General Motors. These are the venerated emblems of the burgeoning economy, easier to identify than the names of battlefields or dead presidents. Not that Jackie's in the mood to scan a magazine. He is sunk in deep inertia, a rancid sweat developing, his mouth filled with the foretaste of massive inner shiftings.

Branca takes the last of his warm-up tosses, flicking the glove to indicate a curve. Never mind the details of manner or appearance, the weight-bearing body at rest. Out on the mound he is strong and loose, cutting smoothly out of his windup, a man who wants the ball.

Furillo watching from right field. The stone-cut profile.

The bushy-haired man still pacing in the bleachers, moaning and shaking his head—call the men in the white suits and get him outta here. Talking to himself, head-wagging like a street-corner zealot with news of some distant affliction dragging ever closer. Siddown, shaddap, they tell him.

Frank keeps putting pages in Gleason's face.

He tells him, "Eat up, pal. Paper clears the palate."

When in steps Thomson.

The tall fleet Scot. Reminding himself as he gets set in the box. See the ball. Wait for the ball.

Russ is clutching the mike. Warm water and salt. Gargle, said his mother.

Thomson's not sure he sees things clearly. His eyeballs are humming. There's a feeling in his body, he's digging in, settling into his stance, crowd noise packing the sky, and there's a feeling that he has lost the link to his surroundings. Alone in all this rowdy-dow. See the ball. Watch and wait. He is frankly a little fuddled is Bobby. It's like the first waking moment of the day and you don't know whose house you're in.

Russ says, "Bobby Thomson up there swinging."

Mays down on one knee in the on-deck circle half leaning on his cradled bat and watching Branca go into a full windup, push-pull click-click, thinking it's all on him if Thomson fails, the season riding on him, and the jingle plays in his head, it's the radio embrace of the air itself, the mosaic of the air, and it will turn itself off when it's ready.

There's an emergency station under the stands and what the stadium cop has to do is figure out a way to get the stricken man down there without being overrun by a rampant stomping crowd. The victim looks okay considering. He is sitting down, waiting for the attendant to arrive with the wheelchair. All right, maybe he doesn't look so good. He looks pale, sick, worried and infarcted. But he can make a fist and stick out his tongue and there's not much the cop can do until the wheelchair arrives, so he might as well stand in the aisle and watch the end of the game.

Thomson in his bent stance, chin tucked, waiting.

Russ says, "One out, last of the ninth."

He says, "Branca pitches, Thomson takes a strike called on the inside corner."

He lays a heavy decibel on the word strike. He pauses to let the crowd reaction build. Do not talk against the crowd. Let the drama come from them.

Those big rich pages airing down from the upper deck.

Lockman stands near second and tries to wish a hit onto Thomson's bat. That may have been the pitch he wanted. Belt-high, a shade inside—won't see one that good again.

Russ says, "Bobby hitting at two ninety-two. He's had a single and a double and he drove in the Giants' first run with a long fly to center."

Lockman looks across the diamond at home. The double he hit is still a presence in his chest, it's chugging away in there, a body-memory that plays the moment over. He is peering into the deltoid opening between the catcher's knees. He sees the fingers dip, the blunt hand make a flapping action up and left. They'll give him the fastball high and tight and come back with the curve away. A pretty two-part scheme. Seems easy and sweet from here.

Russ says, "Brooklyn leads it four to two."

He says, "Runner down the line at third. Not taking any chances."

Thomson thinking it's all happening too fast. Thinking quick hands, see the ball, give yourself a chance.

Russ says, "Lockman without too big of a lead at second but he'll be running like the wind if Thomson hits one."

In the box seats J. Edgar Hoover plucks a magazine page off his shoulder, where the thing has lighted and stuck. At first he's annoyed that the object has come in contact with his body. Then his eyes fall upon the page. It is a color reproduction of a painting crowded with medieval figures who are dying or dead—a landscape of visionary havoc and ruin. Edgar has never seen a painting quite like this. It covers the page completely and must surely dominate the magazine. Across the red-brown earth, skeleton armies on the march. Men impaled on lances, hung from gibbets, drawn on spoked wheels fixed to the tops of bare trees, bodies open to the crows. Legions of the dead forming up behind shields made of coffin lids. Death himself astride a slat-ribbed hack, he is peaked for blood, his scythe held ready as he presses people in haunted swarms toward the entrance of some helltrap, an oddly modern construction that could be a subway tunnel or office corridor. A background of ash skies and burning ships. It is clear to Edgar that the page is from Life and he tries to work up an anger, he asks himself why a magazine called Life would want to reproduce a painting of such lurid and dreadful dimensions. But he can't take his eyes off the page.

Russ Hodges says, "Branca throws."

41

Gleason makes a noise that is halfway between a sigh and a moan. It is probably a sough, as of rustling surf in some palmy place. Edgar recalls the earlier blowout, Jackie's minor choking fit. He sees a deeper engagement here. He goes out into the aisle and up two steps, separating himself from the imminent discharge of animal, vegetable and mineral matter.

Not a good pitch to hit, up and in, but Thomson swings and tomahawks the ball and everybody, everybody watches. Except for Gleason who is bent over in his seat, hands locked behind his neck, a creamy strand of slime swinging from his lips.

Russ says, "There's a long drive."

His voice has a burst in it, a charge of expectation.

He says, "It's gonna be."

There's a pause all around him. Pafko racing toward the left-field corner.

He says, "I believe."

Pafko at the wall. Then he's looking up. People thinking where's the ball. The scant delay, the stay in time that lasts a hairsbreadth. And Cotter standing in section 35 watching the ball come in his direction. He feels his body turn to smoke. He loses sight of the ball when it climbs above the overhang and he thinks it will land in the upper deck. But before he can smile or shout or bash his neighbor on the arm. Before the moment can overwhelm him, the ball appears again, stitches visibly spinning, that's how near it hits, banging at an angle off a pillar—hands flashing everywhere.

Russ feels the crowd around him, a shudder passing through the stands, and then he is shouting into the mike and there is a surge of color and motion, a crash that occurs upward, stadium-wide, hands and faces and shirts, bands of rippling men, and he is outright shouting, his voice has a power he'd thought long gone—it may lift the top of his head like a cartoon rocket.

He says, *"The Giants win the pennant."*

A topspin line drive. He tomahawked the pitch and the ball had topspin and dipped into the lower deck and there is Pafko at the 315 sign looking straight up with his right arm braced at the wall and a spate of paper coming down.

He says, *"The Giants win the pennant."*

Yes, the voice is excessive with a little tickle of hysteria in the upper register. But it is mainly wham and whomp. He sees Thomson capering around first. The hat of the first-base coach—the first-base coach has flung his hat straight up. He went for a chin-high pitch and coldcocked it good. The ball started up high and then sank, missing the facade of the upper deck and dipping into the seats below—pulled in, swallowed up—and the Dodger players stand looking, already separated from the event, staring flat into the shadows between the decks.

He says, *"The Giants win the pennant."*

The crew is whooping. They are answering the roof bangers by beating on the walls and ceiling of the booth. People climbing the dugout roofs and the crowd shaking in its own noise. Branca on the mound in his tormented slouch. He came with a fastball up, a pitch that's tailing in, and the guy's supposed to take it for a ball. Russ is shouting himself right out of his sore throat, out of every malady and pathology and complaint and all the pangs of growing up and every memory that is not tender.

He says, *"The Giants win the pennant."*

Four times. Branca turns and picks up the rosin bag and throws it down, heading toward the clubhouse now, his shoulders aligned at a slant—he begins the long dead trudge. Paper falling everywhere. Russ knows he ought to settle down and let the mike pick up the sound of the swelling bedlam around him. But he can't stop shouting, there's nothing left of him but shout.

He says, "Bobby Thomson hits into the lower deck of the left-field stands."

He says, "The Giants win the pennant and they're going crazy."

He says, "They're going crazy."

Then he raises a pure shout, wordless, a holler from the old days—it is fiddlin' time, it is mountain music on WCKY at five-thirty in the morning. The thing comes jumping right out of him, a jubilation, it might be *heyyy-ho* or it might be *oh-boyyy* shouted backwards or it might be something else entirely—hard to tell when they don't use words. And Thomson's teammates gathering at home plate and Thomson circling the bases in gamesome leaps, buckjumping—he is forever Bobby now, a romp-

43

ing boy lost to time, and his breath comes so fast he doesn't know if he can handle all the air that's pouring in. He sees men in a helter-skelter line waiting at the plate to pummel him—his teammates, no better fellows in the world, and there's a look in their faces, they are stunned by a happiness that has collapsed on them, bright-eyed under their caps.

He tomahawked the pitch, he hit on top of it and now his ears are ringing and there's a numbing buzz in his hands and feet. And Robinson stands behind second, hands on hips, making sure Thomson touches every base. You can almost see brave Jack grow old.

Look at Durocher spinning. Russ pauses for the first time to catch the full impact of the noise around him. Leo spinning in the coach's box. The manager stands and spins, he is spinning with his arms spread wide—maybe it's an ascetic rapture, a thing they do in mosques in Anatolia.

People make it a point to register the time.

Edgar stands with arms crossed and a level eye on Gleason folded over. Pages dropping all around them, it is a fairly thick issue—laxatives and antacids, sanitary napkins and corn plasters and dandruff removers. Jackie utters an aquatic bark, it is loud and crude, the hoarse call of some mammal in distress. Then the surge of flannel matter. He seems to be vomiting someone's taupe pajamas. The waste is liquidy smooth in the lingo of adland and it is splashing freely on Frank's stout oxford shoes and fine lisle hose and on the soft woven wool of his town-and-country trousers.

The clock atop the clubhouse reads 3:58.

Russ has got his face back into the mike. He shouts, "I don't believe it." He shouts, "I don't believe it." He shouts, "I do *not* believe it."

They are coming down to crowd the railings. They are coming from the far ends of the great rayed configuration and they are moving down the aisles and toward the rails.

Pafko is out of paper range by now, jogging toward the clubhouse. But the paper keeps falling. If the early paper waves were slightly hostile and mocking, and the middle waves a form of fan commonality, then this last demonstration has a softness, a selfness. It is coming down from all points, laundry tickets, envelopes swiped from the office, there are crushed cigarette packs and sticky wrap from ice-cream sandwiches, pages from memo pads and pocket calendars, they are throwing faded dollar bills, snapshots torn to pieces, ruffled paper swaddles for cupcakes, they are tearing up letters they've been carrying around for years pressed into their wallets, the residue of love affairs and college friendships, it is happy garbage now, the fans' intimate wish to be connected to the event, unendably, in the form of pocket litter, personal waste, a thing that carries a shadow identity— rolls of toilet tissue unbolting lyrically in streamers.

They are gathered at the netting behind home plate, gripping the tight mesh.

Russ is still shouting, he is not yet shouted out, he believes he has a thing that's worth repeating.

Saying, "Bobby Thomson hit a line drive into the lower deck of the left-field stands and the place is going crazy."

Next thing Cotter knows he is sidling into the aisle. The area is congested and intense and he has to pry his way row by row using elbows and shoulders. Nobody much seems to notice. The ball is back there in a mighty pileup of shirts and jackets. The game is way behind him. The crowd can have the game. He's after the baseball now and there's no time to ask himself why. They hit it in the stands, you go and get it. It's the ball they play with, the thing they rub up and scuff and sweat on. He's going up the aisle through a thousand pounding hearts. He's prodding and sideswiping. He sees people dipping frantically, it could be apple-bobbing in Indiana, only slightly violent. Then the ball comes free and someone goes after it, the first one out of the pack, a young guy in a scuttling crawl with people reaching for him, trying to grab his jacket, a fistful of trouser-ass. He has wiry reddish hair and a college jacket—you know those athletic jackets where the sleeves are one color and leathery looking and the body is a darker color and probably wool and these are the college colors of the team.

Cotter takes a guess and edges his way along a row that's two rows down from the action. He takes a guess, he anticipates, it's the way you feel something will happen and then you watch it uncannily come to pass, occurring almost in measured stages so you can see the wheelwork of your idea fitting into place.

He coldcocked the pitch and the ball shot out there and dipped and

45

disappeared. And Thomson bounding down on home plate mobbed by his teammates, who move in shuffled steps with hands extended to keep from spiking each other. And photographers edging near and taking their spread stances and the first of the fans appearing on the field, the first strays standing wary or whirling about to see things from this perspective, astonished to find themselves at field level, or running right at Thomson all floppy and demented, milling into the wedge of players at home plate.

Frank is looking down at what has transpired. He stands there hands out, palms up, an awe of muted disgust. That this should happen here, in public, in the high revel of event—he feels a puzzled wonder that exceeds his aversion. He looks down at the back of Jackie's glossy head and he looks at his own trouser cuffs flaked an intimate beige and the spatter across his shoe tops in a strafing pattern and the gumbo puddle nearby that contains a few laggard gobs of pinkoid stuff from deep in Gleason's gastric sac.

And he nods his head and says, "My shoes."

And Shor feels offended, he feels a look come into his face that carries the sting of a bad shave, those long-ago mornings of razor pull and cold water.

And he looks at Frank and says, "Did you see the homer at least?"

"I saw part and missed part."

And Shor says, "Do I want to take the time to ask which part you missed so we can talk about it on the phone some day?"

There are people with their hands in their hair, holding in their brains.

Frank persists in looking down. He allows one foot to list to port so he can examine the side of his shoe for vomit marks. These are handcrafted shoes from a narrow street with a quaint name in oldest London.

And Shor says, "We just won unbelievable, they're ripping up the joint, I don't know whether to laugh, shit or go blind."

And Frank says, "I'm rooting for number one or number three."

Russ is still manning the microphone and has one last thing to say and barely manages to get it out.

"The Giants won it. By a score of five to four. And they're picking Bobby Thomson up. And carrying him off the field."

If his voice has an edge of disquiet it's because he has to get to the clubhouse to do interviews with players and coaches and team officials and the only way to get out there is to cross the length of the field on foot and he's already out of breath, out of words, and the crowd is growing over the walls. He sees Thomson carried by a phalanx of men, players and others, mostly others—the players have run for it, the players are dashing for the clubhouse—and he sees Thomson riding off-balance on the shoulders of men who might take him right out of the ballpark and into the streets for a block party.

Gleason is suspended in wreckage, drained and humped, and he has barely the wit to consider what the shouting's about.

The field streaked with people, the hat snatchers, the swift kids who imitate banking aircraft, their spread arms steeply raked.

Look at Cotter under a seat.

All over the city people are coming out of their houses. This is the nature of Thomson's homer. It makes people want to be in the streets, joined with others, telling others what has happened, those few who haven't heard—comparing faces and states of mind.

And Russ has a hot mike in front of him and has to find someone to take it and talk so he can get down to the field and find a way to pass intact through all that mangle.

And Cotter is under a seat handfighting someone for the baseball. He is trying to get a firmer grip. He is trying to isolate his rival's hand so he can prise the ball away finger by finger.

It is a tight little theater of hands and arms, some martial test with formal rules of grappling.

The iron seat leg cuts into his back. He hears the earnest breathing of the rival. They are working for advantage, trying to gain position.

The rival is blocked off by the seat back, he is facedown in the row above with just an arm stuck under the seat.

People make it a point to read the time on the clock atop the notched facade of the clubhouse, the high battlement—they register the time when the ball went in.

It is a small tight conflict of fingers and inches, a lifetime of effort compressed into seconds.

He gets his hands around the rival's arm just above the wrist. He is working fast, thinking fast—too much time and people take sides.

47

The rival, the foe, the ofay, veins stretched and bulged between white knuckles. If people take sides, does Cotter have a chance?

Two heart attacks, not one. A second man collapses on the field, a well-dressed fellow not exactly falling but letting himself down one knee at a time, slow and controlled, easing down on his right hand and tumbling dully over. No one takes this for a rollick. The man is not the type to do dog tricks in the dirt.

And Cotter's hands around the rival's arm, twisting in opposite directions, burning the skin—it's called an Indian burn, remember? One hand grinding one way, the other going the other, twisting hard, working fast.

There's a pause in the rival's breathing. He is pausing to note the pain. He fairly croons his misgivings now and Cotter feels the arm jerk and the fingers lift from the ball.

Thomson thrusting down off the shoulders of the men who carry him, beating down, pulling away from grabby hands—he sees players watching intently from the clubhouse windows.

And Cotter holds the rival's arm with one hand and goes for the ball with the other. He sees it begin to roll past the seat leg, wobbling on the textured surface. He sort of traps it with his eye and sends out a ladling hand.

The ball rolls in a minutely crooked path into the open.

The action of his hand is as old as he is. It seems he has been sending out this hand for one thing or another since the minute he shot out of infancy. Everything he knows is contained in the splayed fingers of this one bent hand.

Heart, my heart.

The whole business under the seat has taken only seconds. Now he's backing out, moving posthaste—he's got the ball, he feels it hot and buzzy in his hand.

A sense of people grudgingly getting out of his way, making way but not too quickly, dead-eye sidewalk faces.

The ball is damp with the heat and sweat of the rival's hand. Cotter's arm hangs lank at his side and he empties out his face, scareder now than he was when he went over the turnstile but determined to look cool and blank and going down the rows by stepping over seat

48

backs and fitting himself between bodies and walking on seats when it is convenient.

Look at the ushers locking arms at the wrists and making a sedan seat for the cardiac victim and hauling him off to the station under the grandstand.

One glance back at the area above, he allows himself a glance and sees the rival getting to his feet. The man stands out, white-shirted and hulking, and it's not the college boy he thought it might be, the guy in the varsity jacket who'd been scrambling for the ball.

And the man catches his eye. This is not what Cotter wants, this is damage to the cause. He made a mistake looking back. He allowed himself a glance, a sidewise flash, and now he's caught in the man's hard glare.

The raised seams of the ball are pulsing in his hand.

Their eyes meet in the spaces between rocking bodies, between faces that jut and the broad backs of shouting fans. Celebration all around him. But he is caught in the man's gaze and they look at each other over the crowd and through the crowd and it is Bill Waterson with his shirt stained and his hair all punished and sprung—good neighbor Bill flashing a cutthroat smile.

The dead have come to take the living. The dead in winding-sheets, the regimented dead on horseback, the skeleton that plays a hurdy-gurdy.

Edgar stands in the aisle fitting together the two facing pages of the reproduction. People are climbing over seats, calling hoarsely toward the field. He stands with the pages in his face. He hadn't realized he was seeing only half the painting until the left-hand page drifted down and he got a glimpse of rust brown terrain and a pair of skeletal men pulling on bell ropes. The page brushed against a woman's arm and spun into Edgar's godfearing breast.

Thomson is out in center field now dodging fans who come in rushes and jumps. They jump against his body, they want to take him to the ground, show him snapshots of their families.

Edgar reads the copy block on the matching page. This is a sixteenth-century work done by a Flemish master, Pieter Bruegel, and it is called *The Triumph of Death*.

A nervy title methinks. But he is intrigued, he admits it—the left-hand page may be even better than the right.

He studies the tumbrel filled with skulls. He stands in the aisle and looks at the naked man pursued by dogs. He looks at the gaunt dog nibbling the baby in the dead woman's arms. These are long gaunt starveling hounds, they are war dogs, hell dogs, boneyard hounds beset by parasitic mites, by dog tumors and dog cancers.

Dear germ-free Edgar, the man who has an air-filtration system in his house to vaporize specks of dust—he finds a fascination in cankers, lesions and rotting bodies so long as his connection to the source is strictly pictorial.

He finds a second dead woman in the middle ground, straddled by a skeleton. The positioning is sexual, unquestionably. But is Edgar sure it's a woman bestraddled or could it be a man? He stands in the aisle and they're all around him cheering and he has the pages in his face. The painting has an instancy that he finds striking. Yes, the dead fall upon the living. But he begins to see that the living are sinners. The cardplayers, the lovers who dally, he sees the king in an ermine cloak with his fortune stashed in hogshead drums. The dead have come to empty out the wine gourds, to serve a skull on a platter to gentlefolk at their meal. He sees gluttony, lust and greed.

Edgar loves this stuff. Edgar, Jedgar. Admit it—you love it. It causes a bristling of his body hair. Skeletons with wispy dicks. The dead beating kettledrums. The sackcloth dead slitting a pilgrim's throat.

The meatblood colors and massed bodies, this is a census-taking of awful ways to die. He looks at the flaring sky in the deep distance out beyond the headlands on the left-hand page—Death elsewhere, Conflagration in many places, Terror universal, the crows, the ravens in silent glide, the raven perched on the white nag's rump, black and white forever, and he thinks of a lonely tower standing on the Kazakh Test Site, the tower armed with the bomb, and he can almost hear the wind blowing across the Central Asian steppes, out where the enemy lives in long coats and fur caps, speaking that old weighted language of theirs, liturgical and grave. What secret history are they writing?

There is the secret of the bomb and there are the secrets that the bomb inspires, things even the Director cannot guess—a man whose own sequestered heart holds every festering secret in the Western world—because these plots are only now evolving. This is what he knows, that the genius of the bomb is printed not only in its physics of particles and rays but in the occasion it creates for new secrets. For every atmospheric blast, every glimpse we get of the bared force of nature, that weird peeled eyeball exploding over the desert—for every one of these he reckons a hundred plots go underground, to spawn and skein.

And what is the connection between Us and Them, how many bundled links do we find in the neural labyrinth? It's not enough to hate your enemy. You have to understand how the two of you bring each other to deep completion.

The old dead fucking the new. The dead raising coffins from the earth. The hillside dead tolling the old rugged bells that clang for the sins of the world.

He looks up for a moment. He takes the pages from his face—it is a wrenching effort—and looks at the people on the field. Those who are happy and dazed. Those who run around the bases calling out the score. The ones who are so excited they won't sleep tonight. Those whose team has lost. The ones who taunt the losers. The fathers who will hurry home and tell their sons what they have seen. The husbands who will surprise their wives with flowers and chocolate-covered cherries. The fans pressed together at the clubhouse steps chanting the players' names. The fans having fistfights on the subway going home. The screamers and berserkers. The old friends who meet by accident out near second base. Those who will light the city with their bliss.

Cotter walks at a normal pace in the afterschool light. He goes past rows of tenements down Eighth Avenue with a small solemn hop in his stride, a kind of endless levered up-and-down, and Bill is positioned off his shoulder maybe thirty yards back.

He sees the Power of Prayer sign and carries the ball in his right hand and rubs it up several times and looks back and sees the college

51

boy in the two-tone jacket fall in behind Bill, the guy who was involved in the early scuffle for the ball.

Bill has lost his buckaroo grin. He barely shows an awareness that Cotter exists, a boy who walks the earth in high-top Keds. Cotter's body wants to go. But if he starts running at this point, what we have is a black kid running in a mainly white crowd and he's being followed by a pair of irate whites yelling thief or grief or something.

They walk down the street, three secret members of some organized event.

Bill calls out, "Hey Cotter buddy come on, we won this game together."

Many people have disappeared into cars or down the subways, they are swarming across the walkway on the bridge to the Bronx, but there are still enough bodies to disrupt traffic in the streets. The mounted police are out, high-riding and erect, appearing among the cars as levitated beings.

"Hey Cotter I had my hand on that ball before you did."

Bill says this good-natured. He laughs when he says it and Cotter begins to like the man all over again. Car horns are blowing all along the street, noises of joy and mutual salute.

The college boy says, "I think it's time I got in this. I'm in this too. I was the first one to grab ahold of the ball. Actually long before either one of you. Somebody hit it out of my hand. I mean if we're talking about who was first."

Cotter is watching the college boy speak, looking back diagonally. He sees Bill stop, so he stops. Bill is stopping for effect. He wants to stop so he can measure the college boy, look him up and down in an itemizing way. He is taking in the two-tone jacket, the tight red hair, he is taking in the whole boy, the entire form and structure of the college boy's status as a land animal with a major brain.

And he says, "What?" That's all. A hard sharp *what*.

And he stands there agape, his body gone slack in a comic dumbness that's pervaded with danger.

He says, "Who the hell are you anyway? What are you doing here? Do I *know* you?"

Cotter watches this, entertained by the look on the college boy's face. The college boy thought he was part of a team, it's us against him. Now his eyes don't know where to go.

Bill says, "This is between my buddy Cotter and me. Personal business, understand? We don't want you here. You're ruining our fun. And if I have to make it any plainer, there's going to be a family sitting down to dinner tonight minus a loved one."

Bill resumes walking and so does Cotter. He looks back to see the college boy following Bill for a number of paces, unsurely, and then falling out of step and beginning to fade down the street and into the crowd.

Bill looks at Cotter and grins narrowly. It is a wolfish sort of look with no mercy in it. He carries his suit jacket clutched and bunched in his hand, wadded up like something he might want to throw.

With advancing dark the field is taking on a deeper light. The grass is incandescent, it has a heat and sheen. People go running past, looking half ablaze, and Russ Hodges moves with the tentative steps of some tourist at a grand bazaar, trying to hand-shuffle through the crowd.

Some ushers are lifting a drunk off the first-base line and the man warps himself into a baggy mass and shakes free and begins to run around the bases in his oversized raincoat with long belt trailing.

Russ makes his way through the infield and dance-steps into an awkward jog that makes him feel ancient and extraneous and he thinks of the ballplayers of his youth, the men with redneck monickers whose endeavors he followed in the papers every day, Eppa Rixey and Hod Eller and old Ivy Wingo, and there is a silly grin pasted across his face because he is a forty-one-year-old man with a high fever and he is running across a ball field to conduct a dialogue with a pack of athletes in their underwear.

He says to someone running near him, "I don't believe it, I still don't believe it."

Out in dead center he sees the clubhouse windows catch the trigger-glint of flashbulbs going off inside. He hears a shrill cheer and turns and sees the raincoat drunk sliding into third base. Then he realizes the man running alongside is Al Edelstein, his producer.

Al shouts, "Do you believe it?"

"I do not believe it," says Russ.

They shake hands on the run.

Al says, "Look at these people." He is shouting and gesturing, waving a Cuban cigar. "It's like I-don't-know-what."

"If you don't know what, then I don't know what."

"Save the voice," says Al.

"The voice is dead and buried. It went to heaven on a sunbeam."

"I'll tell you one thing's for certain, old pal. We'll never forget today."

"Glad you're with me, buddy."

The running men shake hands again. They are deep in the outfield now and Russ feels an ache in every joint. The clubhouse windows catch the flash of the popping bulbs inside.

In the box seats across the field Edgar sets his hat at an angle on his head. It is a dark gray homburg that brings out the nicely sprinkled silver at his temples.

He has the Bruegel folded neatly in his pocket and will take these pages home to study further.

Thousands remain in the stands, not nearly ready to leave, and they watch the people on the field, aimless eddies and stirrings, single figures sprinting out of crowds. Edgar sees someone dangling from the wall in right-center field. These men who drop from the high walls like to hang for a while before letting go. They hit the ground and crumple and get up slowly. But it's the static drama of the dangled body that Edgar finds compelling, the terror of second thoughts.

Gleason is on his feet now, crapulous Jack all rosy and afloat, ready to lead his buddies up the aisle.

He rails at Frank. "Nothing personal, pal, but I wonder if you realize you're smelling up the ballpark. Talk about stinko. I can smell you even with Shor on the premises. Usually with Shor around, blind people are tapping for garbage cans in their path."

Shor thinks this is funny. Light comes into his eyes and his face goes crinkly. He loves the insults, the slurs and taunts, and he stands there beaming with balloonhead love. It is the highest thing that can pass between men of a certain mind—the stand-up scorn that carries their affections.

But what about Frank? He says, "It's not my stink. It's your stink, pal. Just happens I am the one that's wearing it."

Says Gleason, "Hey. Don't think you're the first friend I ever puked on. I puked on better men than you. Consider yourself honored. This is a form of flattery I extend to nearest and dearest." Here he waves his cigarette. "But don't think I am riding in any limousine that has you in it."

They march toward the exit ramp with Edgar going last. He turns toward the field on an impulse and sees another body dropping from the outfield wall, a streaky length of limbs and hair and flapping sleeves. There is something apparitional in the moment and it chills and excites him and sends his hand into his pocket to touch the bleak pages hidden there.

The crowd is thinning quickly now and Cotter goes past the last of the mounted police down around 148th Street.

"Hey Cotter now let's be honest. You snatched it out of my hand. A clear case of snatch and run. But I'm willing to be reasonable. Let's talk turkey. What do you say to ten dollars in crisp bills? That's a damn fair offer. Twelve dollars. You can buy a ball and a glove for that."

"That's what you think."

"All right, whatever it takes. Let's find a store and go in. A fielder's glove and a baseball. You got sporting goods stores around here? Hell, we won the game of our lives. There's cause for celebration."

"The ball's not for sale. Not this ball."

Bill says, "Let me tell you something, Cotter." Then he pauses and grins. "You got quite a grip, you know. My arm needs attention in a big way. You really put the squeeze on me."

"Lucky I didn't bite. I was thinking about it."

Bill seems delighted at the way Cotter has entered the spirit of the moment. The side streets are weary with uncollected garbage and broken glass, with the odd plundered car squatting flat on its axle and men who stand in doorways completely adream.

Bill runs toward Cotter, he takes four sudden running steps, heavy and overstated, arms spread wide and a movie growl rolling from his throat. Cotter sees it is a joke but not until he has run into the street and done a loop around a passing car.

They smile at each other across the traffic.

"I looked at you scrunched up in your seat and I thought I'd found a pal. This is a baseball fan, I thought, not some delinquent in the streets. You seem to be dead set on disappointing me. Cotter? Buddies sit down together and work things out."

The streetlights are on. They are walking briskly now and Cotter isn't sure who was first to step up the pace. He feels a pain in his back where the seat leg was digging in.

"Now tell me what it's going to take to separate you from that base-ball, son."

Cotter doesn't like the tone of this.

"I want that cotton-pickin' ball."

Cotter keeps walking.

"Hey goofus I'm talking to you. You maybe think this is some cheapo entertainment. String the guy along."

"You can talk all you want," Cotter says. "The ball's not yours, it's mine. I'm not selling it or trading it."

A car comes veering off the avenue and Cotter stops to let it go by. Then he feels something shift around him. There's a ripple in the pavement or the air and a scant second in a woman's face nearby—her eyes shift to catch what's happening behind him. He turns to see Bill coming wide and fast and arm-pumping. It seems awful heavy traffic for a baseball. The color coming into Bill's face, the shiny fabric at his knees. He has a look that belongs to someone else entirely, a man out of another experience, desperate and propelled.

Cotter stands there for one long beat. He wastes a head-fake, then starts to run down the empty side street with Bill right on his neck and reaching. He cuts sharp and ducks away, skidding to his knees and wheeling on his right hand, the ball hand, pressing the ball hard in the tar and using it to pivot. Bill goes past him in a drone of dense breath, a formal hum that is close to speech. Cotter sees him stop and turn. He is skewed with rage, face bloated and quirked. A sleeve hangs down from the jacket in his hand and brushes softly on the ground.

Cotter runs back up to the avenue with the sound of rustling breath behind him. They are past the ballpark crowd, this is unmixed Harlem here—all he has to do is get to the corner, to people and lights. He sees barroom neon and bedsheets strung across a lot. He sees Fresh Killed Chickens From The Farm. He reads the sign, or maybe gathers it whole, and there's an odd calm completion in it, a gesturing of safety. Two women step aside when he gets near—they glance past him to his pursuit and he notes the alertness in their faces, the tapering of attention. Bill is close, banging the asphalt in his businessman's shoes.

Cotter goes south on the avenue and runs half a block and then he turns and does a caper, he does a physical jape—running backwards for a stretch, high-stepping, mocking, showing Bill the baseball. He's a cutup in a sour state. He holds the ball chest-high and turns it in his fingers, which isn't easy when you're running—he rotates the ball on its axis, spins it slowly over and around, showing the two hundred and sixteen raised red cotton stitches.

Don't tell me you don't love this move.

The maneuver makes Bill slow down. He looks at Cotter backpedaling, doing a danceman's strut, but he doesn't detect an opening here. Because the maneuver makes him realize where he is. The fact that Cotter's not scared. The fact that he's parading the baseball. Bill stops completely but is too smart to look around. Best to limit your purview to straight ahead. Because you don't know who might be looking back at you. And the more enlightened he becomes, the more open grows the space for Cotter's anger. He doesn't really know how to show it. This is the second time today he has taunted someone but he doesn't feel the spunky rush of dodging the cop. The high heart of the gate-crash is a dimness here—he is muddled and wrung out and can't get his bad-ass glare to function. So he stands there flatfoot and looks at Bill with people walking by and noticing and not noticing and he spins the ball up and over the back of his hand and catches it skipping off his wrist with a dip and twist of the same hand, like fuck you mister who you messing with.

He looks at Bill, a flushed and panting man who has vainly chased along a railroad track for the five-oh-nine.

Then he turns his back and walks slowly down the street. He begins to think about the game's amazing end. What could not happen actually happened. He wants to get home, sit quiet, let it live again, let the home run roll over him, soaking his body with a kind of composure, the settled pleasure that comes after the thing itself.

A man calls from a window to a man on a stoop.

"Hey baby I hear she put your nightstick in a sling."

Cotter turns here, looks there, feeling a sense of placeness that grows more familiar.

He sees a kid he knows but doesn't stop to show him the ball or brag on the game.

He feels the pain from the seat leg.

He sees a street-corner shouter making a speech, a tall man in a rag suit with bicycle clips nipping his pants at the ankles.

He feels a little bringdown working in his mind.

He sees four guys from a local gang, the Alhambras, and he crosses the street to avoid them and then crosses back.

He gets to his street and goes up the front steps and into the sour air of his building and he feels the little bringdown of fading light that he has felt a thousand times before.

Shit man. I don't want to go to school tomorrow.

Russ Hodges stands on an equipment trunk trying to describe the scene in the clubhouse and he knows he is making no sense and the players who climb up on the trunk to talk to him are making no sense and they are all talking in unnatural voices, failed voices, creaturely night screaks. Others are pinned to their lockers by reporters and family members and club officials and they can't get to the liquor and beer located on a table in the middle of the room. Russ holds the mike over his head and lets the noise sweep in and then lowers the mike and says another senseless thing.

Thomson goes out on the clubhouse veranda to respond to the sound of his chanted name and they are everywhere, they are on the steps with stadium cops keeping them in check and there are thousands more spread dense across the space between jutting bleacher walls, many arms extended toward Thomson—they are pointing or imploring or making victory fists or stating a desire to touch, men in suits and hats down there and others hanging over the bleacher wall above Bobby, reaching down, half falling over the edge, some very near to touching him.

Al says, the producer, "Great job today, Russ buddy."

"We did something great just by being here."

"What a feeling."

"I'd smoke a cigar but I might die."

"But what a feeling," Al says.

"We sure pulled something out of a hat. All of us together. Damn I just realized."

"What's a ball game to make us feel like this?"

"I have to go back. Left my topcoat in the booth."

"We need a walk to settle us down."

"We need a long walk."

"That's the only coat you've ever loved," says Al.

They leave by way of the Dodger clubhouse and there's Branca all right, the first thing you see, stretched facedown on a flight of six steps, feet touching the floor. He's still in uniform except for shirt and cap. He wears a wet undershirt and his head is buried in his crossed arms on the top step. Al and Russ speak to a few of the men who remain. They talk quietly and try not to look at Branca. They look but tell themselves they aren't. Next to Branca a coach sits in full uniform but hatless, smoking a cigarette. His name is Cookie. No one wants to catch Cookie's eye. Al and Russ talk quietly to a few more men and all of them together try not to look at Branca.

The steps from the Dodger clubhouse are nearly clear of people. Thomson has gone back inside but there are fans still gathered in the area, waving and chanting. The two men begin to walk across the outfield and Al points to the place in the left-field stands where the ball went in.

"Mark the spot. Like where Lee surrendered to Grant or some such thing."

Russ thinks this is another kind of history. He thinks they will carry something out of here that joins them all in a rare way, that binds them to a memory with protective power. People are climbing lampposts on Amsterdam Avenue, tooting car horns in Little Italy. Isn't it possible that this midcentury moment enters the skin more lastingly than the vast shaping strategies of eminent leaders, generals steely in their sunglasses—the mapped visions that pierce our dreams? Russ wants to believe a thing like this keeps us safe in some undetermined way. This is the thing that will pulse in his brain come old age and double vision and dizzy spells—the surge sensation, the leap of people already standing, that bolt of noise and joy when the ball went in. This is the people's history and it has flesh and breath that quicken to the force of this old safe game of ours. And fans at the Polo Grounds today will be able to tell their grandchildren—they'll be the gassy old men leaning into the next century and trying to convince anyone willing to listen, pressing in with medicine breath, that they were here when it happened.

The raincoat drunk is running the bases. They see him round first, his hands paddling the air to keep him from drifting into right field. He approaches second in a burst of coattails and limbs and untied shoelaces and swinging belt. They see he is going to slide and they stop and watch him leave his feet.

All the fragments of the afternoon collect around his airborne form: Shouts, bat-cracks, full bladders and stray yawns, the sand-grain manyness of things that can't be counted.

It is all falling indelibly into the past.

PART 1

LONG TALL SALLY

Spring–Summer 1992

1

I was driving a Lexus through a rustling wind. This is a car assembled in a work area that's completely free of human presence. Not a spot of mortal sweat except, okay, for the guys who drive the product out of the plant—allow a little moisture where they grip the wheel. The system flows forever onward, automated to priestly nuance, every gliding movement back-referenced for prime performance. Hollow bodies coming in endless sequence. There's nobody on the line with caffeine nerves or a history of clinical depression. Just the eerie weave of chromium alloys carried in interlocking arcs, block iron and asphalt sheeting, soaring ornaments of coachwork fitted and merged. Robots tightening bolts, programmed drudges that do not dream of family dead.

It's a culmination in a way, machines made and shaped outside the little splat of human speech. And this made my rented car a natural match for the landscape I was crossing. Heat shimmer rising on the empty flats. A bled-white sky with ticky breezes raking dust across the windshield. And the species factually absent from the scene—except for me, of course, and I was barely there.

Let's just say the desert is an impulse. I'd decided in a flash to switch planes and get a car and hit the back roads. There is something about old times that's satisfied by spontaneity. The quicker you decide, the more fully you discharge the debt to memory. I wanted to see her again and feel something and say something, a few words, not too many, and then head back into the windy distance. It was all distance. It was hardpan and sky and a wafer trace of mountain, low and crouched out there, mountain or cloud, cat-shaped, catamount—how human it is to see a thing as something else.

The old road bent north, placing the sun approximately abeam, and I wanted to feel the heat on my face and arms. I turned off the air conditioner and lowered the windows. I reached for the tube of sunblock, protection factor fifteen, a thing I keep nearby even though I'm olive-skinned, dark as my father was.

I slowed the car to a no-hands crawl and applied the stuff to half my face and one arm, the exposed person, because I was fifty-seven years old and still learning how to be sensible.

The musky coconut balm and the adolescent savor of heat and beach and an undermemory of seawater rush, salt scour in the eyes and nose. I squeezed the tube until it was sucked dry. It sucked and popped and went dry. I glimpsed something, a mental image, a sort of nerve-firing, a desert flash—the briefest puddled color of an ice-cream vendor weaving through high sand.

Later the wind died and a cloudreef rimmed in pale rose hung low and still. I was on a dirt road now, spectacularly lost, and I stopped the car and got out and scanned the landscape, feeling pretty dumb, and I thought I saw some funk holes out among the yucca—old concrete bunkers from a mining operation or military test site. It would be dark in forty-five minutes. I had a quarter tank of gas, half a can of iced tea, nothing to eat, no warm clothes, a map that scanted the details.

I would drink my tea and die.

Then a scatter of dust, a hazy mass rising from the sundown line. And an approaching object that made me think of a hundred movies in which something comes across the wavy plain, a horseman with scabbarded rifle or a lone cameleer hunched in muslin on his dumbheaded beast. This thing was different, raising twin kicks of sand, coming at a nice clip. But not your everyday average all-terrain vehicle. It had a roof light and a gleam of yellow paint and it was brassy and jouncing, with a cartoon shine. The happiest sort of apparition, coming down the rutted path like a pop-art object. Less than fifty yards away. It seemed to be, it clearly was a New York taxi, impossible but true, yellower than egg yolk and coming fast.

What better gesture might I devise than an outstretched hailing hand?

But the damn thing did not slow down. Windows open, music ripping out—a surge of steroid rock. I stepped back out of the way, my arm still raised, the suntan arm, sleek with chemicals. I saw the cab was jammed with people and I called out as they went by—a person's name, a password in the throbbing air.

"Klara Sax," is what I shouted.

And there were answering shouts. The taxi slowed briefly and I could hear them cheering. Then arms came jutting from two or three windows, waving and beckoning, and a single smiling yellow head, a blond woman sunny and young and looking back at me—the driver serene in all that ruckus, driving blind—and the taxi springing away, hightailing through the studded vegetation and out across the desert.

I got in my silent car and followed.

The volunteers were mainly art students but there were others as well, history majors and teachers on leave and nomads and runaways, coming and going all the time, burnt-out hackers looking for the unwired world, they were people who heard the call, the whisper in the ear that sends you out the door and into some zone of exalted play.

Working with the hands. Scraping and painting. Stirring the indolent mixture. Seeing brushstrokes mark a surface. *Pigment*. The animal fats and polymers that blend to make this word.

They were nice to me. They ate and slept in a set of abandoned barracks at the edge of an enormous air base. Toilets, showers, cots and an improvised commissary. They were a good-humored workforce with an array of skills. They fixed things, sang songs, they told funny stories. When their numbers grew beyond the capacity of the barracks, they slept in pup tents or sleeping bags or in their dusty cars.

I told a student with a welcome badge that I was not here to wield a brush or sandblaster but only to see the piece—the artwork, the project, whatever it was called—and to say hello if that was possible to Klara Sax.

I told him I didn't want to take up space and he gave me directions to a motel where I might spend the night, maybe twenty-five miles away, and then asked me to meet him later at a place he called the paint shop.

I washed the sunblock off my hands and face and got in a food line, sandwiches and kiwis and fruit juice. Then I sat and talked with five or six others. They were all nice. I asked about the taxi and they said it was someone's car that they'd decided to paint and ornament, a gift for Klara on her birthday earlier in the week. Not the car itself, which had been returned to the owner in its taxified form, but the paint, the gesture, the sense of her ancestral New York.

They asked where I was from and I replied with a line I sometimes used.

I live a quiet life in an unassuming house in a suburb of Phoenix. Pause. Like someone in the Witness Protection Program.

I hated the line by this time but it seemed to bend the edge of inquiry, to set a patently shallow tone. All the while we were talking I looked around for the taxi driver with the honey-blond hair.

A number of people wore T-shirts inscribed *Long Tall Sally*.

I thought I could guess Klara's age within a year or two and when I asked which birthday she was celebrating somebody said seventy-two. This sounded about right.

It was a clear night with swirled stars burning low and close and a sweet breeze skimming the earth. I drove for about a minute and a half—don't walk, they'd said—and followed a line of road reflectors stuck in the dirt. There were strung lights and a cluster of jeeps and vans and a single long concrete structure about ten feet high and divided along its length into a dozen compartments, room-sized, open at the front and rear.

This was the operation center, where the project was coordinated—designs created, daily assignments made, most of the material stored.

One of the spaces was filled with people and I spotted a mike boom suspended over the massed heads. Lights, a camera, a woman with a clipboard—and spectators from the workforce, maybe forty of them, some with protective face masks dangled on their chests, many wearing shirts or jackets with the same inscription I'd seen earlier. I parked nearby and walked to the edge of the group. It took me a moment to find the subject. She was seated in a director's chair with a cane alongside and one leg propped on an overturned bucket. She smoked a black cigarette and talked to people while the crew set up.

Now that I was a word or two away, a name away, the oddness of the trip pressed in on me. Seventeen. That's how old I was last time I saw her. Yes, that long ago, and after all this time it might seem to her that I was some invasive thing, a figure from an anxious dream come walking and talking across a wilderness to find her. I stood and watched, trying to generate the will to make an approach. And maybe it was stranger still, odder than the years between meetings, that I was able to see her retrospectively. I could lift the younger woman right out of the chair, separate her from the person in the dark plaid pants and old suede blazer who sat talking and smoking. I'd seen photographs of Klara but could never quite isolate the woman I'd known, straight-bodied and pale, with a little twist about the mouth, the turned mouth that made her seem detached from what she said. And the evasive eyes, the look that seemed to bend the question of what it was we wanted from each other.

She looked famous and rare, famous even to herself, famous alone making a salad in her kitchen. Her hair was white, a mineral glisten, cropped close about her oblong face with a decorative fringe across the forehead. She wore a floppy orange T-shirt under the blazer and a necklace and several rings and one white running shoe and a sock the color of Kool-Aid grape. The injured foot was wrapped in a tan elastic brace.

Somebody passed with a paper cup and she dropped her cigarette in.

She'd rubbed some dark rouge high on her cheeks and it made her look severe and even deathly in an impressive way. But I could see the younger woman. I could make her rise in some sleight of mind to occupy the space I'd prepared, eyes faintly slanted and papery hands and how she used to smile privately and unbelievingly at the thought

67

of us together and how she seemed to move in time-delay—the mind clocks in and the body follows.

I watched her. These first thirty seconds had a compressed power. I could feel my breathing change.

The crew was from French television and they were ready to start filming. The spectators grew still. The woman with the clipboard crouched just out of camera range, the spot from which she would ask her questions. She was in her willowy middle forties, streaked hair and antique jeans, a denim tote bag splay-handled at her feet.

She said, "It is all right we begin I think. I am allowed to be stupid because we edit my questions out of the film. Those are the rules okay? I choke on my English no problem."

"But I must be smart, funny, profound and charming," Klara said.

"It would actually be very nice. We start with the injury of your left leg. You can tell us what happened okay?"

"I fell off a ladder. Very minor. Missed a rung somewhere along the way. We use whatever devices we can find. We don't have a roof over our heads, a hangar or factory. We don't have the scaffolding, the platforms they have in assembly halls where they do construction and repair work."

I moved closer and found myself standing a few feet behind the student with the welcome badge, the young man who'd offered to arrange a room for me.

The interviewer said, "So you are climbing, you are working."

"It's a sprained ankle. Take an aspirin. Yes, I get up there sometimes if it's not too fierce, if the heat's bearable, you know. I've got to see it and feel it. We have many able-bodied volunteers. But I need to pitch in now and again."

"I was at the site tonight the first time and saw many ladders and people crawling on the wings. They're wearing masks. They have strapped to their backs these enormous tanks."

"We have automotive spray guns we use to prime the metal. We have industrial guns that spray oil paints, enamel, epoxy and so on. We use air compressors that are portable. We even use brushes. We use brushes when we want a brush effect."

People in the audience shifted a bit, trying to get a better look at

Klara as she spoke or edging nearer to hear the conversation more clearly. Klara's voice had a slight rasp and a kind of wobble, the loose liquid texture of something sliding side to side.

"We scrape and sandblast," she said. "We have many blasting machines with guns and nine-gallon hoppers, I think they are. We have some pressure blasters, big things on wheels. Most of the planes have only one coat of paint to remove because they were painted originally with weight considerations foremost in mind. They were built to carry bombs in other words, not beautiful coats of paint. Of course this is impossible work. Working outside in heat, dust and wind. Completely impossible. Too much dust we don't paint. A little dust we paint. We're not looking for precision. We spray it on, grit and all. Spray it, shoot it, throw it."

She said, "Of course the planes have been stripped of most components that might still be useful or salable to civilian contractors. But the wheels are still there, the undercarriages, because I don't want planes that sit flat on their bellies. So we need a great deal of elevation to work on the fuselage and the massive fin. We have people standing on ladders with twelve-foot pole guns, we have people on the stabilizers spraying away at the damn tail."

"But you have cooperation."

"We have cooperation from the military up to a point. We can paint their deactivated aircraft. They let us paint and they promise to keep the site intact, to isolate it from other uses and to maintain the integrity of the project. No other objects, not a single permanent object can be located within a mile of the finished piece. We also have foundation grants, we have congressional approval, all sorts of permits. What else? Materials donated by manufacturers, tens of thousands of dollars' worth. But we still have to scratch and steal to get many of the things we need."

"And the dry air of the desert this keeps the metal safe."

"It is dry and it is hot."

"It is very hot okay?"

"Abandoned aircraft. Like the end of World War II," Klara said. "The one difference is—two differences. The one difference is we haven't actually fought a war this time. We have a number of postwar conditions without a war having been fought. And second we are not going to let these great machines expire in a field or get sold as scrap."

"You are going to paint them."

"We are in the process of painting them. We are saving them from the cutter's torch. And it's very strange let me tell you because thirty years ago when I gave up easel painting and started doing my castoffs they attacked me for it. And I don't recall when the term first came into use but they eventually started calling me the Bag Lady, which I said funny ha-ha, figuring it would last a month. But the name trailed me for quite a long time and I was not amused anymore."

"Now you are here in the desert."

"Back to castoffs. This time it is not aerosol cans and sardine tins and shampoo caps and mattresses. I painted a mattress and some sheets. It was the end of marriage number two and I painted my bed in effect. Anyway, yes, I am now dealing with B-52 long-range bombers. I am painting airplanes that are a hundred and sixty feet long with wingspans even longer and total weight operating on full tanks maybe half a million pounds, I don't know about empty—planes that used to carry nuclear bombs, ta-da, ta-da, out across the world."

"This is not a mattress."

"I'll tell you what this is. This is an art project, not a peace project. This is a landscape painting in which we use the landscape itself. The desert is central to this piece. It's the surround. It's the framing device. It's the four-part horizon. This is why we insisted to the Air Force—a cleared area around the finished work."

"Yes it is true the landscape."

"Wait. I'm not finished. I want to say in this passage from small objects to very large ones, in the years it took me to find these abandoned machines, after all this I am rediscovering paint. And I am drunk on color. I am sex-crazed. I see it in my sleep. I eat it and drink it. I'm a woman going mad with color."

And she looked toward her audience, her workers, briefly, and they stirred and laughed.

"But the beauty of the desert."

"It's so old and strong. I think it makes us feel, makes us as a culture, any technological culture, we feel we mustn't be overwhelmed by it. Awe and terror, you know. Unconducive"—and she waved a hand and laughed—"to industry and progress and so forth. So we use this place to test our weapons. It's only logical of course. And it enables us to show our mastery. The desert bears the visible signs of all the detonations we set off. All the craters and warning signs and no-go areas and burial markers, the sites where debris is buried."

The interviewer asked a series of questions about young conceptualists working with biological and nuclear waste and then called for a short break. The spectators applauded lightly and folded into chatty clusters or went outside to watch the night sky build and thicken.

I reached for the guy with the welcome on his chest.

"Can you approach her now? Tell her it's Nick Shay. From New York, tell her. Tell her if she can spare a minute," I said. "We lived near each other in New York."

He was blinking at me.

I told him my name again and watched him head for the director's chair. He had to wait until she was unoccupied and then he spoke to her, gesturing in my direction.

I watched her face, waiting for the name to register, for light to strike her eyes. She paused, then began to look around for me. Her face showed—what? A certain concern, a solicitude on my behalf, grave and memoried. Are you really here? Are you all right? Are you alive?

I walked over there and grabbed a folding chair and set it down alongside her and waited for the kid to go away.

"So this is Nick."

"Yes."

"Talk about surprises."

"You remember."

"Oh yes," she said, and there was the fadeaway smile, the look that says how did this happen.

"I was in Houston."

"You're leading a regular life."

"Shave every day."

"Pay taxes—good."

"I had business in Houston. There was a magazine I took with me that had a story about your project. So I thought why not."

"Nick exercises, I think."

"Well, let's see. I drink soy milk and run the metric mile."

I waited for her to smile. Then I said, "But the story didn't say exactly where the site was located. So I flew to El Paso and rented a car and thought I would drive home to Phoenix and pay a visit along the way."

"And you found us."

"Wasn't easy."

She was looking at me, openly evaluating. I wondered what she was seeing. I felt there was something I ought to explain about the intervening years. I had that half dread you feel when someone studies you after a long separation and makes you think that you've done badly to reach this point so altered and drawn. Unknown to yourself, you see. To reach this point so helpless against your own connivings that the truth has been obscured from you.

"And you're well? You look well," she said.

She was saying I looked well but she was staring in a certain way and there was something in her voice, you see, that made me wary. People kept interrupting to tell her things, to relay messages. Someone came by with a message about some administrative matter and she introduced us.

"An old friend from the cherished past," she said. "Well, cherished in memory maybe. Rough going at the time."

Then she turned to me again.

"Married?"

"Yes. Two children. College-age. Although they're not in college."

"I've married out of impulse, out of a cozy evening with a nice wine. Not lately, though. Lately I've been crazy with work. It took me a long time to realize I was careful and logical about affairs, really sort of scrupulous about who and where and when, and completely reckless when it came to marriage."

I wanted to say, You weren't always careful about affairs. But then it wasn't an affair, was it? Just an occurrence, a thing in two episodes, a few hours only, measured in hours and minutes and then ended. Of course I said nothing. I didn't know how to handle the subject. We could not be wry, considering the difference in our ages, about growing old and deaf and hobbled, and I despaired a little, I began to think we'd already stretched the visit past bearable limits and what a mistake I'd made, coming here, because the subject was not speakable—too secret, still, even between the secret-keepers, after forty years.

"I thought I owed us this visit. Whatever that means," I said.

"I know what it means. You feel a loyalty. The past brings out our patriotism, you know? We want to feel an allegiance. It's the one undivided allegiance, to all those people and things."

"And it gets stronger."

"Sometimes I think everything I've done since those years, everything around me in fact, I don't know if you feel this way but everything is vaguely—*what*—fictitious."

It was an offhand remark that didn't begin to interest her until she got to the last word.

"This is a long way, Nick. We're a long way from home."

"The Bronx."

We laughed.

"Yes. That place, that word. Rude, blunt—what else do we call it?"

"Crunching," I said.

"Yes. It's like three words they've crunched together."

"It's like talking through broken teeth."

We laughed again and I felt better. It was wonderful to laugh with her. I wanted her to see me. I wanted her to know I was out of there, whatever crazy mistakes I'd made—I'd come out okay.

"So strong and real," she said. "And everything since then—but maybe that's just a function of getting older. I don't read philosophy."

"I read everything," I told her.

She looked at me with something like renewed surprise.

"Maybe I should save this for the French," she said. "But didn't life take an unreal turn at some point?"

"Well, you're famous, Klara."

"No. It's not unreal because I'm famous." Annoyed at me. "It's just unreal."

She pulled a box of Nat Shermans out of her blazer and lit one up.

"I'm not pregnant so I can do this."

Another person came and went, a young woman with a schedule change, and Klara's face went distant and tight but not at this news at all. Something else upset her, something stirred and entered and she tilted her head as if to listen.

"Strange you should turn up now. God, how strange and awful in a way. And I didn't make the connection until this minute. What in God's name is wrong with me? Did I forget he died? Albert died two weeks ago. Three weeks ago. Teresa called me, our daughter."

"I'm sorry."

"We were not in touch, he and I. Three weeks ago. Congestive heart failure. It's one of those illnesses, you sort of know what it means even if you don't."

"Where was he living? Back there?"

"Yes, back there," she said. "Where else would Albert die?"

Albert was Klara's husband when I knew them both. He was a science teacher in my high school. Mr. Bronzini. Years after I'd seen him for the last time I found myself thinking of him unexpectedly and often. You know how certain places grow powerful in the mind with passing time. In those early morning dreams when I come back to bed after a sleepy pee and fall quickly into the narrow end of the night, there is one set of streets I keep returning to, one dim mist of railroad rooms, and certain figures reappear, borderline ghosts. Albert and Klara among them. He was the husband, she was the wife, a detail I barely thought about at the time.

Two people leaned over Klara muttering something simultaneously and then one of the crew asked if she was ready to resume.

She said to me, "Your brother."

"Living in Boston."

"Do you see him?"

"No. Rarely."

"What about his chess?"

"I don't see anyone. He gave it up a long time ago."

"But what a pity."

"We couldn't have two geniuses coming out of the same little neighborhood."

"Oh bullshit," she said.

I put a hand on her arm and felt a softening. She looked at me again, eyes protuberant, bloodshot with seeing. I found it deeply agreeable to

74

sit there with my hand on Klara's arm and to recall the younger woman's turned mouth, the kind of erotic flaw that makes you want to lose yourself in the imbalance—mouth and jaw not quite aligned. But this was the limit of reflective pleasure. These were all the things I could put through the squeezer. We'd said what we were going to say and exchanged all the looks and remembered the dead and missing and now it was time for me to become a functioning adult again.

Another person said something and I got up and moved away, feeling Klara's hand trail along my forearm and across my palm. I found a place farther back this time, nearer the opening. It took the audience a moment to assemble and settle down.

The interviewer crouched and spoke.

"Maybe you can tell us why you want to do this thing."

"It's a work in progress, don't forget, changing by the day and minute. Let me try, I'll try to circle around to an answer and maybe I'll get there and maybe I won't."

She held her right hand near her face, the cigarette tilted up, eye-high.

"I used to spend a lot of time on the Maine coast. I was married to a yachtsman, my second husband this was, a dealer in risky securities who was about to go bust any day but didn't know it at the time and he had a lovely ketch and we used to go up there and cruise the coastline. We sat on deck at night and the sky was beautifully clear and sometimes we saw a kind of halo moving across the star fields and we used to speculate what is this. Airliners making the North Atlantic run or UFOs you know, that was a popular subject even then. A luminous disc slowly crossing. Hazy and very high. And I thought it was too high for an airliner. And I knew that strategic bombers flew at something like fifty-five thousand feet. And I decided this is the refracted light from an object way up there, this is the circular form it takes. Because I wanted to believe that's what we were seeing. B-52s. War scared me all right but those lights, I have to tell you those lights were a complex sensation. Those planes on permanent alert, ever present you know, sweeping the Soviet borders, and I remember sitting out there rocking lightly at anchor in some deserted cove and feeling a sense of awe, a child's sleepy feeling of mystery and danger and beauty. I think that is

75

power. I think if you maintain a force in the world that comes into people's sleep, you are exercising a meaningful power. Because I respect power. Now that power is in shatters or tatters and now that those Soviet borders don't even exist in the same way, I think we understand, we look back, we see ourselves more clearly, and them as well. Power meant something thirty, forty years ago. It was stable, it was focused, it was a tangible thing. It was greatness, danger, terror, all those things. And it held us together, the Soviets and us. Maybe it held the world together. You could measure things. You could measure hope and you could measure destruction. Not that I want to bring it back. It's gone, good riddance. But the fact is."

And she seemed to lose her line of argument here. She paused, she realized the cigarette had burned down and the interviewer reached for it and Klara handed it over, delicately, butt-end first.

"Many things that were anchored to the balance of power and the balance of terror seem to be undone, unstuck. Things have no limits now. Money has no limits. I don't understand money anymore. Money is undone. Violence is undone, violence is easier now, it's uprooted, out of control, it has no measure anymore, it has no level of values."

And she paused again and thought.

"I don't want to disarm the world," she said. "Or I do want to disarm the world but I want it to be done warily and realistically and in the full knowledge of what we're giving up. We gave up the yacht. That's the first thing we gave up. Now I've got these airplanes down out of the sky and I've walked and stooped and crawled from the cockpit to the tail gun armament and I've seen them in every kind of light and I've thought hard about the weapons they carried and the men who accompanied the weapons and it is awful to think about. But the bombs were not released. You see. The missiles remained in the underwing carriages, unfired. The men came back and the targets were not destroyed. You see. We all tried to think about war but I'm not sure we knew how to do this. The poets wrote long poems with dirty words and that's about as close as we came, actually, to a thoughtful response. Because they had brought something into the world that out-imagined the mind. They didn't even know what to call the early bomb. The thing or the gadget or something. And Oppenheimer said, It is merde. I will

76

use the French. J. Robert Oppenheimer. It is merde. He meant something that eludes naming is automatically relegated, he is saying, to the status of shit. You can't name it. It's too big or evil or outside your experience. It's also shit because it's garbage, it's waste material. But I'm making a whole big megillah out of this. What I really want to get at is the ordinary thing, the ordinary life behind the thing. Because that's the heart and soul of what we're doing here."

The wobble in her voice. And the way the sound came cornering out of the side of her mouth. It was scary-seductive, it made us think she might trail into some unsteady meander. And the pauses. We waited out the pauses, watching the match tremble when she lit another cigarette.

She said, "See, we're painting, hand-painting in some cases, putting our puny hands to great weapons systems, to systems that came out of the factories and assembly halls as near alike as possible, millions of components stamped out, repeated endlessly, and we're trying to unrepeat, to find an element of felt life, and maybe there's a sort of survival instinct here, a graffiti instinct—to trespass and declare ourselves, show who we are. The way the nose artists did, the guys who painted pinups on the fuselage."

She said, "Some of the planes had markings painted on the nose. Emblems, unit insignia, some with figures, an animal mascot snarling and dripping juices from the mouth and jowls. Wonderful, actually, cartoons. Nose art, they call it. And some with women. Because it's all about luck, isn't it? The sexy woman painted on the nose is a charm against death. We may want to place this whole business in some bottom pit of nostalgia but in fact the men who flew these planes, and we are talking about high alert and distant early warning, we are talking about the edge of everything—well, I think they lived in a closed world with its particular omens and symbols and they were young and horny to boot. And one day I came across one of the oldest planes in the ranks, very weathered, with a nice piece of nose art that was faded and patchy and showed a young woman in a flouncy skirt and narrow halter and she was very tall, very blond, she had amazing legs and her hands were on her hips very sort of aspiring-pinup—you knew she didn't have quite the skill to bring it off—and her name was lettered under the painting and it was Long Tall Sally. And I thought, I like this girl because she is not amazonian or angelic or terrifically idealized. And I thought about her some more and this is what I thought. I thought even if she has to be painted over, and maybe she will be and maybe she won't, I thought we will definitely have to salvage her name. I thought we will title our work after this young woman, after the men who fixed her image to the aircraft, after the song that inspired them to do it. Which I recall only vaguely, the song. But there was a song and I thought there is probably a real and original Sally somewhere in the mix. She inspired the songwriter or the nose painter or the crew that flew the plane. Maybe she was a waitress in an airman's bar. Or somebody's hometown girl. Or somebody's first love. But this is an individual life. And I want this life to be part of our project. This luck, this sign against death. Whoever she is or was, a waitress bedraggled you know, hustling a ketchup bottle across the room, and never mind the bomb, I want to keep our intentions small and human despite the enormous work we've done and the huge work we have ahead of us and I'm sitting here with a propped foot and talking endlessly about my work when I'm completely aware of Matisse and what he said, that painters must begin by cutting out their tongues."

I could see her on television in France, dotted down to reconverted waves. I could hear her voice distanced behind a monotone translation. People watching in every part of the country, their heads clustered in the dark. I could see her flat-screen face buzzing at the edges, her eyes like lived-out moons, half a million Klaras floating in the night.

She said, "Not long ago I saw an old photograph, a picture taken in the midsixties, and there is a woman at the edge of the picture. The picture is crowded with people and they are in the doorway, it looks like the entranceway to a grand ballroom, and they are all wearing black and white, men and women both, and they are wearing masks as well, and I looked at the picture and I realized this was the famous party, the famous event of the era, Truman Capote's Black & White Ball at the Plaza Hotel in New York in the dark days of Vietnam, and I was completely sort of out-of-body looking at this scene because it took me maybe half a minute to understand that the woman at the edge of the frame was me. Absolutely. And I'm standing next to a man who is either Truman Capote or J. Edgar Hoover, one or the other because they had heads that were shaped alike, and the mask and the angle and the shadows make it hard to tell which one it is, and I am wearing a long black sheathy dress that I simply can't believe I ever wore although there I am, it's me, and a little white feline mask. And I thought, What is it about this picture that makes it so hard for me to remember myself? I thought, I don't know who that person is. Why is she there exactly. What is she thinking about? What sort of underwear is she wearing under the stupid dress and I can swear to you that I don't know. Surrounded by famous people and powerful people, men in the administration who were running the war, and I want to paint it over, paint the photograph orange and blue and burgundy and paint the tuxedos and long dresses and paint the grand ballroom of the Plaza Hotel and maybe this is what I'm doing, I don't know, it's a work in perpetual progress. And let's not forget pleasure. The senses, the pleasures, the body juices. But strata blue yes. But yellow and green and geranium red. Maine geraniums that thrive on cool damp air. But magenta yes. But orange and cobalt and chartreuse."

And someone in the small crowd called out, "Better red than dead."

And we all laughed. The remark had a resonance that seemed to travel on our voices, caroming off the facing walls of the space we shared. We stood and listened to our own laughter. And we all agreed together that the evening was done.

I was walking to my car when I saw the New York taxi. Someone was getting in and when the light came on I saw it was the same young woman who'd been driving.

"Hey thanks," I said. "Back there."

"You're the Lexus."

"Lost and wandering. Good thing you came along."

"We were saying I bet he thinks this is the Texas Highway Killer getting ready to claim another victim."

"I knew you weren't the Texas Highway Killer because this isn't Texas."

"Plus I doubt if he drives a yellow cab."

"That's the other reason."

"Here to help out?" she said.

"Wish I could. But I'm due back at the office tower in the great capital city."

"Could be your last chance to make art history."

"Or whatever it is you're doing here."

"Or whatever it is we're doing here."

She sat in the driver's seat with the door open, broad-bodied, not quite the levitated sylph she'd appeared to be in the bucking dust of that earlier moment.

"This your car?"

"I volunteered it more or less," she said, "so I guess I'm stuck with a taxi, which is slightly inconvenient. But to see the look on Klara's face I'd have to say yeah it was worth it."

Broad and open like a summer waitress who says *There you go* when she deposits the food in front of you.

"Been here long?"

"Going on seven weeks and I'm sticking it out if it takes forever, which it actually could."

"Not homesick?"

"Now and then. But this is a one-chance thing. You been out there yet?"

"In the morning," I said.

"Go early. The heat is mean."

"I know about heat. I like heat."

"Where you from?"

I didn't tell her I lived a quiet life in an unassuming house and so forth. Instead I told her where I was spending the night and I let her tell me how to get there although I already knew.

I let her tell me about her hometown.

I asked her about the work she did at the site and she said she applied a metal primer and sometimes she hand-scraped paint and sometimes she sanded with a machine.

She sat high in the seat, reciting details, and wagged her head, mock-girlish but also girlish.

I asked her about school and she said she'd dropped out several years earlier but was thinking of going back to get a degree in retailing and I let her tell me about it.

We talked about her brother, who had a rare blood disease.

I let her tell me about a white-water trip she took one summer when she was seventeen.

She said deteriated for deteriorated. When she said okay it sounded like okai.

She sat on a beaded cushion. Her hair was cut short, bulking out her face. I saw that the taxi's details and fittings, up close, and the paint job itself, had more amateurish charm than accuracy. But then it's not easy to get New York right.

"But here's the joke that's going round," she said. "Except no one seems sure it's a joke. We're painting these old planes as a celebration in a way but how do we know for sure the crisis is really over? Is the breakup of the USSR really happening? Or is the whole thing a plot to trick the West?"

She sounded out a laugh from her sinuses. It was oral and it was nasal and it came out harsh and moist, a curious noise designed to ridicule the idea while conceding its dark appeal.

"They're making it seem like they're falling apart so we'll lower our guard, okai?"

I let her tell me about it.

She made the noise again. A long wet whinnying letter *k*. And I found the more she talked, the more she owed me. But I didn't say a word. It was in my heart to speak, to make a breach in her self-absorption, in the solid stuff of her hometown and dying brother. I wanted to reduce these things to rubble. It was just a passing mood, a thing that erupts out of the formed core of one's middle-minded resolve.

I let her talk. And the more I listened and the more unappealing she became, the more I wanted to get inside her pants, for reasons no one comprehends under heaven.

But I didn't say word one. It was in my heart to talk her into spending the night in my room, or half the night, or an hour and ten minutes. I didn't know why I wanted her but I knew why I didn't want her. It would have been disloyal to Klara, to our shared memory, our own brief time in that small room back there in the narrow streets that were the borders of the world.

"Well, getting late," I said.

"Hey, big day tomorrow."

"Best," I said, "be on my way."

She told me again how to get there and then drove off. All the other vehicles had left the area and I went looking for my car in the dark.

It is interesting to think of the great blaze of heaven that we winnow down to animal shapes and kitchen tools.

I watched TV in my motel.

I lived responsibly in the real. I didn't accept this business of life as a fiction, or whatever Klara Sax had meant when she said that things had become unreal. History was not a matter of missing minutes on the tape. I did not stand helpless before it. I hewed to the texture of collected knowledge, took faith from the solid and availing stuff of our experience. Even if we believe that history is a workwheel powered by human blood—read the speeches of Mussolini—at least we've known the thing together. A single narrative sweep, not ten thousand wisps of disinformation.

A man sat in a contour chair in a living-room set with a coffee table in front of him and books or the covers of books arrayed on the wall behind.

I believed we could know what was happening to us. We were not excluded from our own lives. That is not my head on someone else's body in the photograph that's introduced as evidence. I didn't believe that nations play-act on a grand scale. I lived in the real. The only ghosts I let in were local ones, the smoky traces of people I knew and the dinge of my own somber shadow, New York ghosts in every case, the old loud Bronx, hand-to-mouth, spoken through broken teeth—the jeer, the raspberry fart.

The man in the chair said, "Down's syndrome. Your toll-free number is one, eight hundred, five one five, two seven six eight. Korsakoff's psychosis. One, eight hundred, three one three, seven five eight one. Alzheimer's disease. Call toll-free. One, eight hundred, eight one three, three five two seven." He said, "Kaposi's sarcoma. Twenty-four hours a day. One, eight hundred, six seven two, nine one six one."

∙ ∙ ∙

I drove out to the site at sunrise. I parked near an equipment shed and began to climb a small rise that would place me at a natural vantage in relation to the aircraft. I heard them before I saw them, an uneasy creaking, wind gusts spinning the movable parts. Then I reached the top of the sandstone ledge and there they were in broad formation across the bleached bottom of the world.

I didn't know there would be so many planes. I was astonished at the number of planes. They were arranged in eight staggered ranks with a few stray planes askew at the fringes. I counted every last plane as the sun came up. There were two hundred and thirty planes, swept-winged, finned like bottom creatures, some painted in part, some nearly completed, many not yet touched by the paint machines, and these last were gunship gray or wearing faded camouflage or sanded down to bare metal.

The painted aircraft took on sunlight and pulse. Sweeps of color, bands and spatters, airy washes, the force of saturated light—the whole thing oddly personal, a sense of one painter's hand moved by impulse and afterthought as much as by epic design. I hadn't expected to register such pleasure and sensation. The air was color-scrubbed, coppers and ochers burning off the metal skin of the aircraft to exchange with the framing desert. But these colors did not simply draw down power from the sky or lift it from the landforms around us. They pushed and pulled. They were in conflict with each other, to be read emotionally, skin pigments and industrial grays and a rampant red appearing repeatedly through the piece—the red of something released, a burst sac, all blood-pus thickness and runny underyellow. And the other planes, decolored, still wearing spooky fabric over the windscreen panels and engines, dead-souled, waiting to be primed.

Sometimes I see something so moving I know I'm not supposed to linger. See it and leave. If you stay too long, you wear out the wordless shock. Love it and trust it and leave.

She wanted us to see a single mass, not a collection of objects. She wanted our interest to be evenly spaced. She insisted that our eyes go

83

slowly over the piece. She invited us to see the land dimension, horizonwide, in which the work was set.

I listened to the turboblades rattle in the wind and felt the sirocco heat come blowing in and my eyes did in fact go slowly over the ranks and I felt a kind of wildness all around me, the grim vigor of weather and desert and those old weapons so forcefully rethought, the fittingness of what she'd done, but when I'd seen it all I knew I wouldn't stay an extra second.

Three vehicles moved toward the site, the day's first sturdy workers. I went down to my car and uncapped the tube of sunblock I'd spotted on a rack near the front desk in the mom-and-pop motel, next to the postcards and Indian dolls—the kachina dolls and snack packs of tortilla chips that are part of some curious neuron web of lonely-chrome America. I stood by the car and rubbed the lotion over my arms and face, pausing to read the label again. I'd been reading the label all morning. The label said the protection factor was thirty, not fifteen. I knew this subject well. I'd read up on this subject, seen the research studies, I'd compared the products and the claims. And I knew with total certainty that a protection factor of fifteen was the highest level of sunblock scientifically possible. Now they were selling me a thirty.

And it made me think of something strange. I got in the car and headed out toward the interstate. It made me think of the Teller story. The Teller story was about Dr. Edward Teller and the world's first atomic explosion, which occurred about two hundred miles northeast of my present position. And the story said how Dr. Teller feared the immediate effects of the blast at his viewing site twenty miles from zero point and how he decided it might be helpful to apply suntan lotion to his face and hands.

These thoughts, these flashes of light, that innocent winsome gesture, this Japanese car—all more or less appropriate to the landscape.

I hit the switch, lowering the windows, and saw mountains reared near Mexico, lyrical in themselves and beautifully named, whatever their names, because you can't name a mountain badly, and I looked for a sign that would point me home.

2

My mother was living with us at the time. We finally got my mother to come out from the East and we set her up in a cool room at the back of the house.

My wife was good with her. They knew how to talk to each other. They found things to talk about. They talked about the things I did not talk about with Marian, the things I shrugged off when Marian asked, early girlfriends maybe or how I got along with my brother. The small shrewd things Marian used to ask me. I broke my arm when I was eight, falling out of a tree. This is what they talked about.

From the shimmering bronze tower where I worked I used to gaze at the umber hills and ridges that defined the northeast view. Maybe it was a hundred and eight degrees out on the street. Maybe it was a hundred and ten, a hundred and twelve, and I looked out past the miscellaneous miles of squat box structures where you took your hearing aid to be fixed or shopped for pool supplies, the self-replicating stretch I traveled every day, and I told myself how much I liked this place with its downtown hush and its office towers separated by open space and its parks with jogging trails and its fairy ring of hills and its residential streets of oleanders and palms and tree trunks limed white—white against the sun.

We brought her out from the East. We took her out of the daily drama of violence and lament and tabloid atrocity and matching redemption and how the city is hard and how the city is mean and how the city is nice to a tourist from Missouri who leaves her handbag in a cab and we fixed her up in a cool room where she watched TV.

Marian wanted me to tell her about the old streets, the street games, the street fights, the alley sex, the petty theft. I told her about the car, not so petty, but she wanted to hear more. She wanted to hear about the execution now and then of some wayward member of whatever organized group she imagined might be operating thereabouts, the projectile entering the back of the head and making a pathway to the brain. She thought my mother's arrival might yield the basic savor she could not get from laconic Nick. But my mother only talked about the lazy grades I got in school and how I fell out of a tree when I was eight.

And I liked the way history did not run loose here. They segregated visible history. They caged it, funded and bronzed it, they enshrined it carefully in museums and plazas and memorial parks. The rest was geography, all space and light and shadow and unspeakable hanging heat.

I drank soy milk and ran the metric mile. I had a thing I clipped to the waistband of my running trunks, a device that weighed only three and a half ounces and had a readout showing distance traveled and calories burned and length of stride. I carried my house keys in an ankle wallet that fastened with a velcro closure. I didn't like to run with house keys jiggling in my pocket. The ankle wallet answered a need. It spoke directly to a personal concern. It made me feel there were people out there in the world of product development and merchandising and gift cataloguing who understood the nature of my little nagging needs.

They also talked about my father. That's the other thing they talked about in the deep lull after dinner. It's the kind of subject Marian seized on, trying to fill in gaps, work out details. I used to sit in the living room and listen fitfully through the urgent sexual throb of the dishwasher. I used to half listen, listen with my face in a magazine, hearing scumbled voices coming from the back room, a cluster of words audible now and then above the dishwasher and the TV set. The TV set was always on when my mother was in her room.

Travel was an important part of my job. Leaving the reflecting surfaces of the bronze tower, the way people modeled themselves on someone else, a few people, it's only natural, mostly mimicking up, repeating a superior's gestures or expressions. Think of a young man or woman, think of a young woman speaking a few words in a movie gangster's growl. This is something I used to do for pointed comic effect to get things done on time. I made breathy gutter threats from the side of my mouth and then I'd walk past an office a day or two later and hear one of my assistants speaking in this voice.

We fixed her up with a television set and a humidifier and the dresser that used to be Marian's when she was growing up. We emptied and cleaned the dresser and resilvered the mirror and put a plentiful supply of hangers in the closet.

Or I picked up the phone in the middle of a meeting and pretended to arrange the maiming of a colleague, a maneuver that drew snide laughter from the others in the room. I tried not to laugh a certain way myself, the way Arthur Blessing laughed, our chief executive, with articulated ha-has, a slow nod of the head marking the laugh beat. Going away, flying away freed me from the signals that bounced off every waxed and spanking surface.

He went out to get a pack of cigarettes and never came back. This is a thing you used to hear about disappearing men. It's the final family mystery. All the mysteries of the family reach their culmination in the final passion of abandonment. My father smoked Lucky Strikes. The pack has a design that could easily be called a target but then maybe not—there's no small central circle or bull's-eye. The circle is large. There's a large red circle with a white border and then a narrower tan border and finally a thin black border, so unless you expand the definition of a bull's-eye or the definition of a target, you probably can't call the Lucky Strike logotype a target. But I call it a target anyway and fuck the definitions.

Marian believed this is the crucial thing you have to consider when making a person feel at home. If you don't provide enough hangers, she will think she is not wanted.

87

My firm was involved in waste. We were waste handlers, waste traders, cosmologists of waste. I traveled to the coastal lowlands of Texas and watched men in moon suits bury drums of dangerous waste in subterranean salt beds many millions of years old, dried-out remnants of a Mesozoic ocean. It was a religious conviction in our business that these deposits of rock salt would not leak radiation. Waste is a religious thing. We entomb contaminated waste with a sense of reverence and dread. It is necessary to respect what we discard.

I saw a man on the via della Spiga standing in front of a mirrored column smoothing his hair, running both hands over his hair, and the way he did it, the cast of his eyes, the slightly pitted skin, both hands guiding the flow of his hair—this was half a second in Milan one day—reminded me of a thousand things at once, long ago.

The Jesuits taught me to examine things for second meanings and deeper connections. Were they thinking about waste? We were waste managers, waste giants, we processed universal waste. Waste has a solemn aura now, an aspect of untouchability. White containers of plutonium waste with yellow caution tags. Handle carefully. Even the lowest household trash is closely observed. People look at their garbage differently now, seeing every bottle and crushed carton in a planetary context.

My son used to believe that he could look at a plane in flight and make it explode in midair by simply thinking it. He believed, at thirteen, that the border between himself and the world was thin and porous enough to allow him to affect the course of events. An aircraft in flight was a provocation too strong to ignore. He'd watch a plane gaining altitude after taking off from Sky Harbor and he'd sense an element of catastrophe tacit in the very fact of a flying object filled with people. He was sensitive to the most incidental stimulus and he thought he could feel the object itself yearning to burst. All he had to do was wish the fiery image into his mind and the plane would ignite and shatter. His sister used to tell him, Go ahead, blow it up, let me see you take that plane out of the sky with all two hundred people aboard, and it scared him to hear someone talk this way and it scared her too because she wasn't completely convinced he could not do it. It's the special skill of an adolescent to imagine the end of the world as an adjunct to his own discontent. But Jeff got older and lost interest and conviction. He lost the paradoxical gift for being separate and alone and yet intimately connected, mind-wired to distant things.

At home we separated our waste into glass and cans and paper products. Then we did clear glass versus colored glass. Then we did tin versus aluminum. We did plastic containers, without caps or lids, on Tuesdays only. Then we did yard waste. Then we did newspapers including glossy inserts but were careful not to tie the bundles in twine, which is always the temptation.

The corporation is supposed to take us outside ourselves. We design these organized bodies to respond to the market, face foursquare into the world. But things tend to drift dimly inward. Gossip, rumor, promotions, personalities, it's only natural, isn't it—all the human lapses that take up space in the company soul. But the world persists, the world heals in a way. You feel the contact points around you, the caress of linked grids that give you a sense of order and command. It's there in the warbling banks of phones, in the fax machines and photocopiers and all the oceanic logic stored in your computer. Bemoan technology all you want. It expands your self-esteem and connects you in your well-pressed suit to the things that slip through the world otherwise unperceived.

Marian drove the car with a pencil in her hand. I don't think I ever asked her why. I don't think we talked the way we used to talk when the kids were growing up. What a richness of subject, two living things changing before our eyes, going from dumb clamor, from milk slop to formed words, or starting school, or just sitting at the table eating, little crayoned faces pumped with being. But they were grown people now with a computer after all, with rotating media shelves and a baby on the way and a bumper sticker (this was my son) that read *Going Nowhere Fast*. The days of the marriage were no longer filled with dialogues about Lainie and Jeff. We hung on the birth of the grandchild.

I ran along the drainage canal wearing a wireless headphone. I listened to Sufi chanting while I ran. I ran along the palm alleys and through the winding streets of orange trees and handsome stucco homes—streets of westward dreams, the kind of place my father could have taken us half a century earlier, lightward and westward, where people came to escape the hard-luck past with its gray streets and crowded flats and cabbage smells in the hallway.

Lainie was an entrepreneur, a hard driver, a bargainer, our huckster daughter, we called her, and she was living in Tucson with husband Dex. They made ethnic jewelry and sold it over a shopping channel, bracelets, chains, the works, and they did interviews and traveled to festivals and other cultural events. Her pregnancy gave us a lift and she sent photos of her changing shape and we drove down there often to see the booming body.

I rearranged the books on the shelves. I stood in the room looking at the books. Then I strapped my ankle wallet to my ankle and ran.

The larger she got, the happier we became. We never knew how happy we were supposed to be until we turned off Interstate 10 and followed the sweeping traffic on one of those mall arteries that resemble a marathon of headlong metal and found her little street and saw her posing in the doorway in stately profile.

I call the Lucky Strike logotype a target because I believe they were waiting for my father when he went out to buy a pack of cigarettes and they took him and put him in a car and drove him somewhere near the bay, where the river goes into the bay or where the lagoon lies silent in the dark and there are marshes and inlets, remote spits of land, and then they gave it to him good, the projectile entering the back of the head and making a pathway to the brain. And, besides, if it's not a target, why did they name the brand Lucky Strike? True, there's a gold-rush connotation. But a strike is not only the discovery of some precious metal in the ground. It is also a penetrating hit from a weapon. And isn't there a connection between the name of the brand and the design of concentric circles on the package? This implies they were thinking target all along.

3

We sat in the Stadium Club with our sour-mash whiskey and bloody meat, pretending to watch the game. I'd been to Los Angeles many times on business but had never made the jaunt to Dodger Stadium. Big Sims had to wrestle me into his car to get me here.

We were set apart from the field, glassed in at press level, and even with a table by the window we heard only muffled sounds from the crowd. The radio announcer's voice shot in clearly, transmitted from the booth, but the crowd remained at an eerie distance, soul-moaning like some lost battalion.

Brian Glassic said, "I hear they finally stopped ocean dumping off the East Coast."

"Not while I'm eating," I said.

"Tell him," Sims said. "Describe it in detail. Make him smell the smell."

"I also hear the more they dumped in a particular area, the richer the sea life."

Sims looked at the Englishwoman, who alone ate fish.

"Hear that?" he said. "The sea life thrived."

And Glassic said, "Let's eat fast and get out of here and go sit in the stands like real people."

And Sims said, "What for?"

"I need to hear the crowd."

"No, you don't."

"What's a ball game without crowd noise?"

"We're here to eat a meal and see a game," Sims said. "I took the trouble to book us a table by the window. You don't go to a ballpark to hear a game. You go to see a game. Can you see all right?"

Simeon Biggs, Big Sims, was famous in the firm for his midbody girth. He was fat, bald and fifty-five but also strong, with a neck and arms resembling rock maple. If he liked you enough he might trade chest thumps or invite you to race him around the block. Sims ran the operational end of our Los Angeles campus, as we called it, and designed landfills that were prettier than pastel malls.

Glassic looked at me and said, "We need video helmets and power gloves. Because this isn't reality. This is virtual reality. And we don't have the proper equipment."

Sims said, "We can't take our drinks with us if we go to our seats."

"That's a forceful point," I said.

The only time I ate the wrong food, just about, or drank too much, if ever, was when I was out with Sims, who was a living rebuke to the tactics of moderation.

The Englishwoman said, "Now as I understand it the pitcher gets a signal from the catcher. This pitch or that pitch. Fast or slow, up or down. But what happens if he ardently opposes the catcher's selection?"

"He shakes off the sign," Glassic said.

"Oh I see."

"He waggles his glove or shakes his head," Sims said. "Or he stares down the catcher."

The Englishwoman, Jane Farish, was a BBC producer who wanted to do a program about the salt domes we were testing for the storage of nuclear waste, under the direction of the Department of Energy. She'd been busy for some years devouring American culture, leaving the earth scorched with interviews, she said—porno kings, contemplative monks, blues singers in prison. She'd just finished a sweep of

California and was headed to a poker tournament in Reno and then into the desert to interview Klara Sax.

The Dodgers were playing the Giants.

Sims looked at Farish and said, "You know these two teams go way back. They were New York teams until the late fifties."

"They moved west, did they?"

"Moved west, taking Nick's heart and soul with them."

Farish looked at me.

"There was nothing left to take. I was already a nonfan by that time. Burnt out. This is my first ball game in decades."

"And it turns out to be silent," Glassic said.

Big Sims ordered another round and told Farish about the old Brooklyn Dodgers. Sims grew up in Missouri and he got some of it right, some of it wrong. No one could explain the Dodgers who wasn't there. The Englishwoman didn't mind. She was absorbing things chemically, sometimes shutting her eyes to concentrate the process.

"Nick used to take his radio up to the roof," Glassic said.

Farish spun in my direction.

"I had a portable radio I took everywhere. The beach, the movies— I went, it went. I was sixteen. And I listened to Dodger games on the roof. I liked to be alone. They were my team. I was the only Dodger fan in the neighborhood. I died inside when they lost. And it was important to die alone. Other people interfered. I had to listen alone. And then the radio told me whether I would live or die."

It isn't easy to be smart about baseball if you didn't grow up with the game but Farish asked decent enough questions. It was the answers that came hard. We must have resembled three mathematicians so lost in their highly refined work that they haven't noticed how quaint and opaque the terminology is, how double-meaning'd. We argued the language and tried to unravel it for the outsider.

"Does anyone want wine?" Farish said. "I wouldn't mind trying a local white."

"Wine is a copout," Sims told her. "We clean toilets for a living."

Glassic pointed out that an inning was an inning if we were speaking from the viewpoint of a pitcher getting three outs but it was only half an inning in the broader scheme of a nine-inning game with top halves and home halves. And the same half inning is also two-thirds of an inning if the pitcher is lifted with one out remaining.

I asked the waiter to get a glass of wine for our guest. Glassic returned to the paradox of the innings but Big Sims waved him off.

"Let's go back to the Dodgers," he said. "We left the kid on the roof with his radio."

"Let's not," I said.

"You have to tell Jane what ended your career as a die-hard rooter."

"I don't remember."

"Killed you so dead you never went back."

"These are local afflictions. They don't travel."

"Tell her," Sims said, "about the Bobby Thomson homer."

Farish looked politely hopeful. She wanted someone to tell her something that made sense. So Sims told her about Thomson and Branca and how people still said to each other, more than forty years later, Where were you when Thomson hit the homer? He told her how some of us had stopped the moment and kept it faithfully shaped and how Sims himself had gone running in the streets, a black kid who didn't even root for the Giants—heard the game on good old KMOX and ran out of the house shouting, *I'm Bobby Thomson, I'm Bobby Thomson.* And he told Farish how people claimed to have been present at the game who were not and how some of them honestly insisted they were there because the event had sufficient seeping power to make them think they had to be at the Polo Grounds that day or else how did they feel the thing so strongly in their skin.

"You're not saying like Kennedy. Where were you when Kennedy was shot?"

Glassic said, "When JFK was shot, people went inside. We watched TV in dark rooms and talked on the phone with friends and relatives. We were all separate and alone. But when Thomson hit the homer, people rushed outside. People wanted to be together. Maybe it was the last time people spontaneously went out of their houses for something. Some wonder, some amazement. Like a footnote to the end of the war. I don't know."

"I don't know either," Sims said.

Farish looked at me.

"Don't look at me," I said.

"But you were on the roof, were you, when the blow was struck?"

"I didn't have to rush outside. I was already outside. I rushed inside. I closed the door and died."

"You were anticipating Kennedy," Farish said, and got a little laugh.

"The next day I think it was I began to see all sorts of signs pointing to the number thirteen. Bad luck everywhere. I became a budding numerologist. I got pencil and paper and wrote down all the occult connections that seemed to lead to thirteen. I wish I could remember them. I remember one. It was the date of the game. October third or ten-three. Add the month and day and you get thirteen."

"And Branca's number," Sims said.

"Of course. Branca wore thirteen."

"They called it the Shot Heard Round the World," Sims told Farish.

"A little bit of American bluster?"

"But what the hell," Sims said.

Glassic was looking at me in a strange way, almost tenderly, the way someone regards a friend who is too dumb to know he is about to be exposed.

"Tell them about the baseball," Glassic said.

He reached across the table and took some food from Sims' plate.

Glassic was supposed to be my pal. I'd known Sims and Glassic a long time and Glassic, freckled free-style Brian, a man of shambling charm, was the guy I talked to when I talked about something. I talked to Big Sims but maybe I talked to Glassic more readily because he did not challenge me with his own experience, he did not narrow his eyes as Sims did and fix me in his gaze.

"Let's change the subject," I told him.

"No. I want you to speak about this. You owe it to Sims. It's a crime that Sims does not know this. He's the only one here who still loves the game." Glassic turned to the Englishwoman. "I go to ball games when I go at all for the sake of keeping up. It's a fall from grace if you don't keep up. Nick has fallen from grace. Only Sims is completely, miserably in touch. We had the real Dodgers and Giants. Now we have the holograms."

Farish said, "What baseball?"

95

Sims was looking at me. He was finished with his food and was untubing a panatela, a simple exercise that he surrounded with detailed ceremony.

Glassic gave me a final melting look and turned to Sims.

"Nick owns the baseball. The Bobby Thomson home-run ball. The actual object."

Sims took his time lighting the cigar.

"Nobody owns the ball."

"Somebody has to own it."

"The ball is unaccounted for," Sims said. "It got thrown away decades ago. Otherwise we'd know it."

"Simeon, listen before you make pronouncements. First," Glassic said, "I found a dealer on a trip I took back east some years ago. This guy convinced me that the baseball in his possession, the ball he claimed was the Thomson home run, was in fact the authentic ball."

"Nobody has the ball," Sims said. "The ball never turned up. Whoever once had the ball, it never surfaced. This is part of the whole— what? The mythology of the game. Nobody ever showed up and made a verifiable claim to this is the ball. Or a dozen people showed up, each with a ball, which amounts to the same thing."

"Second, the dealer told me how he'd traced the baseball almost all the way back to October third, nineteen fifty-one. This is not some fellow who turns up at baseball shows looking for bargains. This is pathological obsession. A completely committed guy. And he convinced me to a probability of ninety-nine and nine-tenths percent that this is the baseball. And then he convinced Nick. And Nick asked how much. And they worked out a deal."

"You got rooked," Sims told me.

I watched the Dodger shortstop field a grounder and make a wide throw to first.

Glassic said, "The guy spent many years tracing the thing. He probably spent more money in phone calls, postage and travel miles, I'm exaggerating, than Nick paid for the baseball."

Sims had a derisive smile, a fleer, and it grew meaner by the second.

"Whole thing's phony," he told me. "If that was the authentic ball, how could you afford to buy it?"

"I will count the ways," Glassic said. "First, the dealer wasn't able to provide absolute final documentation. That cut the price. Second, this was before the market boom in memorabilia and the auctions at Sotheby's and the four hundred thousand dollars that somebody paid for an itty-bitty baseball card."

"I don't know," Sims said.

"I don't know either," I said.

Farish finally got her wine. She looked at me and said, "How much did you pay?"

"My shame is deep enough. Let's not examine the details."

"What shame?"

"Well, I didn't buy the object for the glory and drama attached to it. It's not about Thomson hitting the homer. It's about Branca making the pitch. It's all about losing."

"Bad luck," Glassic said, spearing a potato on my plate.

"It's about the mystery of bad luck, the mystery of loss. I don't know. I keep saying I don't know and I don't. But it's the only thing in my life that I absolutely had to own."

"A shameful secret?" Farish said.

"Yes. First to spend serious money on a souvenir baseball. Then to buy it for the reason I bought it. To commemorate failure. To have that moment in my hand when Branca turned and watched the ball go into the stands—from him to me."

Everyone laughed but Sims.

Glassic said, "Even his name. Somber Ralph Branca. Like a figure out of an old epic. Somber plodding Ralph slain in something something dusk."

"Dark-arrowed," said the woman.

"Very good. Except it's not a joke of course. What's it like to have to live with one awful moment?"

"A moment in a game," she said.

"Forever plodding across the outfield grass on your way to the clubhouse."

Sims was getting mad at us.

"I don't think you fellows see the point." The way he said fellows. "What loss? What failure are we talking about? Didn't they all go

97

home happy in the end? I mean Branca—Branca's got the number thirteen on his license plate. He wants us to know he was the guy. Branca and Thomson appear at sports dinners all the time. They sing songs and tell jokes. They're the longest-running act in show business. You fellows miss the point." Making us sound like scrubbed boys in preppy jackets. "Branca's a hero. I mean Branca was given every chance to survive this game and we all know why."

A little pall fell across the table.

"Because he's white," Sims said. "Because the whole thing is white. Because you can survive and endure and prosper if they let you. But you have to be white before they let you."

Glassic shifted in his chair.

Sims told the story of a pitcher named Donnie Moore who gave up a crucial home run in a play-off game and ended up shooting his wife. Donnie Moore was black and the player who hit the home run was black. And then he shot and killed himself. He shot his wife several times, nonfatally, and then shot himself. He took a dirt nap in his own laundry room, Sims said. Sims told this story to the Englishwoman but it was completely new to me and I could tell that Glassic barely remembered. I'd never heard of Donnie Moore and missed the home run and didn't know about the shootings. Sims said the shootings came a few years after the home run but were directly traceable. Donnie Moore was not allowed to outlive his failure. The fans gave him every grief and there weren't any skits at the baseball dinners.

Sims knew a lot about the shootings. He described the shooting of the wife in some detail.

Farish shut her eyes to see it better.

"We hear what you're saying," Glassic said. "But you can't compare the two events on the basis of color."

"What else is there?"

"The Thomson homer continues to live because it happened decades ago when things were not replayed and worn out and run down and used up before midnight of the first day. The scratchier an old film or an old audiotape, the clearer the action in a way. Because it's not in competition for our attention with a thousand other pieces of action. Because it's something that's preserved and unique. Donnie

Moore—well I'm sorry but how do we distinguish Donnie Moore from all the other ball games and all the other shootings?"

"The point is not what we notice or what we remember but what happened," Sims said, "to the parties involved. We're talking about who lived and who died."

"But not why," Glassic said. "Because if we analyze the reasons honestly and thoroughly instead of shallow and facile and what else?"

"Unhistorical," I said.

"Then we realize there were probably a dozen reasons why the guy started shooting and most of them we'll never know or understand."

Sims called us fellows again. I switched sides several times and we ordered another round of drinks and went at it some more. We were not talking to Jane Farish now. We didn't notice her reactions or encourage her interest. Sims called us fellows many times and then he called us chaps. It began to get a little funny. We ordered coffee and watched the game and Farish sat in a thoughtful knot, arms and legs crossed, body twisted toward the window, yielding to the power of our differences.

"Buying and selling baseballs. What heartache. And you never told me," Sims said.

"It was some time ago."

"I would have talked you out of it."

"So you could buy it yourself," Glassic said.

"I deal in other kinds of waste. The real stuff of the world. Give me disposable diapers by the ton. Not this melancholy junk from yesteryear."

"I don't know," I said again.

"What do you do, take the ball out of the closet and look at it? Then what?"

"He thinks about what it means," Glassic said. "It's an object with a history. He thinks about losing. He wonders what it is that brings bad luck to one person and the sweetest of good fortune to another. It's a lovely thing in itself besides. An old baseball? It's a lovely thing, Sims. And this one's got a pedigree like no other."

"He got taken big-time," Sims said. "He's holding a worthless object."

99

We paid the bill and started filing out. Sims pointed to a photograph over the bar, one of dozens of sporting shots. It was a recent photo of a couple of gray-haired ex-players, Thomson and Branca, dark-suited and looking fit, standing on the White House lawn with President Bush between them, holding an aluminum bat.

We went out and sat in the company box for ten minutes so Glassic could hear the crowd noise. Then we walked down the ramp and headed for the parking area. Farish had some questions about the infield fly rule. Sims and Glassic were able to get together on this by the time we got out to the car. It was an unexpected boon for the BBC.

I sat in back and looked at the city flowing past and I thought of Sims the kid running down a street in St. Louis. He's wearing dungarees with the lower legs rolled into bunchy cuffs that are paler than the dark denim twill of the outer cloth. He's waving his arms and shouting that he's Bobby Thomson.

4

I sat with my mother in her room and we talked and paused and watched TV. We paused to remember. One of us said something that roused a memory and we sat together thinking back.

My mother had a method of documentary recall. She brought forth names and events and let them hang in the air without attaching pleasure or regret. Sometimes just a word. She spoke a word or phrase that referred to something I hadn't thought about in decades. She was confident in her recall, moving through the past with a sureness she could not manage to apply to the current moment or hour or day of the week. She made fun of herself. What day is it? Do I go to mass today or tomorrow? I drove her to mass and picked her up. This was the steadiest satisfaction of my week. I learned the mass schedule and the types of mass and the length of service and I made sure she had money for the basket. We sat in the room and talked. She seemed untouched by sentiment. She'd summon a moment that struck me with enormous force, any moment, something ordinary but bearing power with it— ordinary only if you haven't lived it, if you weren't there—and I saw how still she sat, how prudent she was in her recollecting.

I used to tell my kids when they were small. A hawser is a rope that's used to moor a ship. Or, The hump in the floor between rooms, I used to say. This is called the saddle.

We set her up with the dresser and the air conditioner and a hard mattress that was good for her back. She brought forth names from the family passional, the book of special suffering, and we paused and thought. Her hair was still partly brown in places, gone wiry and iridescent, goldshot in bright light, bobby-pinned, and we sat there with the TV going. I knew she would not say too much or remember carelessly. She was in control here, guiding us safely through the pauses.

After the riots in Los Angeles my son started wearing baggy shorts and a cap turned backwards and sneakers with bloated tongues. Before this he used to be nondescript, sitting in his room with his computer, a quiet kid just turned twenty. He dressed the same way all the time. He dressed for a job interview the way you'd dress to walk your dog—it was one continuous thing to him.

We designed and managed landfills. We were waste brokers. We arranged shipments of hazardous waste across the oceans of the world. We were the Church Fathers of waste in all its transmutations. I almost mentioned my line of work to Klara Sax when we had our talk in the desert. Her own career had been marked at times by her methods of transforming and absorbing junk. But something made me wary. I didn't want her to think I was implying some affinity of effort and perspective.

Famous people don't want to be told that you have a quality in common with them. It makes them think there's something crawling in their clothes.

My father's name was James Costanza, Jimmy Costanza—add the letters and you get thirteen.

At home we removed the wax paper from cereal boxes. We had a recycling closet with separate bins for newspapers, cans and jars. We rinsed out the used cans and empty bottles and put them in their proper bins. We did tin versus aluminum. On pickup days we placed each form of trash in its separate receptacle and put the receptacles, from the Latin verb that means receive again, out on the sidewalk in front of the house. We used a paper bag for the paper bags. We took a large paper bag and put all the smaller bags inside and then placed the large bag alongside all the other receptacles on the sidewalk. We ripped the wax paper from our boxes of shredded wheat. There is no language I might formulate that could overstate the diligence we brought to these tasks. We did the yard waste. We bundled the newspapers but did not tie them in twine.

Sometimes we used the pauses to watch TV. We looked at reruns of "The Honeymooners" and my mother laughed when Ralph Kramden flung his arms and bellowed great complaints. It was about the only time I could expect to hear her laugh. She must have felt a certain clean release, looking at the sadly furnished apartment, at wife Alice in her apron or dowdy cloth coat, at Norton the neighbor with a bent fedora on his jerky head—things that were close to what she knew. Superficially of course. Close to what she knew in an apparent rather than actual way. A closeness that was shallow but still a bit touching and maybe even mysteriously real. Look at the picture on the screen, flat and gray and staticky with years, not unlike memories she carried to her sleep. She slept in a room in Arizona and how strange this must have seemed to her. But Jackie Gleason on the screen made the place more plausible—he drew her toward a perceptible center.

A hawser is the thing you tie around a bollard.

I noticed how people played at being executives while actually holding executive positions. Did I do this myself? You maintain a shifting distance between yourself and your job. There's a self-conscious space, a sense of formal play that is a sort of arrested panic, and maybe you show it in a forced gesture or a ritual clearing of the throat. Something out of childhood whistles through this space, a sense of games and half-made selves, but it's not that you're pretending to be someone else. You're pretending to be exactly who you are. That's the curious thing.

Marian wanted to know me at seventeen, see me at seventeen, and there were small shrewd things she asked about, and they talked about my father and I listened, in the deep lull after dinner. My mother said things I already knew but I listened from the living room with a magazine in my face. He was a bookmaker famous for his memory, never wrote a number on a piece of paper. This was the legend of the street. I was eleven years old when he walked out the door and I heard the story later, that he remembered everything, made his rounds of the barbershops and sweatshops, downtown, in the garment district, the street corners, the hotel lobbies, strictly small-time, and that he never had to commit a figure to paper because he was able to retain the details of every bet. This is the story that settled around his name. It was part of the awe that trails a violent death or an unexplained disappearance.

She posed in the doorway in stately profile and we turned off Interstate 10 and entered one of those death marathons of mall traffic and finally found their little street and there she was, pregnant to beat the band.

My mother said things to Marian, a story now and then in her Bronxy half brogue, and I sat and listened fitfully behind the body-throb of the dishwasher. We gave her room a coat of fresh green paint, Lainie's old room, pale and restful. We fixed her up with the TV set and the resilvered mirror and the good hard healthy bed and we laid in a case of flavored seltzer—lemon-lime, I think.

In my office in the bronze tower I made gangster threats that were comically effective. I said to a consultant who was late with a report, "I'm telling you once and for all that I, me, Mario Badalato, I'll sever your fucking family's head off." This in a scraped-raw voice faithful to the genre and evilly appreciated by the others in the room.

In Holland I went to VAM, a waste treatment plant that handles a million tons of garbage a year. I sat in a white Fiat and went past windrows of refuse heaped many stories high. Down one towering row and around to another, waves of steam rising from the tapered heaps, and there was a stink in the air that filled my mouth, that felt deep enough to singe my clothes. Why did I think I was born with this experience in my brain? Why was it personal? I thought, Why do bad smells seem to tell us something about ourselves? The company manager drove me up and down the steaming rows and I thought, Every bad smell is about us. We make our way through the world and come upon a scene that is medieval-modern, a city of high-rise garbage, the hell reek of every perishable object ever thrown together, and it seems like something we've been carrying all our lives.

He was the kind of person you'd have trouble describing if you saw him in the commission of a crime. But after the riots he put on an L.A. Raiders hat and an ultralong T-shirt that had a pair of sunglasses slung from the pocket. Nothing else changed. He lived in his room, disappearing into chips and discs, the same shy boy but physically vivid now, a social being with a ghetto strut.

We sat in the room watching reruns, my mother and I. He left her for a time before I was born. This is why I carry her name, not his. She didn't think he'd ever come back and she told me she saw a lawyer, who did some finagling. The courts tend to rule that a child must retain his father's name until he reaches legal age, at which time he can choose for himself. But the lawyer finagled an exception out of some judge and this is why my birth certificate says Shay. Then he came back and stayed a long time before he went out for cigarettes, ten years or so. He was a man from nowhere, she said, slightly resigned, as if this was all she could expect fate to offer us—her and me and my brother—or maybe I misread the tone and she meant this is where he came from and this is where he went, inescapably, given the rhyming slang of life.

Coming home, landing at Sky Harbor, I used to wonder how people disperse so quickly from airports, any airport—how you are crowded into seats three across or five across and crowded in the aisle after touchdown when the captain turns off the seat belt sign and you get your belongings from the overhead and stand in the aisle waiting for the hatch to open and the crowd to shuffle forward, and there are more crowds when you exit the gate, people disembarking and others waiting for them and greater crowds in the baggage areas and the concourse, the crossover roars of echoing voices and flight announcements and revving engines and crowds moving through it all, people with their separate and unique belongings, the microhistory of toilet articles and intimate garments, the medicines and aspirins and lotions and powders and gels, so incredibly many people intersecting on some hot dry day at the edge of the desert, used underwear fistballed in their bags, and I wondered where they were going, and why, and who are they, and how do they all disperse so quickly and mysteriously, how does a vast crowd scatter and vanish in minutes, bags dragging on the shiny floors.

I used to say to the kids. I used to hold up an object and say, The little ridged section at the bottom of the toothpaste tube. This is called the crimp.

Gleason dead but also in the room with us, Irish like her and camped in a stale sweatbox, dressed in a busman's suit, arm-waving, flailingly fat, the only person who could make her laugh. He stalked across the floor pumping his fist. *You're goin' to the moon, Alice.* My mother liked the familiar things best. The more often he used a line, the more she laughed. She waited for certain lines. We both waited and he never let us down. We felt more closely bound with Gleason in the room. He gave us the line, gave us the sure laugh, the one we needed at the end of the day. Gleason aggrieved. Pounding the table-top and bending his knees and tilting the great head skyward. He was the joke that carried a missing history—the fat joke, the dumb joke, the joke about the rabbi and the priest, the honeymoon joke, the dialect joke, the punch line that survives long after the joke is forgotten. We felt better with Jackie in the room, transparent in his pain, alive and dead in Arizona.

I dropped her off and picked her up and made sure she had money for the basket.

We built pyramids of waste above and below the earth. The more hazardous the waste, the deeper we tried to sink it. The word pluto-nium comes from Pluto, god of the dead and ruler of the underworld. They took him out to the marshes and wasted him as we say today, or used to say until it got changed to something else.

I liked to hurry home from the airport and get into my trunks and T-shirt. I ran along the drainage canal with Sufi voices tracking through my head and sometimes I saw a plane taking off, all light and climb and calculus, and I thought of my son Jeffrey when he was younger—the gift he thought he possessed to take an aircraft out of the sky, the mastery of space and matter, a power and control that rose damnably from the curse of unbelonging.

And sometimes I sat with her through the mass, the mass in English, what a stark thing it was, without murmur or reverberation, but still the best part of my week, and I took her arm and led her out of the church and she was not a small woman but seemed to be dwindling, passing episodically out of flesh—she felt like rice paper under my hand.

He used to shave with a towel draped over his shoulder, wearing his undershirt, his singlet, and the blade made a noise I liked to listen to, a sandpaper scrape on his heavy beard, and the brush in the shaving cup, the Gem blade and the draped towel and the hot water from the tap—heat and skill and cutting edge.

Dominus vobiscum, the priest used to say, and we'd push our way out of the vestibule, several kids chanting, Dominick go frisk 'em. What was Latin for if you couldn't reduce the formal codes to the jostled argot of the street?

It was science-fiction stuff or horror-movie stuff except that Jeff was too shy and frightened to test it in the world, even with his sister whistling in his ear to make the thing explode.

5

Brian Glassic called late sometimes. He called in streaks, late at night, four calls in one weekend maybe, and what did he talk about when he called? The office, of course, bringing up matters he could not easily discuss in the tower itself, or the latest national scandal maybe, with anatomical details, or he'd carry on about a movie he wanted me to rent, guns and drugs—he thought it made us better buddies.

He also did it as a provocation. Brian believed I was safely encased, solid, with a house and family folded around me, surer than he was, older but also physically superior, physically fit, a man of hardier stuff, this was his own stated theme—a man who keeps his counsel. And it greatly fazed him, it made him want to chip away, make boyish forays, place claims on my attention.

When the phone rang at a certain hour, Marian and I exchanged the Brian look—had to be him.

"You will not believe where I am. Get over here right away. This place is astonishing. You're the only person I can bear to share it with. Come alone," he said.

It took me a while to find the place. I kept crossing I-10, out where the map begins to go white, low stucco buildings with satellite dishes—tractor parts and diesel tune-ups, sand and rock and self-defense. Then I spotted a cluster of shops that matched Brian's description, a neat clean minimall, painted sort of rancho pink and green, three of the outlets not yet open for business, and I parked near the last shop on the left, the only going concern, called Condomology.

College kids, gently unkempt. They stood between the shelves talking and browsing, going through the catalogs and reading the small print on the product boxes, and others mixed in, slightly older men and women, they had professions and soft slacks with knife pleats and a certain ease of bearing and belonging, the package of attitudes and values known as lifestyle.

Brian pushed me into a corner so I could scan the area. Wide aisles, the carpeting was soft and pale and the aisles were wide and there were wall paintings, five panels on each of the two long walls showing scenes of an ice-cream parlor of the nineteen-forties and -fifties. A soda jerk behind a marble counter making a strawberry float for a couple of girls in school jerseys and bobby socks—that was one mural, flat-painted, painted in a style not current to the scene, and the effect was interesting, completely undreamy. Brian was studying my lower jaw for some reaction. I heard music in the deep distance, a crooner doing lost songs, the kind of ballad that sometimes included a verse or two in slurred Italian, and it was all nicely subdued, I thought, unaffected, without patronizing humor.

Brian whispered at me sharply, as if I hadn't noticed.

"*Condoms.*"

That's what it was all right, condoms, the whole place was condoms, shelves filled with a hundred kinds of protection, male and female, spermicides, body butter, latex gloves, silicone lubricants, with books, manuals, videos, special displays, with novelty items of the big-dick little-dick type, and T-shirts of course, and baseball caps with condom logos.

"And the place is strategically located, out at the new frontier," he said. "I can see a satellite city growing out from this one shop, a thousand buildings, this is my vision, sort of spoked around the condom outlet. Like some medieval town with the castle smack at the center."

"They built their castles on the periphery."

"Fuck you. Show some amazement. They have peach-flavored rubbers. And kids come here to socialize, to hang around and see what's doing. I'm waiting to hear Al Hibbler sing 'Unchained Melody.' "

"Al Hibbler was good."

"Good? Fuck you good. He was amazing. You think Ray Charles is blind? Al Hibbler, *that* was blind. Show some response."

He led me down an aisle. My response was, Look at all these condoms. Studded, snug, ribbed, bareback. We used to say, Don't go in bareback. Meaning wear a rubber or you'll knock her up. Now there were rubbers called barebacks, electronically tested for sheerness and sensitivity.

"These will replace running shoes," Brian said. "Kids will shoot each other for expensive lambskin condoms."

There were loose condoms sold in bowls, in candy jars—grab a handful. A woman looked at a display model of a polyurethane sheath with flexible rings at either end. Brian knew her from the automated teller machine at his bank—hello, how are you, hi, hello. There were finger condoms and full-body condoms, oral condoms with a minty savor. There were condom cases, pocket-sized, and a condom you could wear as a hat.

Brian said, "My brother carried a rubber in his wallet all through adolescence. He showed it to me once, I think I was twelve. Flipped open his wallet and showed me this little wizened thing like a deflated penis and I don't think I ever recovered. This was a world I wasn't ready to enter. I could understand sex on the animal level. This was something else entirely. Something about the material, the plasticky sort of rubber, the look and touch, he made me touch it, and the whole nature and function of the thing, I don't know, it was alien and unsettling. Sex alone was tough enough to encounter. This was technology they wanted to wrap around my dick. This was mass-produced latex they used to paint battleships."

"You were a sensitive boy."

"I was scrawny and mute, barely human. You were a strapping kid who beat the crap out of kids like me."

"We didn't have any kids like you," I told him.

110

"You carried a rubber?"

"In the little slit pocket in my dungarees."

"By the time I was sixteen they weren't doing that anymore."

"They're doing it now," I said.

"I don't think my brother ever used the condom in his wallet. When he got a car he put it in the car. He put it in the glove compartment. That's when I think he finally got to use it."

A man was singing softly along, crooning the lyrics on the sound system. He moved haltingly toward us, pushing a cylinder of oxygen on wheels, a gray-haired guy, with tubes from the tank running all the way up into his nose. The tank was the size of a dachshund in a custom case. And he sang, he crooned in a rasping voice—he had the phrasing, the timing just right, the lazy line endings, some insipid lyric about a farewell letter, only altered in his gnawed voice to a life's own shape, felt in the deepest skin.

We moved out of the way to let him pass.

Behind the products and their uses we glimpsed the industry of vivid description. Dermasilk and astroglide and reservoir-tipped. There were condoms packaged as Roman coins and condoms in matchbook folders. Brian read aloud from the copy on the boxes. We had natural animal membranes and bubblegum scenting. We had condoms that glowed in the dark and foreplay condoms and condoms marked with graffiti that stretched to your erection, a letter becoming a word, a word that expands to a phrase. He did a little Churchill—*We shall wear them on the beaches*. We had lollipop condoms, we had boxer shorts printed with cartoon characters shaped like condoms standing on end, sort of floaty and nipple-headed, who spoke a language called Spermian.

A young woman stood near the door, a Ramses logo tattooed on her earlobe.

"My kid's got one of those," Brian said. "Only it says Pepsi. Should I be grateful?"

"Which kid?"

"Which kid. What's the difference?"

Brian was wary of his family. He adopted the put-upon pose of the father complaining routinely about kids who are careless with money and forgetful of every caution, we all have this act we perform, it amounts to a second language, the dad's easy-to-master lament, and Brian did scornful solos of high animation, but he also harbored something deeper and sadder, a sense that these were his enemies, forces loose in his own house prepared to drain him of self-worth, a stepdaughter, a daughter and a son, all in high school, and a wife, he said, who was a couple of bubbles off center.

"That's not the only thing she's got planted on her body."

"Which kid?" I said.

"Brittany."

"I like Brittany. Be nice to her."

"Be nice to her. Listen to this, she wears an armband, you won't believe this—they had Apartheid Simulation Day at her school."

"What's that?"

"What it says. They attempt to simulate the culture of apartheid. A lesson for the kids. They all wore armbands. You wore gold if you were the oppressed class and I think red if you were the military and green if you were the elite. Brittany volunteered for the oppressed class and now she won't take her armband off. The official simulation lasted one day but she's been doing this for weeks now. Nobody else is doing this but her. She restricts her access to the lunchroom, ten minutes a day. She only rides certain buses at certain times. She sits in a specified area of the classroom."

"How do the other kids react?"

"She gets spat upon and shunned."

He made a TV screen with his hands, thumbs horizontal, index fingers upright, and he looked out at me from inside the frame, eyes crossed, tongue lolling in his head.

We took a final turn around the room. A boy and girl in one of the murals sat in a booth with ice-cream sundaes and frosty glasses of water and long-handled spoons for the sundaes and the scene was not contrived to be charming but was close to documentary in tone and the whole place was a little museumlike, I thought, with time compressed and objects arrayed of evolutionary interest. And a woman sang a ballad about a chapel in the moonlight, vaguely familiar to me, and I turned to see if the man with the oxygen tank was still singing along.

Brian bought a package of condoms to give to his son David, a buddy-buddy thing, a token of communication and accord. We went outside and stood in the empty plaza and he opened the box and removed a single sheath in its foil wrap. He looked at it. He had a sputter-laugh he saved for certain occasions, like a semidrowned man bitter about being rescued, and he looked at the thing and laughed.

"Everybody talked about VD then. The clap was a term with a very decisive ring to it. The clap."

"The siff."

"All those terms, one worse than the other. But I couldn't detect a saving element in a condom. Maybe because it brought to mind another term."

"Scumbag."

"And in my little retard sort of twelve-year-old brain, maybe I sensed a secret life in this object in my brother's wallet, this scumbag—how could a thing called a scumbag be safe to use?"

"We're waste managers," I told him. "Scumbags are things we deal with."

"But think of the contempt we invest in this word. It's an ugly word. Full of self-loathing."

"Never mind the words. You bought a rubber for your kid because it's important for him to use it. I hate to be sensible. I know it's thankless to be sensible in the face of someone's primitive distrust."

"You're right."

"People have to use these things."

"You're right," he said. "It's thankless."

He unwrapped the condom and shook it out until the nipple end swung lightly in the breeze. Then he crumpled the thing in his fist and held it to his nose.

He said, "What does it smell like? Is it shower curtains? Is it car upholstery or lampshade liner? Is it those big blocky garment bags where you store the clothes you never wear?"

He was inhaling deeply, trying to absorb the odor, retain it fully so he might mark its nature. His lean head flared, red-roostered. He thought it might be the smell of the bubble wrap around your new computer when you take it out of the shipping container. Or the shipping container itself. Or the computer itself. Or the plastic baggies that have been in your freezer too long, collecting Freon fumes. He thought it might be a hospital smell, a laboratory smell, a discharge from a chemical plant. He couldn't place it exactly. The insulation in your walls. The filter in your air conditioner.

"I thought they were odor-free. Modern condoms," I said. "Except when flavor is added."

"That's the new type that's odor-free. I bought him the old cheap latex that binds the sex member and reduces the sensation and smells bad. Because I want him to pay a price for being sensible."

Marian sat in Jeff's room watching a movie on TV. I had to adjust to the sight of someone else in his room. His room was his animal den, his pelt and smell, and I thought she was committing some breach of species, sitting in there.

She wore beat-up jeans and an old tank top that drooped in front, the kind of woman who grows into her beauty, I think, who becomes beautiful over time and then one day you see it, sort of suddenly and all together—it becomes a local scandal of surprise and comment.

"When did you start smoking again?"

"Shut up," she said.

I told her about Condomology. I stood in the doorway and talked above the noise from the movie. She was fine-skinned, assertive in a way that was all featural—slightly angular of face, straight-nosed, dark-haired, no-nonsense-looking, very near classical in an American way, a certain sort of old-fashioned way that doesn't stray drastically from plainness, like the face cut in raised relief on the old soap bar, maybe it was Camay, I'm not sure, the woman's head in profile, with marcelled hair, although Marian's was straight.

"Where's Jeff?"

"Went out. I'm watching this."

I told her about Apartheid Simulation Day, standing in the doorway. She said, "I'm watching this."

"Want something? I want something."

"Mineral water be nice," she said.

I went to the kitchen and got all the things out of all the compartments. I poured the mineral water over ice in a tall glass and dropped a wedge of lemon in. Got the potato vodka from the freezer, smoky cold, and remembered what it was I wanted to say to her. I cut a lune of lemon skin and dropped it in a port glass.

I wanted to say something about Brian.

I'd tried drinking port for a while just to see how it would feel, how it would sound, a port glass, a fortified wine, and now I used the port glass for my vodka, pouring it syrupy cold and opal.

I heard the dialogue from the movie at the other end of the house.

Her skin was Camay-pure and her hair was dark and straight and she usually wore it short because short was easy. Her voice was shaped, it was deep and toned, sort of vowel round and erotic, particularly over the phone or in the bedroom dark, with brandy static in it or just the slightest throaty thing of night desire.

She used to sing in a church choir in her Big Ten town, she liked to call it, but quit over some belittlement, some perceived slight—how she would hate to hear me say perceived.

I handed her the mineral water and she said something about Brian. I thought she might be trying to preempt my own Brian remark. She'd felt it coming in the routine reading of signals in the marriage sensurround.

"Did he recommend another movie where everybody ends up in a storm sewer shooting each other?"

"This is how Brian relieves the pressure of being Brian."

I remembered a party where she stuck herself in a corner of the room with a man we both knew slightly, a university poet with long raked hair and stained teeth, laughing—he talked, she laughed, innocent enough, you say, or not innocent at all but completely acceptable, a party's a party, and if the huddle went on far too long, who is to notice but the husband? And I said to her later. This was a long time ago when the kids were small and Marian drove a car without a pencil in her hand. I said to her later, self-importantly because this was the point, to speak with exaggerated dignity, to speak to the depths of my being and make fun of myself at the same time because this is what we do at parties.

I said, I suffer from a rare condition that afflicts Mediterranean men. It's called self-respect.

I stood in the doorway watching the movie with her.

"Will Jeff be living with us forever, do you think?"

"Could happen."

"The job at the diet ranch. Fell through?"

"I guess."

"He didn't say?"

"I'm watching this," she said.

"Did you do the newspapers?"

"I did the bottles. Tomorrow's bottle day. Let me watch this," she said.

"We'll both watch it."

"You don't know what's going on. I've been watching for an hour and a quarter."

"I'll catch up."

"I don't want to sit here and explain."

"You don't have to say a word."

"The movie's not worth explaining," she said.

"I'll catch up by watching."

"But you're interfering," she said.

"I'll be quiet and I'll watch."

"You're interfering by watching," she said.

The remark pleased her, it had a tinge of insight, and she stretched smiling in a sort of coiled yawn, hips and legs steady, upper body bent away. I guess I knew what she meant, that another's presence screws up the steady balance, the integrated company of the box. She wanted to be alone with a bad movie and I was standing judgment.

"You work too hard," I told her.

"I love my job. Shut up."

"Now that I've stopped working too hard, you work too hard."

"I'm watching this."

"You work unnecessarily hard."

"If he tries to kill her, I'm going to be very upset."

"Maybe he'll kill her off camera."

"Off camera, fine. He can use a chain saw. As long as I don't have to see it."

I watched until my glass was empty. I went back to the kitchen and turned off the light. Then I went into the living room and looked at the peach sienna sofa. It was a new piece, a thing to look at and absorb, a thing the room would incorporate over time. It took the curse off the piano. We had a piano no one played, one of Marian's Big Ten heirlooms, an object like a mounted bearskin, oppressing all of us with its former life.

I turned off the light in the living room but first I looked at the books on the shelves. I stood in the room looking at the peach sienna sofa and the Rajasthani wall hanging and the books on the shelves. Then I turned off the light. Then I checked the other light, the light in the back hall, to make sure it was still on in case my mother had to get up during the night.

I stood in the doorway again. Marian watched TV, body and soul. She lit another cigarette and I went into the bedroom.

I stood looking at the books on the shelves. Then I got undressed and went to bed. She came in about fifteen minutes later. I waited for her to start undressing.

"What do I detect?"

"What do you mean?" she said.

"Between you and Brian."

"What do you mean?" she said.

"What do I detect? That's what I mean."

"He makes me laugh," she said finally.

"He makes his wife laugh too. But I don't detect anything between them."

She thought about ways to reply to this. It was an amusing remark perhaps, not what I'd intended. She looked at me and walked out of the room. I heard the shower running across the hall and I realized I'd done it all wrong. I should have brought up the subject standing in the doorway while she was watching TV. Then I could have been the one who walks out of the room.

6

We laid in a case of the flavored seltzer she liked and we set her up in a quiet room, Lainie's old room, with the resilvered mirror and the big-screen TV.

It wasn't long before Jeff stopped wearing the baggy shorts and turnaround cap and began to resemble himself again. His personal computer had a multimedia function that allowed him to look at a copy of the famous videotape showing a driver being shot by the Texas Highway Killer. Jeff became absorbed in these images, devising routines and programs, using filtering techniques to remove background texture. He was looking for lost information. He enhanced and super-slowed, trying to find some pixel in the data swarm that might provide a clue to the identity of the shooter.

The device weighed only three and a half ounces and it showed the distance I ran and the calories I burned and even the length of the strides I took—clipped to the waistband of my trunks.

I was eleven years old when he went out for cigarettes, a warm evening with men playing pinochle inside a storefront club and radio voices everywhere on the street, someone's always playing a radio, and

they took him out near Orchard Beach, where the shoreline is cran-
nied with remote inlets, and they dropped him into the lower world,
his body suspended above the rockweed, in the soft organic murk. Not
that I really recall the weather or the cardplayers. There's always a
radio and someone playing cards.

At home we wanted clean safe healthy garbage. We rinsed out old
bottles and put them in their proper bins. We faithfully removed the
crinkly paper from our cereal boxes. It was like preparing a pharaoh for
his death and burial. We wanted to do the small things right.

He never committed a figure to paper. He had a head for numbers,
a memory for numbers.

We fixed her up with the humidifier, the hangers, the good hard
bed and the dresser that belonged to Marian when she was growing
up, a handsome piece with a history behind it.

In the bronze tower I looked out at the umber hills and felt assured
and well defended, safe in my office box and my crisp white shirt and
connected to things that made me stronger.

In the bronze tower a fellow executive cleared his throat and I
heard something go by in the small hoarse noise, a secret linger of
childhood, the game he played inside his life. Maybe it was a hundred
and eight degrees out on the street. He was spying on himself. The
third person watches the first person. The "he" spies on the "I." The
"he" knows things the "I" can't bear to think about. Maybe it was a
hundred and ten, a hundred and twelve, telephones warbling in mod-
ulated phrases. The third person sends his nobody to kill the first person's somebody.

I used to say when they were small. I told them more than once.
This is the washer, this is the packing, this is the spout.

In the bronze tower we used the rhetoric of aggrieved minorities to
prevent legislation that would hurt our business. Arthur Blessing
believed, our CEO, that true feeling flows upward from the streets, fully
accessible to corporate adaptation. We learned how to complain, how
to appropriate the language of victimization. Arthur listened to gangsta
rap on the car radio every morning. Songs about getting mad and getting laid and getting even, taking what's rightfully ours by violent
means if necessary. He believed this was the only form of address that

made an impact on Washington. Arthur recited lyrics to me once on the company plane and together we laughed his wacko laugh, those enunciated ha-has, clear and slow and well spaced, like laughing with words.

Coming home I liked to put suntan lotion on my arms, face and legs and go running down the quiet streets of oleanders and palms and along the drainage canal banked with red dirt. I ran in dense heat and strong light and I thought about the protection factor bumping up to sixty now, I wondered about this even though I'm olive-skinned, dark as my old man—from fifteen to thirty to sixty, where once upon a time a factor fifteen was the absolute maximum sunblock scientifically possible. Running past tree trunks limed white against the unrelenting sun.

You have to cut it thick. That's what he said about the bread, the round crusty loaf he called Campobasso bread, after the name of the store, which itself was named for a mountain town on the spine of Italy. The best bread, you cut it too thin, he said, it's worthless. I watched him shave and I watched him cut bread, holding the loaf on its side with one hand, thumb of the other hand, the knife hand, edged over the haft onto the back of the blade to guide the slicing, down through the crust and into the springy middle of the bread.

When Lainie had her baby, her girl, I felt a soft joy settle in my chest. Or a solace, maybe, an easing of some perennial clutch or grab, some taunt of malehood. All these women now, from my mother in her pale green room to this raw arrival kicking in mortal fret, all gathered near the chimneypiece. It was a kindness that the child should be a girl. I felt an expansive ease, an unthrobbing of some knot in my body. I watched her naked in her mother's arms, swimming in a ribbon of light.

Tuesdays only we did plastic, minus caps and lids. Waste is an interesting word that you can trace through Old English and Old Norse back to the Latin, finding such derivatives as empty, void, vanish and devastate.

Residents of Phoenix are called Phoenicians.

They talked about the things I did not talk about, although I told her about the stolen car, and we said to each other, Marian and I, we said if people ever saw our son in the commission of a crime they wouldn't know how to describe him except for his skin color and the jokey sticker fastened to the rear bumper of his Honda, if in fact his

Honda was an element in the crime, the bumper sticker someone gave him—*Going Nowhere Fast*.

Marian and I saw products as garbage even when they sat gleaming on store shelves, yet unbought. We didn't say, What kind of casserole will that make? We said, What kind of garbage will that make? Safe, clean, neat, easily disposed of? Can the package be recycled and come back as a tawny envelope that is difficult to lick closed? First we saw the garbage, then we saw the product as food or lightbulbs or dandruff shampoo. How does it measure up as waste, we asked. We asked whether it is responsible to eat a certain item if the package the item comes in will live a million years.

According to street legend he never wrote a number on a piece of paper.

Night after night we sat in the stale glow, my mother and I, and watched reruns of "The Honeymooners." Ralph Kramden wailing his unstoppable pain. Maybe my mother identified with wife Alice. The apron and cloth coat and underfurnished flat and food smells in the hallway. But Alice had a bus-driver husband who kept walking in the door instead of going out. He drove a vehicle licensed by society. And Ralph and Alice had no kids to worry and torment them. You had the kids without the husband. Not even a body risen from the rock-weed and found floating by two guys early one Sunday in a rented row-boat with a cage for trapping crabs—the nibbled body of Jimmy Costanza, age whatever.

I went back to the coastal lowlands of Texas and did an interview with the BBC wearing a hard hat and miner's lamp and standing in a salt passage two thousand feet under the earth. The producer stood off camera and asked questions and I tasted salt dust stirred up by the forklifts and tried to frame responses that would please her.

You had the man who did the job unlicensed by society. In the hall-ways and alleys you heard the footfalls at night and must have wondered if that was Jimmy coming back. From the dead or the dark or maybe just New Jersey. And that was you dressing quickly at first light before the heat came whistling up the pipes—early mass among the Italians in their graveclothes. You had the kids with their taut nerves, the little woodpushing wonder who was harder to love than a handful

121

of coffee dregs. Alone those cold mornings going to mass. And the older son with his distance and dimmed moods and undimmed rage, up on the roof in the evening sleet to smoke a cigarette.

I look at the Lucky Strike logotype and I think target.

I watched men in moon suits bury drums of nuclear waste and I thought of the living rocks down there, the subterrane process, the half-life, the atoms that decay to half the original number. The most common isotope of uranium is bombarded with neutrons to produce plutonium that fissions, if we can generate a verb from the energy of splitting atoms. This isotope has the mass number two three eight. Add the digits and you get thirteen.

But the bombs were not released. I remember Klara Sax talking about the men who flew the strategic bombers as we all stood listening in the long low structure of sectioned concrete. The missiles remained in the rotary launchers. The men came back and the cities were not destroyed.

7

Marian leaned into me and laughed, watching the land surface expand around us. It was first light, a foil shimmer at desert's edge. At three hundred feet we caught a mild westerly and drifted toward the eyelid slice of sun. But we didn't think we were moving. We thought the land was gliding by beneath us, showing a cluster of mobile homes, a truck on a blacktop to the south. And dogs barking up at us—they barked and leaped and ran yapping into each other as we strayed across the trailer park, passed from dog to dog, new dogs appearing at the fringes, twisting in midleap, dogs from nowhere, multiplying yaps and howls, a contagion to wake the known world.

Then we were out over open earth, bone brown and deep in shadow, and we hung in the soft air, balanced in some unbodied lull, with a measure of creation spilling past.

The pilot yanked the blast valve and we heard the burners pulse and roar and this made Marian laugh again. She talked and laughed incessantly, happy and scared. The basket was not large, barely taking the three of us plus tanks, valves, wires, instruments and coiled rope.

Every propane wallop sent a man-sized streak of flame into the open throat of the nylon that bulbed out above us.

Jerry the pilot said, "We need this wind to hold just like it is. Then we make it okay, I think. But we got to be boocoo lucky."

This made us both laugh. We were lighter than air, laughing, and the balloon did not seem like a piece of science so much as an improvised prayer. Jerry spaced the burns and kept an eye on the pyrometer, adding just enough heat to make up for routine cooling inside the envelope. It was a game, a larger-than-life toy we'd found ourselves wickered into, and our eyes went big at the whooshing flames.

The balloon was candy-striped and when Jerry pointed south we spotted a road and a car, the chase car, a matching candy van that towed the small open trailer used to convey the balloon and basket.

The surge of flame, the delayed rise and Marian saying, "Greatest birthday present ever."

"Ain't seen nothing yet," I said.

She said, "What made you think of it? This is something I've always wanted to do without knowing it exactly. Or knowing it but not at the level of ever making plans. You must have read my mind."

Then she said, "I didn't know how much I needed to get out and see this landscape again. Too cooped up with job. But I never dreamed I'd be doing it from here. When you said four a.m. I thought what sort of birthday are we talking about."

"Now you know," I said. "But you only know the half of it."

We leaned close, my arm around her, our thighs pressing, and we were rocked and whirled, although not turning—whirled within ourselves, blood-whirled into quickened sense. I had my free hand around an iron bar, part of the rigid frame connecting the basket to the load cables, and I could feel the metal breathe in my fist.

About twenty minutes later Jerry touched me on the shoulder and pointed straight ahead and I saw the first splash of sunlight on wingtips. The piece began to emerge out of distance and haze, the mesh rectangle completed now, ranks of aircraft appearing as one unit of fitted parts, a shaped weave of painted steel in the monochrome surround.

Jerry said, "Now if the Air Force don't shoot our asses off, we'll just mosey on over."

And that's what we did, approaching at an altitude of four hundred feet. I felt Marian hanging a sort of tremulous gawk over the padded edge of the basket. It was a heart-shaking thing to see, bursts and serpentines of color, a power in the earth, and she pulled at my sweater and looked at me.

Like where are we and what are we seeing and who did it?

The primaries were less aggressive than they'd seemed earlier. The reds were dampened, taken down by weather or more paint, deeper permeations, and this brought them ably into the piece. There were orderly slashes across the fuselages in one section, beautifully mixed blues and flat blues and near blues. The piece had a great riverine wash, a broad arc of sage green or maybe mustard green with brushy gray disturbances, and it curved from the southeast corner up and across the north edge, touching nearly a third of the massed aircraft, several planes completely covered in the pigment—the work's circulating fluid, naming the pace, holding the surface together.

Like my god Nick, how could this be here without my knowing?

The tension of our pressed bodies was heightened by the physical fact of color, painted light pouring toward us. The sun burned high on the line divide. We'd dropped to two hundred feet and Jerry ran a blast of flame. When we were nearly on it the work grew rougher and frontal. I could see unpainted intervals, dead metal strips across the wings of several planes, peroxide white, scabby and gashed, and a trace of stenciled safety instructions apparent on one fuselage. The piece looked hard-won. It lost its flow and became more deeply grained, thick paint in uneven sheets, spray-gunned on. I saw the struggle to make it, scores of people in this chalk heat, muscles and lungs. And I looked for the blond girl in the flouncy skirt painted on a forward fuselage and was elated to spot her, long and tall and unretouched, the nose art, the pinup, the ordinary life and lucky sign that animated the work.

I could see Marian try to absorb the number. She was not counting but wanted to know, simply as a measure of her amazement. And when I whispered two hundred and thirty at last count, she concentrated more deeply, testing the figure against the dense array, the giddiness of general effect. We passed directly over. The planes were enormous of course, they were objects of hulking size, stratofortresses, thick and massy, slab-finned, wings set high on the fuselage, a few missile pylons still intact, a few outrigger wheels suspended, the main wheels chocked on every plane.

And truly I thought they were great things, painted to remark the end of an age and the beginning of something so different only a vision such as this might suffice to augur it.

And we moved toward the blank flats that framed the aircraft and saw how the work lost vigor at the fringes, giving way, melted by intention in the desert.

Marian said, "I can never look at a painting the same way again."

"I can never look at an airplane."

"Or an airplane," she said.

And I wondered if the piece was visible from space like the land art of some lost Andean people.

The breeze took us past and the pilot yanked the blast handle, giving us a final inchmeal rise. We saw a cloudwall hung many miles to the east and hawks floating in the unforced motion that makes you think they've been up there, the same two birds since bible times. There were stones tumbled in a field, great bronze rocks with carved flanks. I felt my wife at my side. We saw dust blowing off the dark hills and a pair of abandoned cars flopped in forage grass, convertibles with shredded tops. Everything we saw was ominous and shining, tense with the beauty of things that are normally unseen, even the cars gone to canker and rust. The pilot pointed to an object some miles away and we saw it was the chase car, a droplet nosing down a long road toward the place on earth where we would light.

That night we had friends over for dinner and the talk was swift and funny, flying cross-table well past midnight, and when they were gone but also while they were there—they were still there when I felt the distance and stillness of that sprawled dawn like some endless sky waking inside me, flared against the laughter.

When they were gone we lay in bed. We slept in a bookwalled room with creamy shelves and deep carpets and lighting that had a halftone

126

density, warm and whiskeyish. Marian looked at a magazine, turning pages with a crispness that might have seemed short-tempered to someone who didn't know her habits.

"The long day."

"The long drive. The drive was oh boy," I said, "a killer."

"Is this the longest day of my life?"

"The drive was the screaming meemies. I hate those trucks, man."

"I still feel the drive. But it was marvelous, all of it."

"It was unmarvelous. It was marvelous because you slept."

She turned a page.

"Did you notice how they finish each other's sentences?"

"I drove, you slept."

"She says, Da da da. He says, Dumdy dum."

"It's not the worst fate. I mean even strangers do it. Everybody does it to somebody."

"And I didn't sleep. I was one level down for ten minutes."

"It's the only way to get certain sentences finished."

"They ate the roasted corn relish."

"Of course they ate the roasted corn relish. The roasted corn relish was great. Speaking of maps. I'd like to get some old maps. I hate our maps."

"Look at this. The Rapture is approaching. October twenty-eight. They give the exact date."

"I saw that."

"The mark of the beast. Did you see that? It's on the universal product code. Every product."

"That's right. Every box of Jell-O they put through the scanner."

"I'm having one of those nights," she said.

"What?"

"One of those nighty nights."

"What?"

"I'm having that sort of thing where I know I won't sleep. It's the knowing that does it. It's not the tired. Because I'm actually very tired."

"Restless."

"No, it's a tired but not sleepy type thing. Six six six. So the supermarket is a weird sort of place."

"We always knew it was."

I turned off my light and looked into the deep cream ceiling with my hands behind my head.

"She's got a great body for how many kids? Alison. Four kids?" I said.

"Which means I'm either half as great or twice as great but let's not pursue it. What's-his-name Terry was here. The heavyset one."

"Been years since I looked at a real map. It's a sort of Robert Louis Stevenson thing to do. We have maps of highways and motels. Our maps have rest stops and wheelchair symbols."

"Just tell me what his name is."

"For what, the faucet?"

"Day before yesterday or yesterday. Today's been so long I don't know anymore. No, the showerhead."

"The hell's wrong with the showerhead? Our maps have pancake houses."

"What's-his-name with the orange pickup."

"Which shower are we talking about?"

"Terry, right?"

She turned a page. She used a book pillow to read when she was in bed. I ordered it for her out of a catalog, jewel-tone jacquard, a wedge-shaped cushion that nestles in the lap and holds your book or maga-zine at the proper angle, with tasseled bookmarks built in and a slot in back for your reading glasses.

"I'm going Tuesday. I tell you that?"

"This is, what, Moscow? Or Boston. Too soon for Moscow. Which is the heavyset one? I get them completely."

"I need to get these shoes resoled before I go. Remind me to do that tomorrow."

"I have this thing on my leg."

"It's not Boston," I said.

"It's not Boston."

"It's Portland."

"It's Portland."

"What thing?" I said.

"On the inside of my thigh."

128

"Call Williamson."

"It could be an irritation."

"Call Williamson. When did you get it?"

"I don't know. I think it comes and goes."

She turned a page.

"Lainie had the wallpaper today."

"About time."

"That was her that called."

"I hope you didn't tell her."

"Of course I didn't tell her. What was I going to tell her? Sweetheart, we drove right past but didn't stop."

"Stopping would have been."

"We saw them when was it. Recent recent recent. Not that recent actually."

"Recent enough. We don't want to overdo it."

"Paperhangers. One was a woman, she said."

"I'm still not completely over this motherfucking cold. Why is that?" I said.

She turned a page.

"Why is that?" I said.

"Take some of those antihistamines you take. They're hard to buy."

"The tablets."

"The caplets."

"You're all revved up. I can feel the energy."

"I'm not revved up. I'm tired. My mind is in that sort of place. You can forget about sleep, it's telling me."

I selected the jewel-tone jacquard over the ivory because the weave went well with our carpets.

"I saw him in that orange truck he drives. The heavyset one. Last time I installed it myself but this time nothing fit."

"Because the universe is expanding. It expands in warm weather. Remind me we need some sixty-watt bulbs."

"I pulled alongside and he said he could be here in an hour and he showed up exactly on time and he installed the thing in exactly ten minutes and that was the end of that."

She turned a page and then another. She had a way of sounding

129

grim when she was actually showing satisfaction, showing completion—the finishing of a task or the telling of a story with a moral.

"Did you tell her to spackle?"

"They did the baby's room first."

"Because this is not something Dex is going to figure out for himself. I only hope they spackled."

"Take the twelve-hour antihistamines. The four-hour make you
drowsy."

"What's wrong with drowsy? Remind me we need bulbs for the
pantry."

"Just tell me his name. The heavyset kid is the one whose father,
right?"

"And had to be subdued by four or five cops."

"Heavyset."

"Can't you call him fat? Call him fat. He is tremendously fat,"
I said.

"He has rolls of fat. It's true."

"Maybe the bulb's loose. Remind me to tighten the bulb. Too soon
for Moscow."

She turned a page.

"Is it a lump?" I said.

"What? No, I wouldn't use that word. No, it's an irritation."

"Maybe it's the estrogen."

"No no no no no."

"Call Williamson," I said.

I turned on my side and heard a plane in a landing pattern, a late
flight from somewhere.

"Eight hours of solid sleep. That's what I need."

"It's true actually. You've got one good pair of shoes and they need
fixing."

"I almost bought some shoes in Italy. I almost bought some shoes
in Italy."

She turned a page.

"What's the name of that stuff I wanted to tell your mother to
use?"

"Wait a second. I know."

130

"It's on the tip of my tongue," she said.

"Wait a second. I know."

"You know the stuff I mean."

"The sleep stuff or the indigestion?"

"It's on the tip of my tongue."

"Wait a second. Wait a second. I know."

About three hours later I sat in the armchair in a corner of the bedroom feeling damp and cold, a chill sweat across my back and neck and under my arms. I'd come out of a dream deep-breathing and clammy, breathing fast and loud—so odd and loud and fast it woke me up, or something did.

I had the baseball in my hand. Usually I kept the baseball on the bookshelves, wedged in a corner between straight-up books and slanted books, tented under books, unceremoniously. But now I had it in my hand. You have to know the feel of a baseball in your hand, going back a while, connecting many things, before you can understand why a man would sit in a chair at four in the morning holding such an object, clutching it—how it fits the palm so reassuringly, the corked center making it buoyant in the hand, and the rough spots on an old ball, the marked skin, how an idle thumb likes to worry the scuffed horsehide. You squeeze a baseball. You kind of juice it or milk it. The resistance of the packed material makes you want to press harder. There's an equilibrium, an agreeable animal tension between the hard leather object and the sort of clawed hand, veins stretching with the effort. And the feel of raised seams across the fingertips, cloth contours like road bumps under the knuckle joints—how the whorled cotton can be seen as a magnified thumbprint, a blowup of the convoluted ridges on the pad of your thumb. The ball was a deep sepia, veneered with dirt and turf and generational sweat—it was old, bunged up, it was bashed and tobacco-juiced and stained by natural processes and by the lives behind it, weather-spattered and charactered as a seafront house. And it was smudged green near the Spalding trademark, it was still wearing a small green bruise where it had struck a pillar according to the history that came with it—flaked paint from a bolted column in the left-field stands embedded in the surface of the ball.

Thirty-four thousand five hundred dollars.

How the hand works memories out of the baseball that have nothing to do with games of the usual sort.

Bad luck, Branca luck. From him to me. The moment that makes the life.

Marian caught me once looking at the ball. I was standing at the bookshelves with the ball in my hand and she thought it was like Hamlet gazing on Yorick's skull or maybe Aristotle, even better she said, contemplating the bust of Homer. That was nice, we thought. Rembrandt's Homer and Thomson's homer. We smiled at that.

I thought of the old radio voice, Russ Hodges, dead now twenty years or more, disbelief and thrill, the force of a single human voice coming out of a box.

She didn't ask whether it was Portland, Maine or Portland, Oregon when I said it was not Boston, it was Portland, and I'd felt the question coming, layered in the sequence of our exchange, waiting to edge out, but one of us fell asleep before she could ask which Portland by the way in those words exactly, I think I fell asleep first but maybe not—the light was out, the last light was out.

Then I came up out of a dream and felt my way to the armchair, breathing funny, and switched on the small reading lamp.

And the crowd noise behind the voice, the incessant smash and tension, the thickness, the sort of bristle and teem that deepened at a turn in play—a noise so dense it might have had a flash point, a heat to blow out the radio.

I heard my mother in the next room getting up to go to the toilet. I listened to her come out of the room. I waited and listened, nearly breathless. I waited for the shuffle of slippers along the hall, for the pace, the familiar rate and pace of the shuffle, and then I listened for the sound of water flushing—fully intent, listening in the fiercest kind of concentrated stillness until she was safely back in bed.

I hefted the weapon and pointed it and saw an interested smile fall across his face, the slyest kind of shit-eating grin.

Maybe that was the dream—I wasn't sure.

Then I got the baseball from the bookshelves and sat in the armchair and looked into the whiskey-cream ceiling.

132

I didn't listen to the Dodger station that day. I listened to Russ Hodges instead, trying to work a reverse kind of luck. Never occurred to me at the time—I didn't think of it in fact until I sat in the armchair squeezing the baseball—but Russell Hodges, if you count the letters, if you're odd enough to think of doing such a thing, spinning out the full name and counting the characters, you may be amused to see old thirteen.

I felt calmer now. I felt all right. My arm hung over the side of the chair and I squeezed the baseball, listening to Marian sleep-breathe—squeezed it hard, the veins leveling on the back of my hand, going dead flat.

Maybe we fell asleep simultaneously. Then I felt my way to the armchair and switched on the lamp. I stood there, pulling my pajama shirt away from my body where the sweat made it cling. Then I went to the bookshelves and got the baseball.

She was sitting up. She wasn't exactly sitting up, she was propped—I realized she was awake, propped on an elbow looking at me, rubbing her temple with her right hand.

"Nick?"

"I'm here."

"You all right?"

"Yes. I'll be there in a minute."

"Come back to bed."

"I'm all right. Go to sleep."

"It was a lovely birthday, wasn't it?"

"Do you want me to turn out this light?"

"No. Just come to bed."

"I'll be there in a minute."

"I want you next to me," she said.

I stood on the roof with my radio placed on the ledge and sometimes I squatted and took the radio down with me, down behind the ledge, surrounding it sort of, taking hope from it, suffering the game's slides and veers, rooting from the gut—an Emerson, maroon, that I took everywhere. But when I stood I faced southwest, looking beyond the hospital for the incurable and past the elevated tracks on Third Avenue, looking toward the river that cuts the boroughs. That's where the Polo Grounds stood, west by southwest, and I imagined the field and the players, the crisp blues and elysian greens on that great somber-skied day—great and terrible, a day now gone to black and white in the film fade of memory.

MANX MARTIN 1

Then he remembers his books and goes back down the stairs because you can't come home from school without your schoolbooks, fool. He forces the baseball into his side pocket and leans into the dim triangle behind the stairs, where the bottom of the first flight meets the floor, and he scoops the three books he left there in the morning, slides them out and scoops them up, plus a composition book with a mottled cover, and he blows away the dust and smut and sourness.

The janitor comes in the back door from the yards, the new janitor, he limps so bad you're not even sure you feel sorry for him—maybe you wonder why he's walking around at all.

"What's this?"

"Dropped something," Cotter says.

"I need to talk to your father."

"When I see him."

"Tell him," the man says.

Cotter can't figure out how the janitor knows who he is. The last janitor left in a hurry and the new man just arrived and he has four buildings he takes care of and a limp that's hard to look at and he already knows which son belongs to the matching father and it's probably not a mistake. People always want to talk to his father. His father spends hours every day in flight from these conversations.

He climbs to four and goes inside. His sister is there, Rosie, poring over her homework at the kitchen table. Rosie's sixteen, always blasting away at the books, and he has two older brothers, one in Korea with the infantry and one in the airborne stationed in Georgia. This is the peach state. But if Cotter had to choose between these two forms of employment he thinks he'd rather face a weaponed enemy in snow and mud than walk out a door into the balmy evening air with a snatch of bundled silk hanging on his back.

"What's he carrying in his pocket? Makes a person wonder," Rosie says. "Looks like an apple to me. Maybe he went to an orchard on his day off."

"What day off?"

"Traveled upstate on a bus to pick some apples. Of course we have apples right here. But that's for after school. No school, no apples. Is that why he found his own apple?"

"If I didn't go to school, where did I go?"

"I don't know but when I saw you from the window you had no books and when you walked in the door, lo and behold."

"Then you know that's not an apple in my pocket."

He takes out the ball and does his flip trick, back-spinning the thing over his hand and wrist and catching it with a sort of gearshift motion, elbow in reverse. This gets Rosie smiling and she plants her face in the book again, which tells Cotter he has won a little victory because it is only when this girl goes wordless that you know she is showing respect.

In his room he looks out the window, the room he used to share with his brothers, remarkably his own now, and then he drops the ball on the khaki blanket in the lower bunk, it is the only military touch, the sturdy olive drab, and he grabs a sweater off the chair back. He fits the sweater over his head and looks out the window again, watching people move through the streetlights and into the partial dark. Gets dark too soon. He stands and looks, just watching, being nobody in a window, and then he hears his mother pushing through the door.

He snaps to, thinking what he has to say if he is challenged about missing school. But he knows Rosie will not snitch on him. He thinks he knows this. He is confident more or less. He thinks he feels her loyalty through the walls and he goes into the kitchen where his mother is putting away groceries and he drops a hand on Rosie's shoulder and stands at the table with an eye fixed on the bright boxes and cans his mother is placing on the shelves.

His mother says, "How many times?"

"What?"

"You have to be told. Don't wear that sweater. I need to clean that sweater."

"Plunge it in something strong," Rosie says.

"That's a filthy sweater."

"Take it to the cleaner, they'll give it back," Rosie says. "Rejected."

See, the world is filled with things he's not supposed to do and not supposed to wear. But maybe he likes it when they array against him, it's different from his brothers, who bossed him a little and teased him a little but did not show this picky interest, this endless searching concern. His sister's head poked forward so she can study the particular jut of his dumbness. He likes running his fingers over the edge of the fruit bowl, over the specked glaze, with Rosie's books sprawled on the table and the fruit in the bowl and his mother doing things at the stove or cabinet, the way his mother talks to him and never looks in his direction but knows where he is and measures her voice to his sliding whereabouts, room by room. Maybe he wants them to figure him out so they can let him in on the secret.

"The sweater's got burrs," Rosie says. She seems to like that word and puts a teasey nonchalance in her voice. "He's full of burrs from some apple orchard he must have visited sometime or other."

He runs his fingers over the inside edge of the bowl, feeling the sort of spatter of whirled material, the bubbly pinpoint warps. His mother tells him to wash his hands. She is not looking at him but knows the state of his hands from the position of the sun and moon. He must be walking dirt. Walking talking filthman from the planet Dirt.

At dinner they are quiet. This is because his father is not here and might walk in any time and then again might not and they are in a state of involuntary waiting. Funny how his mother pushes through the door, shouldering in with shopping bags and bundles and her purse that she wears on a long strap over her head and across her body, maybe dragging a handled bag or nudging it out of the hallway with a peg-leg motion and making six kinds of noise even when she's not carrying something, bringing the streets in with her, the subways, buses and streets, all the noise and labor of getting uptown and downtown, that's his mother, and his father usually sliding in unannounced, standing and glaring, stuck to the wall like he wandered in the wrong door and needs to work out the details of his mistake.

His mother is tall and slightly lopsided and she is strong. He knows this because he has lifted things she has lifted, he has come up four flights with things she often carries, and poker-faced—it takes her half a minute to work a smile out of those unused muscles.

She says, "I saw that man who preaches in the street. Same place every time."

"I did too," Cotter says.

"I said to myself this man has a life even if we can't imagine it. This man goes home somewhere. But where does he go? How does he live? I try to imagine what does he do when he's not out there preaching."

Rosie says, "I see these people lots of places."

"But this man's steady. Same place. I don't think he cares if people listen. He'll preach to cars going by."

"What was he preaching?"

"How no one knows the day or the hour. Seems there's been the Russians exploding an A-bomb. So no one knows the day or the hour. They announced it on the news."

Rosie says, "I can't get worked up."

"I got worked up until I started up the stairs with those shopping bags. Thought I was going to pull my shoulder out of the socket."

"Back to normal," Rosie says.

"But I stood and listened to him. I have to say. First time I listened to the man."

"He's always there," Cotter says.

"First time I listened. No one knows the day or the hour. I believe this is Matthew twenty-four."

"I can't get worked up," Rosie says.

140

"But the man has a life and it's a mystery to me how he lives it."

"People always preaching," Rosie says.

"Those clothes he wears. I think it's a shame. And he's not a crazy man. He knows his scriptures."

"You can know your scriptures," Cotter says. "There's people know their scriptures they're crazy as a loon."

"Amen," says his sister.

After dinner he's back in his room looking out the window. He's supposed to be in his room doing his homework and he's in his room all right but he doesn't know what his homework is supposed to be. He reads a few pages ahead in his world history book. They made history by the minute in those days. Every sentence there's another war or tremendous downfall. Memorize the dates. The downfall of the empire and the emergence of detergents. There's a kid in his class who eats pages from his history book nearly every day. The way he does it, he places the open book under the desk in his crotch and slyly crumples a page, easing it off the spine with the least amount of rustle. Then he has the strategy of wait a while before he brings his fist to his mouth in a sort of muffled cough with the page inside the fist, like whitesy-bitesy. Then he stuffs in the page and the tiny printed ink and the memorized dates, engrossing it quietly. He waits some more. He lets the page idle in his mouth. Then he chews it slowly and carefully and incomplete, damping the sound by making sure his teeth do not meet, and Cotter tries to imagine how it tastes, all the paper points and edges washed in saliva, becoming soft and limp and blottered so you can swallow smooth. He swallows not so smooth. You can see his adam's apple jerk like he just landed a plane on a foreign shore.

War and treaties, eat your Wheaties.

Rosie's in the shower now. He sits on his bunk and hears water beating on the other side of the wall and he thinks about the game. He remembers things he didn't know he'd seen or heard, people on the exit ramp—he sees shirt colors and hears voices coming back to him. A cop on a horse, the boot shine and animal heat, and he hears water beating on the galvanized walls of the shower, the rattling stain-walled shower that someone added to the bathroom years before.

When his father comes in, there is no doubt of the entrance, the singing of the hinges when the door opens slowly, the way he does not carry sound with him out of the entranceway—there's no shaking out of clothes or heavy breath from the climb up the stairs. Not that you can't hear him at all. He maintains a presence near the door, a hearable something, maybe just the tension of a man standing on a linoleum floor or some tone that comes off his body, a tightness that says he's home.

Cotter sits on the lower bunk and waits. His father comes through the kitchen and appears in the doorway, Manx Martin. He's a working man, a furniture mover when he's employed and a whiskey swigger when he's not. He looks at Cotter and nods pointlessly. He stands there nodding, a gesture that has no point, that seems to mean *Oh yeah it's you* if it means anything at all. Then he comes in the room and sits on the unused bed, the cot. They listen to the water beating on the shower walls.

"Had your dinner?"

"Meat loaf."

"Leave some for me?"

"I don't know."

"You don't know. Why, you left the table early? You had an appointment downtown?"

He sees the man is kidding. His father's eyes go narrow and he does his pencil-line smile. He is a man with high cheekbones sort of poxed in the hollows, rough-graded, and a thin mustache that he keeps well above his lip, tended and particular. He looks around the room. He studies things. He seems to believe this is the right time to see what kind of surroundings his sons grew up in. He is average size, a little developed in the chest, a little bowlegged, and Cotter would not have thought he had the brawn to move heavy pieces up and down long flights of stairs. But he has seen his father lift and hoist with much bigger men.

"Which one's in there?"

"Rosie."

"Washing up a storm."

"The way she does homework. To the last ounce."

"Finishes what she starts, that girl."

142

It bothers Cotter in some lurking way, to sit here with his father talking about Rosie while they hear her in the shower. Just then the water stops.

"Because I need to take a leak, you see."

"Super wants to talk to you."

"He's a yard dog. Pay no mind."

"How come he knows us if he just got here?"

"Maybe we're famous, you and me. Two hombres that they put out the word these guys be mighty tough."

Cotter relaxes a little. He thinks maybe this is going to be all right. The man is feeling no pain as they say and there's something he can get from his father that he can't get from his mother.

Manx calls out, "Rosie baby. Your daddy needs to use the fa-cil-i-tees."

They hear a smothered word or two and then she goes across the hall barefoot in a towel and Manx stands and hitches his pants and clicks his tongue and walks out of the room.

Cotter thinks without knowing it, without preparing the thought—he sees Bill Waterson on Eighth Avenue with his jacket bunched in his hand. He picks up the baseball and looks at it and puts it down. His father is taking a king leak. You don't usually hear anything but the shower in there and noises from the pipes but his father is taking a leak that is the all-time king. It is quickly becoming funny, the time span and force of the leak, and Cotter wishes his brothers were here so they could all be amazed together.

He comes back in and sits down. He's still wearing his jacket, a corduroy windbreaker that used to belong to Randall, speaking of brothers.

"There now. We feeling better."

"How'd you like to write a letter for me? I need it for school," Cotter says.

"Oh yeah? That says what?"

"That says I missed a day due to illness."

"Dear so-and-so."

"That's right. Like that."

"Please excuse my son."

"That's the way."

"Due to he was ill."

143

"Tell them it was a fever."

"How feverish'd you get?"

"Say one hundred ought to do it."

"We don't want to be too modest. If we're gonna do this thing."

"Okay. As he had a fever of a hundred and two."

"Of course you look to me like you're in the pink."

"Recovering nicely, thanks."

"Except what's that on your sweater?"

"I don't know. Burrs."

"Burrs. This here's Harlem. What kind of burrs?"

"I don't know. I guess I get around."

"And where did you get around to that you missed a day of school?"

"I went to the game."

"The game."

"At the Polo Grounds. Today."

"You were at that game?" Manx says. "That made that fuss in the streets?"

"That's nothing. I was there is nothing. I got the ball he hit."

"No, you didn't. What ball?"

"The home run that won the pennant," Cotter says softly, a little reluctantly, because it is such an astounding thing to say and he is awed for the first time, saying it.

"No, you didn't."

"I chased it down and got it."

"Lying to my face," Manx says.

"Not a lie. I got the ball. Right here."

"Know what you are?" Manx says.

Cotter reaches for the ball.

"You're a stick that makes a noise once in a while."

Cotter looks at him. He sits in the lower bunk with his back to the wall, looking out at the man on the opposite bed. Then he picks up the baseball, he takes it off the khaki blanket where it is sunk beside his thigh. He holds it out, he spins it on the tips of his fingers. He holds it high in his right hand and uses the other hand to spin it. He doesn't give a damn. He sports it, he shows it off. He feels anger and bluster come into his face.

144

"Are you being straight-up with me?"

Cotter does a little razzle, shaking the ball in his hand like it's too magical to hold steady—it's giving him palsy and making his eyes pop. He's doing it nasty and mad, staring down his old man.

"Hey. Are you being straight-up with your dad?"

"Why would I lie?"

"Okay. Why would you? You wouldn't."

"No reason for it."

"All right. No reason. I can see that. Who else you tell?"

"Nobody."

"You didn't tell your mother?"

"She'd tell me give it back."

Manx laughs. Puts his hands on his knees and peers at Cotter, then rocks back laughing.

"Damn yes. She'd march you up to the ballpark so you could give it back."

Cotter doesn't want to go too far with this. He knows the worst trap in the world is taking sides with his father against his mother. He has to be careful every which way, saying this and doing that, but the most careful thing of all is stick by his mother. Otherwise he's dead.

"All right. So what do we want to do? Maybe we go up to the ballpark in the morning and show them the ball. We bring your ticket stub so at least they see you were at the game and sitting in the right section. But who do we ask for? Which door we go to? Maybe seventeen people show up saying this one's the ball, no this one's the ball, I got it, I got it, I got it."

Cotter is listening to this.

"Who pays attention to us? They see two coloreds from nowhere. They gonna believe some colored boy snatch the ball out of them legions in the crowd?" Manx pauses here, maybe waiting to hear an idea develop in his head. "I believe we need to write a letter. Yeah. We write you a letter for school and then we write us both a letter and send it to the ball club."

Cotter is listening. He watches his father lapse into private thought, into worries and plots.

"What are we saying in this letter?"

145

"We send it registered. Yeah, give it the extra touch. We send it with your ticket stub."

"What are we saying?"

"We offering the ball for sale. What else we possibly be saying?"

Cotter wants to get up and look out the window. He feels closed in and wants to be alone doing nothing but watching the street from the window.

"I don't want to sell it. I want to keep it."

Manx tilts his head to study the boy. This is a thought he has to adjust to—keeping the ball around the house so it can gather dust and develop character.

He says quietly, "Keep it for what? We sell it, we buy you a wool sweater and throw away that hermit shirt you got on. Look like you're living in a tree. We buy something for your mother and sister. Crazy to let the thing sit here and do nothing and earn nothing." His voice is sensible and thought-out, defining things for the teachable son—we are responsible to our family, not to the vanity of keepsakes and souvenirs. "We buy your mother a winter coat. Winter's coming and she needs a heavy coat."

Cotter wants to be manly here, equal to the issues.

"What kind of money they give us?"

"Don't know. Plain and simple do not know. But they want this ball. They put it on display somewhere. I believe a letter is the thing that we send them registered mail. And we include your stub. What's it called, your rain check."

"I don't have a stub."

His father gets the look, the injured surprise—injury into the depths.

"What you trying to do to me?"

"I didn't get a stub."

"Why not?"

"I didn't buy a ticket. I went over the gate."

"What you doing to me, son?"

"I didn't have money for a ticket. So I went over the gate. If I had the money, I'd a bought the ticket." And he adds helplessly, "No money, no tickee."

His father's eyes get that drifty look. Cotter sees a kind of panic building, an intimate guilt that he has brought about by mentioning money, the ancient subject of being broke. His father is in retreat, his eyes treading inward, escaping the place he has just built for them both, the world of responsible things. This is a terrible moment, one of those times when Cotter realizes he has won a struggle he didn't know was taking place. He has beat his father into surrender, into awful withdrawal.

He says, "And anyway the ticket stub doesn't say what section you're sitting unless it's reserve seat or box seat. So the ticket's no good for anything. People pick up tickets off the street."

His father says, "We sleep on it. How's that?" Grimly getting to his feet. "Nothing we can do tonight so let's just get some sleep."

Cotter doesn't mention the letter his father is supposed to write, the excuse for missing school. Maybe in the morning it will be all right. And maybe he'll change his mind about selling the baseball. Or forget the whole thing. Cotter knows if he can delay any action on the matter for a day, a day and a half, his father will completely forget. This is one of the things they count on in this house, unspokenly— they sit around and wait for him to forget.

He stands by the window and looks down at the street. In school they tell him sometimes to stop looking out the window. This teacher or that teacher. The answer is not out there, they tell him. And he always wants to say that's exactly where the answer is. Some people look out the window, others eat their books.

He gets undressed and goes to bed. He sleeps in his shorts and polo shirt. His mother comes in and says good night. Good night's fine as long as she doesn't want to know what he and his father talked about. That's another trap that opens out of nowhere. She tells him she has to get up extra early to go to work, which is a long trip by subway down to 21st Street, she's a seamstress in a noisy loft with tall fans going— he worked there four hours a week last summer sweeping fabric off the floor and rolling those cardboard barrels in and out and they joked and teased him, forty or fifty women, and said some very direct things.

"Rosie will get you up."

"I don't need any help," he says.

147

"If anybody in this *world* needs help getting up, you're the one."

"She throws things at me."

"Catch them and throw them back."

"Then I'll never get dressed. Because she throws my clothes."

His mother leans into the bunk and kisses him, which she hasn't done in a long time, and then she rubs his head roughly, sort of knuckle-rubbing, and squeezes his cheeks so it hurts, twisting sizable sums of flesh, and he hears his father pass by on his way to the kitchen and hopes he missed the damn kiss.

In the dark he thinks about the game. The game comes rolling over him in a great warm wave of contented sleep. The game was lost and then they won. The game could not be won but then they won it and it's won forever. This is the thing they can never take away. It is the first thing he will think of in the morning and one part of him is already there even as he falls asleep, waking up to think about the game.

Manx Martin stands at the refrigerator. He's looking in at the meat loaf. She saved him some meat loaf that's sitting in a plate like the last meal of Prisoner X. He takes it out and sits at the table, eating slowly. His mind is in the throes of this and that. He sees the food in the plate and has to remind himself what it's there for.

He puts the plate in the sink when he's finished and then decides to wash it and dry it and he does this fastidiously, plus utensils. He knows he ought to fix the drip in the faucet but we can save that for a day when there's a little free time. He puts the plate in the cabinet, whisper soft.

Ivie comes in and does not look at him. She has a way of not looking at him that ought to be studied by science. That's how good she is at doing it, sweeping the room with her look but missing him completely—a thing science ought to investigate for military use.

She says, "You were talking to him."

"Whose business is it?"

She says, "What for?"

"I don't need any what for."

She says, "Talking an awful long time."

"He's my son. Whose business is it?"

"Leave him alone. My business," she says. "That's what he wants. Left alone to grow up without advice from you. Only he won't say it himself."

"Let him tell me."

She says, "I'm telling you."

She's moving through the kitchen doing things.

She says, "I'm leaving early in the morning. They have a rush order, which they're paying time and a half."

He hears the radio playing faintly in their bedroom.

"So I'm giving you fair warning. That alarm's going off well before six."

"Before six," he says, and checks his watch, which doesn't work, and what's the difference anyway, and he says the words in a voice unconnected to the facts.

She's in her housecoat and house slippers moving through the kitchen like a sleepwalker and a sleeptalker, not giving him the barest glance. But she's connected to the facts all right. And he is not. He is drifting out of range of the whole damn thing, the morning chill, the working wife, the harsh alarm that's getting ready, even as he stands here, to populate his meager sleep.

She finds the pills she's looking for and goes back down the hall. He stands and waits. He turns off the overhead light and stands in the dim glow of the lamp in the corner.

He stands there for fifteen minutes. A lifetime of thinking into a thing, trying to straighten out the mental involvements.

Okay. He goes and stands in the doorway of Cotter's room. He is looking into the room, getting accustomed to the dark. The boy is sleeping dead away. Manx steps into the room and sees the baseball almost at once. It is sitting in the open on the unused bed. This is what gets him every time. They obtain a valuable thing and don't even bother to hide it. Trust fairies to watch over their valuables. He told them how many times? Protect what's yours. Because the way things are changing, you have to live defensive.

He tries to recall which son slept in which bed when Cotter was a little kid in the top bunk. They came and went so damn fast.

149

He stands in the dark room. He is arguing out the thought should he do it or not. Then he does it. He takes the baseball. He does it before the argument ends. He does it to end the argument. He takes the ball and walks quietly through the kitchen to the door. The ball fits nice and easy in the roomy pocket of his windbreaker, his oldest son's windbreaker. He opens the door, squinching his face to draw off the noise. Need to oil the hinges when our mind's all clear and we have a little free time at our disposal. He eases the door shut and goes down the stairs and out onto the stoop, wondering how it happened that they're not wearing his hand-me-down jacket—he's wearing theirs.

He looks both ways because he always looks both ways. Then he walks down the steps and into the street.

PART 2

ELEGY FOR
LEFT HAND ALONE

Mid-1980s–Early 1990s

1

It shows a man driving a car. It is the simplest sort of family video. You see a man at the wheel of a medium Dodge.

It is just a kid aiming her camera through the rear window of the family car at the windshield of the car behind her.

You know about families and their video cameras. You know how kids get involved, how the camera shows them that every subject is potentially charged, a million things they never see with the unaided eye. They investigate the meaning of inert objects and dumb pets and they poke at family privacy. They learn to see things twice.

It is the kid's own privacy that is being protected here. She is twelve years old and her name is being withheld even though she is neither the victim nor the perpetrator of the crime but only the means of recording it.

It shows a man in a sport shirt at the wheel of his car. There is nothing else to see. The car approaches briefly, then falls back.

You know how children with cameras learn to work the exposed moments that define the family cluster. They break every trust, spy out the undefended space, catching mom coming out of the bathroom in her cumbrous robe and turbaned towel, looking bloodless and plucked. It is not a joke. They will shoot you sitting on the pot if they can manage a suitable vantage.

The tape has the jostled sort of noneventness that marks the family product. Of course the man in this case is not a member of the family but a stranger in a car, a random figure, someone who has happened along in the slow lane.

It shows a man in his forties wearing a pale shirt open at the throat, the image washed by reflections and sunglint, with many jostled moments.

It is not just another video homicide. It is a homicide recorded by a child who thought she was doing something simple and maybe halfway clever, shooting some tape of a man in a car.

He sees the girl and waves briefly, wagging a hand without taking it off the wheel—an underplayed reaction that makes you like him.

It is unrelenting footage that rolls on and on. It has an aimless determination, a persistence that lives outside the subject matter. You are looking into the mind of home video. It is innocent, it is aimless, it is determined, it is real.

He is bald up the middle of his head, a nice guy in his forties whose whole life seems open to the hand-held camera.

But there is also an element of suspense. You keep on looking not because you know something is going to happen—of course you do know something is going to happen and you do look for that reason but you might also keep on looking if you came across this footage for the first time without knowing the outcome. There is a crude power operating here. You keep on looking because things combine to hold you fast—a sense of the random, the amateurish, the accidental, the impending. You don't think of the tape as boring or interesting. It is crude, it is blunt, it is relentless. It is the jostled part of your mind, the film that runs through your hotel brain under all the thoughts you know you're thinking.

The world is lurking in the camera, already framed, waiting for the boy or girl who will come along and take up the device, learn the instrument, shooting old granddad at breakfast, all stroked out so his nostrils gape, the cereal spoon baby-gripped in his pale fist.

It shows a man alone in a medium Dodge. It seems to go on forever.

There's something about the nature of the tape, the grain of the image, the sputtering black-and-white tones, the starkness—you think this is more real, truer-to-life than anything around you. The things around you have a rehearsed and layered and cosmetic look. The tape is superreal, or maybe underreal is the way you want to put it. It is what lies at the scraped bottom of all the layers you have added. And this is another reason why you keep on looking. The tape has a searing realness.

It shows him giving an abbreviated wave, stiff-palmed, like a signal flag at a siding.

You know how families make up games. This is just another game in which the child invents the rules as she goes along. She likes the idea of videotaping a man in his car. She has probably never done it before and she sees no reason to vary the format or terminate early or pan to another car. This is her game and she is learning it and playing it at the same time. She feels halfway clever and inventive and maybe slightly intrusive as well, a little bit of brazenness that spices any game.

And you keep on looking. You look because this is the nature of the footage, to make a channeled path through time, to give things a shape and a destiny.

Of course if she had panned to another car, the right car at the precise time, she would have caught the gunman as he fired.

The chance quality of the encounter. The victim, the killer and the child with a camera. Random energies that approach a common point. There's something here that speaks to you directly, saying terrible things about forces beyond your control, lines of intersection that cut through history and logic and every reasonable layer of human expectation.

She wandered into it. The girl got lost and wandered clear-eyed into horror. This is a children's story about straying too far from home. But it isn't the family car that serves as the instrument of the child's curiosity, her inclination to explore. It is the camera that puts her in the tale.

You know about holidays and family celebrations and how somebody shows up with a camcorder and the relatives stand around and barely react because they're numbingly accustomed to the process of being taped and decked and shown on the VCR with the coffee and cake.

He is hit soon after. If you've seen the tape many times you know from the hand wave exactly when he will be hit. It is something, naturally, that you wait for. You say to your wife, if you're at home and she is there, Now here is where he gets it. You say, Janet, hurry up, this is where it happens.

Now here is where he gets it. You see him jolted, sort of wire-shocked—then he seizes up and falls toward the door or maybe leans or slides into the door is the proper way to put it. It is awful and unremarkable at the same time. The car stays in the slow lane. It approaches briefly, then falls back.

You don't usually call your wife over to the TV set. She has her programs, you have yours. But there's a certain urgency here. You want her to see how it looks. The tape has been running forever and now the thing is finally going to happen and you want her to be here when he's shot.

Here it comes all right. He is shot, head-shot, and the camera reacts, the child reacts—there is a jolting movement but she keeps on taping, there is a sympathetic response, a nerve response, her heart is beating faster but she keeps the camera trained on the subject as he slides into the door and even as you see him die you're thinking of the girl. At some level the girl has to be present here, watching what you're watching, unprepared—the girl is seeing this cold and you have to marvel at the fact that she keeps the tape rolling.

It shows something awful and unaccompanied. You want your wife to see it because it is real this time, not fancy movie violence—the realness beneath the layers of cosmetic perception. Hurry up, Janet, here it comes. He dies so fast. There is no accompaniment of any kind. It is very stripped. You want to tell her it is realer than real but then she will ask what that means.

The way the camera reacts to the gunshot—a startle reaction that brings pity and terror into the frame, the girl's own shock, the girl's identification with the victim.

You don't see the blood, which is probably trickling behind his ear and down the back of his neck. The way his head is twisted away from the door, the twist of the head gives you only a partial profile and it's the wrong side, it's not the side where he was hit.

And maybe you're being a little aggressive here, practically forcing your wife to watch. Why? What are you telling her? Are you making a little statement? Like I'm going to ruin your day out of ordinary spite. Or a big statement? Like this is the risk of existing. Either way you're rubbing her face in this tape and you don't know why.

It shows the car drifting toward the guardrail and then there's a jostling sense of two other lanes and part of another car, a split-second blur, and the tape ends here, either because the girl stopped shooting or because some central authority, the police or the district attorney or the TV station, decided there was nothing else you had to see.

This is either the tenth or eleventh homicide committed by the Texas Highway Killer. The number is uncertain because the police believe that one of the shootings may have been a copycat crime.

And there is something about videotape, isn't there, and this particular kind of serial crime? This is a crime designed for random taping and immediate playing. You sit there and wonder if this kind of crime became more possible when the means of taping an event and playing it immediately, without a neutral interval, a balancing space and time, became widely available. Taping-and-playing intensifies and compresses the event. It dangles a need to do it again. You sit there thinking that the serial murder has found its medium, or vice versa—an act of shadow technology, of compressed time and repeated images, stark and glary and unremarkable.

It shows very little in the end. It is a famous murder because it is on tape and because the murderer has done it many times and because the crime was recorded by a child. So the child is involved, the Video Kid as she is sometimes called because they have to call her something. The tape is famous and so is she. She is famous in the modern manner of people whose names are strategically withheld. They are famous without names or faces, spirits living apart from their bodies, the victims and witnesses, the underage criminals, out there somewhere at the edges of perception.

Seeing someone at the moment he dies, dying unexpectedly. This is reason alone to stay fixed to the screen. It is instructional, watching

159

a man shot dead as he drives along on a sunny day. It demonstrates an elemental truth, that every breath you take has two possible endings. And that's another thing. There's a joke locked away here, a note of cruel slapstick that you are willing to appreciate even if it makes you feel a little guilty. Maybe the victim's a chump, a sort of silent-movie dupe, classically unlucky. He had it coming in a sense, for letting himself be caught on camera. Because once the tape starts rolling it can only end one way. This is what the context requires.

You don't want Janet to give you any crap about it's on all the time, they show it a thousand times a day. They show it because it exists, because they have to show it, because this is why they're out there, to provide our entertainment.

The more you watch the tape, the deader and colder and more relentless it becomes. The tape sucks the air right out of your chest but you watch it every time.

2

Marian Shay drove up to Prescott on business, allowing herself one cigarette for the two-hour trip, which she managed not to smoke until she was ten miles from town, where the mobile homes began to gather and the fast food blazed, and she felt good about this, controlled and disciplined and clean deep through.

There was something going on in the courthouse square. She parked a block away and walked back down to the square and it was one of those days in the high pines when the sun and sweet breeze get into your underwear. There were cars arrayed on a closed-off street, four rows of vintage machines extending two city blocks along the edge of the plaza, and loudspeakers on the lawn did dance-party rock-and-roll.

She had fifteen minutes to spare and walked among the cars, many with hoods raised for the pleasure of connoisseurs. It was early, not yet eleven, and only a dozen people wandered about. She saw a red-haired man who looked faintly familiar and watched him bend under a hood and then stand back to appraise a customized Buick with a black lacquer chassis.

He stood donnishly posed with jutted elbow and cupped hand and she realized after a moment that he worked with Nick at Waste Containment and that his name, which took another moment, was Brian Glassic, which rhymes with classic, which describes these cars.

He saw her and showed a beam of recognition. Then he did a little dance from half a block away, the slowest of clinging fox-trots from out of the fifties.

About two hours later they met for lunch in the dining room of an old hotel just up the street. The room was close and warm and she held the glass of ice water up against her face.

He said, "You are here?"

"For a job interview. There's a small design firm here that renovates old structures. They want to open a Phoenix office. I would be it."

"How did it go?"

"All right, I think."

"You've done this kind of work?"

"Not exactly. Before the kids I helped manage a small real estate operation. Since the kids I've done part-time things now and then."

"Your own office. This is a fantasy of mine. To come wandering in just before lunch. Like a private detective. Hungover, a faceful of stubble. Riffle through the mail. Throw it down."

"Do you get stubble?" she said.

"Yes, eventually. Why do you ask?"

"I don't know. I thought maybe the smoother and fairer the complexion."

"We do shave," he said.

"I don't think my office will resemble a private detective's."

"You want light and air."

"Great thick proposals in strong binders."

"You want scale models, with trees."

"Maybe."

"And little bland people on the sidewalk."

"Multiracially bland."

"Brava. Want a drink?"

"Why not?" she said.

Brian ordered drinks from an old fellow who probably doubled as hall porter.

She said, "And you are here?"

"For the cars. I read about the show last night and felt a sort of schoolboy itch."

"Couldn't even wait for the weekend."

"Crowded. I deserve a day off anyway."

"You had to wait around for lunch. I'm sorry. I thought you had a business appointment."

"I'm not finished with the cars. They're worth a second look. And what could be nicer than sitting here waiting for someone to bring our drinks and fix the air conditioner and do something about the stuffing in the banquettes?"

"Is that what smells?" she said.

She smoked of course. Once she ordered the drink she knew the facade would crumble. It took very little to bring it down. She would smoke all she had and then find more. He made her laugh a few times and was funny even when he wasn't trying to be. She thought he probably had a rabbit for a pet when he was small but she wasn't sure why this made sense.

"You're tall, aren't you?"

He asked this suspiciously, as if she'd been concealing it.

"No taller than you."

"My wife is small. Have you met her?"

"I'm not sure."

"She wants me to take her to New York next month. I have to consult with engineers at the Fresh Kills landfill, which is sort of the King Kong of American garbage mounds."

"Does Nick like this kind of work?"

"You're asking me?" he said.

"Yes, I'm asking you."

"I think he likes it more than I do. I think he sees it in purer terms. Concepts and principles. Because this is Nick—the technology, the logic, the esthetics. Whereas I, in my little gringo mind-set."

"You're moving into new quarters. That may help your self-image."

"Yes, a great bronze tower. Just like an investment firm or media giant. Of course the structure resembles a geometric turd but that's only fitting, no?"

163

The man brought their drinks and they looked at the menus in the nearly empty room, they talked and looked, not really looking—looking and forgetting. Marian felt the nice bite of the gin and wondered what it was about Brian that made him so easy to talk to. She thought he went around scared most of the time but did not try to hide it from women, some women anyway, maybe the rare woman he runs into a hundred miles from home, and he falls all over himself with honesty and self-scathing insight, the things he does not normally show the boys.

To reciprocate perhaps. She didn't know why else she'd tell the dog story if not to strut her own confessional skills. They had another drink and ordered lunch.

"The dog barked and whined incessantly, Dukey, but the kids were small and they loved their dog and he barked, he cried, he went bye-bye in the house, he yapped at other kids and the neighbors complained and I secretly tried to give him away but no one would take him and so I finally, on an impulse—this is awful, why am I telling you this?"

"Because the story haunts you. Because you see mercy in my eyes."

"Yes, a frantic impulse. I convinced myself the dog was miserable and sick and suffering some irreversible thing and I drove out on 85, I think it is, down past some dam into stark stony desert, much farther than I absolutely had to go, and I just kept going and going and finally stopped the car and opened the door and set Dukey out on the ground and then drove home and told Lainie, Sweetheart the dog ran away and I'm so sorry. But I did not let it go at that. I went reeling out of control. I started driving them through the streets, both kids, day after day, calling out the windows for Dukey, Dukey, and it haunts me, yes, like something I only dreamed and what a relief it is to realize it didn't actually happen."

"And then you realize it did happen."

Brian was enjoying this immensely and so she began to enjoy it too, which was probably the point, she thought.

"Driving through the dead summer streets in the long afternoons. I can hear their voices. Dukey, Dukey. They were five and three, I think. Calling out the windows for their dog."

She was nearly laughing-crying, looking at Brian's mug alight with pleasure and feeling the misery and shame of her act and smoking in the middle of a meal in an empty dining room where the air conditioner is not responding.

He said, "Dukey, Dukey."

"Duchino actually. Little Duke. Nick came up with the name. Do you know he's half Italian?"

"Our Nick? When did this happen?"

"You don't see it in his face?"

"I hear it in that voice he does."

"What voice?"

"The gangster making threats."

"What gangster?"

"It's a voice he does. Expert, stereotyped, pretty funny."

"Speaking of backgrounds," she said. "And if this is too personal, you don't have to answer. But did you ever have a rabbit for a pet?"

They were having a fine time. When he talked she found herself sorting through the responses, getting them ready, one after another, and sometimes she broke in irresistibly and watched his face go bright. She told him she played field hockey in school and missed it. She missed drinking from a garden hose. She missed her mother and father more than ever and they'd been dead nine years and six years and were stronger forces now, so deeply present in her life that she understood completely how people see ghosts and have conversations with the dead. She had a garden hose but did not drink from it and did not allow her kids to drink from it and this was the difference, less in lost things than in knowledge become suspicious and alert. She told him she missed smoking even though she hadn't been able to stop.

When they were finished they walked up a stairway to the lobby and in her mind she kept ascending to a shadowed room at the end of a long empty hall and saw herself folding down the bedspread and standing above the cool sheets waiting for a knock at the door. Then they heard plaintive falsettos from the loudspeakers on the courthouse lawn and they walked down to the cars in the easy heat.

Brian went into a state of body rapture over a lime sherbet Chevrolet, a '57 Bel Air convertible with white upholstery. He draped himself over the hood and pretended to lick the hot metal. Marian thought this is what men get instead of fatty deposits around the thighs. But she had to admire the car, which was carefree and racy and even great in a way, the chromium sweep of it and the funny and touching music that bared its innocence.

Brian detached himself from the hood.

"Did you own one?"

"Too young," he said. "My oldest brother had one for a while. Brendan's Bel Air. We still talk about it in awed tones. It was the high point of his life. It meant everything to him. Girls, love, personality, power. It meant the moment. All those cars had the so-called forward look. Sleek as jet fighters. But it turned out that forward didn't mean the future. It meant do it now, have your fun, because the sixties are coming, bow wow bang bang. The engine had a throaty roar. We couldn't know it at the time but it's been downhill for Brendan ever since."

They walked under the elms at the edge of the square. His car was parked by the old city jail, which was the chamber of commerce now. They spoke oddly polite goodbyes. She thought maybe they felt guilty about something and needed to prepare their faces for the journey home, get the noise out of the system. She walked up the street to her car and felt the liquid pulse of the sun in every step.

3

Brian drove due north, looking for a sign that would lead him to the bridge. A sludge tanker moved downriver, funky and low-slung. He felt the old foreboding. It wasn't widely known, it was narrowly known that he experienced terrible things every time he crossed a bridge. The longer and higher the span, the greater his sense of breathless abyss. And this was a major bridge over a broad and historic body of water. The truth of bridges is that they made him feel he was doing some möbius gyration, becoming one-sided, losing all purchase on name and place and food-taste and weekends with the in-laws—hanging sort of unborn in generic space.

Then he saw it in the distance, steel-beamed and cabled, sweeping to the palisaded bank. He followed the signs, made the loops and started out across the bridge, choosing the upper level because the long gray Lincoln in front of him went that way. Lincoln and Washington, keep me safe. The radio was ablast with call-in voices, they're griping, they're spraying spit, it's the sidewalk salvo and rap, and he imagined a long queue of underground souls waiting to enter the broadcast band and speak the incognito news. He listened in solemn gratitude. It was a clamor so strong it amounted to a life force, carrying this Ohio boy through his white anxiety and across to the Jersey side.

He was looking for 46 west. He'd written out directions that the man had recited over the phone. The man had recited the routes and streets in a manner so automatic that Brian realized many pilgrims had made the trip across the river.

He had the directions written on hotel stationery and he kept the page on the seat next to him, snatching a look every ten seconds. After a mile on 46 west he spotted the Exxon station and made the maneuver onto 63 south, racing along the three-mile stretch to the Point Diner. Then he made a left turn out of the howl of highly motivated traffic and into residential streets, beginning to relax at last, approaching the circle on Kennedy Drive, another dead president.

Down a side street to an old frame house. Marvin Lundy opened the door, a hunched fellow with a stylized shuffle, in his late sixties, holding a burnt-out cigar. Brian thought he resembled some retired stand-up comic who will not live a minute longer than his last monopolized conversation. He followed the man through two rooms steeped in aquarium dimness. Then they went to the basement, a large finished room that held Marvin Lundy's collection of baseball memorabilia.

"My late wife, she would serve us tea with popovers that she made fresh, all other things being equal."

The room was filled with objects on tasteful display. Flannel jerseys draped along the walls, caps with souvenir buttons pinned to the visors, there were newspaper pages framed and hung. Brian did a reverent tour, examining autographed bats ranked on custom wall fittings, game bats beautifully grained, some with pine tar on the choke. There were stadium seats labeled like rare botanical specimens—Ebbets Field, Shibe Park, Griffith Stadium. He nearly touched an old catcher's mitt set on a pedestal, the object gashed yellow, spike-gashed and sun-smoked and patriarchal, but he managed to hold back. He looked at autographed baseballs in plexiglas globes. He leaned over display cases that held cigarette cards, ticket stubs, the signed contracts of famous players, nineteenth-century baseball board games, bubblegum wrappers that carried the pinkish likenesses of men from Brian's youth, their names a kind of poetry floating down the decades.

168

"You would put strawberry preserves on the popovers, which forget it, all life from the Renaissance onward it pales by compare."

None of this amounted to an astonishment. It was interesting, even moving in a way, but not great or memorable. The wondrous touch, the outlandish and surpassing fancy was the large construction along the far wall, a replica of the old Polo Grounds scoreboard and clubhouse facade. It covered an area about twenty-two feet long and twelve feet high, floor to ceiling, and included the Chesterfield sign and slogan, the Longines clock, a semblance of the clubhouse windows and parapet and finally a hand-slotted line score, the inning by inning tally of the famous play-off game of 1951.

"You would have to eat them hot. She made a strict rule of no dawdling, Eleanor, because lukewarm you lose the whole experience."

Brian stood near the scoreboard, looking at Marvin for permission to touch.

"I had a draftsman, a carpenter, an electrician and a sign painter, not a house painter, very temperamental. I showed them photographs and they did measurements and sketches so they could respect the proportions and get the colors. The hit sign and the E light up, for error. Where do you live?"

"Phoenix."

"I was never there."

In the stronger light down here he could see that Marvin Lundy's hair was a swatch of loomed synthetic, ash-brown, combed sleekly forward, and it made Brian think of Las Vegas and pinky rings and prostate cancer.

He said to Marvin, "I grew up in the Midwest. Cleveland Indians, that was my team. And I was flying in on business last night and saw an article in the airline magazine, the piece about you and your collectibles, and I felt a strong compulsion to get in touch with you and see these things."

He fingered the silky lapel of Babe Ruth's smoking jacket.

"My daughter talked me into doing the interview," Marvin said. "She thinks I'm turning into a what-do-you-call."

"A recluse."

"An old recluse with half a stomach. So now my picture's in twenty thousand seat pouches. This is her idea of get out and meet people. They put me in with the vomit bags."

Brian said, "I went to a car show and it did something to me."

"What did it do?"

"Cars from the nineteen-fifties. I don't know."

"You feel sorry for yourself. You think you're missing something and you don't know what it is. You're lonely inside your life. You have a job and a family and a fully executed will, already, at your age, because the whole point is to die prepared, die legal, with all the papers signed. Die liquid, so they can convert to cash. You used to have the same dimensions as the observable universe. Now you're a lost speck. You look at old cars and recall a purpose, a destination."

"It's ridiculous, isn't it? But probably harmless too."

"Nothing is harmless," Marvin said. "You're worried and scared. You see the cold war winding down. This makes it hard for you to breathe."

Brian pushed through a turnstile from an old ballpark. It creaked sort of lovingly.

He said, "Cold war? I don't see the cold war winding down. And if I did, good. I'd be happy about it."

"Let me explain something that maybe you never noticed."

Marvin was sitting in an armchair alongside an old equipment trunk bearing the stenciled inscription *Boston Red Stockings*. He gestured toward the chair on the other side of the trunk and Brian went over and sat down.

"You need the leaders of both sides to keep the cold war going. It's the one constant thing. It's honest, it's dependable. Because when the tension and rivalry come to an end, that's when your worst nightmares begin. All the power and intimidation of the state will seep out of your personal bloodstream. You will no longer be the main—what do I want to say?"

"I'm not sure."

"Point of reference. Because other forces will come rushing in, demanding and challenging. The cold war is your friend. You need it to stay on top."

"On top of what?"

"You don't know on top of what? You don't know the whole thing is geared to your dominance in the world? You see what they have in England. Forty thousand women circling an air base to protest the bombs and missiles. Some of them are men in dresses. They have Buddhists beating drums."

Brian didn't know how to respond to these remarks. He wanted to talk about old ballplayers, stadium dimensions, about nicknames and minor league towns. That's why he was here, to surrender himself to longing, to listen to his host recite the anecdotal texts, all the passed-down stories of bonehead plays and swirling brawls, the pitching duels that carried into twilight, stories that Marvin had been collecting for half a century—the deep eros of memory that separates baseball from other sports.

Marvin sat staring at the scoreboard, his cigar slightly shredded at the burnt end.

"I thought we were going to talk baseball."

"We're talking baseball. This is baseball. You see the clock," Marvin said. "Stopped at three fifty-eight. Why? Is it because that's when Thomson hit the homer off Branca?"

He called him Branker.

"Or because that's the day we found out the Russians exploded an atom bomb. You know something about that game?"

"What?" Brian said.

"There were twenty thousand empty seats. You know why?"

"Why?"

"You'll laugh in my face."

"No, I won't."

"It's all right. You're my guest. I want you to feel at home."

"Why so many empty seats for the most important game of the year?"

"Many years," Marvin said.

"Many years."

"Because certain events have a quality of unconscious fear. I believe in my heart that people sensed some catastrophe in the air. Not who would win or lose the game. Some awful force that would obliterate—what's the word?"

"Obliterate."

"Obliterate. That would obliterate the whole thing of the game. You have to understand that all through the nineteen-fifties people stayed indoors. We only went outside to drive our cars. Public parks were not filled with people the way they later became. A museum was empty rooms with knights in armor where you had one sleepy guard for every seven centuries."

"In other words."

"In other words there was a hidden mentality of let's stay home. Because a threat was hanging in the air."

"And you're saying people had an intuition about this particular day."

"It's like they knew. They sensed there was a connection between this game and some staggering event that might take place on the other side of the world."

"This particular game."

"Not the day before or the day after. Because this was an all-or-nothing game between the two hated rivals of the city. People had a premonition that this game was related to something much bigger. They had the mental process of do I want to go out and be in a big crowd, which if something awful happens is the worst place to be, or should I stay home with my family and my brand-new TV, which common sense says yes, in a cabinet with maple veneer."

To his surprise Brian did not reject this theory. He didn't necessarily believe it but he didn't dismiss it either. He believed it provisionally here in this room located below street level in a frame house on a week-day afternoon in Cliffside Park, New Jersey. It was lyrically true as it emerged from Marvin Lundy's mouth and reached Brian's middle ear, unprovably true, remotely and inadmissably true but not completely unhistorical, not without some nuance of authentic inner narrative.

Marvin said, "Which the whole thing is interesting because when they make an atomic bomb, listen to this, they make the radioactive core the exact same size as a baseball."

"I always thought it was a grapefruit."

"A regulation major league baseball no less than nine inches in circumference, going by the rule book."

He crossed his legs, he stuck a finger in his ear and jigged an itch. Marvin had enormous ears. For the first time Brian became aware of music playing somewhere in the house. Maybe he'd been hearing it all along at the assimilated edge, music blended with the room tone, the airplanes drifting into Newark, the faint wail of bullet traffic on the speedways out there—a moderated sorrow, piano work that had the texture of something old and gentled over, a pressed rose faded in a book.

"People sense things that are invisible. But when something's staring you right in the face, that's when you miss it completely."

"What do you mean?" Brian said.

"This Gorbachev that walks around with that thing on his head. It's a birthmark, what he's got?"

"Yes, I think so."

"It's big. You agree with this?"

"Yes, it's quite big."

"Noticeable. You can't help but notice. Am I right?"

"Yes, you are."

"And you agree that millions of people see this thing every day in the newspaper?"

"Yes, they do."

"They open the paper and there's the man's head with that amazing mark high on the dome. Agreed?"

"Yes, of course."

"What does it mean?" Marvin said.

"Why does it have to mean something?"

"You take it at face value."

"It's his face," Brian said. "It's his head. A blemish, a birthmark."

"That's not what I see."

"What do you see?"

"You asked so I'll tell you."

Marvin saw the first sign of the total collapse of the Soviet system. Stamped on the man's head. The map of Latvia.

He said this straight-faced, how Gorbachev was basically conveying the news that the USSR faced turmoil from the republics.

"You think his birthmark? Wait a minute."

"Excuse me but if you rotate the map of Latvia ninety degrees so

173

the eastern border goes on top, this is exactly the shape that's on Gorbachev's head. In other words when he's lying in bed at night and his wife comes over to give him a glass of water and an aspirin, this is Latvia she's looking at."

Brian tried to conjure the shape of the winestain mark on Gorbachev's head. He wanted to match it with a memory of geography tests on mellow afternoons, his limbs faintly aching with biological drives and the sweetness of school's end. The old melodic line came lullabying back, Latvia, Estonia, Lithuania. But the map shapes escaped him now, the precise silhouettes of those nestled anatomies.

Marvin was looking at the scoreboard again.

"People collect, collect, always collecting. There's people they go after anything out of wartime Germany. Naziana. This is major collectors looking for big history. Does that mean the objects in this room are total trivia? What's the word I'm looking for that sounds like you're getting injected with a vaccine in the fleshy part of your arm?"

"Innocuous."

"Innocuous. What am I, innocuous? This is history, back-page. From back to front. Happy, tragic, desperate." Marvin shifted his gaze. "In this trunk right here I have the one thing that my whole life for the past twenty-two years I was trying to collect."

Brian had an inkling.

"I tracked, I searched and finally I found it and bought it, eighteen months ago, and I don't even put it on display. I keep it in the trunk, out of sight."

Now it was Brian who looked at the scoreboard.

Marvin said morosely, "It's the Bobby Thomson home-run ball, which I traced it back starting with rumors in the business. It wasn't even a business back then, just a few interested parties with someone's telephone number or first name, the skimpiest kind of lead that I pursued with a fury."

He paused to light his cigar. It was old and stale and looked like a soybean sausage from the school cafeteria. But Brian understood that a cigar was tribally required, even if the smoke stung his eyes.

For the next three hours Marvin talked about his search for the baseball. He forgot some names and mangled others. He lost whole cities, placing them in the wrong time zones. He described how he followed false leads into remote places. He climbed the stairs to raftered upper rooms and looked in old trunks among the grandmother's linen and the photographs of the dead.

"I said to myself a thousand times. Why do I want this thing? What does it mean? Who has it?"

Through the narration, the whole wandering epic, skimmed here, protracted there, Brian was confident that the man was slipshod only in the telling. The search itself had clearly been hard, fierce, thorough and consuming.

At one point Marvin hired a man who worked in a photo lab and had access to special equipment. They studied news photographs of the left-field stands at the Polo Grounds taken just after the ball went in. They looked at enlargements and enhancements. They went to photo agencies and burrowed in the archives. Marvin had people sneak him into newspaper morgues, into the wire services and the major magazines.

"I looked at a million photographs because this is the dot theory of reality, that all knowledge is available if you analyze the dots."

There was a slight crackle in his voice that sounded like random radio noise produced by some disturbance of the signal.

He acquired original film. He brought in darkroom equipment. He ate his meals with a magnifier around his neck. The house was filled with contact sheets, glossy prints, there were blowups pinned to clotheslines rigged through several rooms. His wife and child fled to England to visit relatives because Marvin somehow married English.

He hired a private detective with an intermittent nosebleed. They placed ads in the personal columns of sporting magazines, trying to locate people who'd sat in section 35, where the ball went in.

There was the photographic detailwork, the fineness of image, the what-do-you-call-it into littler units.

"Resolution," Brian said.

And then there was the long journey, the suitcase crawl through empty train stations, the bitter winter flights with ice on the wings, there was the weary traipse, a word he doesn't hear anymore, the march into people's houses and lives—the actual physical thing, unphotographed, of liver-spotted hands and dimpled chins and the whole strewn sense of what they remember and forget.

1. The widow on Long Island turning a spoon in her cup.

2. The gospel singer named Prestigious Booker who kept a baseball in an urn that held her lover's ashes.

3. The ship on the dock in San Francisco—don't even bring it up.

4. The man in his car in Deaf Smith County, Texas, the original middle of nowhere.

5. A whole generation of Jesus faces. Young men everywhere bearded and sandaled, bearded and barefoot—little peeky spectacles with wire frames.

6. Marvin's sense of being lost in America, wandering through cities with no downtowns.

7. The woman on Long Island, what's-her-name, whose husband was at the game—she served instant coffee in cups from a doll museum.

8. The Coptic family in Detroit—never mind, it's too complicated, riots and fires in the distance, tanks in the streets.

9. The detailed confusion of Marvin's narrative, people's memories mixed with his own, shaped to bending time.

10. A tornado touching down, skipping along the treetops in an evil weave, the whole sky filthy with flung debris.

11. Whose husband was in the footage Marvin analyzed, scrambling for the baseball, and all she had in the house was instant.

12. Riding up the side of a building in an elevator that's transparent.

13. The ship on the dock—please not now.

14. What a mystery all around him, every street deep in some radiant amaze.

Brian listened to all this and he heard the music end and begin again, the same piano piece, and this was not the second time he was hearing it but maybe the eighth or ninth, and he listened to Marvin's dot theory of reality and felt an underlying force in this theme of the relentless photographic search, some prototype he could not bring into tight definition.

"A thousand times I said. How long do I look? Why do I want it? Where is it?"

He advertised for amateur film footage of the game and acquired a few minutes of crude action that showed a massive pulsing blur above the left-field wall shot by a man in the bleachers. He brought in an optical printer. He rephotographed the footage. He enlarged, repositioned, analyzed. He step-framed the action to slow it down, to combine several seconds of film into one image. He examined the sprocket areas of the film searching for a speck of data, a minim of missing imagery. It was work of Talmudic refinement, zooming in and fading out, trying to bring a man's face into definition, read a woman's ankle bracelet engraved with a name.

Brian was shamed by other men's obsessions. They exposed his own middling drift, the voice he heard, soft, faint and faraway, that told him not to bother.

Marvin's wife and child came home and went away again. The house had become a booby hatch of looming images. The isolated grimace, the hair that juts from the mole on the old man's chin. Every image teeming with crystalized dots. A photograph is a universe of dots. The grain, the halide, the little silver things clumped in the emulsion. Once you get inside a dot, you gain access to hidden information, you slide inside the smallest event.

This is what technology does. It peels back the shadows and redeems the dazed and rambling past. It makes reality come true.

Marvin Lundy opened the trunk.

The baseball was wrapped in tissue paper inside an old red-and-white Spalding box. There were deep stacks of photographs and correspondence and other material related to the search. Birth certificates, passports, affidavits, handwritten wills, detailed lists of people's possessions, there were bloodstained garments in Ziploc bags.

He took some still frames out of a manila envelope and showed them to Brian.

This was a sequence that involved the scramble for the ball, people in bevies, Marvin said, scratching and grabbing, and a man in the last photo standing starkly alone, white-shirted, looking down at the exit ramp, looking hard, glaring at someone, probably at the person who'd come away with the ball, but Marvin could not find a way, for all his mastery of the dots, to rotate the heads of the people on the ramp so he could see the face of the individual in question.

"But you identified the man in the white shirt."

"From running the picture in the back of magazines where they did waterbeds and dirty personals."

"And you went to see the wife."

"This is many years after the game. What happened he died. The widow sits in a cold house turning a spoon in her tiny cup. I try to find out what he might have said to her about the game, the ball, anything. What game, she says. I try to explain the extenuations of the thing. But it's more than twenty years later. What game, what ball?"

A woman came down the stairs carrying coffee and cheesecake on a tray. She seemed to issue from Marvin's story, a recollected figure taking material form. Marvin shut the trunk so she could place the tray on top. She was his daughter, Clarice, determined to tend to dad whatever his objections.

"I didn't hear you come in. She comes in like she's Chinese, with muffled feet."

"You were talking. I could be an armed robbery in progress, you wouldn't hear a thing."

She was in her late twenties, blondish and gym-fit. She told Brian she lived ten minutes away by car and worked as a court stenographer. He thought he could easily fall in love with the sitcom tilt in her voice and the swerve of her thigh lines under the linen skirt.

"We're almost finished here, Clarice."

"In a hundred grueling hours. Your guest may have other things he needs to do."

"What could he have?"

"It'll be dark soon."

"Dark, light. These are words."

The baseball box was on its side among scattered photographs on the floor and the ball had dribbled out, still crinkled in tissue. Clarice pulled up a chair and she and Marvin finished the story, more or less, through mouthfuls of cheesecake.

"For how many years, Clarice, I'm looking for a man named Jackson or Judson?"

"Get to the point," she said.

"Because there were roundabout hints that pointed to him as

someone I should be interested in. And the ball has a history by this time that I've been inching along, where different things match and join. But I can't locate the man or even—what?"

"Ascertain," Brian said.

"His correct name. By this time, forget the footage—I'm using rumors and dreams. There's an ESP of baseball, an underground what, a consciousness, and I'm hearing it in my sleep."

"Faster, daddy, faster."

"Meanwhile there's this woman. I'm trying to find Judson Jackson Johnson and there's this woman who got my name from the memorabilia market and she's been calling me long-distance collect day and night. She says she used to own the thing I'm looking for. Mysteriously missing for years, she says, from the little locked box where she used to keep it."

"Genevieve Rauch."

"Whose name I can never."

"Genevieve Rauch," his daughter said. "And the two of them try to establish the basic, you know."

"Indicators," Brian said.

"That would make her baseball at least a remote possibility."

"The marks and scratches," Marvin said. "The trademark if it's correct. The signature of the league president who was in office at the time. Her memory is iffy. I make some leeway, then she talks about something else. This is a woman she has an extra chromosome for changing the subject. A thousand times I'm tempted to hang up the phone."

"Then it happens," Clarice said.

"A man in his car."

"A man's driving along in his car, someone shoots him dead. Turns out the victim is the long-lost former husband of Genevieve Rauch. Turns out further his name is Juddy Rauch, Judson Rauch. So the two rivers meet. Took a homicide to reveal the connection."

Marvin lowered his head to the trunk top to sip his coffee and Brian stared into the weave of his woeful toupee.

"When I had my stomach I used to eat this cheesecake unconscious."

179

Clarice explained how he went to Deaf Smith County, Texas, where he hired a local lawyer on behalf of Genevieve Rauch and finally located the baseball sealed in a baggie and vouchered and numbered and stored in the property clerk's office. Impounded by the police along with the body, the car, all the things in the car, of which this was one, crammed in a cardboard box filled with junky odds and ends.

Marvin puffed on his stogie.

"I go all the way to the Bronx to buy this cheesecake. A kosher bakery that you couldn't find it if I gave you a road map, a guidebook and whatever he's called that speaks five languages."

"An interpreter."

"An interpreter," Marvin said.

The cheesecake was smooth and lush, with the personality of a warm and well-to-do uncle who knows a hundred dirty jokes and will die of sexual exertions in the arms of his mistress.

"And so finally," Brian said, "you bought the baseball."

"And I traced it all the way back to October fourth, the day after the game, nineteen hundred and fifty-one."

"And how did you finance this operation for so many years? The travel, the technical end, all of it."

"I had a local chain of stores, dry cleaning, which I sold after my wife passed away because I didn't need it anymore, the aggravation."

"Marvin the Clothes King," his daughter said with a little affection, a little regret, some irony, a certain pride, a touch of rueful humor and so on.

She talked to her father about a doctor's appointment he had in the morning and he listened the way you listen to the TV news, staring indifferently into India. She took the tray and headed up the stairs. Brian imagined following her in his car and pulling alongside and catching her eye and then accelerating loudly and leading her to a wayside inn where they get a room and undress each other with their teeth and tongues and never say a word.

He listened to the music drifting through the house, the keyboard lament, and he finally identified the lurking presence in the story of Marvin's search, the strange secondhandedness of all that exacting work, the retouching, the enhancements—it was an eerie replay of the investigations into the political murders of the 1960s. The attempt to reassemble a crucial moment in time out of patches and adumbrations—Marvin in his darkroom borrowing a powerful theme and using it to locate a small white innocent object bouncing around a ballpark.

Brian said, "So we know the lineage of the thing in the later stages. Rauch to Rauch to Lundy. But how did it all begin?"

"You asked so I'll tell you. With a man named Charles, let me think, Wainwright. An advertising executive. I have the complete sequence back to him. The line of ownership."

"But not back to the game itself."

"I don't have the last link that I can connect backwards from the Wainwright ball to the ball making contact with Bobby Thomson's bat." He looked sourly at the scoreboard clock. "I have a certain number of missing hours I still have to find. And when you're dealing with something so many years back, you have to face the mortality rate. Wainwright passed away and his son Charles Jr. is forty-two years old now and stuck with the name Chuckie and I've been trying to talk to him for a long time. He was last seen working as an engineer on a freighter that plied—you like that word?"

"Plied."

"The Baltic Sea," Marvin said. "Speaking of which."

"Yes?"

"You should train an eye on the mark on this Gorbachev's head, to see if it changes shape."

"Changes shape? It's always been there."

"You know this?"

"What, you think it recently appeared?"

"You know this? It's always been there?"

"It's a birthmark," Brian said.

"Excuse me but that's the official biography. I'll tell you what I think. I think if I had a sensitive government job I would be photographing Gorbachev from outer space every minute of the day that he's not wearing a hat to check the shape of the birthmark if it's changing. Because it's Latvia right now. But it could be Siberia in the morning, where they're emptying out their jails."

He looked at his cigar.

"Reality doesn't happen until you analyze the dots."

Then he got to his feet with a certain effort.

"And when the cold war goes out of business, you won't be able to look at some woman in the street and have a what-do-you-call-it kind of fantasy the way you do today."

"Erotic. But what's the connection?"

"You don't know the connection? You don't know that every privilege in your life and every thought in your mind depends on the ability of the two great powers to hang a threat over the planet?"

"That's an amazing thing to say."

"And you don't know that once this threat begins to fade?"

"What?"

"You're the lost man of history."

It seemed the visit was done. But first the host led his guest to a shelved alcove near the stairway. This is where he kept his collection of taped ball games, radio and TV, hundreds of slotted cassettes going back to the earliest broadcasts.

"People who save these bats and balls and preserve the old stories through the spoken word and know the nicknames of a thousand players, we're here in our basements with tremendous history on our walls. And I'll tell you something, you'll see I'm right. There's men in the coming years they'll pay fortunes for these objects. They'll pay unbelievable. Because this is desperation speaking."

Brian wished the man could be lighter and sweeter. He looked at the scoreboard one last time. He thought finally it was an impressive thing but maybe a little funereal. It had that compact quality of preservation and exact proportion and respectful history that can produce a mood of mausoleum gloom.

They went up the stairs and walked through the shadowed rooms to the front door. Marvin stood there with his dead cigar.

"Men come here to see my collection."

"Yes."

"They come and they don't want to leave. The phone rings, it's the family—where is he? This is the fraternity of missing men."

"I understand."

"What's your name?"

182

"Brian Glassic."

"Nice to meet you," Marvin said.

Brian asked about a way back to Manhattan that did not include the George Washington Bridge. There was a tunnel here and a tunnel there and Marvin gave both sets of directions with a number of choices attached to each. Brian the fool narrowed his eyes and nodded yes although he knew he would retain none of this once he was in the car.

He drove along turnpikes and skyways, seeing Manhattan come and go in a valium sunset, smoky and golden. The car wobbled in the sound booms of highballing trucks, drivers perched in tall cabs with food, drink, dope and pornography, and the rigs seemed to draw the little car down the pike in their sheering wind. He drove past enormous tank farms, squat white cylinders arrayed across the swampland, and he saw white dome tanks in smaller groupings and long lines of tank cars rolling down the tracks. He went past power pylons with their spindly arms akimbo. He drove into the spewing smoke of acres of burning truck tires and the planes descended and the transit cranes stood in rows at the marine terminal and he saw billboards for Hertz and Avis and Chevy Blazer, for Marlboro, Continental and Goodyear, and he realized that all the things around him, the planes taking off and landing, the streaking cars, the tires on the cars, the cigarettes that the drivers of the cars were dousing in their ashtrays—all these were on the billboards around him, systematically linked in some self-referring relationship that had a kind of neurotic tightness, an inescapability, as if the billboards were generating reality, and of course he thought of Marvin.

When he went past Newark Airport he realized he'd overshot all the turnoffs and their related options. He looked for a friendly exit, untrucked and rural, and found himself some time later on a two-lane blacktop that wended uncertainly through cattail mires. He felt a bitey edge of brine in the air and the road bent and then ended in gravel and weeds.

He got out of the car and climbed an earthen bank. The wind was stiff enough to make his eyes go moist and he looked across a narrow body of water to a terraced elevation on the other side. It was reddish brown, flat-topped, monumental, sunset burning in the heights, and Brian thought he was hallucinating an Arizona butte. But it was real and it was man-made, swept by wheeling gulls, and he knew it could be only one thing—the Fresh Kills landfill on Staten Island.

This was the reason for his trip to New York and he was scheduled to meet there with surveyors and engineers in the morning. Three thousand acres of mountained garbage, contoured and road-graded, with bulldozers pushing waves of refuse onto the active face. Brian felt invigorated, looking at this scene. Barges unloading, sweeper boats poking through the kills to pick up stray waste. He saw a maintenance crew working on drainpipes high on the angled setbacks that were designed to control the runoff of rainwater. Other figures in masks and butylene suits were gathered at the base of the structure to inspect isolated material for toxic content. It was science fiction and prehistory, garbage arriving twenty-four hours a day, hundreds of workers, vehicles with metal rollers compacting the trash, bucket auger digging vents for methane gas, the gulls diving and crying, a line of snouted trucks sucking in loose litter.

He imagined he was watching the construction of the Great Pyramid at Giza—only this was twenty-five times bigger, with tanker trucks spraying perfumed water on the approach roads. He found the sight inspiring. All this ingenuity and labor, this delicate effort to fit maximum waste into diminishing space. The towers of the World Trade Center were visible in the distance and he sensed a poetic balance between that idea and this one. Bridges, tunnels, scows, tugs, graving docks, container ships, all the great works of transport, trade and linkage were directed in the end to this culminating structure. And the thing was organic, ever growing and shifting, its shape computer-plotted by the day and the hour. In a few years this would be the highest mountain on the Atlantic Coast between Boston and Miami. Brian felt a sting of enlightenment. He looked at all that soaring garbage and knew for the first time what his job was all about. Not engineering or transportation or source reduction. He dealt in human behavior, people's habits and impulses, their uncontrollable needs and innocent wishes, maybe their passions, certainly their excesses and indulgences but their kindness too, their generosity, and the question was how to keep this mass metabolism from overwhelming us.

The landfill showed him smack-on how the waste stream ended,

184

where all the appetites and hankerings, the sodden second thoughts came runneling out, the things you wanted ardently and then did not. He'd seen a hundred landfills but none so vast as this. Yes, impressive and distressing. He knew the stench must ride the wind into every dining room for miles around. When people heard a noise at night, did they think the heap was coming down around them, sliding toward their homes, an omnivorous movie terror filling their doorways and windows?

The wind carried the stink across the kill.

Brian took a deep breath, he filled his lungs. This was the challenge he craved, the assault on his complacency and vague shame. To understand all this. To penetrate this secret. The mountain was here, unconcealed, but no one saw it or thought about it, no one knew it existed except the engineers and teamsters and local residents, a unique cultural deposit, fifty million tons by the time they top it off, carved and modeled, and no one talked about it but the men and women who tried to manage it, and he saw himself for the first time as a member of an esoteric order, they were adepts and seers, crafting the future, the city planners, the waste managers, the compost technicians, the landscapers who would build hanging gardens here, make a park one day out of every kind of used and lost and eroded object of desire.

The biggest secrets are the ones spread open before us. This was Marvin Lundy talking, filling Brian's head with that dry staticky voice that seemed to come out of a surgical slit in his throat.

The wind carried the stink from the mountain of wrack.

Specks and glints, ragtails of color appeared in the stratified mass of covering soil, fabric scraps from the garment center, stirred by the wind, or maybe that teal thing is a bikini brief that belonged to a secretary from Queens, and Brian found he could create a flash infatuation, she is dark-eyed and reads the tabloids and paints her nails and eats lunch out of molded styrofoam, and he gives her gifts and she gives him condoms, and it all ends up here, newsprint, emery boards, sexy underwear, coaxed into high relief by the rumbling dozers—think of his multitudinous spermlings with their history of high family foreheads, stranded in a Ramses body bag and rolled snug in the deep-down waste.

185

He watched several gulls veering near and saw a hundred other gulls positioned on a slope, all facing the same way, motionless, regardful, joined in consciousness, in beautiful empty birdness, waiting for the signal to fly.

4

Marvin was out of his basement, wincing in the light. He steered his car tenaciously, choosing a lane and sticking to it. He wore a tan windbreaker with a plaid lining because this is what he always wore when the leaves began to turn. It was the faithful change of apparel, an adjustment to the cosmos that made his life seem regular. He wore the jacket through the decades, giving the old one to the Salvation Army and buying another just like it, the everyman tan that he could spot on a store hanger from fifty yards in one of those vast hushed areas just before closing time where ranks of suits are arrayed like executives in hell.

He also wore a pair of latex gloves, a precaution he took whenever he went to the city.

When he got to the Lower East Side he drove through the streets a number of times before he found a space that looked okay, where he wouldn't get towed and he wouldn't get broken in, and he locked the car and then stood back and studied the parking job he'd done and the street in general, old furniture sold cheap and a truck lot in which every inch of every truck was covered with graffiti. The humans walked by looking touchy and unbeloved. He saw two men in wheelchairs who scooted after cars stopped at the light to scrounge a little change.

Marvin walked in his sliding step, his sort of explanatory shuffle, it was a comment on the literature of shuffles. He went down Orchard Street looking at the clothes in the windows and stalls, dry goods by the mile. He stopped to read the writing on a collection of what-do-you-call, T-shirts, a nasty remark on nearly every item, words unprintable through history wearing shirts in a window. A young man stood next to him, thin-limbed and tattooed, a mustache that's half finished, glaring at him. He felt the glare, a tapered look directed straight into the side of his head.

Marvin glanced over.

"What? I'm looking in the window," he said.

"I look means you gotta look?"

"I can't look? What? It's a window."

"You seen me looking. Means you gotta look?"

"What? So I can't look?"

"I'm looking."

"It's a public window," Marvin said.

"You want window? I give you window."

"All of a sudden, this?"

"You think you want to look? I show you look."

Marvin walked away because what else could he do, flexing his fingers inside the latex gloves. It was impossible to live. You couldn't walk down the street one foot follows another. Because what happens? They kill you. They come out of a door and stab you because you look at them. This is the latest word in death and menace. You look at them, they kill you. One look where you catch their eye, it gives them the right to end your life.

Later he crossed Essex Street and found the bakery. What he likes, the backroom business right up front, the ovens and mixing table where they make bialys in front of your eyes, a man in a white shirt and a white apron with sifted meal on his hands and arms, and Marvin was struck by the force of the moment, a simple drama in a window, the whiteness of bread and work. He thought he could stand here all day and watch the baker shape the pasty mass. He bought for later, for his daughter, flat rolls, onion-flaked, that were a thing you eat and a city and a religion and a war.

He walked down the street with the bakery bag warm against his ribs. He passed a playground, kids crouched and darting on the hand-ball court, and half a block later it was all Chinese.

When he had his stomach he used to come here with Eleanor.

It was the old mystery of Chinese things, food on steam tables, vegetables he could not identify, the secret minds of the people. He stood and watched the living fish toss in homemade tanks. He bought a fried dumpling and took a bite, more for the gesture than the taste because he didn't taste the way he used to. It was like the memory of food, the ghost of ginger and minced chives.

He shuffled back to the car. He saw the wheelchair beggars with their scraggle beards, they raced each other to a stopped car, bodied forth, hands screwing and cranking. It was a competition of gyrating arms, their eyes peering through the dusty glass for some sign of contact within. But the drivers looked away. The drivers shut their windows against the window washers, the flower sellers, the carjackers, against the medium mad intent on conversation.

You look at them, they kill you.

He drove home, leaning tensely toward the wheel. An English girl from Somerset, you couldn't make it up. He played the piano elegy that was Eleanor's favorite music, once a month or so, hitting the repeat button so it never stopped. It was her voice he heard at this time of year, reminding him to get out the tan windbreaker. Time to don the old McGregor, Marv. In that simple little sentence, word for word through the years, was all the what, the deep dependency of two people who met during the war, wrote letters back and forth, finally got married, had a child after a while, it took some doing, two hearts joined in the habit of the days. Dry cleaning. He dry-cleaned McGregors by the ton.

The phone was ringing when he walked in the door. He went into the kitchen, put the bakery bag on the table, took off his jacket, the phone was ringing, he opened the refrigerator and got out the celery tonic and took a swig from the bottle, he was free to do that now, there are compensations too. He took off the gloves, so tight they resisted separation, peeling them down to the wide part of his hand and then yanking each clinging finger, a process that made him feel part artificial. Then he went across the room to the phone, which was a white wall model with a photograph next to it showing President Reagan standing in the Oval Office between Bobby Thomson and Ralph Branca, which was the only baseball reference anywhere in the house above the basement, a tasseled flag behind them. Because she could be a pain in the ass, Eleanor, on the subject of drinking from the bottle.

The phone was ringing. He looked at it and lifted the receiver, they call it a handset now. He was finally selling the house to go live in Clarice's apartment building, the daughter and son-in-law up on four, the father down on three in an easy-to-manage flat with bananas going brown on the windowsill. He would take showers sitting down while Clarice and Carl went running on their running machine upstairs, they were training to live forever.

"I'm calling from Phoenix," said the voice.

"The city or the bird?"

"Some months ago a man I know. Ten or eleven months ago. Paid you a visit."

"I wouldn't recall."

"Named Brian Glassic."

"If you tortured me, I wouldn't remember. I have people they come here half a dozen times. I see them on the street they could be garment bags on their way to the airport. I function inside my mind."

"In any case he recently mentioned the visit. I wonder what you can tell me about the baseball in the trunk."

They would knock on his door to see if he was all right. He'd poke his head past the shower curtain. All right, I'm fine, all right.

"You're a loyal fan retired in Arizona with a heart valve they implanted with dacron cuffs and you developed a sweetness for the old days. You spent your career in mergers and what, acquisitions. Made millions but you're still dissatisfied. You want one last acquisition that's personal from the heart."

"Brian said it might go like this."

"You want to talk about the ball, you get approximated first. The fact is I'm ready to sell. People know this. I get calls from men with

190

grainy voices. They have polymer packed in their gums. They have openings that were drilled in their sides for human waste to detour. They come home from the hospital echo-dopplered. I hear from men with quadruple bypass, with nitroglycerin in their bloodstream that you manufacture dynamite."

"I'm not a fan anymore. I don't follow the teams."

"I'm in the category myself where I'm undergoing tests. This means I have cancer recurring in so many parts of my body the doctor gives me group rates. Don't worry, you're not supposed to laugh. I'm trying to make you feel bad."

"And you're a Dodger fan, yes?"

"From before I was born."

"Raised in Brooklyn?"

"Raised in Brooklyn, get my cheesecake in the Bronx, go to the Lower East Side for this and that."

"A Dodger fan. But you've reproduced the Polo Grounds scoreboard in your basement."

"To remind me," Marvin said. "Or prepare me. I forget which."

"I'm not retired. And I haven't made millions. And I don't know exactly why I want to buy the ball."

This was good. Marvin liked this. It was good to hear from someone who was not palpitating in his mind for the old Giants or the old New York. They have stools you can buy in surgical supply outlets that you place in your shower so you can sit and do the far-flung parts of your body without falling and breaking a hip, which he saw one day on the hip replacement channel, with molded seats and nonskid legs. They have a channel for every body part.

"You call me out of nowhere," Marvin said. "And you want to do a deal. But you don't know why."

"That's right," said the voice.

Good. Because this was Marvin's situation for a long time. This was Marvin's exact status. For years he didn't know why he was chasing down exhausted objects. All that frantic passion for a baseball and he finally understood it was Eleanor on his mind, it was some terror working deep beneath the skin that made him gather up things, amass possessions and effects against the dark shape of some unshoulderable

191

loss. Memorabilia. What he remembered, what lived in the old smoked leather of the catcher's mitt in the basement was the touch of his Eleanor, those were his wife's eyes in the oval photographs of men with handlebar mustaches. The state of loss, the fact, the facticity in its lonely length. This was a word he never thought he'd need to use but here it was, crouched for years in his secluded brain, coming out to elongate the loss.

"I have a mushroom-shaped tumor."

"Yes."

"The doctor calls it a fungating mass."

"I don't know that term."

"I don't know it either. It's not in the dictionary because I looked in two dictionaries. When they get their terms outside the dictionary, it means they're telling you goodbye."

They went to Chinatown. They went to the Jersey shore and ate harpooned swordfish, which it's tastier when the fish dies unstrangled by a net, with olive oil and capers, the last great fish thing on the planet.

"I have to tell you first thing. I don't have the what-do-you-call completely established."

"The lineage."

"The lineage. I don't have the lineage all the way."

He told the caller some things about the ball. He said he would make a long story short. Then he made it long. He entertained the man, why not? And he saw it coming even as he did the bits and routines, delivered the reliable lines. Clarice would have to rent a hospital bed for the apartment, high sides so he wouldn't tumble to the floor. Strangers would come to wash his genitals, immigrants from countries on the travel channel, they had lives of their own that he could not imagine a single minute of. He would forget how to eat, how to say simple words. His body would lie there trying to put together the needed elements to take a breath. An oxygen tube in his nose and bananas on the windowsill, he hates them when they're spotted and soft. Clarice speaking slowly, putting a cool cloth to his naked head. All right, I'm fine, all right. Carl in his pressed white shorts and tube socks, a stockbroker disguised as a boy.

"Do we want to talk about price?" said the voice.

The word for water is water but he wouldn't be able to say it. The body forgets the basic things. He talked on the phone to Phoenix and looked at his windbreaker hanging on a chair.

They went to the Jersey shore. They made love, they made salads. This was when the terms were in the dictionary.

That night he ate half a cantaloupe with grapes clustered in the scooped-out part. This is how they sold it in the supermarket, packed in clinging wrap.

5

When people tell rat stories, the rat is always tremendous. It's a drag-belly rat the size of a cat because this is a satisfying rhyme. There was a fair amount of rat lore in these streets when Nick Shay was growing up. Not that rats were frequently seen. They were heard in the walls and down the yards, indelible half fictions, running across rooftops in the moon. Enormous rats with rat-brown fur. There were rats in sewers and demolition sites and coal bins, a rustling in the flung garbage of empty lots.

He got out of a taxi near the building where his mother lived. The building was not here thirty, forty years ago, a large brown structure, tall and broad and defined by a sense of fortification—fences and ramps, cameras angled from the brickwork.

This used to be a row of five-story buildings, tenements, and that's where he saw the rat, wet and dead, lying next to a coal pile on the sidewalk. He was nine or ten at the time and the incident came back to him, taxi easing from the curb, with a detailed directness. Just a dead rat but he could see it clearly, feeling a kind of doubleness, a shaped transparency, die-cut, that fit him to the moment. He remembered how he'd studied the limp body, feeling a grisly thrill to be so close, able to trace a faint pink line down the underside of the tail, and the rat was brown and gray and pink and white all together and separate but he was disappointed by its size—he would have to exaggerate the rat, put some heft and length in his story, some mouth drool and yellow eye.

There was a man in a plexiglas booth. Nick signed a register and was buzzed into the lobby, which was occupied by kids, small and smaller, playing, milling, their voices shrieky in the bare space. He took the elevator to twelve. The other rat was later, when he was in his twenties, also ordinary in size, your common Norway brown, but ordinary is big enough when you talk about rats.

Matt opened the door, his brother Matty, still looking a little boyish, short and blocky, cowlicked, with thick glasses and a fresh haircut and some gray, maybe, on top, that seemed extraneous. Midforties he would be. They hadn't seen each other in a few years and it was only an accident of timing that brought them together today.

They shook hands and exchanged the wry smile of adversaries who are enjoined from mauling each other by some inconvenience of context.

Nick said, "Where is she?"

They talked about their mother, about medications, doctors' appointments, not unusual matters, but there was a rigor in the older brother's questions, a particularity of interest and concern that amounted to a kind of challenge.

Matt said finally, "She's okay, she's good, she eats and sleeps normally. You want to know about her natural functions, you'll have to ask her yourself."

"You're staying over?"

"Two nights. You've totally forgotten what it's like, Nick. A night in the Bronx."

But Matty had long since filled out the small boy's sketchy torso, developed some mass in his upper body, a certain sturdiness of bearing.

Nick said, "I have to go to Jersey in the morning or I'd take her to the doctor myself."

"What's in Jersey? Chemical waste eating people's houses?"

"Personal business."

"How's Marian?"

"Fine, they're all fine."

They drank seltzer and took turns looking out the window. There was a picture window with a broad view west. El Bronx. People sat on lawn chairs on the roof of a motel nearby. Nick could tell these were local men and women who'd gained entry to the roof from an adjacent building, carrying their chairs and newspapers. He knew it was evidence of brisk improvisation, people extracting pleasure from the grudging streets, but it made him nervous, it was a breach, another opening, another local sign of instability and risk.

"I took her to the zoo," Matt said. "She has the zoo across the street but it's the first time in twenty years I could get her to go. Practically forced her out the door."

"You're on a mission."

"She says she has more animals on television than she can handle. I can't make her see the point of living breathing creatures."

"I'm getting her out of here," Nick said.

"Is that right?"

"To Phoenix. That's right. There's no reason anymore for her to be here."

"She has friends here. You know this."

"I know this? How many friends? What friends?"

"To Phoenix," Matt said.

"How many friends?"

"We haven't done a head count lately. But if she wanted to go, we'd take her gladly."

"You don't have room."

"We have room," Matt said.

"Listen to me. You don't have room. We have room. We also have climate."

"Climate."

"This is important at her age."

"Janet's a nurse. You want to make a contest out of it? Janet's a nurse."

"This is stupid."

"Of course it's stupid. This is why we're doing it," Matt said.

Nick was at the window again.

"Why would they put a motel in a place like this?"

"I don't know."

"It's a convenience, this motel, for sex and drugs. Because what else is it here for? Or homeless. A shelter for homeless people. They put them in motels now."

"She likes it here, Nick. It's her life, it's what she's used to. She has her church, her stores, all the familiar things. And the friends that are still alive. Ask her for a list."

"You don't know. I know. It's a convenience, this motel, for what they're doing."

Nick went into the kitchen and started opening cabinets. He inspected the area under the sink. Kids were riding tricycles in the hallway. He poured another seltzer and went into the living room. The bike bells sounded down the hall.

"How's Janet? Janet's all right?"

"She had a lump removed from under her arm."

"Did I know this?"

"It's okay. She's doing okay. The kids are okay."

"These lumps are everywhere. Everybody's looking for lumps."

"I read something in the paper not long ago. Made me think of you," Matt said. "Remember those machines they had in shoe stores? Tall consoles sort of like old radios, but with a slot down near the bottom."

"Jesus, yes. I haven't thought of that."

"The clerk puts shoes on the kid's feet and then the kid goes and stands with his feet inside the slot."

"I haven't thought of that since I was, what. They stopped making them."

"And the clerk looks into a viewer at the top of the device and can see the feet inside the shoes."

"To check the fit," Nick said.

"To check the fit. Well, the machine was a fluoroscope and what it did was transmit x rays through the shoe and into the foot, it's called differential transmission and it makes a shadowy greenish image. I just barely remember this. Jimmy's buying you a pair of shoes and then he's lifting me up so I can look into the machine and see your feet inside your shoes and your bones inside your feet."

"The question is, Where are those shoes now?"

"No, the question is, Did you do this enough times to suffer bone damage because the machine was basically spraying your feet with radiation."

They heard the key in the lock.

"I have healthy feet," Nick said.

"I'm relieved."

"But thanks for the scare. I'll do the same for you someday."

Rosemary Shay came through the door with a shopping bag in each hand, her body slanted toward the heavier bag. She saw that Nick was here. She stood and looked at him, eyes alive and searching. She was always searching him for something, some sign, some change. He moved toward her to help with the bags. Her face had furrows nearly everywhere, gathers and tucks, little parchment pleats above the mouth. Her hands were old, they were long and worked, milky blue veins lapping the scored knuckles.

They took the bags away from her, complaining that she did not allow them to help her sufficiently. They warned of back strain and heat exhaustion. She told them to shut up even as she tried to take the groceries away, items passing hand to hand. Nick embraced her, laughing, and she felt unpersuadable in his arms.

They ate and talked, took second helpings, corn on the cob, enormous tomatoes the grocer kept in the back room for special customers, grown in his yard on City Island—the old deep tomato taste, summery and blood-buttery and voluptuous.

"Tell him about the job," Rosemary said.

"He doesn't want to know."

"He's your brother. Tell him."

"Another job change?" Nick said.

"Yes. A research institute."

"Then this is not a change."

"A different one. Nonprofit. We draw up studies to help third world countries develop health services and banking facilities."

"Goody-goody stuff."

"Yes," Matt said happily. "We produce paper. We smoke pipes, those of us who smoke."

"A think tank," Rosemary said.

They let this term hover above the salad. Year by year, job by job, Matt was separating himself from the science he did in the 1970s, work whose precise nature eluded Nick, government work that involved classified projects and remote locations. Not that Nick was eager to reach him. It was strange, that's all, for younger brother to be the tight-lipped guy for a change, not inclined to answer questions readily.

"My kid's learning the game. Jeffrey."

"What game?" Matt said.

"What game. What game would I be talking about? Your game."

"My game."

"He plays against his computer. His computer has a chess program with a take-back option so he can undo his dumber moves."

Matt said nothing.

The cats came out of hiding. They curled around the chair legs, hooked their backs, rubbing against the legs of the people, undulant in the mazy space down there, and they went swaybacked and yawned, asses up.

"We have room for you," Nick said to his mother.

"Where did this come from?"

"It was always here. You know that. We've been waiting for you to say you're ready."

"Well I'm not. We have dessert. Who wants coffee?" she said. "I have the decaf. I know Matty takes it."

Then she told them a story about Jimmy downtown. She told it over coffee and they listened with a shared intensity that no other subject could remotely provoke. It was the thing that made them a family, still, after all the silences and distances—the father in his lost glory, making book.

"It was a funny thing, funny-strange I mean, but the first bets he ever took were from cops. He was a plumber's helper at the New Yorker Hotel. Then he was moved into the security office, which I visited several times, we were keeping company then, a big noisy office in the freight delivery area, and the security chief had made a space for the local bookmaker to come and do his tally every morning. He charged him rent, very reasonable, I'm sure. Soon the bookie makes Jimmy his runner. Jimmy loved this. He made payoffs to winners, he collected money from losers. He did the rounds every day, all through the garment district this was. He was light on his feet, dodging the boys who pushed the racks. He started picking up extra action, action for himself, sitting on bets it was called—he selected carefully, a bet here and there. And it was often the police he was getting his business from. So you have the security people and the police and what else is new? Then once a month a detective, this is the bagman, he went to the Solomon Brothers car dealer and he picked up the protection money to distribute in the precinct house. So the money's flowing back and forth and everybody's happy. The Solomon brothers ran the bookie operation for the whole area, Arthur and I forget the other Solomon, Arthur and Bernie, and Arthur and Bernie wore beautiful suits and had a box at the Polo Grounds and knew ballplayers and show people, and eventually Jimmy got his own small piece of action, on the up-and-up, and the Solomons paid him eighty dollars a week, this is after you're born," she said to Nick, "and after he already left me once, plus a bonus for a good business month."

Matt said, "But who kept other gambling interests from moving in? A couple of car dealers couldn't do that, could they? They must have imported real gangsters."

"They didn't have to. The money they paid the police was double coverage money. They paid the police to let them operate. And they also paid them to roust the competition. When competition showed up, the borough detectives or precinct detectives came down on them like a holy terror."

"Gangbusters," Matt said.

"Like gangbusters. Which is the story I started out to tell before I got involved in the fine print. The police making arrests. They even had to arrest the bookies who were paying them off. They got pressure when people complained, upstanding citizens, you know, or straight from City Hall. These were called accommodation arrests. The sergeant would apologize, he would book you at the precinct on Thirtieth Street and then you went to Centre Street, where the lawyer for the Solomons was waiting, and you said, Guilty, judge, and paid a twenty-five-dollar fine and went back to work. And the day you were born," she said to Matt, "your father was arrested twice. Confusion inside the precinct. They arrested him in the morning and when he finally got released he took the subway to the Bronx, where I was in the hospital getting ready to deliver, it was one of those steamy sticky days and he came in the room and mopped my brow and fanned me with the racing form and said, Did you have it yet, and after a while he said he has to see a man, very important, be right back, and he went downtown and got arrested again, different cop, same desk sergeant, I don't know about the judge, and when he got back to the hospital, with the running around and the heat and the subway, he looked worse off than I did but he got no sympathy, you can believe it, from me."

Matt said, "Interesting day."

"It was a dizzy comedy but we had no one to share it with because it was one thing to take bets but not so acceptable to get arrested for it and I've never told this story until now."

Nick watched her carefully, absorbing every gesture and expression. A depth in her eyes that she dared her sons to interpret—the gnaw, the rankling pain that sits inside the good-natured telling. And the voice in its factual carry, vowels extended and bent a bit, a sound out of the old streets, the old demotic song gone to the near suburbs now, and a slight Irish pitch teasing the piece from somewhere deep in childhood.

There was a noise in the street, a customized car speaker bombing the night with music, a car that was all sound, a mobile sound bomb, and Nick glanced sharply at his brother, who shrugged and grinned.

"He wants you to sit on his patio, Mama. Bright stars above. Cactus outlined in the moonlight."

"Imagine me and cactus."

"No noise in the street. They arrest people for noise out there. If your front yard isn't neat and clean, your neighbor's kids won't talk to your kids."

Nick waited for her to speak again. He opened himself to everything inside her, to the past that never stops happening, and the passing minute, and what she feels when she scratches the back of her hand, pulling at the skin, then scratching. He tried to hear the rustle of her life, the fly buzzing in the room of the woman who lives alone.

One of the cats rubbed against his ankle, the orange tom his mother had found in the street. He shook it off and poured coffee all around.

They sat at the table talking in low tones.

Rosemary was in the bedroom and they talked across the dishes and cups and the flick of spilt milk.

"Where do you sleep?"

"I make up the sofa," Matt said. "Where do you sleep?"

"Park Avenue South. The Doral. You drove down?"

"Took the shuttle. Tell me in all seriousness. Do you really want to take her out there?"

"More than ever."

"You have to understand this woman is not afraid. She lives a free life. People know her. They respect her. The neighborhood's still a living thing."

"Lower your voice."

"Lower my voice."

"Did you see the hallways?" Nick said.

"The hallways. These hallways? Which hallways?"

Matt stacked some dishes and took them to the kitchen.

"Listen to me. Stand at the elevator. Look to your left. Then look to your right. What do you see?"

"I don't know. What do I see?"

"You see the longest, saddest, scariest, most depressing—that feeling, you know?"

"It's a hallway," Matt said.

"It's that feeling. A nightmare out of some Stalinist—all right, I'm overreacting."

"It's a hallway. Filled as a matter of fact with little kids most of the time."

"Lower your voice."

"Look, it is well within your experience to invent a fantasy of events as you think they transpired or are transpiring. This is not un-up your alley."

202

Nick could not look at his brother without wanting to pop him a shot across the mouth. Same reason as ever—the father, not the mother. The deep discordance, the old muscling of wills, that ungiving thing in the idea of brothers.

"No one came for him, Nicky. No one got him and took him away. He left because of us basically. He didn't want to be a father. Being a husband was bad enough, what a burden, you know, full of obligations and occasions he couldn't handle. He was a loner, to use the romantic word, only worse than that, clinically self-involved, not out of vanity or stupidity but out of some fear, some inbred perspective, some closeness of perspective that amounted to fear. It made him unable to see other people except as encumbrances, little hazy shapes that interfered with his solitude, his hardness of being. He should have joined the French Foreign Legion when he was twenty. Not that I'm ready to renounce my existence. But speaking honestly and realistically. That's what he should have done."

"You know a lot. How do you know so much?"

"She tells me things. She tells me things she never told you."

"I'm looking at you saying this."

"You're looking at me."

"That's right."

"You're giving me the look."

"That's right, I am."

Matt was at the sink doing dishes now, running the tap at low volume so they could hear each other, and he didn't turn to check his brother's look.

"He had some trouble. Some sharpshooter hit a long shot on him. A big bet at long odds. Jimmy had his own operation by then, independent of the Solomons. I even know the horse's name."

"You know a lot. How come I'm not impressed?"

"It was the final weight, the final pressure, and it pushed him out the door."

"Listen to me. I'm confused here. Help me out. First he leaves because of us. Then he leaves because somebody hits a long shot and he can't pay off."

"Terra Firma. Jimmy hadn't laid off the bet with bookies who could

203

handle those sums. Maybe it was a late bet and he didn't have time to shop it around."

"You know this and I don't?"

"She protects you."

"I am completely fucking unimpressed. Why is that?"

"There was no drama of men pushing him into a car and speeding away. He owed money he couldn't pay. He was a small operator. He paid a buttonmaker ten dollars a week to help figure out his tally. He dealt in small numbers."

"Listen to me. This is not an invitation to violence? When you owe money to someone and can't pay off? In that environment?"

"What environment? You heard her. They didn't need enforcers."

"No, they had cops. But not for this kind of situation."

"He left before a situation could develop. He had one foot out the door for years. You heard her. He left her once before. He was looking for an excuse to make it permanent."

"You know all this. And I don't. And yet I'm remarkably unimpressed. Help me out. Explain this to me."

Matt turned off the tap and looked at his brother, who sat leaning over the table.

"He did the unthinkable Italian crime. He walked out on his family. They don't even have a name for this."

"He didn't walk out. They came and got him."

"Keep believing it," Matt said.

He turned on the tap, sponging and rinsing the dishes. The car came back, the car-sized boom box, causing a fuzz storm out there. Nick leaned heavily over the table, lazy-eyed now, brows lowered and mouth open just a chink, forming a lifeless grin. He resembled a man who'd started out drinking hours ago determined to reach a point of particular abandon.

No one spoke. Matt washed and dried a dish, then tried to find the place in the cabinet where it belonged. The car moved off now, finally. Then Nick got up. He took the remaining objects from the table and carried them into the kitchen area. He didn't walk, he moved. It was heavy movement, sluggish and brooding.

"She has her church," Matt said.

"What?"

"She has her church. Her priest."

"We'll get her a new church."

"It won't be the same."

"We don't want it to be the same. We want it to be different. That's the point."

Matt handed him a glass to dry. They worked quietly for a time, doing the dishes and putting them away, finding the right place for each item.

"How's the waste business?"

"Booming. The waste business. Bigger by the minute."

"I'll bet it is."

"We can't build enough landfills, dig enough gaping caverns."

"You get in there? See the stuff up close?"

"I drive by sometimes. Inspect from a distance."

"You smell the smell?"

"I've done this, yes."

"You see the rats? It must be the Planet of the Rats."

Nick found the place in the cabinet for dessert dishes.

"Did I ever tell you about the rat downtown?"

"I don't think so," Matt said.

"I was thinking about it coming up here. I had a date, a jazz date, we went to see Charles Mingus. I'm trying to think. I think I was living in Palo Alto then, doing textbook work. Came back for a conference. Maybe I was twenty-six. And my date was a German woman, a philosophy student, yes, and a sort of future, now that I think of it, terrorist type, and we went to see Mingus on Hudson Street somewhere, and Mingus stood up there rocking his bass and glaring down at the cash register every time it rang. Mingus was big and he was wide. He looked like three men sharing a suit. And I walked her home, we walked way across town and then downtown and we get to her place, a basement apartment in an old building, and we walk in the door. The second we walk in the door she turns on the light. And then this rat. I'm standing there thinking whatever I'm thinking. Sex is not external to these thoughts. And then this rat. I see this rat go right up the wall. It runs up the wall, a very tremendous rat, and it makes a sound I can still hear,

205

like a whistling corpse. And my date. My date says something in German and picks up something from a table and goes after the rat. I stand there dead still. I'm immobilized by frozen desire. My desire has frozen in my loins. And my date is charging across the room after the rat."

Matt placed a wet cup in the dish towel that Nick held in his hand. Nick could see the pleasure of the kid brother who is invited into the action, given the privileged details of some infamous event. All the more dimensional, the rarer and sweeter when the narrator allows an element of foolery to attach itself to his sober persona, some haplessness or slippery shame. All the more intimate and appealing.

"And the rat runs down the other side of the wall and goes zip into the bathroom like a toy on a string, only a thousand times quicker. A phenomenal rat, big and fast, and my date goes right after it, wielding whatever she was wielding that I never actually identified. She turns on the bathroom light and goes right in. I'm feeling frankly a little neglected. But never mind. I stay where I am. I think, What is happening to my jazz date? It's disintegrating into a rat hunt. And then she sticks her head out the door."

Matt studied his brother's face, perceptibly moving his lips to Nick's account, anticipating a word, changing expression when Nick did.

"I am standing as far from the bathroom door as I can stand and still be said to occupy the apartment. I have the front door open. My date is battling the rat in the bathroom and I can hear the rat's sick whistle. And my date sticks her head out the door and says, I am not believing this! I am killing this fucking rat two times already! Rat poison with skulls! And now it is coming back! And she goes back in and resumes the hunt. And I feel totally unworthy. Sleep with her? I have no right being in the same city. I can hear the rat running across the bathtub. Did you ever hear a rat run across a tub? I'll tell you, man, it's awesome."

Matt was strangling with pleasure. He made a sound in his throat, an involuntary quaver. Nick finished the story—the rat squeezing neatly through a vent in the wall, the evening completely queered. They drank another cup of coffee and then his brother found the phone book and called a cab. Nick stood by the window in the living room. He was looking for hookers in spandex tights on the motel roof.

· · ·

The Italians. They sat on the stoop with paper fans and orangeades. They made their world. They said, Who's better than me? She could never say that. They knew how to sit there and say that and be happy. Thinking back through the decades. She saw a woman fanning herself with a magazine and it seemed like an encyclopedia of breezes, the book of all the breezes that ever blew. The city drugged with heat. Horses perishing in the streets. Who's better than me?

She heard them talking out there.

He wants me to go to the zoo because the animals are real. I told him these are zoo animals. These are animals that live in the Bronx. On television I can see animals in the rain forest or the desert. So which is real and which is fake, which made him laugh.

It would have been easier to believe she deserved it. He left because she was heartless, foolish, angry, she was a bad housekeeper, a bad mother, a cold woman. But she could not invent a reliable plot for any of these excuses.

But it was the sweetest intimacy, his whispered stories of the gamblers and the police, lying in bed the two of them, his days with the garment bosses and bellhops. He made her laugh, telling these stories late at night, love nights, whispering to her afterward, lying close in bed, and even when he was flat-pocket broke he told her funny screwy stories in the night.

She began to drift into sleep now and said a Hail Mary because this is what she always did before she went to sleep. Except she wasn't always sure anymore whether the last Hail Mary she said was a Hail Mary from last night or from two minutes ago and she said this prayer and said this prayer because she mixed up the time and didn't want to go to sleep without being sure.

She had more material things than most people she knew, thanks to sons who provided. She had nicer furniture, a safer building, doctors left and right. They made her go to a gynecologist, with Janet calling and then Marian calling, women of the world hooray. But she still couldn't say, Who's better than me?

She got the Italian without the family, the boy who just showed up, like a shadow off a wall. She didn't mind that at first. She liked it. She didn't want relatives turning up with pastry in white boxes. She liked his slimness, his lack of attachments. But then she began to see what this meant. The only thing preserved in the man's dark body was a kid in empty space, the shifty boy on the verge of using up his luck.

Then she slept and then the car music woke her up. She heard their voices again, the cupboard doors shutting.

She did not show her love. She showed it but not enough. She was not good at that. But it was partly his doing. The more she loved him, the scareder he got. He was scared in his eyes, telling funny stories in the night.

She heard them opening and shutting the cupboard doors. They'd never known where things belonged. Why should they know now? Jerks. She scratched the back of her hand, fiercely, and said another Hail Mary in case the last one she said was last night.

This is how she was brought up. Go to mass, mind your parents, marry the hardworking boy, the ordinary boy, the ham-and-egger they used to say. And the nuns used to say, You're a child of Mary and you don't have to kiss him. But he wasn't ordinary and she kissed him.

She could not bear to think that Nick might be right. Someone came and got him. This would make her Jimmy innocent. Which Nick believed from an early age. But maybe the other was worse, the truth was worse. It did not happen violent.

She slept and then woke up. She listened and knew that Nick had left and Matty had gone to bed and then she listened for noises in the street and she thought of the animals in their cages and habitats, lions near Boston Road coughing in the night.

They were showing the videotape again but Nick wasn't watching. He stood by the window in his hotel looking at cars move soundlessly on the avenue, sparse traffic in the sodium glow of the streetlamps.

He was waiting for room service to show up with his brandy.

On the trip down here the cabbie had driven left-handed all the way, a Dominican in a net shirt, his right arm extended across the seat back. He told Nick about the murders of gypsy drivers, a regular event lately, a game of chance you play every night.

Nick did not like cats. Once he got her to say yes, the cats would have to be sent into retirement.

Either they rob you and kill you or they rob you and let you live or you take them somewhere very efficient, the man said, and either they pay you or they don't.

I live a quiet life in an unassuming house in a suburb of Phoenix.

Once he got her to say yes, they'd be able to spend untrammeled time remembering together.

He'd tipped the man nicely. What do you tip a man who risks his life when he answers a call? Nick was confident he'd tipped him nicely, handsomely, but not ridiculously, not in a way that would have exposed him as a stranger here.

He looked at the TV screen, where the tape was nearing the point when the driver waves, the crisp wave from the top of the steering wheel, and he waited for room service to knock on the door.

6

When Matty was real small and his brother used to sit on the pot and read comics to a peewee audience, neighbor kids ages four and five supposedly being minded by a grown-up somewhere near, with Matty in the doorway ready to shout out *chickie*, which was the warning word, and there's Nick on the pot reading to them from Captain Marvel or the Targeteers, his pants hanging limp from his kneecaps, and he did lively dialogue, declaimed and gestured, developed a voice for villains and for women and an airy stabbing screech for gangster cars cornering tightly in the night, scaring the kids at times with his intensity of manner, then pausing to loose a turd that would splattingly drop, that would plop into the water, the funniest sound in nature, sending a happy awe across the faces of his listeners—it was the creepiest delight of all, better than anything he might deliver from the paneled pages.

Matt walked through the neighborhood to see the old building, number 611, and wondered idly who lived in their third-floor apartment, what language spoken, how many grinding lives, but mainly he thought of nine-year-old Nicky asquat the glory seat. Who else would read the comics to them, acting out those vibrant dramas of crime fiends and bounding heroes?

He went to see Bronzini, his old chess mentor, a sweet-natured man and not-so-willing drillmaster. Living now in a sad building with an entranceway marked by specimens of urban spoor—spray paint, piss, saliva, dapples of dark stuff that was probably blood. The elevator was not working and Matt made his way up five flights. A child's sandal on the landing. He knocked and waited. He sensed an eyeball on the other side of the peephole and he thought of his own street and house and the life of the computer suburb, those huddled enclaves off the turnpike, situated to discourage entry, and the corner store that sells eleven kinds of croissants and twenty-seven coffees, which are somehow never enough, and the life he led before this, the weapons he studied and helped perfect, the desert experience, so completely unconnected to root reality, compared to this man, he thought, on the other side of the peephole, who watches the ruin build around him on the actual planet where he was born.

The man's smile was in his eyes, a warm fizz that had an eagerness in it, a desire to know. This is what remained, his curiosity. He looked too old, too spare, his face a boxy outline, an underdrawing of the original likeness, the fleshed-out and tinted-in Bronzini. A couple of days of gray stubble surrounded his untrimmed mustache and Matt thought the man had seized upon old age, embraced it with a kind of reckless assent.

"Please, no misters. It's Albert now. And you look well. Robust, I'm surprised. I remember a matchstick. A matchstick with a fiery head."

Evidently the man had forgotten more recent meetings. They sat at a table near the window and drank brewed tea. Bronzini lived with his sister now, who'd never married, who sat in her room and spoke in chants, he said, of reduced informational range. Such compression. But once he'd learned to be patient with her repetitions and attenuations he began to find her presence a source of enormous comfort. A rest, he said, from his own internal rant.

He said, "Sometimes I take the train downtown. There's a chess club that's also a coffeehouse, in the Village, and I play a game or two. I lose but I don't get embarrassed. Or I play down there, in the playground, with a neighbor. We share a bench. They leave us alone, the kids."

"I don't play," Matt said in a voice emptied of any shading.

"I used to wonder about your father. He taught you the moves but was he a serious player, I used to wonder. I didn't know him well enough to bring up the subject, any subject. He was not a man who encouraged, shall we say, inquiries."

The eyes fizzed like carbonated water.

"He taught me quite a bit. We practiced openings and played many games. We played speed chess for fun. He called it rapid transit."

When his father went out for cigarettes Matty was finishing first grade. He found a book of chess problems Jimmy had kept in a bureau. It was a major discovery and he worked his way through the book and sat in front of the board, squares and pieces, pushing wood. His brother used to walk into the room and knock the pieces off the board and walk out of the room without a word. Matty picked up the pieces and set them on the board exactly as positioned earlier. He'd study black's defense. His brother would walk into the room, knock the pieces off the board and walk out again.

"Your mother petitioned me. But you were a problem," Bronzini said. "I needed help to deal with you."

"Hard to handle."

"Volatile, yes, and very quick to dismiss my advice. Of course you saw things I did not. You had remarkable skills and insights. It was exhilarating for me but also humbling. I lacked the deep feel of the master player."

"As a team we were maybe a little shaky. But we managed to last a few years. We tasted a little glory, Albert. I can tell you I don't like that little boy. I don't like thinking about him."

"I study theory now and then. I read a little in the history of the game. The personality of the game. This is a game of enormous hostility."

"I came to hate the language," Matt said. "You crush your opponent. It's not a question of win or lose. You crush him. You annihilate him. You strip him of dignity, manhood, womanhood, you destroy him, you expose him publicly as an inferior being. And then you gloat in his face. All the things that gave me such naked pleasure, I began to hate."

"Because you began to lose," Albert said.

It was true of course and Matt laughed. All that concentrated power, the implosive life of the board, black and white, the autocratic beauty of winning, what a chestful of undisguisable pride—he defeated men, boys, the old and wise, the vigorous and quick, the bohemian café poets, friendly and smelly. But then at ten or eleven he saw his edge begin to muddy and he took some losses, suffered consistent reversals that made him sick and limp.

"The competition changed. We found better opponents for you to play."

"And I slowed down."

"Your development hit a wall. Not a wall. But it no longer grew exponentially."

Matt looked out at the playground, surprised at the desolation, the basketball court potholed and empty, only one backboard still standing. Directly below him the old boccie court grown over with weeds. Everything empty. Up on the second level the softball field empty and tar-hot, a heavy sweltry indolence, the dark surface flashing with broken glass, two or three men, he sees them now, standing out near the left-field fence, sort of mortally posed like figures in spaghetti westerns, lean, nameless, unshaved—he didn't think they were acquainted with the language of life expectancy.

He said, "I've been walking around. It's a complicated thing. I find myself trying to resist the standard response."

"You don't want to be shocked. You're reluctant to blame anyone. But you went to the old streets."

"Yes."

"You saw your building. The squalor around it. The empty lot with the razor wire."

"Yes."

"The men. Who are they, standing around doing nothing? Poor people. They're very shocking."

"Yes, they are," Matt said.

"And these were your streets. It's a curious rite of passage, isn't it? Visit the old places. First you wonder how you lived so uncomplainingly in such cramped circumstances. The streets are narrower, the buildings smaller than you ever remembered. It's like coming back to Lilliput. And think of the rooms. Think of the tiny bathroom, shared by the family, by the grandparents, by the uncle who's slightly *u'pazz'*. But what else do you see? These people that you barely glance at. How can you see them clearly? You can't."

"No, I can't."

"And you want to ask me why I'm still here. I see your mother in the market and we talk about this. We want nothing to do with this business of mourning the old streets. We've made our choice. We complain but we don't mourn, we don't grieve. There are things here, people who show the highest human qualities, outside all notice, because who comes here to see? And I'm too rooted to leave. Speaking only for myself, I'm too rooted, too narrow. My mind is open to absolutely anything but my life is not. I don't want to adjust. I'm an old Roman stoic. But then I was always too old, too narrow. Klara used to attack me on this subject. Not attack me. Chide me, urge me to see things differently."

"Do you talk to her at all?"

"No. Go to Arthur Avenue, Matty. Look at the shops and the people shopping and the people weighing the fish and cutting the meat. This will restore your spirits. I took your mother into the pork store the other day to show her the ceiling. Hundreds of hanging salamis, such bounty and fullness, the place teeming with smells and textures, the ceiling covered completely. I said, Rosemary, look. A gothic cathedral of pork."

They shook hands at the door.

"You used to wear glasses, Albert."

"I didn't absolutely need them. I needed them a little. They were part of my schoolteacher's paraphernalia. My accoutrements. Take the elevator."

"It's not working."

"It's not working. Then I guess you'll have to walk. But don't tarry," Bronzini said, eyes bright. "There are dangers in the woods."

Matt went shopping for dinner and then headed back to his mother's building, walking directly toward the western end of the zoo. Out over the trees he saw the residue of a jet contrail, the vapor losing its shape, beginning to spread and rib out, and he thought of the desert of course, the weapons range and flypaths and the way the condensation in the sky was the only sign of human endeavor as far as he could see, a city boy out camping, taking his soul struggle to the backcountry, and the mach-2 booms came skyclapping down and the vapor formed an ice trail in the heavens.

They were showing the tape again. The TV set was on in the empty room and they had the tape going, they had the victim at the wheel, the random man in the medium Dodge, alive again in sunlight—they were running it one more time.

Matt came in, surprised to find the TV on, and he sat on the footstool near the screen. When it was running he could not turn away from it. When it wasn't running he never thought about it. Then he'd get on line at the supermarket back home and there it was again on the monitors they'd installed to keep shoppers occupied at the checkout—nine monitors, ten monitors, all showing the tape.

But this time something was different. There was a voice-over, barely audible, and he looked around for the remote control device. He hit the button a couple of times and the voice came up and it had something in it that matched the tape. The voice was naked the way the tape was naked. A man's voice, flat and stripped, saying something about the weather.

A set of words appeared, superimposed across the bottom of the tape.

LIVE CALL-IN VOICE OF TEXAS HIGHWAY KILLER.

The voice was asking about the weather in Atlanta. They cut from the videotape to a live shot of a face above a desk, a woman with red hair and amazing green eyes. The anchorwoman. The anchorwoman was telling the caller that the weather desk said rain.

Then she said, "And clearly this is not a true voice we are hearing over the phone lines. This is a manipulated voice, an altered voice."

And the voice said, "Well, it is a device that disguises the sound. It is a device that's a little more than three inches by two inches and you fit it to the talk part of the telephone and it makes the sound hard to identify as an individual."

Then she said, "Just to recap. We are taking a call from an individual who identifies himself as the Texas Highway Killer. He has given us information known only to the real killer and to the authorities and we have checked this information with the authorities in order to verify the caller's credentials."

Then she said something to the caller about his reason for calling.

Matt looked at her, half mesmerized. Those eyes were an amazement, like offshore green you see from an airplane.

The voice said, "Why I'm calling is to set the record straight. People write things and say things on air that I don't know from day one where they're coming from. I feel like my situation has been twisted in with the profiles of a hundred other individuals in the crime computer. I keep hearing about low self-esteem. They keep harping about this. Use your own judgment, Sue Ann. How does an individual with this kind of proven accuracy where he hits targets in moving vehicles where he's driving with one hand and firing a handweapon with the other and he's not supposed to be aware of his personal skills?"

The anchorwoman looked into the camera. She had no choice of course. The camera was on her, not on the caller. She was a live body and he was just a voice, or not a voice. The odd sound, the devoicing, with contour and modulation strained out. Electronically toned but not without a human quality, Matt thought, a trace of jerkwater swerve. The struggle to speak, the bare insides of the simplest utterance.

The anchorwoman listened.

"I keep hearing about history of head trauma whereby an individual, you know, can't control their behavior."

They cut to the tape again. It showed the man at the wheel of the medium Dodge.

"Let's set the record straight. I did not grow up with head trauma. I had a healthy, basically, type childhood."

The car approaches briefly, then falls back.

"Why are you doing it?"

"Say what?"

"Why are you committing these murders?"

"Let's just say it's a nice seasonal day where I'm located here, with scattered clouds, and if that's a hint to my location, then take it as a hint, and if this is all a game, then take it as a game."

On the screen the man at the wheel does his little wave, the friendly understated wave to the camera and the future and all the watching world, his hand wagging stiffly from the top of the wheel.

"You are aware, are you not, that one of these crimes is said to have been the work of a copycat killer. Can you comment on that for us?"

Now here is where he gets it. Matt could not look at the tape without wanting to call out to Janet. Hurry up, Janet, here it comes. Getting her mad. Mad at the tape and mad at him. And the more often they showed it, the more singsong he put in his voice. Hur-ree u-up, here it co-omes. An anxious joke, a joke in somebody else's voice, not meant to be funny. Janet swore at him and said enough. But it wasn't enough. It was never enough.

"Let's just say, okay, the police have their job and I have mine."

The eeriness of the car that keeps on coming after the driver is shot. It approaches briefly, then falls back.

"Which the correct term for this is not sniper by the way. This is not an individual with a rifle working more or less long-range. You're mobile here, you're moving, you want to get as close to the situation as humanly possible without bringing the two vehicles into contact, whereby a paint mark might result."

The car is drifting toward the guardrail now. The odd sound of the caller's voice, leveled-out, with faint tremors at the edges, odd little electronic storms, like someone trying to make a human utterance out of itemized data.

They cut to the face above the desk. The anchorwoman live. Her elbows rested on the desk now, hands tucked together beneath her chin. Matt wondered what this meant. Every shift of position meant a change in the state of the news. The green eyes peered from the screen. And the altered voice went on, talking in that flat-graphed way, he was actually chatting now, confident, getting the feel of the medium, the format, and the anchorwoman listened because she had no choice and everybody watched her as she listened. They were watching her in Murmansk in the fog.

The voice said, "I hope this talk has been conducive to understand the situation better. For me to request that I would only talk to Sue Ann Corcoran, one-on-one, that was intentional on my part. I saw the interview you did where you stated you'd like to keep your career, you know, ongoing while you hopefully raise a family and I feel like this is a thing whereby the superstation has the responsibility to keep the position open, okay, because an individual should not be penalized for lifestyle type choices."

They began to run the tape again. It showed the man at the wheel of the medium Dodge.

When his mother came in he was scouring a frying pan with a short-handled brush. She stood there and looked at him.

"You'll wear it out," she said.

"I did this in the army. I liked doing it. It was the best thing about the army."

"That was a long time ago. Besides, the pan is already clean. Whatever you think you're doing, you're not getting the pan any cleaner."

"The TV was on. When I walked in," he said. "You normally leave the TV on?"

"Not normally. But if you say it was on, I guess it was on. Abnormally."

"I always thought you were careful."

"I'm pretty careful. I'm not a fanatic," she said. "You're wearing out the steel. You'll clean right through it."

He made dinner for them and they kept a fan going because the air conditioner seemed to be running at half strength.

"I walked over there today. Quite a few buildings are gone. Nothing in their place. Parking lots without cars. It's very strange to see this. There's a skyline, suddenly."

"I don't go over there," Rosemary said.

"Good. Don't."

"I don't like to go."

"I looked at 611."

"I don't want to see it."

"No, you don't. Eat your asparagus," he said.

He heard thunder in the west, the promise of rain on stifling nights, one of the primitive memories.

"I caught Nick just before he left the hotel. Told him the doctor said you were in great shape."

"Don't get carried away."

"They'll send me printouts of all the tests."

"Does he ever say anything to you?"

"Nick?"

"Does he ever say anything?"

"No."

"Not to me either."

"He erased it," Matt said.

"I guess what else could he do."

"What else could he do?"

"I don't know," she said.

They ate quietly for a while. Two of the cats came out of the bedroom. They slipped past the chairs like liquid fur.

"I went to see Mr. Bronzini."

"Albert. He's the last rose of summer. I told him last time I saw him. See a barber. He goes out in his house slippers. I said to him."

"He lost weight."

"What did I say? You're turning into an old eccentric."

They finished eating and Matt went into the kitchen and got the fruit he'd bought, huge ruby grapes that did not have the seeds bred out of them, and peaches with leafy stems.

"What time do you want me to wake you up?"

"Don't bother," he said.

"What time is your plane?"

"When I get there."

"You have your ticket all set?"

"I'm taking the shuttle."

"The shuttle."

"I don't need a ticket."

"What's the shuttle?"

"I go to the airport, I get on the plane and we go to Boston. Unless I get on the wrong plane. Then we go to Washington."

"Where was I when they stopped using tickets?"

"I pay on the plane."

219

"What if all the seats are taken?"

"I get the next plane. It's the shuttle. One plane goes, there's another waiting."

"Where was I when they did this? The shuttle. Everybody knows this but me."

He waited for her to say something about the enormous grapes bunched in the ceramic bowl, or to eat one, rinsed and glistening.

"What about Arizona?"

"What about it?" she said.

"I don't know. What about it?"

The last cat came out of the bedroom, the shy white one, and Matt scooped it onto his thigh.

"Scrubbing pots and pans."

"That was the best part of basic training," he said. "Because it was the most civilian part."

"I don't know how many nights I stayed awake when they sent you over."

"How many letters did I write saying I was nowhere near the combat zone?"

"You were in the country. That was near enough for me."

"The country's not that small. If they fired a shot in Khe Sanh, I wasn't about to get hit wherever I was sitting, comfortably indoors, doing my drudge work."

"You were luckier than a lot of others."

"You sure you don't want to go?"

"I'm staying here," she said.

They sat there with the fruit between them. He heard rain glancing off the window, sounding cool and fresh, and he looked at his mother. She didn't see peaches with leafy stems as works of art.

"I'm going to early mass."

"Say hello to God for me. I'll have coffee waiting when you get back."

"He erased it," she said. "Because what else was he supposed to do?"

She said good night and went inside. The cats vanished while he made up the sofa. Nick was always the subject, ultimately. Every subject, ground down and sifted through, yielded a little Nicky, or a version of the distant adult, or the adolescent half lout looking to hit someone. These were the terms of the kinship. He lay in the dark and listened to the rain. He felt little. He felt small and lost. His wife was little. He had undersized kids. They did nothing in the world that would ever be noticed. They were innocent. There was a curse of innocence that he carried with him. Against his brother, against the stature of danger and rage he could only pose the fact of his secondness, his meek freedom from guilt.

There was a noise near the door. He didn't move for a moment. He lay there listening. The rain hit hard now, splashy, rattling the window. He heard the noise again and got up. He put on his glasses and looked through the peephole. He edged the door slowly open. He looked into the hallway, long and prison-lit, left and right, rows of closed doors, all blank and still, and he was a grown man in his mother's house, afraid of noises in the hall.

7

How deep is time? How far down into the life of matter do we have to go before we understand what time is?

The old science teacher, Bronzini, moved through the snow, slogging, dragging happily, head down, his cigar box tucked under his arm—the scissors, the combs, the electric clipper to do the nape of Eddie's neck.

We head out into space, we brave space, line up the launch window and blast off, we swing around the planet in a song. But time binds us to aging flesh. Not that he minded growing old. But as a point of argument, in theory only, he wondered what we'd learn by going deeper into structures beneath the standard model, down under the quantum, a million billion times smaller than the old Greek atom.

The snow came down, enormous star-tipped flakes, feathery wet on his lashes, stuck and gone, and he raised his head to see parked cars humped and stunned, nothing moving in the streets, snow on the back of his hand—touches flesh and disappears.

He climbed the stairs to Eddie's apartment and rang the bell. No ding or buzz, no sawtooth whine. He knocked on the metal sheath that covered the door and heard Mercedes approach in her slappy shoes.

She opened up, calling back to Eddie, "You'll never guess who is it."

Bronzini handed her the cigar box, Garcia y Vega, fine cigars since 1882. He took off his checked cap and gave it to her. He got out of the old belted greatcoat he'd bought cheap at Freight Liquidation, where you go for factory discounts, for irregular suits and dresses, cardigans hijacked by mistake—they thought they were getting cigarettes. He gave her the coat. He wiggled his hands to show no gloves. Then he bent to unbuckle his galoshes, stepping out of them half dizzy from the bending.

"Eddie, look, he wears slippers under his boots. The man is undescribable."

He embraced the woman and the coat and then moved into the living room rubbing his hands like a man treading across a Persian rug toward a birch fire and a snifter of rare brandy. Eddie sat there smiling, the real Eddie Robles who lived inside the imposter, inside the haunted likeness, arthritic, emphysemic, with ulcerated veins in his legs, retired more or less from everything.

"I woke up this morning and I knew it," Bronzini said.

"You knew it."

"Time for Eddie's haircut."

"In a blizzard. You woke up but you didn't look out the window."

"It's a gentle snowfall. Old-fashioned. You should go walking."

"Walking," Eddie said. "You have any idea what you're saying? Sit down, you're making me nervous."

"I can't give you a haircut sitting down. Where are my tools of the trade?"

"I should give *you*. You're the one who needs his hair cut. You should carry a violin, Albert."

"You don't want to play chess with me anymore. There's no one left in the world I can defeat in chess, trounce—I can trounce the way I trounce you. So you have to submit to the barber's moves. It's a beautiful snowfall from out of the past. Incidentally, Mercedes. Where is she? Your doorbell's not working."

They sat drinking hot chocolate. What Albert wanted was a shot of hootch from an imported bottle. He imagined the warm wincing sting of a trickle of scotch. Durable, that was the beauty of the thing. It hit you so it lasted. The chairman scotched rumors of a takeover. A wedge you stick behind a wheel to keep a vehicle from rolling. That's a scotch. So is a line drawn on the ground, as in hopscotch, he thought.

"Doorbell. Only the doorbell?" Mercedes said.

"The elevator of course. But we know about the elevator."

"You know about the plaster?" she said. "I put newspapers in the cracks. Someday they find this place and they know exactly when the trouble started, from the newspapers."

"Let the man live," Eddie said. "Talk about something else."

"My own elevator, this is a problem," Bronzini said. "Periodic breakdowns."

"Four flights?"

"Five flights." ˙

"Let the man live," Eddie said.

"Five flights with his heart?"

"Talk about something else."

Mercedes was heavy, disposed to gesture, swaying in the chair, hand-sweeping, but ably taking care of feeble Eddie, the imposter, the aching and stiff-jointed and gasping man. The old Eddie of the subways was a robust guy, selling tokens from a booth in that cinema dimness of bad air and sprocketing trains, immune to the hell rattle of the express, and she tended him now with expert love, with knowledge and command, and when she got mad at something it made Albert want to hide because he was a coward of blunt emotion, things met head-on and direct.

"They put up the bobwire to save us from drug dealers. But what about the water when it rains? Comes right in. I don't want to see winter end. I rather be cold. I rather jam newspapers in the cracks. Because when the snow melts."

"The man is happy. Let him live," Eddie said.

She got a kitchen chair for Eddie to sit on. She got the cigar box and put it on the table and opened it. She went away and came back with a bath towel, which she placed over her husband's upper body and then spread down around his knees. She fastened the two upper corners at the back of his neck, loosely, and then she looked across at Albert, who shared her satisfaction with all the collateral matters, the stir of preparations, crucial to the business of the haircut.

Albert took the implements out of the cigar box. He set them on the table a couple of inches apart. The short black rubberized comb, tapered for sideburns. The tortoiseshell comb with a handle and three missing teeth, called a rake comb. The beautiful pair of scissors, made in Italy, a family possession for generations, one of those things that turns up among the effects of the deceased, suddenly seen anew, an everyday treasure, filigreed shanks and a spur attached to one loop, a curved projection to support the middle finger. You put your index finger in the loop and rest the middle finger against the suitably shaped appendage. What else? The shaving brush, not needed. The nose scissors, let him do his own nose. The electric clipper, heavy and black, Elk Grove, Illinois, blade still a little wispy with Eddie's shorn hair of six weeks ago. What else? Tube of lubricating oil for clipper. Five-and-dime whiskbroom, soft-bristled.

He had no idea how to cut hair. He'd done Eddie's hair a number of times but hadn't worked out a method. He paused often to study the effect, snipping, stepping back. Mercedes did not stay around to watch. Working slowly, snipping. The idea was to get the hair off the guy's head and onto the floor. Mercedes did not seem to think this was a thing she had to see.

"They have a new thing, maybe you heard," Eddie said. "Called space burials."

"I like it already."

"They send your ashes into space."

"Sign me up," Bronzini said.

"They have orbits you can select. There's an orbit around the equator. This is one orbit. The earth turns and you turn. Not you, your ashes."

"Is there a waiting list?"

"There's a waiting list. I saw it on the news. Plus the premium shot. This is way out there."

"Deep space."

"Way out. You and the stars."

"But you don't go up alone."

"You go up with about seven hundred other ashes in the same shot. Humans and their pets. You call the company, they'll put you on the list."

"What if you're already dead?"

"So your children call. Your lawyer calls. The important thing is how much do your ashes weigh. Because this is costing you—guess."

"I can't guess."

"Guess," Eddie said.

"You have to tell me."

"Ten thousand dollars a pound."

Eddie worked this line with a finality that had a grim pleasure in it.

"A pound. What do we weigh, in ashes, when we're dead?" Albert said. "I think it sounds reasonable myself."

"You think it sounds reasonable. Then you ruin my story."

"A pound of ashes, Eddie. That could be a whole family. For burial in space. Preserved forever."

"You ruin my story," he said.

Albert used the rake comb, working the top of his friend's head. He combed in sweeping motions, letting the hair settle, then combing again. He loved this work. He used the scissors sparingly up here because a mistake might show. He moved the comb softly through Eddie's thinning hair. He lifted the hair, then let it fall. Mercedes played the radio in the kitchen, making dinner or maybe lunch. Albert was vague, lately, on the subject of time. A heartbeat, a wrist pulse, a tapping foot. This was discernible time. He lifted the hair, then let it fall.

"You miss the booth, Eddie."

"I liked my job."

"I know you did."

"All those years and never once."

"They never robbed you."

"Never even tried," he said.

That's the genius of New York. Eddie Robles with a miniature chess set practicing moves at two in the morning in his token booth and don't think people didn't pop their faces in the slot and challenge him to a game, and don't think he didn't play them because he did, behind five layers of bulletproof glass, with trains blowing by in the night.

"I never thought today's the day they rob me. I never had this thought. And it never happened. I had a woman vomit in the slot. My worst incident personally. I never thought what I would do if they tried to rob me. I had the psychology you plan for it, then it happens. She puts her hands on the ledge and out it comes."

"Middle of the night?"

"Just her and me. You have to vomit, why can't you do it on the tracks? Her and me alone in the station, she comes right over like the coin slot they intend it just for this."

He plugged in the clipper and did the back of Eddie's neck. He went down under the towel and the shirt collar and did the hair that grew up from the shoulders. He cleared the neck completely and dusted with the brush and asked Mercedes for some talcum powder, which was the one thing he did not have in the cigar box, and he made a mental note to resupply, for next time.

Space burial. He thought of the contrails on that blue day out over the ocean, two years ago if that's when it was—how the boosters sailed apart and hung the terrible letter Y in the still air. The vapor stayed intact for some time, the astronauts fallen to sea but also still up there, graved in frozen smoke, and he lay awake in the night and saw that deep Atlantic sky and thought this death was soaring and clean, an exalted thing, a passing of the troubled body into vapor and flame, out above the world, monogrammed, the Y of dying young.

He wasn't sure people wanted to see this. Willing to see the systems failure and the human suffering. But the beauty, the high faith of space, how could such qualities be linked to death? Seven men and women. Their beauty and ours, revealed in a failed mission as we haven't seen it in a hundred triumphs. Apotheosis. Yes they were god-statured, transformed in those swanny streaks into the only sort of gods he cared to acknowledge, poetic and fleeting. He found this experience even more profound than the first moonwalk. That was stirring but also a little walkie-talkie, with ghosted action, movements that looked computerized, and he could never completely dismiss the suspicions of the paranoid elite, the old grizzled gurkhas of the corps, that the whole thing had been staged on a ranch outside Las Vegas.

•   •   •

In the spring they were still there, Albert and Laura. How was it possible his sister had not fallen into some calamitous illness? You sit there, you let your body go weak and slack, you don't walk, you don't see people, or mingle, or feel the bloodflow of inquisitive interest.

But he was grateful for her presence. There had always been a woman close to him, one woman at least, a woman or a girl, sharing the bathroom, the kitchen, long ago the bed. He needed this company. Women and their pride of time, their vigorous sense of a future. He married a Jew and loved her but Klara's future did not include him. He took care of his mother, a Catholic of the old eloquence, wearing a scapular, blessing herself and touching her thumb-knuckle to her lips, and he loved her and watched her die. He raised his daughter to make her own fate, to be a worthy individual outside compliance with religious rites, and he loved her, she lives in Vermont now, very much. And his sister, drifting in and out of the past but knowing him always in uncanny ways, seeing straight into his unadorned heart, and he loved her for all the stammered reasons you love a sister and because she'd narrowed her life to a few remarks that he found moving.

He had a portable phonograph, sleek-seeming once, advanced design. Now looked drab and squat but still played music after all these years. He found the record he was looking for and polished the vinyl with a treated cloth and placed it hostlike on the spindle. Saint-Saëns, piano works, gentle and pensive, a change of pace from the gorgeous torment of Bronzini's operas, the tabloid sensation that shatters teacups. He turned to make sure Laura was here, shapeless in the armchair, head resting against the hand-knit antimacassar, face lifted to the chords. He clicked the dial and watched the tone arm rise and the record descend, a jerky downslide to the turntable. Then the tone arm shifted laterally and the disc began to spin and this series of laboriously linked actions with their noises and pauses and teeterings, their dimwit delays, seemed to place him in some lost mechanical age with the pendulum clock and hand-cranked motorcar.

The needle slurred some notes but he was used to that. He sat at the edge of the room, where he could feel the kitchen sun and look at

Laura's face. The music joined them edgewise. He believed he could enter her reverie. He could know her, almost know her, feel her innocence through the music, know the girl again, the spinsterly twelve-year-old who walked behind her parents in the street, he could see her in the face of the somber older sister, she was almost there, the girl, in the pouches and moles and smoky hair. There was a brief moment in one of the pieces, after passagework of mellow recollection, when something dark seemed to enter, the soloist's left hand urging the tempo, and it made her raise an arm, slowly, a gesture of half shock, thoughtful and fraught—she'd heard a boding in the bass notes that startled her. And this was the other thing they shared, the sadness and clarity of time, time mourned in the music—how the sound, the shaped vibrations made by hammers striking wire strings made them feel an odd sorrow not for particular things but for time itself, the material feel of a year or an age, the textures of unmeasured time that were lost to them now, and she turned away, looking past her lifted hand into some transparent thing he thought he could call her life.

"You have to tell me, Albert, when you're going out. So I know."

"I did tell you."

"You never tell me."

"I do tell you."

"I don't know if you forget or what's the reason."

"I will tell you."

"If you tell me, then I know."

"I will tell you. I will be sure to tell you."

"But I forget, don't I?"

"Sometimes, yes."

"You tell me and I forget."

"Sometimes. It's not important."

"But you have to tell me."

"I will. I will tell you."

"So this way I know," she said.

•   •   •

He took his coffee black with a stab of rye in the morning, a nip, a pin drop, and with anisette in the afternoon or early evening, a shot, a jolt of the licorice sap, and maybe a beady tongue-taste of rye again before retiring, without coffee this time, medically forbidden of course but just a driblet, a measured snort, the briefest swig in the history of guilty drinking.

"You have to tell me. So I know."
   "I will tell you. I promise."
   "This way I know."
   "This way you know."
   "If you tell me, then I know."
   "That's right."
   "That's right, isn't it?"
   "Yes, that's right."
   "But you have to tell me. That's the only way I know."

He cleaned the kitchen windowsill, dust, hair, fly heads, flakes of plaster—stony little spalls.
   When they made dinner together she hit Albert's hand every time he got in the way, a jurisdictional tap on the back of the hand.
   He set his three pills next to his plate on the table, lined up for consumption. His heart pill, his fart pill and his liver pill.
   He spent more time indoors when there were people in the halls. He'd seen a hypodermic syringe on the second-story landing and now there were people in the halls, busy and inert at the same time, busy inside their eyes but also body-dead, barely able to drag a hand through the air. When it stops raining, he thought, they'll go to the playground or empty lots. And the elevator was stuck between floors so he was better off not leaving the apartment anyway because it was not a good idea for him to be climbing stairs.
   He slipped her glasses off her face and cleaned them with a tissue and put them back.
   And when he went out they were on the front stoop muttering

something that sounded like Wall Street and Albert finally surmised this was a brand of heroin for sale, Wall Street, Wall Street, and he could hear them in the halls, strangers in the building, breathing in and out.

He told her he was calling his daughter Teresa long-distance. He announced every phone call to keep Laura involved, including weather and time, and because he liked to make announcements.

His daughter ran a child-care center in a small city and had expenses and two children of her own and a lapsed husband trying to start a new career and Albert sent her a little money now and then, out of his teacher's pension.

A long-distance call was an act of predeliberation that filled a span in his mind much more extended than the length of the call. He planned an evening around it, waiting for the hour of the rate change and then placing a chair by the telephone and working the numbers carefully, his face down in the rotary dial.

He heard them breathing in the halls and knew he had food for two days easy and when the milk went sour he could open a can of peaches and dump the fruit and syrupy juice on the breakfast cereal. Clingstone, flesh that clings to the pit, to the stone, as with a peach. He heard them late at night and knew he could stretch the chopped meat, bulk up the tomato soup with macaroni, and they didn't live in the building and would find another place.

When his daughter answered the phone he looked across the room to Laura and nodded—contact made, the century of progress marches on.

Apples and cheese, they had apples and cheese, that was a meal in itself.

He was taking a book back to the library, another spring or early summer, a mild-hearted day, and he saw a familiar figure crossing the street and going toward the convent that was part of the Catholic grammar school. Anciently familiar, a figure from the land of the past. He hadn't realized she was still alive, Sister Edgar, how remarkable, the same blade face and bony hands, hurrying, a spare frame shaped by rustling garments. She wore the traditional habit with long black veil and white wimple and the starched clothpiece over the neck and shoulders, an iron crucifix swinging from her waist—she might have been a detail lifted from a painting by some sixteenth-century master.

He watched her open the convent door and disappear. This was a nun who'd been notorious for the terror she spread among the children, fifth-graders or sixth-graders, beatings, vituperations, keep them after school, send them out to clap erasers in a rainstorm. He'd never exchanged a word with Sister Edgar but felt half an urge to knock on the convent door and speak to her now, find out who she was after all these years. He'd been proud to teach in a public school, never mind the lax discipline. He worked among humane colleagues and heard stories about this nun and her routine cruelties.

He walked with a cane now and it gave him a feeling of professor emeritus. At the local library, named after Enrico Fermi, there was a photograph on the wall showing the scientist with an early model of the first atomic bomb. Years ago Albert used to entertain the idea of certain affinities between himself and the great Fermi. Illness in early childhood, marriage to a Jewish woman, science itself of course, cultural heritage—the allowable flush of Italian pride, only not so rousing in this case, attached to such destruction. The library was a movie house then, known to neighborhood kids as the Dumps for its sour odors and unswept debris. Let's not forget how some things get better, he thought. Books now, the hush of decimaled stacks.

He walked to the social club where he played cards sometimes, less than he used to, and took an occasional glass of wine. Some pictures on the wall, old days, fishmongers in aprons and caps, waiters outside a restaurant with sharply parted hair, dignified by time. He heard the church bell at Mount Carmel, half a block away, and poured himself a glass of red. He sat alone at a formica table and studied the legs of the wine, the trickles of swirled liquid that run down the inside of the glass and tell you how much body the wine has. This wine had legs. It was all legs. It had the legs of a sumo wrestler.

The videotape was running on the TV set in the corner. He'd seen the tape only once before, right here, and knew that they would keep running it until everyone on the planet had seen it. And when they started running it again after an interval of not running it, he knew it

232

meant the shooter had shot someone else, someone new, and because there was no film or tape of the new shooting, they had to show the old tape, the only tape, and they would show it to the ends of the earth.

Steve came over, Silvera, one of the Silvera brothers, he wore a suit and drove a hearse. Albert always asked, Who died?

"You *drink* that wine?"

"I tried talking to it but that didn't work," Albert said. "Sit down and join me."

"I got a funeral."

"Who died?"

"What's-his-name, from the fish market."

"Bury or cremate?"

"They put them in a wall nowdays. It's a popular thing."

"Encrypted," Albert said with satisfaction.

When the church bell rang again Steve hurried out. Albert could lean a bit and see the other drivers and pallbearers put out their cigarettes and start up the steps. It was nearly time for them to carry out the coffin. Another fishmonger, one more photograph that will seem decades hence to be an emblem of a certain stately innocence, some old lost sweet-tasting time. How memory conspires with objects of human craft, pressing time flat, inciting a tender reminiscence.

Later he went into the empty church and sat in the last row to spend a moment alone with Eddie Robles. A pigeon flew across the transept and landed on the edge of a swivel window near a bank of candles. He admired this old church. Corinthian columns and niched saints. Lighted candles in rosy glass containers. The neighborhood changes, the church remains the same. In the days that followed Eddie's mass he began to see again how the loss of a friend, how any loss was an aspect of Klara's departure, repeating the impact, the devastation.

The pigeon was aloft again, fluttering up near the dome. He thought he recalled that the Holy Ghost took form as a dove, was it? Every ghost is holy, he supposed, but you'll have to point one out to me before I genuflect. Still, he liked to sit here alone, brood and mourn amid the architectural details, the faith of stone and wood, pigments mixed in glass.

When Klara left him it turned something loose, a rant, an unworded voice that incited feelings so varied and confused and bled-together, so resistant to separation and scrutiny that he felt helpless in its surge. It was a hindrance to living. It made him distrust the man he was supposed to be, soft-spoken, well-spoken, gently reflective. Oh that bitch and how unworthy of him to think of her that way. It was his sister, eventually, who kept him from despair, another kind of voice, a woman marooned in introversion, only oddly loving.

He needed to walk, shake his muscles loose, and he went out into the street. Yes, people talking, eating, the loyal shoppers, they came from other boroughs, other counties, the double-parked cars, the coronary throb of the immediate streets still palpable. He walked west across Arthur Avenue and then edged warily north, an old route lately forsworn, toward the high school where he'd taught for thirty years.

Eddie dead, Mercedes in Puerto Rico now. Stop walking and you die.

When he entered a street behind the high school he was surprised to see it was closed to traffic. A play street, the pavement marked with painted game grids, with the numbered spaces of hopscotch and skelly, bases for slapball, and Albert was delighted. He'd thought this old custom of closing off streets for children's games was long dead, decades dead, a mind relic of life not yet dominated by cars and trucks. He stopped and watched the kids play, holding his cane across his waist as if gripping a stadium rail. Small children, slim and quick, Jamaican cadence in some of the voices and a girl with mottled skin maybe Malaysian or South Indian, he was only guessing, who jumped the hopscotch boxes with a measured deftness, doing a midair whirl so economical her hair was barely ruffled—bronze skin that went darker and lighter, olive-drab beneath the eyes. He wanted to stop her in midjump, stop everything for half a second, atomic clocks, body clocks, the microworld in which physicists search for time—and then run it backwards, unjump the girl, rewind the life, give us all a chance to do it over. He recalled the word for do-it-over, a word that kids used to shout during a game interrupted by a rare passing car or a lady crossing the street with a baby carriage. In-do, someone cried. In-do or hin-du, he wasn't completely sure. The Indian girl in sneakers and jeans.

234

Cheeky chose always goes. That's what the kid said when he got a second chance and did the same thing he'd done before the interruption. Hit a homer, kicked the can, shot a marble on target through the gutter dust. Cheeky chose always goes.

He saw a vendor selling sugarcane from an open-sided van, mangoes in wooden crates and tall cane sheaved with twine. Some things get better, Albert thought. A library, a play street, prods to his optimism block by block.

But what does do-it-over mean? He didn't want to lose his soul over compromises, second chances that turned him inside out. And anyway we don't depend on time finally. There is a balance, a kind of standoff between the time continuum and the human entity, our frail bundle of soma and psyche. We eventually succumb to time, it's true, but time depends on us. We carry it in our muscles and genes, pass it on to the next set of time-factoring creatures, our brown-eyed daughters and jug-eared sons, or how would the world keep going. Never mind the time theorists, the cesium devices that measure the life and death of the smallest silvery trillionth of a second. He thought that we were the only crucial clocks, our minds and bodies, way stations for the distribution of time. Think about it, Einstein, my fellow Albert.

He walked around to the front of the high school, tempted to go up on the portico and talk to the boys and girls standing there—but, no, they didn't know him and didn't care. Then why come here? The old squat pile of limestone and brick held his teacherly corpus, a million words spun into tepid air, and there was no reason to think he'd need to pass this way again. One documentary look to freeze the scene. He made a circuit of the block and headed home.

In one of the bare streets he came across a large stray dog that looked diseased, all ribs and flecked slaver, and he sidled away from it. In a culture of guard dogs there are always a few that fall from grace and end up haunting the streets. The trick is to skirt the animal without publishing your fear. *Festina lente.* Make haste slowly.

He cleaned the windowsills with a damp rag, fly wings, fly parts, the crumbled husks of glassy green beetles.

He had his teacher's pension and a small tax-deferred annuity and an old passbook with interest posted in cozy broken type.

Seasons ran together, the years were a stunned blur. Like time in books. Time passes in books in the span of a sentence, many months and years. Write a word, leap a decade. Not so different out here, at his age, in the unmargined world.

He put a record on the turntable and Laura sat in the chair seeming not to hear the music so much as see it.

Bread was dependable, bread with nearly every meal, bread fresh from the brick ovens. He kept library books stacked by the breadbox so he would be sure to return them by the due date.

"Are we moving, Albert?"

"No. We're not going anywhere."

"Someone told me, I don't remember, we're moving."

"Maybe we'll go see Teresa again. We'll take the bus. It's a beautiful ride. That's the only move we're making."

"Did you tell me you were going out?"

"You like the ride. Vermont. We'll go when the leaves turn. You like it then."

"Albert."

"What?"

"If you tell me, then I know."

Seasons and years. Laura read a soap opera digest to keep track of TV characters even though the TV had gone on the blink so long ago it was another life.

Oatmeal bubbled on the stove.

He came along and took her glasses off and cleaned them with a tissue, then placed them on her face again.

8

The old nun rose at dawn, feeling pain in every joint. She'd been rising at dawn since her days as a postulant, kneeling on hardwood floors to pray. First she raised the shade. That's creation out there, little green apples and infectious disease. Then she knelt in the folds of the white nightgown, fabric endlessly laundered, beaten with swirled soap, left gristled and stiff. Sister Alma Edgar. And the body beneath, the spindly thing she carried through the world, chalk pale mostly, and speckled hands with high veins, and cropped hair that was fine and flaxy gray, and her bluesteel eyes—many a boy and girl of old saw those peepers in their dreams.

She made the sign of the cross, murmuring the congruous words. *Amen*, an olden word, back to Greek and Hebrew, *verily*—the most familiar of everyday prayers yet carrying three years' indulgence, seven if you dip your hand in holy water before you mark the body.

Prayer is a practical strategy, the gaining of temporal advantage in the capital markets of Sin and Remission.

She said a morning offering and got to her feet. At the sink she scrubbed her hands repeatedly with coarse brown soap. How can the hands be clean if the soap is not? This question was insistent in her life. But if you clean the soap with bleach, what do you clean the bleach bottle with? If you use scouring powder on the bleach bottle, how do you clean the box of Ajax? Germs have personalities. Different objects harbor threats of various insidious types. And the questions turn inward forever.

An hour later she was in her veil and habit, sitting in the passenger seat of a black van that was headed south out of the school district and down past the monster concrete expressway into the lost streets, a squander of burnt-out buildings and unclaimed souls. Grace Fahey was at the wheel, a young nun in secular dress. All the nuns at the convent wore plain blouses and skirts except for Sister Edgar, who had permission from the motherhouse to fit herself out in the old things with the arcane names, the wimple, cincture and guimpe. She knew there were stories about her past, how she used to twirl the big-beaded rosary and crack students across the mouth with the iron crucifix. Things were simpler then. Clothing was layered, life was not. But Edgar stopped hitting kids years ago, even before she grew too old to teach, when the neighborhood changed and the faces of her students became darker. All the righteous fury went out of her soul. How could she strike a child who was not like her?

"The old jalop needs a tune-up," Gracie said. "Hear that noise?"

"Ask Ismael to take a look."

"Ku-ku-ku-ku."

"He's the expert."

"I can do it myself. I just need the right tools."

"I don't hear anything," Edgar said.

"Ku-ku-ku-ku? You don't hear that?"

"Maybe I'm going deaf."

"I'll go deaf before you do, Sister."

"Look, another angel on the wall."

The two women looked across a landscape of vacant lots filled with years of stratified deposits—the age of house garbage, the age of construction debris and vandalized car bodies, the age of moldering mobster parts. Weeds and trees grew amid the dumped objects. There were dog packs, sightings of hawks and owls. City workers came periodically to excavate the site and they stood warily by the great earth machines, the pumpkin-mudded backhoes and dozers, like infantrymen huddled near advancing tanks. But soon they left, they always left with holes half dug, pieces of equipment discarded, styrofoam cups, pepperoni pizzas. The nuns looked across all this. There were networks of vermin, craters chocked with plumbing fixtures and sheetrock. There were hillocks of slashed tires laced with thriving vine. Gunfire sang at sunset off the low walls of demolished buildings. The nuns sat in the van and looked. At the far end was a lone standing structure, a derelict tenement with an exposed wall where another building had once abutted. This wall was where Ismael Muñoz and his crew of graffiti writers spray-painted a memorial angel every time a child died in the neighborhood. Angels in blue and pink covered roughly half the high slab. The child's name and age were printed under each angel, sometimes with cause of death or personal comments by the family, and as the van drew closer Edgar could see entries for TB, AIDS, beatings, drive-by shootings, measles, asthma, abandonment at birth—left in dumpster, forgot in car, left in Glad Bag stormy night.

This area was called the Wall, partly for the graffiti facade and partly the general sense of exclusion—it was a tuck of land adrift from the social order.

"I wish they'd stop already with the angels," Gracie said. "It's in totally bad taste. A fourteenth-century church, that's where you go for angels. This wall publicizes all the things we're working to change. Ismael should look for positive things to emphasize. The townhouses, the community gardens that people plant. Walk around the corner you see ordinary people going to work, going to school. Stores and churches."

"Titanic Power Baptist Church."

"What's the difference—it's a church. The area's full of churches. Decent working people. Ismael wants to do a wall, these are the people he should celebrate. Be positive."

Edgar laughed inside her skull. It was the drama of the angels that made her feel she belonged here. It was the terrible death these angels represented. It was the danger the writers faced to produce their graffiti. There were no fire escapes or windows on the memorial wall and the writers had to rappel from the roof with belayed ropes or sway on makeshift scaffolds when they did an angel in the lower ranks. Ismael spoke of a companion wall for dead graffitists, flashing his wasted smile.

"And he does pink for girls and blue for boys. That really sets my teeth on edge," Gracie said.

They stopped at the friary to pick up groceries they would distribute to the needy. The friary was an old brick building wedged between boarded tenements. Three monks in gray cloaks and rope belts worked in an anteroom, getting the day's shipment ready. Grace, Edgar and Brother Mike carried the plastic bags out to the van. Mike was an ex-fireman with a Brillo beard and wispy ponytail. He looked like two different guys front and back. When the nuns first appeared he'd offered to serve as guide, a protecting presence, but Edgar firmly declined. She believed her habit and veil were safety enough. Beyond these South Bronx streets people may look at her and think she is a quaintness of ages past. But inside the strew of rubble she was a natural sight, she and the robed monks. What figures could be so timely, costumed for rats and plague?

Edgar liked seeing the monks in the street. They visited the homebound, ran a shelter for the homeless, they collected food for the hungry. And they were men in a place where few men remained. Teenage boys in clusters, armed drug dealers—these were the men of the immediate streets. She didn't know where the others had gone, the fathers, living with second or third families, hidden in rooming houses or sleeping under highways in refrigerator boxes, buried in the potter's field on Hart Island.

"I'm counting plant species," Brother Mike said. "I've got a book I take out to the lots."

Gracie said, "You stay on the fringes, right?"

"They know me in the lots."

"Who knows you? The dogs know you? There are rabid dogs, Mike."

"I'm a Franciscan, okay? Birds light on my index finger."

"Stay on the fringes," she told him.

"There's a girl I keep seeing, maybe twelve years old, runs away when I try to talk to her. I get the feeling she's living in the ruins. Ask around."

"Will do," Gracie said.

When the van was loaded they drove back to the Wall to do their business with Ismael and to pick up a few of his crew who would help them distribute the food. Ismael had teams of car spotters who ranged across the boroughs, concentrating on the bleak streets under bridges and viaducts. The nuns represented his North Bronx operation. They gave him lists that detailed the locations of abandoned cars along the Bronx River, a major dump site for stolen, joyridden, semistripped, gas-siphoned and pariah-dog vehicles. Ismael sent his crew to salvage the car bodies and whatever parts might still be intact. They used a small flatbed truck with an undependable winch and a motif of souls-in-hell graffiti on the cab, deck and mud flaps. The car hulks came here to the lots for inspection and price setting by Ismael and were then delivered to a scrap-metal operation in remotest Brooklyn. Sometimes there were forty or fifty cannibalized cars dumped in the lots, museum quality, a junkworld sculpture park—cars bashed and bullet-cratered, hoodless, doorless and rust-ulcered, charred cars, upside-down cars, cars with dead bodies wrapped in shower curtains, rats ascratch in the glove compartments.

The money he paid the nuns for their locational work went to the friary for groceries.

When the van approached the building Edgar felt along her mid-section for the latex gloves she kept tucked in her belt.

Gracie parked the van, the only operating vehicle in human sight. She attached the vinyl-coated steel collar to the steering wheel and fitted the rod into the lock housing. At the same time Edgar force-fitted the gloves onto her hands and felt the ambivalence, the conflict. Safe, yes, scientifically shielded from organic menace. But also sinfully complicit with some process she only half understood, the force in the world, the array of systems that displaces religious faith with paranoia. It was in the milky-slick feel of these synthetic gloves, fear and distrust and unreason. And she felt masculinized as well, condomed ten times over—safe, yes, and maybe a little confused. But latex was necessary here. Protection against the spurt of blood or pus and the viral entities hidden within, submicroscopic parasites in their soviet socialist protein coats.

The nuns got out of the van and approached the building.

Squatters occupied a number of floors. Edgar didn't need to see them to know who they were. They were a society of indigents subsisting without heat, lights or water. They were nuclear families with toys and pets, junkies who roamed at night in dead men's Reeboks. She knew who they were through assimilation, through the ingestion of messages that riddled the streets. They were foragers and gatherers, can redeemers, the people who yawed through subway cars with paper cups. And doxies sunning on the roof in clement weather and men with warrants outstanding for reckless endangerment and depraved indifference. And there were shouters of the Spirit, she knew this for a fact—a band of charismatics who leapt and wept on the top floor, uttering words and nonwords, treating knife wounds with prayer.

Ismael had his headquarters on the third floor and the nuns hustled up the stairs. Grace had a tendency to look back unnecessarily at the senior nun, who ached in her movable parts but kept pace well enough, her habit whispering through the stairwell.

"Needles on the landing," Gracie warned.

Watch the needles, sidestep the needles, such deft instruments of self-disregard. Gracie couldn't understand why an addict would not be sure to use a clean needle. This failure made her pop her cheeks in anger. But Edgar thought about the lure of critical risk, the little love bite of that dragonfly dagger. If you know you're worth nothing, only a gamble with death can gratify your vanity.

Gracie knocked on the door.

"Don't get too close to him," Edgar said.

"Who?"

"Ismael."

"Why?"

"He's not well."

"I saw him three days ago. I was here. You weren't, Sister. How do you know he's not well?"

"I can sense it."

"He's well. He's fine," Gracie said.

"I've sensed it for some time."

"What do you sense?"

"AIDS," Edgar said.

Gracie studied old Edgar. She looked at the latex gloves. She looked

242

at the nun's face, emphatic of feature, eyes bird-bright. She looked and thought and said nothing.

One of the kids unlocked the door—latch bolts, dead bolts, steel shafts.

Ismael stood barefoot on dusty floorboards in a pair of old chinos rolled to his calves and a parrot-print shirt worn outside his pants, smoking a whopping cigar and resembling some carefree islander wading in happy surf.

"Sisters, what do you have for me?"

Edgar thought he was quite young despite the seasoned air, maybe midthirties—sparse beard, a sweet smile complicated by rotting teeth. Members of his crew sat around on scavenged sofas, improvised chairs, smoking and looking at comic books. Too young for one, too old for the other. She knew in her heart he had AIDS.

Gracie handed over a list of cars they'd spotted in the last two days. Details of time and place, type of vehicle, condition of same.

He said, "You do nice work. My other people do like this, we run the world by now."

Edgar kept a distance of course. She looked at the crew, seven boys, four girls. Graffiti, illiteracy, petty theft. They spoke an unfinished English, soft and muffled, insufficiently suffixed, and she wanted to drum some hard *g*'s into the ends of their gerunds.

"I don't pay you today, okay? I got some things I'm doing that I need the capital."

"What things?" Gracie said.

Retroviruses in the bloodstream, acronyms in the air. Edgar knew what all the letters stood for. AZidoThymidine. Human Immunodeficiency Virus. Acquired Immune Deficiency Syndrome. Komitet Gosudarstvennoi Bezopasnosti. Yes, the KGB was part of the multiplying swarm, the cell-blast of reality that has to be distilled and initialed in order to be seen.

"I'm making plans I get some heat and electric in here. Plus pirate cable for the Knicks."

Here in the Wall many people believed the government was spreading the virus, our government. Edgar knew better. The KGB was behind this particular piece of disinformation. And the KGB was

243

responsible for the disease itself, a product of germ warfare—making it, spreading it through networks of paid agents.

She'd stopped talking about these things to Gracie, who rolled her eyes so far up into her head she looked like science fiction.

Edgar looked out a window and saw someone moving among the poplars and ailanthus trees in the most overgrown part of the rubbled lots. A girl in a too-big jersey and striped pants grubbing in the underbrush, maybe for something to eat or wear. Edgar watched her, a lanky kid who had a sort of feral intelligence, a sureness of gesture and step—she looked sleepless but alert, she looked unwashed but completely clean somehow, earth-clean and hungry and quick. There was something about her that mesmerized the nun, a charmed quality, a sense of something favored and sustaining.

She gestured to Gracie. Just then the girl slipped through a maze of wrecked cars and by the time Gracie reached the window she was barely a flick of the eye, lost in the low ruins of an old firehouse.

"Who is this girl," Gracie said, "who's out there in the lots hiding from people?"

Ismael looked at his crew and one of them piped up, an undersized boy in spray-painted jeans, dark-skinned and shirtless.

"Esmeralda. Nobody knows where her mother's at."

Gracie said, "Can you find the girl and then tell Brother Mike?"

"This girl she be real quick."

A murmur of assent.

"She be a running fool this girl."

Heads bobbing above the comic books.

"Why did her mother go away?"

"She be a addict. They un, you know, predictable."

All street, these kids. No home or school. Edgar wanted to get them in a room with a blackboard and then buzz their heads with Spelling and Punctuation. She wanted to drill them in the lessons of the Baltimore Catechism. True or false, yes or no, fill in the blanks.

Ismael said, "Maybe the mother returns. She feels the worm of remorse. But the truth of the matter there's kids that are better off without their mothers or fathers. Because their mothers or fathers are dangering their safety."

"Catch her and hold her," Gracie told the crew. "She's too young to be on her own. Brother Mike says she's twelve."

"Twelve is not so young," Ismael said. "One of my best writers, he does wildstyle, age eleven or twelve. Juano. I send him down in a rope to do the complicated letters."

Edgar knew about Ismael's early career as a graffiti master, a legend of spray paint. He was the infamous Moonman 157, nearly twenty years ago, and he told the nuns how he'd marked subway cars all over the city, his signature running on every line, and Edgar believed this was where he'd started having sex with men, in his teens, in the tunnels. She heard it in the spaces in his voice.

"When do we get our money?" Gracie said.

Ismael stood there coughing and Edgar moved back against the far wall. She knew she ought to be more sympathetic to the man. But she was not sentimental about fatal diseases. Dying was just an extended version of Ash Wednesday. She intended to meet her own end with senses intact, grasp it, know it finally, open herself to the mystery that others mistake for something freakish and unspeakable.

People in the Wall liked to say, When hell fills up, the dead will walk the streets.

It was happening a little sooner than they thought.

"I'll have some money next time," Ismael said. "I make practically nothing on these cars. My margin it's very minimum. I'm looking I might expand out of the country. Don't be surprise my scrap ends up in North, you know, Korea."

Gracie joked about this. But it was not a thing Edgar could take lightly. She was a cold war nun who'd once lined the walls of her room with Reynolds Wrap as a safeguard against nuclear fallout. The furtive infiltration, deep and sleek. Not that she didn't think a war might be thrilling. She often conjured the flash even now, with the USSR crumbled alphabetically, the massive letters toppled like Cyrillic statuary.

They went down to the van, the nuns and five kids, and they set out to distribute the food, starting with the hardest cases in the projects, just outside the Wall.

They rode the elevators and went down the long passageways. Unknown lives in every wallboard room. Sister Grace believed the

245

proof of God's creativity eddied from the fact that you could not surmise the life, even remotely, of his humblest shut-in.

They spoke to two blind women who lived together and shared a seeing-eye dog.

They saw a man with epilepsy.

They saw children with oxygen tanks next to their beds.

They saw a woman in a wheelchair who wore a Fuck New York T-shirt. Gracie said she would trade the groceries they gave her for heroin, the dirtiest street scag available. The crew looked on, angry. Gracie set her jaw, she narrowed her pale eyes and handed over the food. They argued about this and it was Sister Grace against everybody. Even the wheelchair woman didn't think she should get the food.

They talked to a man with cancer who tried to kiss the latexed hands of Sister Edgar. She backed rapidly toward the door.

They saw five small children being minded by a ten-year-old, all of them bunched on a bed, and two infants in a crib nearby.

They went single file down the passageways, a nun at front and rear, and Edgar thought of all the infants in limbo, unbaptized, babies in the seminether, and the nonbabies of abortion, a cosmic cloud of slushed fetuses floating in the rings of Saturn, and babies born without immune systems, bubble children raised by computer, and babies born addicted—she saw them all the time, three-pound newborns with crack habits who resembled something out of peasant folklore.

They handed out food and Edgar rarely spoke. Gracie spoke. Gracie gave advice. Edgar was a presence only, a uniformed aura in regimental black-and-whites.

They went down the passageways, three boys and two girls forming one body with the nuns, a single swaybacked figure with many moving parts, and they finished their deliveries in the basement of a tenement inside the Wall, where people paid rent for plywood cubicles worse than prison holes.

They saw a prostitute whose silicone breasts had leaked, ruptured and finally exploded one day, sending a polymer whiplash across the face of the man on top of her, and she was unemployed now, living in a room the size of a playpen.

They saw a man who'd cut his eyeball out of its socket because it contained a satanic symbol, a five-pointed star, and Edgar talked to this one, he'd popped the eyeball from his head and then severed the connecting tendons with a knife, and she talked to him in English and understood what he said although he spoke a language, a dialect none of them had ever heard—finally flushing the eye down the communal toilet outside his cubbyhole.

Gracie dropped the crew at their building just as a bus pulled up. What's this, do you believe it? A tour bus in carnival colors with a sign in the slot above the windshield reading *South Bronx Surreal*. Gracie's breathing grew intense. About thirty Europeans with slung cameras stepped shyly onto the sidewalk in front of the boarded shops and closed factories and they gazed across the street at the derelict tenement in the middle distance.

Gracie went half berserk, sticking her head out the van and calling, "It's not surreal. It's real, it's real. Your bus is surreal. You're surreal."

A monk rode by on a rickety bike. The tourists watched him pedal up the street. They listened to Gracie shout at them. They saw a man come along with battery-run pinwheels he was selling, brightly colored vanes pinned to sticks—an elderly black fellow in a yellow skullcap. They saw the ailanthus jungle and the smash heap of mortified cars and they looked at the six-story slab of painted angels with streamers rippled above their cherub heads.

Gracie shouting, "Brussels is surreal. Milan is surreal. This is real. The Bronx is real."

A tourist bought a pinwheel and got back in the bus. Gracie pulled away muttering. In Europe the nuns wear bonnets like cantilevered beach houses. That's surreal, she said. A traffic jam developed not far from the Wall. The two women sat and waited. They watched children walk home from school, eating coconut ices. Two tables on the sidewalk—free condoms at one, free needles at the other.

"Granted, he may be gay. But this doesn't mean he has AIDS."

Sister Edgar said nothing.

"All right, this area is an AIDS disaster. But Ismael's a smart man, safe, careful."

Sister Edgar looked out the window.

A clamor rising all about them, weary beeping horns and police sirens and the great saurian roar of fire-engine klaxons.

"Sister, sometimes I wonder why you put up with all this," Gracie said. "You've earned some peace and quiet. You could live upstate and do development work for the order. How I would love to sit in the rose garden with a mystery novel and old Pepper curled by my feet." Old Pepper was the cat in the motherhouse upstate. "You could take a picnic lunch to the pond."

Edgar had a mirthless inner grin that floated somewhere back near her palate. She did not yearn for life upstate. This was the truth of the world, right here, her soul's own home, herself—she saw herself, the fraidy child who must face the real terror of the streets to cure the linger of destruction inside her. Where else would she do her work but under the brave and crazy wall of Ismael Muñoz?

Then Gracie was out of the van. She was out of the seat belt, out of the van and running down the street. The door hung open. Edgar understood at once. She turned and saw the girl, Esmeralda, half a block ahead of Gracie, running for the Wall. Gracie moved among the cars in her clunky shoes and frump skirt. She followed the girl around a corner where the tour bus sat dead in traffic. The tourists watched the running figures. Edgar could see their heads turn in unison, pinwheels spinning at the windows.

All sounds gathered in the dimming sky.

She thought she understood the tourists. You travel somewhere not for museums and sunsets but for ruins, bombed-out terrain, for the moss-grown memory of torture and war. Emergency vehicles were massing about a block and a half away. She saw workers pry open subway gratings in billows of pale smoke and she knew she ought to say a fast prayer, an act of hope, three years' indulgence, but she only watched and waited. Then heads and torsos began to emerge, indistinctly, people coming into the air with jaws skewed open in frantic gasps.

A short circuit, a subway fire.

Through the rearview mirror she spotted tourists getting off the bus and edging along the street, poised to take pictures. And the schoolkids going by, barely interested—they heard shootings all the time out their windows at night, death interchangeable on the street and TV. But what did she know, an old woman who ate fish, still, on Friday, beginning to feel useless here, far less worthy than Sister Grace. Gracie was a soldier, a fighter for human worth. Edgar was basically a junior G-man, protecting a set of laws and prohibitions.

She had a raven's heart, small and obdurate.

She heard the yammer of police cars pulsing in stalled traffic and saw a hundred subway riders come up out of the tunnels accompanied by workers in incandescent vests and she watched the tourists snapping pictures and thought of the trip she'd made to Rome many years ago, for study and spiritual renewal, and she'd swayed beneath the great domes and prowled the catacombs and church basements and this is what she thought as the riders came up to the street, how she'd stood in a subterranean chapel in a Capuchin church and could not take her eyes off the skeletons stacked there, wondering about the monks whose flesh had once decorated these metatarsals and femurs and skulls, many skulls heaped in alcoves and hidey-holes, and she remembered thinking vindictively that these are the dead who will come out of the earth to lash and cudgel the living, to punish the sins of the living—death, yes, triumphant.

But does she really want to believe that, still?

After a while Gracie edged into the driver's seat, unhappy and flushed.

"Nearly caught her. We ran into the thickest part of the lots and then I was distracted, damn scared actually, because bats, I couldn't believe it, actual bats—like the only flying mammals on earth?" She made ironic wing motions with her fingers. "They came swirling out of a crater filled with red-bag waste. Hospital waste, laboratory waste."

"I don't want to hear it."

"Dead white mice by the hundreds with stiff flat bodies. You could flip them like baseball cards."

"Cars starting to move," Edgar said.

"Ever wonder what happens to amputated limbs after the doctor saws them off? They end up in the Wall. Dumped in a vacant lot or burned in the waste incinerator."

"Drive the car."

"And Esmeralda somewhere in those shrubs and junked cars. I bet anything she's living in a car," Gracie said.

"She'll be all right."

"She won't be all right."

"She can take care of herself."

"Sooner or later," Gracie said.

"She's quick. She's blessed. She'll be all right."

Gracie looked at her and drove and looked again, hearing the engine knock, and said nothing. Edgar was never known to take an optimistic position. Maybe this worried her a little.

And that night, under the first tier of scratchy sleep, Edgar saw the subway riders once again, adult males, females of childbearing age, all rescued from the smoky tunnels, groping along catwalks and led up companion ladders to the street—fathers and mothers, the lost parents found and gathered, shirt-plucked and bodied up, guided to the surface by small faceless figures with day-glo wings.

Weeks later Edgar picked up a copy of Time on her way out of the refectory and there she saw it, a large color photo of a white-haired woman seated in a director's chair beneath the old weathered wing of an Air Force bomber. And she recognized the name, Klara Sax, because she recognized everything, because people whispered names to her, because she felt stirrings of information in the dusty corridors of the convent or the school's supply room that smelled of pencil wood and composition books, because she sensed some dark knowledge floating in the smoke of the priest's swinging censer, because things were defined for her by the creak of old floorboards and the odor of clothes, a man's damp camel coat, because she drew News and Rumors and Catastrophes into the spotless cotton pores of her habit and veil.

All the connections intact. The woman once married to a local man. The man a tutor in chess to one of Edgar's own former students. The boy with necktie ever askew, Matthew Aloysius Shay, fingernails bitten to the pink, one of her brainier boys, male parent missing.

She knew things, yes, chess, all those layers of Slavic stealth, those ensnarements and ploys. She knew that Bobby Fischer had all the fill-

250

ings removed from his teeth when he played Boris Spassky in 1972—it made perfect sense to her—so the KGB could not control him through broadcasts made into the amalgam units packed in his molars.

She put the magazine in her closet with the old fan mags she'd stopped reading decades ago when she lost her faith in movie stars.

The faith of suspicion and unreality. The faith that replaces God with radioactivity, the power of alpha particles and the all-knowing systems that shape them, the endless fitted links.

That night she leaned over the washbasin in her room and cleaned a steel wool pad with disinfectant. Then she used the pad to scour a scrub brush, cleaning every bristle. But she hadn't cleaned the original disinfectant in something stronger than disinfectant. She hadn't done this because the regression was infinite. And the regression was infinite because it is called infinite regression. You see how fear spreads beyond the pushy extrusions of matter and into the elevated spaces where words play upon themselves.

She cleaned and she prayed.

She said brief prayers while she worked, simple pious pleas called ejaculations that carried indulgences numbered in the days rather than years.

She prayed and she thought.

She went to bed and lay awake and thought of Esmeralda. They'd spotted her a number of times but hadn't been able to catch her. Not Gracie or the monks or the agile writers in Ismael's crew. And Edgar's sense of her safety was beginning to grow less assured.

She welcomed every breath of knowledge that came her way, all the better for its element of disquiet, but this time the foreboding shook her strongly. She sensed something out there in the Wall, a muddled shuffling danger that waited for the girl on her lithe passage through car bodies and discarded human limbs and acres of uncollected garbage.

Mother of Mercy pray for us. Three hundred days.

9

Nick was trying to find the magazine he'd been saving to take to Houston. He saved certain kinds of reading for business trips, things he never got around to looking at otherwise, magazines that stacked and nagged and finally went to the sidewalk on the designated day. There was a noise that started, a world hum—you began to hear it when you left your carpeted house and rode out to the airport. He wanted something friendly to read in the single sustained drone that marks every mile in a business traveler's day.

The magazine was Time, missing about a month. He found it finally in the bathroom, stashed in a basket that Marian kept filled with mostly glossy fashion books—every shadow brushed to an anatomical polish, contoured against crumble and waste. Just the thing to browse when your body is squatted and your pants are down. The copy of Time had an article on Klara Sax he wanted to read, not the first such piece he'd spotted through the years but maybe more interesting than most, some desert project she'd started, bristling with ambition.

His suitcase was on the bed, small enough for the overhead bin, and he zippered the magazine into an outer pocket and finished packing. Marian walked in wearing her catwoman shades. They came with the job. She worked for the city's arts commission now and wanted a sleeker look.

"Don't you need to hurry?"

"The car's not here. I trust the car," he said.

"The car is dependable."

"The car knows things we don't know."

"The car is never late."

"The car and the plane are in constant touch."

She always looked great when he was walking out the door. Why is that, he thought. Some soft-bodied mood, some tone that half insisted on being noticed but was also a shy secret, afraid of disturbing the air between them.

He moved her into the wall and put his hands on her thighs, kiss-biting her mouth and neck. She said something he didn't quite catch. He put his hands between her ass and the wall and moved her into him. Her skirt slid against her parted legs, fabric stretched out and up, the tensile whisper of friction he counted on to carry him through life. He stepped back slightly and looked at her.

"Why is that?" he said.

"What are we talking about?"

"And why is it that when I get back, the whole thing's gone and lost and forgotten?"

"What thing?"

He took off her sunglasses and handed them to her. When he walked out the door, seconds later, the company car was waiting.

A few hours later Marian stood in a small room in a two-story pale brick building near Jack in the Box and Brake-O. Cars were parked under a lopsided shed out back and there was a man's abandoned shoe in one of the empty slots. She stood naked in the room by the edge of the window. Then she walked to the long mirror and edged her hip against the surface of the glass, feeling some small coiled chill of body and object. She looked all right. All the exercise, the diet, the diet, the exercise. All the butt repetition, the toilsome boredom she endured in the name of keeping fit. She was not the twisted perfect woman she used to be but she still kept fit. Fuck you, keep fit. She stood squared up to the glass. Nothing she could do about the needle nose but otherwise not bad. She never looked at herself so closely at home. It was easier to see herself out here, inside strange walls. She let her nipples touch the glass and when she backed away she saw they'd left a moistness, a pair of pressed kisses like winter breath.

When Brian arrived she was wearing a robe she'd found in the closet.

"I shouldn't be here," he said.

"Neither should I. This is the point, isn't it?"

He sat on the edge of the bed taking off his shoes, a little like the class crybaby undressing for gym.

"Whose place is this?"

"My assistant's."

"Are you serious?"

"Why not? We need a safe place," she said.

"But your secretary?"

"My assistant. And it's better than a hotel."

"I shouldn't be here."

He walked around the room barefoot, unbuttoning his shirt. He had clown feet, long and bunioned, and he didn't loosen his tie until he'd pulled his shirt out of his trousers.

"Is she young?"

"How do you know it's a woman?"

"Seriously. Young?"

"Yes," she said.

He walked around touching things, looking at photographs and matchbooks.

"Good-looking?"

"You want to check out her underwear? Look, I'm wearing her robe. Fuck me fuck me fuck me," she said drily.

"She can't afford better?"

"We're underbudgeted."

"It's a roomette."

254

"Small but intense," Marian said.

She was standing against the wall, arms folded, and he stepped into her. She freed her hands and worked at his pants. She liked having sex with Brian because she could handle him, turn him, get him to match her mood, rouse him easily or make him talk, talk—acid candid shameful stuff, bitter-funny.

"I think he knows," she said.

"What?"

"I think he knows."

"He doesn't know."

"I think he knows."

She had her hands in his pants and a smile on her face. He moved the robe off half her body, smeared it—rubbed it against her shoulder and breast before he got it off her, almost off her, pulling her arm through the hole and letting the garment drag.

They eased onto the bed. She tried to get clear of the rest of the robe but he wouldn't let her. He wanted a woman in half a robe. The phone rang and they stopped to listen. Every time a phone rang in a borrowed apartment they stopped and thought about the thing they were doing and maybe at some level about the life of the person whose apartment they were using. It made them feel the wrong kind of guilty trespass, she thought. The bed. The mystery of the other person's life and medicine cabinet and bed. It was the one thing she didn't like about this, one among others, and she couldn't have sex to a ringing phone.

She felt around for her handbag, which was on a chair at the side of the bed. The ringing stopped. Brian got off the bed and finished undressing.

"You trust her to keep quiet?"

"She keeps quiet about everything else."

"This isn't everything else."

Marian found her cigarettes and lit one up and he handed her an ashtray.

"I thought you stopped."

"I'm down to five a day."

"I thought you were wearing the patch."

255

"I'm not," she said.

He stretched out next to her, on his side. The ringing phone had brought them prematurely to a lazy state of small caresses and mellow bends of conversation and streams of smoke.

He said, "This job of yours. Real or fake?"

"I work with structural engineers, urban designers. I fight with citizens' groups all the time. But I get things done, pretty much."

"I had lunch in a mechanical mist the other day. In some mall somewhere."

"We don't do malls. We do parkways."

"What do you do to a parkway?"

"Make it livable, bearable. Tell little stories. Sculpture on the road dividers. Piers that are shaped like animals."

"What's your secretary's name?" he said.

She tipped a length of ash onto his pubic hair.

"Long hours, single-minded devotion. Stuck in that Japanese thing," he said. "Death from overwork."

"Disappear in the company and die. Only I don't do it to disappear. I do it to be visible and audible. And I'm not sure what you mean by real or fake."

He picked the ashes out of his crotch and blew them off the tips of his fingers.

"Most jobs are fake," he said.

They'd been late starters and had never developed a reliable pace. Only three or four apartments in all this time and they'd used each apartment only once or twice. She'd learned not to notice her disappointment. This was an aspect of being twistedly perfect. But Brian's reluctance was fairly maddening. She had to arrange the apartments, make the assurances, calibrate the timing and then wonder if he'd show. They talk about demon lovers. She had a demon husband. Her lover was a loose-jointed guy with a freckled forehead and nappy hair. But this was the dare she had to take, a way into some essential streak of self, some possibility that felt otherwise sandy and scanted and unturned. These times were hers, however brief and infrequent. And he was enormously easy to be with and growing dear to her. She liked to tease and scare him but did not want to think about giving him up.

256

"Blow smoke my way," he said. "I want all the aromas. Tobacco, bedsheets, women."

She was herself with Brian, whatever that meant. She knew what it meant. Less enveloped in someone else's figuration, his self-conscious shaping of a life.

"And don't let me forget, I have a meeting at three," he said.

"I'm a little put off by the fact that you haven't, you know," sort of dangling the words, "fallen in love with me, Brian."

"You're my age, you're my height. I fall in love with small brisk women I see from a distance."

"And they have to be young."

"They have to be young. You and I, we're buddies. And I'm too guilty to fall in love with you. I'm very guilty. I'm guilty as shit."

"Then why are you doing it?"

"Because you want it so much," he said.

She bent the cigarette into the ashtray.

"And you're that accommodating? Because I want it? You're willing to do it?"

"I want it too. But you want it like life and death."

She didn't like him when he was serious. It was outside the rules. He let his head flop toward her, whispering.

"It's stupid and it's reckless and we shouldn't do it anymore. Because if he finds out," he whispered.

"What if your wife finds out? She's the one who'll cut your balls off."

"Nick will only kill me."

"And he doesn't have to find out. He already knows."

"He doesn't know."

"I think he knows."

He whispered, "Let's make this one last happy farewell fuck."

She started to tell him something but then thought no. They fell together, folded toward each other, and then she leaned back, arching, shored on her back-braced arms, and she let him pace the occasion. At some point she opened her eyes and saw him watching her, measuring her progress, and he looked a little isolated and wan and she pulled his head down to her and sucked salt from his tongue and heard the sort of breast-slap, the splash of upper bodies and the banging bed. Then it was a matter of close concentration. She listened for something inside the bloodrush and she spun his hips and felt electric and desperate and finally home free and she looked at his eyes stung shut and his mouth stretched so tight it seemed taped at the corners, upper lip pressed white against his teeth, and she felt a kind of hanged man's coming when he came, the jumped body and stiffened limbs, and she ran a hand through his hair—be nicer if we did it more often.

She waited for their breathing to settle so she could ease free and get her handbag off the chair.

He went to the kitchen and drank a glass of water.

It was a fairly large bag, a drawstring bag, and she pulled out a length of aluminum foil and unrolled it and spread it on the bed. Brian stood watching from the kitchen entrance. Then she took out a small transparent packet. It looked like a pleated sandwich bag, only smaller, and it carried a stick-on label reading Death Trip #1.

"Come here," she said.

She opened the packet and let the contents, half the contents, spill onto the aluminum sheet. It was a resinous substance, chunked up, nubbed up. She told Brian to sit on the bed and pick up the sheet and hold it straight, hold it by the edges so the stuff, the tarlike chunks, didn't run off the ends.

"What the hell is it? And how can it run off if it's solid?"

Then she went into the handbag again and took a small rolled-up straw of some kind, a foil straw a few inches long.

"Yo, Marian, what are we doing here?"

Then she reached for her matches and lit one and held it under the aluminum sheet in Brian's hands, heating the substance on the sheet.

"It's heroin," she said, watching the tar slowly begin to liquefy.

"It's heroin," he said. "What am I supposed to say to that?"

When the tar started evaporating and smoking up, she shook out the match and put the foil straw in her mouth and trailed the curling smoke, sucking it up and holding it in her lungs, conscientiously.

"Okay. Where'd you get it?"

She watched the tar melt and run and evaporate and she followed the smoke off the stretched foil and sucked it through the straw.

"Mary Catherine."

"Who's that?"

"My assistant."

"Whose bed we're on? Your secretary's your dealer? When did you start doing this?"

"I never actually thought of her."

She trailed the smoke off the sheet and put her head right into it and sucked it through the straw.

"I never thought of her as my dealer but I guess she's my dealer and I'm her whatever."

"This is something new?"

"Fairly new yes. Here, take a chase."

"No, thanks."

She trailed the smoke into the air.

"I'm, you know, completely prudent. I use it rare, rare, rare. I don't get out of bed puffy-eyed, or pain, or nausea. Take a chase."

She sucked up the smoke.

"Nick knows this? He can't know this."

"Are you crazy? He'd kill me. Take a chase."

"Get the hell away from me."

"I want to get you in deeper. Take a chase. I want to get you in so deep you'll stop eating and sleeping. You'll lie in bed thinking about us. Doing our things in a borrowed room. You'll be able to think about nothing else. That's my program for you, Brian."

"Mary Catherine. I like the name," he said. "Sexy."

They sat on the bed, side by side, listening to traffic roll by on Thomas Road. When she was finished they cleared the things away and brushed off the bed and lay back talking.

"I think he knows," she said.

"Where is he?"

"On his way to Houston or there already. Then he drives out to that nuclear waste site wherever it is exactly."

"The salt dome."

"At the mercy of the Texas Highway Killer."

"He doesn't know," Brian said. "But we ought to think about ending it. We ought to make this the end."

"I'm not nearly ready. So just keep quiet. You're making me feel like some old dowd barely hanging on."

"You're not a dowd. You're a bawd."

"Be nice to me," she said.

The day had slipped down to a drowsy pulse located somewhere near her eyes. When she stretched she felt the jismic crust in her pubic hair speck out and crackle slightly.

He whispered, "Let's have a civilized final fuck and get out alive."

She listened to the traffic and wondered what she would say in the movie version.

He whispered, "Let's fuck the sayonara fuck and get into our suits and dresses."

She smiled faintly. The air had the feel of some auspicious design. She was feeling faintly L.A.ish and she rolled over on Brian and talked while they were doing it, on and off, sweetness, dearness, blowing the words, sensing an unseen design of completely auspicious things.

When they were side by side he raised up on an elbow and looked at her.

"You have that molten ball of defiance in your eye."

"Just don't talk about ending. It's not yours to end."

He laughed. When Brian laughed he became semitransparent. You could see blood racing under his skin, a freshet of rose pink. He got up and began to dress. He picked up a fashion magazine and held it open to a looming photo of some casually muscled bisexual, maybe a white guy, maybe not—dangled it over the bed as if to indicate how dated he was in his own body, his very life, Brian himself, a man without a fitness video to sling in the oblong groove.

"Underwear. Everything, suddenly, is underwear," he said. "Tell me what it means."

He checked the time and got a little panicky. She attempted to help, handing items of apparel across the bed, and he fumbled things intentionally, he wore a sock inside out and tied his shoes together so he could scuttle and lurch to the door. The later it got, the more he capered. It was Brian at his best.

"But what if he knows?"

"He doesn't know," she said.

She had a demon husband if demon means a force of some kind, an attendant spirit of discipline and self-command, the little flick of distance he'd perfected, like turning off a radio. She knew about his father's disappearance but there was something else, hard and apart. This is what had drawn her in the first place, the risky and erotic proposition.

Brian was looking at the photographs on the wall by the door.

"Which one is her?"

"Get out," she said.

She made the bed and bagged the dope and put the robe back in the closet. She washed the glass Brian had used, standing naked in the kitchenette, and it seemed completely reasonable and natural, all of it, earned, needed, naked, and she took a shower and got dressed.

She was feeling pretty good. She felt lazy-daisy, you know. You know the way something's been nagging and dragging and then it gets unexpectedly sort of settled.

She felt all the good things would find her, which they usually don't. She would know them when she saw them with her L.A.-type eyes.

She stood before the mirror adjusting her sunglasses. Because if she didn't have this thing to do, to plan and maneuver and look forward to, this far-too-infrequent Brian, and this is what she'd almost told him earlier, she would become lonely and shaky, driving along the decorated highway under the burning sky, and maybe a little indistinct.

She felt well liked. She liked who she was today. She felt a little lazy-souled. She thought anything L.A. seemed right today. She'd even say she was more or less euphoric, although she wasn't ready to commit to that completely.

Before she left she inspected the room one last time. These were the things that opened the world to secret arrangements, the borrowed flat and memorized phone number and coded notation on the calendar. Childish spy games really that made her feel guiltier than the sex did, a sheepish kind of self-reproach. She patted down a pillow to remove the indentation. She wanted things to have an untouched look so Mary Catherine would not mind when she asked to use the place again.

10

He spread the mayonnaise. He spread mayonnaise on the bread. Then he slapped the lunch meat down. He never spread the mayonnaise on the meat. He spread it on the bread. Then he slapped down the meat and watched the mayo seep around the edges.

He took the sandwich into the next room. His dad was watching TV, sitting in that periscope stoop of his, crookback, like he might tumble into the rug. His dad had infirmities still waiting for a name. Things you had to play one against another. If one thing required a certain medication, it made another thing worse. There were setbacks and side effects, there was a schedule of medications that Richard and his mother tried to keep track of through the daily twists of half doses and warning labels and depending on this and don't forget that.

Richard ate about half the sandwich and left the rest on the arm of the chair. In the kitchen he called his friend Bud Walling, who lived forty miles into nowhere and wasn't really his friend.

He drove out to Bud's place through old fields marked off for development, with skivvy strips on narrow posts running stiff in the wind. Out here the wind was a force that seized the mind. You left the high school a quarter of a mile behind still hearing the big flag snapping and the halyard beating nautically on the pole and you powered your car into the wind and saw dust sweep across the road and you drove into a white sky feeling useless and dumb.

Bud's place could have been something blown in from the hills. It had a look of being deposited in a natural spree, with lumber warping in the yard and sprung-open doors and an unfinished porch on cinder blocks, one of those so-low porches the house looks sunk in sand. Bud had a coydog that lived in chains in a ramshackle hut out back, part coyote, part alley mutt. Richard thought this dog was less dangerous than legend would have it. Richard thought Bud kept this dog basically for the juvenile thrill of having a chained beast that he could feed or starve according to his whim.

He realized he'd forgotten to give his dad two glasses of water to take with the blue and yellow capsule despite the bold-faced reminder on the prescription bottle. These little failures ate away at his confidence even when he knew it was his father's fault for not managing his own intake or his mother's for not being around when she was needed. There were constant little wars of whose fault is it and okay I'm sorry and I wish he'd die and get it over with, all taking place in Richard's inner mind.

He did the dumb-joke thing of knocking on Bud's door and saying, "Alcohol, Tobacco and Firearms."

Nothing happened. He went in and saw Bud in a large open room sawing a two-by-four that he'd set between benches of unmatching height. The house was still mainly framework although Bud had been working for many months in a conscientious struggle that Richard thought had less to do with gutting and reshaping a house than destroying some dread specter, maybe Bud's old drug habit, once and for all.

"Your phone's out of order," Richard said. "I thought I'd drive on out, see if everything, you know's, okay."

"Why wouldn't it be okay?"

"I reported it to the phone company."

"My only feeling about the phone."

"Sometimes they correct the problem from the office."

"It brings more grief than joy."

Bud finally looked up and noted his visual presence.

"It brings personal voices into your life that you're not prepared to deal with."

Richard kept to the edges of the room, running his palms over the planed sills, examining the staples that kept plastic sheeting fastened to the window frames. It was empty distraction of the type that forestalls the pain of ordinary talk.

"I'm putting in parquet," Bud said. "Herringbone maybe."

"Should be good."

"Better be good. But I probably won't ever do it."

The sound of the wind in the plastic sheeting was hard on the nerves. Richard wondered how an ex-addict could work all day in this scratching and popping. The sheeting popped out, it whipped and scratched. Crack cocaine fools the brain into thinking dope is good for it.

He thought of something he could say.

"Tell you, Bud. I'm forty-two years old next week. Week from Thursday."

"It happens."

"And I still feel like I'm half that, pretty much."

"That's because it's obvious why, you living as you do."

"What do you mean?"

"With your folks," Bud said.

"They can't manage alone."

"Who can? My question to you is."

Bud tossed half the length of sawed wood into a corner. He studied the other half as if someone had just handed it to him on a crowded street.

"What?" Richard said.

"Don't they smell?"

"What?"

"Old people. Like bad milk."

Richard heard the plastic windows pop.

"Not so I notice."

"Not so you notice. Okay. You want to feel your correct age. Get yourself a wife. That'll do it for you. It's horrible but true. A wife is the

264

only thing that can save guys like us. But they don't make you feel any younger."

Richard fidgeted happily in his corner. He liked the idea of being included in the female salvation of wayward men.

"Where is she?" he said.

"Working the late shift now."

Bud's wife worked on the line at Texas Instruments, mounting microchips on circuit boards, Bud said, for the information highway. Richard thought he was half in love with Bud's wife. It was a feeling that came and went, secret and sort of semipathetic, like his heart was made of some cotton product. If Aetna ever had a clue to what he felt, what would she think? The fear this question carried made him experience actual physical symptoms, a heat, a flush across his upper back, and a tightening at the throat.

He thought of something else to say.

"Left-handers, I read this the other day." And he paused here trying to recall the formal sentences in the narrow column of type. "Left-handers, which I am not one of, live typically shorter lives than right-handers. Right-handed men live ten years longer than left-handed men. You believe that?"

"We're talking this is mean life span."

"Left-handed men die typically at age, I think, sixty-five."

"Because they jerk off facing the North Pole," Bud said in a remark that Richard could not analyze for one shred of content.

He watched Bud pry nails out of the old floorboards and offered to help, looking around for a claw hammer.

"So, Richard."

"What?"

"You drove fifty miles to tell me my phone's not working."

Richard didn't know if this was a setup for a scathing type of Bud Walling remark or maybe just an ordinary thank-you.

"Forty miles, Bud."

"Well that's a relief. I'd offer you a beer, but."

"No problem."

"Maybe it's Aetna who drives fifty miles. I forget exactly."

It was not outside Bud's effective range to say something personal about his wife, maybe her sex preferences or digestive problems, and whenever he mentioned her name old Richard caught his breath, hoping and fearing something intimate was coming, and even though he knew Bud did this to shock and repel him, Richard absorbed every word and image and smell description, watching Bud's long creased face for signs of mockery.

"She'll be sorry she missed you," Bud said, looking up from the wood rot and hanging dust.

He was not left-handed but taught himself to shoot with the left hand. This is what Bud would never understand, how he had to take his feelings outside himself so's to escape his isolation. He taught himself based on the theory that if you are driving with your right hand and sitting snug to the door it is better practically speaking to keep the right hand on the wheel and project the left hand out the window, the gun hand, so you do not have to fire across your body. He could probably talk to Bud about this and Bud might understand. But he would never understand how Richard had to take everything outside, share it with others, become part of the history of others, because this was the only way to escape, to get out from under the pissant details of who he was.

Bud was saying, "So cop says, Feet together, head back, eyes shut please. Which Aetna starts to laugh when he says please. Now spread your arms wide, he says. Now bring your left hand around and touch your nose with your index finger. Which I'm standing there in sheets of rain and he's advising from the car. Touch your nose with your index finger, he tells me."

"You're a left-hander driving a car you're five times likely to die in a crash."

"Than a right-hander."

"Than a right-hander," Richard said, religiously convinced.

Bud ripped a board out of the floor.

"Not my problem."

"Mine neither."

"I die from stress," Bud said. "I'll tell you where my stress level's at."

Richard waited for the rest. He used to sit in a glass booth at the supermarket batching personal checks and redeemed coupons and giving out rolled nickels to the checkout personnel but he seemingly messed up somehow and was out at the counters again, running items over the scanner, keying fruit and vegetables into the register, subject to the casual abuse of passing strangers in the world.

"We have to do our business outside because the toilet's not ready for human habitation. So I built a thing outside where this is the only workable method pending I figure out the toilet. And Aetna, well you can imagine."

"Coming home from work."

"The stress builds up real personal."

"Driving that drive," Richard said.

"And she has to go. And then she remembers. There's no working toilet in the house. And she looks at me outright murderous."

They said unbelievable things, obese women in the express line, with him having two sick parents at home, or one sick and one bad-tempered, like that's sixteen cents off on the tomato paste or that's not a red pear that's a an-jew. They forced him to ask across the aisle. Can't you see it's not red? He charged me for red, this here's a an-jew. He had to speak across the aisle to the other checkout, where any person on either line could hear what he said.

"For myself I don't mind," Bud said. "Because it makes a certain amount of sense to take your business outside. When you think about what's involved."

They talk about head trauma. They talk about is he adopted or was he abused? The problem is all in the spacing. If you fire out the window on the driver's side, which you have to do if you don't want to shoot across the width of your own car and the space between your car and the other car, you still face the problem of having to fire across the space between cars and the width of the other car because the other driver's side is the far side in relation to your position at the wheel. You are not going to shoot a passenger. If you shoot a passenger, then the driver is liable to take evasive action and note your license number and make of car and color of hair and so on. So you are going to shoot lone drivers and you are going to fire out the window on your side using the left hand to hold the weapon. But the fact is, as he eventually figured out, that if you shoot with the right hand, the natural hand, your projectile travels the same distance across the same spaces, pretty much, as the self-taught method of the left hand. He figured this out after victim five or six, he forgets which, but decided to stick with the left hand as the shooting hand even though it made more sense to steer with the left hand and shoot with the right. Because the right hand was the born hand.

"I just noticed what it was I couldn't figure out," Bud said.

They heard the dog barking and Richard looked through the dusty sheeting and saw the animal thrust up on hind legs at the end of its chain, dog balls taut, and he hoped it might be Aetna come home early. Aetna made a pie for them once that had a latticed crust. This was something he remembered. Seeing it wasn't her coming home but likely some critter in the woods that roused the dog, he felt a sadness out of all proportion. But then everything was out of all proportion. The wind beat at the sheeting, making it shiver and pop. Crack cocaine is supposedly the cravingest form of substance abuse, according to studies made over time.

"You're wearing a tie," Bud said.

Richard paused, wary about how to take this, peering inwardly ahead for a setup, a possible remark.

"Well that's from work," he said. "I went home from work and didn't change."

"But you wear ties? To check out groceries?"

"It's a company regulation, statewide, pretty much."

Be calm, he thought.

"And there's the thing Aetna said, which she's right for a change. That you look like a guy that wears glasses. Except you don't. Except when she said it, we weren't sure. We said, Does he or doesn't he?"

"Never did," Richard said.

When he first walked in the house and Bud barely noticed him, it was like the normalcy of dying. It was the empty hollow thing of not being here. A forty-mile drive into being transparent, awful but not unaccustomed. But now this scrutiny as to what he wears and what he looks like. A panic set in. He tried to think of what to say. There might be something he could say about the dog. He searched for a glimpse of the dog through the sheeting. How nothing gets dirtier than plastic sheeting, retaining, absorbing the dirt.

"Well maybe you should. Glasses give appearance to a person. Get yourself some thick dark frames that match your tie."

He didn't know why Bud would want to talk to him this way. Bud sat cross-legged over the narrow rent in the floor. He held the hammer at rest on his shoulder and looked directly into Richard's face. Richard tried to smile, make the whole thing humorous. He felt the stupidity of the look on his face, as if a turn of the mouth can alter the outside world.

"I can think about it."

"You do that."

"I should probably be getting back."

"She'll be sorry she missed you."

"Tell her I said."

"I'll be sure and do that."

The only person he ever talked to from the heart was Sue Ann. She made him feel real, talking on the phone. She gave him the feeling he was taking shape as himself, coming into the shape he'd always been intended to take, the thing of who he really was. It was like filling out—did you ever feel things pouring out from the center of who you are and taking the shape of the intended person? Well that's what Sue Ann did and you can disbelieve it or disrespect it but he was never really who he was until he talked to her.

He heard Bud ripping up wood as he walked out the door to his car.

With mental killers roaming the earth, the checkout boys wear neckties.

That's what he thought Bud might say.

He made the call to Sue Ann from a house he broke and entered. Switched on the TV and called the superstation in Atlanta and touched things with a hanky and placed the voice device on the phone that he'd ordered from the back pages of a mercenary magazine. This was not a publication Richard normally perused. He was not a surveillance man or gun lover. His gun was his father's old .38. It did not have massive knockdown power and it did not shoot through concrete blocks or make fist-size holes in silhouette targets. It just killed people.

He drove out of the wooded area and into the open sky, where the road dropped down to the floodplain and he felt the true force of the wind.

He made the call and turned on the TV, or vice versa, without the sound, his hand wound in a doubled hanky, and he never felt so easy talking to someone on the phone or face-to-face or man to woman as he felt that day talking to Sue Ann. He watched her over there and talked to her over here. He saw her lips move silent in one part of the room while her words fell soft and warm on the coils of his secret ear. He talked to her on the phone and made eye contact with the TV. This was the waking of the knowledge that he was real. This alien-eyed woman with raving hair sending emanations that astonished his heart. He spoke more confidently as time went on. He was coming into himself, shy but also unashamed, a little vain, even, and honest and clever, evasive when he needed to be, standing there in a stranger's house near a lamp without a shade and she listened and asked questions, watching him from the screen ten feet away. She had so much radiance she could make him real.

This was an untraveled road. Travel thirty miles on this road and you may not see another car. You see power lines extended to the limits of vision, sinking toward the earth as a matter of perspective. When the wind dies there's a suspense that falls across the land and makes you think about the hush before the Judgment.

Then they cut away to the tape. He was suspicious of the tape because it had a vista different from his experience and he kept thinking the girl was going to move the camera and get him in the picture. He'd watched the tape a dozen times sitting with his pain-racked dad and every time he watched the tape he thought he was going to turn up in his own living room, detached from who he was, peering squint-eyed over the wheel of his compact car.

He called Sue Ann twice after that but the switchboard would not put him through because many others were trying to reach her now and the switchboard was leery and abrupt and unbelieving. He needed her to keep him whole. He probably would have told her his name. She would have broken him down completely over a number of calls over a number of days, watching him from the screen. He would have surrendered to her in a blaze of lights, Richard Henry Gilkey, hustled down a hallway with Stetsoned men all around him and Sue Ann Corcoran by his side.

He drove past the flagpole with the banging halyard. The wind was banging the halyard against the pole and it made him weak somehow, the repeated meaning of this noise.

He went in the house and saw his dad twisted whole in front of the TV set. Mother was in the kitchen running a beater inside a white bowl.

"Look what got dragged in by the scruff."

"I went out to Bud's."

"Do we have time for you to go out to Bud's?"

"We need to give daddy his Nitrospan."

"Well go ahead and do it."

"Well aren't we supposed to call about the new dosage?"

"I didn't call. Did you call?" she said.

The glass booth had a talk hole where you talked. But they sent him out to the checkout and forced him to talk across the aisle.

"I'll call," she said, "but he's not there."

"You'll get the answering service."

"I'll get the answering service and they'll tell me he's not there."

"I meant to call," he said.

"I'll call," she said, "and you do the ointment."

After dinner he did the ointment on his father's chest. His father lay back on the bed with the stubbled look of an old man turning into a castaway, a reject of the islands, except for his eyes—they were moist and deep, pleading for time. Richard spread the ointment and buttoned his father's pajama tops and he thought about the time, any day now, when he would have to wipe his behind.

Pending notification of next of kin.

He came alive in them. He lived in their histories, in the photographs in the newspaper, he survived in the memories of the family, lived with the victims, lived on, merged, twinned, quadrupled, continued into double figures.

He stood at the kitchen door watching her stir some solution for his father's first intake of the next day.

"Well you have a good night now."

"You sleep well," she said.

He went to his room and sat in a chair to take off his shoes. All the

271

meaning of a given life was located in the act of leaning over to untie your shoes and set them in a designated place for the start of the following day.

He thought about the other person.

When he was stationed in the booth he had the talk hole to talk through. But when they put him back at the checkout he had to talk in the open space where anyone could hear.

He kept the gun hidden in the car and he thought about this as he drifted near sleep and he thought about the other person who'd shot a driver on one of the highways where he had shot a driver, just one day later. The so-called copycat shooting. He did not like to think about this but found it was lately, more and more, a taunting presence in his mind.

He was an early riser. He heard the rain on the roof and he dressed and ate a muffin standing up, a hand cupped under his chin to catch the crumbs. He had three and a half hours before it was time to report to work. He heard the rain dripping off the eaves and hitting the pie tin where he left food for a stray cat when he remembered.

I know who I am. Who is he?

He zipped up his jacket. Then he put the glove on his left hand, a woman's white glove, and he went out to the empty street, where his car sat waiting under the sheet-metal sky.

PART 3

THE CLOUD
OF UNKNOWING

Spring 1978

1

I've always been a country of one. There's a certain distance in my makeup, a measured separation like my old man's, I guess, that I've worked at times to reduce, or thought of working, or said the hell with it.

I like to tell my wife. I say to my wife. I tell her not to give up on me. I tell her there's an Italian word, or a Latin word, that explains everything. Then I tell her the word.

She says, What does this explain? And she answers, Nothing.

The word that explains nothing in this case is *lontananza*. Distance or remoteness, sure. But as I use the word, as I interpret it, hard-edged and fine-grained, it's the perfected distance of the gangster, the syndicate mobster—the made man. Once you're a made man, you don't need the constant living influence of sources outside yourself. You're all there. You're made. You're handmade. You're a sturdy Roman wall.

I was in Los Angeles thinking about these things. People say L.A. is only half there and maybe that's why I was thinking about my father. And also because my brother Matt—it was Matt's endless premise, his song of songs, that our old man Jimmy was living somewhere in southern California under the usual assumed name.

I told him Jimmy was dead under his own name. We were the ones with assumed names.

But the curious thing, the contradiction, is that I was standing in the middle of a fenced enclosure in a bungalow slum looking up at the spires of the great strange architectural cluster known as the Watts Towers, an idiosyncrasy out of someone's innocent anarchist visions, and the more I looked, the more I thought of Jimmy. The towers and birdbaths and fountains and decorated posts and bright oddments and household colors, the green of 7-Up bottles and blue of Milk of Magnesia, all the vivid tile embedded in cement, the whole complex of structures and gates and panels that were built, hand-built, by one man, alone, an immigrant from somewhere near Naples, probably illiterate, who left his wife and family, or maybe they left him, I wasn't sure, a man whose narrative is mostly blank spaces, date of birth uncertain, until he ends up spending thirty-three years building this thing out of steel rods and broken crockery and pebbles and seashells and soda bottles and wire mesh, all hand-mortared, three thousand sacks of sand and cement, and who spends these years with glass specks crusting his hands and arms and glass dust in his eyes as he hangs from a window-washer's belt high on the towers, in torn overalls and a dusty fedora, face burnt brown, with lights strung on the radial spokes so he could work at night, maybe ninety feet up, and Caruso on the gramophone below.

Jimmy was an edge-seeker, a palmist, inferring the future out of his own lined flesh, but he looked at his hand one day, according to my little brother, and it was blank. And did he become, could I imagine him as a runaway eccentric? In a way, yes, a man who doesn't wash or change his clothes, bummy looking, talks to himself on the street, and in another way, maybe, I could imagine him rising this high, soaring out of himself to produce a rambling art that has no category, with cement and chicken wire.

This was the contradiction. Jimmy's future closed down the night he went out for cigarettes. Why would I even try to imagine him in an alternative reality, coming out here, half here, escaping to the Angeleno light, the Mediterranean weather?

I walked among the openwork towers, three tall, four smaller ones, and saw the delftware he'd plastered under a canopy and the molten glass and mother-of-pearl he'd pressed into adobe surfaces. Whatever the cast-off nature of the materials, the seeming offhandedness, and whatever the dominance of pure intuition, the man was surely a master builder. There was a structural unity to the place, a sense of repeated themes and deft engineering. And his initials here and there, SR, Sabato Rodia, if this was in fact his correct name—SR carved in archways like the gang graffiti in the streets outside.

I tried to understand the force of Jimmy's presence here. I saw him shabby and muttering but also unconstrained, with nothing and no one to answer to, in a shoe-box room somewhere, slicing a pear with a penknife. Jimmy alive. And then I thought of a thing that happened when I was about eight years old and it was a memory that clarified the connections. I saw my father standing across the street watching two young men, greenhorns, trying to lay brick for a couple of gateposts in front of someone's modest house. First he watched, then he advised, gesturing, speaking a studied broken English that the young men might grasp, and then he moved decisively in, handing his jacket to someone and redirecting the length of string and taking the trowel and setting the bricks in courses and leveling the grout, working quickly, and I didn't know he could do this kind of work and I don't think my mother knew it either. I went across the street and felt a shy kind of pride, surrounded by middle-aged men and older, the fresh-air inspectors, they were called, and you've never seen happier people, watching a man in a white shirt and tie do a skillful brickwork bond.

When he finished the towers Sabato Rodia gave away the land and all the art that was on it. He left Watts and went away, he said, to die. The work he did is a kind of swirling free-souled noise, a jazz cathedral, and the power of the thing, for me, the deep disturbance, was that my own ghost father was living in the walls.

The waitress brought a chilled fork for my lifestyle salad. Big Sims was eating a cheeseburger with three kinds of cheddar, each described in detail on the menu. There was a crack in the wall from the tremor of the day before and when Sims laughed I saw his mouth cat's-cradled with filaments of gleaming cheese.

We heard the test flights shrieking out of Edwards. Sims said they had aircraft that bounced off the edge of space and came back born-again.

We were at Mojave Springs, a conference center some distance from Los Angeles. I'd recently gone to work for Waste Containment, known in the industry as Whiz Co, and I was here in the spirit of freshmen orientation, to adjust to the language and customs, and my unofficial advisor was Simeon Biggs, a landfill engineer who'd been with the firm for four or five years. There were a number of waste-handling firms represented at the Springs and we were sharing seminar space with a smaller and more committed group, forty married couples who were here to trade sexual partners and talk about their feelings. We were the waste managers, they were the swingers, and they made us feel self-conscious.

Sims said, "The ship's been out there, sailing port to port, it's almost two years now."

"And what? They won't accept the cargo?"

"Country after country."

"How toxic is the cargo?"

"I hear rumors," he said. "This isn't my area of course. Happens in some back room in our New York office. It's a folk tale about a spectral ship. The Flying Liberian."

"I thought terrible substances were dumped routinely in LDCs."

An LDC, I'd just found out, was a less developed country in the language of banks and other global entities.

"Those little dark-skinned countries. Yes, it's a nasty business that's getting bigger all the time. A country will take a fee amounting to four times its gross national product to accept a shipment of toxic waste. What happens after that? We don't want to know."

"All right. But what makes this cargo unacceptable? And why don't we know what the shipment actually consists of?"

"Maybe we're trying to spare ourselves a certain amount of embarrassment," Sims said.

The tremor had hit at cocktail time when I was standing in the hospitality suite with a number of colleagues, who peered over their drinks in the slow lean of the world. The room whistled and groaned. I worked at controlling the look on my face, waiting for the situation to define

278

itself. It was not a mild shock. It was in the middle fives, we later learned, a five point four, and I felt justified in my sense of potential alarm, seeing the crack in the restaurant wall when we sat down to lunch.

"You think what, it's a drug shipment? Disguised as toxic waste? Because I hear rumors too."

"Tell me about it," Sims said.

He sat across the table, meat face and wide body, the jut underlip, the odd little unlobed ears, round and perfectly worked, the tiny mannered ears of a sprite child.

"I'm eager to hear your version," he said, a trace of sweet condescension in his voice.

"One, it's a heroin shipment, which makes no sense. Two, it's incinerator ash from the New York area. Industrial grade mainly. Twenty million pounds. Arsenic, copper, lead, mercury."

"Dioxins," Sims said agreeably, biting into the middle of his mesquite-grilled beef.

Four couples took the round table nearby and Sims and I observed a pause. We wanted to be amused and slightly derisive. These were swingers, of course, dressed assertively, in the third person, and they leaned back in sequence when the boy poured water.

"They take time out for lunch. I respect that," Sims said.

"I hear things about the ship."

"The ship keeps changing names. You hear that?"

"No, I don't."

"The ship left a pier on the Hudson River with one name, I don't know what it was but it got changed three months later off the West African coast. Then they changed it again. This was somewhere in the Philippines."

"Enormous quantities of heroin, I hear. But why would heroin get shipped from the U.S. to the Far East? Makes no sense."

"Makes no sense," Sims said. "Except it ties in with another rumor. You know this rumor?"

"I don't think so."

"Mob-owned."

He liked saying this, he rounded out the words, popped his eyes a little.

"What's mob-owned?"

"The company that owns the ships we lease. The mob has a lot of involvement in waste carting. So why not waste handling, waste shipment, waste everything?"

"There's a word in Italian," I said.

"Maybe it's not just the shipping company. Maybe it's our company. We're mob-owned. They're a silent partner. Or they own us outright."

He liked saying this even more. Not that he believed it. He didn't believe it for half a second but he wanted me to believe it, or entertain the thought, so he could ridicule me. He had a hard grin that mocked whatever facile sentiments you might be tempted to shelter in the name of your personal conspiracy credo.

"There's a word in Italian. *Dietrologia*. It means the science of what is behind something. A suspicious event. The science of what is behind an event."

"They need this science. I don't need it."

"I don't need it either. I'm just telling you."

"I'm an American. I go to ball games," he said.

"The science of dark forces. Evidently they feel this science is legitimate enough to require a name."

"People who need this science, I would make an effort to tell them we have real sciences, hard sciences, we don't need imaginary ones."

"I'm just telling you the word. I agree with you, Sims. But the word exists."

"There's always a word. There's probably a museum too. The Museum of Dark Forces. They have ten thousand blurry photographs. Or did the Mafia blow it up?"

This is where Sims laughed, showing a mouth crisscrossed with cheddar.

I checked the round table. Two of the women smoked. Two of the women wore studded western vests. One was nearsighted, sticking her head in the menu, and one had an accent I couldn't place. All the women were ornamented, decked in chains, bracelets and breastpins, in hoop earrings with bead pendants, jewelry with a hammered look, a pounded look, and one chewed a carrot stick and talked about her kids.

"You know Italian?" he said.

"I studied Latin for a while. In school, then on my own, pretty intensively. And dabbled in German and Italian."

"My wife is German," he said. "Met her when I was stationed there."

"A GI with a swagger."

"That pretty much says it. Except I was Air Force."

"She speaks German around the house?"

"A little bit. Yeah. Quite a lot."

"You understand?"

"I better understand," he said.

The men wore broad-collared print shirts unbuttoned to the thorax. The men were all hair. Not the protest hair of the sixties of course. Chest hair, mustaches, brushy sideburns, great heads of Hollywood hair—real hair that resembled toupees in bad taste, wish-fulfilling rugtops, sort of spit-curled and heavily surfed.

Big Sims called for the check.

"But we like our jobs, don't we, Nick? Whoever owns the ships we use."

"I like my job."

"I like my job."

His sport coat was draped over the back of his chair, too broad to fit snugly over the palmettes that adorned the top rail. He wore a white short-sleeved shirt with a dark tie and a tie clip shaped like a scimitar.

He gave me a tight-eyed look.

"Want to go to a Dodger game?"

"No," I said.

It did not seem surprising, all these ghost-ship stories, even if they were only elusive hearsay, because we'd been told the night before that waste is the best-kept secret in the world. This is what Jesse Detwiler said, the garbage archaeologist who'd addressed the massed members about an hour after the tremor—an address that did not go down well with the grilled squab and baby Zen vegetables.

Our faces showed a pristine alertness, back there at cocktail time, when the room shook around us. It was a look that trailed a self-awareness in its wake, a sheepish sense of our own glimpsed fear, of being caught unaware, just before we gained control, and this is the face that traveled through the suite, above the vodka tonics, creating an ironic bond among the managers, in the indoor wind.

We saw Detwiler in the lobby after we paid the bill. Sims went over and collared him, literally, got him in a headlock and mock-pummeled his shaved dome. They were acquaintances, it seemed, and the three of us made a date to drive out to a landfill that Sims had designed, a massive project still in development.

A man and woman walked across the lobby and I watched her carefully. Maybe it was the hip-sprung way she moved, high-assed and shiny, alert to surfaces, like a character in a B movie soaked in alimony and gin. I went over and checked the schedule of events on the easeled board near the revolving doors, registration and coffee, licensing laws, spent fuel storage, all the topics and speakers in movable white type, ten to twelve and two to five and on into the night, and I thought about the swingers and their arrangements.

Whiz Co was a firm with an inside track to the future. The Future of Waste. This was the name we gave our conference in the desert. The meeting was industry-wide but we were the firm that provided the motive force, we were the front-runners, the go-getters, the guys who were ready to understand the true dimensions of the subject.

I was in my early forties, hired away from a thin-blooded job as a corporate speechwriter and public relations aide, and I was ready for something new, for a faith to embrace.

Corporations are great and appalling things. They take you and shape you in nearly nothing flat, twist and swivel you. And they do it without overt persuasion, they do it with smiles and nods, a collective inflection of the voice. You stand at the head of a corridor and by the time you walk to the far end you have adopted the comprehensive philosophy of the firm, the *Weltanschauung*. I use this grave and layered word because somewhere in its depths there is a whisper of mystical contemplation that seems totally appropriate to the subject of waste.

I went running with Big Sims and we ran along trails that hikers used, backpackers with rugged boots, and we ran on bridle paths that went into the hills. We wore sunglasses and peaked caps and ran on stony rubble and red sand and Sims didn't stop talking, he talked and ran across the desert scrub and I labored to keep up.

"You know, it's funny, I took this job four years ago and it's a good job and pays well and has the benefits and provides for my widow when I die from overwork but I find—you find this, Nick? From the first day I find that everything I see is garbage. I studied engineering. I didn't study garbage. I thought I might go to Tunisia and build roads. I had a romantic idea, you know, wear a safari jacket and pave the world. Turns out I'm doing fine. I'm doing real work, important work. Landfills are important. Trouble is, the job follows me. The subject follows me. I went to a new restaurant last week, nice new place, you know, and I find myself looking at scraps of food on people's plates. Leftovers. I see butts in ashtrays. And when we get outside."

"You see it everywhere because it is everywhere."

"But I didn't see it before."

"You're enlightened now. Be grateful," I said.

Our sneakers were flimsy things against the slabstone and tuff. We ran on trails littered with straw shit from the rented horses and we ran gasping and panting, panting as we talked, and the sweat came down Sims' face in intersecting streams. I kept up with him. It was necessary to keep up, keep running, show you can talk while you run, show you can run, you can keep up. The sweat came down our bodies and plastered our shirts to our backs.

"We get outside and we're waiting. The guy's bringing our car around. I peer into the alley meanwhile. And I see something curious. An enclosure, a barred enclosure set along the wall. A cage basically. Three sides and a top. Wrought iron bars and a big padlock." He's talking and pausing, the words are pumping out of his chest. "And I have to step a little ways into the alley. Before I can see exactly what this is. And I smell it before I see it. The cage is filled with bags of garbage. Food waste in plastic bags. A day and a night of restaurant garbage."

He was looking at me as we ran.

"Why do they cage it?" I said.

He looked at me.

"Derelicts come out of the park and eat it."

We turned back toward the compound of rose stucco buildings burning in the light. It was not easy keeping pace with Sims. He had the plodding force of a fleshy ex-boxer who still has reserves of deep endurance, oil reserves, fossil fuel—he had calories to burn, sweat to yield in abundance.

"Why won't the restaurant let them eat the garbage?"

"Because it's property," he said.

Five fighter jets went over in tight formation, flying low, a haunted roar spilling through the valley, and Sims jerked his thumb at the sky as if to signal something that had slipped my mind.

I kept seeing my own face of the evening before, when the fiver shook the room, all the work it took to reconcile the forces that pressed against each other.

We pounded down past the golf course and guest cottages, a cropped world of people in soft pastels, alive by the handful, by the orderly foursome, and I felt relieved the run was nearly over.

"Ask me about the ship," he said.

"Is the ship Liberian register?"

"It was when it started out. I hear it's registered in Panama now."

"Is that possible? Change registry in midcourse?"

"I don't know. It's not my area," Sims said. "But the rumors about the ship don't only concern what the ship is carrying in its hold. Or who owns the ship. Or where the ship is headed."

"Okay, what else is there?"

"Is this an ordinary cargo ship? Or is there some degree of confusion about this?"

"What kind of ship would it be if it carries cargo but isn't a cargo ship?"

"Remind me to give you a lesson in sludge sometime."

He laughed and ran, capering a little, bop-running, elbows out and fingers snapping, and he surged ahead of me. I felt a flare of competition, a duress of the spirit that warns against the shame of losing, and I hurried to catch up.

And interesting that later this business of picking through garbage, old winos and runaway kids slipping into an alley to get at broken bread chunks and slivers of veiny beef—later, with Detwiler, the subject would reoccur, but differently, with a touch of the renegade theater of the sixties.

The three of us went out to the landfill in the early evening, half an hour's drive to the east, some of this on roads restricted to military use. Sims had a permit that allowed entry at select times, an arrangement worked out between Whiz Co and some agency buried in the Pentagon, and this saved us the trouble of taking the long way around.

The construction crew had gone for the day. We stood above a hole in the earth, an engineered crater five hundred feet deep, maybe a mile across, strewn with snub-nosed machines along the terraced stretches and covered across much of the sloped bottom by an immense shimmering sheet, a polyethylene skin, silvery blue, that caught cloudmotion and rolled in the wind. I was taken by surprise. The sight of this thing, the enormous gouged bowl lined with artful plastic, was the first material sign I'd had that this was a business of a certain drastic grandeur, even a kind of greatness, maybe—the red-tailed hawks transparent in the setting sun and the spring stalks of yucca tall as wishing wands and this high-density membrane that was oddly and equally beautiful in a way, a prophylactic device, a gas-control system, and the crater it layered that would accept thousands of tons of garbage a day, your trash and mine, for desert burial. I listened to Sims recite the numbers, how much methane we would recover to light how many homes, and I felt a weird elation, a loyalty to the company and the cause.

Sims spoke to both of us but mainly to Jesse Detwiler because this was the visionary in our midst, the waste theorist whose provocations had spooked the industry. And Sims was eloquent, he loved his subject and gestured sweepingly, hand-shaping the layers of plastic and earth, the shredding of tires, the mixing of chemicals with kiln dust. I hadn't seen these things yet, myself, but it was easy to perceive what they meant to Sims, a labor of earth, utterly satisfying in its mingled tempers of technology and old hard useful work, dust in the mouth and a wall of drenching smells.

Detwiler stood at the rim of the crater, looking in.

"What about the hot stuff?"

"We'll drum it and segregate it. But we won't forget it. It'll be logged on three-D computer records. We can find it if we have to."

"What's your approach to bomb waste?"

"Bomb waste. That's why we hired Nick."

I saw the gleam in Simeon's eye and I said deadpan, "I have a background in public relations."

Detwiler tilted his chin, marking the small measure of amusement he might attach to this remark. He had the canny self-assurance of an industry maverick, the outsider who tries to roil the works, japing every complacent rule of belief. And he looked remade, retooled, shaved head and bushy mustache, a guy in firm control, with a workout coach and a nice line of credit, in a black turtleneck jersey and designer jeans. It occurred to me that except for the plucked hair he could have been a swinger.

"I'll tell you what I see here, Sims. The scenery of the future. Eventually the only scenery left. The more toxic the waste, the greater the effort and expense a tourist will be willing to tolerate in order to visit the site. Only I don't think you ought to be isolating these sites. Isolate the most toxic waste, okay. This makes it grander, more ominous and magical. But basic household waste ought to be placed in the cities that produce it. Bring garbage into the open. Let people see it and respect it. Don't hide your waste facilities. Make an architecture of waste. Design gorgeous buildings to recycle waste and invite people to collect their own garbage and bring it with them to the press rams and conveyors. Get to know your garbage. And the hot stuff, the chemical waste, the nuclear waste, this becomes a remote landscape of nostalgia. Bus tours and postcards, I guarantee it."

Sims wasn't sure he liked this.

"What kind of nostalgia?"

"Don't underestimate our capacity for complex longings. Nostalgia for the banned materials of civilization, for the brute force of old industries and old conflicts."

Detwiler had been a fringe figure in the sixties, a garbage guerrilla who stole and analyzed the household trash of a number of famous people. He issued mock-comintern manifestos about the contents, with personal asides, and the underground press was quick to print this stuff. His activities had a crisp climax when he was arrested for snatching the garbage of J. Edgar Hoover from the rear of the Direc-

286

tor's house in northwest Washington and this is what people remembered, what I remembered when I first reheard the name Jesse Detwiler. He'd earned a brief feverish fame in the chronicles of the time, part of the strolling band of tambourine girls and bomb makers, levitators and acid droppers and lost children.

A bird flew across the width of the crater, a finch or wren, moving with the nervous fleetness, the urgency of sundown.

Detwiler said that cities rose on garbage, inch by inch, gaining elevation through the decades as buried debris increased. Garbage always got layered over or pushed to the edges, in a room or in a landscape. But it had its own momentum. It pushed back. It pushed into every space available, dictating construction patterns and altering systems of ritual. And it produced rats and paranoia. People were compelled to develop an organized response. This meant they had to come up with a resourceful means of disposal and build a social structure to carry it out—workers, managers, haulers, scavengers. Civilization is built, history is driven—

He talked in his talk-show way, focused, practiced, generically intimate. He was a waste hustler, looking for book deals and documentary films, and I don't think he cared whether we were two people listening or half a million.

"See, we have everything backwards," he said.

Civilization did not rise and flourish as men hammered out hunting scenes on bronze gates and whispered philosophy under the stars, with garbage as a noisome offshoot, swept away and forgotten. No, garbage rose first, inciting people to build a civilization in response, in self-defense. We had to find ways to discard our waste, to use what we couldn't discard, to reprocess what we couldn't use. Garbage pushed back. It mounted and spread. And it forced us to develop the logic and rigor that would lead to systematic investigations of reality, to science, art, music, mathematics.

The sun went down.

"Do you really believe that?" I said.

"Bet your ass I believe it. I teach it at UCLA. I take my students into garbage dumps and make them understand the civilization they live in. Consume or die. That's the mandate of the culture. And it all ends up in the dump. We make stupendous amounts of garbage, then we react to it, not only technologically but in our hearts and minds. We let it shape us. We let it control our thinking. Garbage comes first, then we build a system to deal with it."

The rim clouds took on a chromium edge and the high sky was still an easy noonish blue. But the pit went dark in a hurry, the vast plastic liner wind-lapped and making the eeriest sort of music, just outside the wave-fold of nature, and the surface was indigo now, still faintly sky-streaked, washed by gradations of shade and motion. We stood a moment watching and then went back to the car. Detwiler sat in the middle of the rear seat, needling us about dumping our garbage on sacred Indian land. And about Whiz Co's vanguard status. He thought the firm had the hard-core appetites of any traditional company.

We drove an empty road.

"You tracking the rumors, Sims? This ship you've got."

"It's not my area."

"Cruising the oceans of the world trying to dump some hellish substance."

"I'm looking the other way," Sims said.

"Look this way. I hear it's headed back to the U.S."

"You know more than we do." Sims hated saying this. "What do we know, Nick?"

"We're not sixties people. We're forties and fifties people."

"We're limited," Sims said.

"We don't know much of anything."

"We listened to the radio," Sims said. "We know the Lone Ranger and Tonto."

"From out of the past," I said.

"The thundering hoofbeats of the great horse Silver."

"A fiery horse with the speed of light."

"This is what we know, Jesse."

"A cloud of dust."

"And a hearty hi-yo Silver."

Deep-pitching our voices to the baritone drama of the old radio show.

"Guys think you're funny," Detwiler said. "Bet you don't know the name of Tonto's horse. Come on, Sims. You know the white man's horse. Why don't you know the Indian's horse?"

I didn't think I liked Detwiler but I liked to listen to him. Sims did not. Sims wanted to get him in another headlock, not so fraternal this time. No, he didn't know the Indian's horse and maybe it bothered him a little.

Jesse kept talking.

"The more dangerous the waste, the more heroic it will become. Irradiated ground. The way the Indians venerate this terrain now, we'll come to see it as sacred in the next century. Plutonium National Park. The last haunt of the white gods. Tourists wearing respirator masks and protective suits."

I said, "What was the name of the Indian's horse?"

"Scout, okay? And I'm amazed and shocked. This is a deep cultural failure, you guys. Tonto's horse. You have to know this."

He leaned toward us, needling.

"A ship carrying thousands of barrels of industrial waste. Or is it CIA heroin? I can believe this myself. You know why? Because it's easy to believe. We'd be stupid not to believe it. Knowing what we know."

"What do we know?" Sims said.

Choppers in formation, ten or twelve, coming at us right over the road, large assault transports lighted like manic angels, and they passed above us with a rackety blast that sucked the air out of the car and left us limp and ducking.

"That everything's connected," Jesse said.

Not that I completely disliked my previous job. I wrote speeches mainly for corporate chairmen, ruddy white-haired guys with big ravaged noses, patriarchs of this or that industry. They tended to be sportsmen who flew in company planes to remote lakes in Canada, where they fished the last unspoiled waters of the continent. I went along on one such trip with a chairman named McHenry, a sweet and decent man in fact who owned a number of software companies that had contracts with the government. And his grandsons were at the lake, a pair of white-browed boys in down vests, primed for blood sport. And I stood and looked at the old lakeside house with its cedar shakes and tall chimneys and all the shabby and splintery porch furniture of a backwoods retreat. I looked at the house and missed it on some curious level. It might have been some object of my own past, some augury in reverse, stately rustic and high-ceilinged and mothballed in the unused rooms, with thick scratchy blankets on the guest beds, bearing college emblems—the promise of things I'd never had but somehow seemed to know, collectively, at the edge of memory. And the way the boys handled their shotguns, born to it, you see—they were kids and I was a man but I think I took a measure of instruction from them, Johno and Todd, not that I joined them in their game stalking. Mostly I sat on the porch and worked on speeches for McHenry but I gleaned from the boys what it must be like to grow into this kind of world, how commensurate to one's expectation of what is due—the world that money makes and erect bearing and clear speech and college emblems on the beds and a sense of birthright and usable history. At dinner we talked about things, about their schools and sports, and I took pleasure in all this effortless youth, rude youth in the best sense, robust and vigorous and unfinished. I took secondary pleasure, felt myself walking in their angled strides, felt what it was like to cast a line in the sun with nothing obtaining in the world but the rub of the boat's burred wood and the early heat on my arms, and even when I felt something drawn up out of me, some cornered shape, I was able to pull it down in the table talk and lose it in the throbbing fires that burned inside the great fieldstone hearth.

I took notes and introduced myself around, walking the floor, a crowded couple of acres—cranes and grapples, hydraulic units for heavy balers and then the hauling equipment, the refuse trucks that seemed toylike for all their bulk, innocent in shiny paint, unprepared for the nasty work ahead.

I was standing by a model of a confidential shredder called the Watergate, talking to a sales rep about some technical matter, educating myself, jotting notes as we talked, and that's when I saw the woman in a row of new computer products, dressed in tense denims and carrying a shoulder bag with a satin appliqué—not one of us.

When she raised her head and looked my way, I knew who she was. I'd watched her walk across the lobby with her husband, a day earlier or two days or whenever it was, walking high on the balls of her feet, camera-selected in the liquid mingle of loiterers and bellmen, and now she stood looking at me dead-on, secretly amused by something.

We had coffee by the pool. It was ten in the morning and the pool man and the gardeners drifted along the edge of the conversation.

"Among the waste machines. Strange way to spend a morning, Donna."

We'd exchanged first names only.

"Change of pace," she said.

"From what?"

"From what. From being here to do what we're doing."

She sat on the shady side of the table, hands flashing when she reached for her coffee, and when the umbrella edge lifted in the breeze her face caught contour and warmth.

"You're beginning to feel restricted?"

A slight twisty smile.

"You think the program's too confining?"

She was dark-haired and had a way of pursing her lips demurely to plant a curse on a remark she didn't like.

"Where's your husband?"

"Sitting around somewhere with a bloody mary."

"How do you know he's not fucking one of the wives?"

"Or he's fucking one of the wives."

"This is what you're here for after all."

"Exactly," she said.

She watched a maintenance man test a sliding door on a balcony.

"Why aren't you there while they're doing it? He's in bed with another woman and you're not allowed to watch? There must be a review board you can talk to."

"It's a nice day. Be quiet."

"They're all nice days."

"What's your name again?" she said flatly, teasing out a casually complex irony—mocking herself and me and the swimming pool and the date palms.

291

"Donna, I like your mouth."

"It's my overbite."

"Sexy."

"So I'm told."

"What if you and I decided? Or do you have to stick to your own kind?"

"Barry saw you watching me yesterday. I didn't see you but he did. And last night at dinner he pointed you out."

"Does he think that you and I?"

"We decided we know who you are. You're the ice-blue Aqua Velva man."

"And who are you?"

"We're two swing clubs getting together."

"No, you. The mouth and eyes."

She watched the maintenance man slide the door back and forth.

"I'm a person if you ask me questions. You want to know who I am? I'm a person if you're too inquisitive I tune you out completely."

She kept looking into the middle distance.

"Private person who fucks strangers."

"Where's the contradiction?" she said, smiling warmly over the spume of her cappuccino, not looking at me. "Actually you sort of hate us, don't you?"

"Not true."

"And I know why. Because we make it public."

"It's business. Why shouldn't it be public?" I said. "We're all businesspeople here to make contacts, expand the range of possibility."

"Yes, it's true, you hate us."

These were movie scenes, slightly elliptical in tone, with the shots maybe a little offhand, slurred by incidental action. First the wordless moment in the exhibit space, where the characters trade looks amid the truck bodies. Then the poolside exchange with close-ups and pauses, the people a bit detached from their own dialogue, and a sense throughout of morning languor in the standard birdsong, in the rhythmic motion of men with hedge clippers and the shimmer of perfect turquoise in the background.

The long lens insinuates a certain compression, a half-lurking anxiety that serves not only the moment but the day and week and age.

And now the scene in the room, my room, where she took off her jeans, mainly because they were too tight, and sat on the bed in her shirt and briefs, legs stretched toward the footboard. I pulled up a chair and sat alongside, in a posture of consultation, my hand around her ankle.

She was not so pretty in direct light, with a sad wash under the eyes and a spatter bruise on her upper thigh, like an eggplant dropped from a roof. But I liked the way she looked at me, curious, with a tinge of challenge. It made me ambitious, this look, eager to decondition the episode, make it intimate and real.

"You hate the fact that it's public. You can't stand us coming out here and saying it and doing it and acting it out. We talked about this at dinner."

"You and Barry."

"We play a game."

"The two of you. You and Barr'."

"Where we study people in a restaurant. And he is really good at this? And we do their habits and secrets and favorite whatever, right down to underwear."

"Want to tell me what I'm wearing?"

"Actually with you."

"You didn't get that far."

"No. Because we found there were more important things. Like why you hate us."

I watched and listened, trying to locate the voice and manner, place her in some small industrial city, maybe, a Catholic girl growing up by the dreary riverfront, in a house that looked falling-down drunk.

"You know what I like about you? You make me aggressive, a little reckless," I said. "I'm having a relapse just sitting here. I'm backsliding a mile a minute."

"What's that supposed to mean?"

"It means all the interesting things in my life happened young."

"If you fuck me, it'll be a hate fuck. This what you want? This what you mean by aggressive?"

"No. But what do you want? You're in my room half undressed."

"Maybe this is what Barry wants."

"To put you in bed with a man who hates you?"

"We're here to stretch ourselves."

"This is for him then."

"Maybe."

"Carry out a command."

"No, share a fantasy, carry out a fantasy."

"What does Barry do for you?"

"None of yer business, bud," and she says this in a rural barroom twang.

I didn't want to understand her too quickly. It was possible she wasn't here for sex at all but only back matter, the kind of supplementary material that fills out an experience. We would talk a fuck but not do it and she would go back happy to her swapmeet. I looked at the bruise on her thigh. It was depressing to think she might be an agent of her husband's will, here to do the thing and run it back for him, and old Barry a sometime screenwriter, probably, who makes his money over the phone, selling real estate to retirees. When I leaned forward to kiss her, she turned away with an expert shrug, minimal, impersonal, that managed to place me on the outer brow of the perceivable.

"Maybe you're not completely wrong about me, Donna. Maybe I have a theory about the damage people do when they bring certain things into the open."

"Go on. We're always interested in constructive criticism."

"But I don't think you want to hear this. Too personal."

"Oh but I do."

"I'll probably make a fool of myself."

"Oh make a fool. I want you to."

She took off her watch and dropped it on the bed beside her. I felt an urge to fuck her now and risk the malaise of bleak bargain sex that might drift into the room from the boat show of the swingers. Because I didn't know how dumb I'd sound, how schoolboy earnest, or what exactly I'd be giving up with this digression into personal history.

"Go on. We want to be enlightened," she said.

I moved into a kiss and she did not lean away this time but returned a certain tepid sip, a hint of distances we'd yet to cross.

"A long time ago, years ago, I read a book called *The Cloud of Unknowing*. Written by an anonymous mystic, I'm not sure, fourteenth century maybe, whenever the Black Death was—he was writing in the days of the Black Death. A priest gave me this book. This was the priestly part of my life. He pressed this book upon me. And I've forgotten most of this book over the years. But I know that it made me think of God as a force that withholds himself from us because this is the root of his power. I remember one sentence."

"Neat title."

"I remember the title and I remember one sentence."

I stopped here, letting the words take shape and sequence, my hand around Donna's ankle, and I sensed a certain receptiveness, a thing I needed to beat back the incongruity. What the hell, I thought. Take a chance.

"The sentence appears near the beginning of the book and it made me feel I was being addressed directly by the writer, whoever he was, a poet maybe, a poet-priest, I like to imagine. 'Pause for a moment, you wretched weakling, and take stock of yourself.' See, that was me, sort of incisively singled out, living in a state of pause and stocktaking, twenty years old and stupider than my fellows and desperate to find a place for myself. And I read this book and began to think of God as a secret, a long unlighted tunnel, on and on. This was my wretched attempt to understand our blankness in the face of God's enormity. This is what I respected about God. He keeps his secret. And I tried to approach God through his secret, his unknowability. Maybe we can know God through love or prayer or through visions or through LSD but we can't know him through the intellect. *The Cloud* tells us this. And so I learned to respect the power of secrets. We approach God through his unmadeness. We are made, created. God is unmade. How can we attempt to know such a being? We don't know him. We don't affirm him. Instead we cherish his negation. We wretched weaklings, you see. And we try to develop a naked intent that fixes us to the idea of God. *The Cloud* recommends that we develop this intent around a single word. Even better, a single word of a single syllable. This was very appealing to me. I became preoccupied with this search for the one word, the one syllable. It was romantic. The mystery of God was romantic. With this word I would eliminate distraction and edge closer to God's unknowable self."

"What kind of word?"

"I searched. I thought about it. I took it seriously. I was young."

"Love would be a word. But not for you. Too namby-pamby," she said.

"Help would be a word. But even for a weakling, this was a little pitiful. And I thought the problem is the language, I need to change languages, find a word that is pure word, without a lifetime of connotation and shading. And I thought of the Italian word for help because this is what my father used to say when we annoyed him, my brother and I, he'd clasp his hands and wag them and roll his eyes toward heaven and he'd say, *Aiuto*. The way his own father or grandfather probably did. A word to penetrate the darkness. *Aiuto*."

"Too many syllables."

"Too many syllables and too comical. Because he did it basically to make us laugh, distract us with laughter. Maybe my father knew twenty words of Italian, I don't know, he was born here, or maybe he spoke the language fairly well, I don't really know. But he did this word. This word was a three-act play the way he did it, drawing it out, croaking like a poisoned duke. Ay-oo-tow. And we laughed because on some level he was making fun of the old country and the old mannerisms. A great and profound word but I couldn't use it."

Oddly now she reached down and took my hand and moved it up along the inside of her thigh and placed it sort of cuppingly snug in her crotch, adjusting her posture to get completely comfy, like a child at story time.

"Where's your father now?"

"Dead."

"Where's your brother?"

"I don't know."

She waited for me to continue.

"But I knew I was right to abandon English. And finally I came upon a phrase that seemed alive with naked intent. Alive with something I knew and felt from my own experience. A beautiful spontaneous prayer. Five syllables but so what. Three words and five syllables but I knew I'd found the phrase. It came from another mystic, a Spaniard, John of the Cross, and for that one winter this phrase was my naked edge, my edging into darkness, into the secret of God. And I repeated it, repeated it, repeated it. *Todo y nada.*"

"*Todo y nada.*"

"Yes. And what does it make you think of? What does it refer to, in your own life? What does it describe?"

"Sex," she said at once. "The best sex. *Todo y nada.*"

"Yes, exactly."

"So what are you saying?"

"I'm not saying sex is our divinity. Please. Only that sex is the one secret we have that approximates an exalted state and that we share, two people share wordlessly more or less and equally more or less, and this makes it powerful and mysterious and worth sheltering."

"Don't take it into the open, you're saying. But this is because you're still the same romantic person, probably, you were at twenty. Sex is not so secret anymore. The secret is out. You know what sex means to most people?"

She put her hand down over mine and shifted her pelvis slightly, working into my palm.

"Sex is what you can get. For some people, most people, it's the most important thing they can get without being born rich or smart or stealing. This is what life can give you that's equal to others or better, even, that you don't have to go to college six years to get. And it's not religion and it's not science but you can explore it and learn things about yourself."

She paused and it was true, she looked a little toneless in here, away from the sundance of poolside light, her face deprived of its unquiet shading, the mica animation that gave her bones a line and edge. All the more interesting, I thought. All the graver, the weightier. I was after real time and an honest reading of the woman.

"And anyway there's all kinds of public sex," she said. "Horny writers write sex scenes."

"Alone. They write them alone. And you read them alone."

"How do we meet people with similar interests?"

"I don't know. Silently, clandestinely."

"Like criminals. But we're not criminals. We want our own conference, with hors d'oeuvres and little napkins. There's too much loneliness in America? Too many secrets? Let them out, open them up. And don't look at me so closely. You're looking too closely."

"How else do I know you?"

"You don't know me. You don't want to know me. We're in the desert here."

"There's another sentence from *The Cloud*. But I only recall a fragment. About the sharp dart of longing love."

"Sounds porno."

"You're porno and your friends are porno. You have your own magazine, right? Like any business. Like the rock and gravel business and the mortician business. Only you show pubic hair. And home movies through the mail."

Head erect, her mouth pursed in mock self-righteousness.

"This isn't about smut, you know. I'm not a smutty person believe it or not"—she began to laugh a little wildly, her voice cracking—"as I sit here with a strange man's hand on my pussy." And she hip-twisted and moaned oohingly at the friction—moaned in parody but also in earnest.

"I'm not a strange man's hand."

"Don't look at me."

"Who will I look at?"

"I didn't come to this freaking outback to be analyzed."

"You're my relapse. Not the first but the first in a very long time. And that's what makes you unsafe."

"What makes you unsafe?"

"I'm your exception to indiscriminate fucking."

"You think you're discriminate? What makes you discriminate? I don't even remember your name."

I told her my name, first and last, and she said it sounded phony.

"More. I need more," she said. "There you were. Weak and wretched."

"Yes."

"Reading books about God."

"Yes."

"Talking to priests."

"Yes."

"So what was your sin? Your secret? The reason for your wretched state?"

She had that original challenge in her eyes but without the knowingness, the amused and slightly tilted—not disdain but unwillingness to allow the possibility of surprise. This was gone and there was a curiosity that was less sheer and frontal.

I withdrew my hand from her body and sat back and folded my arms across my chest, head tilted, as a sign of resignation, of being abject before a mystery, a young man unstatus'd and base.

"I'd been in correction."

"In correction."

"As we called it. A juvenile correction center. They'd sent me away for a time and when I got out, I went to a small Jesuit outpost in northern Minnesota, where they specialized in hardship kids and others of uncommon qualities."

"And you were in correction?"

"For shooting a man. I shot a man."

"Killed him?"

"Killed him. I was seventeen when it happened and to this day I'm not sure whether the intent was express or implied or howsoever the law reads. Or was it all a desperate accident?"

"And you've thought about this a great deal?"

"I've tried, on and off. I retain the moment. I've tried to break it down, see it clearly in its component parts. But there are so many whirling motives and underlying possibilities and so whats and why nots."

"What does that mean?"

"Well at some point, with my finger already moving the trigger, at some micropoint in the action of the mind and the action of the finger and the trigger-action itself, I may have basically said, So what. I'm not really sure. Or, Why not do it and see what happens."

"Who was the man?"

"Who was the man. He wasn't an enemy or a rival. A sort of friend if anything. A guy who helped me out occasionally, an older guy, not an influence in any way, I don't think, except in the sense that he owned a shotgun."

I had a rash inspiration then, unthinking, and did my mobster voice. "In udder words I took him off da calendar."

A voice my wife had never heard and a story I'd never told her and how strange this was and how guilty it made me feel. But not right away. Guilt later in Phoenix—save the guilt for the bookwalled rooms and the Turkish prayer rugs and the fashion magazines in the bathroom basket.

Donna had the sniffles. She'd taken a midnight swim and caught a chill and that was all we talked about for a while. We talked about the night and the chill air and the food in the restaurant.

Then she took off her panties and handed them to me. I tossed them on the bed and got undressed.

I felt a breath of estrangement in the room and thought she might be a voyeur of her own experience, living at an angle to the moment and recording in some state of future-mind. But then she pulled me down, snatched a fistful of hair and pulled me into a kiss, and there was a heat in her, a hungry pulse that resembled a gust of being. We were patched together grappling and straining, not enough hands to grab each other, not nearly sufficient body to press upon the other, we wanted more hold and grip, a sort of mapped contact, bodies matching point for point, and I raised up and saw how small she looked, naked and abed, how completely different from the woman of the movietone aura in the hotel lobby. She was near to real earth now, the sex-grubbed dug-up self, and I felt close to her and thought I knew her finally even as she shut her eyes to hide herself.

I said her name.

We were hollowed out like scooped guava when it was over. Our limbs ached and I had a desert thirst and we'd killed the morning off. I went and peed and watched the fluid splash amber in the sun-washed bowl. What well-being in a barefoot piss after a strenuous and proper screw. In the room she sniffled a little and sounded hoarse and brassy and I rolled a blanket over her. She fell into pretend sleep, leave-me-alone sleep, but I eased onto the blanket and pressed myself upon her, breathing the soft heat of her brow and tasting at the end of

300

my tongue the smallest beadlets of fever. I heard room maids talking in the hall and knew we were gone from each other's life, already and forever. But some afterthing remained and kept us still, made us lie this way a while, Donna and I, in the all-and-nothing of our love.

You withhold the deepest things from those who are closest and then talk to a stranger in a numbered room. What's the point of asking why? Guilt later in Phoenix, where I could evade vexing questions in the daily wheel of work.

I was the juniormost fellow with the fixed smile. There was a spirit of generous welcome, the spirit of one-of-us and how-many-kids and let's-have-lunch. I wanted to be bound to the company. I felt complicit with some unspoken function of the corporation. I stayed late and worked weekends. I corrected my foot-drag step. I heard my own voice and saw my smile and earned an office at the end of the hall, where I wore a crisp gray suit and grew stronger by the day.

It was a long run through a narrow draw on the last day of the conference and we jostled for space, Sims and I, just beginning to forget the tremor in the fives and the way the room spoke to us, and I thought this is when we get the aftershock, after we forget the shock.

The first part of the run was a monologue that Sims delivered with a veteran's artful zest and he stopped talking only to take deep breaths or blow sweat off the edge of his upper lip.

"The thing about raw sewage," he said. "You treat it with loving care. You route it through bar screens way underground. And pump it up to settling tanks and aeration tanks. And you separate it and skim it and nurse it with bacteria."

He went through the process in lushest detail, stroking certain words, drawing them out, oozy, swampy, semisolid, thick, slick, sludge.

"Because this is your medium now. A tarlike substance with a funky savor to it."

What gusto he managed to salvage from our punishing run, eyes wide and voice strong—he made it sound like a personal attack.

"And you wait for a sludge tanker to come and get it. Honey buckets, they're called in the Northeast. The tanker dumps the sludge in the ocean. Like you take a dump in your own home. One hundred and six miles from the Jersey shore, legally. Or less, illegally."

"Interesting."

"Interesting," he said. "Isn't it?"

"Yes it is."

"Never thought about it, did you?"

"I thought about it a little."

"Never thought about it. Say it."

"I thought about it vaguely maybe."

"Vaguely maybe. I see. That's well put. Perfect really."

A delta-wing plane nudged the sun and vanished in the dizzy ozone, climbing dreamily.

"But how is it my medium?" I said.

We ran through the gulley, over the stony surface.

"This is what you and I. And all of us here. Fundamentally deal with. Over and above. Or under and below. Our stated duties."

"You're saying all waste."

"That's what I'm saying."

All waste defers to shit. All waste aspires to the condition of shit.

We poked and elbowed, jockeying for advantage, and Sims blew mist off his upper lip.

"How are things at home? Things all right at home?"

"Things are good. Things are fine at home. Thanks for asking."

"Love your wife?" he said.

"Love my wife."

"Better love her. She loves you."

We went a little faster and he took off his cap and hit me with it and put it back on.

"But this ship thing," I said.

"This ship thing is a dumb rumor that builds on itself."

"The ship is a running joke."

"The crew keeps changing. You know that?" he said. "They change the crew more often than they change the name of the ship."

He laughed and hit me with his hat.

"One crew leaves, they have to press-gang another."

He pulled ahead of me and I caught up and we went hard past the golf course in the bright clean heat.

Later we drove back together and went directly to the campus, our Los Angeles headquarters, a series of bridge-linked buildings with mirrored facades, high above a freeway, and I could see it all shatter in slow motion in my mind.

A cobbled road took us past ponds and blond sculpture and cinnamon trails for jogging.

"You see these buildings breaking apart and coming down?"

He looked at me.

"You don't think this is what we're supposed to see when we look at these buildings?"

He wanted nothing to do with this idea.

"You don't think it's a new way of seeing?"

We walked along hallway mazes fitted with electronic gates that Sims opened by inserting a keycard in a lockset. This was the smart new world of microprocessors that read coded keys. I liked the buzz and click of the card in the lock. It signified connection. I liked the feeling of some power source accessible to those of us with coded keys. In the elevator he spoke his name into a voiceprint device, Simeon Branson Biggs, suitably sonorous, and the machine lifted instantly to three.

We sat in his office.

"Nobody dies here. I get blood pressure readings right down the hall. We have exercise rooms. They measure my body fat and tell me what to eat in grams and ounces."

He lit a cigar and looked at me through the skeptical smoke.

"People come to work in tennis shoes and blond beards. Play tennis and volleyball. I go to sleep black every night and come back white in the morning."

He wore shoes we used to call clodhoppers, great heavy things with squared-off toe caps.

"You believe in God?" he said.

"Yes, I think so."

"We'll go to a ball game sometime."

Sims had calls to make and mail to read. I spent some time with other people and then took a taxi to my hotel—I'd be here for a couple of days. And the taxi driver said something odd. We were driving along. I didn't know where we were. You come to a city and you go where the driver takes you—you go on faith. And he said something either to me or to himself. He was an old guy with nervous hands and a catch in his voice, a half gasp like a splice that wasn't working.

He said, "Light up a Lucky. It's light-up time."

Neither one of us had a cigarette in hand or showed any sign of reaching for one. Maybe he was just recalling the old slogan, idly, reciting the thing simply because he'd thought of it, because it had shot to mind out of some nowhere in the memory, but it was odd and unsettling. You come to a city and hear a thing like that and you don't know what to think. I looked at him. I leaned to the side and looked at his profile and I tried to figure out what he meant.

2

He was waiting for Chuckie Wainwright. The broad-backed work of the waterfront went on around him, a sense of enormous tonnage and skyhook machinery, tractor-trailers crooking into marked slots and containered goods stacked on the decks of tremendous ships, you almost can't believe how big, and the what-do-you-call, the booms of dockside cranes swinging cargo through the mist. And farther out in the bay an aircraft carrier easing toward the Golden Gate, sent on its way by a mongrel fleet of small craft and three fireboats spritzing great arcs of water like a champagne farewell.

Marvin checked his watch for the tenth time in the last hour. He stood near a transit shed where he was safe from the action. He resembled a gentile lost in a fog, wearing a suede touring cap and a double-breasted raincoat with epaulets, gun flaps, raglan sleeves, he knows these terms from years in dry cleaning, broad-welt pockets, belt loops, sleeve straps and so many buttons he felt dressed for life.

He carried a telescopic umbrella enclosed in a sheath that belonged to a different umbrella, he has kelly green inside sky blue, not that it mattered to anyone but his wife.

Eleanor was here, the first time she'd ever accompanied him on a trip in search of the baseball. This was San Francisco, don't forget, which she didn't want to live a life and miss it.

And that was the Bay Bridge over his right shoulder, flashing a million cars a minute that never heard of Marvin Lundy and his baseball mania.

He checked his watch again and peered across the bay.

Chuckie Wainwright was a crewman on a tramp steamer coming down the coast from Alaska. Marvin had communicated with shipping companies, harbormasters and actual captains on matters pertaining to the whereabouts of the ship and the roster of the crew, making phone calls and sending radiograms. And it was confirmed more than once, it was determined and duly documented that Charles Wainwright Jr., known as Chuckie, was aboard the Lucky Argus steaming out of Anchorage with a load of sand and pulverized rock.

Chuckie was his key to the chain of possession. Marvin had gathered a thousand tidbits of information that connected the baseball to previous owners and finally, what is the word for the thing that is not ultimate but next to ultimate—finally the Wainwright name came into play.

He waited half an hour and then went to the Ferry Building to ask about the Lucky Argus, should he be worried or not, and they told him it would put in at pier 7 in about an hour and a half.

Outside he caught a whiff in the air, a faint sort of stinkhole odor, barely detectable but odd in its emotional force. Then it passed, gone on the breeze, and he heard the watery shush of traffic on the bridge and saw his Eleanor approach, alight with her strawberry smile, under a sky blue umbrella.

"Thought I'd find you here. I came to see this lovely old building."

Marvin looked behind him to fathom what was lovely that he'd missed.

"Did you know this building survived the great earthquake but the clock stopped dead and stayed that way for a whole year?"

"There's always a clock somewhere that's stopping," Marvin said morosely.

"As if to remind everyone in visual range."

"Remind them of what?"

She waved her guidebook at him.

"Sometimes bad luck is writ large and plain."

"What do you mean?"

"The clock stopped at seventeen minutes past five in the morning. Five one seven, dear. Add the digits and you get thirteen."

Maybe there was a shift in the breeze. He noted the smell again and found it moved him in strange ways, one of those smells that traces back through memory, musty and earthy in this particular case, and he felt an unaccountable urge to follow it to its source.

"Where is your Mr. Wainwright?"

"Boat's late," he said.

"Don't be so pessimistic."

"Where's pessimistic? I'm standing here having a conversation."

"You're hunched and slumped."

"I'm always hunched and slumped. This is how it came from the factory."

"You're more hunched than usual when the subject is the baseball."

Eleanor was not wrong. Was Eleanor ever wrong? He grouched at her sometimes but they both knew she was almost always right. She had her English accent, her popovers she baked that he felt the anticipation a day in advance, her excruciating neatness of dress that he thought might be a disease, he caught her talking to her closet a couple of times—but always seemly is a word he likes, tastefully matching this to that. She had a stern determination that she soft-pedaled but made sure he got the point. And now that their daughter was on her own, with a nice job and an apartment on a safe street, Eleanor stood guard over Marvin's obsessiveness and joke-spattered gloom.

They were walking now, taking an amble along the Embarcadero, and Marvin realized the pier numbers were getting higher as they walked—high numbers and even numbers, which meant they were moving away from pier 7. But this is where the odor seemed to be leading him, a stinky wisp intermittent on the wind.

"And you need this fellow Wainwright to tell you what?"

"How his father acquired the ball, who's dead and buried."

"And in this way you will complete the what?"

"The what-do-you-call."

"The lineage."

"The lineage," Marvin said.

1. The ex-wife of Chuckie Wainwright, Susan somebody—never mind the details.

2. The one-eighth Indian, Marvin forgets the tribe, who led him to the former wife.

3. The shock of other people's lives. The truth of another life, the blow, the impact.

4. Chuckie in the Air Force, in Greenland, in Vietnam, and going AWOL, which is a what, an acronym, and drifting afar and growing a beard and fathering a child and naming it Dakota.

5. Which is where Marvin found the ex-wife, coincidentally, in Rapid City, walking sick people across a swimming pool in four feet of water.

6. The shock, the power of an ordinary life. It is a thing you could not invent with banks of computers in a dust-free room.

"Marvin, you know what I'm going to say."

"There's a three-hour time difference. I don't think I can wait."

"Pick up your feet when you walk. You're a healthy man who tries to look sick."

"This is chitchat on the people channel."

She did not quibble or carp, she spoke gently to him, she was better than he deserved, writing postcards when she went back home to visit—imagine getting a postcard from your wife.

Then she stopped dead, going rigid in her brilliant slicker.

"What's that I smell?" she said.

Marvin began to understand why the odor was so compelling. It came, in a way, from him. He recalled the trip they'd made through Europe six years after the war, he and Eleanor, newly wed, a girl of modest background, taking a long honeymoon by the cheapest means possible, slow trains and old hotels squeezed of every convenience, but they were also embarked on a mission important to Marvin's family. He was trying to find his half brother, Avram Lubarsky, who'd served in the Red Army, who was wounded at Leningrad, who was wounded at Stalingrad, who shot himself in the toe at Grodno, who rowed a boat across the Volga under a strafing attack by Stukas, who was captured by the Germans and escaped, who fled south wearing newspapers for shoes and married a gypsy in the Carpathians and ate whitefish from the Black Sea and disappeared somewhere in the Urals.

Such Russian stuff, and here was Marvin today looking for a base-ball. But he wasn't inclined to make light of his preoccupation. It had its own epic character, its history of comebacks and sweet memories and family picnics and buggy evenings on the back porch and hopes that rise and fall and the song of loss that goes unwritten in the records.

"Let's turn back, shall we? I don't think I want to get any closer to that smell."

She said the word with a grimace of suspicion, the response reserved for certain smells, clutching up the mouth and nose, beading the eyes against the sight of criminal matter at the source.

"Just some sewer work probably. Comes and goes. Let's walk a little more."

"I'm on holiday," she said.

"This makes you squeamish? People eat camel meat barehanded, they're back at work in the morning."

"Make a deal. We'll walk as far as that construction site up ahead. Then we'll come back."

"What's a little smell?" he said.

But it wasn't a little smell anymore. It grew stronger and drew him nearer and he recalled those old hotels and their toilets, the toilets down the hall, fortunately, and he thought of the public toilets in rail-road stations, a stranger in the next stall with his own autobiography of foreign foods and personal smells, through England, France and Italy, but it wasn't other people's smells that began to overwhelm him—only his own.

Marvin's bowel movements seemed to change, gradually, in grim stages, as he and Eleanor moved east through Europe. The smell grew worse, deeper, it acquired a kind of density, it ripened and aged, and he began to dread the moment after breakfast every day when it came time for him to haul himself to the toilet.

What is the word, ignoble?

Marvin thought of his bowel movements as BMs, a phrase he'd heard an army doctor mutter once. His BMs were turning against him, turning violent in a way. He and Eleanor went through the Dolomites and across Austria and nipped into the northwest corner of Hungary and the stuff came crashing out of him, noisy and remarkably dark. But mainly it was the smell that disturbed him. He was afraid Eleanor would notice. He realized this was probably a normal part of every early marriage, smelling the other's smell, getting it over and done with so you can move ahead with your lives, have children, buy a little house, remember everybody's birthday, take a drive on the Blue Ridge Parkway, get sick and die. But in this case the husband had to take extreme precautions because the odor was shameful, it was intense and deeply personal and seemed to say something awful about the bearer.

His smell was a secret he had to keep from his wife.

They entered Czechoslovakia, where the toilets flushed so weakly that he had to flush and wait and then flush some more and he opened windows and waved towels, feeling guilty and trapped. There was something cold and hard in the streets, a breathable tension, many arrests, people on trial. The newlyweds argued with an ironworker in a café, he was proud of the smoke and filth that hung over the landscape, this was progress, this was industrial might and drive— the darker the skies and the more property owners in prison, the greater the future of the socialist state.

Who are they, Marvin thought, that it drives me crazy not to convince them that they're wrong?

His BMs grew steamier as they traveled up through eastern Poland. They argued with workers in a stand-up bar, men drinking morning mugs of beer. They argued with a woman who did ticket prices on an abacus. Marvin returned to a toilet for a newspaper he'd left behind, he was looking vainly for baseball scores in a Warsaw daily, and he was surprised by the heat in the little room, the steamy aura he'd established there, it was heavy and humid, an air mass of sweltry stench— all that radiant energy from a single BM.

Lucky for him that Eleanor went first every day. Because she shouldn't have to confront this, an English girl with hair that's nearly blond. He made sure she never passed a toilet he'd just used.

"This is as far as I'm going," she said now.

"We're not at the construction site."

"I will die gasping if I take another step."

Ahead a hundred yards was an area of halted roadwork, there were unmanned bulldozers and dump trucks, the pavement heaved-up and rubbled and not a living soul in sight except for a lone figure asleep in a mail sack, one of those draggled men Marvin sees everywhere these days—where have they been hiding all this time?

"I'll just go ten, twenty yards," he told her. "Just to see what's causing this, some ruptured pipe probably, out of curiosity."

He had to conceal the memory from her just as he'd once concealed the smell. And the strain of evacuation grew worse, they had their passports, they had their visas, they went to Pinsk, they went to Minsk, he grunted on the seat until all the elements issued—earth, air, fire and water.

The deeper into communist country, the more foul his BMs.

They were accompanied everywhere they went by an Intourist guide. A guide dropped them off, another guide met them, someone sneaked a look in their luggage, a guide made sure they did not cast a passing glance at certain sensitive buildings, at rivers with dams a hundred miles upstream, at roads that led to military sites a thousand miles away. It was like sharing every breath with your personal policeman. Even the weather was a secret, unpublished in newspapers and never mentioned in tones above a whisper.

He had names and addresses and talked to a dozen people and followed a trail that led to Gorki, where a cousin many times removed told him to go to a street of unfinished buildings and that's where they found Avram, the first time he and Marvin had ever set eyes on each other, he's living in a tiny flat with his second wife and his second, third and fourth children. They embraced and wept, maybe it was real, maybe partly for effect, speaking smidgens of Russian, English and Yiddish, and soon they were arguing strenuously. Avram was a dedicated communist with a beetled brow and he spat little word-flecks of contempt at the U.S., the system is corrupt, we will eat you for lunch, you are a what-do-you-call-it kind of culture, a mickey mouse culture, and that night Marvin had to make an emergency visit to the hotel toilet, where he unleashed a firewall of chemical waste. The smell that surrounded him was infused with what, with geopolitics, and he waved a towel for five minutes and propped open the window, it kept closing, with a rolled-up copy of Pravda, he was still looking for baseball scores, and then he went and stood in their room and watched Eleanor sleep—she came from a gentle rural place and could easily perish from his reek.

He walked to the edge of the construction debris and realized this was not the source of the smell. The smell was still distinct, completely reminiscent of his Soviet experience, only less farshtinkener than his personal output, a bit toned down, and it was not coming from a sewer main break or a communal toilet of the homeless.

Then he saw the ship. It was docked at a remote pier up ahead, between a number of empty slips and a wide basin, and it appeared to be abandoned, with bridge and deck deserted and rust stains running down the sides and graffiti spray-painted on the smokestacks in languages he did not recognize and in alphabets unknown.

He turned and looked at Eleanor. She had a thing she did to show impatience, where she dipped her body and tilted her head and went half limp, her mouth showing a yawny oh.

The name of the ship was unreadable, covered with rust and graffiti. Such a woebegone thing, an oceangoing vessel that carries a public funk of portable toilets in a field.

Marvin and Avram argued for three days. They ate meals in the little unheated flat where you had to unscrew the tap from the kitchen sink and take it down the hall to the bathroom when you wanted to take a bath because construction of this block of flats ended on a certain date, finished or not. The two men traded many family stories but always with an undercurrent of contention and with intervals of open insult, Us and Them, and it grated on Marvin to hear these things from a man so self-assured who's a total nobody, a little guy who pushed upward when he talked, with two false teeth made of stainless steel, he's the shiniest appliance in sight. The flat came without windows. Avram had to install the windows himself, they came from the plate-glass factory where he worked, glass so thin you had to come away from the window to talk. A word with too many consonants might shatter the glass.

He said to Marvin, We're making bigger bombs than the West can even dream. That's why the windows break so easy.

Yes, it galled Marvin to think of a man living under these circumstances, carrying a kitchen tap back and forth, the spout and two valves but only the cold gives water, the family crowded up the walls and he's so cocky and flushed, this was the thing that drove Marvin nuts, how the guy gets along without the basic whatevers, Eleanor knows the word, the things that contribute to material comfort—she says it so refined.

She called out to him now, "Come away."

And on the way back to Western Europe his system slowly returned to normal, branny BMs, healthful and mild.

And they were on a train in Switzerland, a normal neutral place, going through tunnels and past moonlit lakes, and Marvin heard a familiar voice up ahead, a radio crackle and yak, and he followed the sound to the front of the car, where two GIs were huddled over a little portable radio with a stunted antenna, listening to Russ Hodges on the Armed Forces Network, his account of the game interrupted whenever the train entered a tunnel, and that's where Marvin was when Thomson hit the homer, racing through a mountain in the Alps.

Eleanor was just out of the shower when Marvin walked in, collapsing the room with his mood. She stood in a towel, pink-toed, and looked at him.

"The ship came in. Lucky Argus. Pier seven. Exactly when they said to the minute."

"But Wainwright," she said.

"Not on board."

"Stand up straight."

"Jumped ship in Vancouver."

"Do they know where he went?"

"Signed on some other ship. Going north somewhere. He's a cold-weather person, this Chuckie."

"You'll find him."

"It doesn't matter."

"Actually it does. I used to think you were mad. But I understand now. Yes, you're mad but there's a certain reasoning behind it. There's a little childlike spot of logic. A little bedtime thing. You need to finish the story. Dear Marvin. Without the final link to the baseball there's no way to be sure how the story ends. What good's a story without an ending? Although I suppose in this case it's not the ending we need but the beginning."

He liked her in a towel. They'd first met near the end of the war, said hello–goodbye but corresponded, she was an air-raid warden with a torch, they called it, and he was a quartermaster handing out condoms for D-day that the troops fixed to the muzzles of their rifles to keep out sand and water and he still liked her in a towel or slip, married twenty-seven years to this point.

He sat in his shorts at the edge of the bed, taking off his ribbed socks. They would do like tourists in commercials, have marital sex in a nice hotel. Their room had a view of a view. From their window they could look across the courtyard to office towers and reflected clouds in the picture window of the hotel restaurant.

"Marvin, do you plan to wear it?"

She was talking about his toupee.

"I need it for how I see myself."

He also needed it because it took the edge off his large ears and sorrowful Marvin nose. He wanted to look nice for her even if she didn't think it mattered. Tonight he'd wear his best shirt, with cuffs so French he wanted to hum the what-do-you-call.

"You're my man, with or without."

A thing she said with a half-fake quiver of her mouth that made him feel he owned the earth.

She slipped off the towel and placed a knee on the end of the bed. They were honeymooners still, shy but eager, and Marvin in his Brooklyn-bornness, his religion of skeptical response—he was only now beginning to see how hard it was to persist in the sentimental myth, after all these years, of their dissimilarity, a thing he'd fabricated out of her accent and complexion. He was glimpsing his Eleanor truth by truth, that she matched him in appetite, that her ambitions for the business were bigger than his own, that her main ambition was

America, a fact he'd managed to miss—the things, the places, the bright buzz of products on the shelves, the sunblast of fortune's favor.

Here they were in a strange bed in California, what twists to life, how uncertain go the turns, an English girl in his arms, pink and innocent even if she's not, and Marvin's polymerized hairpiece secure on his head.

She wanted Japanese but that wasn't enough. They had to go to a place where the guidebook said tatami seating.

Marvin thought if he lived all his life for a hundred years before meeting Eleanor, he would have done the same three or four things in the same order every day and as soon as he met Eleanor, at the age of a hundred and one, he would be sitting on the floor to eat seaweed.

They faced each other over the low table, in their stocking feet.

"What's the word for the thing that's not ultimate but next to ultimate?"

"Penultimate."

"Penultimate. See, that's what I've got in Chuckie Wainwright."

"Sit up straight," she told him.

"Greenland. I always had my suspicions about that place."

"What do you mean?"

"That's where he was stationed in the Air Force if he was actually there."

"Why wouldn't he have been there?"

"Do you personally know anybody who's ever been there?"

"No, I don't," Eleanor said.

"Let me advise you. Neither do I. And neither does anyone I've talked to lately."

"I think there's a main city."

"You think there's a main city. Do you know the name of this place?"

"No, I don't."

"Did you ever look at Greenland on a map?"

"I guess I have, once or twice perhaps."

"Did you ever notice that it's never the same size on any two maps? The size of Greenland changes map to map. It also changes year to year."

"It's large," she said.

"It's very large. It's enormous. But sometimes it's a little less enormous, depending on which map you're looking at."

"I believe it's the largest island in the world."

"The largest island in the world," Marvin said. "But you don't know anyone who's ever been there. And the size keeps changing. What's more, listen to this, the location also changes. Because if you look closely at one map and then another, Greenland seems to move. It's in a slightly different part of the ocean. Which is the whole juxt of my argument."

"What's your argument?"

"You asked so I'll tell you. That the biggest secrets are staring us right in the face and we don't see a thing."

"What's the secret about Greenland?"

"First, does it exist? Second, why does it keep changing its size and its location? Third, why can't we find anyone who's personally been there? Fourth, didn't a B-52 crash about ten years ago that the facts were so hush-hush we still don't know for sure if there were nuclear weapons aboard?"

He pronounced it nucular.

"You think Greenland has a secret function and a secret meaning. But then you think everything has a secret function and a secret meaning," she said.

"The bigger the object, the easier it is to hide it. How do you get to Greenland? What boat do you take? Where do you find an airport that has a flight to this main city that nobody knows the name of and nobody has ever been to? And this is the main city. What about the outlying areas? The whole enormous island is one big outlying area. What color is it? Is it green? Iceland is green. Iceland's on TV. You can see the houses and the countryside. If Iceland is green, is Greenland white? I'm only asking because nobody else is asking. I have no personal stake in this place. But I watch the nature channel and I see tribes they wear mud on their body in New Guinea and I see those thingabeests, they're mating in some valley in Africa."

"Wildebeests," Eleanor said.

"But I never hear a peep from Greenland."

The waitress brought saki for her, beer for him. She called the drinks beverages and Marvin thought he was on an airliner. All the traveling he'd done, baseball-related, the unsheveled lives, the words and sentences.

Wait-listed passenger Lundy please present yourself at the podium.

1. The mother of twins in what's that town.

2. The man who lived in a community of chemically sensitive people, they wore white cotton shifts and hung their mail on clotheslines.

3. The woman named Bliss, which he was younger then, Marvin was, and maybe could have, with eyes as nice as hers, done a little something, in Indianola, Miss.

4. The shock of lives unlike your own. Happy, healthy, lonely, lost. The one-eighth Indian. Lives that are blunt and unforeseen even when they're ordinary.

5. Who knew a Susan somebody who spoke about a baseball with a famous past. Marvin forgets the tribe.

6. Stomach acting up again.

7. The chemically sensitive man, his whole body vibrated when somebody snapped a photo a mile and a half away.

8. And Chuckie Wainwright gone to sea, leaving a woman and child behind, a hippie Christian cluster, barefoot with beads, and Marvin tracking him ship by ship.

9. And the bone cancer kid in Utah, which his mother blamed the government.

10. Marvin often lost, setting out one day for Melbourne, Florida and nearly ending up Down Under.

11. And the woman with the chipped tooth—a whole long story, you shouldn't ask.

12. And the chemicals in the core of the ball that made the man run in place after breakfast every day.

"Tell me what we're going to do after dinner."

"Me you're asking?"

"You've been to this city before. I haven't," she said.

"What's left to do by the time I pick myself off the floor? I've got a knot in my leg a cannibal would spit it out."

"Come on. Show me a good time."

"She wants to go gallivanting."

"Let's make this our city, Marv."

Strange how he was compiling a record of the object's recent forward motion while simultaneously tracking it backwards to the distant past. Sometimes he thought he was seeing the ball sort of fly by. He wanted to find Chuckie and establish the last link, the first link, the connection to the Polo Grounds itself, but if he couldn't find the guy he would probably buy the ball anyway, the reputed ball, once he located it, and keep looking for Chuckie till he died.

"I want you to show me the seamy underside," Eleanor said.

The ball brought no luck, good or bad. It was an object passing through. But it inspired people to tell him things, to entrust family secrets and unbreathable personal tales, emit heartful sobs onto his shoulder. Because they knew he was their what, their medium of release. Their stories would be exalted, absorbed by something larger, the long arching journey of the baseball itself and his own cockeyed march through the decades.

All right. Marvin was not a night person but he knew one place he might take her, one street really, that's all it was, called the Float, out near the old hippie district, shops that came and went overnight, buildings without house numbers, an area catering to very select desires that changed with the phases of the moon.

He lifted himself off the floor mat in stages, joint by joint, and they called a cab and went outside.

Twenty minutes later they walked along the street, umbrellas up, it was raining lightly, a few panhandlers about, a woman in a mohawk and white makeup punching a doomsday leaflet into the belt buckle of Marvin's raincoat. PEACE IS COMING—BE PREPARED. Most of the shops were open despite the hour or because of the hour and they were almost all below street level so you peered over a guardrail to see what they were selling, Role-Reversal Rubber Goods, or Endangered Fashions—jackets made from the skin of disappearing species.

They went into a hole-in-the-wall place, a lot of cracked plaster and roachy baseboards and a stock of rare recordings. But you're not talk-

318

ing about old jazz 45s. These were phone taps you could buy, or bugs in the wall, recordings of organized crime figures discussing their girlfriends or their lawyers, he's a hard-on with a briefcase—you're talking about men on the eleven o'clock news in cashmere overcoats with enough material you could clothe a Little League team from Taiwan. And phone taps of ordinary anonymous men and women, even more repellent-addictive, your next-door neighbor maybe, and Marvin understood how such a purchase could lead to stupefied hours of listening, could take over a person's life, all the more so for the utter sucked-dry boredom of the recordings and how they provided the lure of every addiction, which is losing yourself to time.

The Float had an edge, it had a midnight finish.

They stepped briefly into shops that sold autopsy photos, that sold movie stars' garbage, the actual stuff deep-frozen in a warehouse—you looked in a catalog and placed an order.

Eleanor was delighted by the ambiance, a word she pronounced a little French. Bare-board floors and stained walls. She took Marvin's arm and they went down the street, spotting a sign in a first-floor window, Foot Fetish Cruise of Spanish Ports.

Floating zones of desire. It was the what, the dismantling of desire into a thousand subspecialties, into spin-offs and narrowings, edgewise whispers of self. There was a dive with a back room where they showed sex movies involving people with missing limbs. They had gay nights and straight nights. If you were open to suggestion you could float through the zone, finding out who you were by your attachments, slice by slice, tasting the deli specials of the street. You were defined by your fixation.

A boy walked by in clothes so raggedy he could have been a tickertape parade.

There was a place called the Conspiracy Theory Café. Shelves filled with books, film reels, sound tapes, official government reports in blue binders. Eleanor wanted to have a coffee and browse but Marvin waved the place off—a series of sterile exercises. He believed the wellsprings were deeper and less detectable, deeper and shallower both, look at billboards and matchbooks, trademarks on products, birthmarks on bodies, look at the behavior of your pets.

Something's staring you straight in the face.

The largest shop was at street level, a dozen men standing around, furtive, in raincoats, looking at old copies of National Geographic. These were used magazines, used and handled, lived-with, and the address labels were attached, machine-stamped and ink-smudged and skin-greasy, and printed on the labels were the names and addresses of real people out there in magazine America, and the men in raincoats stood by tables and bins and read the labels and leafed through the magazines, heads never lifting.

A man bought a magazine and left quickly, slipping it under his coat.

Marvin did not think these men were interested in photos of wolf packs on the tundra at sunset. It was something else they sought, a forgotten human murmur, maybe, a sense of families in little heartland houses with a spaniel flop-eared on the rug, a sense of snug innocence and the undiscovered world outside, the vast geographic. A pornography of nostalgia, maybe, or was it something else completely?

And was there a back room, because isn't there always a back room, another splintering of desire, a little more refined and personalized, and in the back room weren't the magazines cased in acetate folders, maybe these were rare issues or rare labels, or maybe the folders themselves were the fetish items here, dust-veneered, handled, nearly opaque some of them, a dullish sort of plastic with a faint odor and prophylactic feel, like condoms for reading matter, and maybe there's another room where you need to whisper a password and this is the room with folders only, empty folders, handled a thousand times, and Eleanor was completely creeped out by this place, it was more than she'd bargained for, raincoated men with National Geographics, furtively thumbing the labels.

Across the street they saw a tall woman's shop, called Long Tall Sally, but not for dresses and coats. Fantasy Enhancements, the sign read. Books, movies, appliances—tall women only.

You see a few funny things in some off-street on a rainy night and you wonder why they seem significant. Marvin thought there was something here that might be an early sign of some great force beginning to tremble awake, he didn't know what exactly, he didn't know for good or ill, he didn't know where in the world—a shaking in the earth that could alter everything.

"All right, Marv. I'm ready to go to bed now."

One more place. The one place on the street he'd been to before, run by an acquaintance, you could call him a colleague, Tommy Chan, maybe the country's first baseball memorabilist if that's an actual word.

They went down a grimy set of steps into a dark cubby stacked with scorecards and old songbooks and a thousand other baseball oddities, whole slews of records and documents in tottering columns.

Eleanor sighed in her chest like a shot partridge.

And there was Tommy in his high chair, the chair and cash register platformed, islanded higher than the surging mass of old paper that was going chemically brown, and it made Marvin think of all the game footage he'd seen during his search, fans in the Polo Grounds throwing scorecards and newspapers onto the field as the day waned and the Dodgers approached their doom. All that twilight litter. Maybe some of it was sitting here today, preserved by the stadium sweepers and eventually entering the underground of memory and collection, some kid's airplaned scorecard, a few leaves of toilet tissue unfurled in jubilation from the upper deck, maybe autographed delicately by a player, the scatter of a ball game come to rest all these years later, a continent away.

"This is my wife."

"We don't see many women," Tommy said like a Buddhist monk in a backcountry compound, polite and wise.

"It's a wonder you see anybody. Because frankly who would come here?" Marvin said. "You have to make the place halfway presentable."

"Presentable." Nice word. "Marvin, think. What am I selling here? I'm not selling housewares in a regional mall."

He was a smart guy and would-be likable but ageless in the face, which disconcerted Marvin because you like to know how old a man you're talking to.

"What did you sell today?"

"You're the first people in the shop."

"Don't look so smug."

"I've been here since noon. These other merchants don't open till very late."

"Since noon. And no one."

"How interesting to see a woman," Tommy said.

Eleanor stood motionless, maybe part paralyzed by her exotic status.

She said, "Don't you have to give people an incentive to buy? Not that it's any of my."

"An incentive." What a novel idea. "The incentive is within, I think. These materials have no esthetic interest. They're discolored and crumbling. Old paper, that's all it is. My customers come here largely for the clutter and mess. It's a history they feel they're part of."

Marvin said to Eleanor, "I always thought the people who preserved these old things, baseball things, I always thought they lived in the East. I thought this is where all the remembering is done. Tommy is the first collector I found anywhere west of Pittsburgh."

Tommy had a smile so slight and fleeting it could only be photographed on film stock developed by NASA. His little knickknack face floated in the gloom and Marvin had a childlike urge to reach up and touch it, just to see if it felt like his, the rough dull surface he washed and shaved every day.

"Did you find your man?" Tommy said.

"I found my ship. The man, forget about."

"You must give it up."

"Who's talking?"

"You can't precisely locate the past, Marvin. Give it up. Retire it. For your own good."

"Who's talking?"

"Free yourself," Tommy said.

"You sit here inhaling dust like what kind of statue."

"Equestrian," Eleanor said.

"An equestrian statue in the park."

"True. My situation is even more unreal than yours. At least you move about. I sit here with my crumbling paper. There's a poetic revenge in all this."

"What revenge?"

A hummingbird's breath of a smile brushed across Tommy's lips.

322

"The revenge of popular culture on those who take it too seriously."

The remark had an impact. Marvin felt a thing in his chest like a Korean in pajamas who's crushing a brick with the striking surface of his hand. But then he thought, How can I not be serious? What's not to be serious about? What could I take more seriously than this? And what's the point of waking up in the morning if you don't try to match the enormousness of the known forces in the world with something powerful in your own life?

He knew Eleanor wanted to leave. He knew Eleanor was thinking, At least Marvin keeps the basement neat.

There was something he had to buy first. A small empty box semi-discarded in a corner, marked Spalding Official National League Number 1—it once held a new baseball, many years ago. And he would save it for the time when the old used bruised ball came into his possession, if and when.

He reached up to pay the man. Hung on the wall was a photograph of President Carter and his daughter what's-her-name standing in the Rose Garden with Bobby Thomson and Ralph Branca, a strained smile on every face.

They went out to the street. A woman in rags pushed her belongings in a shopping cart, seemingly bent on a specific destination. Was there a family waiting, was she a commuter of the future, did people live unknown to us in the crawlspaces of the what, the infrastructure, down the tunnels and under the bridge approaches?

"Tommy looks so happy. How is that possible, living in the dark?"

"Pick up your feet, Marv. You're healthy, not sick."

"Alone in that dungeon every day."

"Does he have a wife and children?"

"I don't know. Who would ask? That's not a question we ask in the memorabilia field."

"Does he enjoy the amenities, do you think, of our basic way of life?"

"You say that word terrific."

"Does he have a little backyard where he grows Jersey tomatoes every summer?"

"I look at him I don't think I see a tomato looking back."

"Does he take his bride on business trips?"

Eleanor knew how to make him feel lucky. And she was right, she was nearly always right, the tomatoes, the cleaning business, the house with the spacious basement, the daughter who hadn't caused them major aggravation by doing something stealthy out of wedlock. Think of Tommy eating Cambodian takeout in his shop at midnight. Think of Avram in Gorki walking down the hall with the kitchen tap every time he wanted to take a bath.

They found a taxi idling in front of an old flophouse.

But in truth, let's be honest, it was Marvin who shuffled, Marvin who was the true schlimazel, bad-lucked in his own mind, Marvin the Dodger fan, doomed in ways he did not wish to name.

A police car went by with its siren going, a rotary slurping noise, it sounded like the blender in their kitchen—she made fruit shakes compulsively that they felt morally bound to drink.

Time to think about going to bed. But first he took her dancing in the penthouse lounge of their hotel, an intimate room with a combo, well past midnight.

They moved across the floor, swayed and dipped—not really dipped but only showed a pause, a formal statement that such a thing as a dip could happen here. They liked to dance, were good together, used to go dancing but forgot, let the habit slip away through the years the way you forget a certain food you used to devour, like charlotte russes when they were popular.

She ran her hand through his fire-resistant hair.

And Marvin held her close and felt the old disbelief of how they'd found a life together, such fundamentally different people even if they weren't, and he knew the force of this disbelief was the exact same thing, if you could measure it, as being stunned by love.

But in the deep currents, in the Marvinness of his unnamed depths, there was still an obscure something that caused disquiet.

And when they danced past the window he looked out at the lights of the Bay Bridge spotting through the mist and saw the old forlorn tanker snug in its berth, pungent and shunned, and he counted over to pier 7 and found that the Lucky Argus was already off-loaded and gone, borne on the tide, a dark shape going at what, flank speed, in the great deep danger of night.

3

The club was not exactly jumping. There were seven patrons, counting Sims and me, and four guys on the bandstand—a goateed sax and his hunchy sidemen.

I didn't know where we were, it might have been Long Beach or Santa Monica or some blurry suburban somewhere. This was the third club we'd stopped at and my scant sense of bearing lay in ruins. Big Sims was not talkative tonight, racing through the landscape with dark determination, half a drink and out the door, like a man assigned a task in an epic poem.

"Hey Sims. Go home, okay? You're not enjoying the music. I don't want you to think."

"The music's okay. It's music."

"But don't think you have to show me the sights. Go home. I'll stay a while and grab a cab."

"Go home."

"Go home. That's right. But first tell me who you're mad at."

"This isn't mad. If you think this is mad," he said.

An elderly fellow brought our drinks, a guy with a wad of cotton in one nostril. He had a T-shirt that read Monday Night Football at Roy Earley's Loins and Ribs. It wasn't Monday and we weren't there.

I said, "What happened?"

"What happened. What happens at home?"

"You had a fight with Greta."

"Forget it," he said. "Drink up."

"These guys ain't half bad."

"It's music. Drink up," he said.

"Your stomach's knotted up."

"The fact is we never fight."

"You never fight. Marian and I never fight. So when it happens."

"You retain it in the body."

"You feel a knot, a weight."

"We never frigging fight."

"We never fight, Marian and I. Go home and make up. I'll call a cab. Can I call a cab from here?"

"You're going a little gray," he said.

"You're going a little bald."

"I'm going a lot bald. But you're going a little gray."

The tenor was hitting cubist notes and we'd had a number of half drinks and the drummer was firing rim shots or whatever they do and in the local noise and the wider dislocation of a nightscape that was unfamiliar, I tried to understand what Sims was saying.

"Seriously, go home. I'm fine. I like these guys. It's hard-driving stuff."

"It's race music," he said.

"It's hard-driving free-wheeling jazz."

"It's race music. You like it for what you want to like it for. I'll like it for what I want to like it for. I'll show you this picture I've got at home. Great photograph, circa I don't know, nineteen-fifties. Charlie Parker in a white suit in some club somewhere. Great, great, great picture."

"A club in New York."

He gave me a flat-eyed look.

"You know this?"

"Great picture," I said.

"Wait. You know this? A club in New York?"

"He's wearing a white suit and those shoes I can never remember what they're called."

Out of nowhere I thought about how our faces changed, how I tried to spy out a sign in another man's eye that would tell me how worried I ought to be but at the same time how I avoided eye contact until I'd had a chance to gain a certain purchase on the situation and how we seemed to agree together, as the room whistled and groaned, that if we all carried the same face we would be free from any harm.

"Can I call a cab from here? Go home. Make up with her. Don't subject the episode to ten hours of neurotic scrutiny."

"Go home."

"Go home. What are those shoes called that I'm trying to think of? Tell her you're sorry. Don't let it fester. Old-fashioned two-tone shoes."

He looked at me, measuring.

"We'll go to a ball game sometime. You're coming back in a few months, right? We'll go to a game."

"I don't want to go to a game."

"We'll go to a game," he said.

We drank up and left. In less than fifteen minutes we were in another club listening to hornplayers rake the walls, four guys in fezzes and caftans with a physical sound and a drummer who's making mostly vocal noise, off-pitch wails and cries.

We ordered drinks and listened a while and then Sims leaned in closer.

"Happen to me twice since I been out here. Pull their guns. My life held in some cop's bent finger because I resemble a suspect or my taillight's out. And he's out of the car. And he gets me out of the car. He says, I need you to get out of the car right now. And I get out of the car. And he says, I need you to hit the roof and spread them wide. But I just look at him. And he looks at me. We look at each other with a longing to kill that's completely puzzling in one sense and completely natural in another."

I nod and wait. He sits very serious over his drink, Sims.

"You want to be my friend, you have to listen to this," he said.

The walls were decorated with old Pacific Jazz album covers and we turned our heads toward the bandstand and felt the force of the music, a sophisticated jazz that had the texture of life-and-death argument.

I told him, "Yes." I said, "Yes, I'm going a little gray. But I don't understand why this is worse than all-out bald. Which is your own admitted destiny."

"That's the point."

"What point? A little gray is not the most ominous thing that happens to a man."

"Let's get rolling, okay?"

"Why?"

"There's a place."

"I'm enjoying this place."

"I'm showing you some things, okay? You have to accept this," he said. "I'm here, you're not."

"All right. But you ought to go home. Tell her you're sorry."

"I want you to know something about us."

"What?"

"We never fight."

"We never fight either. Our friends fight."

"That's why I'm twisted up inside."

"I hear you talking."

"Then let's roll," he said.

The next place was in downtown L.A. Downtown L.A.—the term had a secret life I couldn't clearly read. The group was between sets and a haze of ten-year-old smoke hung over the room.

"I played the horn. You know that?"

"Still play?"

"An old hockshop horn. Threw it away finally."

"But you still have it."

"Threw it away," he said.

"But you kept it. You still have it."

"Threw it away."

"You didn't keep it?"

"What for? It sounded like hell."

"Great thing to have. An old trumpet? They're not called saddle shoes by the way. Those aren't the shoes I mean when I talk about two-tone shoes."

"It sounded like the death and burial of music."

"Jerk. You should have kept it."

"Wait. I'm a jerk?"

"Great thing to have. You keep things like that. A secondhand horn? Great thing."

"Wait."

"Big mistake, Sims."

"I'm a jerk?"

The pianist came out first, then the bass. The drummer wore a headband and dark glasses.

"The ship's back," he said. "You know that?"

"No."

"Up the coast in San Francisco."

"Who tells you these things?"

"You know how rumors work. Nobody tells you. You just hear."

"What do you hear about the cargo?"

"That's a whole other deal," Sims said, slipping into the forced-air voice of a used-car salesman, and a cracker at that, and a laugh shot out of me. "That's real innerestin. That's the sweetest deal about this whole buncha rumors."

The horn finally showed, a rangy man with a gold chain and a gap in his front teeth, wearing resort clothes and sandals.

"They said it was heroin. They said it was the CIA moving heroin to finance some covert operation. But we didn't believe this, you and I."

"Because we're responsible men."

"And we were right," Sims said. "Because it's not heroin. It's not toxic chemicals, it's not industrial ash and it's not heroin."

"What is it?"

"It's a mixup over a word. That's what it is."

"Which word?"

"You know what heroin's called. It's called scag, it's called horse, it's called H, it's called smack, it's called this, it's called that. And what else, Nick?"

"Called shit."

"See, it's not a boatload of heroin. It's a boatload of shit."

We were momentarily alert and uncircling. It was one of those episodes of heightened clarity in a night of talking and drinking.

"At one point, am I right, the rumor suggested it wasn't an ordinary cargo ship."

"A sludge tanker. Turns out the rumor was correct."

"Carrying treated human waste."

"Port to port, it's nearly two years," he said.

We listened to the music, a cash register ringing at the end of the bar and a trace of a radio voice, radio or TV, coming from a back room somewhere.

"Tell her you're sorry. Go home, Sims."

"Maybe she ought to tell me."

"Tell her first."

"Maybe I'm not the guilty party. Ever think of that? The instigator."

"Doesn't matter, you jerk."

"That's the second time," he said, showing me two fingers.

We got out of there and went somewhere else, zebra walls and small tables, a fairly crowded room with a body hum, people in aviator glasses and silver shirts.

"He's wearing a white suit."

"Right."

"He's playing his alto."

"Right."

"And he's facing out of the picture, out of the frame."

"And he's wearing white and brown shoes. Two-tone shoes. But they're not saddle shoes."

"I didn't ask what kind of shoes. I don't care about his shoes."

"I'm just saying."

"I'm not interested in his shoes."

"They have a name I'm trying to think of."

"Do it somewhere else."

"In a club in New York," I said.

"You know this? And I don't? And it's my photograph? In my house we're talking about?"

The waiter brought drinks.

"Look. Go home, tell her you're sorry, take a bath and go to bed."

He looked at me, underlip jutting.

"There's something else."

"What's that?" I said.

"A judge issued an order, an injunction that they couldn't dump the sludge because there's a body buried there," Sims said, and took a drink, and pulled a cigar out of his pocket.

"Whose body?"

"Whose body. Whose body do you want it to be? That's whose body. Some mobster, I hear. Shot in the head execution-style."

A trio with a singer. She had streaky reddish hair and copper skin, holding the mike at her spangled thigh while the sidemen cued the next verse.

"We never fight. Our friends fight," I said.

When the set ended a fatigue passed over us, a staleness. Sims blew smoke past my shoulder. I jabbed an ice cube in my drink, poked it with a finger and watched it bob.

"There's this man I knew once. I didn't know him, I met him once. I was young," I said. "He came around the poolroom."

"You're speaking in reference to what?"

"To the body in the sludge."

"A mob figure. Who was he?"

"I was young, high-school age. I only talked to him that one time. But my father had known him years earlier, which he told me about. Badalato told me, not my father. They weren't friends, they were acquaintances. They might run into each other somewhere."

"This is Mario, you're talking about, Badalato? Who I saw one time on TV," he said, "when they're putting him in an unmarked car to take him to be arraigned and some detective places a hand on his head to keep him from bumping his head on the door frame and I sit there thinking why is it the police put so much effort into keeping these criminals from bumping their heads when they get into police cars, it's a major concern of the police, lately, this hand on the head."

"You're talkative all of a sudden."

"He's always being photographed on the courthouse steps. He's the king of the steps."

"You're right. Let's leave," I said.

"Your father knew him. This means—what?"

"It means he knew him."

"In other words I have to show respect. I have to be reverent when I mention his name. This guy who runs a criminal enterprise in narcotics, extortion, what else. Murder, attempted murder, what else."

"Waste carting," I said.

"Could be. Why not? And I have to respect him. Because he was nice to your father."

"You're right. Let's leave," I said.

"I didn't say I wanted to leave. I don't want to leave."

"Tell her you're sorry and take a bath," I told him.

Half an hour later we were in the last club of the night, a blues room with an air of desperation, and the waiter resembled the old guy from two or three places ago, facially resembled—he wore a standard waiter's getup but looked a lot, I thought, like the other guy, in the football T-shirt, three or four places ago, or whenever it was, the T-shirt and cotton nose plug.

"This place reminds me. You know how they're always saying, Where were you when such and such? Where were you when Kennedy? Well, remember the time the lights went out. This place reminds me. The great Northeast blackout."

"Am I supposed to ask where you were?" he said.

"Thirty million people affected."

"I was in Germany. I never knew what caused it. What caused it?"

"Nobody remembers. Thirty million people. Not one of us remembers."

"But you remember where you were."

"Ask me where I was. I was in a bar that was a little like this place," I said. "Dead souls, sad jazz. Palm trees painted on the wall."

"This place doesn't have palm trees on the wall."

"Even better, even more similar. And the lights went out."

"They made a movie. I was in Germany," he said.

"Maybe they didn't have jazz at this other place. Maybe they used to have jazz but stopped. They had a jazz policy that became a policy of no jazz, which is much the same thing if you examine it closely."

He didn't resemble the old guy from three or four places ago. That's not who he resembled at all. He resembled the cabdriver I'd hailed earlier in the day, or the day before, the guy who'd said, "Light up a Lucky. It's light-up time."

When they put me in the squad car, or maybe they called it a radio car then, it was a green and white vehicle in any case and the cop who drove was smoking, which he wasn't supposed to do, a uniformed cop on duty was not supposed to smoke, and it surprised me to see this, I remember, an officer cupping a smoke between his knees, because I'd shot a man dead and thought I was being taken into a system where the rules were consistent and strict, and the other thing I remember is that no one put a hand on my head and folded me into the car because evidently this was not something they did at the time, this was something they developed later, preventing the felon from bumping his head when they took him in.

This happened back east of course. I've heard that term a lot since coming to this part of the country. But I never think of the term as a marker of geography. It's a reference to time, a statement about time, about all the densities of being and experience, it's time disguised, it's light-up time, shifting smoky time tricked out as some locus of stable arrangement. When people use that term they're talking about the way things used to be before they moved out here, the way the world used to be, not just New Jersey or South Philly, or before their parents moved, or grandparents, and about the way things still exist in some private relativity theory, some smoky shifting mind dimension, or before the other men and women came this way, the ones in Conestoga wagons, a term we learned in grade school, a back-east term, stemming from the place where the wagons were made.

The room was very nearly empty and they were playing blues.

"Be nice to her," I said. "Go home, talk to her, make nice. You know this phrase? Make nice. They use this phrase when you were a Negro child in St. Louis, Sims?"

"They came to take the census."

"Yes, and what?"

"And my mother told me to hide."

"What for?"

"What for. That's the point. I didn't know what for. She thought, I don't know what she thought. I went and hid, you know. Two people at the door with clipboards. She said, Get inside, stay down."

"Stay down."

"She said, Stay down. I don't know what I thought and I don't know what she thought."

"It was only the census."

"Don't say only the census."

"You tell me I'm going a little gray. And I'm supposed to understand how this is worse than total baldness."

"Because it's in my history, it's in my family," he said. "I'm supposed to go bald. It's expected of me. Stay down, she said."

"Stay down."

"You believe the census, Nick?"

He sat there with his loosened tie and wrinkled jacket, relighting the discontinued cigar, a line of sundown pink visible above the jut of his lower lip.

"What do you want me to say? Yes, I believe it. No, I don't believe it."

"I want you to say what you believe."

"Because I can sense we're about to enter some touchy area."

"What do you believe?" he said.

"I believe the census. Why shouldn't I believe it?"

He gave me a flat-eyed look with a nice tightness to it.

"You believe it."

"Why shouldn't I believe it?"

"You believe the numbers. You believe there's only twenty-five million, for example, black people in America."

"Why shouldn't I believe it?"

"You believe it then."

"If that's the number, that's the number."

"And you don't think they might be underplaying the true number."

"Wait a minute."

"You don't think."

"Wait wait wait wait wait wait."

"Think about it," he said.

He plucked his shirt, he did a thing big men do, he used both hands to pluck his shirt away from his chest and then he shook it, half dainty, letting his upper body breathe.

"Sims, you and I."

"Just think about it."

"We're not, remember, we don't have a word, you and I, for the science of dark forces. For what is behind an event. We don't accept the validity of this word or this science. Remember that conversation?"

"This is another conversation. And in this conversation I'm saying, Think about it."

"But you and I. We go against the tide, Sims. The tide is easy, it's irresponsible. We're responsible men. We've established this. We don't believe there are secret forces undermining our lives."

"Thirty million people affected by your local blackout. But only twenty-five million, they're saying, black people in the whole huge country."

"If that's the number, that's the number."

"And this is all you can say. We have an issue that's crying out for, really, scrutiny, to use one of your words."

"Go ahead, scrutinize it."

"You're willing to accept this number."

"Twenty-five million. Yes, why not?"

"You don't think this number is way too low."

"Twenty-five million's not so low. It's twenty-five million," I said.

"You don't think this number is totally underreported."

"Why do you say scrutiny is my word?"

"Because you used it."

"This makes it my word?"

"I didn't use it. You used it."

"I believe the number. It's a believable number to me."

"You don't think somebody's afraid that if the real number is reported, white people gonna go weak in the knees and black people gonna get all pumped up with, Hey we oughta be gettin' more of this and more of that and more of the other."

"You and I," I said.

"You don't think the number is underinflated by maybe forty percent."

"We don't indulge ourselves in cheap and easy delusions, Sims."

"Cheap and easy."

"Am I right? You and I. We don't believe that what is behind an event is so organized and sinister that we have to make a science out of it."

"You don't think white people gonna be so depressed, so, I hate to say it, menaced by the true number."

He didn't hate to say it at all.

"You think the census bureau is hiding ten million black people," I said.

"Not hiding the people. They're hiding the number. This is an easy thing to hide."

"But a number so large. What a tremendous manipulation. And it's going on in front of our eyes. Maybe it's the mothers," I said. "Ten million mothers telling their kids to stay down. Stay down," I said.

A brief smile from Big Sims, a reflex smile minus the ensuing brightness of eye.

"Face the issue," he said.

"What's the issue?"

"We have a right to know how many of us there are."

"But you do know."

"We don't know. Because the number is too dangerous. How threatened do you feel by the real number? I'm talking to you. Think into your own heart."

"All right, I'm thinking."

"Tell me in your heart you don't think there's something genuine in what I'm saying."

"There's genuine paranoia. That's the only genuine anything I can see here."

He seemed to take pleasure in this. He sat back and looked off to the side, grimly happy, examining what there might be in the nature of human exchange that makes people so smoothly predictable.

I listened to the blues trumpet, a young guy in a beat-up suit, he had an African blackness, you know the saturate blacking of a bandwidth somewhere on the continent, some nomad swath of high desert grace and shape, but in gesture and stance, I saw, the way he tongued some spittle off his lip between riffs, a body demotic that was locally made—he was another scuffling trumpet from an inner city somewhere.

"Charlie Parker in a white suit in a club in New York," I said.

"Now how many references to New York have I heard from you tonight?"

"And I know what kind of shoes he's wearing."

"I don't care what kind of shoes he's wearing."

"Spectator shoes."

"I don't care what kind of shoes he's wearing."

"They're not saddle shoes. They're called spectator shoes."

"I don't care what they're called."

"Look. Here's what you do," I told him. "You go home, you say you're sorry, you put some fizzy stuff in your bathtub and you take a bath and go to bed."

Ten minutes later we were standing outside the club waiting for someone to bring the car around and Sims put his hands on my shoulders and head-butted me.

I didn't know how to take this.

He gave me a tight grin and butted me high on the forehead and I didn't know if this was an impulsive gesture at the end of a long night when you're muzzy with booze and hoarse with talk and smoke, a thing that brings an evening to a formal close, or something a little more deliberate.

I pushed his arms away and butted him back, put my hands on his shoulders and butted him back and he looked at me with interest and did it again.

It hurt of course, it set off a throb, it was a monosyllabic thing, a butt, a blow, a downward driving shock that sent an electric pain through the back of the head and into the neck and shoulders.

And it was up close, eyeball tight, a combat space without maneuvering room or finer points, a certain amount of acted rancor filling the visual field, a scowl and glare, or a hooded look, a sort of sleepy killer thing, lidded and dumb.

I was taller than Sims but not so solid and volumed and I'd never used my head as an instrument of medieval siege.

I butted him just above the nose, driving down, and it stung him, I could tell, it sent a message unit ringing through his skull.

He jolted me good. He hit me so hard I was stunned backwards half stumbling, right out of his grip on my shoulders, and the guy showed up with the car and stood by to watch.

The pain was electric and compact, reducing everything to its own sort of benumbment, making the world beyond my head seem small and dazed.

This is what we did, we hairlined in, blocking out everything but the butting and glaring and pain.

When he butted me again I moved my head, eased back a quarter inch, trying to tone the blow a little, and he jutted his chin and glared.

Pain is just another form of information.

We knocked heads one more time, one time each, and the guy stood there with the car keys, watching.

In my hotel room I looked in the mirror above the washbasin. I put both hands to the wall and leaned into the mirror and saw bruises and welts, deep discolorations, and a slash of dried blood with a winy flush around it. I used cold water to clean the wounds and then I went to bed. But I felt dizzy as soon as my head hit the pillow and I had to sit in a chair for an hour before the feeling passed.

The thing kept coming back to me and I tried to get inside it, inside the tremor, our faces sort of double-framed over the ice cubes in our drinks, flying out of focus, then in again—not to detail my own feelings but only to understand the hidden triggers of experience, the little delves and swerves that make a state of being.

We ran through smogged-out hollows past houses stilted over raw defiles and we ran into wooded areas that had the look of tinder, a dry white dusty stillness, a sense of combustible edge, but maybe not—I might have been devising my own newsreel.

338

"What do you hear about the body in the sludge?"

"They won't find a body. The body's just another embellishment," he said. "The main thing is the ship itself."

"What about it?"

"A ship being on the high seas for two years, changing names and crews—that's just a story too. The ship made one recent voyage, East Coast to West Coast. Carrying sludge to California to deliver to a composting operation. Ordinary simple shipment."

We ran along city streets, landscaped avenues of a certain fallen aura, an out-of-timeness that was ravishing in its open regret.

"Look, Sims, here's the thing."

"Let's run," he said.

"I don't know. I'm a little, and I shouldn't say this, I know, to someone like you."

"Love your kids, right?"

"Yes of course."

"Then run," he said.

"How close I am, some of the time, I sometimes think, as much as I love them all, to feeling like an imposter. Because it has not fucking, ever, been something I am comfortable with."

We stood in the kitchen wasted by miles of hills and hot pavement, reluctant to move about for fear of dripping sweat on something, two men in shorts, and Greta gave us glasses of water, a brown-haired woman with long hands and a half-hidden gauntness, a sort of lean and angular suchness, an x-ray Greta that probably showed itself in argument or stress.

"You like this place?" I said.

"I think I'm at the ends of the earth. Four years we are here and I am waking up every morning and trying to remember where I am. So far from everything."

"We are backed up," Sims said, "to a very big ocean."

And the son, the five-year-old, sitting at the table with his cereal bowl and oversized spoon, Loyal Branson Biggs, a boy so softly handsome, so offhandedly blessed with expressive beauty that I could not stop looking at him, I looked at him while I spoke to his parents and they looked at him too and they looked because I was looking—I reminded them to renew their sense of amazement in the child.

"What happened to your face?" Greta said to me.

I looked at Loyal work his spoon through the lumpy milk.

"Well, this is a good question actually."

"And what is the answer?" she said.

"Well, I had a little scuffle in the elevator. It's noticeable? At my hotel. I didn't know the marks still showed. Two drunks. A white guy and a black guy."

I could feel Sims enjoy this in his hot Reeboks.

"Nick started the fight," he told her.

"This is true?"

She said it to me but she was looking at the child eat his breakfast. We were all looking at Loyal.

"They told him he was going a little gray and he went berserk," Sims said.

Greta had to take the child to school and then she had to go to her own school where she taught chemistry three days a week with the ocean at her back.

Sims and I stood on our spots, drinking water.

"You two still mad?" I said.

"She's still mad. I got over it."

"I have a plane to catch," I told him.

He showered and dressed and took me to my hotel and I hurried through a shower and got dressed and grabbed my bag and got back in the car and there was a man on the freeway, a man on an embankment, nodding his head to drive-time radio, and he sat on the grass with an object across his knees and Sims said it was a rifle and I said it was a crutch, one of those metal crutches with a forearm brace, and it took me a couple of seconds to understand that Sims was kidding—this was just the language of the freeway.

I found southern California too interesting. The experimental aircraft, the fault systems, the inferno of cars and smog, the women from nowhere, even the street gangs that were coming into prominence at the time, adopting varsity colors. I made business trips but kept them brief and blinkered, after the first one. The place had that edge-of-everything quality that creeps into innocuous remarks and becomes the vanguard of estranged feeling.

When I shot George Manza I began to understand the nature of this kind of feeling. They put me in a radio car with a cop who smoked and they sent me eventually to a facility in upstate New York, a place that featured one of the oddities of the penal system. This was a miniature golf course, nine holes, with cartoon turrets and windmills—we were youthful offenders, you see, and maybe the guidance counselors thought we'd take snug comfort in the nursery shapes and bright colors or in the anal stuff of balls and holes. I don't know. I didn't know then and I don't know now. But my mates and I, the D-felonies, the E-felonies, the head breakers, the thieves in the night, a mixed group as you'd imagine, with races, creeds, cries in the dark— we used to amble past the windows in the mess and look at the layout down there with its loopedy-loops and tunnels and puddle lakes, its sward of tinsel grass, and we called it California.

Phoenix was a neater package for me. I needed a private life. How could you have a private life in a place where all your isolated feelings are out in the open, where the tension in your heart, the thing you've been able to restrict to small closed rooms is everywhere exposed to the whitish light and grown so large and firmly fixed that you can't separate it from the landscape and sky?

I walked in the door and Marian said, "What happened to your face?"

I walk in the door and this is what I hear, children playing, radio playing, the news, the traffic, the phone is ringing, the washer is pumping through a cycle.

I smiled and kissed her and she picked up the phone. The kids were making noise out back, our kids and the neighbor's kids, a game made up by Lainie—I knew this from the quality of the shrieks. Lainie made up fiendish games, inventive shrill spectacles of torture and humiliation.

"What did you do to your hair?"

"Had it cut. You like?" she said, still on the phone with someone. "What happened to your face?"

I walk in the door and see light strike the cool walls and bring out

341

the color in the carpets, the apricots and clarets, the amazing topaz golds.

I told Marian the next night about the thing I'd done, or the night after that, the thing with Donna at Mojave Springs. I thought I had to tell her. I owed it to her. I told her for our sake, for the good of the marriage. She was in bed reading when I told her. I'd anguished about the right time to tell her and then I told her suddenly, without immediate forethought. I didn't tell her what I'd said to Donna, or why Donna was at the hotel, and she didn't ask. I stood near the armchair with my shirt in my hand and I thought she took it well. She understood it was an isolated thing with a stranger in a hotel, a brief episode, finished forever. I told her I felt compelled to speak. I told her it was hard to speak about the matter but not as hard as withholding the truth and she nodded when I said this. I thought she took it fairly well. She didn't ask me to tell her anything more than I'd told her. There was an air of tact in the room, a sensitivity to feelings. I stood by the chair and waited for her to turn the page so I could get undressed and go to bed.

And the first available Saturday, the first Saturday I didn't go to the office, we drove south with the kids to see an ancient ruin.

We had sunscreen and hats and drinking water, which was Marian's idea, the water was, because this was desert scrub and the heat was intense.

Lainie stood behind the front seat, sometimes elbowed forward between Marian and me, leaning toward the windshield, quick to point out stupid maneuvers by other drivers. She reacted angrily to this, a habit that drained my own anger, and Marian's too, and prompted us to make excuses for the stupid and dangerous moves she pointed out.

Jeff was two years younger, he was six and liked to curl in a corner of the backseat, curl and twist, slide toward the floor in an astral separation from everything around him, using his body to daydream.

Even if it wasn't a rifle, what was he doing on the freeway, on the grassy verge, sitting there with a metal crutch in his lap just yards from that madman traffic?

The ancient ruin was over six hundred years old, a single major structure with smaller scattered remains and a trace of a wall somewhere. We stood in the late morning heat and listened to a park ranger for a few minutes before we drifted off, one by one, although there was nothing else, essentially, to see.

I read a plaque and then watched Jeff stalk a ground squirrel. He wasn't wearing his hat but I didn't say anything, I just thought, Tough shit kid, don't say we didn't warn you. Then I relented and called him over and gave him the car keys. The effort to relent, the effort to slacken and yield, to love him in his careless slouch, this was a brutally difficult thing to do, small as it seems, small and fleeting—it was surprisingly hard. But I called him over and gave him the car keys, I knew he would like this idea, and told him to get his hat and lock the car and bring me the keys, and off he went, happy as I'd ever seen him.

I drifted back to the main structure and stood among a dozen tourists and listened to the ranger talk, a heavyset woman who scratched her elbow. No one knew the purpose of this structure, she told us, which was three stories high with a faint trace of graffiti near the top. I found I was more interested in the protective canopy than I was in the ancient structure. The ranger said the building was abandoned about a hundred years after it was built, the building and the whole settlement abandoned for no discernible reason, one of those mysteries of a whole people who disappear. But I found myself studying the protective canopy with its great canted columns, maybe seventy feet tall, and the latticed framework that supported the roof.

Lainie came and stood next to me, sort of collapsed against my haunch in a way that meant she was irreversibly bored.

The ranger listed some reasons why the people might have disappeared, the desert dwellers. She named flooding, she named drought, she named invasion, but these were only guesses, she said—no one had a clue to the real reasons.

I thought of Jesse Detwiler, the garbage archaeologist, and wondered if he might suggest that the people abandoned the settlement because they were pushed out by waste, because they had no room to live and breathe, surrounded by their own mounting garbage, and it was nice in a way to think it was true, one of those romantic desert mysteries and the answer's staring us in the face.

I was becoming Simslike, too soon, seeing garbage everywhere or reading it into a situation.

I told Lainie to go find her brother and see what he'd done with the car keys. Then we started home like a ragged band of pilgrims who'd failed to see the statue weep.

We were in the car ten minutes when Marian began to cry. She was at the wheel and her face lit up and she started crying softly. Lainie backed off from her standing station just behind us and took a seat by the window, hands folded in her lap. Jeff got interested in the scenery.

I said, "Want me to drive?"

And she shook her head no.

I said, "Let me drive, I'll drive."

And she gestured no, she preferred to drive, this is what she wanted.

We were on a back road flanked by saguaros and wildflowers, notched saguaros, pecked by birds that nested there, and then we reached the interstate and edged into the windblast of streaming traffic.

No last names, no echoing second thoughts. This is the pact of casual sex. But I told her my last name and it wasn't casual, was it? That's the odd dominant of the piece, that I wanted to reach her, still her breathing, to make her breathless, yes. There was something about Donna that untongue-tied me. Guilt later, feeling Marian next to me, asleep in the dark.

When we disliked each other, usually after an evening out, driving home, feeling routinely sick of the other's face and voice, down to intonation, down to the sparest nuance of gesture because you've seen it a thousand times and it tells you far too much for all its thrift, tells you everything, in fact, that's wrong—when we experienced this, Marian and I, we thought it was because we'd exhausted our meaning, the force that drives the alliance. Evenings out were a provocation. But we hadn't exhausted anything really—there were things unspent and untold and left hanging and this is where Marian felt denied.

Marian in her Big Ten town, raised safely, protected from the swarm of street life and feeling deprived because of it—privileged and deprived, an American sort of thing. All the scenes she recoiled from when she watched TV, the narrative of local crime, we see the body in the street, the lament of the relatives, the suspect doubled over to conceal himself—

344

Marian could not even watch the detective's hand on the suspect's head, bending him into the unmarked car. It was all a violence, a damage to the spirit. But she wanted my stories, my things, the fiercer the better.

I was selfish about the past, selfish and protective. I didn't know how to bring Marian into those years. And I think silence is the condition you accept as the judgment on your crimes.

She said it was her mother, she said it was two years ago today that her mother died and I repeated it for the kids and the kids relaxed a little. I reached back and got a stick of gum from Lainie. Two years ago today and of course Marian knew this and we didn't, I didn't, I hadn't kept track, and I felt relieved and the kids did too because at least there was a reason, at least it wasn't a thing where the parents act funny and the children learn to make their faces blank.

She shone brilliantly, she glowed in her weeping, she smiled, I think—a smile that was a wince but also a real smile, with her mother in it somewhere.

After a while the kids started to sing.

And I was relieved, I was goddamn glad because I'd sat there thinking I was to blame or thinking maybe she does it all the time because how the hell do I know what goes on when I'm not home.

And the kids were singing, "Ninety-nine bottles of beer on the wall, ninety-nine bottles of beer, if one of the bottles should happen to fall, ninety-eight bottles of beer on the wall. Ninety-eight bottles of beer on the wall, ninety-eight bottles of beer."

She looked at me and looked at the road and the kids kept singing, counting backwards all the way to one as Marian drove—cried and drove.

MANX MARTIN 2

The super comes gimping toward him. Before he takes five steps along the street the super comes gimping toward him from a building down the block, moving with that hip-lurch of his that takes up half a sidewalk.

"Been looking for you," the man says.

Manx Martin stands with folded arms, not bothering to cock his head just yet—a little early for gestures of the superior type.

"You seen those shovels?"

"What shovels?" Manx says.

"Because they're missing out of the basement."

"Things always missing. Bought a new pair of socks missing in the wash."

"Two snow shovels from the utility room standing against the wall this morning."

"We expecting snow?" Manx says.

And he looks heavenward. Look like snow to you? Don't look like snow to me. Weatherman say snow?

349

"Gone by noon, right out the door. And I'm asking up and down the street."

"You ought to be more careful who you ask. Because some people touchy on the subject."

"I'm asking you because I hear things."

The super is wearing a light shirt in this chill. Manx smells the change of season, the bite of wet and the cutting wind, and the man's standing here with his sleeves rolled up, getting on in years, the super, with stubble specked a little white.

"Somebody tells me straight out," he says to Manx. "Talk to the klepto."

"You're saying to my face."

"I'm saying what I hear."

"Who you hear it from?"

"And I'm saying those shovels worth good money. Those are tools I need to do my job. Those blades, understand. Try pushing snow with a coal shovel."

Manx is surprised by the super's attitude, knocked a little off-balance. The super seems determined. Should be the landlord's problem. Why run around doing detective work? Let the landlord go into his pocket for replacements. Those pockets so deep the man's knees get skinned by rattling change.

Someone stands on the corner preaching to the wind.

Manx is also surprised by the super's forearms. Got some strength in those arms, wrestling garbage cans, you know, rolling the cans diagonal across the pavement.

"I think you got your business backwards," Manx says. "Because what we see in this block of buildings is buildings getting robbed, not shovels getting robbed. They breaking in left and right."

"I'm telling you what I hear."

"And I'm saying this is the thing you ought to be occupying your time. Jimmy guards on the doors."

"I find out you took those shovels I go to the landlord and you're out on the street, brother."

Awful biggity for a cripple.

"Because he will listen when I talk."

350

Most janitors around here are floaters who work in one neighborhood and then another, come and go, staying one step ahead of something. This man's dug in like infantry.

"You and me, we're through passing the time," he says. "You show up at my door with a shovel in your right hand and a shovel in your left, then I listen to what you say."

Manx cocks his head, makes his eyes go tight in phonied concentration. He's looking to stare the man down, put the man in his place.

But the super pushes on past. Manx is leaning into the man but the man pushes on past, clumsily, every step a contortion and a labor, and Manx is fazed once more—he was just getting set to make a major statement.

He walks over toward Amsterdam Avenue. Three kids run by, going like hellfire, and he sees Franzo Cooper in a suit and tie, standing by the shoe repair.

"Who died? You're all dressed up, Franzo."

Turning as he speaks, wanting one last look at the super, he's not sure why, to shoot a beam of evil, maybe.

"You seen my brother?" Franzo says.

He's wearing a hat with a little feather in the band and his shoes have a military shine. The neon shoe is out of juice.

"I'm going to Tally's."

"You see him, tell him I need his car."

"Who died, Franzo?"

"I need to go to Jersey to see a lady. Else I die. What you doing?"

"Nothing much."

"I die of lovesick, man. Tell him to get over here with that junkheap. Be worth his while."

There's the beauty school, the shoe repair, the furnished rooms and over the door of the shoe repair there's a neon highshoe and the neon, he sees, is dark and cold, which brings him down a ways, a little sag in his mood.

The traffic stops and rolls at the corner, rolls on into the night, and a man stands by the rib joint preaching. Three or four people stop a minute and get the drift and stand another minute and go where they're going and two or three others come and listen and leave and the cars roll past and the light changes and the cars roll on.

The preacher says, "They say that only insects survive."

He's an old man with a hungry head, veined at the temples, and his hands are coming out of his sleeves. The sleeves of his jacket are so shrunk down that you can see way up his wrists. Long flat fingers marking his words and bicycle clips on his pants.

Three kids race by, like fleeing the scene.

"This is what they say and I believe them because they study the matter. All the creatures God put on earth, only insects survive the radiation. They have scientists studying the cockroach every second of his life. They watch him when he sleeps. He comes through a crack in the wall, there's a man with a magnifying glass been waiting since dawn. And I believe them when they say the insects still be here after the atom bombs will fell the buildings and destroy the people and kill the birds and the animals and masculate the dogs and cats so they can't begat their young. I believe them in and out and up and down. But I also got news for them. I know this before they do. We all know this, standing here right now, because we veterans of a particular place. Do we need somebody telling us how insects survive the blast? Don't we know this from the morning we born? I'm talking to you. Nobody here need scientific proof that insects be the last living things. They already pretty close. We dying all the time, these roaches still climbing the walls and coming out the cracks."

Manx glances back the other way. He'd like to get one last look at the super to nourish his grudge.

People stop to get the street preacher's drift, six or seven folks standing in the wind. Manx looks at the old man in his cuffed pants like some uniform a boy invents, playing army. There's something thin-skulled about him, his head is naked and veined and papery. A man listens, interested, in a French hat, a black beret, and two women in those sister outfits, sister so-and-so from the storefront church, glad to meetcha, with napkins on their heads and frown faces.

"Nobody knows the day or the hour."

Two men in suits and their well-dressed wives, the men want to listen, the ladies say no thanks—cockroach talk is not their deedly-dee.

"Russians explode an atom bomb on the other side of the world. You got your radio tuned to the news? I'm telling you the news. Clear across the world. And you're standing there saying don't mean nothing to me. Old business, you're saying. The business of the generals and the diplomats. But right now, this here minute, while I'm talking and you're listening, officials making plans to build bomb shelters all over this city. Building bomb shelters that hold twenty-five thousand people under the streets of this city. And guess what you don't hear on today's news. You have to stand in the wind and hear it from me. Every one of those people standing in those shelters while the bombs raining down is a white person. I'm talking to you. Because not one single shelter's being built in Harlem. All right. They're putting shelters on the Upper East Side. They're putting shelters down lower Sixth Avenue. They're sheltering Forty-second Street all right. They're putting shelters out in Queens all right. They're sheltering Wall Street deep and dry. A-bombs raining from the sky, what are you supposed to do? Take a bus downtown?"

Manx has a faint grin.

A girl's standing there with her boyfriend and she says, "He's a agitator, let's go."

Manx can appreciate the man's argument but it's a little removed. The argument is satisfying because it's the multiplying into millions of the little do's and don'ts he carries around every day.

She says, "He's a agitator, let's go."

But it's the do's and don'ts he has to live with, not the news of the world with that rooster that goes scraw scraw in the movie house down the street.

The man's still talking, standing tall and with a whippy kind of bend in his body, a head like a hatched egg that's all veined out, and three kids race by, and a face so naked you think you've known him all your life, pants cuffed tight, and some kids race by.

"Where's your bicycle, man?"

And the boyfriend's got his cap slung low, not moving from the spot, and the girlfriend's saying, "He's a agitator, let's go."

The man's swiveling his head to catch an eye somewhere.

"They say stop paying rent. I don't say stop paying rent. I don't say blow up the gas and electric, the power and light. They say walk the landlords to the river. I don't say walk the landlords to the river or

353

stand them up against the wall. I say take a dollar bill out of your pocket where it's folded up tight because you been saving it for this and that. Unfold this dollar bill and turn it over to the backside where they keep their secret messages. They keep their Latin words and their Roman numbers."

And the man takes a wadded bill out of his pocket and unfolds it like a magic trick and then he waves the money at the group in front of him.

"You see the eye that hangs over this pyramid here. What's pyramids doing on American money? You see the number they got strung out at the base of this pyramid. This is how they flash their Masonic codes to each other. This is Freemason, the passwords and handshakes. This is Rosicrucian, the beam of light. This is webs and scribbles all over the bill, front and the back, that contains a message. This is not just rigamarole and cooked spaghetti. They predicting the day and the hour. They telling each other when the time is come. You can't find the answer in the Bible or the Bill of Rights. I'm talking to you. I'm saying history is written on the commonest piece of paper in your pocket."

And he holds the bill by its edges and extends his elbows, showing the thing for what it is.

"I've been studying this dollar bill for fifteen years. Take it to the privy when I do my hygiene. And I worked those numbers and those letters all whichway and I hold the bill to the light and I read it underwater and I'm getting closer every day to breaking the code."

And he draws the dollar to his chest and folds it five times and puts it in his pocket, smaller than a postage stamp.

"This is why they're watching me with that eye that floats over the top of the pyramid. They're watching and they're following all the time."

Manx needs a drink. He hurries up Amsterdam past a TV-radio store where a TV is flickering and half a dozen people are watching in the cold. About a block away he see some guys running toward him, grown men, you know, pounding over the sidewalk, over the iron hatchways that lead to storage cellars, rattling the metal as they come, and he sees they're sort of half laughing, they're embarrassed, must be a crap game down an alley that the police broke up, and they go past him rattling the hatchways and looking back, running and half laughing and looking back.

He almost wants to turn around and run with them. He sees the humor of it. They'll meet in some doorway three blocks away laughing and panting and catching their breath, feeling grown-up stupid, and they'll find a place to do their gambling, the back room of a barbershop or someone's living room if the wife's not there.

But the wife is there.

Because I got a wife can't stand the sight of me even if I'm ten miles away, and will not let me breathe without a comment, and makes more comments in her head, and she is definitely there.

A dog looks out a first-floor window.

Yeah, black men running in the streets. Manx found himself running in the '43 riot and he probably had that same look on his face, conscious of being caught up in something he shouldn't be doing but doing it anyway, running past Orkin's where Ivie bought a sample coat, a coat a dummy used to wear, on sale cheap, and it rankled his mind all right, and all the Orkin's dummies were on the sidewalk now, torsos tumbled in the gutter, and heads without bodies, and slim necks and pale hair, and dummies armless like famous statues. He recalls this now, the big windows busted and dummies in garters, dummy legs in stockings and garters and kids in tuxedos, men running in the streets and a kid maybe twelve years old in a top hat and looted tux and a cop was leading him to a prowl car, funniest damn thing, top hat and tails and dragging pants—even the cop had a sweetheart smile.

He goes the last four blocks with his head turned away from the wind and the wind is whipping off the Hudson and Manx is walking like a horse with a spooked head.

But how different once you step inside the bar. The warm buzz, the easy breathing, the rumps happy on their stools. The buzz in Tally's is special tonight, more bodies than the usual midweek slump and more static in the air—and then he remembers. There's a tone, a telling rustle in the room and he pats the side of his jacket and feels the baseball and understands that they're talking about the game.

He waves to Phil, who's behind the bar, Tally's brother, in his plain

355

shirt and fancy suspenders, and he gestures a question *where*—and Phil nods toward the far corner and there is Antoine Cooper sitting with a drink in front of him and two tall shovels leaned on the wall behind.

Manx sits across from Antoine, sits sideways in his chair so he doesn't have to look at the shovels.

"I seen Franzo standing in the dark."

"I know it. He wants my car. But he can't have it."

"What's that you're drinking?"

"He's looking to make some chick he's better off avoiding. Trust me. I already done her."

Manx looks around the room, takes in the buzz, hears half a sentence fly up out of shared laughter and he decides not to mention the shovels. He is aghast at the shovels. The shovels should not be here in any manner, way, shape or form. But he decides for now he won't say a word.

"What was that riot in forty-three? I'm trying to recall how it started. They filled so many holding cells in so many station houses they had to open an armory."

"Forty-three. I'm in the army, man."

"They had bleeding men carrying their loot under armed guard. Put them in an armory on Park Avenue."

"We had our own riot," Antoine says.

Manx goes to the bar and gets a Seagram's from Phil—he likes his rye in a short glass with a single ice cube.

Phil says, "What's happening?"

"I hear they played a ball game today."

"Goddamn it was something."

Manx carries the drink back to the table with one hand clutching the glass in the usual manner and the palm of the other hand under the glass, supporting it like some polished object in a church.

The ice cube is mainly scenery.

Antoine says, "How the boys doing?"

"The boys. The boys spread far and wide," Manx says. "Randall's in the South somewhere, bivouacking, you know, training in the field. And Vernon."

"I know where Vernon's at."

"Vernon's on the front line is where he's at. They got a quarter million troops they're looking at across the line. Them Chinese."

"What division he's with?"

"What division."

"Second Infantry's in Korea," Antoine says.

"I don't know what division."

"You don't follow the war?"

"What's that you're drinking?"

"I like to follow the war. They plot their strategies."

"They blow horns and whistles, that's their strategy, them Chinese. They come charging down in swoops."

"This here's brandy, my man. Drinking imported tonight."

"It's sitting there a little potent," Manx says.

"Only in the glass. Goes down the hatch real smooth."

"They come in swoops. That's their strategy."

"You say a prayer now and then. That's what you do."

"Sure, Antoine. I kneel by the bedside."

"You done okay with your kids."

"Sure, Antoine. They take care of me in my old age."

"You got some work?"

"They come visit me in the old folks. Slip me a bottle through the gate."

"You done okay, considering."

"Rosie's the one. That's a great girl. That's the only one that shows respect."

"You need some work. Change your temperament around. You're walking on eggs lately."

"They're laying off. They're not hiring. They're laying off."

"You need to get into long-distance moving."

"They bring me a cake on my birthday," Manx says.

"Long-distance, that's the ticket. I got a cousin in Alabama, which he's based in Birmingham, gets plenty of work long-hauling furniture and whatnot."

"I keep that in mind."

"Yellow yams from Birmingham."

"I place that on my list of things I need to think about."

"Greenest greens you ever seen," Antoine says a little croony.

Manx decides he can't contain it any longer. But he doesn't look at Antoine. He looks across the room at one of those wall lamps, the old-fashioned-type lamp bracketed to the wall where the sleeves that hold the bulbs have fake candle wax running down the sides.

And he says, "Shit man you got those shovels in plain sight."

Antoine has a long slick head and narrow neck, a man of schemes and contrivances, called Snake when he was younger, and he determines it is necessary to turn his upper body to the wall behind him so he can identify the objects in question. Oh yeah, these things, for shoveling off the patio after a white Christmas.

And he turns back to Manx real low in his chair so he's peering out confidentially over his drink.

"I don't think there's an FBI bulletin circulating tristate. What do you think?"

"I think they belong in your car, like we stated."

"The point is you got to raise your sights. Because these things don't bring no return."

"We stated beforehand, Antoine."

"Not worth arguing. You're right, I'm wrong. But you got to raise your sights."

They sit drinking a while and Manx thinks about leaving but he doesn't move off the chair. He thinks about taking his shovels and leaving but he sits there because once he gets up and takes the shovels off the wall he is committed to walking the full length of the barroom with two large snow shovels in early October, and no place sensible to take them, and the thought of it, and the sight of it, keeps his ass in the chair.

Instead he takes out the baseball and sets it on the table. Then he waits for Antoine to take some time out of his busy day so he can notice.

"My kid brought it home from the game, my youngest, says it's the home run that won the game."

"That game they played today?"

"That's right," Manx says.

"I seen people on Seventh Avenue hollering up and down. Hands pressed on their horns, hollering out the windows. I said to Willie Mabrey. You know Willie? I said, They must be opening the vaults. The banks opening up their vaults. First come first serve. I said, Let's go get ours."

"My youngest. He come home with the ball. This is the ball what's-his-name hit in the stands. The game winner. Win the pennant."

Manx feels uneasy, he feels separated from what he's saying—it comes out of his mouth like a lie, the way a lie hangs in the air independent of right and wrong, making you feel you're not responsible.

He feels an urge to take the ball off the table and put it back in his pocket.

"This is the ball what's-his-name? What you saying exactly?"

"I'm saying it could be worth something."

"And I'm saying raise your sights. Because the circumstantial fact, you can't prove nothing. And who do you sell it to anyway?"

"I sell it to the ball club. They want it for a trophy. They make a display."

"Let me look at this thing. This thing's all smudged up."

Manx realizes he doesn't want Antoine to touch the ball. Antoine will look at the ball and say something that's a bringdown, something that gets Manx riley and griped, and he is already feeling tense enough, with his stomach acting up.

He takes the ball and puts it in his pocket.

Antoine leans back, hands up and palms facing out, showing his old snakehead smile, cool and mean.

"Tell you something. Maybe you sell the thing somewhere. But I don't think you be buying a sofa from Ludwig Bauman's," he says. "Or a pretty di-*nette*."

Manx goes to the bar to drink in peace. After a while Phil comes over and they talk a while. The place is quieter now, down to serious drinkers, they talk about the game. Phil is a straight-up guy, barn-sized, looks you in the eye. He talks about the game and Manx listens carefully, hoping for an angle, something to go on. The Dodgers are finished for the year. Dead and buried. The Giants play in the World Series starting tomorrow—starting today, Phil says, checking his watch, because it's past midnight now.

359

"Who they playing in the Series?"

"Yankees, who else?"

"All New York in other words."

"All New York series. And people already lining up for tickets. Heard it on the radio. All night they'll be lining up. Sleeping bags, you know. I love to go myself."

"All night?" Manx says.

"People do anything to see this series, the way the Giants got in."

Manx likes the sound of that. People do anything. He tells Phil to pour one for himself, knowing the man will decline, he always declines, and Manx feels a little snakelike, caught it from Antoine.

He goes back to the table with a little shuffle in his step.

"You leave your brother standing in the cold."

"I know it," Antoine says.

"He wants the car one night is all."

"I'm doing him a favor. Because that lady he's looking to make is all kinds of two-faced."

"Let him find out for himself. He's a young guy looking for some action."

"See, you're not a jealous man. Let me explain something. I'm a jealous man. When I say jealous I mean the full meaning of the word. Everybody jealous," Antoine says. "The word don't mean shit unless you give it the full meaning. It needs a adjective. Like crazy jealous or can't-think-straight jealous. So if I say I'm jealous, you have to picture eyeballs filled with blood."

"You already done with her. What do you care? He's a good boy, Franzo. Let him learn."

"Let him find out, you mean. Because he won't learn nothing."

But Antoine seems to soften. He eases toward the tabletop, elbows spread, his chin nearly touching the brandy glass.

"Yeah I like that boy a lot. He's a good boy, Franzo. But I got my car in an awkward position."

"You wrap it around a pole?"

"You know Willie Mabrey?"

"Don't think so," Manx says.

"Willie and I been talking about my car. A way to make some fast cash. I ain't broke per se. But I can use some hurry in my income." Sipping his brandy. "And this here's my first payment in advance. Go down smooth. The cream de la cream."

"Payment for what?"

"Willie opened a restaurant about six weeks ago. Doing okay. But he's got a problem with his garbage. The city's talking about private companies coming in to pick up this trash. But right now the city does it and there's an ordinance about what time of day or night a restaurant can leave garbage on the street. You can't leave it there all night."

"Smells bad."

"Smells bad, attracts vermin. And if you keep it on the premises, you have a situation where the rats talking to the customers."

"So you made an arrangement with the man."

"Me and my car both."

"Which this reminds me," Manx says. "You mind give me a lift?"

"Take you anywhere," Antoine says.

They drain their glasses and get up and sort of shake themselves out, shake off the complacent airs and humors of the tavern and rearouse themselves for whatever's out there, the edgy wind-spooked street.

Antoine gets into his jacket and rolls his shoulders and zips the jacket to the throat. He cuffs his nuts for good measure, aligning for comfort and symmetry, placing them squarely at the center of the world. Manx is already wearing his jacket, he never took his jacket off, he's been wearing his jacket since he left the house in the morning, drinking in it, eating dinner in it, washing the dinner dish, and he zips it to the throat and sinks into the hull, the shell, already a little lightweight for the season.

They wave to Phil on the way out. They walk down to the end of the block, where the car is parked. Manx goes around to the passenger side and puts his hand on the door handle and then he stops and looks.

Antoine says, "Get in, man. Faster you get in, faster we move. Where you want to go?"

Manx is looking. He looks in the window at the rear seat and it is filled with garbage. He'd smelled it when he walked down the street but this is not an unoccurring smell and he took it for the general thing it was, garbage in an alleyway or empty lot. Now he sees it is

Antoine's car that smells, it is Antoine's car packed with mounds of ripe trash.

"Oh man. Sheesh. I misdescribed this in my mind. Because I thought."

"Get in, man. Friggin cold tonight."

There is garbage in paper bags and cardboard boxes. There are two metal garbage cans wedged between the front and rear seats, regulation street-size cans with dented tops sort of erupted up by the pressure. Manx sees garbage stowed on the ledge by the rear window. He sees front-seat garbage in a peach crate smack on the seat, the oozy smell so near you can drink it.

"I thought you were on your way to get the man's trash and take it somewhere."

"Took it here. Trash right here. I filled up the trunk while they were still eating their dinner. Then I started on the inside of the car, working backseat to front seat. Move the crate and get in."

Manx opens the door and sets the peach crate on the mat and sits down, trying to find room for his feet on either side of the crate.

"Where you want to go?" Antoine says.

"Not far. But fast. Up by One Fifty-fifth Street. Where you taking this stuff?"

"Drive it to the Bronx. There's a tower of garbage under the Whitestone Bridge somewhere. I fling the trash out the door and press the gas pedal hard."

"You do me a favor and press it now," Manx tells him. "Because I'm about to die sitting here conferring."

"Be calm. I take you where you going."

Antoine puts the vehicle in motion. He drives steady and unfazed, pointing the car up Broadway like a poison dart.

Manx realizes this is why the snow shovels were not in the car, where he'd told Antoine to put them. No room for shovels in the car.

Then he realizes they left the shovels in the barroom. Good a place as any. Except they won't be there tomorrow. So cross that little caper off the slate.

The last thing he realizes is that Antoine's been telling him all night to raise his sights. And him driving a DeSoto full of garbage.

"You drop me just up ahead there."

"I take you exactly where you're going."

"Broadway be fine," Manx says.

The stink is killing him, lifting him out of the insulated state of a day's slow whiskey burn.

The trash is bumping and mashing around and it has a life of its own, a kind of seething vegetable menace that pushes up out of the cans and boxes, it's noisy and restless, or maybe that's just the vermin moving around, on the verge of being carsick.

"This here's fine," Manx says. "Right at the corner."

"You're not gonna tell me where you're going?"

"I tell you where you're going if you want to take this trash to the Whitestone Bridge. You cross the river and get on One Sixty-first, which I think it runs two ways, and you take it to Bruckner, you be okay, Boulevard."

Antoine looks at him. Manx is already out of the car and he's standing on the sidewalk and Antoine looks at him, sitting unfazed at the wheel. A long lazy snake-eye look.

"Or I could dump it in the street."

"That's what I thought. That's what I said to myself."

"While the city sleeps," Antoine says. "And the cops be eating their chowder."

Manx watches the car move off. The feel of empty streets after midnight and the wind off the Hudson as he walks east. The hawk at his back. The cutting wind that sends loose trash skidding in the street.

Could be Antoine unleashing early.

He'd like to see an Alka-Seltzer is what he'd like to see, sizzling down the length of a cold glass of water.

He walks down the long ramp with the ballpark on his left, the Polo Grounds, and he looks for people standing in line or huddled on the pavement with blankets and food, the all-nighters, the men and boys eager for tickets, the kids who get paid by scalpers to stand in the cold and buy tickets that desperate fans will haggle over next day, paying prices out of sight.

The place is deadly still. And Manx has a stale acid feeling, that fidgety indigestion where you drink too much on an empty stomach, even though he knows he ate a meal, he recalls the dish Ivie left him, he tastes the meat loaf and greens, but there's a wrenching pull like he's all sucked dry.

He's down on Eighth Avenue now wandering the perimeter of the ballpark, looking for a sign that someone's still alive. The place is stone cold quiet.

What's a pyramid doing on a U.S. bill? That's a question you do well to ask.

The only thing he sees is a dog of the slinking type, been kicked so often it decides it's being petted. He can't understand how Phil could be wrong about this. Phil's a straight-up guy. If Phil says the fans will be lining up all night to buy tickets and then you go there and look around and the place is deadly still, you have to wonder who's messing with your head.

It is frankly a fly-by-night moving and storage. They call him and he works, they don't and he don't.

Now he sees a car stopped for a light and he walks on over, sliding his feet the way he does when things get culminated on him. A man sits at the wheel. He sees Manx coming and rolls up the window, a white man with a look on his face like I ain't ready to die. Manx makes a motion with his hands. He shakes his hands in the air, no no no no— I only want to ask a question. And the man hits the pedal and he's gone, never mind the light's still red, burning rubber real impressive.

The sound dies into the night stillness and a deep quiet comes on again. The old ballpark stands over the avenue and makes its own enormous silence, different from the street and the river. Kids still swim in the Harlem River in the summer, way uptown where it turns out of the Hudson, and his own boys used to leap off a dock, arms all flung—he sees them momentarily in midair.

It grieves the bejesus out of him.

He feels a little empty. He feels low and put off and frankly humanly disgusted and he wants to lie down and sleep. He feels a little messed with. He wants to somehow, from someone, make some money.

One chance in ten million the ball club even lets him in the door. He has to find the paying fans. And he only walked toward the car to ask where they are. And the face at the wheel, like don't cut me up in little pieces please.

He looks across 155th Street, south to the tenements, and he sees a woman standing under the Power of Prayer sign, soliciting her trade.

He hears a sound across the river.

What's the point of all the secret codes on a U.S. dollar except to disconnect you from the people who know the facts?

He hears something. He's ready to head home, there's nowhere to go but home unless he finds another bar, and he knows he has to go down the subway and wait for a train in an empty station, another bringdown, stand there on the long platform waiting, half an hour maybe, and he hears a sound from across the river, far away but clear, the way voices travel exact on the water at night.

He stands near the bridge approach and listens. Men singing, the sound of a great many voices, some following behind the others, rambunctious and uneven, and he knows the tune.

They're singing, Riding on a pony.

They're singing, Stuck a feather in his cap.

They're singing, Called it macaroni.

And he hears laughter drift across the river and begins to understand finally. It wasn't the bartender who made the mistake. Phil never said the people would be lining up at the Polo Grounds. He never named the ballpark. It was Manx who made the mistake. Because they're lining up at Yankee Stadium just across the river. It's the Giants versus the Yankees at Yankee Stadium and the voices travel so exact it's like someone's whispering just to him.

He hears a group of fans chanting Say Hey Willie and of course those are Giant fans and that's Willie Mays they're singing his praises.

And he hears the answering chant from the Yankee fans with that old Joltin' Joe DiMaggio song from before the war, he thinks, that they were playing on every radio in the country, *we want you on our side*, and it's all rough-and-tumble and good-natured and his mood picks up and he gives the ball a smack with the palm of his hand where it's tucked in his jacket pocket, the perfect roundness and hardness of an object that's substantial.

He walks across the swing bridge and hears them in the streets and then he begins to see them. They're walking across the public park to the stadium, across the fields and pathways, and they're coming down from the elevated train, men and boys in long streams turning the bends in the high stairways, and they're laughing and singing.

He sees flags waving on the stadium roof and World Series bunting hung high on the outer wall. He sees fires on the pavement, they're building fires in fifty-five-gallon drums, and he is struck a little dumb by the masses of people out to buy tickets at this time of night. His mouth hangs a little open and he is wide-eyed dumb. He paces himself to the crowd, feeling pulled along, feeling frankly happy to be among them, and they're carrying food and chairs, webbed chairs for the beach that fold up light, and they have sleeping bags strapped to their backs, a dozen college boys with their hair clipped short, and they're passing thermos bottles that smoke up when you screw off the lid, strong coffee to keep them awake and warm.

He sees fathers and sons standing around the fires to warm themselves, masses of people if you could count them, and mounted police with horses breathing steam, and he feels a rare elation, a wanting-to-be-among-them, and he is pulled along a little slack-jawed because it's a great thing to see, and they're singing roaring warring songs, they're back-and-forthing on the street with rough-and-tumble humor, all these ball fans striding toward the ticket lines at two or three in the morning or whatever the actual hour.

Manx is wearing a watch that stopped running six weeks ago. This is a situation he will direct his attention to when his life gets back to being regular.

PART 4

COCKSUCKER
BLUES

1

It was the rooftop summer, drinks or dinner, a wedged garden with a wrought iron table that's spored along its curved legs with oxide blight, and maybe those are old French roses climbing the chimney pot, a color called maiden's blush, or a long terrace with a slate surface and birch trees in copper tubs and the laughter of a dozen people sounding small and precious in the night, floating over the cold soup toward skylights and domes and water tanks, or a hurry-up lunch, an old friend, beach chairs and takeout Chinese and how the snapdragons smell buttery in the sun.

This was Klara Sax's summer at the roofline. She found a hidden city above the grid of fever streets. Walk and Dont Walk. Ten million bobbing heads that ride above the tideline of taxi stripes, all brainwaved differently, and yes the street abounds in idiosyncrasy, in the human veer, but you have to go to roof level to see the thing distinct, preserved in masonry and brass. She looked across the crowded sky of ventilators and antennas and suddenly there's a quirk, some unaccountable gesture that isolates itself. Angels with butterfly wings tucked under a cornice on Bleecker Street. Or the mystery of a white clapboard cottage on the roof of an office building. Or the odd deco heads, sort of Easter Islandish, attached to the corners of a midtown tower. She found these things encouraging, dozens such that hung unauthored, with bridge cables in the distance and occasional booming skies, the false storms of summer.

She was fifty-four now, let that number rumble in your head—fifty-four and between projects and humanly invisible and waiting to go back to work, to make and shape and modify and build.

The World Trade Center was under construction, already towering, twin-towering, with cranes tilted at the summits and work elevators sliding up the flanks. She saw it almost everywhere she went. She ate a meal and drank a glass of wine and walked to the rail or ledge and there it usually was, bulked up at the funneled end of the island, and a man stood next to her one evening, early, drinks on the roof of a gallery building—about sixty, she thought, portly and jowled but also sleek in a way, assured and contained and hard-polished, a substantial sort, European.

"I think of it as one, not two," she said. "Even though there are clearly two towers. It's a single entity, isn't it?"

"Very terrible thing but you have to look at it, I think."

"Yes, you have to look."

And they were out of ideas for a while, standing at the ledge and taking in the baleful view together, uncomfortably, she thought, because esthetic judgments feel superficial when you share them with a stranger, and finally she sensed a rustle, a disturbance in his bearing that was meant to mark a change of subject, earnest and determined, and he said to her, still looking toward the towers, he whispered actually, "I like your work, you know."

"Yes?"

"Very sympathetic."

It was so humid some nights you could not close your door. You had to shoulder your door closed. Bridges expanded and sidewalks cracked and there was garbage in the streets and you had to sort of talk to your door before it would close for you.

She loved the nights that were electrical, a static in the air and lightning in soft pulses, in great shapeless beats, you can almost read the rhythmic pattern, slow and protoplasmal, and maybe a Cinzano awning fixed to a table on a higher terrace—you can't identify that gunshot sound until you spot the striped awning, edges snapping in the breeze.

Klara was happy in a guarded way, keeping it folded close. She had a sense of being favored, fairly well-regarded for recent work, feeling good again after a spell of back pain and insomnia, clear-minded after a brief depression, saving her money after a spending spree, getting out and seeing friends and standing at parapets, quietly happy, looking better than she had in years—they all said so.

It was the time of Nixon's fall from office but she didn't enjoy it the way her friends did. Nixon made her think of her father, another man of frazzled mind, rehearsed in his very step, his physical address, bitter and distant at times, with a loser's bent frame, all head and hands.

She stood at parapets and wondered who had worked the stones, shaped these details of the suavest nuance, chevrons and rosettes, urns on balustrades, the classical swags of fruit, the scroll brackets supporting a balcony, and she thought they must have been immigrants, Italian stone carvers probably, unremembered, artists anonymous of the early century, buried in the sky.

She wasn't used to being recognized. She was recognized in certain situations but only rarely and it made her feel that someone was taking measurements of her body in a small mirrored room. She tended to be unseen except by friends. She was mostly invisible, humanly invisible to people in the market down the street and not just youngsters hurrying past a hazy shape in the aisles, the unfocused stuff of middle age, but people in general—okay, men in general—who gave her generic status at best.

It was not an issue. She wasn't lonely or unloved. Well, she was unloved in the deeper senses of the word but that was fine, she'd had enough love of the deeper types, painful and ever echoing, the rancorous marriages that make it hard for you to earn a dependable solitude. It was a curiosity only, and a bracing form of self-awareness, learning to be unseen.

Miles Lightman came around a lot that summer. There was something about Miles that made her think he ate off dirty dishes but she began to get used to him, to like him a lot—he was kinetic and unreflective, essentially artless, blank to the schemes of conceit that ruin many a budding love.

She wore long ruffled skirts, she wore denim skirts with floriated hems.

She stood on the roof of a factory building, a space made available for the evening so that a small theater group might launch a fund drive, and fifty people drank tepid wine out of plastic cups and said, We need theater.

She was near the ledge talking to a woman she didn't know and at some point she understood that the building she was facing, about ten blocks uptown, an oldish tower with a massed midsection and mosaic summit, was the Fred F. French Building.

And she tried to listen to the woman but could not concentrate because the name lit up her brain, one of those deep sheer flashes that take forty years to happen.

Fred F. French. She had to tell the story to Miles because it was funny and screwy and she wanted to give in to it completely, get it out and work it around and pile on the details. Boy-crazy Rochelle and the horny boy in the backseat and she was in it too, of course, Klara Sachs without the *x*, how she walked and talked, how things were real and she was real in ways she'd forgotten how to be.

From the tall windows of her loft she saw fire escapes angled and stepped, this was her principal view, dark metal structures intersecting in depth over the back alleys, and she wondered if these lines might tell her something.

Lofts were maybe dangerous, she thought, but not for fires—spacious and pillared and memoried and grand. She had to watch for ego creeping in. She had to ask herself would you do this piece a truer way if you worked in a stunted garret somewhere. She tried to scale her work to the human figure even though it wasn't figural. She was wary of ego, hero, heights and size.

That was the stuff of rooftop eloquence. Admire but do not emulate.

Her daughter was in town and they walked around the cast-iron district and had lunch in the Village and they shopped a little bit and it was hard. It was always hard with Teresa, she had an air of deprivation and a plainness that seemed obstinate—she was overweight and willfully unpretty and seemed to be saying that daddy loves me exactly the way I am but my mother doesn't, my mother thinks I can be better and smarter and know better and smarter people.

She heard those shots and then looked up and saw the Cinzano awning and realized the fringes were flapping in the river wind.

Teresa was twenty-five but looked ageless and shapeless and the hardest part of the visit for Klara was sitting in the loft talking, or waiting out the silences, or finding out her daughter took sugar in her tea and not having sugar in the house.

"You should visit daddy," Teresa said.

And this is spoken as a provocation, a form of censure that has nothing to do with a train ride to the Bronx.

"That's not a good idea. Trust me."

"I can't believe you live in the same city and you never once."

"Frankly I could live on the same street. It's not a question of where we live, you know? There's nothing to be gained and he knows it and I know it."

She leaves unsaid the fact that Teresa knows it too.

"Why does something have to be gained? Why is there always this thing of a gain?"

"So many years, Teresa. What's the point?"

Another silence now of tea things clinking and trucks at the loading platforms along the street, those trucks with dented metal sides and no company names.

"You don't have any Sweet 'n Low, even?"

Klara looked out the windows at the fire escapes, the backsides of gray buildings, what a gleaning of sheened iron and rust fungus and scaly brick.

"How is he?" she said.

"What? He's all right. He won't move to a new building. That building is getting to be ridiculous that he's in now."

Everywhere they walked there was garbage stacked in black bags. They were seven days into the strike, which included a number of violent incidents and one private hauler nearly beaten to death. Teresa said nothing about the mounds of trash, fifty bags in some places, because she lived in Vermont and what could she say? But she used the trash against her mother. The trash was another form of accusation, it passed telepathically between them, a hundred bags on one corner and a smell so summer-lush it enveloped the whole body, pressing in like a weather system.

In the loft Teresa said, "He listens to opera all day long. All summer until school's back in. He wants Aunt Laura to move in with him. She's getting, I don't know, not senile, just a little shaky, Laura, but I think she'd rather live alone."

Klara could hear the drag in her daughter's voice, the old mauled vowels, and how odd to hear these neighborhood noises so close to hand and from her own child, who seemed to exaggerate the slur, the loitering quality of the accent, a form of inflection and pronunciation her father and mother had escaped—that is the word, escaped—as if the young woman needed to go one boundary farther back, one level deeper into the life of the streets to make some point about constancy and faith.

She'd been pulling color out of her work for years. For a while she used bitumen and house paint. She liked to mix colors in clamshells she'd brought back from Maine a dozen years ago. But there was less color to mix now. It felt right for her to pull it out.

She walked down to the market past another new gallery, there were galleries and shops now but the cast-iron facades were safe from the wreckers, that was the main thing—the old factories where immigrants made buttons and suits, women and girls working eighteen-hour days, and she bought a box of sugar in the market before she forgets and ten months go by and Teresa turns up again.

Art in which the moment is heroic, American art, the do-it-now, the fuck-the-past—she could not follow that. She could look at it and respect it, envy it, even, in a way, but not, herself, place hand to object and make some furious now, some brilliant jack-off gesture that asserts an independence.

She said to a friend on the phone, her friend and dealer Esther Winship, who was always ready to advise a painter or sculptor, to bully the washy artist into a sound strategy, some plan for clear action, when in fact it was Esther who needed help, Esther in her bosslady trousseau, her pearls and pinstripe suits, who was losing painters and getting squeezed by her landlord uptown and feeling sorry for herself, and she said to Esther on the phone, "Hey, look, I'll start working again if you'll invite me to the country."

"Never mind the country. I want you to take me to the Bronx."

"What's in the Bronx?"

"A kid who does graffiti. He does trains, subways, whole trains, he does every car in a subway train. I want to sign him up and show his work. But I have to find him first."

"How do you show his work?"

"I'll give him a wall," she said.

Klara had to admit she liked the sound of that. Maybe it was the first stage of saying, I'll give him a building, I'll give him a city block. That's the way Esther wanted it to sound. You live longer and sleep better if you can say things like that. I'll give him a train with a hundred cars.

"Why do you need help finding him?"

"I don't know his name. I only know his tag. Moonman 157."

"Sounds familiar," Klara said.

"You've seen it. Everybody's seen it. The kid's a goddamn master."

She loved the water tanks she saw from the roofs, perched everywhere, old brown wood with tops like coolie hats. They often built the tanks right on site, the way you make a barrel, grooved staves bound with metal hoops, and of course the twin towers in the distance, a model of behemoth mass production, units that roll identically off

377

the line and end up in your supermarket, stamped with the day's prices.

Miles was younger than Klara, eight or nine years maybe, and looked even younger than that, so free of responsibility, engagement with real things, that he struck her as an ever welcome and weightless state, someone who happens by, almost always late but it almost never matters kind of person.

He was usually in jeans and lizard-skin boots and he had bad skin and a beautiful bent nose and wore his hair raked straight back and lived in a room and a half on the Upper West Side with reels of film and things from his life still packed in boxes—just things, you know, stuff you carry with you and keep because it's a form of mind clutter that you are comfortable with.

He worked for a movie distributor part-time and also produced documentaries, or coproduced, or made phone calls, and it was a process that carried just enough slanting light to make it renewably futile. He arranged screenings for a film society as well. And he saw everything, collected movie posters and lobby cards, could recite the filmographies of the obscurest directors because the more obscure the figure, of course, the more valuable the knowledge. This has always been a point of honor in the business.

And this summer he was trying to put together financing for a documentary about a woman who contracted the illnesses and diseases of celebrities. Through some odd form of neurohypnosis, or whatever the term, this woman, who lived in Normal, Illinois—this made her irresistible—showed the symptoms of whatever illness Elizabeth Taylor was suffering at a particular time, or John Wayne, or Jackie Onassis, or name your star, from a fluey sort of fatigue to the skin eruptions of herpes simplex and the wasted frame of cancer.

It was the modern stigmata. And doctors sponsored by the tabloids were studying her. And Miles wanted to title the film, if he could put it together, nice and simple—*Normal Illinois.*

·　　·　　·

378

Her hair fell freely to both sides of her face, more or less untended to, sort of chop-cut at the bottom and going noticeably gray at the parted top. She had eyes that were set wide and bulged slightly and her brows slanted away toward her temples. She had a shy look—not shy but private and if you'd seen her alone on a roof that summer you might have thought twice before sidling up with small talk.

It was the summer of sheet lightning and red wine, those deep Bordeaux that resemble lion's blood, and she stood on rooftops and terraces and wondered how all these things could have been here so long without her ever knowing.

She loved the biplane sculpture on a roof downtown, an old mail plane maybe, full-scale, with a landing strip and lights. And the stepped pyramid atop a building on Wall Street and the machined-steel spire of the Chrysler Building and the south face of the Hotel Pierre like some scansion of rooftop Paris, only elongated many times, shot versingly skyward.

She realized how rare it was to see what stands before you, what a novelty of basic sensation in the grinding life of the city—to look across a measured space and be undistracted by signs and streetlights and taxis and scaffolding, by your own bespattered mind, sorting the data, and by the energy that hurrying people make, lunch crowds and buses and bike messengers, all that consciousness powering down the flumes of Manhattan so that it becomes impossible to see across a street to the turquoise tiles of some terra-cotta facade, a winged beast carved above the lintel.

Klara conducted dialogues with her body, reminding herself before she got out of a chair where it was she wanted to go, to the kitchen maybe for a spoon, and exactly how she would have to get there. She needed to locate her body in a situation, tell herself where she was, sometimes looking back as if she might still be sitting in the chair.

She had a full mouth that was too bunched and puckered and also slightly askew, designed to speak asides, and her voice had tonal changes that were interesting, it had dips and hollows and husky undertows.

Me and my friend Rochelle, who taught me how to smoke.

She had drinks with a few people on a high roof planted with fruit trees and scarlet runner and they watched a woman jogging on a track on top of an office tower and it made them all feel happy, the jogger in day-glo sweats and the medieval turrets in the distance and the smoke-stacks beyond that and then the river lying silky just off Brooklyn.

Klara had a slender neck and wore a chain with an amulet from North Africa, a charm against bad luck, which her second husband gave her, Jason, when they were divorced.

Miles had a fancy deck of Italian cards and taught her a game called *scopa*. They played it late at night after a dinner somewhere and a session in her bed beneath the tall windows of her loft with the intersecting steps of the fire escapes running a deep perspective down the alleys.

He asked her about the stack of floorboards in the far corner. Floorboards, burlap, lengths of rope.

She had a former student who gathered materials for her. She'd taught a class in sculpture for some years and one of her young men went to abandoned buildings, to boatyards, glazieries, he scoured the outer boroughs, went to garages and bowling alleys and came back once with a dozen old pillows from a condemned hotel, stained gray by how many transient heads—such sad and eerie objects to have around.

"You don't mind working and living under one roof?"

"It's one thing," she said.

"But don't you have to get away from it? All this stuff in here. You can't escape it. It's everywhere and it's work and you have to look at it all the time."

"I am lying here with someone whose own abode."

"I know but I don't work there. I talk on the phone at most. That's the actual extent of what I do workwise. We're screening a thing you'll want to see. Next week. I'll call you."

"Good. The movies."

She loved to swim, she went to the Y nearly every day and stroked invisibly through the water, delivering herself to the laps, the soothing pool lengths, monotonous and restoring, like the rote recitations in early school—stiffens your sense of who you are.

"The thing about summer is you feel you have the city to yourself."

"I'd like to take a few days in Sagaponack. But Esther wants me to show her the Bronx before she invites me out there."

At some point she realized that the card game she played with Miles, the game they played with the expensive deck of attenuated knaves and queens, figures of a certain sinister minimalism—she understood gradually that *scopa* was the same game she'd seen boys playing on the stoop of the building where she lived when she was married to Albert, they were Albert's own students, some of them, Mr. Bronzini's boys, and they played the game with an ordinary dog-eared deck, of course, and called it sweep.

"What's in the Bronx?" he said.

"There's a kid she's looking for. Graffiti artist."

"Graffiti writer."

"Yes, well, it's so completely everywhere, this writing."

"Tell me when you find him," Miles said.

"What for?"

"I've been thinking about a film where we follow a kid day and night into the paint stores, into the train yards, into the trains."

"Sounds like a film they've already done even if they haven't."

"They haven't," he said.

"What happened to Normal, Illinois?"

"We're going ahead, pushing to get a grant. But she's sick now."

"Of course she's sick. This is what she does, isn't it?"

"I mean sick-sick. Independent of other sources," he said.

But the laps were more effective when she was busy on a project. She didn't love swimming nearly so much when she was idle. The laps were an attachment to rigorous work, the interval that completes the octave.

When Esther gave advice and Klara submitted to it, there should have been an element of reciprocal condescension. Because Esther was usually overbearing and Klara a little offhand and glib. But in fact she needed to hear whatever Esther had to say. Esther said a number of useless things but she needed to know someone was out there preparing a space, making time for her and uttering her name and passing on stray accolades from whatever shadowy source.

It didn't always help. When Klara heard praise it sounded weak and tentative to her, badly rehearsed, and when she was criticized in the press or through the intimate roundabouts of rumor and half news, she had to struggle against the feeling that they might be right, she was doing shallow and meek and dismissable work.

"This is the Darwin dog-eat-dog," Esther liked to say, said incessantly, enjoyed saying because she knew it scared people like Klara.

She loved the floorboards stacked in the corner. Streaked brown wood, sort of drenchingly dark brown like the staved towers on the rooftops, the tanks filled with water and mostly bare to the elements but sometimes enclosed in elaborate churchly structures with lancet arches and great eagled ornamentation.

People weren't saying *Oh wow* anymore. They were saying *No way* instead and she wondered if there was something she might learn from this.

She watched her friend Acey Greene on TV, a new friend, young and talented, interviewed late at night on a local cable outlet. She looked great—you look so great, Klara thought. Modestly afro'd, in a torn dinner jacket and red bow tie.

Miles called and she met him at an old sail-making loft downtown. The film group he belonged to showed rare things, mostly unrunnable in theaters for one reason or another, and the screenings were a floating affair—wherever Miles could secure a space.

Fifty or sixty people were here to see a Robert Frank film, *Cocksucker Blues*, about the Rolling Stones on tour in America.

Klara sat in the dark and spooned yogurt from a carton. She realized she'd been seeing Mick Jagger's mouth everywhere she went for some time now. Maybe it was the corporate logo of the Western world, the leer and pout that follows you down the street—she liked to watch him dance and devil-strut but found the mouth a separate object, sort of added later for effect.

She told Acey, who sat next to her, she said, "I think everything that everybody's eaten in the last ten years has gone into that mouth."

She loved the washed blue light of the film, a kind of crepuscular light, a tunnel light that suggested an unreliable reality—not unreliable at all in fact because you have no trouble believing what you see but a subversive reality maybe, corruptive and ruinous, a beautiful tunnel blue.

"You have to interpret the mouth like it's satire," Acey said.

Coke sniffing backstage or in the tunnels and people sitting around a room or sleeping on a plane, that edge-of-time feeling, remarks half uttered, a cigarette in someone's mouth, people not yet ready to stir, and she liked the glancing sound, the way documentary sound, this kind of flyby movie, bounces off the tile walls, the cinder-block walls in dressing rooms and stadium tunnels.

Someone saying, Often he will shoot me in an unfavorable way.

And she realized yes, his mouth was completely satirical, it was caricaturish, a form of talking anus from the countercomics of the sixties, and all the jeers and taunts we'd uttered, all the half sentences we'd mumbled had come out of the same body opening, more or less.

Acey said, "I saw them in San Francisco, this is the same tour, has to be, two years ago this was."

Throwing the hotel TV off a balcony.

Interviews mumbled and blotted, the simplest of earnest rehearsed queries lost and pondered and lost again, the tour is a series of unfinished remarks, and a man and woman fucking on the plane, and the mouth chewing food, the paste-on peel-off mouth, Mick strobed and flashed in concert like some multimouth de Kooning female, sucking on the hand mike.

The camera phalanx in the tunnels. People sitting around, two people asleep in a lump or tripped out or they could be unnoticeably dead, the endless noisy boredom of the tour—tunnels and runways.

Acey said, "I went to the show and there's this bodyguard, maybe I can spot him in one of these shots, a black guy with a T-shirt that says Stones, you know, Security, only something else completely but along those similar lines."

And Klara loved the tunnel blue light and the nothing-happening parts, everybody's got cameras and they're shooting nothing happening, and the sound that gets lost in the ceiling tiles.

Someone saying, I hate those motherfuckers. Those in-between schmucks.

Saying, What state are we in?

Two mumbling junkies on a bed, a man and woman equally sort of squintingly attentive to the needle that's angled in her arm.

Saying, How come you wanted to film that?

Saying, It hadn't occurred to me to film that.

Oh Indiana.

It just happened.

Mick standing slack-jawed in room. The mouth gargling and spitting, licking ice-cream cone. And the concert footage that's gelled red, bodies bioluminescent, what we all love about rock, Klara thought, the backlit nimbus of higher dying.

Excedrin on TV, significantly more effective than common aspirin.

"And he's following me," Acey said, "down this long tunnel and he's saying, Brown sugar you wait for me because there's something I got here which I definitely want you to look at. Hey brown sugar. And I turned, which was admittedly, you know, completely dumb-ass, and he didn't have it out but he had his hand on it."

Two white men in room and one white man talking in black voice about, Put the brothers in touch with their cultural heritage. And second white man threads needle into arm and first white man talking black says, Tomb of the Unknown Junkie, a Hundred and Thirty-seventh Street and Lenox Avenue, made top to bottom, he says, from discarded spikes.

Someone saying, They took my child away from me because I was on acid.

Where's my room key?

Tunnels and runways and washed blue light and then the opening to the stage, the loud white glare and prehistoric roar.

You suck him off?

No. Just took a picture with him.

Saying, The state comes along and takes my kid from me.

And nude woman caressing herself on bed in hotel room who rubs hand on pussy then licks it. And Acey interrupting her story to say, "Mmmm."

The whole jerk-off monotonic airborne erotikon.

And Klara thought it was interesting that this was the only woman

384

who didn't seem like a girl. It was interesting, she thought, how all the women in the film were girls or became girls. The men and women did all the same things, dope, sex, picture taking, but the men stay men and the women become girls except maybe the woman who rubs her pussy and licks it and says something inaudible because the whole point of sound in a film like this is to lose it in the corners of the room.

I don't care—it's only San Diego.

Acey was telling her story and meanwhile looking for the guy in the story up there on the screen.

"And I wanted to say something to, you know, disabuse him of every wishful thought in his head. Hey brown sugar. But we were alone in this big roaring echoing place, the concert's in full roar somewhere above us and, Brown sugar, he's, Brown sugar, brown sugar."

"This show we're looking at now?" Klara said.

"I don't know if it's the same night but it's the same show, the same city, the same motherfucking band of emaciated millionaire pricks and their Negro bodyguards."

It was the rooftop summer and the air was filled with heroes, the dusty sky that burned with stormlight. Oblong gods braced in narrow corners and a pair of seated pharaohs that flank an air conditioner. And she loved the mermaided columns she saw on lower Fifth and all the oddnesses, the enigmatic figures she could not place in particular myth, mainly downtown, atop the older banks, on the parapets and setbacks—robed oracles jutting over the streets or helmeted men of unrevealing aspect, lawgivers or warriors, it was hard to tell.

And it was down there on a roof one Sunday, the streets hot and dead, that the gentleman reappeared, the European she'd talked to once before, gazing into the unfinished grid of the World Trade Center.

Yes, hello, we meet again.

And he told her that the figures she'd been wondering about with their cultic look, faces in shadow under the streamlined headgear, were called the Titans of Finance. And how suitably dour they were, as if measuring the Depression's effects on the streets below—she guessed the building had been erected around that time.

"Some kind of secret fraternal order, sounds like to me."

"Perhaps," he said. "But all banking is secret, I think."

And she could believe it, with all the granite and limestone massed around them, and the newer towers, curtained sheer, of reflecting glass and anodized aluminum, and every office empty of human trace today, except in basements maybe where paper was spun through microfilm machines, a billion checks a second.

His name was Carlo Strasser. He lived on Park Avenue and collected art with an amateur's clumsy passion, he said—an apartment on Park and an old farmhouse near Arles, where he went to do his thinking.

And of course she said, "What do you think about?"

And he said, "Money."

She laughed.

"I sometimes wonder what money is," she said.

"Yes, of course, exactly. This is the question. I will tell you what I think. It is becoming very esoteric. All waves and codes. A higher kind of intelligence. Travels at the speed of light."

He was dressed very well, he was turned out, he had presence and manner and she felt a little shambly, but not uncomfortably so, in her denim and old sandals. The man confirmed her in her partialities and she was marvelously, in fact, at ease, talking to him.

They heard foghorns in the bay and paused to listen and the sound had an element of formal awe, it rolled and caromed down the narrow streets, collided with itself, an organ work that swelled the air and sent pigeons beating out of the tower clocks.

He asked questions about painters and she did something she almost never did—she expounded, she did detailed analysis, a thing she'd tended to avoid even when she used to teach. She heard herself go into explanations so ardent and newly struck that she realized she'd been withholding them from herself.

"Louise told me once, Nevelson, that she looked at a canvas or a piece of wood and it was white and pure and virginal and no matter how much she marked it up, how many strokes and colors and images, the whole point was to return it to its virgin state, and this was the great and frightening thing."

Klara could not connect this remark to her own work but she liked to repeat it to herself anyway—she liked the idea of a famous artist being frightened by what she does.

"I have a small Nevelson," he said. "Very small piece, I bought it years ago, and now you have given me a reason to look at it in a different way, and this is something I will do with pleasure."

"I'd go into her studio and she'd show me a black sculpture, a wood sculpture painted black, and I'd comment on the color and I'd comment on the material and she'd look at the thing and she'd say, 'But it's not black and it's not wood.' She thinks reality is shallow and weak and fleeting and we're very different in that regard."

Miles showed up later and Carlo Strasser faded gracefully into the cluster, eight or nine people standing around a table filled with cheese and fruit and wine, those lion-blood Bordeaux, those damson plums and blue-black nights and how the thunder sounded dry and false.

Standing in someone's kitchen, slicing a lemon, she understood that the knife would slip and she would cut herself and she did.

It was one of those microseconds that's long and slow and nuclear-packed with information and she knew it would happen and kept on slicing and then it happened, she cut her finger and watched the blood edge out from the knife line and slide unevenly down her knuckle.

She watched people sunbathing, they did it so completely, dominating the experience, a woman flopped on a ledge with a blanket and a pitcher of iced tea and a child's drinking glass appliquéd with flowers and a paperback book that Klara tried to spy the title of—they did it without conceding anything to the stone ledges or pitched roofs or breathless tar surfaces, it was the spectacle of here I am, and there's a window washer's empty rig scaling the side of a slab tower. She saw a brick facade flushed with coral light, more or less on fire with light, and the brick seemed revealed the way only light reveals a thing—it is baked clay of some intenser beauty than she'd ever thought to notice. And there's the old lady again sitting in her webbed chair with the Sunday papers scattered, so familiar and encouraging—she holds a reflector under her chin and faces sacrificially into the sun, a plattered head going mummy-brown in the deeps of a summer day.

She watched the blood slide out from the cut and noticed the creases and whorls in her finger and heard the music in the next room, it's Esther's husband Jack playing one of his old 45s, the swing-band music that drives his guests out onto the roof.

The garbage was down there, stacked in identical black plastic bags, and she walked home past a broad mound that covered a fire hydrant and part of a bus sign and she saw how everyone agreed together not to notice.

Miles Lightman showed up late for dinner on a roof uptown, carrying a box of the black cigarettes she smoked, queen-sized and extra-mild and slow-burning, and a baggie of marijuana, which he liked to call boo, a term he'd heard in some bar in Harlem maybe twenty years ago.

They were on the roof of a new building, forty stories, it loomed over the reservoir in the park and they stood a while watching runners in the night. The runners went around the reservoir in fair numbers, faintly lamplit, and Miles thought they resembled fleeing crowds in a Japanese horror film. He had a thing for fleeing crowds. He wanted to do a picture book on the subject. He collected publicity stills from obscure productions—fleeing crowds of Asiatics looking up at something awesome.

They stood on the roof and looked across the park to the silhouetted buildings named like ocean liners. The Beresford, Majestic and Eldorado. The Ansonia and San Remo.

Fleeing crowds always included a mother with a baby and a woman with bulging breasts and a man with his arms flung up to shield him from some terror in the sky.

Miles looked at the runners going around the reservoir and he came up with a name for the forty-story building that loomed over the park, so tall and massive it made its own weather, downdrafts nearly strong enough to topple people walking by.

Godzilla Towers, he thought they ought to call it.

It's women, usually, who take the lead in recovering lost careers. When you begin to hear about a writer reemergent or a painter lovingly disinterred, it's usually because women have shown extraordinary interest, even when the artist is a man. Usually the artist is a woman, but even a man—we specialize in forgotten lives, Klara said.

She was talking to Acey Greene. Acey did not need to be reclaimed, of course. She was young, smart, ambitious and so on, and interestingly sweet-mean, playing with juxtapositions as a form of ironic dialogue with herself—a device to help her confront the prospect of being famous.

Acey grew up in Chicago, where both parents were teachers, and she began to do pen-and-ink sketches, she began to do West Indian collages pretty much in the tritest manner possible, according to her own account, and had a sexual adventure with a member of the Blackstone Rangers, a very sizable street gang, and eventually packed a bag and went to Los Angeles, where she married a professor of sociology and enrolled at Cal Arts and got a divorce and found her karma as a painter.

When Klara first saw her work she told people how good it was and word reached Acey on the Coast. Eventually she followed her paintings east. She was living at the Chelsea Hotel for the time being and sharing studio space in Brooklyn somewhere.

"What about you?" she said.

"Me, I had to make a career before I could worry about losing it. That was not easy. I pay and pay."

"A family," Acey said.

"I broke up a family, yes. I went away, I came back, I took my daughter for a while. She was better off with her father and I understood that but it consumed me, being separated like that. I had a very bad time. Of course we all did. She came down to see me on weekends or whenever. He rode the subway with her and left her at the door because he didn't want to set eyes on me."

"What would it do to him?"

"And then he came and picked her up and I was not allowed to walk all the way down the stairs. I walked her down to the first floor. I was living in a ramshackle building way downtown and it was arranged and agreed that I would walk her to the first floor and let her go the rest of the way herself because he might otherwise set eyes on me. What would it do to him? Something, I don't know, catastrophic."

"But you talked on the phone."

"We talked on the phone. In monosyllables. We sounded like spies passing coded messages. It was a very hateful time. But once she was older, that stopped, the phone calls. She and I made our own arrangements. Albert was gone for good."

"And her?"

"Teresa doesn't hate me. Maybe worse. I think she hates herself. She was part of the failure somehow. Let's not talk about this."

"We'll go for a walk."

"We'll walk across the bridge. Ever do that?"

"I'm new here, lady. You forget."

Acey's best work was part of a series about the Blackstone Rangers. Chicago winters, young men in hooded sweatshirts, morose and idly violent, hunched in front of barred windows or sitting on a broken sofa in the snow, and Klara thought these pictures were utterly modern in one sense only, that the subjects seemed photographed, overtly posing or caught unaware, sometimes self-consciously aloof, a housing project massed behind them or here's a man with lidded eyes and a watch cap and one of those bloated polyester jackets and a gun with banana clip—you see how Acey belies the photographic surface by making the whole picture float ineffably on the arc of the cartridge clip.

People on the roof, Esther's guests fleeing the swing band on the record player in the apartment and Esther's husband coming out as well, Jack, because he's the kind of man who melts away if he's left alone for twenty seconds.

She loved the little temple across the street, a top-floor facade with a set of recessed windows between the fluted columns, and does someone actually live there?

She felt good. She felt lucky for a change. She was sleeping well and saving money and seeing friends again.

"What's she reading?" someone said, talking about the woman on the ledge with the child's drinking glass and paperback book.

"Looks like detective fiction from here," Jack said. "Lots of moral rot. That's what people read in summer."

He was a tall florid guy, Jack Marshall, a Broadway press agent who was on the perennial edge of dropping dead. You know these guys. They smoke and drink heavily and never sleep and have bad tickers and cough up storms of phlegm and the thrill of knowing them, Klara thought, is guessing when they'll pitch into their soup.

She wore a bandage on her finger and waited for Miles to show up with her cigarettes because he was more reliable than she was.

She grubbed one from Jack for now.

And people on the street, when did Klara begin to notice how people talked to themselves, spoke aloud, so many of them and all of a sudden, or made threats, or walked along gesturing, so that the streets were taking on a late medieval texture, which maybe meant we had to learn all over again how to live among the mad.

"You have a boo-boo, Klara."

"You can't kiss it, so go away."

"I don't want to kiss it. I want to lick it," Jack said.

"Does someone live, I'm very curious about the thing across the street there."

"Inside the little Greek temple? I think it's an office."

"I would love to get a job there."

"Import-export."

"I could do either."

"So could I. But I want to lick it," he said.

Acey had an oval face and high forehead. Her hair had the barest cinnamon tinge. If you looked at her, if she sat across the aisle on a bus and you sneaked a glance every other stop, it was probably because of her mouth. She had a tough mouth, a smart mouth—it had a slight distortion of shape you'd probably call a sneer although the look shifted and moderated all the time and gave her smile a windfall quality, like a piece of unexpected news.

"I didn't have to leave my husband to paint," she told Klara. "I had to leave him because I didn't want to be with him anymore."

"What was the problem?"

"He's a man," Acey said.

391

Klara noticed, midbridge, how the younger woman checked the human action, the bike riders and runners and what they wear and who they are and the thing they develop together of a certain presentational self. Not like Chicago, Acey said, where the action near the lake is all unself-conscious sweat, people who are busting to run, to shake off the film of office and job, the abnormal pall of matter. Here the film is what they're in, the scan of crisp skyline, and she seemed ready for it, Acey did.

"And you're here now. And maybe for good. So the sense of starting over must be doubly strong."

"I probably started over a long time ago. Unbeknownst, basically, to everyone but me."

"You worry about the consequences?"

"Of breaking up? Had to happen. I'd worry if it hadn't."

"What about the husband?"

"What about him?" Acey said.

"I don't know. What about him? Does he know you have women lovers?"

"He gets off on dykes. I told him. I said, James, I'll send you some action snaps, baby."

"You're a gangster," Klara said.

"Gangster's moll. Gang moll. That's what they called me in L.A. You know, the Blackstone paintings. Middle-class Negro groupie."

"Very nice. They called me the Bag Lady."

They laughed and crossed to the Brooklyn side, where Acey worked in an old warehouse not far from the bridge approach. She did not want to show her current work prematurely and they only did a tour of the space. There was a Marilyn Monroe calendar on the wall, the famous early pinup called Miss Golden Dreams, a high-angle shot of the nude body posed on a velveteen blood-red bedsheet.

"This can't be here accidentally, can it?"

"Okay, it's something I'm looking at," Acey said.

"And thinking about."

"Something I'm working out for myself, little by little by little."

"Interesting. But I hear you're doing something completely different."

"Oh yeah? What do you hear?"

And Klara swung an arm toward the far wall, where canvases stood on a low shelf or were bracketed on easels, some with strips of construction paper she'd glimpsed earlier—paper taped to unfinished work as color-mapping guides.

"I hear you're doing a Black Panther series."

Acey did her scornful smile, slow and elaborate.

"Oh yeah? Well you know what? That's what I hear too."

This was supposed to be a postpainterly age, Klara thought, and here was a young woman painting whole heat, a black woman who paints black men generously but not without exercising a certain critical rigor. The frontal swagger of the gangs, a culture of nearly princely hauteur but with bodings, of course, of unembellished threat, and this is what Acey examined surgically, working the details, looking for traces of the solitaire, the young man isolated from his own moody pose.

They walked back across the bridge.

"They still call you that? The Bag Lady?"

"Not so much anymore," Klara said. "There were a few of us then. We took junk and saved it for art. Which sounds nobler than it was. It was just a way of looking at something more carefully. And I'm still doing it, only deeper maybe."

"It's not my thing. Maybe I don't trust the need for context. You know what I mean?"

"I guess."

"Because I understand up to a point. You take your object out of the dusty grubby studio and stick it in a museum with white walls and classical paintings and it becomes a forceful thing in this context, it becomes a kind of argument. And what it is actually? Old factory window glass and burlap sacking. It becomes very, I don't know, philosophical."

They reached the other side and Acey wanted to walk some more and Klara was nearly beat. They looked at old sailing ships moored off South Street. She was trying to dispel the little hurt, the small delayed disappointment of Acey's casual slighting of her work. First she delayed her reaction, then she tried to smother it.

"I was the type girl," Acey said, "I was always in a hurry to grow up. Now I guess I'm here, officially. This city is the ticking clock. Makes me panic but I'm ready."

What Klara admired most was the seeming ease of address, the casually ravishing way Acey laid down paint. Saturated undercoats and beautiful flesh browns, skin strokes in every sort of unnameable shade and many grays as well, glaucous and sky smoke, because it's always winter in Chicago and the gang members belong to their terrain, to the pale brick and iced-over windows, and in this sense they could be brothers to the olive-skinned men in the frescoed gloom of some Umbrian church—Acey had the calm and somber eye of a cinquecentist.

She was talking on the phone to Esther Winship.

Esther said, "Dear god why?"

"Because it's easier and quicker."

"But I haven't been on a subway in thirty years."

"Good. I want to feel superior."

They took the Dyre Avenue line. The train was marked with graffiti outside and in, slapdash and depressing, Klara thought. She did not like the idea of tagging trains. It was the romance of the ego, poor kids playing out a fantasy of meretricious fame.

"I thought it would be stifling hot," Esther said. "I thought I'd suffocate in my seat."

She said this in a grim whisper, afraid that someone might overhear and take offense somehow. In the subway, words have a charged quality they don't carry elsewhere.

"It's called air conditioning," Klara whispered back.

"I'm completely stunned."

Esther liked to sound stupidly out of touch—it sealed her in a safer frame of reference.

Two stops into the Bronx their train took on passengers and another train pulled into the downtown side and Klara felt a poke in the ribs. It was Esther, thrusting an elbow to get her attention because the other train was one of his, Moonman's, every car spray-painted top to bottom with his name and street number. And Klara had to admit this particular kid knew how to make an impact. The train came bopping into the old drab station like some blazoned jungle of wonders. The letters and numbers fairly exploded in your face and they had a relationship, they were plaited and knotted, pop-eyed cartoon humanoids, winding in and out of each other and sweaty hot and passion dancing—metallic silver and blue and cherry-bomb red and a number of neon greens.

Esther whispering out of her clenched jaw.

"That's him, that's him, that's him."

That was his train all right but they never found the young man himself. They looked for the address Esther had acquired from a reporter who'd done a story on graffiti writers. Moonman had not told the guy what his real name was or where he lived—only his age, sixteen. The address came from another kid, who claimed to be in Moonman's crew, and the two women searched it out, walking across a terrain of torched buildings, whole blocks leveled by arson, and there were buildings still burning in the distance. They stopped and watched. Three or four buildings oozing lazy smoke. No sign of fire engines or anxious people grouped behind barricades. Just a few passersby, it seemed from here, routinely occupied. They watched in silence and it was hard to bridge the distance. They couldn't quite place the thing in context. It was like a newsreel of some factional war in a remote province, where generals cook the livers of their rivals and keep them in plastic baggies. A thing totally spooked by otherness.

Esther finally spoke. "This is where you used to live?"

"No. I lived about a mile north of here."

"Still, I have to show you more respect."

"Thank you, Esther. But it wasn't like this at the time."

"Still, I have to make an effort to be nicer to you."

"You do that," Klara said.

They knew it wasn't a good idea to stand around indefinitely and when they reached 157th Street and looked for the young man's address, they found there was no such number.

They went into a couple of bodegas and asked at the check-cashing place.

People said, "Mooney, who's Mooney?" They said, "What kind of Mormon? There's no Mormons here."

And the women said, "No, no, no, no. Moonman. Moonman uno cinco siete." And they made spray-paint gestures and said, "Graffiti, graffiti."

And Esther wore a safari jacket like some network correspondent looking for rebels in the smoky hills and who could blame her, really.

"You look a little Chinese tonight," Miles said.

"Jason used to call me the chink."

She said this in her small voice. She looked and sounded small to herself. People were getting bigger, she was getting smaller, going more or less invisible. If Miles were not here, how long would it take the waiter to wait on her?

"Jason. I know a Jason?"

"Jason my second husband. Jason Vanover."

They were eating seafood on Mulberry Street in a place Miles liked to come to because a mobster had been killed here, shot in the head by a couple of guys from a rival family, or his own family maybe, or a family from out of town.

"You're always mentioning people that I don't know and that I never heard of and you mention them," he said, "in a way that makes me think I'm supposed to know who you're talking about when as a matter of fact I couldn't possibly."

"It's true, I do that."

"People go by me in a blur."

"It's just that I feel if I know someone, it's automatic that the person I'm talking to about that individual should also know him, by some human arithmetic," she said.

Miles had a cold, he always had a cold, it went unnoticed, went without saying, he had coughing jags and slightly woozy eyes, completely unremarked by people who knew him—it was part of the irregular life, the general unhealth, half meals and travel and erratic sleep.

He looked around for particular silhouettes, hefty men in suits who might be connected.

"I used to look more Chinese when my hair was shorter," she said.

"What did he do?"

"He was a market analyst, a risk-taker with his own and other people's money, and a sailor, we used to sail for weeks at a time, a yachtsman. That was the best thing about our marriage. When we shared the ketch everything fell into place. He had a ketch he named High Finance."

"You on a boat?"

"We knew we had to cooperate. We had to live in close quarters. Take turns at the wheel, in the galley, share the head, stow the equipment, coil the lines, keep things in their place. Yes, me on a boat. We were disciplined. We respected the boat and the elements. We had a pretty good marriage as long as we were aboard."

They walked over to the loft. A supermarket cart stood in the middle of the street and cars went around it and a man rose from the shadow of a loading platform murmuring a plea to Jesus.

They shared a joint and watched a newsclip of Nixon waving on TV.

"Acey told me she was at a party and she said to a man, What do men really want from women, and he said, Blowjobs, and she said, You can get that from men."

"In six months Acey will be too famous to live," Miles said. "She'll be assassinated walking out of a disco."

It wasn't quite the time for her to go back to work but it was beginning to be the time. Something in her skin began its anxious leap, some need to handle and shape, only deeper really—some need so whole she could sit alone in the loft and be a little wary of it.

"Yes, walking out of a disco," she said. "And then you'll want to take me dancing there."

Her mother took her downtown, her and Rochelle, her best friend, and they ate lunch at the automat near Times Square, where the front window was stained glass and the milk came out of the mouth of a bronzed fish. They watched matinee crowds enter theaters and her mother made comments on the ladies' hats. They looked in shop windows of the better sort. Her mother took them into fine hotels and office buildings, marched them right in and showed them the moldings and engravings in the lobbies, the carved wood on elevator doors. And they stood outside a skyscraper on Fifth Avenue, it was probably 1934 and the Japanese were entrenched in Manchuria and they looked straight up the face of the building and walked through the polished lobby and it was the Fred F. French Building, which intrigued the girls because who on earth was Fred F. French, and Klara's mother, who knew things, who worked for a social service agency and studied child psychology, who followed world events and worried about China, who planned these outings systematically, did not have a clue to the identity of Fred F. French, and this intrigued the girls even more, intrigued and amused them, they were thirteen and fourteen and everything amused them. They rode home on the Third Avenue el, rattlebanging up Manhattan and through the Bronx, looking out the train windows into tenement apartments on both sides, hundreds of film-flickering lives shooting past their eyes forty feet above the street, and Rochelle might see an undershirted man leaning tousled out his window and, Maybe that's Fred F. French, she'd say, he's had a streak of bad luck, ha ha, and that was the end of that, Klara said to Miles—they were in bed playing cards in the loft, until three or four years later when the girls left a high school dance with two boys who weren't even in their high school, interlopers from the north, and the four of them slipped into somebody's parked car at the dark end of the street and they puffed a couple of cigarettes and talked and smooched and necked and petted. Klara and one boy were huddled in the front seat and Rochelle had the other boy in the roomy rear, boy-crazy Rochelle putting on a show of tonguing and seat-slithering, actually raising dust from the upholstery, and she wore a smoky look that distracted the front-seat partners and made them stop and watch. There was just enough light to watch. And it went on toward the outer limits of what a girl is willing to commit herself to, even a boy-crazy minx like Rochelle. The boy in the backseat was in a bundled frenzy by now and Rochelle's look contained a complicated betrayal, it was smoky and deadly and cool and it seemed to be saying to Klara that their friendship, the best and deepest there could ever be, was about to enter a strange and disturbing phase, the intricate thing of men and sex and personal needs. There was a flurry of hands and knees, there was all that stuff of backseats and body angles and what you're wearing, the whole grabby flare-up of sex in the dark. She heard panty-band elastic snapping. She thought she heard the boy's finger actually enter the fleshy pocket between Rochelle's legs, a palpatory sea suck, the wetness, the slaver of long stupefying kisses, that whole thing of having a strand of his hair in your mouth that you can't exactly locate, and it was abruptly and bitterly clear that Rochelle had done this before, gone this far and more, and what a shock to Klara, detecting such experience in her best friend's eyes, and she watched in a clinical spell, she looked and listened—what a stark thing a secret is when it belongs to someone else.

Now she knew what people meant by experience, the way they used the word experience, and the form it took was not sex but knowledge, and the knowledge was not hers but her friend's—how it twisted her insides and made her feel puppyish and dumb.

She heard Rochelle mutter something like, Time to take the rubber out of your wallet, Bob, or she might have said Rob, but instead of a pale flexible sheath the boy took out his living thing, stiff and pulsing and ultraviolet, there it was, suddenly unbuttoned and in the world, pretty much the configuration Klara had imagined but so hot and real, independently alive, unyoked to the host, to the bearer, the wearer, and Rochelle was nervous because the boy did not have a rubber and Klara was nervous because the Japanese might invade China.

Miles cut the cards and listened.

And at the all-crucial moment Rochelle Abramowicz looked over the boy's shoulder into the eyes of Klara Sachs and said to her, thoughtfully, What do you think the F stands for?

And Klara said, What F?

And Rochelle said, The F in Fred F. French.

This was a good thing to say, maybe it was the best thing anyone had ever said, then or now, under the circumstances, and it made them friends again. They dissolved, as the saying goes, in laughter, they practically disappeared into their constituent elements, into atoms and molecules, a couple of girls in a gangster Packard, blown forward in time, and Klara stood on the roof sipping tepid wine and hearing people say, We need theater, and she knew she would tell this story to Miles and she also knew she could never again have a friend like Rochelle or a mother like her mother for that matter and she looked across ledges and parapets to the old skyscraper with the massed midsection and the sunburst paneling, ten blocks north, and thought how wonderful it was, what an accidental marvel to come upon a memory floating at the level of a glazed mosaic high on a midtown tower—the old spoked sun that brings you luck.

2

The poets of the old nations of the basin told stories about the wind.

Matt Shay sat in his cubbyhole in a concrete space about the size of a basketball court, somewhere under the gypsum hills of southern New Mexico.

This operation was called the Pocket.

There were people here who weren't sure whether they were doing weapons work. They were involved in exploratory research and didn't know exactly what happened to their findings, their simulations, the results they discovered or predicted. This is one of the underlying themes of the systems business, where all the work connects at levels and geographic points far removed from the desk toil and lab projects of the researchers.

Matt used to do consequence analysis, figuring out the lurid mathematics of a nuclear accident or limited exchange. He worked with data from real events. There was the thing that fell to earth on Albuquerque in 1957, a thermonuclear bomb of jumbo tonnage mistakenly released from a B-36—*nobody's perfect, okay*—and landing in a field within the city limits. The conventional explosives detonated, the nuclear package did not. The incident remained a secret to this day, seventeen years later, as Matty sat in his cubicle reading a camping guide.

He'd been in the Pocket for five months and was definitely doing weapons work but of the soft-core type, involved with safing mechanisms mainly, his face pressed to a computer screen. He wasn't sure how he felt about this. He'd wanted to do weapons, he'd wanted the edge, the identity, the sense of honing his silhouette, knowing himself a little better—a secret installation in the desert.

They named it the Pocket after a creature called the pocket gopher that lives in tunnels it frantically digs under the furrowed dunes.

The dune fields, the alkali flats, the whiteness, the whole white sea-bottomed world, the lines of white haze in the distance, the six-thousand-year-old mummified baby found in a cave near White City, yes, and there were animals that bleached themselves white over the eons, a once-brown mouse that color-matched itself to the gypsum drifts to escape the gaze of predators.

The wind blew out of the Organ Mountains, busting up to fifty miles an hour, refiguring the dunes and turning the sky an odd dangerous gray that seemed a type of white gone mad.

And the men and women of the Pocket, mainly men and mainly single, with only a small cluster of marrieds and their albino, was the joke, children—they lived in semiattached bungalows at the edge of the missile range and listened to the wind that the sages of the old nations spoke about, evolving metaphors and philosophies, and it recrested the dunes, blowing steadily, sometimes, for days.

Do you work with sound waves? Do you gauge the effects of blast on delivery aircraft? Do you do physics packages and dream about a girl back in Georgia, the one who put her hand in your pants at the drive-in near the swamp? Do you long to see a fireball, an actual test shot—

they are outlawed of course by now, atmospheric blasts, but you wish you'd seen one of the monster shots that vapored an atoll way back when.

He ate lunch in the underground mess with Eric Deming, a tall shuffly man in his early thirties, a couple of years younger than Matt, and one of the bombheads.

There was a droop to Eric's shoulders and clothes. He tended to eat with his hands—french fries, sure, but also lettuce, beets, boiled rice, corn niblets, anything he could pincer and lift in units.

"When's Janet coming?"

"Soon. We're working out the details," Matt said.

"Will you show her to us? We haven't seen a woman from the outside world."

"You're in Alamogordo all the time."

"That's not outside. You have to go a thousand miles before you're outside. You know that. In this state, Matty."

"She's not coming here."

"Okay but in this state do you know the percentage of people who have security clearance? Isn't that why we love it?"

"We're meeting somewhere west of here and then we're going camping. Remote remote remote. If I can talk her into it. She's not eager to do this, Janet."

Eric worked in a lab area that Matt was not cleared to enter. He used to work with radioactive materials inside a sealed glove box. He wore protective gloves, he wore overgloves attached to his sleeves, he wore layers of treated clothing equipped with a number of film badges and rad-detectors and he worked with bomb components—the neutron initiator, the detonators, the subcritical pieces, the visceral heat inside the warhead.

He was doing something else now and Matt didn't know what it was. He wore a Q badge with yellow edges and spread astounding rumors.

•   •   •

The bombheads loved their work but weren't necessarily pro-bomb, walking around with megadeath hard-ons. They were detail freaks. They were awed by the inner music of bomb technology. Matt watched them. He went to their parties and learned their language. They carried an afterglow of sixties incandescence, a readiness to give themselves compulsively to something.

They thought he was angling for a transfer in, ready to become one of them, wear the coded badge, the Q-sensitive access that would get him through the last gate and into the tunnel that led to bomb design.

But Matty was sneaking looks at outdoor magazines, at camp bags and dome tents, because he needed time to get away and think.

He had doubts about the rightness of his role.

Down route 70 a ways, near the sign for the missile range, an area that is white on your map—this is where the protesters stood, seven or eight men and women, sometimes only two or three, and they carried a sign stretched between wooden uprights, *World War III Starts Here*, and base personnel taunted them, or just smirked, or were flattered by the sign, or felt sorry for the sign carriers because they were windswept and unattractive.

Matt liked seeing them. He counted on it in a way. It began to be important to him, knowing they were there, four, five, six people, usually women outnumbering men, or maybe two grim figures clinging to the uprights, never saying a word as military vehicles passed, or flatbed trucks with draped objects, or civilian workers and construction crews, the odd finger flipped their way.

The white places on your map include the air base, the army base, the missile range, the vast stretch to the northwest called the Jornada del Muerto and the interdunal flats as well—the flats were map-white, on the page and in living fact, and a few low buildings were situated here, fenced structures with propane tanks, to service the underground operation in the Pocket, where weapons were conceived and designed.

•   •   •

404

They worked to strict deadlines. There were always deadlines to meet. The bombheads complained about this. They were the people of superior sensibility, the ones who'd gained a rational mastery over themselves, who were not subject to moral ambivalence, to the sentimental babyshit of consequence and anguish. They were the ones who understood the hard-ass principles of the conflict and they did not like bureaucratic pressures exerted from the surface.

But the deadlines persisted. There were deadlines all the time. There was the urgency of war without a war.

Eric said, "Hear the latest secret?"

They were walking beyond the bungalows at sunset, totally alone on the sand plain, and Eric kept looking around for eavesdroppers, comically of course, and he affected a side-of-mouth murmur that might frustrate even a lip-reader recruited to study surveillance tapes.

"It's an old thing just now surfacing," he said, "in the form of very faint rumors."

"What old thing?"

"Workers at the Nevada Test Site in the days of aboveground shots."

"What about them?"

"And people living downwind. These people have a name, incidentally, that totally defines their existence."

"What is it?"

"Downwinders," Eric said.

They ambled out past low growths of saltbush toward the electrified fence.

"What about them?" Matt said.

"Nobody's supposed to know this. It's something that's more or less out in the open but at the same time."

"What?"

"Secret. Untalked about. Hushed up."

"What's the secret?" Matt said.

"Multiple myelomas. Kidney failures. Or you wake up one morning and you're three inches shorter."

"You mean exposure to fallout."

"Or you start throwing up one day and you throw up every succeeding day for seven, eight weeks."

"But isn't this something we have to expect? Occasional miscalculations. It's dangerous work, you know?"

Eric seemed to enjoy this remark. No, he seemed to expect it, he seemed to find it encouraging. They walked out past a large parabolic dune and it was so draggingly hot out here that the air seemed a form of physical hindrance.

"Little farm communities downwind of the tests. Nearly all the kids wear wigs," Eric whispered.

"Doing chemo?"

"Yeah. And here and there a kid that's born with a missing limb or whatnot. And a healthy woman that goes to wash her hair and it all comes out in her hands. She's a ravishing, you know, brunette one minute and totally bald the next."

"Where?"

"Mainly southern Utah, I hear, because it's downwind. But other places too. Adenocarcinomas. Old Testament outbreaks of great red boils. Great big splotches and rashes. And coughing up handfuls of blood. You look in your cupped hands and you see a pint of radded blood."

They walked along the electrified fence past a warning sign graffiti'd by a protester or some apostate working slyly in the Pocket.

"You think the stories are true?"

"No," Eric said.

"Then why do you spread them?"

"For the tone, of course."

"For the edge."

"For the edge. The bite. The existential burn."

Matty was six years old when his father went out for cigarettes.

Eight days later, when his father hadn't come back and hadn't called or sent a message through a friend, the boy took all the change he could find in the apartment and started walking.

He'd never gone alone past the Third Avenue el in this particular direction but that's where he walked. Then he crossed the avenue where the trains ran through the long corridor below street level from the suburbs all the way down to Grand Central Station. That Nicky

406

would one day throw rocks at. That Nicky would stand at the railing in plain sight throwing rocks at the trains running right below him.

Then he climbed the long set of steps up to the streets near the Concourse. He'd climbed these steps with his mother to go to the movies and get a sundae at the ice-cream parlor nearby and now he climbed the steps alone, going to the Grand Concourse, where the movie theater stood, the Loew's Paradise, and there were sixty or seventy steps and buildings on iron stilts, like another country altogether.

He sees himself from this distance in the white sands standing across the street looking at the great Italianate facade of the Paradise.

He sees himself staring up at the clock and the roof balustrade and the ornate stone cupola.

He sees himself buying a ticket, barely able to reach the window hole, and he pushed the coins through the hole and watched the ticket woman hit a thing that sent the ticket out of a slit.

He walked into the lobby. He felt an enveloping sort of warmth rise from the thick carpet like the happy repose of a stroked dog. There were goldfish swimming in marble basins. He looked at the etched glass chandeliers. There were a number of jutting balconies where paintings hung in gilded frames. He thought this was a thousand times more holy than church.

He is sitting in his half bungalow near the missile range and he sees himself climb the carpeted staircase because he wanted to sit high up, close to the theater ceiling.

He saw the usher standing with a flashlight held across his belt. The usher wore braiding on his shoulders and a row of brass buttons set aslant his chest and he flashed the light repeatedly on and off just to hear it click. Matty thought the usher would tell him he could not sit in the balcony because it was grown-ups only here, for smoking, or boys and girls who want to neck. But the usher clicked the thing and stood there and Matty walked right by.

He climbed to seats near the ceiling, where stars twinkled and moved. The whole sky moved across the ceiling, stars and constellations and misty blue clouds. His mother wanted him to be an altar boy when he was old enough but this was more tremendous than church.

He sees all this as a grown-up who has never smoked a cigarette, who barely drives a car and no longer plays chess and loves a woman who's a nurse in Boston.

He sees himself sitting in the balcony at the Paradise. The light from the movie glowed or faded depending on the nature of the scene. He looked at the wall nearest him and then at the other wall and when the light flared and leaped there it all was, the whole tremendous thing, arches, porticos, statues, the urns and marble busts, the vines trained through balusters, the pedestaled heroes with long swords, the columns in the shape of draped figures, both walls crowded with stacked anatomies and structures, too much to take in, and angels that stood halo'd atop the pediments, and he sat there and waited for his father, for the ghost or soul of his father to make a visitation.

He took off his glasses, he put on his glasses. Then he took them off and wiped them with a pale cloth and sat in front of his screen blinking at a display of data that pertained to an arming system, to that element of the weapon designed to send signals that will arm or safe or resafe the firing system. He heard a faint boom somewhere over the desert, the blast wave of mach speeds, and it thrilled him, moved him. It always did, no matter how often he heard it or how far he was situated from the source. The sound woke him some mornings when the planes flew right over and sometimes he stood outside his quarters before nightfall and watched the matched contrails of half a dozen aircraft in tight formation, the planes themselves long gone, but it was the drag and sonic shock, this is what awed and moved him, and then the afterclap rolling off the mountains, like they were blowing out a seam in the world.

There were people here who didn't know where their work ended up, how it might be applied. They didn't know how their arrays of numbers and symbols might enter nature. It could conceivably happen in a flash.

Everything connected at some undisclosed point down the systems line. This caused a certain select disquiet.

But it was a splendid mystery in a way, a source of wonder, how a brief equation that you tentatively enter on your screen might alter the course of many lives, might cause the blood to rush through the body of a woman on a tram many thousands of miles away, and how do you define this kind of relationship?

Matt did not like to drive. He'd been driving only six months and knew he'd never feel natural at the wheel. The best he could do was mimic a driver. He borrowed a four-wheel-drive vehicle from one of the bombheads and drove it with the instruction booklet in his lap. The roads, the road signs, the other cars made him self-conscious, exposing his crime of driving.

But he wanted to practice for his camping trip with Janet and he went for drives on his days off and there were signs for runaway truck ramps and dangerous crosswinds and there was the Jesus is Lord sign and the lines of whitish haze in the deep distance that he now knew to be sea-bottom sand and the Do not enter sign When road is flooded and the slat-back shadows on the flats formed by the crossbars of power lines that stretched hellbent to Texas.

Returning one day from a drive he saw the protesters, as always, positioned in the wrong place. They should have been standing by the third gate to the air base, the unmarked gate, because that's where scientists from the Pocket entered and left, and they were the most susceptible presence, and he half wanted to tell the protesters to move their operation up the road.

Matt looked slightly Jewish, a little Hispanic maybe. He'd lifted weights in his late teens, remaking the soft flimsy body that used to function as an adjunct to the Univac head. Back in the Bronx, people said he looked a little everything. Mexican, Italian, Japanese even—his friendliest smile could look like a ceremonial grimace. A police sketch made from seven different descriptions—that was Matt. He never stopped resembling the student he was at City College in the late fifties, hardworking, nearsighted, smart and poor, riding the subway to class.

·   ·   ·

He sat with Eric Deming in the mess. Eric took a strand of spaghetti in his fingers and slow-lowered it down his throat with a certain amount of snakely constriction.

Matt said, "All right. These are things we have to expect. We're not naive. Mistakes are part of the process. There's a sudden wind shift and the fallout blows the wrong way. Or the blast and shock are larger than anyone anticipated."

"The placid nineteen-fifties. Everybody dressed and spoke the same way. It was all kitchens and cars and TV sets. Where's the Pepsodent, mom? We were there, so we know, don't we?"

"You know. I don't know," Matt said.

"You were there. We were both there."

"You were there. I was somewhere else."

"Dad's in the breezeway washing the car. Meanwhile way out here they were putting troops in trenches for nuclear war games. Fireballs roaring right above them."

"Positioned too close, you mean."

"That's the story I hear. You look at your arm and see right through it. Basically your arm becomes an x ray of your arm. You can see right through the uniform cloth and the skin. The light's so white. You can see blood, bones and whatnot. But that's not all. You can see all this with your eyes shut. You don't have to open your eyes. You see right through the lids. Ha!"

"Well was it officially acknowledged?"

"You wake up one day a few years later, all your inner organs are fused. It's one big jellied lump."

"But did the men get compensated?"

"I don't know," Eric said.

"That's not part of your rumormongering."

Eric stuck a finger in Matty's creamed spinach and hooked a shreddy morsel toward his mouth.

"What good's a rumor that deals with bureaucratic details? The point is this," he said. "It happened right out in the open but it's still a huge secret to this day. That's the story anyway. Which I don't happen to believe. They did major shots off towers or dropped devices from planes and they put troops too close to the blast and they let the

410

fallout drift to Utah, where kids are getting born with their bladders backwards."

Matt wanted to like Eric. The guy was smart, friendly, sort of semi-charismatic in a physically awkward and too-tall way. But his motives were sometimes lost to observers in the inward drifts of his smile. You saw the shadow action around the mouth and wondered if you were being set up for something.

"You know about the school not far from here. This is not rumor now but fact. I've been there and seen it. The Abo Elementary School and Fallout Shelter. A real place down in the ground."

"Just like us."

"We're not real," Eric said. "They're only kids. It's a grade school. They still have a chance to be real. I was sent there to speak to them."

"As a bombhead."

"As a clean-cut younger member of the military industrial complex. A diversion at recess type thing."

"What did you say to them?"

"There's a water tank at the edge of town. State Champs in bright new paint. And rows of neat homes. Then you come upon the school but just barely. Some trailerlike structures and a couple of basketball courts and finally you spot an entrance and you open the steel door and go down the stairs and there's a lot of concrete and steel and the lighting's slightly eerie. The classrooms, the bedding, the canned food, the morgue. No window breakage. That's one of the features. Because there aren't any windows of course. But the point is. What's the point, Matty?"

"I don't know. Tell me."

"Did they do all this to protect the kids from Soviet bombs or from our bombs and our fallout?"

"I don't know. Both. What did you say to the kids?"

"I spoke in tongues," Eric said. "I mean think about it. I'm standing in an underground room at the northern edge of a great desert with filtering systems for fallout and a fully equipped morgue and there are crayon drawings pinned above the blackboard of piglets and cows. Incidentally."

"What?"

"I have a chess set in my room. What about a game?"

411

The Pocket was one of those nice tight societies that replaces the world. It was the world made personal and consistently interesting because it was what you did, and others like you, and it was self-enclosed and self-referring and you did it all together in a place and a language that were inaccessible to others.

Janet Urbaniak was Matt's girlfriend, a registered nurse. They were off-and-on serious, mostly on, often impatient with each other but always strongly joined, the kind of star-matched couple born to meet and disagree.

He called Janet on her days off and she told him where she'd gone and what she'd seen or bought, and who with, and for how long, and he listened and commented and asked for details.

She worked in a trauma unit now. She told him about her nights there but he said almost nothing about his own work and of course she understood and did not probe.

Janet called his mother twice a week to find out how she was doing and then she called Matt to give him a report and then Matt called his mother to confirm everything, to clarify the particulars of an ache or pain, and he liked all these calls, the ones he made and the ones he heard about—they gave him a life outside the Pocket.

He drove his borrowed jeep past a protester alone, a woman struggling to keep the sign upright in a dry stiff wind that beat across the flats. He wanted to stop and talk to her. Give her a hand, have a chat. He wanted to show his tolerance of her viewpoint, allow himself to be convinced by some of her arguments, make certain trenchant points of his own and then drive her to the nondescript room where she lived at the edge of this or that town, with a partial view of the mountains, and have soft, moaning and mutually tolerant sex in her rumpled bed, but he slowed only slightly as he drove past.

Later someone told him the protesters lived in a ruined school bus in the Sacramento Mountains. Matt kind of liked that. He liked the idea of people leaving everything behind to pursue an idea. He thought of Sister Edgar in sixth grade talking about desert saints, pillar saints, stylites, and she hoisted herself up on her desk and crossed her legs under the habit, a saint lotused on a column in the Sinai, and spoke to the class in snatches of Latin and Hebrew and he remembered liking that—he liked to think of a godstruck band of wanderers haunting the test ranges and silos of the West.

It was part of the reason he'd come here in the first place. For the questions and challenges. For the self-knowledge he might find in a sterner life, in the fixing of willful limits.

Did you do grad work on solar energy? Did you do a paper on the trigger principle of nuclear fission? Do you go to the dentist every six months for a prophy and a polish? Are you a physicist with a grudge against your mother? Are you a systems engineer who masturbates in secret while your wife is watching reruns of "The Honeymooners"? Do you wish to hell you could see a tower shot with all the special effects, with the sun coming up ass-backwards and the trees casting shadows in the wrong direction, the spectacle of the unmattered atom, the condensation cloud arranged split-secondly on the shock disc, sort of primly place-centered, and the visible shock approaching, and the biblical wind that carries sagebrush, sand, hats, cats, car parts, condoms and poisonous snakes, all blowing by in the desert dawn?

Eric kept after him to play chess. But he didn't want to play chess. He didn't talk about his chess. His chess was old dark difficult history, suppressed forever. The history of a chess homunculus. No one knew about his chess. Janet knew a little and only Janet and no one else but his mother and brother and Mr. Bronzini, of those who might tend to remember.

"You don't get the point," Eric said in the jeep.

"You're spreading rumors you don't even believe. That's the point," Matt said.

413

"They had to throw up roadblocks because the cloud was moving into populated areas. Neuroblastomas. Beta burns. Two-headed lambs. Or entire herds of sheep dead in the fields. Or you wake up one morning and your teeth start flipping out of their sockets, painlessly and bloodlessly."

Two or three teeth, say. Sort of gently expelled with the faintest kind of squishy sound, Eric said. And you wrap them in cold wet gauze and jump in your car and drive to the dentist's office confident that he'll be able to reinsert the teeth because don't doctors do amazing things with severed limbs. Or he will not reinsert the teeth. He will send the teeth to a lab at the new medical center where they have equipment so advanced it can learn more about you in a passing glance than you could figure out yourself if you lived to be a thousand.

But at the first red light you take the gauze out of your pocket and unfold it for a brief peek, Eric said, and there's nothing there but a small mound of powder because your teeth have completely crumbled. These hard strong reliable structures designed for biting and gnawing, for tearing flesh. These things that last a million years in the jaws of prehistoric people, in the skulls that we dig up and study. Turned to dust in your pocket in six frigging minutes.

He called Janet and talked. He talked and listened. The smaller the talk, the better he felt. He took satisfaction in the details of her day, the matters of barely passing interest that struck him in his lonely love as items of privileged witness.

Sometimes she talked about her work, trauma duty deep in the night, and she was matter-of-fact about it, bodies flopping on the just-mopped floor of the corridor, relatives dragging in a knife victim or OD, the uncle and mother gripping the man's head and legs and a cluster of small kids at the edges, two to each arm.

She described scenes that were like paintings of the European masters, the ones who did miracles and wars.

Her strength in these matters made her beautiful to him. She was a smallish woman, they were both fairly short and Janet was slight as well, and he liked to imagine her in a scrub suit plunging a fist into someone's chest cavity and coming out with a bullet or a chicken bone. Her shyness did not conceal her eloquence of mettle and will. He saw and heard it often. She clung to him persistently to make a point.

He thought they were too damn earnest. They wanted a family and each other but were periodically beset by the complexity of the undertaking, the plans, the chances, the cities, the idea of marriage and children and jobs and how hard it is to do everything right, and they agreed and bargained and argued, they planned and fought.

He looked at Landsat photos shot from space a year or two earlier. The pictures were false-color composites that revealed signs of soil erosion, geological fracture and a hundred other events and features. They showed stress and drift and industrial ravage, billion-bit data converted into images.

He saw how remote sensors pulled hidden meanings out of the earth. How sweeps and patches of lustrous color, how computer fuchsias or rorschach pulses of unnamed shades might indicate a change in water temperature or where the dwindling grizzlies go to forage and mate. He looked at spindly barrier beaches that showed white as shanked bone. He found sizable cities pixeled into mountain folds and saw black lakes high in the ranges, kettle holes formed by glacial drift.

He could not stop looking.

The photo mosaics seemed to reveal a secondary beauty in the world, ordinarily unseen, some hallucinatory fuse of exactitude and rapture. Every thermal burst of color was a complex emotion he could not locate or name.

And he thought of the lives inside the houses embedded in the data on the street that is photographed from space.

And that is the next thing the sensors will detect, he thought. The unspoken emotions of the people in the rooms.

And then he thought inevitably of Nick.

•   •   •

He wanted to call his brother many times. He thought he'd like to talk to him about the work he was doing here. He'd be able to give Nick a general sense of things, let him know that the kid was doing important work but that it troubled him now and then.

One day he might find himself putting together a physics package, the explosive components of a nuclear device—true-blue bombhead country.

Matt wasn't sure he could deal with this himself. He could if he had to, and Janet would help, she'd have a clear position he could set against his doubts, but he wanted to talk to Nick. He wanted to hear his brother's voice coming down the phone line, the slightly bent stresses that carried a literal lifetime of associations.

Nick had a graveness that was European in a way. He was shaped and made. First unmade and then reimagined and strongly shaped and made again. And he was somber and self-restrained at times and not free-giving but maybe he would give the kid advice about the moral and ethical aspects of this kind of work. Mainly what Matt wanted was a show of interest. This was more important than outright counsel, a recommendation or judgment, but he wanted that too—a judgment in his brother's voice.

He didn't know what his brother might say. He might say this is the way you define yourself as a serious man, working through the hard questions and harrowing choices, and if you stick with it you'll be stronger in the end. Or he might say, Fool, what kind of mark will this make on your soul when you become a father like me? Think of the guilt of raising children in a world you've made—your talent put to such desolate use. Speaking softly now. And who knows the ticklish business of weapons better than I do, brother?

But he'd never make that last remark, would he? And Matt didn't make the call. They didn't often talk, or they talked about their mother, or they hassled each other routinely, but maybe he'd call later when he felt the urge again.

When the wind gusted out of the mountains it rebodied the dunes and if you were up out of the Pocket and sitting around at home with a beer and a snack you saw your laundry go horizontal on the backyard line, all of it, sheets, hankies, boxer shorts, pajama bottoms, like people of all sizes and shapes snapping from the pressure, letting their souls fly forth to the gypsum hills.

"But that's not the point," Eric said. "You keep mi, mi, missing the point."

It was raining in the mountains.

Eric had a fake stutter he liked to use to texture the conversation, a thing he'd developed to mock himself or his listener, although neither one of them stuttered, or maybe he was imitating some nightclub comic or simpy character on TV—it wasn't clear to Matt.

He looked out a window of Eric's bungalow. The rain was a wall of smoky shimmer that hung across the limestone bluffs. Eric sat on a sofa that was still wrapped in warehouse plastic amid a mess of scientific journals, UFO monthlies, supermarket tabloids, half a dozen Playboys and some lost food.

"Even though huge amounts of territory were affected and large numbers of people were exposed, it remains a major secret to this day."

"So secret it may not be true," Matt said.

"Do you believe it's true?"

"I believe mistakes were made."

Eric enjoyed this. His shadow smile appeared at the far end of the sprawled body. It came and went, like some inner dialogue he was conducting that ran parallel to the spoken lines, a thing of elusive drift.

"But the point is, pure and simple."

"What's the point, Eric?"

He picked up a magazine and leafed through it aimlessly, speaking in a tone that was slightly impatient but mostly, now that he was finally coming to the point, a little weary and bored.

"It was done deliberately," he said. "They knew the tests weren't safe but they went ahead anyway. They marched troops to zero point after the detonations. They sent manned aircraft through radiation clouds. They injected people with plutonium to track its course through the body. They did this deliberately, without telling people what the risks were. They exposed troops to the atomic flash and some of them were given protective eye filters and some were not. They experimented on children, infants, fetuses and mental patients. They never told the Navahos who worked in uranium mines what the dangers were. The dangers were considerable as it turned out. They zapped the testicles of prison inmates. They basically grabbed you by the balls and zapped you full of x rays. This is the story I hear. Do you believe it?"

"It's awfully, I don't know."

"Of course. It's very hard to believe. That's why I don't believe it," Eric said. "Not for a tenth of a second."

The rain line came dragging across the flats and the wind kicked up. The poets of the desert nations told stories about the wind. It bucks and swirls and turns you around and knocks you flat. But it also speaks so softly only your inner spirit can hear it and this is how you correct your path.

Eric said, "They never told the test subjects they were sub, sub, sub, sub."

"Subjects."

"I don't believe it," Eric said. "But you may feel differently."

Matt didn't know how he felt. But he didn't think the story was completely far-fetched. He'd served in Vietnam, after all, where everything he'd ever disbelieved or failed to imagine turned out, in the end, to be true.

Then one day he stopped to talk to her, the woman alone with the protest sign. He parked the car on the opposite side of the road and walked on over. She held one post cradled in her arms, one eight-foot-long upright piece, and the other was planted in the dirt with rocks piled around the base, and the sign itself, a spray-painted sheet, extended wind-whipped between the posts.

He stood there and started talking. He talked to her in a reassuring, trite and slightly compulsive way, like a first-timer nervous in a singles bar. He realized her wrist was padlocked to the post. He'd never noticed this before and it seemed, well, a little self-dramatizing maybe. Or fanatical and irrational and victim-wishful. She looked at him briefly as he spoke. He'd finished the get-acquainted part and was

418

talking about the need for readiness and the folly of being naive about the other side's intentions.

He didn't use words such as American and Soviet. They seemed provocative somehow. Or NATO and Europe and the East Bloc and the Berlin Wall. Too soon to be so intimate.

She looked at him only briefly. It was not a hostile look but it was brief. There was something scoured about her, a sense of rubbed surfaces, a willing away of normal accretions and gleanings, and he thought she carried the countermarks of the rural poor.

He talked to her about the need to match our weapons to theirs, even when the numbers become absurd, because this is the only seeming safeguard against attack by either side.

She was fair-skinned, etched and fixed, with lank hair, string hair, and he thought she was true and impressive and unreachable.

They stood on a stretch of flat straight highway, beautiful and lonely, and if you're going to do this kind of work, isn't it necessary, he thought, to be fanatical? *World War III Starts Here.* Isn't this exactly what he wanted from these people, a kind of sunstruck religious witness?

He told her he was completely willing to listen. But she would not talk to him. She stood padlocked to the post and looked off down the road somewhere. He could not despise her arrogance because she wasn't arrogant. She wasn't smarter or more sane or less guilty. They are armed, he said, and so we have to be armed. She clutched the upright and looked down the road, blue-eyed, with an inbuilt wince, and he went back to the car and drove away.

Eric's laundry jumped on the line. It shot straight out and held stiff in the wind.

"I think of my days in the glove box," he said. "Handling that hot pluto. Mistakes were made even in the small narrow sealed limits of the box. Better believe it. With all the safety procedures and data sheets and supervisors, people still made amazing mistakes. And I'd stick my hands in the gloves and think oddly of my mom, who was a super sensible lady and used to wear rubber gloves to do the dinner dishes back in the placid days when we were bombing our own people."

"I'm leaving tomorrow," Matt said.

"Let me have that jacket when you go."

Matt wore a lightweight calfskin jacket, the kind of soft leather that scuffs and unscuffs at a touch, and Eric often remarked his wish to own it whatever the difference in their sizes.

"I think I'll probably take it with me for the not so rugged parts of the trip."

"The taste is metallic according to downwinders. You open the door and step outside to get the newspaper that the newsboy on his bike has tossed on the porch and you taste a kind of metallic grit in the air, like salt made of metal shavings. Coming to our party tonight?"

"Wouldn't miss it," Matt said.

"Your child is born with eyes that are pure white. No discernible pupil or iris. Just a large white eyeball. Two if you're lucky."

Eric lifted the Playboy off the sofa and held it sideways, letting the centerfold swing open so he could see the monthly subject full-length.

He said, "Where are you going exactly?"

"Someplace remote."

"Remoter than this?"

"I've been looking at maps."

"But remoter than this?"

"Where the paved roads end."

"You're a city kid, Matty."

"I've been looking at southwest Arizona maybe."

"I want that jacket if you die."

When the bombheads threw a party you couldn't expect to emerge into the world you'd always known. And last night's affair seemed to overlay the landscape as Matty drove west on Interstate 10 through a town called Deming, which was Eric's last name of course, and how clammy was the hand of coincidence—faces, places and provocative remarks all running through his mind.

He'd smoked something that had made him immobile. But not just immobile. Matt was not a user except at parties, where he'd go through the sociable motions, taking a pull on a long-stemmed pipe

420

with a clay bowl that was tamped with grassy substance. But the thing he'd toked last night was either a rogue strain of hashish or standard stuff laced with some psychotomimetic agent. And he was not just immobilized. And somebody sat in front of him and spoke thickly into his face in a ridiculous movie accent evidently meant to be Prussian.

"You can never underestimate the willingness of the state to act out its own massive fantasies."

It was Eric of course. But even if Matt understood this, he could not place it in the jocular context of broad bombhead sport. Because he was not just immobile—he couldn't think straight either. He was surrounded by enemies. Not enemies but connections, a network of things and people. Not people exactly but figures—things and figures and levels of knowledge that he was completely helpless to enter.

The villingness of the shtate.

You can never unterestimate the villingness of the shtate.

Eric went on in his stupid voice, talking about problem boxes and minimax solutions, all the kriegspielish stuff they'd studied in grad school, theory of games and patterns of conflict, heads I win, tails you lose, and Matty sat there stoned totally motionless.

He was locked to his chair, mind-locked and gravity-trapped, aware of the nature of the state he was in but unable to think himself out. He was bent to the weight of the room, distrustful of everyone and everything here. Paranoid. Now he knew what it meant, this word that was bandied and bruited so easily, and he sensed the connections being made around him, all the objects and shaped silhouettes and levels of knowledge—not knowledge exactly but insidious intent. But not that either—some deeper meaning that existed solely to keep him from knowing what it was.

To ahkt out its own massif phantasies.

Eric was still talking, stirring a drink with his finger, and it occurred to Matt in the morning, driving his car through Deming, that maybe the accent was not supposed to be Prussian at all but Hungarian. Eric was paying tribute to the original bombheads, all those emigrés from Middle Europe, thick-browed men with sad eyes and roomy pleated pants. They came to do science in New Mexico during the war, an overnight sprawl of trailers and hutments, and they ate the local grub and played poker once a week and went to the Saturday square dance and worked on the thing with no name, the bomb that would redefine the limits of human perception and dread.

He sat in the chair studying someone's shoe.

He knew he wasn't part of some superficial state that people like to borrow from when they say they're feeling paranoid. This was not secondhand. This was real and deep and true. It was all the one-syllable words that mean we aren't kidding. It was also familiar in some strange paleolithic root-eating way, a thing retained in the snake brain of early experience.

He studied the shoe on the foot of someone seated near him. It was an Earth shoe, one of those functional, sensible, unsexy, shallow-heeled and vaguely Scandinavian items of fad footwear, the shy, androgynous and countercultural shoe, unthreatening to the environment or the species, and he wondered why it looked so sinister.

Eric was stuttering now.

He didn't know who was wearing the shoe. The idea of connecting the shoe to the person who was wearing it required such an immensity of effort, there was such encumbrance and complication that he could only bend his head to the weight of the room. Maybe the shoe looked sinister because all its meanings and connections and silhouettes were outside Matty's faculties of knowing.

And maybe it looked sinister because it was the left shoe, on the left foot, and this is what sinister means of course—unlucky, unfavorable, leftward—and the word was asserting its baleful roots, its edible tubers and stems, through the medium of someone's shoe.

Eric was still there, talking in a normal voice interrupted by stutters. He seemed to be in another time frame, Eric did, cut and edited, his words in stop-start format and his position frequently altered in relation to the background, and here he was again on the sign for Deming, his name floating out of the soft dawn as Matt drove west, deeper into the white parts of the map, where he would try to find a clue to his future.

3

The statue in the marbled niche had the thighs and calves of a man, a man's bundled muscles in the forearms, but the figure in fact was biblical Eve, tight-breasted, with an apple in her hands and the sloping shoulders of a fullback.

And why not. The evening had the slightly scattered air of some cross-referenced event. Klara wandered through the grand foyer, among the early arrivals, and what a happy buzz they generated, mostly men in fact, and this was interesting. Look at the lean sleek geometry and gunmetal surfaces, the draped mirrors and long chandeliers, it was an art deco palace, burnished steel and chrome, a sense of machine-age completion, and fairly refined in tone except for the mural.

The lobby crowd loved the mural. An enormous mystical vision, sixty feet by forty, with a sort of Lost Horizon motif, situated above the staircase and contoured in a gentle curve so that the craggy peaks of the painting were captured in the towering mirrors, extending the enchanted effect over much of the lobby. Amber mists, a cloaked old man with a staff, a cluster of flamingos standing in the alpenglow—a vision so steeped in kitsch you could die just by buying the postcard.

Yes, this was Radio City Music Hall, a place Klara had last visited when she was thirteen probably, about a year after the doors opened—showplace of the nation. She remembered the soaring walls and carpeted stairs. She remembered the powder room, that's what she remembered, downstairs, in the grand lounge.

She watched Miles Lightman weave through the crowd, doing a couple of pirouettes as he approached, taking in the full 360, eyes slightly popping.

"Where are we, in a model room at Bloomingdale's?"

"We're in 1932, that's where we are."

"It's sort of I-don't-know-what, isn't it?"

"Jazz moderne," Klara said.

"Can you believe I've never been here?"

She was surprised to see that Miles had dressed for the occasion. Many people had and so had Miles, to the extent that he dresses. He wore his scuffed boots and jeans but also had a leopard shirt and mustard tie and a black corduroy jacket with an Edwardian flare.

They watched a man come down the grand staircase, feigning injury as he went past the mural. Miles had a package of cigarettes for Klara. While they waited he gave her further background on the event.

The event was a showing of the legendary lost film of Sergei Eisenstein, called *Unterwelt*, recently found in East Germany, meticulously restored and brought to New York under the aegis of the film society Miles belonged to, a remarkable coup for the group. After a period of maneuvering, infighting and hard bargaining they managed to reach an agreement with several rock impresarios and arranged to cosponsor this one-time screening, with orchestral accompaniment, in a house seating nearly six thousand people.

"How do you explain the turnout?" Klara said. "A lot of gay men in this lobby."

"I think you ought to see the film and figure it out for yourself. I'll only tell you that word got around, early on, that Eisenstein made a film with a powerful theme and the footage has been hidden away all these decades because the theme deals on some level with people living in the shadows, and the government, or the governments, the GDR and the Soviets, have suppressed the film until now."

Probably shot in the midthirties, sporadically and in secret, during a period of acute depression for Eisenstein. Ostensibly idle at the time, goaded by fellow Soviet directors to discard his theories and conceits. Called eccentric, called myth-ridden and politically unsound, accused of being out of touch with the people. Stories began to circulate that he'd been executed.

Esther Winship showed up waving her handbag and saying, "I don't need to see the movie. I already love it. This hall is so wonderful. I'd forgotten it was here. Miles, you look like a mod-and-rocker reunion."

"Where's Jack?" Klara said.

"Where could he be? Is it your shirt or tie that gives me vertigo?"

"Thank you, Esther."

"He's having a drink around the corner," she said.

There was an ambivalence that vitalized the crowd. Whatever your sexual persuasion, you were here to enjoy the contradictions. Think of the relationship between the film and the theater in which it was showing—the work of a renowned master of world cinema screened in the camp environment of the Rockettes and the mighty Wurlitzer. But a theater of a certain impressive shapeliness, a breathtaking place, even, for all its exaggerations and vanities, with roundels of enameled brass on the outer walls and handsome display cases in the ticket lobby and nickel bronze stair rails here in the foyer, a space that resembled the hushed and sunken saloon of an ocean liner. And possibly a film, you're not likely to forget this, that will be riddled with mannerisms whatever the level of seriousness. At least you hope so. Didn't *Ivan the Terrible* contain scenes so comically overwrought, amid the undeniable power of the montage, that you laughed and caught your breath more or less simultaneously?

"Nobody, practically, has seen the film up to this point," Miles said. "Four of us have seen it in our group and half a dozen promoters and theater brass and that's about it on this side of the Iron Curtain."

Miles knew Eisenstein inside and out. He knew more than was humanly healthy. He knew the shot sequence in *Potemkin* just about cold. The deadly cadence of black boots. The white jackets of the soldiers. The mother clutching weakly at her waist. The rear wheels of the baby carriage rolling out of the frame.

425

But there were things nobody seemed to know about this movie. Where it was made. How it was made—he didn't have official backing obviously. And why he didn't use sound. One theory pointed to Mexico. The enormous amount of footage he shot openly for his Mexican epic was a cover for a subversive venture, went the theory, and this was it.

"Actually I haven't seen a single thing he's ever done," Esther said. "But I met him once, you know."

Miles turned his head slowly to look at her.

"You knew Eisenstein?"

It was a look of total reevaluation.

"Met him briefly."

"Where?"

"Here. I was very young, of course. New York. Barely twenty, I think. And he was sitting for a portrait and my parents knew the painter and I went along."

"We have to talk about this," Miles said.

"That's all there is, I'm afraid. He asked me to call him Sergei."

"What else?"

"He drank a lot of milk. He said it was breakfast."

"What else?" Miles said.

"Actually he showed up with the milk, in a bottle. I got him a glass and he thanked me."

"What else?" Miles said.

The other thing nobody knew was where the title came from. Eisenstein knew German and may have had a reason for choosing a title in that language. But it's more likely the film acquired the title during its long repose in an underground vault in East Berlin.

"Gnomelike sort of fellow, as I recall."

"What else?"

"Large head. Sort of very high forehead. Milk came in bottles then, remember?"

It became the movie people had to see. A nice tight hysteria began to build and there were tickets going for shocking sums and counterfeit tickets and people rushing back from the Vineyard and the Pines and the Cape to engineer a seat.

Just a movie for godsake and a silent movie at that and a movie you probably never heard of until the Times did a Sunday piece. But this is how the behavioral aberration, once begun, grows to lavish panic.

"But will we actually be able to sit through it?" Esther said. "Or is it one of those things where we have to be reverent because we're in the presence of greatness but we're really all sitting there determined to be the first ones out the door so we can get a taxi."

"You're thinking of theater," Miles said. "This is film."

Jack Marshall turned up with peanuts on his breath, Esther's husband, and they went into the auditorium.

Klara remembered it now, suddenly so familiar, the feeling of plush and mothered comfort, it felt like her mother hovering, a space soothingly wombed and curved, and the way the proscenium arch rayed out into the ceiling, about eight stories at its highest point, and the spoked rows of downy seats, and the choral staircases that softened the side walls, and the overvastness that seemed allowable, your one indulgence of this type, shrinking everyone in the hall to child size, heads turning and lifting, a rediscovered surprise and delight floating over the crowd, not the last such emotion that people would share this evening.

It developed that the show had a pace and theme and it started with the sound of chase music, offstage, a tinny piano doing the familiar sort of ragtime score that used to accompany silent movies. Then the house lights went down and the great motorized curtain slowly lifted and the full orchestra appeared. A rustle in the audience. Moments after the musicians began to play, the whole unit commenced moving, sliding nicely in its band car to the front of the stage. How wondrously funny and odd. The music became suspenseful now, a series of diminished chords, perhaps a scary moment pending—and sure enough the orchestra reached the stage apron and dropped rather dramatically into the pit and then completely out of sight, elevatored down like so many geeks in tuxedos, a maneuver of a certain farcical bravado, greeted with cheers.

Gone but not inaudible. They were playing patriotic music now, a medley of familiar marches with drum ruffles and sousaphones, and the curtain descended halfway, recontoured in flag format and starred and striped by colored floods, and just as the audience began to wonder what the point was, out came the Rockettes, what a toothsome shock—did anyone know there was a stage show in the works?

They were wearing West Point gray and came out saluting, thirty-six women remade as interchangeable parts, height, shape, race and type, with plumed dress hats and fringed titties and faces buttered a christmassy pink but isn't it odd they're wearing bondage collars—saluting and high-kicking in machine unison and Klara thought they were kind of great and so did everyone else. Snapping into close formation, tap-dancing in a wash of iridescent arcs, all symmetry and drill precision, then fanning open in kaleidoscopic bursts, and she passed a question along the aisle to Miles, who sat at the far end of the foursome.

"How do we know it's really the Rockettes and not a troupe of female impersonators?"

And this droll notion seemed to travel through the audience because isn't it unlikely that the real Rockettes would be wearing slave collars and doing routines with such pulsing sexual rhythm? In fact it's probably not unlikely at all, it's probably what they do all the time. You don't know for sure, do you? And if they are the real Rockettes, what you're seeing are three dozen women in close-order cadet formation, or women done up like men and not the reverse—but it's a cross-dressing event either way.

Klara realized the flag curtain was gone. And when a camera in the flies took a live video shot of the dancers that was projected on a back screen she understood, you all did, how a crowd is reconfigured, teased into methodical geometry, into slipknots and serpentines. And it was funny of course because the routines were so impeccably smooth and serious, so nineteen-thirties in their dynamic alignments, and isn't that when the movie was made?

The dancers spread across the stage and in a single dexterous swipe, like unholstering a gun, they pulled off their tearaway trousers and went into a final rousing kick, gams flashing, and drew several waves of applause. Then they dissolved their kick line and formed a star, clearly depicted in the high-angle shot on the screen above them, and the footlights painted them solid red. They marched in place as the orchestra lifted solemnly into the pit and began to play, what—something Russian, Klara thought. And how strange it was to see a thing like this, a red star of such political and military moment, plunked down here, the grim signet of the Soviet Union, in the Music Hall of all places—think of all the Easter shows and Lassie movies.

The dancers stood white-faced now, upstage, transfixed by beams of light from mammoth spots high in the rear of the auditorium. The curtain began to fall, covering first the video image of the dancers and then the dancers. The music grew weepy and frilled and then the curtain lifted to reveal the vast movie screen bearing a single word, *Unterwelt*, and finally the borders at each end of the curved screen folded in to accommodate the small squarish frame of the old movie, and images poured from the projection booth, patchy and dappled with age.

Of course the film was strange at first, elusive in its references and filled with baroque apparitions and hard to adapt to—you wouldn't want it any other way.

Overcomposed close-ups, momentous gesturing, actors trailing their immense bended shadows and there was something to study in every frame, the camera placement, the shapes and planes and then the juxtaposed shots, the sense of rhythmic contradiction, it was all spaces and volumes, it was tempo, mass and stress.

In Eisenstein you note that the camera angle is a kind of dialectic. Arguments are raised and made, theories drift across the screen and instantly shatter— there's a lot of opposition and conflict.

It seems you are watching a movie about a mad scientist. He sweeps through the frame, dressed in well-defined black and white, in layered robes, wielding an atomic ray gun. Figures move through crude rooms in some underground space. They are victims or prisoners, perhaps experimental subjects. A glimpse of a prisoner's face shows he is badly deformed and it is less shocking than funny. He has the sloped head, shallow jaw and protuberant lips of an earthworm—but a worm with a human pathos about him.

In a scene that was extravagant, silly, off-kilter and technically impressive all at the same time, the scientist fires the ray gun at a victim, who begins to glow in the dark, jerking and dancing and then looking rather wanly at his arm, which starts to melt away.

Other victims appeared, muscles and bones reshaped, slits for eyes, shuffling on stump legs.

Klara thought of the radiation monsters in Japanese science-fiction movies and looked down the aisle at Miles, who was a scholar of the form.

Was Eisenstein being prescient about nuclear menace or about Japanese cinema?

She thought of the prehistoric reptiles that came mutating out of the slime and the insects with chromosome damage poking from the desert near some test site, ants the size of bookmobiles—these were movies for the drive-ins of the fifties, a boy and girl yanking at each other's buckles and snaps while the bomb footage unfurls and the giant leeches and scorpions appear on the horizon, all radioactive and seeking revenge, and the fleeing crowds, of course, because in the end these creatures not only come from the bomb but displace it, and the armies mobilize and the crowds flee and the sirens wail like sirens.

Eisenstein's creatures were fully human and this complicated the fun. They humped and scuttled through the shadows, hump-lurched with hands dragging, and you can always convince yourself it's okay to laugh at cripples and mutants if everybody else is laughing, it's a way to play off your aversion, and it wasn't just the twisted features and elaborate gestures and the curious sort of lip-gloss effect you've noticed on the faces of male actors in silent movies but the music as well, this was pretty broad too—string sections of soaring melodrama.

A title now and then, in Russian, untranslated, not that it mattered—it made in fact for a giddy kind of total confusion.

Jack said, "Getting claustrophobic, are you?"

And it was true, the film was embedded so completely in the viewpoint of the prisoners that Klara was beginning to squirm.

Jack said, "I bet you'd give a hundred dollars to stand in the rain right now and smoke a cigarette."

"Is it raining?"

"Does it matter?"

The plot was hard to follow. There was no plot. Just loneliness, barrenness, men hunted and ray-gunned, all happening in some netherland crevice. There was none of the cross-class solidarity of the Soviet tradition. No crowd scenes or sense of social motive—the masses as hero, colossal crowd movements painstakingly organized and framed, and this was disappointing to Klara. She loved the martial architecture of huge moving bodies, the armies and mobs in other Eisenstein films, and she felt she was in some ambiguous filmscape somewhere between the Soviet model and Hollywood's vaulted heaven of love, sex, crime and individual heroism, of scenery and luxury and gorgeous toilets.

All you have to do is think of the other *Underworld*, a 1927 gangster film and box office smash.

Esther said, "I want to be rewarded for this ordeal."

Admit it, you're bored. Klara tried to take encouragement from Miles. He was in a state of rapt elation, that pure surrender he undertakes, able to lose himself in the eye and mind of the movie, totally drawn and charmed—charmed at some level even when he doesn't like what he's watching. But she knew he liked this. It was remote and fragmentary and made on the cheap, supposedly personal, and it had a kind of suspense even as it crawled along.

How and when would it reveal itself?

She wondered why the film was silent. Maybe it was shot earlier than the experts surmised. But she thought it was more likely that Eisenstein knew he'd have an easier time doing the film in secret if he did not use sound. And maybe silence suited the development of his themes.

What about the politics? She thought this film might be a protest against socialist realism, against the party-minded mandate to produce art that advanced the Soviet cause. Was he in secret rebellion? He'd been condemned for earlier work, according to Miles, and had seemed to capitulate. But what was this murky film, this strange dark draggy set of images if not a statement of outrage and independence?

Even better. Doesn't this movie seem to anticipate the terror that was mounted against Russian artists in the late nineteen-thirties? The secret police. The arrests, the torture, the disappearances, the executions.

The mad scientist aims the gun.

A figure stands against a wall, his body going white.

The scientist shows a tight smile.

The victim is transfigured, pain-racked, his lower lip dribbling off his face, a growth appearing at the side of his neck, a radiant time-lapse melanoma.

The scientist approaches and touches the man, tenderly, on the cheek.

Abruptly the screen went dark. Intermission seemed a timely idea and Klara thought she'd take Esther on a tour of the powder rooms, there were quite a few, she thought, on several levels, and well worth beholding—murals, sculpture, furniture, things she'd seen through her mother's eyes, suddenly free in space, independent of memory.

Miles went up to a private viewing room in the third mezzanine to confer with his colleagues. The two women left Jack in a chair in the grand lounge, downstairs, a carpeted area about two hundred feet in length, and they went into the nearest powder room.

"I've got a question," Esther said.

Klara lit a cigarette. Esther, who'd stopped smoking, bummed one and lit it and inhaled and then looked away to protect the sensation, to guard it from distraction.

They heard a rumble. They felt something shaking under their feet and Klara studied the white parchment wall, listening carefully.

Then she took a drag and said, "S'okay, friend. Only the subway. The IND plowing under Sixth Avenue with its cargo of human souls."

They went up to the mezzanine levels and peered in at the walnut and pigskin in the men's smoking rooms and Klara said, "So what's your question?"

"Do we have to stay for the rest of it?"

"Miles went to a certain amount of trouble. Besides I want to see what happens."

"What could happen?"

"I don't know. But it's an interesting movie to look at from time to time."

"There's something about the tone," Esther said. "The photography. The glances that get exchanged. It's awfully shrouded of course. And the way the scientist."

"Touched the victim."

"What do you know about Eisenstein?"

"He was your friend, not mine," Klara said.

They made their rounds of the powder rooms and went back down

432

to find Jack on the lower level, sitting above the rattle of another sub-way run.

The train was one of his, Moonman's, he had a dozen pieces running through the system, top-to-bottom burners, and it just so happens he was aboard tonight, under the water mains and waste pipes, under the gas and steam and electric, between the storm sewers and telephone lines, and he moved from car to car with each stop and checked out the people who stepped inside, wearing their retractable subway faces, and the doors went ding dong before banging shut.

Ismael Muñoz, dark and somber, watching people come aboard. Sparsely stubbled Ismael reading lips and faces, hoping he might catch a bravo comment. Hey this guy is lighting up the line. This was his newest piece so here he was going uptown on the Washington Heights local, every car tagged with his own neon zoom, with high-lights and overlapping letters and 3-D effect, the whole wildstyle thing of making your name and street number a kind of alphabet city where the colors lock and bleed and the letters connect and it's all live jive, it jumps and shouts—even the drips are intentional, painted supersharp to express how the letters sweat, how they live and breathe and eat and sleep, they dance and play the sax.

This was not a window-down piece. This was a whole-train burner with windows painted over and each letter and number bigger than a man.

Moonman 157.

Ismael was sixteen, not too old and not too young, and he was determined to kill the shit of every subway artist in town.

Nobody could take him down.

And he sat there in his khaki jacket with his eyes ever moving, wait-ing for someone to say something that would make his day.

He knew he was getting fame. He had imitators now, a couple of fairy-ass kids who tried to outking him in his own country. One of them got busted by the vandal squad, sentenced to clean graffiti from the station walls with an orange juice mixture because there's an acid in the juice that eats into paint.

Serves the *chulo* right for biting my style.

And he sat there with his longish face and misaligned teeth, an old man's worried head, and he studied the platform people at every stop. They reacted to the train, their heads went wow. Some shocked looks too, they're seeing hell on wheels, but mostly the eyes go yes and the faces open up. And he studied the riders as they shuffled in, carrying umbrellas, some of them, and concealed weapons, others, and gum wrappers and phone numbers and crushed Kleenex and hankies wrapped around house keys all wadded together on their mulatto bodies because the subway's where the races mix.

It made him think he was an unknown hero of the line, riding a train he'd maximum tagged. Revealing himself in a cartoon glow. Hey it's Moonman in our midst.

Once a man stood on the platform and took a picture of one of Moonman's top-to-bottoms, a foreigner by the look of him, and Ismael sidled to the open door so he could be in the picture too, unknown to the man. The man was photographing the piece and the writer both, completely unknown to himself, from someplace like Sweden he looked.

The whole point of Moonman's tag was how the letters and numbers told a story of backstreet life.

At Columbus Circle he changed to the Broadway train because he had business at the end of the line. He got on a train that was bombed inside and out by Skaty 8, a thirteen-year-old writer who frantically tagged police cars, hearses, garbage trucks, who took his Krylon satin colors into the tunnels and tagged up the walls and catwalks, he hit platforms, steps, turnstiles and benches, he'd tag your little sister if she was walking by. Not a style king, no way, but a legend among writers for the energy he put forth, getting his tag seen by major millions and then two weeks ago, and a genuine regret went through Ismael as he recalled being told, he slumped and sagged all over again and felt the deepest kind of soldierly sadness—Skaty 8 hit by a train while he's walking on the tracks under downtown Brooklyn.

People moved along the car, they skated to a seat, they looked at display ads above the heads across the aisle, all without eye motion that you could detect with the most delicate device.

Ismael used to walk the tracks when he felt sorry for himself. Those were foregone times. He'd pop an emergency hatch in the sidewalk and climb down into a tunnel and just, like, go for a walk, be alone down there, keeping the third rail in sight and listening for the train and getting to know the people who lived in the cable rooms and up on the catwalks, and that's where he saw a spray-paint scrawl, maybe five years ago, down under Eighth Avenue. *Bird Lives*. It made him wonder about graffiti, about who took the trouble and risk to walk down this tunnel and throw a piece across the wall, and how many years have gone by since then, and who is Bird, and why does he live?

And the guy who reached around saying excuse me please.

He rode up the edge of Manhattan headed for the Bronx. There was no art in bombing platforms and walls. You have to tag the trains. The trains come roaring down the rat alleys all alike and then you hit a train and it is yours, seen everywhere in the system, and you get inside people's heads and vandalize their eyeballs.

The doors went ding dong before banging shut.

He saw a thin black male standing at the end of the car, disregard-ful, he's acting out the birth of the cool, and Ismael thought he was an undercover cop. It made him go low profile in his mental makeup, willing himself to be unnoticed in his seat, because he believed they were closing in on him. There was a big push out of City Hall to wipe out graffiti once and for all, to cork these ghetto crews and the middle-class white boys that came biting in behind them, and writers were being careful and playing safe.

He did not fear arrest, only the complications that would follow. Arrest would be good for his notoriety. It might even mean a story in the Post. But then the matter of the family begins to be important. It's not that he didn't want to be a father. He liked the idea of father and family. But there were so many things in between.

When he walked the tunnels as a kid he used to ask about Bird and he found out this was Charlie Parker. A jazz giant. He used to talk to the men who lived on the catwalks and in the unused freight tunnel under the West Side, they had beds and chairs and shopping carts, they had slippers they put on in the evening, they were mostly ordi-nary men, they washed the dishes and took out the garbage, and they

435

told him about bop, bebop, and how Bird was dead at thirty-four. And one day Ismael, maybe he's thirteen, he's taking a leak against a wall and a guy comes along and stands behind him and reaches around, believe it or not, saying excuse me, and holds Ismael's dick while he pisses.

Dead at thirty-four, that was Bird, which was a ripe old age in the tunnels.

He knew he was getting fame because he had imitators, first, and because other writers did not disrespect him by spraying over his work, except some of them did, and because two women came looking for him in the Bronx.

But, see, this was the way his mind was reasoning at this particular time. Stay totally low and out of sight. Do not get your name or face in the papers. Do not get in trouble with the transit police. Because he had a woman he used to live with who was pregnant head to toe. They used to live with her mother and her mother's part-time man and it isn't that Ismael Muñoz doesn't want to be a father. It's just that this is not the time to get personally involved.

He heard they went into the superettes, two women from the galleries. They went into the bodegas, the church, the firehouse, he pictured them going into the firehouse to ask about graffiti, twenty men in rubber boots eating combination pizzas.

He sat on the Broadway train listening to the way his mind was reasoning.

People from the galleries were all over the Bronx looking for Moonman, for Momzo Tops, for Snak-Bar and Rimester and the whole Voodoo crew.

Forget it, man. He could easily envision a case where the whole gallery scene is a scam by the police to get writers out of the tunnels and train yards and into the open, identified by name and face.

The man held his dick and eventually sucked it, whenever it was, a couple of days later, or weeks, that was the act he performed. And Ismael went down there, feeling sorry for himself, fairly often after that, going through a fence near the West Side Highway and into an opening in a grated emergency exit and down the narrow steps into the freight tunnel, where they had bookshelves, some of them, and

Christmas decorations, and used half names and code names, tags like the writers would develop, and the truth of the matter is that he still goes down there for sex with men because some habits you drop and others you come to rely on.

The train went past City College, then veered east.

They did it herky-jerky in the dark. Or they went to a cable room and did it with sheets and towels. They kept pets down there and ran clotheslines across the tunnel and stole electricity from the government.

Bop, bebop. And how Bird was dead at thirty-four.

And he sat there in his khaki slouch, looking down between his feet, glancing at the feet across the aisle, all the notched and dimpled shoes that did not seem to be things that people bought and wore so much as permanent parts, body parts, inseparable from the men and women sitting there, because the subway seals you durably in the stone of the moment.

The train entered the Bronx and he got off four stops later, at the end of the line, where his crew was waiting faithfully.

There were three of them, ages twelve, eleven and twelve, and they'd spent the day racking paint from hardware stores, which is a pastime, petty theft, that Ismael has long since risen above.

They walked up the steep hill at 242nd Street.

"Where's the rain?" Ismael said.

"Nothing happen," they said.

"I hear rain on the radio all day. I figure we don't work tonight. Ten to one against."

"Nothing happen," they said. "Two, three drops."

They had the spray-paint cans in three gym bags. They had Ismael's sketches in a manila portfolio. They had peaches and grapes in a paper bag inside a plastic bag. They had the French mineral water he liked to drink while he worked, also acquired in the day's little wave of thievery, Perrier, in pretty green bottles. He believed in going elite whenever possible. They had nozzles for the spray cans. They had master keys to open up the cars in case he wanted to work inside, which he did not.

His crew consisted of hopefuls, of course. Up writers of the future. They racked for the master. They kept lookout while he painted. They crossbraced their arms to support his weight when he needed to reach the upper part of a car.

A chain-link fence ran along the street, topped by razor ribbon. The crew paused near the west end of the fence, where there was a section of snipped links, concealed by poison ivy. They held back the fence and Ismael edged through, jump-stepping to the roof that was adjacent. There was a series of equipment sheds with sawtooth roofs. They went to the last roof and shinnied down drainpipes to the wooden planking at track level, which they could do in their sleep by now, and began to look around for a suitable train to tag.

They knew pretty much in advance that they wouldn't be hassled. There were too many trains, too many writers. The city could not afford all the guards that would be needed to patrol the yards and sidings through the night.

They saw Rimester near a light tower, one of the older writers, a black guy wearing a kufi, a skullcap, who did amazing wildstyle window-downs, Ismael had to admit—the letters decorated with love poems and sentiments of heartbreak.

They gave each other ceremonial respect, with precise and detailed flourishes of handshake and phraseology, and they rapped about this and that, and then Rimester described how he'd seen six of his cars going under the acid bath in the large yard about a mile and a half south of here. They run the cars under sprinklers built above the track. All his two-in-the-morning spray-crazy unpaid labor getting buffed away in minutes. Forget orange juice, man. This was the new graffiti killer, some weirdshit chemical from the CIA.

It's like you knock a picture off a shelf and someone dies. Only this time it's you that's in the photo.

That's how some writers felt about their tags.

There were a dozen tracks at the siding here. Ismael and his crew went to the far end, to the last track, overlooking the field where the Irish played Irish football. They picked out a flat—this was an old train with a paintable surface, much better than the ridgies that were coming on the market.

The crew lined up his colors and he went to work. He had a Rustoleum yellow he'd started using, like mad canary, and the crew fitted different nozzles on the can so he could vary the breadth and mass of the strokes.

"We seen Lourdes," they said to him.

Lourdes was the woman he used to live with, two years older than Ismael, more or less, and maybe twenty pounds heavier right now.

"Who asked you who you seen?"

"She say she want to talk to you."

"*Maricón*, who asked? I ask?"

Ismael rarely got angry. He was not an angry guy. He had the reflective head of an elder of the barrio, playing dominoes under a canopy while the fire engines idle up the street, but if the crew expected to do the fill-in once he set the style and faded the colors, they'd better learn the manners of the yard.

"Where's my Perrier, okay? You want to work with Ismael Muñoz, you give him his Perrier and forget about messages from whoever."

They worked through the night without unnecessary talk. They handed him the spray cans. They shook the cans before handing them over and the clicking sound of the aerosol ball was basically the only noise in the yard except for the spray itself, the hissy wash of paint folding over the old iron flanks of the train.

The man who reached around and said excuse me.

Moonman 157. Add the digits and you get thirteen. But that's the street where he lives, or used to live, he lives a lot of places now, so it's properly part of his tag, it's what they know him as, and bad luck is an ego trip you can count on, and think of a train coming out of the tunnels and going elevated—think of your tag in maximum daylight rolling over the scorched lots where you were born and raised.

The crew shook the cans and the ball went click.

He stood on the door edge of one train and leaned across to the train parked adjacent and tagged it from the windows up.

And he went down the slate stairway that crumbled to the pressure of his weight, his hand on the rusty pipe that was the banister, and he felt the mood of the tunnel on a given day. It might be a coke mood one day, Ismael did not do drugs, or a mood of speed that's traveling through the tunnel, someone made a buy and shared it, or a mood of mental illness, which was often the case. And always a brown rat mood because they were there in pack rat numbers, an endless source of stories, the size of the rats, the attitude of unfearing, how they ate the bodies of those who died in the tunnels, how they were eaten in turn by the rat man who lived in level six under Grand Central, he killed and cooked and ate a rat a week—track rabbits, they were called.

In other words to muralize a whole train you need a full night and part of the next night and no shuffling bullshit talk.

And a mood of who you are in your head day by day, which he did not share with anyone at street level, and going to sleep in a cousin's bed at night or in the supply cellar of some bodega where they knew Ismael Muñoz and gave him a place that was adequate and hearing the doors go ding dong and seeing the man from Stockholm, Sweden, who took pictures of his piece.

He liked to watch the eyes of platform people to see how they reacted to his work.

His letters and numbers told a story of tenement life, good and bad but mostly good. The verticals in the letter N could be drug dealers guarding a long diagonal stash of glassine product or they could be schoolgirls on a playground slide or a couple of sandlot ballplayers with a bat angled between them.

Nobody could take him down. He kinged every artist in town.

They had dozens of cans out and ready, all by prearrangement, and he called a color and they shook the can and the ball went click.

"Where's my Perrier?" he said.

But you have to stand on a platform and see it coming or you can't know the feeling a writer gets, how the number 5 train comes roaring down the rat alleys and slams out of the tunnel, going whop-pop onto the high tracks, and suddenly there it is, Moonman riding the sky in the heart of the Bronx, over the whole burnt and rusted country, and this is the art of the backstreets talking, all the way from Bird, and you can't *not* see us anymore, you can't *not* know who we are, we got total notoriety now, Momzo Tops and Rimester and me, we're getting fame, we ain't ashame, and the train go rattling over the garbagy streets and past the dead-eye windows of all those empty tenements that have people living there even if you don't see them, but you have to see our tags and cartoon figures and bright and rhyming poems, this is the art that can't stand still, it climbs across your eyeballs night and day, the flickery jumping art of the slums and dumpsters, flashing those colors in your face—like I'm your movie, motherfucker.

They came funneling out of the lobby and moved down the aisles and found their seats, the anticipation of early evening largely depleted by now, and they settled in quickly, all business, and the second half of the film began.

Klara looked around for Miles. But Miles didn't show. He'd evidently sensed the impatience of his guests and decided to stay with the cineastes in the private booth upstairs.

"Does this mean we're unworthy?" Esther said.

It seems you are witnessing an escape. Figures moving upward through gouged tunnels into a dark rainy night. A long scene of silhouettes and occasional tight shots, eyes peering in the dark.

Then a spotlight swung across the orchestra pit and came to rest on a side curtain on the north wall, set slightly higher than the stage and some yards distant. And you knew what you were going to see half a second before you saw it and what a mood-booster, absolutely. The curtains parted and the horseshoe console of New York's last great theater organ, the mighty Wurlitzer, stood framed and gleaming in the dark hall.

The organist was a slightish man, white-haired, who seemed to hover in the alcove, his back to the audience, wizardly in his very smallness, and he hit the thunder pedal just as a figure on the screen drew back cowering from some danger above, and laughter swept the auditorium.

The prisoners continued their climb, moving in grim proximity to each other.

The organist hit a series of notes that had an uncanny familiarity. The sort of thing that takes you hauntingly back to your bedside radio and the smells in your kitchen and the way the linoleum used to ripple near the icebox. It was a march, sprightly is the word, and it worked in ironic counterpoint to the foreground silhouettes on the screen, figures climbing in rote compliance, and Klara felt the music in her skin

441

and could practically taste it on her tongue but wasn't able to name the piece or identify the composer.

She gave old Jack a poke in the arm.

"What's he playing?"

"Prokofiev."

"Prokofiev. Of course. Prokofiev did scores for Eisenstein. I knew that. But what's this march?"

"It's that Three Oranges thing, whatever it's called. You've heard it a thousand times."

"Of course, yes. But why have I heard it a thousand times?"

"Because it was the theme music on an old radio show. Brought to you by Lava soap. Remember Lava soap?"

"Yes, yes, of course."

And Jack chanted in sacramental sync with the organ.

"El-lay-vee-ay. El-lay-vee-ay."

"Of course, yes. It's completely clear to me now. But I don't remember the program," she said.

And Jack kept chanting because he was having such a good time with this, and so was the audience, eyes shifting from the screen to the console and minds locked in radio recall, those of you who were old enough, and somewhere backstage, in a dozen lofts, the enormous organ pipes sounded the tones—pipes, wind chests, shutters and blowers bringing this vintage theme, borrowed from a Russian opera, back home to the past.

And Jack left off his chanting to adopt the bardic voice of a veteran announcer doing the show's opening.

" 'The FBI in Peace and War,' " he spoke ringingly.

It was nice to have friends. Klara remembered now. Neighbor kids used to listen to the show, faithfully, toward the end of the war, and she could almost hear the voice of the actor who played the FBI field agent.

The curtain closed on the organist just as the sun came out and Esther said, "Finally."

Yes, the film has climbed to the surface, to a landscape shocked by light, pervasive and overexposed. The escaped prisoners move across flat terrain, some of them hooded, the most disfigured ones, and there are fires in the distance, the horizon line throbbing in smoke and ash.

442

You wonder if he shot these scenes in Mexico, or could it be Kazakhstan, where he went to shoot *Ivan the Terrible*, later, during the war?

Many long shots, sky and plain, intercut with foreground figures, their heads and torsos crowding out the landscape, precisely the kind of formalist excess that got the director in trouble with the apparat.

The orchestra was in its covert mode, somewhere under the pit, playing faintly at first, a soft accent edged against the strong visuals.

You study the faces of the victims as they take off their hoods. A cyclops. A man with skewed jaw. A lizard man. A woman with a flap of skin for a nose and mouth.

A series of eloquent largo passages begins to fill the hall.

The audience was stilled. You saw things differently now. If there was a politics of montage, it was more intimate here—not the themes of atomic radiation or irresponsible science and not state terror either, the independent artist who is disciplined and sovietized.

These deformed faces, these were people who existed outside nationality and strict historical context. Eisenstein's method of immediate characterization, called typage, seemed self-parodied and shattered here, intentionally. Because the external features of the men and women did not tell you anything about class or social mission. They were people persecuted and altered, this was their typology— they were an inconvenient secret of the society around them.

Now there is a search party on the prowl, men on horseback strung out across the plain. They recapture some of the fugitives, they shackle and march them in somber lockstep, in tired mindless versions of the stage routines, and Klara saw it retrospectively, how the Rockettes had prefigured this, only it wasn't funny anymore, and they bare the faces of those who are still hooded, and the shots begin to engage a rhythm, long shot and close-up, landscape and face, waves of hypnotic repetition, and the music describes a kind of destiny, a brutish fate that bass-drums down the decades.

Klara was moved by the beauty and harshness of the scenes. You could feel a sense of character emerge from each rough unhooding, a life inside the eyes, a textured set of experiences, and an understanding seemed to travel through the audience, conveyed row by row in that mysterious telemetry of crowds. Or maybe not so mysterious.

This is a film about Us and Them, isn't it?

They can say who they are, you have to lie. They control the language, you have to improvise and dissemble. They establish the limits of your existence. And the camp elements of the program, the choreography and some of the music, now tended to resemble sneak attacks on the dominant culture.

You try to imagine Eisenstein in the underground of bisexual Berlin, forty-five years ago, with his domed head and somewhat stunted limbs, hair springing from his scalp in clownish tufts, a man with bourgeois scruples and a gift for sublimation, and here he is in the Kit Kat or the Bow Wow, seamy heated cellars unthinkable in Moscow, and he's dishing Hollywood gossip with men in drag.

I'm terribly fond of Judy Garland, he once said.

But you don't want to be too modishly knowing, do you? He was a dynamo of ideas and ambitious projects but it isn't clear that he had the sexual resolve to realize actual contact with either men or women.

Look at the figures in long shot on the low smoky line of the plain.

All Eisenstein wants you to see, in the end, are the contradictions of being. You look at the faces on the screen and you see the mutilated yearning, the inner divisions of people and systems, and how forces will clash and fasten, compelling the swerve from evenness that marks a thing lastingly.

You realize the orchestra has been silent for a time. All hoods removed, members of the expedition plodding in endless matching step, trailed by distempered dogs oozing from the eyes. Then you hear the melody again, one more time, the familiar march from Prokofiev, not the mock-heroic organ but full orchestra now, and the pitch is very different, forget the amusing radio reminiscence, it is all vigilance and suppression, the FBI in peace and war and day and night, your own white-collar cohort of the law.

The march lasted only a minute and a half but how dark and strong, what fatedness in the rolling brass, and then there was a long silence and a white screen and finally a face that transfigures itself in a series of multiple-exposure shots, losing its goiters and gnarls, a seamed eye reopening, and it was awfully mawkish, okay, but wonderful also, a sequence that occurred outside the action proper, a distinct

444

and visible wish connecting you directly to the mind of the film, and the man sheds his marks and scars and seems to grow younger and paler until the face finally dissolves into landscape.

The orchestra began to rise into the pit and the music now was Shostakovich, you are sure of this, how spacious and skysome, lyrically wheeling, bird-wheeling over the wide plain.

Then it ended. It didn't end, it just stopped dead. A landscape of foreground dogs and distant figures leaning to their march. Klara remained in her seat, you all did, and she felt a curious loss, that thing you used to feel as a child when you walked out of a movie house in the middle of the day and the streets were all agitation and nasty glare, every surface intense and jarring, people in loud clothing that did not fit.

Miles showed up and they went to a bar that Jack knew. Jack knew all the midtown bars, he knew the steak houses and the best cheesecake and where you got onion soup that makes you think you're in Les Halles and he told funny stories about his early days in the theater district, flacking shows up and down the street, but Klara wasn't listening.

The film was printed on her mind in jits and weaves. She felt she was wearing the film instead of a skirt and blouse. She heard Esther laugh and it sounded like someone in a room three rooms away. Miles told a story that required her to join in but she couldn't get the details straight. She smiled and drank her wine. The conversation was over there somewhere. She kept seeing snatched fragments. She saw the marked faces in the great landscape. She had the movie all around her, sitting in a bar under walls of white neon beating in the Broadway heat.

4

In cities you build a language of circumspection and tact, a thousand little intimations, the nuance that has a shimmer of rubbed bronze. Then you go to the wilderness and become undone, lapsing into babble, eating mushroom caps that implode your brain, that make you preternaturally aware and afraid, turn you into an Aztec bird.

Matt Shay sat in the terminal at the airport in Tucson and listened to announcements bouncing off the walls.

He was thinking about his paranoid episode at the bombhead party the night before. He felt he'd glimpsed some horrific system of connections in which you can't tell the difference between one thing and another, between a soup can and a car bomb, because they are made by the same people in the same way and ultimately refer to the same thing.

There was a garbage strike in New York.

There was a man being paged known only as Jack.

A woman with an accent said to someone seated next to her, "I so-call fell in love with him the day he paint my walls."

There was a man in a wheelchair eating a burrito.

446

He sat waiting for Janet's plane to be announced. He wondered if this might be a good time to call his brother. Nick was living in Phoenix now, doing some vague consulting work and teaching Latin once a week at a junior college.

When Nick dies a team of metaphysicians will examine the black box, the personal flight recorder that's designed to tell them how his mind worked and why he did what he did and what he thought about it all, but there's no guarantee they'll find the slightest clue.

Reciting Latin epigrams to business majors in a place called Paradise Valley.

Matt took off his glasses and blew on the lenses, his mouth worked into a whispery ellipse, and then he ran his handkerchief over the steamy surface and held the glasses to the light.

Whenever the ambient voice asked someone to pick up the white courtesy phone, a small girl made a fist and spoke into it.

He put his glasses on. Janet came out of the gate and he laughed when he saw her. Laughed in sheer and healthy delight, in relief that she was finally here and in physical anticipation as well, and he laughed at the shambles they were going to make of the camping trip they were taking and he laughed in the end because he couldn't help it. He was woozy from the long day's drive and didn't have the strength to keep from laughing.

Janet walked briskly toward him wearing a slightly twisted grin, the one that meant she wasn't completely sure what she was doing here.

"The captain said it's a hundred and four."

"Should I call Nick?"

"What for? It was seventy-two in Boston."

"He's right up the road. It seems dumb not to call."

"There's a garbage strike in New York," she said.

He was woozy from driving and she was numbed by confinement and engine noise. They went to the parking area and crammed her bags into the jeep. The jeep was brimful, a consumer cartoon bulging with equipment, clothing, luggage and books.

"Tell me again where we're going," she said.

. . .

They spent the night at the edge of an Indian reservation, in an old adobe lodge with a teenage girl eating popcorn at the desk and the white dome of an observatory visible from their bed.

It was a fine beamed room with creepy suburban furniture and they were shy because they hadn't seen or touched each other in a long time and Janet had to get used to this. They'd only slept together several times, planned always in advance. They didn't have a set of understandings, a pace and glance, the whole hushed protocol of wishes and hints, bodies lightly brushing in the elevator. There was no elevator here. And Janet was a little unsure of herself in a strange room. It wasn't really her, was it?

Another woman might feel the lure of anonymity. Meeting a man in a room of a thousand previous men and women. Shedding the personal past in a faceless sort of motel abandon. But this wasn't a motel and at least there was that to be thankful for.

She was nervous, standing by the window in her jeans and bra. They'd gotten only as far as the bra. That's when she paused to talk, to let him know how she felt. She was not sexually anxious. She was sexually anxious, yes, but mainly unsure in a general way, she said, because it did not seem completely comfortable, meeting a man in a setting that had predetermined expectations—a strange bed in the middle of nowhere. She had a way of seeing herself, a wariness about things that didn't feel right. The place wasn't particularly clean for one thing. The girl downstairs for another, cross-eyed or walleyed, whatever. She talked to him honestly, in her small voice, slightly piping, and he lay in bed and listened, waiting for her to get used to the idea, a flight across country that ends in a random sort of room, making her feel isolated from everything that's familiar.

He listened and waited and finally understood that some of the things she was saying about herself were also true of him. He understood this the way you sneak up on things you've always sort of known.

She stood by the window. Over her shoulder he could see the observatory dome washed in last light at the top of the mountain.

. . .

There were men who walked these deserts a hundred years ago, the penitentes, chanting and fasting, scourging themselves with hemp whips, or whips made from the braided fiber of the yucca plant, or cord whips, *la cuerda*, a small whip of tightly knotted wool.

Janet didn't know how to look at the desert. She seemed to resent it in some obscure personal way. It was too big, too empty, it had the audacity to be real.

They drove and talked.

"Tell me again why we're going there."

"It's a wildlife preserve and gunnery range."

"So if one doesn't kill us, the other will."

He reached over and put his hand on her leg.

"We want to be alone," he said.

"We could be alone in Boston."

"They don't have bighorn sheep there. We want to see bighorns in the wild."

"What will we do when we see them?"

"We'll be happy. It's rare that anyone sees them. And it's very remote, where we're going. We'll rejoice and be glad. They're beautiful animals that no one ever sees."

She moved closer to him. She didn't like public affection and even if they were alone on the road it wasn't her apartment, was it, and it wasn't even a room in a lodge with a locked door and drawn curtains, once she'd gotten around to drawing the curtains, but she moved a little closer anyway and told him if she'd known he was going to stroke her thigh she wouldn't have worn thick coarse jeans, would she?

Matt didn't think he'd ever felt so happy. He was happy when she leaned against him and maybe happier still when she read aloud from the small library he'd amassed in preparation for the trip.

They saw hawks installed on utility poles and she looked them up in the bird book and said they were kestrels—falcons, not hawks, and this made him happier yet.

The landscape made him happy. It was a challenge to his lifelong citiness but more than that, a realization of some half-dreamed vision, the otherness of the West, the strange great thing that was all mixed in with nation and spaciousness, with bravery and history and who you are and what you believe and what movies you saw growing up.

After a while he told her to stop looking at the book and look at the scenery but the scenery was empty spaces and lonely roads and this made her very nervous.

When Nick came back from Minnesota, Matty called him the Jesuit.

His catechism days were well behind him now, Matty's were, his days of blind belief, and he liked to gibe at his brother's self-conscious correctness, his attempts at analytical insight. Whatever Nick's experience in correction and however deftly the jebbies worked him over later in their northern fastness, minting intellect and shiny soul, it was still a brother's right to heckle and jeer.

Their mother also called him the Jesuit but never so Nick could hear.

They filled the tank and bought charcoal, food and bottled water. They found the office of the refuge manager at the far end of town and Matt went in and received a permit and signed a liability release. This was called a hold harmless form and it basically pointed out that if they were killed and/or injured during live-fire exercises while they were in the refuge, it would be the giddiest sort of childlike illusion for either or both of them and/or their survivors to think for even a minute about receiving compensation.

Fair enough. They were allowed to enter the refuge but placed on notice that air-to-air exercises were set to commence three days from now. Friendly fire. It put a little edge in their schedule.

He told all this to Janet, conscientiously. He told her they weren't allowed to handle or take possession of any military items found in the area such as fuel drums, flare casings, tow targets, projectiles carrying real or dummy warheads. He told her there were no human inhabitants of the refuge. He told her there was no gas, food, lodging or other facilities. She had a right to know. He told her there were no paved roads or running water.

But he didn't tell her why this excited him. He didn't say anything about this because he didn't understand it, the stark sort of shudder, the leveling out, the sense of knowing he was headed into remote Sonoran waste, where the interplay of terrain and weapons was a kind of neural process remapped in the world, a hollow sort of craving lifted out of the brain stem, or wherever, and painted over with words and sky and diamondback desert.

Janet said, "All right. Go go go go."

"At's the spirit."

"We're going to do it, let's do it."

"At's what I want to hear."

They drove south through a white space on the map, headed for the entrance to the refuge, and he recalled something Eric Deming had told him about this part of Arizona, a rumor, a sort of twilight zone story about people known as sensitives, men and women who were psychically gifted—telepathists, clairvoyants, metal-benders.

There was a secret facility near the Mexican border where sensitives were tested and experiments carried out. The idea was that psychic commandos might be able to jam the enemy's computer networks and weapons systems, perhaps even read the intentions of the defense minister riding in his chauffeured car in the middle of Moscow.

In fact the Russians were thought to be well ahead of us in this endeavor, Eric said, soulful and mystical as they were, and we were desperate to catch up.

Janet said, "There's something else of course."

"What do you mean?"

"Besides sheep. We're not going all this distance to look at sheep."

"Bighorn sheep. We want to be alone. Undistracted. So we can talk. An extended period. So we can figure things out."

"What things?"

"You know what things."

"What things?"

"Do we get married? Do we have kids, children? Do we wait a while? Do we live here, or there, or somewhere in the middle?"

451

"What else?" she said. "Because I know there's something else."

Matt could believe the story about a closed base where sensitives refined their paranormal skills. Thought transfer and remote viewing. Why not believe it? He'd read many an enemy's mind as a ten-year-old, pushing wood across a game board. This was the supernatural underside of the arms race. Miracles and visions. The final wishful weapon is a middle-aged lady from Decatur who can pinpoint the location of Soviet submarines off the East Coast.

Unreal. This is what disturbed him. It was one of the things he wanted to talk about with Janet.

There were ship ridges, great ship rocks with prows thrust upward, and there were hills that resembled rubble heaps. The land seemed to be in open formation, harsh and scarred, and you could almost read upheaval and convergence. It looked like dinosaur country. They saw white mountains and flesh mountains and slags of glassy matter that turned out to be mountains when they drew near.

It took a long time to get anywhere. There was only the one road, one track, and sections were deep sand and other parts were ruts and gulleys. The sun beat down with a swarming sort of density. They came to flooded stretches where they had to leave the track and maneuver the jeep tenderly around the palo verde and cholla.

He looked up the words. He consulted the books all the time. He drove with a book or two in his lap, or asked Janet to look things up, or asked her to drive so he could read.

The dust powdered the hood and windshield and the sun seemed nearly upon them, burning down so squarely and vastly he wanted to laugh in shitface fear.

"I know you can't tell me about your job."

"I can tell you some things. I work with safing mechanisms, they're called. Timers, batteries, switches, actuators. Electromechanical locks. I run endless computer tests. I drink instant coffee and look at cross-section details of great finned weapons on my screen. Then a

452

bunch of guys in California or Nevada or someplace will take a war-head and rocket-launch it into a hardened target at fifteen hundred miles an hour."

"To test your calculations."

"Splat. Not just mine of course. But, yes, that's the idea."

"You make weapons safer. Safer to handle and use."

"That's right."

"Then what's the problem? It's not exactly criminal activity."

"No but it's weapons work. It's what I wanted. I wanted this and more. But now I'm feeling unsure about it."

"It's important work, Matthew. We need the best people to do this work."

They were camped just yards from the track. He made a charcoal fire and they emptied cans of pork and beans into a pan. They put on sweaters and sat on a blanket.

She said, "What would you do if you left?"

"I'm not sure. Get a doctorate maybe. I know some people who work in think tanks. I'd want to talk to them. Sound them out."

She gave him a sour look. The term made her unhappy—think tank—and he didn't blame her. Passive, mild, middle-aged, ivory-towerish. People rustling papers in redoubts of social strategy. Situation reports, policy alternatives, statistical surveys.

He got the flashlight and led her to a spot where she might pee. The moon was nearly full. He waited while she lowered her jeans and squatted, more or less in one motion, and she looked at him and smiled, a dirty sort of smirk, a dirty-face girl with mucky drawers—didn't we do this once before, in another life? He played the light around them and softly sang the names of bushes and shrubs to the sound of Janet piddling. She laughed and peed in spurts. They thought they heard a coyote and she struggled into her jeans laughing.

They set up the dome tent and got into their mummy-shaped camp bags, nicely lined with flannel, and they realized the coyote was Wolfman Jack on the transistor radio, a howling disc jockey vectored into the desert from some bandit station below the border.

Don't put no badmouth on me, baby, we gon rock tonight. Da Wolf-

man sending Little Richard to climb in your face from out of the glory days of the marcel pompadour and the glass suit. Richard don't need no dry cleaner. He got his Windex wid him.

The sleeping bag had stretch straps that made it possible for you to roll over on your side, if that was your preference, and when Little Richard started bending notes in his primal falsetto, Matty thought he was in bed in the Bronx, a fifteen-year-old capable of trading his brother's old fielder's glove for three or four raunchy rock-and-roll singles, which he played when his mother was out.

Janet called him Matthew. This was her way of separating him from family history, the whole dense endeavor of Mattiness, the little brother and abandoned son and chessboard whiz and whatever else was in the homemade soup.

He'd told Janet the story, how Nick believed their father was taken out to the marshes and shot, and how this became the one plot, the only conspiracy that big brother could believe in. Nick could not afford to succumb to a general distrust. He had to protect his conviction about what happened to Jimmy. Jimmy's murder was isolated and pure, uncorrupted by other secret alliances and criminal acts, other suspicions. Let the culture indulge in cheap conspiracy theories. Nick had the enduring stuff of narrative, the thing that doesn't have to be filled in with speculation and hearsay.

Of course Matt thought his brother was guilty of emotional delusion. But when Janet agreed too readily, dismissing Nick's version, he cut her off quick. He defended Nick. He told her how he himself had thought their father was dead, originally. Not a runaway, a dropout, the grievously weak man who takes a powder. Dead somewhere in untranslated space. And even if he was a little kid at the time. Even if he did the sad-funny fruitcake thing of going to the Loew's Paradise to see the soul of his faithful departed father drift across the starry ceiling. Even if he was unable to make a studied judgment, he told her, consider the episode itself, the journey he'd made to a movie house through strange neighborhoods, alone, at the age of six. The power of an event can flow from its unresolvable heart, all the cruel and elusive elements that don't add up, and it makes you do odd things, and tell stories to yourself, and build believable worlds.

Who the hell was Janet to ridicule his brother?

There were scar lines in the distance, deep arroyos, and stands of tall saguaro on the south slopes of mountains.

The track was white sand and then red dirt, it was cracked playa, drained and baked, and then it turned abruptly to mineral green dust and then again to sand and finally stony rubble.

Janet liked to drive aggressively whatever the surface. The jeep bucked and jumped, leaning badly at times, and when the track went narrow in thick bush she had to tell him to get his dangling arm back inside before the thorny acacia cut him up.

"I don't think you should leave your job out of conscience. Conscience works both ways," she said. "You have duties and obligations. If you're not willing to do this work, the next person may be less qualified."

"How hot do you think it is?"

"Never mind how hot. Too hot to be here. You have special training and a certain kind of skill."

"At some point we have to decide whether to turn around and go back out the way we came in."

"Or what?"

"Or keep going into bighorn country and exit the refuge somewhere in the northwest sector before the exercises start."

Ten minutes after he said this, they saw objects in the distance and he put the binoculars on them. They appeared to be tanks and jeeps, some trucks as well, but they were flimsy somehow, unbulky and perfunctory, showing squared-off contours and a cheap gleam—simulated tactical targets.

"I want us to be together," she said. "You know how much I want a home and family. I want to have a child. I've always wanted these things. I want to be safe, Matthew."

He reached over and fingered some loose hair at the nape of her neck.

"You want to be safe. This is the woman who works half the night treating injured people," he said. "Shocks to the body. One emergency after another."

"There's nothing unsafe about that. That's completely safe to me. It's the thing I do best and I want to keep on doing it. And you should do the thing you do best. That's what safe is."

"If I keep this job, how do we live together?"

"We'll do it. We'll work it out," she said.

The air went taut and the light took a chlorine edge and then it was raining hard. They couldn't see a thing and sat parked on a rise. The storm seemed to originate ten feet above them. They sat there waiting and they talked.

Matt could tell her anything. It was completely easy with her. She knew him before he was born. She could finish a thought he'd only barely started. She had no shaded spaces in her, none of the silences and disguises that can be fascinating, yes, but not for a guy like him, he thought.

They heard name-saying birds such as whippoorwills and phoebes. After the rain the heat came blowing back and he scanned with the glasses for birds of prey. They hung in the burning air, fantailed and soaring and great, and he went scrambling for the book when he spotted a large dark bird nested in the arm-crotch of a tall saguaro.

It was a golden eagle, immature, and he gave Janet the binoculars and took them back and couldn't stop talking. He talked and laughed and looked at the books. He talked less to Janet than to the bird. He checked the book a number of times to confirm for the bird's benefit that it was an eagle, an eaglet, with a bit of flashing on the wings and a wash of honey-gold at the hindneck.

Janet was not caught up in this. He glanced at her and found a complex plea in her eyes. She was asking him something but he wasn't sure what it was. He put the glasses back on the bird. The bird was a flick of the dial to her. You turned on the TV in the nurses' lounge and saw giraffe heads bobbing on the veldt. This was her nature preserve, a cramped room with a couple of sofas and chairs, where she sat and

456

yakked with the night staff about coffee prices and unsafe streets and the burn victim with the smell you can't describe—this was the hand-grip, the safehold she needed to live.

But the look she'd given him was not about what she needed or where she preferred to be. She wanted him to understand something about himself.

Every defeat was a death inside the chest, his little bird-boned thorax. Basically dead at eleven, that was him. Good riddance to little wooden rooks. How many years did it take him to get over the game?

It was Fischer-Spassky that brought him back, and only briefly at that, two years ago, in Iceland, halfway between Washington and Moscow, where they played twenty-one games, Bobby and Boris, a summer's rousing theater of black and white.

Matt checked the newspapers and watched TV. He rooted for Bobby, the gangly boorish boy now pushing thirty. He identified with the public tantrums, all the rude demands, the strokes of unwhole-someness that Bobby consistently delivered, the open show of bitter-ness when he lost.

If the American's eventual victory didn't begin to redeem Matt's own sulky youth, at least it edged the game out of the private migraine of abnormal introversion and into the mingled thing out there, the everyday melee of competing states and material forces.

You need a makeshift word to describe the process. De-ego'd. This is what the game did to Matt. So let our Bobby rant. He was only showing what is always there beneath the spatial esthetics and the mind-modeling rigor of the game, beneath the forevisional bursts of insight—an autoworld of pain and loss.

He told her about mountains hollowed out in New Mexico. These were storage sites for nuclear weapons. He told her about the gouged mountain in Colorado where huge wall screens could display the flight track of a missile launched from a base in Siberia. He knew a few things about Obyekt, the Installation, built by slave labor in a remote part of the USSR, and he told her about it—a center for bomb design.

People went willingly to these places, scientists eager to meet some elemental need. Or was it just a patriotic duty or the standard challenge of doing serious work in physics or mathematics? He thought they went in search, on impulse, almost recklessly, to locate some higher condition.

"You make it sound like God," she said.

He told her what he could about the Pocket. The Pocket was just a cozy donut-dunk in a vast hidden system. A system predicated on death from the sky. He told her about the emergency networks, underground shelters carved out of mountains in Virginia and Maryland where leaders could keep the government running during a major war. He told her about accidents in the Soviet Union, rumored explosions and fires at nuclear plants, and the sense of excitement he felt, the thrill of devastation in the enemy barrens, and his subsequent shame.

You make it sound like God. Or some starker variation thereof. Go to the desert or tundra and wait for the visionary flash of light, the critical mass that will call down the Hindu heavens, Kali and Shiva and all the grimacing lesser gods.

"Maybe I stayed a Catholic too long. Should have got out when I was ten."

He thought about the sensitives, preparing for psychic war, and he thought about the penitentes, men in black hoods dragging heavy wooden crosses through the desert, a hundred years ago, or fifty years, and lashing themselves with sisal and hemp, all that Sister Edgarish stuff, and speaking fabricated words—the maunder of roaming holy men.

"I don't know what you mean by staying a Catholic. I told you what I think about conscience," she said.

"It's only partly that. It's mainly that I feel I'm part of something unreal. When you hallucinate, the point of any hallucination is that you have a false perception that you think is real. This is just the opposite. This *is* real. The work, the weapons, the missiles rising out of alfalfa fields. All of it. But it strikes me, more and more, as sheer distortion. It's a dream someone's dreaming that has me in it."

Maybe Janet was a little annoyed by this. Found it self-indulgent or unconvincing or beside the point.

"I heard a story not long ago," he said. "They did a bomb test in the nineteen-fifties in which a hundred pigs were dressed in custom-made GI field jackets and positioned at well-spaced intervals from the blast site. One hundred and eleven, to be exact, pigs, as the story was told to me. Then they exploded the device. Then they examined the uniforms on the barbecued pigs to evaluate the thermal qualities of the material. Because this was the point of the test."

Janet didn't respond because whatever the point of the test, and whatever the point of the story, it was only making her mad.

"Picture it. Chester whites. A breed of large fat hog with drooping ears. Wearing khaki uniforms with zippers, seams, everything, and with drawstrings drawn because that's how the regulation reads. And a voice on the loudspeaker's going, Ten, nine, eight, seven."

She told him to get his arm inside the jeep.

"Is this when history turned to fiction?" he said.

She looked at him briefly.

"That's not the question you're asking," she said.

"What am I asking?"

"I don't think you're asking that question. That's a large question and I think you're asking a smaller question and it has nothing to do with pigs in uniforms. You're talking about something else completely."

He didn't look at her.

"What am I talking about, Janet?"

"You tell me," she said.

He kept his eyes on the rutted track and didn't say a word. Acacia slapped and twanged on the windshield and doors. They both watched the track.

There was a structure about two hundred yards ahead, concrete and bunkerlike, sand-streaked, with slit windows and brambly growth edging up the walls.

It was nearly sundown and they decided to camp nearby. There was something irresistible about the building, of course, even an unyielding ruin such as this, slabbed private and tight. It stood alone here, with mountains behind it, and carried the tilted lyric of a misplaced object, like some prairie drive-in shut down for years with the audio hookups all askew and the huge screen facing blankly toward a cornfield. It's the kind of human junk that deepens the landscape, makes it sadder and lonelier and places a vague sad subjective regret at the edge of your response—not regret so much as a sense of time's own esthetic, how strange and still and beautiful a chunk of concrete can be, lived in fleetingly and abandoned, the soul of wilderness signed by men and women passing through.

"I'd rather sleep in there," Janet said, "than do the tent again."

There were two slab doors sealed tight and the windows were narrow and high but they went around the back and found an opening at waist height and climbed inside. After all the choppy hours they'd put in, jeep-weaving over rubblestone and sand, the place seemed homey enough. A table, a few chairs, some nude calendars on the wall and a couple of shelves filled with canned food, utensils, safety matches and old magazines.

Matt thought the bunker might have been constructed to accommodate spotters during exercises, a couple of ordnance guys helicoptered in to check firing accuracy, retrieve tow targets and possibly mark the location of unexploded rockets and bombs.

Back outside he started a charcoal fire and they ate quickly and unconversationally and scraped the makings and remains into a plastic bag and stowed it in the jeep because they didn't know what else to do with it.

They carried their camp bags into the bunker and undressed in the moonlight. Janet sat on the nylon shell, one leg flat, one flexed, and she leaned back like a sunbather at lunch break on the library steps. He approached and lowered himself and felt the sun on her body, the residue of deep heat transferred to his hands and mouth and the way their bodies exchanged a sense of the day and the land, all the heat and blowing dust heavy on their breath, tasted again, fingertipped and felt and smelled.

But the act was melancholy and slightly odd, it was calm and sweet

460

and loving but also odd and slightly resigned and they lay together without speaking for a long time afterward.

"I think we ought to turn back in the morning."

"Why?" she said. "We came this far."

"I think we've seen everything there is to see, pretty much."

"You haven't seen the bighorns."

"I don't need to see the bighorns. I don't need to see the pronghorns either. There are pronghorns out there, antelope."

"You barely saw the eagle."

"I saw the eagle."

"From a distance, barely, in its nest," she said.

"The eagle was great. The eagle met every expectation."

She slept, he did not.

He finally told himself the truth, that he'd wanted her to talk him out of his job. This was the question he'd been asking all along. Aren't you going to tell me that you don't want me to do this kind of work, for your sake, and the baby we'll have, and the home we'll own someday?

But Janet did not cooperate.

He understood this finally, that he'd wanted her to think he was making a sacrifice, leaving the Pocket for wife and child. He'd wanted her to say, Come to Boston and marry me.

But Janet did not say it.

He wasn't made for this kind of work. He wanted to leave the job but he didn't want to do it himself. He wanted her to do it for him.

But Janet did not do it. And she knew all along what was in his heart. And she had no patience with his arias of the unreal. Whatever we're doing in secret, she'd say, they're doing something worse.

The wind drove out of the east from time to time and he heard an animal near the jeep, going for the garbage.

No, he was not a weaponeer. But that wasn't the point. He'd wanted her to feel responsible, and guilty, for making him change his life. What an edge that would give him in the years to come.

At Army Intelligence School he did double shifts of classwork, surrounded every edgy minute by combat analysts, language experts, counterintelligence guys snooping out drug use, by agent trainees on simulated missions, a spook for every body function.

They sent him to Vietnam, to Phu Bai, and the first thing he saw when he entered the compound was a flourish of spray-paint graffiti on the wall of a supply shed. *Om mani padme hum.* Matt knew this was some kind of mantra, a thing hippies chanted in Central Park, but could it also be the motto of the 131st Aviation Company?

From this point on he had trouble with the input.

He worked in a quonset hut, cranking rolls of film across a light box. This was the take from aerial recon, an endless series of images sucked up by the belly cameras of surveillance planes. It was all about lost information, how to recover the minutest unit of data and identify it as a truck driven by a man smoking a French cigarette, going down the Ho Chi Minh trail.

He tossed a frisbee to a gook dog and watched the animal leap and twist.

There were rumors about a secret war, bombs in unnumbered tons dropped from B-52s. Laos, Chaos, Cambodia. Except the tons were not unnumbered but conscientiously counted because this is how we earn our stripes, by quantifying the product.

Matt was a spec 5, the same pay grade as a sergeant but less command authority. That was okay with him.

The rocket attacks were not okay, or the mortar rounds that came arcing down out of the rain.

The rains came and the sirens sounded and he went to the nearest entrenchment, a shelter put together with sandbags and construction debris, with an open sewer running through.

The heat and heroin came and there was the odd body found facedown in the muddy company street, a casualty of smack.

Someone hung a photo of Nixon in the quonset hut, two men flanking him, familiar somehow but unrecallable, and there were rumors about a substance stored in black drums near the perimeter of the compound.

In the movie version you'd freeze the frame with the dog in midleap about to snare the frisbee. A park on a summer's day somewhere in America—that would be the irony of the shot, with a solo guitar producing the bitter screech of feedback.

This is what happens when part of a system's output is returned to the input.

Yes, someone tacked up a magazine page and Matt could not quite identify the two men who flanked the President but they weren't politicians or corporation heads. A curly-haired man, handsome and smiling. And a sad-eyed guy with a honker nose and the leaden aspect of an immigrant in a borrowed suit.

He cranked the film across the light box. When he found a dot on the film he tried to make a determination. It was a truck or a truck stop or a tunnel entrance or a gun emplacement or a family grilling burgers at a picnic.

It was hot and monotonous and planes came and went all the time, gunships, transports, medium bombers, stratotankers, fighter jets, executive jets, a little pink Piper carrying an instructor and a student and finally converted cargo planes spraying the jungles with a herbicide stored in black drums that had identifying orange stripes.

There were rumors about whole other wars, just to the east, or was it west?

The drums resembled cans of frozen Minute Maid enlarged by a crazed strain of DNA. And the substance in the drums contained, so the rumor went, a cancer-causing agent.

He heard the rumors and the mortars and felt the monsoon heat and heard the universal slogan of the war.

Stay stoned, man.

He'd wanted to come to Vietnam. He'd been back and forth in his mind about the war but thought this was a thing he had to do, a form of self-reckoning—stay straight, be brave, answer when your country calls. But there was also something else, the older blood-borne force known as family.

He could not evade the sense of responsibility. It was there to be confronted. He did not want to slip away, sneak through, get off cheap, dodge, desert, resist, chicken out, turn tail, flee to Canada, Sweden or San Francisco, as his old man had done.

When he found a dot on the film he translated it into letters, numbers, coordinates, grids and entire systems of knowledge.

Om mani padme hum.

In fact the dog didn't leap at all but only watched the frisbee sail past, more or less disdainfully.

A dot was a visual mantra, an object that had no properties except location.

The jewel in the heart of the lotus.

He was in his sleeping bag but wasn't asleep. He wanted company and woke up Janet. He stuck his arm out of the bag and reached over and shook her awake.

"I want the same things you want."

"All right, Matthew."

"I want us to be surrounded by familiar things. I'm excited about it. I want to start right away."

"You ought to wait. Stay where you are. Work for another year at this job. See what happens," she said.

"I want to think up nicknames for our children. Do you know what I mean? I want us to be surrounded. I want photographs, silverware, things we'll pass on some day. I want to talk about what we're having for dinner. You like baked clams? We've barely ever talked about food, you and I."

"Stay where you are," she told him. "Don't do anything in a hurry."

"I'm excited about this. I wish it wasn't going to take so long to get out of here. I'd like to start driving basically right now."

"Go to sleep," she told him.

"There are so many things to talk about."

She was asleep inside a minute. Matt lay there helpless against his racing mind. He understood finally that he wouldn't be able to sleep and he decided to watch the sun come up over the desert.

He put on his pants and a sweater and went out behind the bunker about fifty yards, where he switched off the flashlight.

Then he sat in the dirt and waited.

He remembered how he'd felt sitting in a chair at the bombhead party, locked in a gravitational field, his head buzzing with suspicion.

He thought of the photograph of Nixon and wondered if the state had taken on the paranoia of the individual or was it the other way around.

He remembered how he felt cranking film across the light box and wondering where the dots connected.

Because everything connects in the end, or only seems to, or seems to only because it does.

At the light box he was a parody of the traditional figure in the basement room, the lone inventor stooped over his worktable, piecing together the pins, springs and wires of some eccentric contraption, the lightbulb idea that would change the world.

And the voice with the Hungarian accent, Eric Deming speaking into his face in the crowded room.

The dots on the film might have been trucks going down the supply route or new model cars coming off the line or condoms that look like fingers on a latex glove.

And someone in the quonset hut had to tell him who they were. Nixon flanked by a couple of ballplayers, old-time guys, a winner-loser sort of thing, joined at the hip for life.

He sat in the dust with his eyes closed and smelled the wet resin of a creosote bush and began to sense light about to break somewhere.

People hide in their basement rooms. They take to the bunkers and tunnels as weapons roll identically off the line and begin to light up the sky.

And how can you tell the difference between orange juice and agent orange if the same massive system connects them at levels outside your comprehension?

And how can you tell if this is true when you're already systemed under, prepared to half believe everything because this is the only intelligent response?

People hide in dark dank places, where mushrooms grow, sprouting quickly.

The dots he marked with his grease pencil became computer bits in Da Nang, Sunday brunch in Saigon and mission briefings in Thailand, he guessed, or Guam.

When you alter a single minor component, the system adapts at once.

465

Somebody had to give him the names. The president flanked by Thomson and Branca, Bobby and Ralph, the binary hero-goat inseparable to the end.

A mushroom with a fleshy cap that might be poisonous or magical. In Siberia somewhere the shamans ate the cap and were born again. What did they see in their trance state? Was it a cloud shaped like a mushroom?

He was in the Pocket even then, cranking film all night long, waiting for the mortar rounds to come raining down. They made a crunch like a kid eating cereal on TV.

And how can you tell the difference between syringes and missiles if you've become so pliant, ready to half believe everything and to fix conviction in nothing?

And how can you know if the image existed before the bomb was invented? There may have been an underworld of images known only to tribal priests, mediums between visible reality and the spirit world, and they popped magic mushrooms and saw a fiery cloud that predated the image on the U.S. Army training film.

Watched from a safe distance, says the narrator, this explosion is one of the most beautiful sights ever seen by man.

He was in the Pocket even then, in a way, but did not think along the systems track to the culmination of his tedious little labors. The thousand-pound bombs clustering out of the bays of B-52s like finned pellets of excrement, cratering the jungle trail.

But they were the enemy so what the hell.

And they're the enemy still, or someone is, and he opened his eyes and saw the sky go an odd sort of mad granny gray.

Ideas used to come from below. Now they're everywhere above you, connecting things and grids universally.

The binary black-white yes-no zero-one hero-goat.

And the two men flanking the president in the photo tacked up on the quonset wall. The tallish handsome fellow and the bushy-browed immigrant. Could just as easily be Oppenheimer and Teller, their bodies greased with suntan oil as they quote Hindu scriptures to each other.

Om does not rhyme with bomb. It only looks that way.

Death and magic, that's the mushroom. Or death and immortal

life. Psilocybin is a compound obtained from a Mexican mushroom that can turn your soul into fissionable material, according to scholars of the phenomenon.

They are everywhere at the same time, endlessly connected, and you half believe the most implausible things because you'd be stupid not to.

All technology refers to the bomb.

He sat in the dust with his eyes opened and realized the sun was rising behind him and wondered what this meant.

It meant he'd been facing in the wrong direction all along.

Matt drove the jeep, Janet drowsed next to him, drowsed a while and got bounced awake and nodded off again.

He felt good, clear-minded, he drove and thought, he saw everything, he identified plants without the book.

The sun was still very low and the track would take them right into it for a time before veering gradually north.

He saw the rubble turn to sand.

He saw the silty limestone bottoms of dried-out creeks that paralleled the track.

He heard the wing-whir of mourning doves breaking out of the bush.

He saw a dust devil on a level stretch of desert doing slow-motion spirals.

There was an odd charged pause.

Then the roar descended on them, so close it stopped his blood, and Janet grabbed an arm. No, first she fell against him, knocked sideways by the force of the noise, a flat cracking boom, and then she snatched his arm and missed and grabbed again. He sat there with his head hammered into his shoulders. The jeep left the track but he freed his arm from Janet's clutch and steered it back. He realized his other arm was raised just over his head, curled above him in defense.

The noise broke over them and washed past, nearly taking them with it, and Janet was looking at him. Her mouth made a small smooth lonesome oval.

Matt was intently absorbing the news. He was sorting through. He was looking toward the mountains, ready to be happy. Then he saw the twin glint just before they disappeared, a pair of F-4 Phantoms in silver skin reaching the top of their arc before leveling off—just thought they'd skim the desert on a quiet morning.

He was happy, hearing the echo carom off the ranges now, a remnant thunder that cross-called from the Little Ajo Mountains to the Growler Mountains to the Granites and the Mohawks and out into the towns and truck stops. Yes, he loved the way power rises out of self-caressing secrecy to become a roar in the sky. He imagined the sound waves passing over the land and lapping forward in time, over weeks and months, cross-country, eventually becoming the gentlest sort of rockabye rhyme in a small safe room where a mother nurses a baby and a man stands with his arm over his head, a research fellow, not in fear of shattered plaster and flying glass but only to draw down the shade—the sky is going dark, and a tangy savor drifts from the kitchen, and there is music in the house.

But it was the steroid jolt he experienced now, the gooseflesh, the prickling thrill that traveled over his body as they sat trembling in the little jeep. They were not yet ready to talk to each other. They needed a moment to collect themselves, speechless in the wake of a power and thrust snatched from nature's own greatness, or how men bend heaven to their methods.

5

First there was an empty room. Then someone appeared and began to put things on a table, to move the magazines and picture books and put out bowls and crocks and cut flowers and then to reinstate some of the picture books but only the ones that claimed a status of a certain sumptuous kind. Then a few people arrived and there was sporadic conversation, a little awkward at times, because not everyone knew everyone. Then the room slowly filled and the talk came more easily and the faces shed some layers. Klara spoke with someone in a corner, half aware that the spirit of being friendly and funny and well-met was overtaking the place, and isn't it one of those things you never consider but might find amazing if you did, how the details of contact, the eye movement and hand waves, the smiles of recognition, the catch-up lives that propel the early dialogue— how this becomes an energy that moves among the guests like a circulating angel, inspiring stories, rumors, flirtations and misconstrued remarks, basically the makings of human history, even though people don't drink the way they used to, so you can't say it's the gin that makes them happy and natural. It's mainly the encouragement of others.

It was the rooftop summer, the summer of sheet lightning, and she watched thunderheads go white in the gunned flash. Threat of rain, said the Weather, but it rarely rained. She waited for Miles to show up with her cigarettes and thought that being alive had never seemed such luck, although she was getting nervous about her work because it just wasn't coming.

In a corner of the room she talked to a man who complained about people keeping large dogs in small apartments and after guests began to leave she took the elevator to the roof and a young woman said, "I semi lost my mind"—I sem-eye lost my mind—and there was a man, a painter Klara knew, with a great-looking necktie, and she thought that keeping dogs in small apartments was one of those subjects nobody talks about and then everybody does, abruptly, it comes flowing out of doors and windows, should you or shouldn't you, only to stop one day with a ruthless sort of suddenness, leaving the dogs undiscussed, rare Siberian breeds in studio walk-ups.

She watched the runner on the track on top of an office tower, a woman in day-glo sweats, at sundown, with smokestacks in the distance. Three or four people stood at the ledge with drinks, watching with matched pleasure, and the jogger went around the track, alone, thirty stories up, and it was a beautiful thing to see, the woman's lightsome stride and the great faded day that shows burningly in the glass slabs and then the power-company smokestacks down near the river, blowing gorgeous poisons.

She walked through Times Square with Miles and he made her stop to admire a pimpmobile parked in a towaway zone outside a topless pinball parlor. The car was painted rose and mauve and the side windows were protected by iron grillwork—guy's got an urban sense of humor. Tourists took pictures, posing each other in front of the car, taking turns snapping and posing, and there were Krishna skinheads with handbells, young and pale in ocher robes and high-top sneakers, jumping devoutly up and down.

Acey Greene had a grandmother act she did, mostly vocal, in which she referred to Klara as child. Reprimandingly. Oh child please, don't be such a fool.

They were in a SoHo bar.

"It's impossible," Klara said. "A woman doesn't even think of marrying someone like Miles."

"Who you wouldn't want to marry whether you thought about it or not."

"Give him a little credit."

"That's what I give him," Acey said.

"No, Miles is great. But you'd have to be crazy to try something permanent or even halfway binding. Can't be done, either from your viewpoint or his."

"Just the word cohabitation."

"That's right." And Klara laughed. "The word alone."

"He's a little evasive would be my general, you know."

"He's a little unready," Klara said, and the more she talked about his irresponsibility, the more affection she felt for the man. "There is always a plot potential, you see." And she laughed again. "He sees things closing in and becomes defensive and withdrawn. But it's not an issue. There are no issues between him and me. We get along great."

Things flew out of her hand. A coffee mug flew right out of her hand and over the kitchen counter. She could not find the veal cutlets she'd just bought. Then she looked around for the extra key to the downstairs door. The key could only be in one of two places, there were no other possibilities, worldwide, but it wasn't here and it wasn't there and she stood at one end of the loft staring through the tall windows opposite and she wondered if the fire escapes, if those dark lines intersecting in depth over the back alleys could tell her something about her work.

"You be whistling dixie, child," said Acey in the bar.

For a while she used house paint, radiator paint. She liked rough surfaces, flaked paint on metal, she liked puttied window frames, all the gesso textures, the gluey chalks and linseeds that get mixed and smeared, that get *schmeered* onto a weathered length of wood. And it took her years to understand how this was connected to her life, to the working-class grain, the pocked sidewalks, beautiful blue slate in fact, cracked and granuled at the corners, and the tar roofs, and the fire escapes of course, painted green and then black and how the flowoff of drips and trickles became elements of memory, and the aluminum paint on the whistling radiators, and the paint her father carried home to recoat the kitchen chairs, a chair upended on a newspaper page, and the spidery plash of white paint on the inked page, and the spattered page on the old linoleum.

At Esther and Jack's she held a glass of wine and listened to Jack talk in his friendly sandpaper voice. She liked his voice and she liked his jokes. Old ruddy grayhair Jack, somehow still alive, waving his cigarette and ever on the verge of forgetting your name. Jack was greatly given to robust jokes that Esther hated and Klara kind of liked, the kind of joke you're supposed to like in spite of yourself, outdated stories with stupid stereotypes and a range of dialects, but sly in the manner in which they welcome the listener's complicity—Jack told jokes in which nothing ever changes.

At some point she realized she was putting down paint mainly to take it off, scrape it with a kitchen tool—she liked the veiny residue.

And her radius of endeavor, her smallish ambition, what she saw as a clustering in her work, a familial thing, determinedly modest. She was only now beginning to wonder if she wanted to ensure herself a life unlaureled, like her father's.

Albert used to tell her in his slightly didactic way that the Italians of his experience, his Harlem and Bronx upbringing, his Calabrian heritage, tended to be wary of certain kinds of accomplishment, as immigrants, people who needed protection against the cold hand of the culture, who needed sons and daughters and sisters and others because who else could they trust with their broken English, their ten thousand uprooted tales, and he came home one day, the thirteen-year-old son, and saw his parents huddled on the sofa in one of those dolorous southern states of theirs, his mother's eyes dark-pocketed, drained by betrayal, and his father helpless and bent, a forty-year-old man who could double his age, in an eyeblink, through membership in some cooperative of sorrow, and they were looking at Albert's report card, just mailed from school, and he thought he'd failed everything, flunked out, been expelled, D's at best and funereal F's, but it was just the reverse, wasn't it, a row of A's with little gold stars stuck to the margins of the card, and young Bronzini eventually understood the nature of their distress, that they didn't want to lose him, the shop-keeper and the shopkeeper's wife, to the large bright world that began at some floating point only blocks away.

Klara did not see herself sharing this state of mind even remotely, until now, sitting alone in the loft, knowing how guarded she was about certain accomplishments, not other people's but her own—how distrustful and slightly shamed. She needed to be loyal to the past, even if this meant, most of all if this meant incorporating her father's disappointments, merging herself with the many little failures he amassed like faded keepsakes. She thought of his View-Master reels of the Grand Canyon and the great West, the unreachable spaces he clicked into place on his stereoscope, and she recalled so clearly the image of the Hopi scout posed on the edge of some rimrock, and whatever it was out there in the 3-D distance, the Painted Desert or Zion Park, and how her own smallness, her unnoticeability was pre-cisely the destiny she'd assigned herself.

Acey was drinking tequila and Klara took her usual humdrum ration of white wine because she liked white in the afternoon on the days when she had a glass before six or so and red with dinner, and a dead afternoon in a dark bar was not the worst of fates.

"What are you doing that I should know about, workwise?" Acey said.

"I'm going to Sagaponack to hide out."

"Hide out. You don't hide out there. You hide out here."

"Depends on what you're hiding from."

"Start working. Just start working. What are you sitting here for?" Acey said. "You ain't making history looking at me."

It was so humid you had to put your shoulder to the door or it would not close. She heard those shots on a terrace somewhere and then she saw the striped awning, Cinzano, and knew the sound was only canvas snapping in the wind.

Klara talked about her early days painting, trying to paint, and how it was small-scale hell in a number of ways but was beginning, now, to seem late bohemian and sort of pastel-edged until she made herself remember more rigorously.

"Men treated us, male painters, let's face it, the big names, as if we were dumb little would-be artists. Students forever, you know, in kneesocks. At best," she said. "And speaking of work."

"What?"

"I gave you some public praise the other day. I was talking to a woman doing a piece on younger artists. I told her who to watch. And in return."

"And that's not the first time and I want you to know it means a lot."

"Shut up. In return," Klara said, "you're required to give me a verbal preview because if I'm going to sit here and be envious of someone who's working, at least you can tell me what you're doing."

Acey's mouth did its sneery lift and curl. She looked at Klara and finished her drink and issued a kind of scorched sigh.

"Okay. You remember the Marilyn Monroe calendar you saw in my studio."

"Sure."

"And you know how it is when you're starting on a project, how you sometimes have to start with a series of misunderstandings."

"I always start that way."

"I thought and worked and sketched and did small oils and large charcoals and finally I realized. It's not Marilyn I want, it's fake Marilyn. I wanted a packaged look. I didn't want Monroe, I wanted Mansfield. All bloated lips and total boobs. I mean it was so obvious and it took me fucking forever."

"Have I ever seen a Jayne Mansfield movie?"

"Nobody has. Doesn't matter. She was uncontainable in a movie," Acey said. "And there were all the other Marilyns. On the one hand you can never have too many Marilyns. On the other hand the minute Marilyn died, all the other sexpots died with her. They were like philo-

474

sophically banned from existing. Jayne outlived Marilyn by only five years and for about four and a half of those years she was bummed-out, washed-up, beat up by husband number whatever-he-was and there was nothing left but exploitation movies and heavy drinking."

"You're crossing over. White women," Klara said.

"Jayne was a white whale. I had to shake off a lot of higher-minded shit before I got to where I am with this work. And I'm doing some things with color I want your opinion of."

"Anytime."

"Because you're the one I trust."

"Paying phony compliments is hard work," Klara said. "That's why I don't do it."

It was the summer of Nixon waving on TV, clutching Ike's wrist in the fifties clips, or the hand-jerk over the head, sudden and neurologically odd, or the final wave from the helicopter on the lawn, arms shooting out, fingers shaping a sad pair of V's, or the clips of the late sixties that showed his arms wantonly flung in the winged gesture of victory, of resentful writhing triumph—here I am, you bastards, still alive and kicking.

Miles talked her into going to Bloomingdale's to help him buy a gift for his mother because she'd be thrilled and slightly shamed, his mother would, wrapped in happy chagrin, outside Toledo, to own a thing from Bloomingdale's. They went through a vast area of reflecting surfaces and little knobby bottles and the cling of a hundred teeming essences and Klara finally found something, a batik blouse and vaguely Persian slippers, and they were headed out through the menswear area, touches of autumn decor and many tables and displays, racks of field coats and fleece liners, and Miles said, "Wait."

What is it, she wondered, and he put a hand to her arm—wait, look, do not speak. Then she saw what he meant. Eight or nine boys, black kids moving among the suits and knit sweaters, maybe a dozen now, adolescents mostly but some no older than ten. Then she saw a guard coming from the perimeter, summoned by walkie-talkie, and the younger kids were trying to go unnoticed, among the mirrored surfaces, somewhat comically, their eyeballs doing surreptitious scans, and they must have felt the pressure by now, the full weight of observation. One of them grabbed a jacket, half hurried, and one of them said something and they all moved now, converging on one display. They grabbed and ran, jackets flying off hangers and hangers bouncing on the floor, and they grabbed what they could, two-three jackets, some of them, or only one, or two kids snatching the same jacket, and ran for different exits. There were two guards coming fast and another semicrouched by the main door. The customers stood motionless and alert, fixed in neutral zones, and one kid was pinned by a guard and Klara had a sense of half a dozen others scatter-running through the store, weaving and shying off, all the jacket arms flapping.

And Miles said, "Leather," in a voice that rang with broadest joy.

He said, "They take the subway down to Fifty-ninth Street and come up the stairs right into the store and they flood one area and grab what they can and then they're outta here, man, in a dozen directions."

He said, "Security gets ahold of two, maybe three kids at most."

He said, "Notice, they didn't take the big insulated parkas, they didn't take the warm stuff or the hooded stuff or the down vests. Only leather. They took the leather," and his voice was musical with admiration.

Acey leaned over her empty glass.

"How old was he?"

"I don't know. Seventeen, eighteen. I don't think I wanted to know."

"Seventeen's a man."

"I was teaching kids to draw, part-time. And I had a baby, two or three years old, and this was awesome enough, and my husband's mother who was bedridden, although maybe she'd died by then, and my husband of course as well."

"And this juvenile delinquent in his what—did they wear pegged pants? He came on to you."

"I don't know who came on to whom. Only thing I know, we're in the spare room next to where my mother-in-law just died."

476

Acey's eyes went humorously wide and she let her mouth hang open.

"Maybe you're right. Seventeen's a man," Klara said. "Because one thing this was not. This was not a case of sexual initiation. It wasn't at all tender. And he didn't need instruction especially. And you're also right about juvenile delinquent. Except the term doesn't do justice to the thing he eventually did."

She looked down the cornice line of Park Avenue to the New York Central Building with its traffic arches and great clock and floodlit summit and she wasn't sleeping well lately and someone stood next to her looking at the same thing she was looking at and she went inside to watch Nixon wave.

Esther Winship's apartment was lavishly understated, beiges, off-whites, great staid sofas that did not give when you sat, and expanses of dunnish rug, deep-piled, and almost no pictures, and the few pictures Esther elected to hang were self-effacing to the point of who cares, and the place had so much attitude, all tension and edge, that Jack seemed largely lost here.

Esther said, "I haven't given up, you know. I've sent agents into the field."

"For what?"

"Moonman."

"I thought we'd forgotten all that. Besides, didn't somebody do a graffiti show?"

"It didn't include him."

"I think it's just as well you don't find him."

"Why's that, sweetie?"

"You'll sign him and dump me."

Esther liked that. She had a laugh that was two thousand years old, salty and hoarse. And Klara found it strange to feel the way she did about graffiti writers. It should have been Esther who decried the marked-up trains—defaced, ugly, like mobile dumpsters. Esther in her flawless suits and face powders and lightly clanging jewelry. Esther, she thought, and not for the first time, her dealer and friend and enemy.

"That is the utterest nonsense of course."

"Just tell me when we're going," Klara said.

"Out to my place?"

"So I can stop the mail."

"You're invited, you know. We're all going. It's official. Friday week."

"I love stopping the mail," Klara said.

And it should have been her who defended the graffitists, daredevil kids who put color and spunk into the seismic blur of a rush-hour Monday.

Chance of rain, said the Weather, but it didn't rain. The garbage was down there in identical black plastic bags, leaching out, beginning to burn its way out of the bags, and she looked and did not look for rats, passing the mound on her way to the Y. She swam nearly every day at the Y and then not so often and then only once a week because the point of swimming was to take the edge off work, return her to the offsetting rhythms, the agreeable mild monotony of what is left of you after a long pull of work and isolation.

It was the summer of damson plums, juicy and bluish, and she loved the water towers that hung at dusk, raised on pillars and stilts, like oddments of the carpentered city, the least likely things to survive, dowels and staves, the old streaked wood hooped in its delicate bulk.

In a little roof garden with a cheapo copy of a marble from the Acropolis, a male figure minus arms and head and most of one leg, and with a ravaged cock and birdblown shit on his left pec, and why was he so sexy, Klara thought—it was here that she saw the man for the third time in about seven weeks, Carlo Strasser, the amateur art collector and whatever else he was, in his splendid Italian shoes, with a farmhouse, she recalled, near Arles.

It turned out the host had been meaning to invite the two of them to dinner for the longest time. And it turned out Carlo was in solid-state electronics, traveled to Hong Kong and Taiwan on business and had once flown to Mexico City to see a soccer game.

"Actually I'm supposed to be in Dus-sel-dorf today"—he pronounced it comically—"but I thought, you know, life is short and I get on too many planes lately and besides."

"Besides you can pick up the phone."

"I can pick up the phone, absolutely. Someone is there at the other end."

All around them on brownstone roofs were skylights and tall vents with spiral caps and new metal fencing that extended past the roof edge to discourage cat burglars.

And late at night she woke up in the loft and thought she was somewhere else—not somewhere else but in a place that wasn't hers because even after years here she could not wake up without feeling she was in alien space, in dreamspace still. The height and breadth of the area, the pillars and tall windows were out of some early dream, not quite nightmarish, of a child located at the edge of a room, or a child dreaming the room but not in it herself—a room surreally open at one end, where the child stands or the dream begins, a room where things, where objects are called chairs and curtains and beds but are also completely different, unsupported by the usual guarantees, and she shifted in the bed and woke up Miles.

They went to the Fulton Fish Market and Miles took photographs, it was four in the morning, of a row of enormous swordfish chucked down on the pavement, what an epic of misplacement, these great sea creatures beached on a New York street, and then they found an all-night diner and had bacon and eggs and coffee.

Miles wanted to talk about Acey Greene.

"This stuff she's doing. You know what she's doing, don't you? A group of paintings on the Black Panthers. More crap being dumped on black males."

She let him talk.

"You overrate her about two hundred percent. Her stuff is all show. It's a cut above total shit. You need to look again. It's all surface. She's catering, she's pandering to white ideas about scary blacks."

Klara realized that in her praise of Acey's work she'd been waiting all along for someone to disagree. Now here it was. The moment sat in her stomach in a lump with the egg yolk and rye toast.

"You know how it works. She got what she wanted from you. Approval, publicity, whatever. Now she's greasing other wheels."

Klara sat there in an odd kind of thoughtful silence. She wanted him to keep talking. Say it all whether it's true or not. She felt completely ungenerous but thought he might have a point about Acey's work. He had useful intuitions about art. It was one of the things between them, of course, how he'd stand before one of Klara's pieces and let her know with a few well-placed words and with his general surrender to the object that he saw what she was doing.

"She loves the slippers," he said.

"She loves the slippers. What are we talking about? Oh your mother."

"She loves the slippers."

"She loves the slippers. Good. I'm happy."

Or possibly the case could be stated thus. He was totally wrong about Acey's work but maybe she wanted him to be right.

In Sagaponack she dropped her bag in the guest room and went to visit painters all over the local map. They painted in sheds, white-washed studios and renovated potato barns and she went mostly alone, borrowing Esther's car because Esther was on the phone trying to deal with landlords and lawyers.

At dinner Jack got dizzy and lay on the sofa and the evening more or less went on around him.

She stood on the sand and watched the waves barrel up and come snugging beachward.

She called Miles, who was leaving the next day for Normal, Illinois.

She met a sculptor with a face full of burst capillaries, English, his wife was dying, and she had a long talk with him, a completely intense conversation about the way in which their work exposed them, layer by layer, as inadequate, and they took solace one from the other, seeing how such things can be shared no matter how seemingly unique. And embraced when she left.

480

Esther said, "You're looking sexy lately, you know that?"

"Says who?"

"Old Jack."

Klara typically grew tired of old Jack and then took his side, sympathizing, saying Jack has a point and finding him funny and then finding him tiresome again, even pathetic at times, but he loved Esther in the sweetest way, spoke about it openly and didn't care who heard and told waiters and doormen how good she was in bed and Esther knew it wasn't possible to stop him and probably didn't want to. They both needed the drama of public avowals because how else could their vividness survive?

Things flew out of her hand. A glass flew out of her hand when she was standing on someone's deck. Alone in Esther's car she talked about left turn and right turn, reciting directions aloud, telling herself to stop on red.

On the phone Miles said, "People don't think it's totally, you know, bizarre that a woman can get sick every time Henry Kissinger gets sick, a thousand miles away. We the ungreat have to get our diseases any way we can."

A wind started blowing and would not stop and it carried a faint taste of summer's end and Esther said, "It's like the *tramontana*," and Klara thought oddly of Albert, or not so oddly—he loved the Italian words for different kinds of winds blowing off the Alps and up from the African littoral.

And she didn't really like the English sculptor's work if we're going to be honest about it, whatever their affinity of ominous doubt.

"No, seriously, you look great," Esther said.

The nights so breezy and clean. Shadows, whispers, a man's chin-line, his hair, how he holds a wineglass.

Esther said, "Jack's a baby of course. That's why he stayed on the sofa when he was feeling out of sorts the other night."

"He wanted to be with people."

"He's the biggest baby ever but if he dies on me I'll go to pieces in a tenth of a second."

She loved them both and told them when she left and meant it the way you always mean it after four blowy days and nights and good food and talk and the potato fields running clear to the dunes under high swift skies.

Such luck to be alive, she thought, and took the train back, humanly invisible in her roomy seat, where she smoked a cigarette and looked forward to being home—home alone, surrounded by all the things and textures that make you familiar, once again, to yourself.

Her father used to say, The best part of a trip is coming home.

But when did they ever go away? Only rarely, and briefly, a rented bungalow on a lake, with another family, because godforbid we shouldn't feel crowded, her mother said, and let's hurry back before someone steals the note we left for the milkman.

When Klara's mother found a business card in his jacket—she was taking his suit to the cleaner and found a business card with his name but no company and the name was spelled Sax and of course she asked him about it.

He told her it was for trips he might take. He wanted to have a card to give to someone he might meet on a train.

Her mother said, That's not what I'm asking. Never mind such a trip is strictly I don't want to say what.

So then what you are asking?

I'm asking the spelling. Her mother said, Sachs is not a hard name.

He said, It's not a question hard or easy.

Her mother said, What is *s-a-x*? This is what? You're changing careers, this means? We have a jazz musician in the house?

He said, It's a small thing, never mind.

Her mother said, It's not so small.

He said, The names are pronounced the same. It's a small thing. I only changed the spelling so it's easy for someone to pronounce on a train who's accustomed to easy names. Which most names in business they're easy if you'll notice.

Sachs is an easy name. Her mother said, This is not a hard name unless the train you're talking about is full of people who are a little funny, let's say, in the head.

Her mother's maiden name was Soloveichik.

He said, It's not the name is easy or hard. It's what the letters say. That whole business of the *c-h*.

Her mother said, What whole business?

And her father made a sound that Klara would not forget. She thought about it many times in the years since he made the sound. He made a sound, a harsh guttural produced at the back of the mouth, rattling and metallic, filled with rancor, and at first she thought he had the card printed because he did not want people to make the mistake of thinking he was German and then she thought he had the card printed because he did not want people to know he was a Jew.

People on trains. Businessmen with their own cards and shaving kits and private compartments on the most important trains out of Grand Central Station.

And how curious, what a distance he sought to travel from the grating sound of that *c-h* with its breadth of reference, its guttural history and culture, those heavy hallway smells and accents—from this to the unknown *x*, mark of mister anonymous.

And the change provoked Klara's loyalty precisely because it made no practical sense, because it exposed the mind spirals of a certain kind of torment.

Her father was a billing clerk in a department store. Then he was an insurance agent working on commission in the drearier reaches of the Bronx. They gave him the Negro neighborhoods and Chinese laundries and the immigrants from everywhere, just off the boat. He painted signs for a while, company names on frosted glass doors, applying gold leaf with a sable brush, a thing he did well but hated.

It's only a business card, he said. I didn't go to a judge and get my name changed. On my tombstone you can carve the regular spelling to your heart's content.

Her mother said, How come I never knew you played an instrument?

And when Klara's divorce from Albert became final, she changed her name from Bronzini back to Sachs but made a point of spelling it with an *x*, if only publicly in her emerging identity as an artist—it was how she signed her work.

•   •   •

483

"Yes, well, maybe it's true. Seventeen's a man," Klara said. "And I've asked myself was the thing more important than I was willing to admit?"

"In other words did it show you a way out?"

"Did it point a way out?"

"Which you didn't want to think about at the time."

Acey didn't want another drink and Klara still had half a glass of wine and they talked away the afternoon, one of those dead summer days in a dark and empty bar.

"And he didn't seem to make too much of it himself. He was, I thought, remarkably unconfused and even-keeled was my impression. My second husband sailed a yacht but was not so even-keeled and I don't know why I'm bringing that up."

She laughed and sipped her wine.

"He drank Tanqueray martinis, Jason did. He took a bottle of Tanqueray every time we went to Maine, or a couple of bottles, I guess. We were allowed to forget the vermouth but not the gin but we didn't forget the vermouth either and I loved going up there but I used to wonder sometimes in the most detached sort of way."

"How it happened."

"How did it happen that I'd marry a man who says what he says and thinks what this man thinks?"

"And drinks martinis," Acey said.

They talked about other things. They talked about work.

"See, Marilyn hated being Marilyn. But Jayne loved it," Acey said. "She was born to be Marilyn. She lived in a pink palace that had a sizable zoo. And the way these things happen, the discount sex queen becomes famous and famous and famous and finally she's the most photographed woman in the world."

"And she died how?"

Acey lowered her head to her chest, doubling up her chin and doing a southern sheriff's voice.

"Ho-rrific car crash. Like Jimmah Dean."

"Are you painting the wreck?"

"No, I want a Jayne that's a living threatening presence. This is one greasy peroxide blond. Constant secretions from every quarter. This is a woman with a heavy flow. Atomic Jayne."

"Anytime you're ready to show it," Klara said, and the sun had cleared a building nearby and was beating on the street.

"You worry too much," Acey said. "You worry about the work you're not doing because you feel deeply obliged to justify. I think you're always justifying in your mind. And you also worry about the work you've done because considering what you gave up and took away, considering the damage you caused, if we tell it like it is, child, you need to convince yourself your work is good enough to justify this."

They paid the bill.

Acey put her hands on the older woman's shoulders and pressed tight, sort of macho motherly, and the bartender brought their change.

In Sagaponack Esther wore safari outfits and talked on the phone.

She said to Klara at breakfast, "Who cuts your hair? Did they arrest the mass murderer who cuts your hair?"

At someone's house Klara talked with a woman it turned out she used to know, a painter from the early days, the industrial spaces on the East River, near the ferry terminal, where Klara lived after her divorce, with a makeshift shower and no stove, fifty dollars a month, and met painters and sculptors, people who worked with found material, and the street was paved with old stone blocks, once used as ballast perhaps, and they used to gather on the roof sometimes, three or four painters and a wife or husband and a couple of kids and a dog someone was keeping for someone else, and the two women remembered how Klara never sat on the sloped part of the roof, on the tarpaper surface that sloped up to the edge because she was afraid of edges, and there was a sense of sea passage and new work, and off to the north, situated beyond the rooftop, between the rooftop and the great bridge, was the polyhedral mass of towered downtown.

The wind blew day and night and Jack said, "I'm reasonably sure that's what's-his-name over there who used to be married to the paper bag woman. It was a great scandal. She was the paper bag heiress and I sat next to her at dinner—this was, godhelp me, twenty-five years ago. Esther knows who I'm talking about. It was a major scandal. Esther, help me out here."

485

The thing about Jack is that he sounded drunk when he wasn't and then made beautiful and courtly sense absolutely blotto.

They were in a small basement place in Chinatown eating broad noodles that were very tasty, chow fun or chow fon, the menu was spattered—a place with formica tables and spattered menus and no liquor license and Miles with a mint toothpick in his mouth.

"I've got a movie to show you that you're going to hate me for this movie."

"We can't be talking about Normal," she said.

"We shot about eleven hours in Normal. She was inexhaustible, this woman, because she was born that way. She comes across like a law of physics but I still don't know what we've got. Could be crap."

"And in the meantime."

"You're going to hate this other thing but there's no question of not seeing it because you have to see it."

He deferred to Klara in a number of ways, sometimes subtle, sometimes not, and forced soft arguments he knew he could not win and played certain subjects toward her strength, which should have annoyed her but didn't, and was otherwise thoughtful, carrying her brand of cigarettes and talking her through this dormant period in her work, a time of small despair.

He had his cold, it was always there, voice a little woofy, his eyes dimmed by medications, and after Acey's show they all went to a disco somewhere and she watched Miles and Acey dance and they looked completely great together and how curious, of course, because there was no love lost, or maybe not so curious—the lights were flashing and the music shook the walls.

It was the rooftop summer, still, and she sat in the dense shade of a grape arbor on a Chelsea roof, redwood posts and rafters and a latticework of cedar that was weathered bony gray.

A poet walked across the roof, he came from the far end of the roof over the thin slate surface.

486

He said, "They're writing the name Marie."

And Klara looked out through the opening at the front of the arbor, fringed with broad puckered leaves, grape leaves of whatever variety of native grape, and she saw the smoke from a skywriting plane, spelling the name Marie.

And the World Trade Center rising at the southern rim, the towers siamesed when you see them from this angle, joined at the waist by a transit crane.

What an encouragement it was that someone built this thing, lugging so much wood and soil up five narrow flights, raising the posts and joists, and vines growing out of half barrels, old whiskey barrels great-girthed and stained, and she sat with three others at the table eating nachos and drinking sangria, the others did—Klara liked her wine unmixed.

It was the summer of blue-black nights, ambiguous thunder to the east, hoarse and false, and the city grid below—a guy beheads his lover, puts the object in a box and takes it on the train to Queens.

And don't forget the poet drunk on a cast-iron bench and the small strange woman who photographed him obsessively.

Klara watched the skywriter's smoke begin to attenuate and drift. A cat walked along the ledge at the far end, a stray from the alleys and back gardens, and she didn't know why, you never know why, but her mother was part of this moment, angry about something, and a neighbor with a special shoe, a man with a high shoe, an orthopedic shoe, things, shapes, masses, memories, all the braidwork of unmatching states.

Even the poisoned air floats a woman's name.

Miles took her to the studio of a video artist he knew. Not a studio, okay, but an ordinary set of rooms packed with equipment and TV sets, where the guy lived and worked. People started arriving. There were people already there and others started arriving and there was a pungent trail in the air, the root aroma of marijuana rolled and toked communally, and a sense of some event not unlike the showing of a midnight film, only not so loose a group—a little beady-eyed, these people, wary of their own anticipation.

They sat on the floor mainly. There were a few folding chairs and a sofa in one room and a number of people stood huddled in corners but most of them sat on the floor, which was covered with soda stains and unspeakable scuz. TV sets were arranged in stacks everywhere in the flat and other sets were parked individually on TV tables with copies of TV Guide and there were sets with rabbit ears and a few old mahogany consoles and every size screen from the smallest imported eyeball to the great proscenium face of the household god.

And one whole wall in one room—there was a TV wall, maybe a hundred identical sets banked floor to ceiling.

Klara and Miles stood in a corner and she'd begun detaching herself from the event long before she got here because she'd been told what it was at some point but still had to see it, whatever the level of misgiving.

The event was rare and strange. It was the screening of a bootleg copy of an eight-millimeter home movie that ran about twenty seconds. A little over twenty seconds probably. The footage was known as the Zapruder film and almost no one outside the government had seen it.

Of course the event had a cachet, an edge of special intensity. But if those in attendance felt they were lucky to be here, they also knew a kind of floating fear, a mercury reading out of the sixties, with a distinctly trippy edge.

The footage started rolling in one room but not the others and it was filled with slurs and jostles, it was totally jostled footage, a home movie shot with a Super 8, and the limousine came down the street, muddied by sunglint, and the head dipped out of the frame and reappeared and then the force of the shot that killed him, unexpectedly, the headshot, and people in the room went ohh, and then the next ohh, and five seconds later the room at the back went ohh, the same release of breath every time, like blurts of disbelief, and a woman seated on the floor spun away and covered her face because it was completely new, you see, suppressed all these years, this was the famous headshot and they had to contend with the impact—aside from the fact that this was the President being shot, past the outer limits of this fact they had to contend with the impact that any high-velocity bullet of a certain lethal engineering will make on any human head, and the sheering of tissue and braincase was a terrible revelation.

And oh shit, oh god it came from the front, didn't it?

And that was the other thing, all these things in the sequence that begins with frame 313, and wouldn't you know, Miles would say later, there had to be a thirteen somewhere in the case.

She was getting backaches again and sleeping episodically and it hurt to sit in a chair sometimes. They told her to go to a yoga class. They told her about herbal teas and holistic massages.

She went to the hospital to see Jack Marshall, who was recovering from heart surgery, and she went with Esther, who thought that a hospital visit was a thing out of pharaonic antiquity, where you fixed your face and arrayed yourself sedately and you carried books, puzzles and flowers and brought along a priest to utter certain phrases.

Esther didn't seem to know what went on in hospitals and she moved at a cringing gait, leaning away from doors to patients' rooms, afraid she'd glimpse something or catch something, taking it all personally—a challenge to her remoteness from such matters.

Jack said that catheter was the ugliest word in the language.

They told her to eat whole grains, take warm baths, to see a man in Finland who did the lower back.

She went to Acey's opening, of course, in a hot new gallery uptown, in the early fall, and Acey looked sensational in a white linen suit with a sequined bandeau and the work was all breasts and heart-shaped asses, a raunchy assault in which a woman's body parts, her skintight gowns and full mouth and bazoomy tits become a kind of politics.

There was no comfort here, Klara thought. If women have a condition called incompleteness, and some recover nicely and some don't, then these paintings were flaunting it, loving it, shoving it in your face. And Acey located her arguments in composition and perspective, in the odd bodiness, the massive off-center ass, the misalignments, the relationship of breasts to body, the way Jayne came angling out of her Jaguar, all avid excess, her knees and dimpled crotch bursting out of their package.

It was a question of lines of force. Here was a woman who lived outside the bureaucratic needs of male desire, outside the detailed ceremonies and horny hands.

Acey used off-tones, flesh tones, completely nonpop, a lot of sand and amber and a beautiful burnt rose, a sunburnt strip that ran across the top of every canvas, a little sad and frayed, and all of it slightly blurry and doubled, color-xeroxed, that was the telling touch—you have copycat Jayne, the reproduced goddess, and she is all the more strong for being unoriginal.

They went to a disco somewhere and she watched Miles and Acey dance and they looked totally great together and she felt a little jealous, of course, and she still felt jealous half a minute later—not jealous but begrudging—when Acey danced with a woman.

She watched them weave and shimmer in the flashing lights and she was admiring and begrudging both, taken by the sight of them, the other woman in jeans and braided sandals, some diplomat's daughter, Klara thought, hair hung down in spiral curls, and how completely easy they were in their physical mien, a grace of a certain passing abandon, searching each other's eyes in the fever strobes, and she was stung by her reaction.

Acey's ascent, Acey's name in the air, her brash talent and sense of freedom and her self-asserting manner and how she wants it all and'll probably get it and dancing sort of striped in the lights with her jacket flying open and the music shaking the walls.

The funny thing is, Esther wasn't kidding. A priest showed up, from some actor's chapel, arranged by Esther, although Jack hadn't been to church in forty years except for midnight mass at Christmas, which he attended, as they say, religiously.

They sat around and talked about Broadway show tunes. Jack was too weak to sing or tell jokes. He was a great splayed length of pounded veal. Esther held his hand until she had to go out for a smoke. She'd stopped and started again and the priest went with her and Klara adjusted the pillow for Jack.

And when she embraced Acey at the end of the evening—it was the end of Klara's evening because the music in that place was a form of brain seizure and she had to get out fast and when she embraced Acey and told her the show was great and wished every blessing on her head, it was an experience of shadings and half meanings and an awful sort of feeling, to extend love to a friend with reluctance.

She decided to go to Los Angeles with Miles. He'd run out of money for Normal, Illinois and was trying to get financing from an Israeli gangster who lived in L.A. Or there were two men maybe, she wasn't sure, one Israeli and one gangster, and she decided she'd go. She didn't like the idea of going but she thought she'd go out of a sense of loose ends or whatever the exact state of mind—she wasn't sure of that either.

And the poet drunk on a cast-iron bench, the visiting Romanian on the roof, and how a woman no one knew shot seven rolls of film and left without a word.

In the three days she was there. She was there to small and passing purpose so it wasn't supposed to matter what she saw and heard but at some point in the three days someone mentioned the Watts Towers and Klara thought she probably ought to see this place because she'd known about the towers for years and thought maybe if there's time and then forgot about it.

At another point she got a call from New York and who was it, someone eager to read reviews of Acey's show, the first to appear, and they were bad, they were stinging and grim, and Klara called a few people who said word around town was even worse.

They spoke with controlled excitement, that tone of breathy documentary where you code your pleasure to the formal pauses.

They waited for her to respond in kind. This made her feel sleazy as hell. They waited for her to rejoice in kind, on cue, with due observance of the protocols.

That was the next-to-last day. On the last day she went to see the

Watts Towers. Miles dropped her off and said he'd come by an hour later. She had no idea. She didn't know a thing so rucked in the vernacular could have such an epic quality. All she knew about the towers was that the man worked alone, an immigrant, for many years, a sort of unimaginable number of years, and used whatever objects he could forage and scrounge.

She went around touching things, rubbing her palms over the bright surfaces. She loved the patterns made by jute doormats pressed in cement. She loved the crushed green glass and the bottle bottoms that knobbed an archway. And one of the taller towers with its tracery of whirling atoms. And the south wall candied with pebbles and mussel shells.

She didn't know what this was exactly. It was an amusement park, a temple complex and she didn't know what else. A Delhi bazaar and Italian street feast maybe. A place riddled with epiphanies, that's what it was.

Cats passed through, they were everywhere, asleep in the sun or trying to mooch a knuckle rub, strays from the hot streets, ghetto cats, and she felt a kind of static in her body, seeing columns inlaid with broken glass, shards of discarded mirrors, and the crazy-quilt tiles, and the arc he'd shaped over the front gate with cans of Canada Dry.

She felt a static, a depth of spirit, she felt delectation that took the form of near helplessness. Like laughing helplessly as a girl, collapsing against the shoulder of your best friend. She was weak with sensation, weak with seeing and feeling. She touched and pressed. She looked up through the struts of the tallest tower. Such a splendid independence this man was gifted with, or likely fought for, and now she wanted to leave. She didn't need to stay any longer. An hour was too long and she stood by the entrance, buzzing, and waited for Miles to arrive.

That night she got on the phone and tried to find Acey, she called around for an hour, waking people up, and Miles came in, dragging, and pulled off his boots where he stood, a seamless swipe of the hand, repeated.

She said, "Look, your socks are the color of the rug. That must mean it's time to leave."

He told her about his afternoon, which was spent around a pool drained of water, speaking of which—there was a guy there who described how he'd faked his own suicide by drowning and managed to effect a clean disappearance.

"You're talking a mile a minute," she said.

And there's Yankel saying, the Israeli with the bankroll, Some people fake their death, I'm faking my life.

She called New York again and found out Acey had gone somewhere or just didn't want to talk.

Miles wanted to talk. Miles was beat, he was dragging but also amped-up, jangled by caffeine and freeway traffic and whatever else he was inhaling in the way of controlled substances. Three days of whatever else on the fringes of the business. They were in a borrowed apartment and he had to get up early to go to Normal and there was a space between his weariness and his sparky nerve ends and they filled it persuasively with sex. They did it and did it and talked and did it. They had a thumping time, or she did—she wasn't sure what he was having. He was intense and a little feverish and had his indigenous common cold and when he talked it was on a polyphonic plane, steep and desperate, and when he fucked it was strong and aloof—not aloof but rootless, a kind of any-fuck in the sense that there was nothing outside the act, they lived for the strokes, for the nasal drone, and finally he slept, and then she did, and they barely made their flights in the morning.

From the air, what was it like? The vast swept West, basin and range, you could almost detect the mineral content, the badland shale—it was the kind of immense and unsparing beauty that left you slightly subdued because you didn't know the natural language, the names of formations and mountain folds.

And her father with his Hopi scout, Hopi or Navaho—his View-Master slides of a headbanded scout at the edge of a canyon. Sitting in the kitchen clicking his slides through the handheld device. He specialized in slides of the great West. He called it the great West and it was, it is, look at it, his 3-D slides of the trail ride down the canyon on muleback, or the Canyon Dons the Velvety Cloak of Twilight, and that's exactly what it did, his completely unreachable West, and he sat in the kitchen because the light was better there.

She didn't know the West and she'd never flown above it in weather so clear. It looked young and untouched, it had the strangeness of worlds we'd never seen, it was not ours from up here, it was too flowingly new and strange—we hadn't settled it yet.

Klara remembered who she was. She pulled away from the window and she was a sculptor, although she didn't always believe it, an artist—she believed them sometimes when they said she wasn't.

She thought of her work, the skewed meter of putty and junk, the crambo clink, she thought of rust rot and wadded cotton batting. She wanted to feel the urge to work again. She wanted to be rushing out of the airport to take a taxi home. She needed to feel that thing begin to happen, suddenly, that faithworthy feeling, that newness, a freshet of life behind the eyes.

She called around looking for Acey and reached her a few days later, she was bitter and tight and didn't want to talk. But Klara talked to her. She was good at this. She'd talked like this to Teresa a thousand times, the daughter determined to be unhappy.

They had dinner that night and talked some more. Klara was in control. She cajoled and encouraged. She was good at this. She was eager to help and she was helping.

The waiter stood there reciting the specials. There was a fire down the street, or a false alarm, and an amplified voice erupted from one of the trucks, absorbing everything around it, and the days got darker earlier, and the streets began to acquire a medieval texture with strange draped women, scarfed like Tuaregs, living in junked cars, watchful and silent, and the ones who danced in subways for loose coins, and the ones with their own radio programs that you didn't need a radio to listen to because they followed you down the street in the endless inspired catastrophe of New York.

After a while some people got up and walked around. They didn't leave, almost nobody left. The footage kept repeating and they walked around, they stirred from their corners and visited the other rooms or stood in front of the TV wall. They were like tourists walking through the rooms of some small private collection, the Zapruder Museum, one item on permanent display, the twenty-some-odd seconds of a home movie, and it runs continuously.

It ran continuously, men who carried the power of the state, the film muddied by sunglint, riding in a car with their confident wives, all the jostled quality of birthday footage.

Or they stayed on the floor and passed a joint and just kept looking in an acquired sort of awe, here comes the car, here comes the shot, and it was amazing that there were forces in the culture that could out-imagine them, make their druggiest terrors seem futile and cheap.

The footage ran at normal speed on some sets, slow motion on others, and the car moved down Elm Street and past the freeway sign and the head dipped out of the frame and reappeared and the shot was unexpected.

Different phases of the sequence showed on different screens and the spectator's eye could jump from Zapruder 239 back to 185, and down to the headshot, and over to the opening frames, and on the TV wall the sets and frames were geared to patterns. The TV wall was a kind of game board of diagonals and verticals and so on, interlocking tarots of ele-mental fate, or synchronous footage running in an X pattern, and whatever the mathematics of the wall there were a hundred images run-ning at once, here comes the car, here comes the shot, and even though it wasn't part of the footage Klara was sure there was a Hertz sign on top of the Book Depository—she'd seen it in photographs, forgotten about it until now and thought it was another passing strangeness, however minor, a rent-a-car sign brooding over the motorcade.

A man and woman stood in a closet with the door open, seemingly stoned and not especially noticeable, remotely making out—Klara happened to glimpse them when she went by.

She knew she'd hear from Miles at dinner about the secret manip-ulation of history, or attempts at such, or how the experts could not seem to produce a clear print of the movie, or whatever. But the movie in fact was powerfully open, it was glary and artless and completely steeped in being what it was, in being film. It carried a kind of inner life, something unconnected to the things we call phenomena. The footage seemed to advance some argument about the nature of film itself. The progress of the car down Elm Street, the movement of the film through the camera body, some sharable darkness—this was a death that seemed to rise from the streamy debris of the deep mind, it came from some night of the mind, there was some trick of film emulsion that showed the ghost of consciousness. Or so she thought to wonder. She thought to wonder if this home movie was some crude living likeness of the mind's own technology, the sort of death plot that runs in the mind, because it seemed so familiar, the footage did—it seemed a thing we might see, not see but know, a model of the nights when we are intimate with our own dying.

Someone passed her a joint, she passed it back.

On a large console the screen was split four ways and the headshot ran in every sector and, "It's outside language," Miles said, which was his way of saying far-out, or too much, or the other things they used to say, and here was an event that took place at the beginning of the sixties, seen belatedly, that now marked the conceptual end, carrying all the delirium that floated through the age, and people stood around and talked, a man and woman made out in a closet with the door open, remotely, and the pot fumes grew stronger, and people said, "Let's go eat," or whatever people say when a thing begins to be over.

It ran continuously, a man in his forties in a suit and tie, and all the sets were showing slow motion now, riding in a car with his confident wife, and the footage took on a sense of elegy, running ever slower, running down, a sense of greatness really, the car's regal gleam and the murder of some figure out of dimmest lore—a greatness, a kingliness, the terrible mist of tissue and skull, so massively slow, on Elm Street, and they got something to eat and went to the loft, where they played cards for a couple of hours and did not talk about Zapruder.

She married Carlo Strasser in his Park Avenue apartment before a justice of the peace and twenty-five friends of the couple. Carlo's daughter was there, the youngest of his three children, a beautiful spindly girl, fifteen, who lived with her mother in Brussels. It was one of those autumn days in New York. And Klara's daughter also appeared, about half an hour late but lively and bright, completely unmorose—she embraced people left and right and danced after the ceremony with Jack Marshall.

It was one of those taut autumn days. The bride wore an old brocade vest that had once been her mother's, and someone's before that, a second cousin or great-aunt, and maybe someone's before that, before America. People ate wherever they found a space, standing up or sitting primly in hall chairs, and the dancing did not last long—it wasn't meant to be a drawn-out affair.

When the guests were gone they decided to take a walk, the bride and groom and their daughters, and after a night of stiff winds the air was rinsed clean and the light was so precise that distances in the park seemed diminished. Clouds began to build, fair-weather cumulus, high-prowed and drifting. It was one of those days in Central Park when there's a distilled sense of perception, a spareness, every line firm and unredundant, and the leaves were beginning to turn, the dogwoods and sumacs, and nothing was wasted or went unseen.

How nice to be a family again, even if fleeting and incomplete, with parceled-out children and children on tight schedules and who knows when they'll all see each other next. Carlo's daughter spoke a clipped efficient English. She stuck to her father's side and followed his wagging hand to particular vistas. They could look over the treetops to the buildings on Fifth Avenue, the unbroken taupe facade, and then to the mansards and temple-tops at the western edge of the park, and Klara imagined the whistling doormen, the taxis hotfooting past—she loved the showy yellow coats of New York cabs.

It was one of those days of light and scale when everything you see has the full breadth of intention. She held Teresa's hand and talked about visits here and there, and they made promises and resolutions, they made mental notes. And how nice, how strange to be doubly paired like this, husband and wife, mother and daughter, and she saw that Carlo walked with a slight limp and was amused to think she'd never noticed—felt free to be amused, felt what the hell it's only marriage.

They walked behind a man with a wolfhound, a dog as grand as any in a vodka ad.

Klara laughed for no reason. Maybe she laughed for no reason and maybe because she'd noticed her husband had a limp. The others thought she was laughing in relief, laughing in the spirit of a swirling day, and it made them all smile benignly. They thought she was laughing in the aftermath of checking on planes that were late and hearing complaints from the caterer and finding the right receptacles for all the goddamn flowers. And finally just unwinding on a walk, they thought. Laughing in ragged relief. They thought they knew the mystery of living in her skin.

PART 5

BETTER THINGS
FOR BETTER LIVING
THROUGH CHEMISTRY

Selected Fragmaent Public
and Private in the 1950s
and 1960s

1

You looked at the hills and they were rolling hills that made you wonder who you were and how you got here. The hills had no more connection to your life than a calendar with a picture of hills, old rolling hills set above a river, fixed to some kitchen wall.

I sensed the river was out there somewhere, a briskness in the wind, and I took deep breaths because I was upstate and it was supposed to be healthy here.

Staatsburg was seventy-five miles from home, farther than I'd ever been, and I got settled in the dorm and took classes for a high school certificate and never missed an afternoon in the old barn where the makeshift gym was located, a boxing ring at one end and a backboard at the other.

You commit your crimes in the city and they send you upstate to take deep breaths and get a perspective on your life.

I played basketball with members of a street gang named the Alhambras after a movie theater in Harlem. They were doing nigger

501

time, they said. They'd come up through Youth House and a number of reformatories, raised on the felony alphabet, and we pounded up and down the floor in that dusty gym, working off the effects of our transgressions.

We were all juvies, under eighteen. I was an E-felony, criminally negligent homicide, reduced from a charge of manslaughter in the second degree, and we played game after game of half-court, going all-out and taking deep and healthy breaths and having a tussle or two.

You could fight a guy here and then forget it, leave it on the court or in the ring, because you'd already mind-whipped yourself repeatedly for what you'd done out there in the streets, whatever misfit thing of rage or bleakness or stupendous aberration, and maybe you'd reached an early maturity on the subject of running a grudge—how important it is to be selective.

When I entered correction I wanted things to make sense. I kept my bed neat, corners squared, and stacked my clothes sensibly in my cubicle.

The minute I entered correction I was a convert to the system. I went out on work crews that did road repair and I was the eagerest hand, giving myself up to the rote motions of breaking asphalt, leaky-eyed and sneezing in the ragweed brush.

I believed in the stern logic of correction. I did my study assignments every night and pounded the floor and pounded the boards in the old gym, good riddance to bad beginnings, blood beginnings, and I was ready for this, hammering hard surfaces on some country road in the julepy haze of a midsummer day, feeling the dead soul slowly drain out of me, the sedimentary stuff of who I was, gone in the dancing air of insects and pollen.

The hills took on color in the fall and they had about as much meaning in your life as a poem on a calendar, four lines about rolling hills in Ronald Colman English.

At Staatsburg I heard many stories about doojee, which was one of the ninety-nine names of heroin, but I didn't tell them my own weak-kneed story, about how I was scared of needles and drugs.

At Staatsburg they had a psychologist who wanted me to talk about the shooting. She thought it was the way to my salvation. I told her,

No, man, forget it, let's talk about the weather. I gave her nothing she could use on my behalf.

I didn't want sweetheart treatment. I was here to do time, one and a half to three, and all I wanted from the system was method and regularity. When the kitchen caught fire I was disappointed. I took it personally. I didn't understand how a well-trained staff could allow this to happen. When three kids went out the gate in the rear of a bakery truck, fifteen-year-olds, junior Alley Boys as the Alhambras were sometimes called, I thought it was a tremendous, what, a dereliction, a collapse, bunched in the back of a Silvercup truck—I was shocked at the level of neglect.

In the gym that day we played half-court with our customary combat skills, hacking the shooter, wheeling off the boards with elbows jutting, but the intensity wasn't there and the game stopped cold a couple of times so the players could talk about the escape. They cracked jokes and bent over laughing but I thought the joke was on us. We weren't worth much if the system designed to contain us kept breaking down.

All that winter I shoveled snow and read books. The lines of print, the alphabetic characters, the strokes of the shovel when I cleared a walk, the linear arrangement of words on a page, the shovel strokes, the rote exercises in school texts, the novels I read, the dictionaries I found in the tiny library, the nature and shape of books, the routine of shovel strokes in deep snow—this was how I began to build an individual.

But before the snows came and the ground hardened they put in the golf course. Miniature golf, novelty golf. They unloaded the equipment in a field near the mess hall on a sweet and clear November day. Plywood castles and ramps. Enough junk for nine holes. Little waterwheels and bridges and whatnot. I watched it all take shape with an odd kind of disbelief. I felt tricked and betrayed. I was here on a serious charge, a homicide by whatever name, destruction of life under whatever bureaucratic label, and this was where I belonged, confined upstate, but the people who put me here were trifling with my mind.

The club was in West Hollywood, called the Troubadour, and the man walked onto the stage and unscrewed the mike from the stand and waved it over the crowd, blessing them, and maybe they felt they needed a benediction, tonight of all nights, because the President had addressed the nation about six hours earlier, four o'clock Pacific time, on a matter of the highest national urgency.

The man looked into the audience, stroking his chin, body set in a hipster slouch, and he wore a charcoal suit, continental cut, with natural shoulders and half lapels, and a dark slim knit tie, and that New York Levantine look—yes, this was the infamous sick comic, Lenny Bruce, and they waited for him to tell them how they felt.

Because the Russians had put missiles into Cuba. And President Kennedy's grim speech still formed a kind of auditory wall running through the room. Nuclear strike capability. Full retaliatory response. Such resonant and carefully crafted terms. This was an audience accustomed to a different level of dread. Out-of-work actors and musicians, screenwriters doing draft number ninety-two, there were agents with eczema, wholesome blond beach-body hookers with their vicious slithering pimps. And Lenny's wearing a little smirk, eyeing this group like he sees right to the tacky nougat center of their collective soul. Always a few literate junkies. Maybe a couple of beehived tourists who'd wandered in by mistake with their siding salesmen husbands. And there has to be one name actor with a dose of clap and another who's been reduced to doing soaps. And they all needed Lenny to help them make the transition to the total global thing that's going on out there with SAC bombers rumbling over the tarmac and Polaris subs putting to sea, like *dive dive dive*, it's dialogue from every submarine movie ever made and it's all factually happening but at the same time they find it remarkably unreal—Titans and Atlases being readied for firing.

Lenny studies them a while, letting the moment draw meaning and portent. It's not at all obvious what he's going to say until he says it, with a thrust to his lower lip and an executive timbre in his voice.

"Good evening, my fellow citizens."

And once he says it, the remark is retroactively inevitable because this was the President's opening line of course and it gets a medium laugh but Lenny kills the bit before it begins. He's not about to do a Kennedy imitation.

He leaned back to distance himself further from the line. Smoke rose from the crowd, hanging in the beam of the baby spot, and he shifted into his own voice with its bent vowels and high nasal shadings.

"I dig it on one level. Being on the brink. It's a rush, man. You can talk all you want about living on the edge. Yeah I know, you smoke some grass on Saturday night. Making the scene. Plus you accidentally drove through Watts one night and can't stop talking about it. Made your shorthairs stand on end. Negroes in porkpie hats. No, yes, this thing here, let me tell you what the edge is. The true edge is not where you choose to live but where they situate you against your will. This event is infinitely deeper and more electrifying than anything you might elect to do with your own life. You know what this is? This is twenty-six guys from Harvard deciding our fate."

He swiveled toward the wings and pointed at some shadow presence as a laugh bubble broke over the massed heads.

"Dig it. These are the guys from the eating clubs and the secret societies. They have fraternity handshakes so complicated it takes three full minutes to do all the moves. One missed digit you're fucked for life. Resign from the country club, forget about the stock options and the executive retreat, watch your wife disappear in a haze of secret drinking. You have to be hip to stay connected. These guys wear boxer shorts with geometric designs that contain the escape routes they've been assigned when the missiles start flying."

Lenny was a handsome guy with dark hair and hooded eyes and he resembled a poolshark who'd graduated to deeper and sleazier schemes. His brows were set at a cosmopolitan arch that seemed to function as an open challenge to his hustler aspect—if you're dumb enough to believe my scam, that's *your* problem, shmucko.

And he said, "Picture it," and snapped his fingers, releasing the genie from the bottle. "Twenty-six guys in Clark Kent suits getting ready to enter a luxury bunker that's located about half a mile under the White House and the faggot decorator's doing a last-minute checklist. Let's see, peach walls, stunning. Found the chandelier in a little abbey outside Paris. None of that Statler Hilton dreck in *my* bomb shelter."

And even those in the audience who were familiar with Lenny's habitual scat, the vocal apparatus with its endless shifts and modulations and assumed identities, the release of underground words and tensions—they felt a small medicinal jolt at the pitch of the decorator's voice.

"Rugs, fabulous, the purest Persian slave labor. Arched windows, okay we're twelve stories underground but the curtain fabric was irresistible so just shut up. Dining table, plantation mahogany, eleven bottles of Lemon Pledge. Centerpiece, designed it himself, the highlight of his career. A huge mound of crabmeat carved in the shape— they're gonna love this, it's so forceful and moving—yes, Kennedy and Khrushchev wrestling in the nude. Lifesize."

And Lenny did a knee dip with his swivel, pausing to let the audience develop the image.

"All right, can't stand around admiring. They'll be down any second. The President, the Secretary of State, the Joint Chiefs, this guy, that guy, the guy with the secret codes for nuclear launch—he's a toilet-trained Jew, incidentally, so there won't be any mix-ups. Let's see now, what else? Flatware he's done, stemware he's done. After-dinner mints, let's see—do I give them the mocha or the café noir?"

He did the opening again, checking the line for style and fit.

"Good evening, my fellow citizens."

A stir of renewed anticipation—maybe they wanted him to pursue the presidential thing but he waved it off again and stood there sort of humming at the hips, doing a little wobble that seemed to get the next thought going.

Then he did the shrillest sort of falsetto.

"We're all gonna die!"

This cracked him up. He bent from the waist laughing and seemed to be using the mike as a geiger counter, waving it over the floorboards.

"Dig it, JFK's got this Russian man-bull staring him down, they're pizzle to pizzle, and this is a guy Jack doesn't know how to deal with.

What's he supposed to say? I shtupped more debutantes than you? This is a coal miner, he's a guy who herded farm animals barefoot for a couple of kopeks. He's been known to stick his fist up a sow's ass to fertilize his vegetable garden. What's Jack supposed to say to him—a secretary gave me a handjob on the White House elevator? This is a guy who craps with the door open on state occasions. He has sex with his bowling trophies."

The seating at the Troubadour consisted mainly of folding chairs and when enough people laughed there was a wheezy groan from the slats and hinges. And the audience sat there thinking, How real can the crisis be if we're sitting in a club on Santa Monica Boulevard going ha ha ha.

"We're all gonna die!"

Lenny loves the postexistential bent of this line. In his giddy shriek the audience can hear the obliteration of the idea of uniqueness and free choice. They can hear the replacement of human isolation by massive and unvaried ruin. His closest followers laugh the loudest. Their fan-fed vanity is gratified. They're included in Lenny's own incineration. All the Lennies. The persecuted junkie. The antihypocrite. The satirist and nose picker. Lenny the hipster fink. Lenny the ass mechanic, girl-spotting in hotel lobbies. Lenny the vengeance of the Lord.

"Powerless. Understand, this is how they remind us of our basic state. They roll out a periodic crisis. Is it horizontal? One great power against the other. Or is it vertical, is it up and down?" He seemed to lose his line of argument here. "The U.S. is putting up a naval blockade. Fine, good, groovy. D'ya hear what he said?" And Lenny did his basso head of state. "Any offensive military equipment being shipped to Cuba gets stopped dead in the water by the U.S. fleet." He jabbed at some imaginary lint on his lapel, signaling a shift, a bit. "And there's this woman sitting out there in Centralia listening to the speech. She hears, Maximum peril. She hears, Abyss of destruction. She has a job dishing out meat patties in the school cafeteria and she comes home exhausted and turns on the TV and it's the President of the United States and he's saying, Abyss of destruction. And she sits there in her cafeteria whites, with her shoes off, picking her feet. Her name is Bitty. She's thinking they preempted Lawrence Welk so this Irish Catholic millionaire can talk about abyss of destruction. Then she thinks, Hey, wait, that's a movie title, right? Sure, it's one of those hard-boiled cynical crime dramas in moody black and white. I saw it with the Muscular Dystrophy Mothers of Central Kansas. The speech goes on and on and Bitty's trying to register the enormous—and the President says something about, Swift and extraordinary buildup. Soviet missiles in Cuba. But she thinks he's talking about the grease in her oven. Yeah that greasy buildup's beginning to bug me, man. She has this oven cleaner she's eager to try. Works fifty-two percent faster than the strongest industrial acid. She tries to concentrate on the President's speech but everything he's saying sounds like a pitch for insect repellent or throat spray. And Bitty's sitting there in Emporia or Centralia and she gets up out of the chair and goes to the phone and calls her friend DeeAnn. DeeAnn is the local movie expert. DeeAnn reviews movies for the cafeteria workers' newsletter, Meat Patty Week. And Bitty says into the phone, Who was in that movie the President's talking about on TV? And DeeAnn says, You're asking me about movies? At a time like this?"

Lenny bent his knees and spread both arms wide, his mouth stretched in a rictus of gaped and grinning terror.

"We're all gonna die!"

He loved this line so much it was a little unnerving, especially in DeeAnn's voice, which could shatter a urinal at fifty feet. An hour later, after all the bits, the scatological asides, the improvised voices, it was this isolated line that stayed in people's mind when they went to their cars and drove home to Westwood or Brentwood or wherever, or roamed the freeways for half the night because they knew they wouldn't be able to sleep and what better place to imagine the flash and burst, where else would they go to rehearse the end of history, or actually see it—this was the meaning of the freeways and always had been and they'd always known it at some unsounded level. And so they drove half the night, at first morose and then angry and then fatalistic and then plain shaking scared, chests tight with the knowledge of how little it would take to make the thing happen—the first night on earth when the Unthinkable crept up over the horizon line and waited in an animal squat, and all the time they drove they heard the keening of that undisguisable Jewish voice repeating the line that had made them bust their guts laughing, astonishingly, only a few hours earlier.

It was a gesture without a history.

You hefted the weapon and pointed it and saw an interested smile fall across his face. But after that you were in unknown country. The slyest kind of shit-eating grin. But after you forced back the trigger. The trigger pull was heavy and rough. And after you force-squeezed the trigger you were in another place, absorbing the noise and movement, the gesture, the way he jerked and fell, although jerked isn't an adequate word—it was a movement beyond your competence as a witness to understand and describe.

At Staatsburg they had the woman in the office, Dr. Lindblad, and I had regular appointments, knock-knock, and she probed the subject of the shooting while I tried to get a look at her legs.

Forget for a minute that you're the one who shot him.

You can't describe the movement properly because it was a level of reality you hadn't rehearsed, either one of you. The unhinged fling of an arm, the right arm whippy and haywire, like a part that runs amuck in a machine, and the whole body spasm, an arrhythmic thing, a thing outside the limits of experience.

You don't want to forget he was sitting in a chair. The chair moved not unlike the man. The chair could have been a version of the man, so drastic was its tumble into the wall.

And of course your own shock, the trauma of perception—how can you tell what's going on if you're in shock yourself?

Dr. Lindblad said, "Do you think you'd like to have a family someday?"

"I don't know. Haven't thought about it. No," I said. "I don't think so. Kids? I don't want kids. I don't want to be a father."

"And why is that?"

"Why is that. I don't know. After what I've done? I don't think I should be a father. Do you?"

"What have you done, Nick?"

I smiled at her. I liked Dr. Lindblad. She wasn't good-looking but she was stacked. The Alley Boys liked her, the gang members, because she listened to their stories without making judgments. She did delicate twirling tricks with their rage and shame and sullen excuses. She did not try to get them to moderate their sense of inevitability. They were at war with society and what's the point of pretending otherwise. I didn't tell her anything but I liked going into her office and smelling the furniture wax and checking the titles of the books and scouting out the bulge of her breasts under the fabric of whatever snug blouse she was wearing that day.

One of the Alley Boys looked out the window of the mess and said, "That's a Disney picture, man." He was talking about the miniature golf course. "And we're the dwarfs that supposed to be in it."

I wanted my correction to be consistent and strong. They'd made an attempt to try me as an adult even though I was only seventeen at the time and I agreed with their reasoning, that there was a cold-blooded element in this crime whatever the shadings. When a judge ruled that the prosecution couldn't do this, they decided to try me for manslaughter and again I thought why not, considering the reckless-ness of the act, but my lawyer Imperato, a man with sallow jowls and a briefcase that was shedding skin, arranged a plea deal and they went for a lesser charge and now I stood looking at the golf course on a soft summer morning a few days before my release and saw that someone had painted names all over the ramparts and windmills, the nick-names of gang members, all hail the Alhambras, and the guys gawked and pointed and bent over laughing and I thought this was the time to start my round of guilty goodbyes.

Because you were the shooter and the witness both and you can separate these roles. The second was helpless to prevent the first from acting. The second could not stop the act, could not manage it and finally did not know how to perceive it. It was too down deep even as it reached his eyes, your eyes. The terrible spasticky thing, the whole groanlike abandon, the resignation of life and breath to this vehement depth of gesture, man and chair going different ways.

Dr. Lindblad might have said, "The gesture is extreme because the

510

mind is closing down. It's the end of consciousness. So the body goes berserk. The body shows you what's happening to the mind. The way a person's grief bends the body. This is how consciousness looks. This is how it flails and thrashes when the end is sudden and violent and the mind is unprepared."

And I might have said, "You're talking about his mind, how the end is sudden, or mine?"

But she didn't say it and I didn't say it because I wasn't talking much. The Alley Boys were talking. They told her they were in a state of total war with society. They told her it would be that way until they were dead. Society wanted them dead. The Alley Boys were too smart not to know this. They told her they'd get released and go back to the street, which was another department of the penal system and vice versa, and they'd go back and do what they'd always done, they told her. They'd deal, steal, get the edge, carry the piece and pursue the conduct of the war.

The book fits the hand, it fits the individual. The way you hold a book and turn the pages, hand and eye, the rote motions of raking gravel on a hot country road, the marks on the page, the way one page is like the next but also totally different, the lives in books, the hills going green, old rolling hills that made you feel you were becoming someone else.

Dr. Lindblad tried to work my soul. She believed in my salvation. She probed all the forces in my history and she gave me books to read, and I read them, and she advanced ideas about what had happened, and I thought about them. But I didn't know if I accepted the idea that I had a history. She used that word a lot and it was hard for me to imagine that all the scuffle and boredom of those years, the crisscross boredom and good times and flare-ups and sameshit nights—I didn't understand how the streaky blur in my nighttime mind could have some sort of form and coherence. Maybe there was a history in her files but the thing I felt about myself was that I'd leaned against a wall in a narrow street serving out some years of mostly aimless waiting.

But you felt some things, didn't you? You felt the strange fascination of his dying fall, so crazy-armed and unmade-up that you didn't know how to look at it.

511

She told me that my father was the third person in the room the day I shot George Manza. This was frankly news to me and I sort of half laughed—you know the way you snicker a nervous draft of air down your nostrils. She told me that one way or another the two events were connected, meaning that six years after Jimmy disappeared I shot a guy who didn't know my father, or barely knew him, or saw him on the street a few times, and this was a link she wanted to probe.

"You have a history," she said, "that you are responsible to."

"What do you mean by responsible to?"

"You're responsible to it. You're answerable. You're required to try to make sense of it. You owe it your complete attention."

She kept talking about history in her tight blouse. But all I saw was the crazy-armed man, his body spinning one way, the chair going another. And all I saw was the rough slur of those narrow streets, the streets going narrower all the time, collapsing in on themselves, and the dumb sad sameness of the days.

Then they came and told me I'd be getting an early release, unexpectedly, one summer day. I wasn't sure how I felt about this. They told me they were sending me to the Jesuits, at the wintry end of the world, somewhere near a lake in Minnesota.

2

The Demings were home this afternoon, busy at various tasks in their split-level suburban house, a long low two-tone colonial with a picture window, a breezeway and bright siding.

Erica was in the kitchen making Jell-O chicken mousse for dinner. Three cups chicken broth or three chicken bouillon cubes dissolved in three cups boiling water. Two packages Jell-O lemon gelatin. One teaspoon salt. One-eighth teaspoon cayenne. Three tablespoons vinegar. One and a third cups whipped topping mix. Two-thirds cup mayonnaise. Two cups finely diced cooked chicken. Two cups finely chopped celery. Two tablespoons chopped pimiento.

Then boil and pour and stir and blend. Fold spiced and chilled gelatin into chicken thing. Spoon into 9×5-inch loaf pan. Chill until firm. Unmold. Garnish with crisp lettuce and stuffed olives (if desired). Makes six entree salads.

Do not reuse this bottle for storing liquids.

Erica did things with Jell-O that took people's breath away. Even

513

now, as she prepared the chicken mousse for final chilling, there were nine parfait glasses in the two-tone Kelvinator. This was dessert for the next three evenings. Each glass was tilted at a forty-five-degree angle either against the wall of the refrigerator or against another object. This tilting method, handed down from her grandmother and her mother, allowed Erica to do Jell-O desserts in a number of colorful diagonal stripes, working the combinations among half a dozen flavors. She might put black raspberry Jell-O, slightly thickened, into a parfait glass. She puts the glass in the fridge, tilting it at forty-five degrees. After the gelatin chills and fully thickens she folds in a swathe of lime Jell-O, and then maybe orange, and then strawberry or strawberry-banana. At the end of the process she has nine multistriped desserts, all different, all so vividly attractive.

Doing things with Jell-O was just about the best way to improve her mood, which was oddly gloomy today—she couldn't figure out why.

From the kitchen window she could see the lawn, neat and trimmed, low-hedged, open and approachable. The trees at the edge of the lawn were new, like everything else in the area. All up and down the curving streets there were young trees and small new box shrubs and a sense of openness, a sense of seeing everything there is to see at a single glance, with nothing shrouded or walled or protected from the glare.

Nothing shrouded or secret except for young Eric, who sat in his room, behind drawn fiberglass curtains, jerking off into a condom. He liked using a condom because it had a sleek metallic shimmer, like his favorite weapons system, the Honest John, a surface-to-surface missile with a warhead that carried yields of up to forty kilotons.

Avoid contact with eyes, open cuts or running sores.

He sat sprawled in a butterfly chair and thought nobody could ever guess what he was doing, specially the condom part. Nobody could ever guess it, know it, imagine it or associate him with it. But what happens, he thought, if you die some day and it turns out that everything you've ever done in private becomes general knowledge in the hereafter. Everybody automatically knows everything you ever did when you thought you were totally and sneakingly and safely unseen.

Prolonged exposure to sun may cause bursting.

They put thermal pads on the Honest John to heat the solid fuel in

514

preparation for firing. Then they remove the pads and launch the missile from a girderlike launch rail in a grassy field somewhere in the Free World. And the missile's infallible flight, the way it sweeps out precise volumes of mathematical space, it's so saintly and sun-tipped, swinging out of its apex to dive to earth, and the way the fireball haloes out above its column of smoke and roar, like some nameless faceless whatever. It made him want to be a Catholic.

Plus she'd have three chicken mousse salads for leftovers later in the week.

Out in the breezeway husband Rick was simonizing their two-tone Ford Fairlane convertible, brand-new, like the houses and the trees, with whitewall tires and stripes of jetstreak chrome that fairly crackled when the car was in motion.

Erica kept her Jell-O molds in the seashell beige cabinet over the range. She had fluted molds, ring molds, crown molds in a number of sizes, she had notes and diagrams, mold techniques, offer forms for special decorative molds that she intended to fill out and mail at her earliest convenience.

If swallowed, induce vomiting at once.

Eric stroked his dick in a conscientious manner, somber and methodical. The condom was feely in a way he'd had to get used to, rubbery dumb and disaffecting. On the floor between his feet was a photo of Jayne Mansfield with her knockers coming out of a sequined gown. He wanted to sandwich his dick between her breasts until it went *wheee*. But he wouldn't just walk out the door when it was over. He would talk to her breasts. Be tender and lovey. Tell them what his longings were, his hopes and dreams.

There was one mold Erica had never used, sort of guided missile-like, because it made her feel uneasy somehow.

The face in the picture was all painted mouth and smudgy lashes and at a certain point in the furtherance of his business Eric deflected his attention from the swooping breasts and focused on the facial Jayne, on her eyebrows and lashes and puckered lips. The breasts were real, the face was put together out of a thousand thermoplastic things. And in the evolving scan of his eros, it was the masking waxes, liners, glosses and creams that became the soft moist mechanisms of release.

515

Intentional misuse by deliberately inhaling contents can be harmful or fatal.

Erica wore a swirly blue skirt and buttercup blouse that happened to match the colors of their Fairlane.

Rick was still in the breezeway, running a shammy over the chromework. This was something, basically, he could do forever. He could look at himself in a strip of chrome, warp-eyed and hydrocephalic, and feel some of the power of the automobile, the horsepower, the decibel rumble of dual exhausts, the pedal tension of Ford-O-Matic drive. The sneaky thing about this car was that, yes, you drove it sensibly to the dentist and occasionally carpooled with the Andersons and took Eric to the science fair but beneath the routine family applications was the crouched power of the machine, top down, eating up the landscape.

Danger. Contents under pressure.

One of Erica's favorite words in the language was breezeway. It spoke of ease and breeze and being contemporary and having something others did not. Another word she loved was crisper. The Kelvinator had a nice roomy crisper and she liked to tell the men that such-and-such was in the crisper. Not the refrigerator, the crisper. The carrots are in the crisper, Rick. There were people out there on the Old Farm Road, where the front porches sag badly and the grass goes unmowed and the Duck River Baptists worship in a squat building that sits in the weeds on the way to the dump, who didn't know what a crisper was, who had iceboxes instead of refrigerators, or who had refrigerators that lacked crispers, or who had crispers in their refrigerators but didn't know what they were for or what they were called, who put tubs of butter in the crisper instead of lettuce, or eggs instead of carrots.

He came in from the breezeway.

"The carrots are in the crisper, Rick."

He liked to nibble on a raw carrot after he'd waxed and buffed the car.

He stood looking at the strontium white loaf that sat on a bed of lettuce inside a cake pan in the middle of the table.

"Wuff what is it?"

"It's my Jell-O chicken mousse."

"Hey great," he said.

Sometimes she called it her Jell-O chicken mousse and sometimes she called it her chicken mousse Jell-O. This was one of a thousand convenient things about Jell-O. The word went anywhere, front or back or in the middle. It was a push-button word, the way so many things were push-button now, the way the whole world opened behind a button that you pushed.

May cause discoloration of urine or feces.

Eric sidled along the wall and slipped into the bathroom, palming the sloppy condom. He washed it out in the sink and then fitted it over his middle finger and aimed the finger at his mouth so he could blow the condom dry. And in the movie version of his life he imagined how everything is projected on a CinemaScope screen, all the secret things he did alone over the years, and now that he is dead it's all available for public viewing and all his dead relatives and friends and teachers and ministers can watch him with his finger in his mouth, more or less, and a condom on his finger, and he is panting rhythmically to dry it off.

He heard his mother call his name.

He had to wash it and reuse it because this was the only one he had, borrowed from another boy, Danny Anderson, who'd taken it from his father's hiding place, under the balled socks, and who swore he'd never used it himself—a thing that wouldn't be fully established until both boys were dead and Eric had a chance to see the footage.

To avoid suffocation keep out of reach of small children.

Eric hid the rubber in his room, pressed into a box of playing cards. He took a long look at Jayne Mansfield's picture before he slipped it into the world atlas on his desk. He realized that Jayne's breasts were not as real-looking as he'd thought in his emotionally vulnerable state, dick in hand. They reminded him of something but what? And then he saw it. The bumper bullets on a Cadillac.

He went into the kitchen and opened the fridge, just to see what was going on in there. The bright colors, the product names and logos, the array of familiar shapes, the tinsel glitter of things in foil wrap, the general sense of benevolent gleam, of eyeball surprise, the sense of a tiny holiday taking place on the shelves and in the slots, a world unspoiled and ever renewable. But there was something else as well, faintly unnerving. The throb perhaps. Maybe it was the informational flow contained in that endless motorized throb. Open the great white vaultlike door and feel the cool breezelet of systems at work, converting current into power, talking to each other day and night across superhuman spaces, a thing he felt outside of, not yet attuned to, and it confused him just a bit.

Except their Kelvinator wasn't white of course. Not on the outside anyway. It was cameo rose and pearly dawn.

He looked inside. He saw the nine tilted parfait glasses and felt a little dizzy. He got disoriented sometimes by the tilted Jell-O desserts. It was as if a science-fiction force had entered the house and made some things askew while sparing others.

They sat down to dinner and Rick carved the mousse and doled out portions. They drank iced tea with a slice of lemon wedged to the rim of each glass, one of Erica's effortless extra touches.

Rick said to Eric, "Wha'cha been up to all afternoon? Big homework day?"

"Hey dad. Saw you simonizing the car."

"Got an idea. After dinner we'll take the binoculars and drive out on the Old Farm Road and see if we can spot it."

"Spot what?" Erica said.

"The baby moon. What else? The satellite they put up there. Supposed to be visible on clear nights."

It wasn't until this moment that Erica understood why her day had felt shadowed and ominous from the time she opened her eyes and stared at the mikado yellow walls with patina green fleecing. Yes, that satellite they put into orbit a few days ago. Rick took a scientific interest and wanted Eric to do the same. Sure, Rick was surprised and upset, just as she was, but he was willing to stand in a meadow somewhere and try to spot the object as it floated over. Erica felt a twisted sort of disappointment. It was theirs, not ours. It flew at an amazing rate of speed over the North Pole, *beep beep beep*, passing just above us, evidently, at certain times. She could not understand how this could happen. Were there other surprises coming, things we haven't

518

been told about them? Did they have crispers and breezeways? It was not a simple matter, adjusting to the news.

Rick said, "What about it, Eric? Want to drive on out?"

"Hey dad. Ga, ga, ga, great."

A pall fell over the table, displacing Erica's Sputnik funk. She thought Eric's occasional stuttering had something to do with the time he spent alone in his room. Hitting the books too hard, Rick thought. He was hitting something too hard but Erica tried not to form detailed images.

Do not puncture or incinerate.

The boy could sit in the family room and watch their super console TV, which was compatible with the knotty pine paneling, and he could anticipate the dialogue on every show. Newscasts, ball games, comedy hours. He did whatever voice the announcer or actor used, matching the words nearly seamlessly, and he never stuttered.

All the other kids ate Oreo cookies. Eric ate Hydrox cookies because the name sounded like rocket fuel.

One of her kitchen gloves was missing—she had many pairs—and she wanted to believe Eric had borrowed it for one of his chemistry assignments. But she was afraid to ask. And she didn't think she looked forward to getting it back.

Yesterday he'd dunked a Hydrox cookie in milk, held it dripping over the glass and said thickly, "Is verry gud we poot Roosian moon in U.S. sky."

Then he took a bite and swallowed.

The men went out to find the orbiting satellite. Erica cleared the table, put on her rubberoid gloves and began to do the dishes. Rick had kidded her about the gloves a number of times. The kitchen was equipped with an automatic dishwasher of course. But she felt compelled as a homemaker to do a preliminary round of handwashing and scouring because if you don't get every smidge of organic murk off the fork tines and out of the pans before you run the dishwasher, it could come back to haunt you in the morning.

Flush eyes with water and call physician at once.

And the gloves protected her from scalding water and the touch of food scraps. Erica loved her gloves. The gloves were indestructible, basically, made of the same kind of materials used in countertops and TV tubes, in the electrical insulation in the basement and the vulcanized tires on the car. The gloves were important to her despite the way they felt, clammy but also dry, a feeling that defied innate contradiction.

All the things around her were important. Things and words. Words to believe in and live by.

Breezeway	Car pools
Crisper	Bridge parties
Sectional	Broadloom

When she finished up in the kitchen she decided to vacuum the living room rug but then realized this would make her bad mood worse. She'd recently bought a new satellite-shaped vacuum cleaner that she loved to push across the room because it hummed softly and seemed futuristic and hopeful but she was forced to regard it ruefully now, after Sputnik, a clunky object filled with self-remorse.

Stacking chairs	Room divider
Scatter cushions	Fruit juicer
Storage walls	Cookie sheet

She thought she'd lift her spirits by doing something for the church social on Saturday to pep up the event a little.

Do not use in enclosed space.

She would prepare half a dozen serving bowls of her Jell-O antipasto salad. Six packages Jell-O lemon gelatin. Six teaspoons salt. Six cups boiling water. Six tablespoons vinegar. Twelve cups ice cubes. Three cups finely cut salami. Two cups finely cut Swiss cheese. One and a half cups chopped celery. One and a half cups chopped onion. Twelve tablespoons sliced ripe olives.

She remembered coming home one day about six months ago and finding Eric with his head in a bowl of her antipasto salad. He said he was trying to eat it from the inside out to test a scientific theory of his. The explanation was so crazy and unconvincing that it was weirdly believable. But she didn't believe it. She didn't know what to believe.

Was this a form of sexual curiosity? Was he pretending the Jell-O was a sort of lickable female body part? And was he engaged in an act of unnatural oral stimulation? He had jellified gunk all over his mouth and tongue. She looked at him. She had people skills. Erica was a person who related to people. But she had to put on gloves just to talk to him.

She set to work in the kitchen now, listening all the while for the reassuring sound of her men coming home, car doors closing in the breezeway, the solid clunk of well-made parts swinging firmly shut.

AUGUST 14, 1964

The charismatic black stood outside the church talking to the crowd.

Downtown the young whites leaned on brick walls and parked cars, crew-cut young men in chinos or jeans, or squatted on the curbstone, some older men among them, most showing a small hard salty grin, eyes tight, watching the marchers move out of the bus terminal.

Past the brick dorms and athletic fields of the campus, a group of black men lounged against a car parked in front of a rickety frame house in an alley off Lynch Street. A man with a cane. A man with blue suspenders. A man in a necktie and white shirt and straw fedora. A couple of younger men sitting on the fenders and talking to a woman eating a peach on the porch steps.

The charismatic speaker said, "They made us run, so we got good at it."

The marchers came into town carrying knapsacks and signs. Some of them walked toward the campus as the sun began to set. A number of white-shirted police stood along the route, smoking, some of them, and seeming to disregard the marchers, who walked in two loose columns toward the sound of the speaker's voice.

The young speaker said, "They made us run until we got so good at it we didn't need their inspiration anymore."

In the Greyhound terminal a number of marchers separated from the others and began to sit on the floor of the whites-only waiting room.

But the porch didn't really have steps. It had a couple of loose cinder blocks set against the brick underpinning and that's where the woman sat.

Students joined the crowd in front of the church, listening to the speaker, and some of the cornerboys came out of Cooper's, where they'd been shooting pool, and stood around to watch the crowd.

Men and women kept marching through the downtown streets and the whites sat on the curbstone and watched them, seemingly unable to stop grinning.

Four highway patrolmen stood outside the bus terminal leaning on a cruiser and talking casually, the butt ends of their shotguns leveraged on their hips, muzzles pointing up.

The young speaker said, "But just about the time we became Olympic-class runners, some of us decided we were gonna sit down."

The woman finished eating the peach and held the pit in her hand and when one of the men leaning on a car fender said something racy or tricky or sly, she threw the pit at his feet with a kind of dismissive motion.

Somebody adjusted the speaker's microphone and his voice began to carry now, reaching the guardsmen who were coming down out of trucks at the end of a blocked-off street.

A black woman stood watching in the bus terminal. She'd come from up north, riding buses all the way, and now she was in the terminal, fittingly, about to sit on the floor. She watched local police move among the demonstrators and lift a young man by an arm and leg, taking him in two directions, briefly, at once, until they got straightened out, a pair of short-sleeved cops, not looking at the youngster, who sat unstruggling in their grip as they carried him out to the street.

The charismatic black said, "There's a certain feeling circulating in the culture that black people ought to develop a willingness to die."

The guardsmen formed up and began to fix bayonets and their commander stood nearby in summer tans and a campaign hat, looking around for the armored van.

The miked voice floated over the heads of the assembled marchers and students and townspeople.

On the floor of the bus terminal the woman waited for the police to reach her and carry her out to the truck and take her to the jail, one

522

Rose Meriweather Martin, known as Rosie, an insurance adjustor from New York City.

"The interesting thing is that this here's not what the white man is saying. It's what the Negro is saying. If they want to kill us, in other words, let's develop a willingness to die. Or was saying. Because we damn well ain't saying it anymore."

There was an armored van moving through the streets, with bullet-proof windows and gunports, and the men inside had submachine guns and tear-gas launchers.

The young whites began moving away from the walls and the parked cars. They got up from the curbstone and dusted off their pants and they went to stand at the far end of the street, uninterested in the marchers now or interested in a different way.

The woman on the porch saw some young men running in the dark, cornerboys or students, looking back as they ran, and the men lounging against the parked car also saw them but did not stiffen or speak or move away. It was their car, their street, and they needed to measure the situation.

The young black man said, "I ain't saying don't resist. I ain't saying assume the fetal position and let them put their cocked revolvers upside your head. Tell you what I'm saying."

The whites didn't look at the marchers as people coming into town to agitate and make trouble. Not anymore. They stopped reading the signs about voter rights and freedom rides. They stopped grinning at white nuns marching with black ministers. It was the armored van they were interested in now, twenty-three feet long, searchlights blazing.

"And I ain't saying you're obliged to love those truncheons they're beating you with."

They watched it go by and began to follow it, some of them, vaguely.

The guardsmen wore standard issue helmets and were putting on gas masks now and the troopers outside the bus terminal wore white ridged helmets that resembled construction hard hats.

Rosie Martin watched them get closer, local police in pairs scooping up the demonstrators and taking them out to flatbed trucks.

Blacks with shirttails flying, looking back as they ran, and maybe the woman on the porch could smell a burning in the air.

The gas masks were bulky devices with goggle eyes and swollen nosepieces. The guardsmen looked insect-eyed, stepping into a flood-lit area near the black college campus. The masks had flap mouths and filtration chambers that bulged out of the left side like pineapple tins.

A man lay spread-eagle outside the terminal, being patted down by troopers.

A man was being tug-of-warred, a young black in a striped shirt, two guardsmen gripping an arm and a leg and a marcher holding the other leg and trying to pull him back into the crowd outside Mount Calvary church.

Somebody threw a bottle and the woman on the porch heard it break in the street. She stood up and tried to see what was happening in the dark out there. Voices, people running, people coming this way and then turning back.

"Tell you what I'm saying. I'm saying there's nothing in the world to worry about despite the evidence all around you. Because anytime you see black and white together you know they are joined in some effort of betterment. Says so in the Constitution."

Another bottle broke.

And in the terminal Rosie Martin saw them drag a woman out the door facedown and headfirst.

The guardsmen moved into the crowd outside the church, holding their bayoneted rifles at port arms, and the gas came blowing in behind them.

In the terminal a cop started clubbing people on the arms and legs. Rosie watched him calmly, counting the number of sit-in marchers before he got to her.

The charismatic speaker said, "They're spraying, I'm talking. I'm gonna keep on talking as long as I got a larynx that can function. Black people love to rap," he said.

The marchers sat down, they scattered, some entered the church, some ran the other way, and the guardsmen dragged others along the ground toward the barricaded street.

At the terminal the cops had their billy clubs out and were moving in a stoop among the demonstrators, who sat hunched forward with their arms over their heads.

The gas rolled through the streets scorching people's eyeballs, making their eyeballs feel sucked out by the heat. The streets were filled with running men and women. The gas rolled in and they strayed down alleys, feeling their way, chests tight, coughing in spasms, or chose to walk, some of them, shambling half blind toward the church.

Rosie knew she'd be taken off to jail on a flatbed garbage truck and then put in a crowded cell and given a piss-smelling mattress because this had been the scuttlebutt for days.

Blacks came running down the dark street and the men who'd been lounging against the car began to stir finally. The man with blue suspenders went into a frame house and the man with the straw hat got into the car and rolled up the windows and then got out again and the other men slid off the fenders and went to stand on the porch where the woman stood looking down the street.

Women wanted the same prison conditions the men got. This was a definite issue.

Guardsmen massed around the armored van, insect-headed, and looked down the dark alleys for students throwing rocks or men out of the bars, the juke joints, still holding cans of Colt 45, and they heard the speaker say, "It's all a question of mind over matter. They don't mind and we don't matter."

Rosie was dragged on her ass out into the street and spun around on her britches and left there. She spotted sawhorse barricades and police cruisers, people milling and scuffling and photographers popping flashcubes, and she thought she caught the first taste of gas.

People stagger-ran toward the church through ranks of guardsmen.

She saw the one-legged man on crutches, a familiar figure over weeks of bus rides and marches across state lines. And the man being beaten. She saw a slim man being struck by a cop with a billy club, hit three, four times, a pause, then hit again, white eyes showing.

The woman on the porch felt the air burning and went inside and the men went inside with her. Young men went running past, students and marchers, and one of them stopped long enough to fling a bottle the other way.

The gas, called CS, made people dizzy almost at once and caused a stinging on the body where the skin was moist.

Rosie smelled the gas, she tasted it before she saw it. A trooper had a man bent over the trunk of the cruiser, in an armlock, and another trooper stood nearby holding two shotguns, his own and his partner's who had the armlock on the marcher.

The armored van moved slowly through the streets, searchlights swiveling on the roof.

The church was filling up with people trying to escape the gas, which rolled through the alleys off Lynch Street in Jackson, Mississippi on a muggy summer night with radios playing and children standing at the windows of shotgun shacks, watching men run through the dark.

Rosie started running. She saw the cop beating the man methodically, three, four blows and then a pause, and she started running toward them.

The gas had a radiance, a night glow, and the men in insect masks came walking out of the cloud, alive and bright.

The man who'd rolled up the windows of the car, a sixty-year-old in a white shirt and straw hat, proceeded to walk down the unpaved street toward his house, tasting the gas and putting his hat over his face and accidentally kicking a pop bottle someone had thrown, lying unbroken in the dust.

She watched the cop strike the man on the head and arms, three, four blows with his billy club and then a pause, and she pushed through a couple of sawhorses and ran directly toward them, feeling fast and light and unstoppable.

The gas rolled through the streets in tides and drifts, narrowing down alleys and fitting into confined spaces.

She had no idea what she planned to do when she got there, about four seconds from now.

DECEMBER 19, 1961

Charles Wainwright was on the phone to a client in Omaha, soothing, stroking, joking, making promises he could not keep. He felt a measure of detachment from the matters at hand, his eyes slightly aswim in the agreeable yield of a long liquid lunch.

He heard himself saying, "Off the top of my head I would estimate, Dwayne, we'll be able to present this campaign, timewise, in four and a half weeks. Four weeks minimum. We just switched our best art director to the account. Three weeks with heavenly intervention. God keeps an apartment in New York, incidentally, because this is a swinging town. Seriously, the guy's an award-winning art director and he's in his office right now doing roughs."

Just then Pasqualini, the art director, stuck his head in the door.

"What is death?" he said.

Wainwright smiled and shrugged.

"Nature's way of telling you to slow down."

Charlie tossed his head to indicate laughter and Pasqualini headed down the hall to tell the joke to some of the other senior account men, Charlie's peers, the guys with the snap tab collars and chromium smiles—they drank gibsons straight up and said, Thanks much.

In fact Charlie thought the joke was beautifully suited to these surroundings. In the Times every morning, wasn't it a fact that the obits and the ad column tended to appear on facing pages?

Charles Wainwright was an account supervisor at Parmelee Lockhart & Keown, a medium-sized agency located in the Fred F. French Building on Fifth Avenue in New York.

The shop had suffered a few setbacks lately. And every time an account went walking out the door, a hush fell over the carpeted halls. People stood in line at the coffee wagons, holding their poignant mugs. The jokes they told had a bitter edge. Executives made phone calls behind closed doors. The pasteup boys sat in the bullpen with the radio off and the lights down low. Copywriters took three-hour lunches and came back stinko. They sat in their cubicles and stared at memos pinned to the corkboard, wondering why they'd sold out if this was how it felt to be a sellout.

Charlie had to fire people sometimes. Once he fired three people in one day, two before lunch and one after. He fired a tall man and a short man in the same week. These were the Mutt and Jeff firings. He fired a man recovering from a heart attack and a woman who'd just died. He didn't know Maxine was dead and he was forced to fire the secretary who'd caused the mix-up.

Charlie said into the phone, "If you want us to do the presentation here, I'll get you a table at the Four Seasons, Dwayne, and you can play footsie with my English secretary. Or I'll schlep the layouts out to Omaha. What a thrill it is to spend time—no, seriously, what do you do on Sundays, Dwayne? Go to the park and look at the cannon?"

This was a line off a Lenny Bruce LP but Charlie didn't think he had to credit the source. He liked Dwayne Sturmer, a decent guy for an ad manager. And the account was fairly sound, the lawn fertilizer division of a giant chemical company. The creative types here in the shop wanted to do a Bomb Your Lawn campaign. A little twist on the fact that these fertilizer ingredients, plus fuel oil, could produce a rather loud disturbance if ignited.

A young copywriter, Swayze, stuck his head in the door.

"Had a date with a Swedish model last night."

Charlie smiled and waited. The kid paused for effect.

"When I touched her Volvo, she Saabed."

It was Charlie who killed the Bomb Your Lawn campaign while it was still in-house. The creative types wanted to use George Metesky as a spokesman. An approach so suicidal Charlie found it somewhat lovable. George Metesky was the Mad Bomber of the 1940s and 1950s, famous for setting off a series of blasts at New York landmarks. They wanted to track him down at the state pen or the funny farm and build the whole campaign around his ancient and fabled deeds and his endorsement of the product.

Bomb your lawn with Nitrotex.

Mad Ave was getting younger all the time and Charlie was forty-six. Almost ready to be placed on an ice floe with his handcrafted English wingtips and his Patek Philippe timepiece. Still, he had solid accounts and a sunlit corner office with a crushed leather sofa. Prints of steeple-chase races and frocked lordlings riding to hounds. A painted sea chest he'd spotted in a London shop. And the thing that gave him away as a regular guy—a sort of baseball shrine, three populist mementoes clustered at the far end of the room.

First, a tenth-anniversary limited-edition lithograph entitled The Shot Heard Round the World. The piece included photos of the Polo Grounds, Ralph Branca delivering the pitch, Bobby Thomson swinging the bat, Thomson's teammates waiting in a conga line to greet him at home plate.

Second, a photo of Thomson and Branca standing on a golf course with Dwight D. Eisenhower, all holding drivers, a couple of Secret Service men shadowing the fringes of the picture—Charlie's wife found the item in a junk shop in Vermont.

And, third, a smudged baseball balanced on the rim of a coffee mug that sat on the credenza—a ball he'd bought from a guy who claimed it was the very object Branca had hurled and Thomson had heroically struck.

His secretary walked in, Sandy, in a Mondrian dress and white shoes.

"Dwayne, my secretary just walked in. She's wearing white shoes. She's got a foot fetish and she's dying to meet you."

He liked to tease Dwayne, who was a bachelor, extremely shy, a large flesh-colored man in a pajama-striped wash-and-wear suit and shoes like Chinese gunboats.

Sandy dropped some status reports in his in-box. He listened to Dwayne talk about ad rates and cost-per-thousand. Sandy walked out of the office and he watched her, buttocks swinging meanly, printed with yellow parallelograms.

They'd wanted to give George Metesky a wig, a mustache and spectacles to make him look like Einstein.

These creative minds with their sublimated forms of destruction. Every third campaign featured some kind of play on weapons. The agency was still in shock over the Equinox Oil campaign. This was a very expensive effort that culminated in a sixty-second commercial shot in the Jornada del Muerto in remotest New Mexico. Site of the first atomic test shot ever made. A white space on the map. Totally closed to the public. Charlie thought the idea would fly, actually. Fill up two cars with premium gasoline. One with Equinox, the other with a leading competitive brand. Run the cars across the barren desert. Shoot the commercial with helicopters, crane shots, tracking shots, slow motion, stop action, all the latest know-how. White car versus black car. Clear implication. U.S. versus USSR. First car to get to the Trinity site wins—this is the monument that marks the spot where the bomb went off. We get permission from the Department of Energy, Department of Defense, Atomic Energy Commission, National Park Service. We shoot the thing. Takes many weeks. Costs, per second, more than a Hollywood epic. But it'll fly, baby. The stark scrub. The heat undulations and cow skulls. The dust storms. The high-angle shots—one car pulling away, the other catching up. A voice-over done by a pompous announcer with a cold war tone. Which car will run out of gas first? Which one will get to the marker? Miles per gallon. A huge consumer issue. Of course the white car outlasted the black car and reached the site first. We air the commercial. Heavy schedule. We thought the Soviet embassy might lodge a complaint. We looked forward to it. Free publicity. What happens? We get complaints all right. But not from foreign governments. We hear from the National Association for the Advancement of Colored People. We hear from the Urban League. We hear from the Congress of Racial Equality. Because the white car beat the black car. An amazing firestorm of protest. Threatened boycotts of all Equinox products. We pull the commercial. We reshoot the entire thing and absorb the cost ourselves. Two cars. Both white. Car with letter A painted on roof. Car with letter B painted on roof. Lesson. Don't mix your metaphors.

"Cost per thou, Dwayne, is an overrated device intended to blind us to the truth of our situation." He waited for Dwayne to ask what the truth of our situation was. "There is only one truth. Whoever controls your eyeballs runs the world."

There were probably two dozen people walking the streets in the days after the game, shysters, heisters, fools and knaves, all claiming they had the one and only baseball. Which Charlie devoutly wanted to believe was the selfsame object on his credenza.

Yes, the baseball that marked him as a regular fellow with a soft streak despite his milled-steel veneer. He got fascist haircuts done by Spadavecchia of Milan—his *school* actually, since Gianni was frequently overbooked. He wore striped shirts with white collars, or white shirts with blue collars. He wore suits so compulsively custom-fit a fart would split a seam. He played squash and handball, did Canadian Air Force exercises, applied bronzing agents to his face and body and sat in front of a sunlamp all winter long. A regular guy with a station wagon heart despite the giddy MG he'd just treated himself to, perfect for tooling the foothills of the Berkshires around their weekend place.

A sentimental weepy white guy.

Yes, the baseball he dearly wanted to entrust to his son Chuckie. To Charles Jr. No longer the bubblegum boy of yore but a failed preppy now, slant-bodied and dissonant, with dumdum eyes and a way of hating you from a distance. Flunked out of Exeter, chased out of Choate, walked out of Andover. Chuckie didn't care. But Charlie did and it was painful. How could he give such an emotional object, whatever ambiguity throbbed in the ball's corked heart, to this aimless wayward aging kid, a displaced person in his own life?

Pasqualini stuck his head in the door on his way back to the art department.

"What do you call a six-foot five-inch two-hundred-and-sixty-pound Negro that you run into in a dark alley?"

Charlie smiled thinly, wary of the new wave of civil rights jokes, and raised his head to indicate, What?

"Mister."

He fired a pregnant woman once. He fired a man related to the Dutch royal family. He fired a Catholic, a Protestant and a Jew in fairly close succession. He fired a man for falling in the water on the company boat ride and another for carrying a gun to a client meeting.

"They're doing research, Dwayne, on what they call retinal discharge. They secretly photograph women in supermarkets. They have sensitive cameras hidden on the shelves that record excitations of the inner eye, motions of the eye far more subtle and telling than a simple blink, and it seems that women go completely crazy eyeballwise when they see certain colors, packages and designs. These are orgasms, basically, of the eye, the brain and the nervous system. How do we use this research? Simple. We correlate high discharge events with the particular items that caused them and then we design our products and packaging accordingly. Once we get the consumer by the eyeballs, we have complete mastery of the marketing process."

Sandy came back in and began to mouth some sort of complicated message.

But if Charlie truly believed the baseball was authentic, would he leave it in plain sight, unguarded, where a cleaning woman might decide to take it home to her kid because she doesn't earn enough money to buy him a baseball, or a delivery boy from the coffee shop around the corner—he pictured a swarthy male drifting through the corridors on a slow afternoon, with creamless coffee and a toasted English in a white bag, looking for something to pinch.

"She wants to talk to us, Dwayne. Yes, my secretary. Did I ever tell you how she types? She likes to fold one leg up under her. Before she began sitting on her foot she did about twenty-five words a minute. Now she does two hundred."

Charlie was fascinated by certain quirks and traits that Sandy brought to her job. She had that distinctive English quality of looking terrifically fresh and crisp even while conveying tawdry intimations of the state of her underwear and the fact that she bathes only under pressure from her roommates, Fiona and Georgina.

Charlie talked to Omaha and deciphered his secretary's mouthed message at the same time.

"She's telling us she needs to leave early, Dwayne. She's been leaving early quite often lately. And taking conspicuously long lunches. We know what that means, don't we? An affair with a married man."

Sandy did a stand-up collapse, aghast at the man's cheek. His temerity, his effrontery, his American facking New York nerve. Charlie gave her his Richard Widmark grin. He had no reason to keep her around the rest of the afternoon but asked her to order him an orange juice before she left.

Charlie wanted to pitch the Minute Maid account. He thought about orange juice all the time. He looked at it, drank it, had fantasies about it. He knew how to advertise orange juice. Forget Florida. Forget the piddling vitamins. You have to go for appetite appeal, for the visual hit, because this is a beautiful and enticing beverage and women's eyeballs reach high levels of excitation when they see bright orange cans in the freezer, gleaming with rime ice. You have to show the pulp. You show the juice splashing in the glass. You show the froth on a perky housewife's upper lip, like the hint of a blowjob before breakfast. Of course there is no pulp in concentrate. And there is only a microtrace of pulp in container juice. But you can suggest, you can

532

make inferences, you can promise the consumer the experience of citrusy bits of real pulp—a glass of juice, a goblet brimming with particulate matter, like wondrous orange smog. You show it. You photograph it lovingly and microscopically. If the can or package can be orgasmically visual, so can the product inside. There was nothing Charlie liked better than a glass of orange juice on a lazy Sunday morning in the country, nicely spiked with vodka.

He wanted to pitch the Smirnoff account. There was an element of Russian chic in the culture these days. Yevtushenko in his black-market jeans. Those Russian hats that sprouted earlier this winter, still going strong in New York and Chicago. Astrakhans. You wake up one morning and every third man earning a salary in a certain range is wearing a lambskin Russian hat.

"Dwayne, she's gone, good buddy. We've lost her to some lech in the copy department. I'd bet anything on that. Sandy thinks writers are moody and glamorous because they're always in danger of getting canned."

The moans of spewing buses rose into the settling dusk. The office lights were on now and all up and down the halls the girls tapped on the squarish keys of their IBM Selectrics. The graved ball kissed the ribbon, the ribbon kissed the paper, a superior grade of bond that was rag-weaved like the oxford shirts worn by the bosses of the typing girls. Every sixteen seconds one of them hit the wrong key and muttered a middling curse.

The married copywriters met their secretaries, or the secretaries of other writers, or the tall and lissome secretaries of account executives, white-shod and well-spoken, and went about the tender regimen of their lunchtime love—the nooner, it was called, or the matinee—meeting in the secretaries' snug apartments, striking in their dimensional similarity to the cubicles the writers worked in, only decorated more touchingly and vulnerably, with posters of Madrid on the off-white walls, or prints of Marino Marini horses or Bernard Buffet lobsters, or in the larger apartments of secretaries with roommates, which complicated the schedule and made the writers yearn for an intimate glimpse of one of the roommates, barefoot in a partially open robe, perhaps, coming from the shower after a late night with a failed date, the apartments situated

533

nearly always in the sunless hindquarters of white-brick buildings in the East 80s, undoormanned, the small elevators inspected every two years by an individual called A. Bear, according to recent entries on the record of inspection that was fixed to the elevator walls.

And yes, it's true, Charlie has practiced this kind of erotic disport himself, off and on, with one or another single young woman working in the production department or somesuch level of the mothership, belowdecks and lonesome and not always, actually, very young. But did he enjoy these interludes or were they sad entertainments he inflicted on himself in the stark space of a convertible sofa turned open to span the room so that he had to walk upon the bedding to go and pee? He had lovely sex with his wife in an antique bed with carved oak posts, so what are you doing here, Charlie, balling this morose media clerk. It was an odd form of mortification for some pattern of behavior, or grain of being, too transparent for this adman to fathom.

"This is the challenge, Dwayne. You have to read the mysterious current that passes in the night and connects millions of people across a continental landmass, compelling them to buy a certain product first thing in the morning. They gotta have it and you gotta be ready for them when they show up."

He said, "Package goods and painkillers. These are the things that keep the country running."

A swarthy male stood in the doorway.

"Jou order oranjuice?"

Charlie fished some money out of his pocket and paid the guy. He took an extra-strength antacid tablet out of the bottle in his desk and washed it down with the watery pulpless half-rancid juice, for whatever calmative effect it might have on his acidic backwash.

He told a dirty joke to Dwayne and sensed the fellow going pink out there on the prairie. There was nothing left to do but leave. Charlie walked through the semiswank lobby, done in Babylonian art deco, and nipped around the corner to his Swedish masseuse, who karate'd his aching lumbar for ten minutes. Then he wheeled into Brooks Brothers and picked up a couple of tennis shirts because what's more fun than an impulse buy? He double-timed it across Madison to the Men's Bar at the Biltmore, where he massively inhaled a Cutty on the rocks and was out the door in half a shake and skating across the vast main level of Grand Central, the Bobby Thomson baseball jammed into the pocket of his topcoat—a Burberry all-weather that he loved like a brother and that went especially well with the suit he was wearing, a slate gray whipcord made for Charlie by a guy who did lapels for organized crime—because he'd decided the ball was no longer safe in his office and he wanted his son to have it, for better or worse, love or money, real or fake, but please Chuckie do not abuse my trust, I could fall down dead passing the stuffed mushrooms at dinner and this is the one thing I want you to take and keep and care for, and he went striding through the gate just in time to make his train, which was the evolutionary climax of the whole human endeavor, and he bucketed up to the bar car, filled with people who more or less resembled Charlie, give or take a few years and a few gray hairs and the details of their evilest dreams.

The last express to Westport.

3

There were stories about the Pope. There were reports, a certain kind of underground rumor that can make its way across a country, parish to parish. Pope Pius was having mystical visions. That was the rumor going round. He was witness to a series of supernatural events, seeing things in the dead of night. That was the story people told, I don't know, nuns, old ladies on novena nights, maybe well-heeled parishioners too, pink and fit, officers of the Knights of Columbus. People hear such a story and feel something turn in their souls, a leap out of dear old singsong life into some other reading altogether.

In class a student mentioned the rumors to Father Paulus in the course of a discussion that touched on the subject of thaumatology, or the study of wonders.

The old priest looked out the window.

"If you'd been drinking dago red until three in the morning, you'd have visions too."

I went to see Father in his office later in the day. It was a three-

536

hundred-yard walk through a billowing white storm. I had the edges of my watch cap unfurled over my ears and kept my forearm raised against the cutting sleet, against the whole hard physical thing, the snowstorms and open spaces, the reality of a mass of land called North America, new to my experience.

Father started talking before I had my jacket off.

"It's when the hair in my nostrils begins going stiff. That's when I want to retire to the south of France."

"The snow on the parade."

"Yes, I know."

"The benches are buried."

"Yes," he said.

"I realized, just out the window there, I was walking over a bench."

"Yes. Sit down, Shay, and tell me how you're doing. A young man's progress. That's the title of this session."

"I borrowed a pair of boots."

He liked that response.

"Do they fit?"

"No."

Even better. When he asked about the state of my mind and soul, which he did only rarely, and when I answered on a practical plane, as I always did, he seemed to think I was devising a down-to-earth reply out of some manly instinct when in fact I was only confused, forever trying to put together a suitable set of words.

"What are you reading?"

I recited a list.

"You understand what's in those books?"

"No," I said.

Again he smiled. I think he was tired of gifted kids. He'd done work with boys of advanced standing and now he wanted to talk to misfits of the other kind, the ones who'd made trouble for themselves and others.

"Some of it maybe. What I don't understand, I memorize."

His arm was propped on the desk and he leaned his head into the canted hand. No smile this time.

"That's not why we started this place, is it?"

"I study like a madman, Father."

"But you can't memorize ideas the way you do the endings of Latin verbs."

His hands were unspotted and small. Some of the other jebbies wore flannel shirts and heavy sweaters but Father Paulus was not influenced by climate or geography or the sense of special freedoms at Voyageur. He went black-suited and roman-collared and I respected this and found it reassuring.

"One of the things we want to do here is to produce serious men. What sort of phenomenon is this? Not so easy to say. Someone, in the end, who develops a certain depth, a spacious quality, say, that's a form of respect for other ways of thinking and believing. Let us unnarrow the basic human tubing. And let us help a young man toward an ethical strength that makes him decisive, that shows him precisely who he is, Shay, and how he is meant to address the world."

You were always afraid of disappointing Father, being unequal to the level of discourse. Being bland when he wanted a more spirited sort of traffic, even a bullshit act, wiseass and slouchy. Bland and plodding when he wanted independence and open argument.

"My own life, I confess—yes, why not, you'll hear my confession, Shay. Who better than you? Took me all these years to understand that I'm not a serious man. Too much irony, too much vanity, too little what—I don't know, a lot of things. And no rage, you see. Or a small ingrown toenail rage, a puny frustration. Eventually you get to know these things. Do you act out of principle? Or do you devise self-justifying reasons for your bad behavior? This is my confession, not yours, so you're not required to come up with answers. Not yet anyway. Eventually, yes. You'll know in your heart how well you've met the calling to be a man."

"No rage," I said. "What do you mean?"

"No rage. Rage and violence can be elements of productive tension in a soul. They can serve the fullness of one's identity. One way a man untrivializes himself is to punch another man in the mouth."

I must have looked at him.

"You can't doubt this, can you? I don't like violence. It scares the hell out of me. But I think I see it as an expanding force in a personal-

538

ity. And I think a man's ability to act in opposition to his tendencies in this direction can be a source of virtue, a statement of his character and forbearance."

"So what do you do? Punch the guy in the mouth or resist the urge?"

"Point well taken. I don't have the answer. You have the answer," he said. "But how serious can a man be if he doesn't experience a full measure of the appetites and passions of his race, even if only to contain them or direct them, somehow, usefully?"

Who better than you to hear me confess? He'd said that, hadn't he? Someone who's been in correction. Someone who has the answer. Of course I had nothing that resembled an answer and wondered why he thought I carried a stain of special knowledge for having done what I'd done.

"Have you come across the word velleity? A nice Thomistic ring to it. Volition at its lowest ebb. A small thing, a wish, a tendency. If you're low-willed, you see, you end up living in the shallowest turns and bends of your own preoccupations. Are we getting anywhere?"

"It's your confession, Father."

His office was in an old barracks building and the force of the wind made the beams shift and crick.

"Aquinas said only intense actions will strengthen a habit. Not mere repetition. Intensity makes for moral accomplishment. An intense and persevering will. This is an element of seriousness. Constancy. This is an element. A sense of purpose. A self-chosen goal. Tell me I'm babbling. I'll respect you for it."

We were about thirty miles below the Canadian border in a rambling encampment that was mostly barracks and other frame structures, a harking back, maybe, to the missionary roots of the order—except the natives, in this case, were us. Poor city kids who showed promise; some frail-bodied types with photographic memories and a certain uncleanness about them; those who were bright but unstable; those who could not adjust; the ones whose adjustment was ordained by the state; a cluster of Latins from some Jesuit center in Venezuela, smart young men with a cosmopolitan style, freezing their weenies off; and a few farmboys from not so far away, shyer than borrowed suits.

"Sometimes I think the education we dispense is better suited to a fifty-year-old who feels he missed the point the first time around. Too many abstract ideas. Eternal verities left and right. You'd be better served looking at your shoe and naming the parts. You in particular, Shay, coming from the place you come from."

This seemed to animate him. He leaned across the desk and gazed, is the word, at my wet boots.

"Those are ugly things, aren't they?"

"Yes they are."

"Name the parts. Go ahead. We're not so chi chi here, we're not so intellectually chic that we can't test a student face-to-face."

"Name the parts," I said. "All right. Laces."

"Laces. One to each shoe. Proceed."

I lifted one foot and turned it awkwardly.

"Sole and heel."

"Yes, go on."

I set my foot back down and stared at the boot, which seemed about as blank as a closed brown box.

"Proceed, boy."

"There's not much to name, is there? A front and a top."

"A front and a top. You make me want to weep."

"The rounded part at the front."

"You're so eloquent I may have to pause to regain my composure. You've named the lace. What's the flap under the lace?"

"The tongue."

"Well?"

"I knew the name. I just didn't see the thing."

He made a show of draping himself across the desk, writhing slightly as if in the midst of some dire distress.

"You didn't see the thing because you don't know how to look. And you don't know how to look because you don't know the names."

He tilted his chin in high rebuke, mostly theatrical, and withdrew his body from the surface of the desk, dropping his bottom into the swivel chair and looking at me again and then doing a decisive quarter turn and raising his right leg sufficiently so that the foot, the shoe, was posted upright at the edge of the desk.

A plain black everyday clerical shoe.

"Okay," he said. "We know about the sole and heel."

"Yes."

"And we've identified the tongue and lace."

"Yes," I said.

With his finger he traced a strip of leather that went across the top edge of the shoe and dipped down under the lace.

"What is it?" I said.

"You tell me. What is it?"

"I don't know."

"It's the cuff."

"The cuff."

"The cuff. And this stiff section over the heel. That's the counter."

"That's the counter."

"And this piece amidships between the cuff and the strip above the sole. That's the quarter."

"The quarter," I said.

"And the strip above the sole. That's the welt. Say it, boy."

"The welt."

"How everyday things lie hidden. Because we don't know what they're called. What's the frontal area that covers the instep?"

"I don't know."

"You don't know. It's called the vamp."

"The vamp."

"Say it."

"The vamp. The frontal area that covers the instep. I thought I wasn't supposed to memorize."

"Don't memorize ideas. And don't take us too seriously when we turn up our noses at rote learning. Rote helps build the man. You stick the lace through the what?"

"This I should know."

"Of course you know. The perforations at either side of, and above, the tongue."

"I can't think of the word. Eyelet."

"Maybe I'll let you live after all."

"The eyelets."

"Yes. And the metal sheath at each end of the lace."

He flicked the thing with his middle finger.

"This I don't know in a million years."

"The aglet."

"Not in a million years."

"The tag or aglet."

"The aglet," I said.

"And the little metal ring that reinforces the rim of the eyelet through which the aglet passes. We're doing the physics of language, Shay."

"The little ring."

"You see it?"

"Yes."

"This is the grommet," he said.

"Oh man."

"The grommet. Learn it, know it and love it."

"I'm going out of my mind."

"This is the final arcane knowledge. And when I take my shoe to the shoemaker and he places it on a form to make repairs—a block shaped like a foot. This is called a what?"

"I don't know."

"A last."

"My head is breaking apart."

"Everyday things represent the most overlooked knowledge. These names are vital to your progress. Quotidian things. If they weren't important, we wouldn't use such a gorgeous Latinate word. Say it," he said.

"Quotidian."

"An extraordinary word that suggests the depth and reach of the commonplace."

His white collar hung loose below his adam's apple and the skin at his throat was going slack and ropy and it seemed to be catching him unprepared, old age, coming late but fast.

I put on my jacket.

"I meant to bring along a book for you," he said.

His hands were still young, though, a soft chalky baby blush. There was a chessboard on a table in a corner, opposing pieces marshaled.

"Come to Upper Red tomorrow and I'll dig it out for you."

Upper Red was the faculty residence. They named the buildings at Voyageur after local landmarks—lakes, towns, rivers, forests. Not after saints, theologians or Jesuit martyrs. The Jesuits, according to Paulus, had been treated so brusquely in so many places for their attempts to convert and transform, decapitated in Japan, disemboweled in the Horn of Africa, eaten alive in North America, crucified in Siam, drawn and quartered in England, thrown into the ocean off Madagascar, that the founders of our little experimental college thought they'd spare the landscape some of the bloodier emblems of the order's history.

"By the bye, Shay."

"Yes," I said.

"Did I see you in that little group yesterday signing a petition in support of Senator McCarthy?"

"I was there, yes, Father."

"Signing a petition."

"It seemed okay," I said.

He nodded, looking past me.

"Do you know why the Senate condemned him?"

"The others were signing," I said. "Some of the South Americans," I said a little desperately, knowing how stupid this sounded but thinking, somehow, this was the way to exonerate myself.

"So you signed. The others were shitting, Father. So I shat."

He looked past me, nodding reasonably, and I turned and left.

I walked back and forth across the parade in the blowing snow. Then I went to my room and threw off my jacket. I wanted to look up words. I took off my boots and wrung out my cap over the washbasin. I wanted to look up words. I wanted to look up velleity and quotidian and memorize the fuckers for all time, spell them, learn them, pronounce them syllable by syllable—vocalize, phonate, utter the sounds, say the words for all they're worth.

This is the only way in the world you can escape the things that made you.

They arrived in the rain, a young crowd except for the columnists from the Chronicle and Examiner and a couple of graybeard poets from City Lights, and they waited for Lenny Bruce to come out onstage.

This was Basin Street West and the small stage had a backdrop of fake fieldstone. The wall was supposed to suggest a homey atmosphere but it resembled a mass of ugly bulging rock and it made the club seem dungeonlike or bunkeresque.

They sat there and waited for Lenny, the jazz musicians emitting a faint reek of weed, a few monosyllabic chicks in existential black, the clean-cut college boys with secret deviant tastes, the entire staff of a little magazine called Polyester Wok, five righteous souls whose anger at the world was being undermined by the events of the past few days.

Suddenly Lenny was there, without an intro, slipping into the spotlight and beginning to talk before he'd even lifted the mike from the stand.

"They're evacuating Norfolk, Virginia. You know about this? Norfolk. The huge naval base where ships have been setting out, destroyers, cruisers, to form the blockade. They're evacuating dependents and all nonessential personnel. The question is," and he turned his head sideways so he could look at the audience obliquely with a sly sense of put-on. "Who moves in when they move out? That's right—there goes the neighborhood. Because all the spade undesirables from three hundred miles around are gonna snatch up those houses and ruin real estate values and the Navy's gonna say, Fuck it, man, never mind the Russian subs and cargo ships, let's aim our guns at Norfolk."

Lenny looked a little bloated tonight, his face puff-pastry white and an extracurricular jitter in his body lingo.

"Everything is real estate. You're a product of your geography. If you're a Catholic from New York, you're a Jew. If you're a Jew from Butte, Montana, you're a totally goyish concoction. You're like instant mashed potatoes. And that's what this crisis is all about, incidentally. Instant mashed potatoes. The whole technology, man, of instant and quick, because we don't have the attention span for normal wars anymore, and in the movie version it's Rod Steiger playing Khrushchev as an Actors Studio chief of state. Dig it, he's deep, he's misunderstood, he's got the accent down pat, the shaved head, he does the screaming fits, he does the motivation—lonely boy from the coal pits ruthlessly fights his way to the top but all he's really looking for is a wisecracking dame who'll give him some back talk and make him laugh once in a while. This is no bumpkin—half man, half sausage. Steiger plays him as a moody and sensitive loner burdened by the whole mishegaas of Russian history. We see his tender feminine side when he has an affair in a coat closet with an American double agent played by Kim Novak in a butch haircut."

Lenny did the voices, the accents. He was not technically sound but mixed in whole cultures and geographies and cross-references to convey the layers of impersonation involved.

There was a beatnik element in the audience, several postbeats in old checked lumberjackets vintage 1950, men with a kind of distance in their gazes but still alert to signs of marvels astir in the universe, and a woman in a patchwork shirt with a baby in a pouch, probably the first and last infant at one of Lenny's shows but this was San Francisco in the week that was.

"Kennedy makes an appearance in public and you hear people say, I saw his hair! Or, I saw his teeth! The spectacle's so dazzling they can't take it all in. I saw his hair! They're venerating the sacred relics while the guy's still alive."

In the beatnik canon it was America's sickness that had produced the bomb. If the beats were receptive to Lenny's take on hypocrisy and related matters and if they regretted his drug busts and obscenity trials, they were probably unmoved by the Russian accents and other ethnic riffs and bits that came shpritzing out of him like seltzer from an old bottling plant in Canarsie. The whole beat landscape was bomb-shadowed. It always had been. The beats didn't need a missile crisis to make them think about the bomb. The bomb was their handiest reference to the moral squalor of America, the guilty place of smokestacks and robot corporations, Time-magazined and J. Edgar Hoovered, where people sat hunched over cups of coffee in a thousand rainswept truck stops on the jazz prairie, secret Trotskyites and sad nymphomaniacs with Buddhist pussies—things Lenny made fun of. Lenny was showbiz, he was suited and groomed and cool and corrupt, the mortician-comic, and the bomb was part of a scary ad campaign that had gotten out of hand.

He was wearing a Nehru jacket tonight, a dark tunic with a high collar, it needed cleaning and pressing, and he had a white raincoat draped over his shoulders—either he'd forgotten to take it off or he was planning to get out of here in a hurry.

He began an impressionistic ramble. Hard to follow. About court cases, lawyers and judges. Like listening to someone who thought he was talking to someone else.

Then he broke off and said, "Love me. That's what I'm here for. Tonight and every night. Stop loving me, I die."

This was not a bit. The bit followed this. It was a bit he'd thought up sitting in the plastic pygmy toilet on the flight from L.A. with a red light near his right eyeball flashing *Return to seat Return to seat*.

"The archangel Gabriel appears in the sky over Havana. Bodyguards wake up Castro and he tells them, Lemme alone, and they tell him it's the messenger of God, and he gets in a helicopter and goes up there. The angel's wearing a white robe and he's holding a flaming trumpet and Castro's intrigued when he sees that Gabriel's a black man. He thinks, Great, an articulate Negro, we can have a real no-bullshit dialogue. He says to the angel, I don't believe in God but lemme ask you. Whose side are you on in this crisis? And the angel says, I'm only gonna say this once. The side that has baseball and jazz. Castro says, We have baseball and jazz. We call it Afro-Cuban music and you'd dig it, man. Swings like crazy. And Gabriel says, Don't patronize me, motherfucker. I blew with Bird, you know. Yeah, we jammed together at Minton's in the old days. Okay, you wanna know which side I'm on. The side that has mom and apple pie. Castro says, No problema. The Russians have mom and apple pie. They call it *yablochy pirog*. The angel says, Okay, you so smart, the side that has Donald Duck, Mickey Mouse and the Mafia. And Castro says, Damn we threw the Mafia out of Cuba. But how come you're siding with them? The angel says, Lawd Jesus has a soft spot for the mob. Castro says, How come? The angel says, What you think, man? He's Italian.

Castro says, Wait a minute. Jesus is Italian? The angel says, Well—ain't he? And he looks a little uncertain. He starts shaking the spittle off the mouthpiece of his trumpet, a thing Gabe does whenever he's insecure. He's very touchy about his education. He says a little defensively, All the popes are wops. Everybody knows this, man. This because Jesus a wop. Jesus a guinea from the word go. Check his complexion, Jim. Castro says, Jesus lived in the Middle East. Gabriel says, You must be crazy, telling me shit like that. The cat's Neapolitan. Talks with his hands. Castro says, He was a Jew if you wanna know the truth. The angel says, I know he was a Jew—an Italian Jew. They have them, don't they? And Castro says, Why am I standing here listening to this? You're totally loco, man. And the angel says, Are you telling me I believed all my life that Jesus changed water into wine at an Italian wedding—and he *didn't*."

Lenny did this bit a little distractedly, slurring lines here and there, but isn't that what he always did, wasn't that part of the whole hipster format—a kind of otherworldly dope-driven fugue.

"I saw his hair! I saw his teeth!"

Then he remembered the line he'd come to love. He went into a semicrouch and put the raincoat over his head and practically stuck the mike down his throat.

"We're all gonna die!"

Yes, he loved saying this, crying it out, it was wondrously refreshing, it purified his fear and made it public at the same time—it was weak and sick and cowardly and powerless and pathetic and also noble somehow, a long, loud and feelingly high-pitched cry of grief and pain that had an element of sweet defiance.

And his voice sent a weird thrill shooting through the audience. They felt the cry physically. It leaped in their blood and bonded them. This was the revolt of the psyche, an idlike wail from their own souls, the desperate buried place where you demand recognition of primitive rights and needs.

Then he gets an idea and flicks it straight out, like a boxer jabbing so well it brings a grin to his face.

"But maybe some of us are more powerless than others. It's a white bomb, dig." And his voice changes here, goes redneck and drawly. "It's our bomb. Moscow and Washington. Think about it, man. White people control this bomb."

The idea delights him.

"You look down at Watts. You look up at Harlem. And you say, Fuck with our chicks, man, we drop the bomb. Better end the world than mix the races."

He goes into a bopster's finger-snapping slouch.

"Because we'd rather kill everybody than share our women."

Then the lights went out. Just like that. The spotlight, the bar lights, the exit signs—all out. A vague shape, Lenny's, could be seen moving sort of experimentally toward the large metal door that opened directly onto the street and the customers up front might have heard him muttering, "Return to seat, return to seat."

A rustle in the audience, a few heads turning, several people standing uncertainly. Were they thinking maybe this is it, a bomb, an airburst? Didn't the electromagnetic pulse from a test shot in the Pacific send massive currents surging through power lines in Honolulu, only recently, blowing out lights and setting off burglar alarms all over the island?

The lights came on. The spotlight shone on an empty stage. The field-stone wall had never looked more naked and fake. And there was Lenny, standing about a yard and a half from the exit. He came walking slowly stageward, mimicking a person sneaking back into a room, relieved and abashed, and they waited for him to say something that would pay off the long tense moment and shake them with laughter and he reached the stage and lifted the dangling mike and put it to his face and it began to screech and crackle and then the lights went out again and the afterimage of Lenny's tallowy face stuck to every retina in the house, half a scared smirk across his mouth, and the baby started crying.

When the lights came back on, a twenty-second lifetime later, the stage was empty, the metal door was ajar, the show was evidently over.

JUNE 14, 1957

There were weeks went by when we barely slept. We were together every hour of the day and night for three or four weeks, much of it, most of it in her car, eating and sleeping there, having sex in her car, sleeping and waking up and looking around and it was still dark, or still light, depending, and finally we'd stop driving for one reason or another, logical or not, and life'd slow down enough so things could happen normally in rooms but only until it was time to go again and she'd rumble up in the 1950 Merc, chassis lowered and driveline slightly souped, and we were headed west again.

"Don't tell me your dreams," I said.

"But you have to hear."

"I don't want to hear."

"Oh you bastard, you have to hear," Amy said, "because everything that happens has to happen to both of us."

"Don't you know people don't want to hear other people's dreams?"

"Oh you bastard, what other people? Who are these other people?"

"Watch the road."

"Every smallest thought we said we'd share."

"Watch the road. Drive the car," I told her.

And once I dropped her off in Santa Fe, where she had family friends, and kept the car myself and didn't play the radio or read the newspaper and she caught up with me a week later in a miners' bar in Bisbee, Arizona and we played a flirty game of liar's poker and climbed the high tight streets and felt a thing so powerful, and knew the other felt it, that we thought our faces might ignite.

"It was a mountain dream. A high clear place near a lake."

"Don't you know dreams are only interesting to the dreamer?"

"Think you're so worldly-wise. You're awful smart for a foreigner."

"Drive the car."

"Who only learned English when he left New York."

Amy was tall and competent and looked good in jeans. She knew how to do things and make things and even her good looks were competent, a straightforward sort of ableness, open and clear-eyed, with a smatter of fading freckles and a dirty-minded smile.

And once we were in Yankton, South Dakota, early on that summer, and the movie theater was just letting out, the Dakota it was called, with a bright tile facade and Audie Murphy on the marquee, and the young people of Yankton got in their cars and drove up and down the main drag and we drove with them, nearly falling asleep, and we went to drive-in movies and talked about life and we rode across prairies and talked about movies and we drove through car washes and read poetry aloud, one of us to the other, and soapy water slid down the windows.

Her car was black and hooded-looking and we thought we were phantoms of the road, djinns who could pee unseen in the country dust. She didn't want me to know her father had given her the car. A graduation gift. But this was a thing I knew because one of her brothers had told me and the other thing I knew was that she'd drop me cold when the trip was done.

"You know what's interesting about you? You say you want to share the smallest thought. But what's interesting about you," I said, "is that you're going to forget everything we said and everything we did and every thought we shared the minute."

"No."

"The minute."

"No."

"The minute we say goodbye. Because you know what you are? A practical hardheaded more or less calculating individual who is planning ten years ahead and knows every passing minute for what it is."

"What is it?"

"A thing you drain every drop of juice from so you can forget it in the morning."

And once we stopped at some stables and she tried to teach me to ride but I got up there and got down again and would not get back up and she rode off with the Indian who led the expeditions, into the cool hills.

She said, "What's wrong with that?"

"I'm just talking."

She said, "Draining every minute. What's wrong with that?"

"I'm talking."

"And I haven't told you everything. So don't accuse," she said.

"You've told me everything twice."

"You are such a bastard."

"Tell me things you haven't told me. Go ahead. Shock me," I said. "You're not shocking me."

She could make and fix things and she liked to talk about the Brookhiser family, the grandparents and pioneer women and gold-panners and all the far-flung offspring of the old rugged stock.

And once we stayed with her oldest brother, an architect, sleeping in separate rooms—she seemed to have brothers everywhere. This one lived near Yuma in a lopsided house he'd built himself, skewed for effect, out of railroad ties and stucco and stamped tin, and Amy was in an elevated state, looking sideways at the place.

We were partly out of our minds from driving and we talked at each other across half a major state, pretty much nonstop, and we had the chemistry of a whole long brutal marriage compressed into weeks, the twang in the air of a thing that stays unadjusted, and we also had the feeling it was wrong to sleep because we could be saying something awful and important.

And once we drove along a dirt road somewhere near Ruby, Arizona and saw four men on horseback driving a bull, a humped bull of amazing size, nearly unreal, and we stopped not only to watch and not only because we thought the animal might charge a moving car but out of a strange and pagan respect, an animal so awesome, a Brahma bull, and the cowboys waved and drove the bull down the red dirt road.

"I have these tantrums in my mind," she said, "where you'd hate me if I told you these raging throwing things of sex and jealousy and spite and wishing the worst kind of pain and slow death on someone who is close."

"Tell me."

"I won't tell you. Not even you. Least of all you."

"I want you to tell me."

"I won't unless you make me," she said

Amy had a danceaway manner at times. She had a ritual thing she did, a reflex, not coy but wary and foxy, pulling away from me the more she showed a need, dancing away, eyes bright, her shoulder rounding against my approach. She could be skittish even in the midst of the act, close to pretending we weren't doing this but something else entirely, I don't know, holding hands in a school corridor maybe, and sometimes she turned me down flat, saying, No you can't, or, No I won't, even as we sprawled on the seat screwing.

I thought our faces might flare up and disappear the night in mid-June when we climbed the narrow stepped streets of Bisbee, Arizona, shocked by love, sort of self-erased, after a beer and a sandwich in a dark bar filled with copper miners and their heartworm dogs. I didn't know it was possible to feel a thing like this, and then to feel it together, our heads half blown away and our minds emptied out, lost to everything but love.

She said, "I know what you do. You stay awake and watch me when I sleep."

"When do you sleep?"

"You want too much. You want to crawl inside me basically. You want to follow your cock right in. Did it ever occur to me?"

"Drive the car."

"No but did it ever occur to me?"

"Don't look at me when you drive."

"No but did it ever occur to me that I would know a man someday who tries to follow me into the bathroom?"

"Drive the car."

She said, "You wanted to crowd into the gas station toilet with me. I just remembered. I almost forgot. Because you thought you might miss something."

And once we were passing through Bakersfield, California and the car overheated and we stopped for water at a trailer camp and this was something I absolutely did not know about. All these rows of trailer homes with people cooking hot dogs in a hundred and seven heat. A woman in a bathing suit ironing clothes on an ironing board outside her trailer with small kids riding tricycles in their underwear. And this was a thing I did not know existed, absolutely, or could ever conceive, a thing I had completely missed, people living permanently in trailers, and Amy called me a foreigner from New York.

I was going to Palo Alto, a textbook editor, fledgling, with an outfit determined to change the nature of the classroom, make it open, fluid, casual and Californian, and she was heading up to Seattle or Portland, she wasn't sure which, or back across to Denver with a master's in earth science and a number of professional connections she wasn't letting on to.

"I don't know what I'm doing here with you. I don't know anything about you. All this time and all this talk and I don't know anything about you, basically," she said, "except for the fact that you know how to make me mad."

"Good. It's good for you. Getting mad cleans the blood," I told her. "According to my Irish mother."

"You have a mother. This is encouraging."

"Get mad. Be mad," I told her.

I didn't want her looking at me while she drove but sometimes I looked at her and invited a look back.

"I want everything that happens to happen to both of us," she said.

"So do I," I said, and meant it, at the time, truly.

She felt the weight of the gaze and looked across at me on the empty road with a mountain of lavender tailings rising above the old sheds that marked a mineworks and it was a look so intimate and reaching, so deep in things we'd done that it became a crazy kind of dare, a form of drag-strip chicken—which one of us would break the lovers' gaze and look away first to see if the car had wandered into the eastbound lane, with a shiny-eye pickup approaching, half a second from dazzling death.

"Who's strange?" I said.

"You stay awake and watch me when I sleep. I know you do. I feel it in my sleep."

"I'm strange or you're strange?"

"You followed me into a ladies' room."

"No, wait wait wait wait. You can feel me watching you while you sleep and you think I'm strange? Who's strange?" I said.

And there were times when you detached yourself from the steepest breathing, even, and felt a kind of white shadow, a sliding away into a parallel person, someone made of mind-light who seemed to speak for you.

Or, "You can't make me do this," she'd say, running her hand up the seam of my fly, and I'm trying to drive the car.

And once when I was alone for a day and a night, not playing the radio or reading the newspaper and driving around aimlessly for hours, I finally stopped and parked and took a walk in a picnic grounds where there were white-barked trees and garbage cans for food scraps and a man who looked disturbed sitting on a bench, outside Fresno somewhere, but maybe he was only deep in thought, or worried about something, and I felt a sadness I could not exactly locate, a feeling that could have been mine or could have been theirs, the little families with food on paper plates, the unhappy man slouched on the bench, the place itself, the bench itself, the trash cans that didn't have lids.

I bought a postcard to send her after she went her way and I went mine, a card that showed a picnic table in the trees, and I slipped it in a book inside my bag until I had time to figure out what kind of message I would write.

4

The first man stood by the window of his stately suite at the Waldorf. He watched the yellow cabs sink into soulful dusk, that particular spendthrift light that falls dyingly on Park Avenue in the hour before people take leave of the office and become husbands and wives again, or whatever people become in whatever murmurous words when evenings grow swift and whispered.

The second man sat on the sofa, legs crossed, looking at Bureau reports.

Edgar said, "Of course you packed the masks."

The second man nodded yes, a gesture that went unseen.

"Junior, the masks."

"We have them, yes. I'm looking at a security memo that's a little, actually, rankling."

"I don't want to hear it. File it somewhere. I feel too good."

"Protest. Outside the Plaza tonight."

"What is it the bastards are protesting? Pray tell," Edgar said in a tone he'd perfected through the years, a tight amusement etched in eleven kinds of irony.

"The war, it seems."

"The war."

"Yes, that," the second man said.

They were staying at the Waldorf, which was J. Edgar Hoover's hotel of choice during his sojourns in New York, but the party was taking place, the ball, the fête, the social event of the season, the decade, the half century no doubt—the ball was in the ballroom at the Plaza.

Edgar changed the subject, if only in his mind. He gazed far up Park, where the earth curved toward Harlem. Maybe the deep and fleeting light was making him nostalgic, or the noise perhaps, the muted clamor of taxi horns below, a sound at this protected distance that was oddly and humanly happy, little toots and beeps that seemed to carry a pitch of celebration.

He said, "Where were you when Thomson hit the homer?"

"Beg pardon?"

"Where were you?"

"Yes?"

"Never mind. An idle thought, Junior."

Clyde Tolson, known as Junior, was Edgar's staunchest aide in the Bureau, his dearest friend and inseparable companion.

They were getting on, of course. Clyde was five years younger than Edgar but not so sharp as he used to be, his flash-card memory a little less prodigious now. But where Edgar was pug-nosed and compact, with brows like batwings, Clyde was long-jawed and tallish, sort of semidebonaire, a fairly gentle fellow who liked conversation—again, unlike his boss, who thought you gave yourself away, word by word, every time you opened your trap to speak.

Edgar held a tumbler of scotch. He checked the glass for smudges, then sniffed and sipped, feeling the charred fumes prickle his tongue. The complimentary suite, the soothing booze, the presence of Junior in the room, the party that everybody'd been talking about for months, famous long before it happened, the uninvited lapsing into states of acute confusion, insomniac, unable to function—yes, Edgar was feeling pretty good tonight.

Talkative or not, he loved a good party. He loved celebrities in particular and there would be an abundance of mammal glamour at the Plaza tonight. Personage and flair and stylish wit. A frail schoolboy still crouched inside the Director's pudgy corpus and this lonely crypto-child came to robust life in the presence of show people and other living icons—child stars, ballplayers, prizefighters, even Hollywood horses and dogs.

Celebrated people were master spirits, men and women who spiked the temper of the age. Whatever Edgar's own claim to rank and notoriety, he found himself subject to anal flutters when chatting with a genuine celeb.

Clyde said, "And this, of course, as well."

Edgar did not turn to see what the second man was reading. He studied the carpet instead. The carpets at the Waldorf were thick and lush, nesting grounds for bacteria of every sort. If you knew anything about modern war, you knew that weapons utilizing pathogenic bacteria could be every bit as destructive as megaton bombs. Worse, in a way, because the sense of infiltration was itself a form of death.

Clyde said, "I knew it was a mistake to publicize our methods regarding organized crime figures."

"What methods?"

"Ransacking their garbage."

"Makes good copy."

"And creates a copycat mentality. Now we have a situation that's a public relations nightmare. To wit, a so-called garbage guerrilla is targeting guess whose garbage, Boss?"

"Please. I'm enjoying my drink. A man enjoys a drink when the day winds down."

"Yours," Clyde said.

Edgar could not believe he'd heard the fellow correctly.

"This is what our confidential source tells us." And Clyde rattled the page he was reading for maximum nuisance effect. "Team of urban guerrillas planning a garbage raid at 4936 Thirtieth Place, Northwest, Washington, D.C."

It was the end of the world in triplicate.

"When is this supposed to happen?"

557

"More or less momentarily."

"You've posted guards?"

"In unmarked cars. But whether we arrest them or not, they will find a way to make public theater of your garbage."

"I won't put the garbage out."

"You have to put it out, eventually."

"I'll put it out and lock it up."

"How will the garbage collectors collect it?"

When FBI agents stole off in the night with some mobster's household trash, they substituted fake garbage, to allay suspicion—aromatic food scraps, anchovy tins, used tampons prepared by the lab division. Then they took the real garbage back for analysis by forensic experts on gambling, handwriting, fragmented paper, crumpled photographs, food stains, bloodstains and every known subclass of scribbled Sicilian.

"Or do this," Edgar said. "Put out simulated garbage. Bland bits and pieces. Unnewsworthy."

"We can't use conventional methods, however clever, on these people. Because what they're doing flies in the face of ordinary confrontation. And no matter how well-guarded the premises, sooner or later they'll snatch a trash can and make off with it."

Edgar walked over to another window. He needed a change, as they say, of scene.

"Confidential source says they intend to take your garbage on tour. Rent halls in major cities. Get lefty sociologists to analyze the garbage item by item. Get hippies to rub it on their naked bodies. More or less have sex with it. Get poets to write poems about it. And finally, in the last city on the tour, they plan to eat it."

Edgar could see part of the east facade of the Plaza, about a dozen blocks away.

"And expel it," Clyde said. "Publicly."

The great slate roof, the gables and dormers and copper cresting. How odd it seemed that such a taken-for-granted thing, putting out the garbage, could suddenly be a source of the gravest anxiety.

"Confidential source says they will make a documentary film of the tour, for general release."

"Do we have a dossier on these guerrillas?"

"Yes."

"Is it massive?" Edgar said.

In the endless estuarial mingling of paranoia and control, the dossier was an essential device. Edgar had many enemies-for-life and the way to deal with such people was to compile massive dossiers. Photographs, surveillance reports, detailed allegations, linked names, transcribed tapes—wiretaps, bugs, break-ins. The dossier was a deeper form of truth, transcending facts and actuality. The second you placed an item in the file, a fuzzy photograph, an unfounded rumor, it became promiscuously true. It was a truth without authority and therefore incontestable. Factoids seeped out of the file and crept across the horizon, consuming bodies and minds. The file was everything, the life nothing. And this was the essence of Edgar's revenge. He rearranged the lives of his enemies, their conversations, their relationships, their very memories, and he made these people answerable to the details of his creation.

"We'll arrest them and charge them," Clyde said. "That's all we can do."

Edgar turned from the window, smiling.

"Maybe I can sympathize with the Mafia over this."

Clyde smiled.

"You were always half a gangster," he said.

They laughed.

"Remember the tommy-guns we carried," Edgar said.

"When photographers were around."

They laughed again.

"You were right there alongside me, posed heroically."

"Edgar and Clyde," said Clyde.

"Clyde and Edgar," said Edgar.

Where the current of one's need for control met the tide of one's paranoia, this was where the dossier was reciprocally satisfying. You fed both forces in a single stroke.

"I liked the thirties," Edgar said. "I don't like the sixties. No, not at all."

The desk at the end of the room was out of the thirties in a way, equipped with items fashioned to Edgar's specifications. Two nibbed black pens. Two bottles of Skrip Permanent Royal Blue Ink, No. 52. Six sharpened Eberhard Faber pencils, No. 2. A pair of 5×8 linen-finish writing pads, white. A new 60-watt bulb in the standing lamp. The Director did not want to breathe the dust of old bulbs used to illuminate the reading matter of total strangers. Newspapers, guide-books, Gideon bibles, erotic literature, subversive literature, under-ground literature, literature—whatever people read in hotels, alone, thumbing and breathing.

Clyde checked his watch. Dinner first, the two of them, alone, a practice spanning the decades—then the short ride to the Plaza.

It was called the Black & White Ball. A godlike gathering of five hundred, a masked affair, invitation only, dinner jacket and black mask for men, evening gown and white mask for women.

The party was being given by a writer, Truman Capote, for a pub-lisher, Katharine Graham, and the factoidal data generated by the guests would surely bridge the narrowing gap between journalism and fiction.

Edgar had not been invited, initially. But arranging an invitation was not difficult. A word from Edgar to Clyde. A word from Clyde to someone close to Capote. They were in the files of course, a number of those involved in planning the event—all catalogued and dossier'd up to their eyeballs and none of them eager to offend the Director.

Clyde took a call from the desk. The mask lady was coming up for a fitting.

Edgar noticed that Clyde was wearing a necktie with a driblet design. The little figures made him think of paramecia, sinister organ-isms with gullets and feeding grooves. At home Edgar sat on a toilet that was raised on a platform, to isolate him from floorbound forms of life. And he'd ordered his lab people to build a clean room at the Bureau with unprecedented standards of hygiene. A white room manned by white-clad technicians, preferably white themselves, who would work in an environment completely free of contaminants, dust, bacteria and so on, with big white lights shining down, where Edgar himself might like to spend time when he was feeling vulnerable to the forces around him.

She walked in the door, Tanya Berenger, in a maxidress and thrift-shop boots, once a well-known costume designer, now ancient and frowzy, living in a room in a sad hotel off Times Square, a place where the desk clerk sits behind a grille eating a tongue sandwich. People tracked her down, three or four times a year, to do masks for special occasions and she found fairly steady work doing sadomasochistic accessories for a private club in the Village.

The two men, as always with a female in the room, someone they didn't know, and without others present, and lacking an atmosphere of sociable cheer—well, they tended to become stiff and defensive, as though surprised by an armed intruder.

Clyde did not stray from Edgar's side, sensing a potential for way-ward behavior on the woman's part. She wore heavy makeup she might have poured from a paint can and cooked. And Clyde noted how one pocket on her dress drooped just a bit, becoming unseamed.

She spoke to Edgar with a sort of rueful affection.

"You know I can't let you wear one of my masks, dear man, without a consultation. I must put my hands on the living head. Bad enough I had to create my *objet* from a set of written specifications, like I'm a plumber installing a sink already."

She had a European accent slashed and burned by long-term residency in New York. And her hair had the retouched gloss of a dead crow mounted on a stick.

Of course Clyde had been briefed on Tanya Berenger. She was in the files in a fairly big way. She'd been accused at various times of being a lesbian, a socialist, a communist, a dope addict, a divorcee, a Jew, a Catholic, a Negro, an immigrant and an unwed mother.

Just about everything Edgar distrusted and feared. But she did exquisite masks and Clyde had been quick to commission her for the job.

He hurried into Edgar's bedroom and fetched the mask.

When she held it in her hands she looked at Edgar and looked at the mask, weighing the equation, and the Director experienced a queer tension in his chest, wondering whether he was worthy.

She held the object at eye level, six inches from her face, and looked through the eyeholes at Edgar.

And Edgar in turn looked at the mask as if it had a life, an identity

561

of its own that he might feel ballsy enough to borrow for a single mid-night on the town.

It was a sleek black leather mask with handlebar extensions and a scatter of shiny sequins around the eyes.

Tanya said, "You want to put it on or have a conversation with it?"

But he wasn't quite ready.

"Do I want to put it on, Junior?"

"Be brave."

Tanya said, "Leather. It's so real, you know? Like wearing someone else's face."

She fitted the mask over Edgar's head, the padded band not too tight and the leather alive on his skin.

Then she took him by the shoulders and turned him slowly toward the mirror over the desk.

Clyde took the whiskey glass from his hand.

The mask transformed him. For the first time in some years he did not see himself as a tenant in an old short popover body with an immense and lumpish head.

"I can call you Edgar—this is okay? I can tell you how I see you? I see you as a mature and careful man who has a sexy motorcycle thug writhing to get out. Which the spangles give a crazy twist, you know?"

He felt creamy, dreamy and drugged.

She made a slight adjustment in the fit and even as he cringed at her touch Edgar felt himself tingle thrillingly. She was insidious and corrupt and it was like hearing your grandmother talk dirty in your ear.

"You are a butch biker to me, you know, riding into town to take over leadership of the sadists and necrophiles."

Clyde watched in civilized alarm as a cockroach crawled out of Tanya's pocket and moved slowly down her flank. It was Spanish-Harlem-sized, with antennae that could pick up the BBC.

"It's a lovely fit, darling. You have savage cheekbones for a full-figure man. I would love to do the total face, you know? Highlights and shadows."

Clyde took her gently by the arm, concealing her roach side from Edgar's view.

"In fact, shall I tell you something? The ball tonight is a perfect setting for you. Because you are very black and white to me. So you'll be totally in character, yes?"

When she was gone the men busied themselves with practical preparations. Clyde made dinner reservations and set out their evening clothes. Edgar set the mask on a tabletop and took a bath.

When he was finished he put on his fluffy white robe and stood by a window sipping the rest of his drink. He heard a sound above the beeping traffic, something strident rising in the night. New York was less genial than it used to be when the saloons and supper clubs were hangouts for lively and charming women and for gentlemen-bums with a comic flair.

"Junior, that noise. Can you hear it?"

Clyde walked into the room in his shirtsleeves, a shoe brush in hand.

"Yes, barely."

"Is it possible?"

"Yes, it could be the protesters at the Plaza."

"The wind."

"Yes, the wind is carrying the sound this way."

They heard the hard rhythmic salvo of voices chanting angry slogans, again, louder, fading when the wind shifted, then audible once more.

"You know what they want, don't you?" Edgar said.

Through the battered century of world wars and massive violence by other means, there had always been an undervoice that spoke through the cannon fire and ack-ack and that sometimes grew strong enough to merge with the battle sounds. It was the struggle between the state and secret groups of insurgents, state-born, wild-eyed—the anarchists, terrorists, assassins and revolutionaries who tried to bring about apocalyptic change. And sometimes of course succeeded. The passionate task of the state was to hold on, stiffening its grip and preserving its claim to the most destructive power available. With nuclear weapons this power became identified totally with the state. The mushroom cloud was the godhead of Annihilation and Ruin. The state controlled the means of apocalypse. But Edgar, by the window, heard the old alarums. He thought the time might be coming, once

563

again, when ideas became insurgent and rebel bands were reborn, longhair men and women, scruffy and free-fucking, who moved toward armed and organized resistance, trying to break the state and bring about the end of the existing order.

"They want the power to shake the world. It's the old bolshevik dream being dreamed again and it's the communists who are behind it all. And you know where it begins, don't you?"

"These are kids, mostly, who lie down in the street and wave flowers at the police," Clyde said. "Vietnam is the war, the reality. This is the movie, where the scripts are written and the actors perform. American kids don't want what we've got. They want movies, music."

Let Junior devise his clever perceptions. He didn't understand that once you patronize the enemy, you begin the process of your own undoing.

"It begins in the inmost person," Edgar said. "Once you yield to random sexual urges, you want to see everything come loose. You mistake your own looseness for some political concept, whereas in truth."

He didn't finish the thought. Some thoughts had to remain unspoken, even unfinished in one's own mind. This was the point of his relationship with Clyde. To keep the subject unspoken. To keep the feelings unfelt, the momentary urges unacted-upon. How strange and foolish this would seem to the young people running in the streets, or living six to a room, or three to a bed, and to many other people for that matter—how sad and rare.

Clyde went back to his duties, leaving the Boss by the window.

Edgar thought there was something noble in a constant companionship that does not fall to baser claims. He assumed Clyde believed likewise. But then Clyde was the second man, wasn't he, and perhaps he only followed Edgar's line of march wherever it led, or didn't.

He heard the chanting intermittently on the wind. Clyde was in the shower now. Edgar turned to see where he'd left the mask and saw himself unexpectedly in a full-length mirror, across the room, in his white robe and soft slippers, and he was startled by the image.

Of course it was him, but him in the guise of a macrocephalic baby, sexless and so justborn as to be, in essence, unearthly.

Mother Hoover's cuddled runt.

He crossed the room and picked up the mask. He noted how the stylized handlebars were simple swirls of cut leather designed to flare from the temples.

He heard Clyde come out of the shower.

When they were younger and on vacation together, or away on business, sharing a suite or taking adjoining rooms and keeping the connecting door open so they could talk from their respective beds well into the night, Edgar sometimes managed to angle the mirrors in such a way that he could catch a glimpse—by taking the free-standing antique in an old inn, the cheval glass, for example, and simply moving it to another part of the floor, or opening the medicine cabinet to a certain position when he shaved and letting the mirror absorb the light from the bed in the next room, or leaving a hand mirror propped on a desk—a glimpse, a passing glance, a spyhole peek at Junior as he busied himself dressing or undressing or taking a bath, the arrangement being such that the moment would seem wholly accidental, should the subject realize he was being watched, and an accident not just from his perspective but to Edgar's own mind as well, Junior's likeness being a thing that might simply float across his ken in the normal course of events, away on urgent Bureau business, his companion's body lean and virile, or at a golf resort, or following the ponies west to Del Mar, when they were both a great deal younger.

Junior was going bald now, and bulb-nosed, and he walked with a stoop. But then Junior had always walked with a stoop in an effort to appear no taller than the Boss.

Edgar was in the bedroom with the door closed. He stood at the mirror, a seventy-one-year-old man wearing nothing but his sequined biker's mask and his wool-lined slippers, listening to the voices in the street.

JANUARY 9, 1967

When her workday was finished Janet Urbaniak put on her running shoes. There was a stretch of four desolate blocks between the hospital complex where she did classroom work and got floor experience and the apartment complex where she lived. Bleak and weedy streets, unshoveled snow going grim with bus exhaust, snow that was drilled and gilded with dog piss, and there were usually a few lurking figures in green fatigues, the last of a straggle battalion of wasted men.

So when her workday was finished Janet took off her lightweight casual slip-ons and got the running shoes out of her locker, a pair of firm padded sneakers with shock-absorbent midsoles and a supple and confident feel. Then she went and stood at the hospital entrance with another student nurse and they waited for the traffic lights to turn green along the semideserted length of the four extended blocks, the kind of heartless boulevard you find in parts of town where the architecture is guarded and tense and it always feels like curfew.

Janet stood and waited in the deep and eerie dusk. Then the lights went green and her buddy said, "*Go, go, go, go,*" and Janet started to run, nonstop she hoped, with the lights in her favor, hitting top speed in a matter of seconds and trying to avoid icy patches, and her buddy watched her all the way.

Some evenings, most evenings it's the men you want to look out for. This is why you're running after all. They see you coming in your bouncy blue-and-white shoes and have things to say and gestures to make or just looks to look, or nothing at all sometimes, you're a ghost, a shadow—a number of men clustered near a chain-link fence or empty lot, and you're never sure whether it's better to veer away in a defensive arc or keep running in a straight line because the first tactic might offend them and the second might tempt them to get familiar or maybe even affront them in its unaffectedness, and some evenings it's the snow.

It's the snow or rain or garbage or the stray dogs you have to look out for.

But you're not running because of the dogs. The dogs make you slow down, ease into a walk. It's the men loitering who make you run and the men who are out of sight in doorways or junked cars—you want them to think you're running for the love of running, you and all the others, the evening stream of students making the four-block sprint.

We're just runners, you want them to think, getting our minutes in.

Janet was dashing now, deep-breathing, concentrating on the snow and on the lights staying green, and she watched for men who might be leaning on a wall or getting out of a car—there were usually a couple of junked cars in the course of a run, used as social clubs in winter.

Four long blocks under a streaky northern sky. When she reached the entrance to her building the keys were already in her hand and she went inside and took the elevator up, still running in a sense, with the apartment keys out now, and fifteen seconds after she was in the living room, door double-locked, the telephone rang. It was only then that her heart stopped racing.

The call was routine procedure, another student back at the hospital checking to see if she'd made it safely. They gave her eleven minutes door-to-door including the elevator up and the keys in the locks. A number of student nurses lived in the same complex and the routine was designed to allow people to switch roles systematically. Janet ran the dash, made the phone call and monitored the progress of the running woman according to a schedule.

They figured it all out and posted it on a board. Then they changed into running shoes and waited for green.

NOVEMBER 29, 1966

The second man made the decision to show up late. It was the kind of firm determination in the type of difficult circumstance that Clyde Tolson liked to make.

It proved his mettle. And when you're a man who is variously described as dutiful, deferential, obsequious, slavish and brown-nosingly corrupt, in descending order of distinction, you need to make a show of character now and then.

But first Clyde had to convince the Boss that missing an hour or two of party time was not going to haunt the twilight years of his directorate.

An FBI security detail at the Plaza had reported that the protest was growing loud and that the party guests, as they entered, were being cursed in rhyming couplets, exposed to obscene signs and gestures, spat upon at close range and forced to duck an occasional flying object.

It did not make sense to Clyde to allow the Director to enter a situation, and Edgar finally agreed, in which the dignity of the Bureau might be compromised.

So it was midnight when the two men rolled through the deserted midtown streets in their bulletproof black Cadillac. They'd had a leisurely dinner, bantering with the wine steward and then enjoying a brandy at the bar with old acquaintances because there were old acquaintances wherever J. Edgar Hoover went, some who were loyal supporters, others residing in the files, a few who were enemies-for-life but didn't know it yet, and Edgar and Clyde were in a mellow enough mood, despite reports from the site, seated in the plush rear seat in black tie of course and wearing their masks, like a suave and jaunty crime fighter out of the Sunday comics, a master bureaucrat by day who becomes dashing Maskman at night, cruising the streets in formal dress with his trusted right-hand man.

The driver activated the intercom to report that a car was tailing them.

Clyde turned to look while the Director slumped in his seat, getting his head below the window line.

"Little Volkswagen bug," Clyde said. "Painted top to bottom in very bright colors. Psychedelic. Big bright swirls and streaks. Can't make out the driver's face."

The Cadillac coasted slowly past the Plaza. The klieg lights were gone, the media pack was gone, there was no trace of the crush of curious onlookers drawn by news of the event. There were still a few demonstrators, listless now, young people in their grimy tie-dyes, and city cops as well, idler still, showing the eternal laden strain of a big meal hustled down the gullet, where it sits for hours earning overtime.

The great dark car circled the block, equipped with an Arpège atomizer that contained room freshener, and Clyde checked the other entrances.

The north steps were empty and he tapped on the glass and the driver pulled up and the two men exited and suddenly there was the VW, cutting in front, and people came scrambling out, three, four, what, six

568

people, it's a circus car debouching clowns, about seven people tumbling onto the sidewalk and hurrying up the steps to flank the doorway.

All wore masks, the faces of Asian kids, some blood-spattered, others with eyes seamed shut, and they commenced their shouting as Hoover and Tolson moved up the stairs.

The first man was clumsy and slow and the second took his arm to assist and they made their plodding way toward the entrance.

They heard, "Society scum!"

They heard, "A dead Asian baby for every Gucci loafer!"

Clyde wasn't sure whether the protesters knew who they were. Was Edgar's mask sufficient cover for his gnarled old media mug?

They heard mottoes, slurs and technical terms.

And they labored upward, step by step, eyes front, outer arms stroking, and the protesters jangled and hissed.

"Vietnam! Love it or leave it!"

"White killers in black tie!"

A young woman stood at the entrance wearing the mask of a child's shattered face and she said somewhat softly to Edgar, blocking his way and speaking evenly, whispering in fact, "We'll never disappear, old man, until you're in a landfill with your trash."

Clyde said, "Coming through," like a waiter with a heavy tray, and a couple of minutes later, after a stop in the men's room to collect themselves, the Director and his aide were ready to party.

But first Edgar said, "Who were those jaspers?"

"I have an idea or two. I'll put someone on it."

"Did you hear what she said? I think they're connected to the garbage guerrillas."

"Straighten your mask," Clyde said.

"I'd like to see them maimed in the slowest possible manner. Over weeks and months, with voice tapes made."

They walked down the hall to the grand ballroom. They'd walked down five hundred halls on their way to some ceremonial event, some testimonial dinner, one or another ritual salute to Edgar's decades in the Bureau, but they'd never heard a sound such as this.

A subdued roar, a sort of rumble-buzz, with a chandelier jingle in the mix and the dreamy sway of dance music and a vocal note of self-delight—the lure, the enticement of a life defined by its remoteness from the daily drudge of world complaint.

"Tapes of cries and moans," Edgar said, "which I would play to help me sleep."

They moved through the ballroom, they circulated, seeing prominent people everywhere. The room was high and white and primrose gold, flanked by Greek columns that caught the lickety amber light of a thousand candles.

Swan-necked women in textured satin gowns. Masks by Halston, Adolfo and Saint Laurent. The mother and sister of one American president and the daughter of another. Crisp little men aswagger with assets. Titled jet-setters, a maharajah and maharani, a baroness somebody in a beaded mask. Famous and raging alcoholic poets. Tough smart stylish women who ran fashion books and designed clothes. Hair by Kenneth—teased, swirled, backcombed and ringleted.

"Did you see?"

"The old dowager," Edgar said.

"In the dime-store mask."

"Decorated with pearls."

They shook hands here and there, daintily, and dropped a flattering remark to this or that person, and Clyde knew how the Director felt, mixing with people of the rarest social levels, the anointed and predestined, aura'd like Inca kings, but also the talented and original and self-made and born beautiful and ego-driven and hard-bargaining, all bearing signs of astral radiance, and the ruthless and brutish as well.

Yes, Edgar was damp with excitement.

He stopped to chat with Frank Sinatra and his young actress wife, a nymph in a boy's haircut and a butterfly mask.

"Jedgar, you old warhorse. Haven't seen you since."

"Yes, I know."

"Tempus fugits, don't it, pal?"

"Yes, it does," Edgar said. "Introduce me to your lovely."

Sinatra was in the files now. Many people in the room were in the files as well. Not a single one of them, Clyde imagined, more accomplished in his occupational strokes than Edgar himself. But Edgar did not carry the glow. Edgar worked in the semidark, manipulating and bringing ruin. He carried the small wan grudging glory of the civil servant. Not the open and confident show, the wide-striding boom of some of these cosmic bravos.

On the stage, under the furled curtain, two bands took turns. A white society band and a black soul group. All musicians masked.

People loved Edgar's leather mask. They told him so. A woman in ostrich feathers ran her tongue over the handlebars. Another woman called him Biker Boy. A gay playwright rolled his eyes.

They found their table and settled in for a spell, sipping champagne and nibbling on buffet tidbits. Clyde uttered the names of people dancing past and Edgar commented on their lives and careers and personal predilections. Whatever anecdotal lore he failed to recall, Clyde was quick to provide.

Andy Warhol walked by wearing a mask that was a photograph of his own face.

A woman asked Edgar to dance and he flushed and lit a cigarette.

Lord and Lady somebody held their masks on sticks.

A woman wore a sexy nun's wimple.

A man wore an executioner's hood.

Edgar spoke rapidly in his old staccato voice, like a radio reporter doing a series of punchy news items. It made Clyde feel good to see the Boss show such animation. They spotted a number of people they knew professionally, administration faces, past and present, men who held sensitive and critical positions, and Clyde noted how the ballroom seemed to throb with crosscurrent interests and appetites. Political power mingling lubriciously with art and literature. Domed historians clubbing with the beautiful people of society and fashion. There were diplomats dancing with movie stars, and Nobel laureates telling chummy stories to shipping tycoons, and the demimonde of Broadway and the gossip industry hobnobbing with foreign correspondents.

There was a self-conscious sense of some profound moment in the making. A dreadful prospect, Clyde thought, because it suggested a continuation of the Kennedy years. In which well-founded categories began to seem irrelevant. In which a certain fluid movement became possible. In which sex, drugs and dirty words began to unstratify the culture.

"I think you ought to dance," Edgar said.

Clyde looked at him.

"It's a party. Why not? Find a suitable lady and spin her around the floor."

"I do believe the man is serious."

"Then come back and tell me what you talked about."

"Do I remember a single step?"

"You were quite a good dancer, Junior. Go ahead. Do your stuff. It's a party."

On the floor the guests were doing the twist with all the articulated pantomime of the unfrozen dead come back for a day. Soon the white band reemerged and the music turned to fox-trots and waltzes. Clyde watched the slowly shuffling mass of careful dancers, barely touching, heedful of hairdos and jewelry and gowns and masks and always on the alert for other fabulous people—heads turning, eyes bright in the great black-and-white gyre.

"Yes, show your true colors," Edgar said with a twisted grin.

So that was it. Tipsy and bitter. All right, thought Clyde. If this was to be a night in which old restrictions were eased, why not a turn around the floor?

He approached a woman not only masked but wholly medieval, it seemed, a cloth wound about the head and a long plain cloak sashed at the waist and a tight bodice girdled high under her breasts.

She smiled at him and Clyde said, "Shall we?"

She was tall and fair and wore no makeup and spoke without awe of the evening and its trappings. A levelheaded young lady of the sort that Edgar might admire, and therefore Clyde as well.

She wore a raven's mask.

Clyde's own mask, an unadorned domino, was in his pocket by now.

"Are we using names," he said, "or shall we abide by strict rules of anonymity?"

"Are there rules in effect? I wasn't aware."

"We'll make our own," he said, surprised by the slightly sexy banter he was generating.

He led her in and out of pairs of bodies ghost-floating to the tune of an old ballad from his youth.

Clyde used to have women friends. But when the Boss started to court other possible protégés, strong-bodied young agents who would serve a social function more than a Bureau function, Clyde knew it was time to submit to Edgar's need for a steadfast and unquestioning friend, a mate of soul and word and unvarying routine. This was a choice that answered Clyde's own deep need for protection, a place on the safe side of the fortified wall.

Power made his suits fit better.

He saw Edgar being photographed with a group at the far end of the ballroom. Clyde recognized most of the people and noticed how eager Edgar seemed to nestle among them.

Edgar's own power had always been double-skinned. He had the power of his office of course. And also the power that his self-repression gave him. His stern measures as Director were given an odd legitimacy by his personal life, the rigor of his insistent celibacy. Clyde believed this, that Edgar had earned his monocratic power through the days and nights of his self-denial, the rejection of unacceptable impulses. The man was consistent. Every official secret in the Bureau had its blood-birth in Edgar's own soul.

This is what made him a great man.

Conflict. The nature of his desire and the unremitting attempts he made to expose homosexuals in the government. The secret of his desire and the refusal to yield. Great in his conviction. Great in his harsh judgment and traditional background and early American right-eousness and great in his quibbling fear and dark shame and great and sad and miserable in his dread of physical contact and in a thousand other torments too deep to name.

Clyde would have done whatever the Boss required.

Knelt down.

Bent over.

Spread out.

Reached around.

But the Boss only wanted his company and his loyalty down to the last sentient instant of his dying breath.

Clyde saw another man, and another, in executioners' hoods. And a figure in a white winding-sheet.

"And that man over there. Having his picture snapped," the young woman said. "That's the person you were sitting with."

"Mr. Hoover."

"Mr. Hoover, yes."

"And with him, let me see. The wife of a famous poet. The husband of a famous actress. Two unattached composers. A billionaire with a double chin." Clyde realized he was showing off. "And a stockbroker-yachtsman, let me think, called Jason Vanover. And his wife, a middling painter called whatever she's called. Sax or Wax or something."

"And you are Mr. Tolson," said the woman.

And how clever, thought Clyde, who was rarely recognized in public and felt a bit flattered and somewhat unsettled as well.

They were dancing cheek to cheek.

He saw another woman in modified medieval dress, a bit more shrouded and hooded, and it brought to mind—no, not the sixteenth-century painting Edgar was so morbidly fond of, the Bruegel, with its panoramic deathscape. (Edgar had postcards, magazine pages, framed reproductions and enlarged details stored and hung in his basement rumpus room. And he'd ordered Clyde to talk to officials in Madrid about the priceless original and how he might acquire it as a gift to the American people from a Spanish nation grateful for the protective shield of U.S. armed might. But when a B-52 and a tanker collided during routine refueling, earlier this year, and four hydrogen bombs came crashing to earth on the Spanish coast, releasing radioactive materials, Clyde had to deinitiate all discussions.) No, not Bruegel. The nunnish woman brought to mind, of all things and all people, the hip sick dopester comic—Lenny Bruce. No, Lenny Bruce was not a guest at the Black & White Ball. Lenny Bruce was dead. Died several months ago, at his home in Los Angeles, of acute morphine poisoning, naked on his toilet floor, limbs gone stiff, mucus trailing out of his nose, his glassy eyes wide open, the syringe still stuck in his arm.

An 8×10 police photo of the bloated body—the picture could have been titled *The Triumph of Death*—was in the Director's personal files. Why? The horror, the shiver, the hellish sense of religious retribution out of the Middle Ages. And only hours after the body was found a buzz began to circulate in the usual places. Dig it. Lenny's been killed by shadowy forces in the government.

Lynda Bird Johnson danced past with a Secret Service agent.

The rumors had not surprised Clyde. He could smell the decade's paranoid breath. And he wondered suddenly about the woman in his arms. Had he in fact approached her on the dance floor or had she subtly stepped into his path?

A man with a skeleton mask and a woman with a monk's cowl. There, standing at the edge of the bandstand.

"You know my name," Clyde said, "but I'm at a loss, I'm afraid."

"Which doesn't happen very often, does it? But I thought our rules tended to favor nondisclosure."

They were dancing to show tunes from the forties. She pressed slightly closer and seemed to breathe rhythmically in his ear.

"Have you ever seen so many people," she whispered, "gathered in one place in order to be rich, powerful and disgusting together? We can look around us," she whispered, "and see the business executives, the fashion photographers, the government officials, the industrialists, the writers, the bankers, the academics, the pig-faced aristocrats in exile, and we can know the soul of one by the bitter wrinkled body of the other and then know all by the soul of the one. Because they're all part of the same motherfucking thing," she whispered. "Don't you think?"

Well, she just about took his breath away, whoever she was.

"The same thing. What thing?" he said.

"The state, the nation, the corporation, the power structure, the system, the establishment."

So young and lithe and trite. He felt the electric tension of her thighs and breasts passing through his suit.

"If you kiss me," she said, "I'll stick my tongue so far down your throat."

"Yes."

"It will pierce your heart."

Then everything happened at once. Figures in raven faces and skull masks. Figures in white winding-sheets. Monks, nuns, executioners. And he understood of course that the woman in his arms was one of them.

They formed a death rank on the dance floor, halting the music and

575

sending the guests to the fringes. They commanded the room, a masque of silent figures, a plague, a spray of pathogens, and Clyde looked around for Edgar.

The woman slipped away. Then the figures trooped across the floor, draped, masked, sheeted and cowled. How had they assembled so deftly? How had they entered the ballroom in the first place?

He looked for old Edgar.

An executioner and a nun did a pas de deux, a round of simple circling steps, and then the others gradually joined, the skeleton men and raven women, and in the end it was a graceful pavane they did, courtly and deadly and slow, with gestures so deliberate they seemed acted as well as danced, and Clyde saw his young partner move silkenly in their midst.

I will stick my tongue so far down your throat.

The guests watched in a trance, five hundred and forty men and women by actual count, and musicians and waiters and other personnel, and men assigned to guard the jewelry of the women, all part of the audience for an entertainment other than themselves—respectful, hushed and half stunned.

It will pierce your heart.

When they were finished the troupe stood in a line and removed their headpieces and masks. Then they opened their mouths, saying nothing, and directed hollow stares at the guests. An extended moment, a long gaping silence in the columned hall.

They departed single file.

A couple of minutes later Clyde found the Boss and they went to the men's room to collect themselves.

"Enjoy your dance, Junior?"

"I think I know who they are."

"Didn't you say that last time we were in here?"

"A group little seen and less known. Campus demonstrations mostly. No one, and this is odd."

"What?" the Boss barked.

"No one in Internal Security has come up with a name for the group. They've been known to act out protests, playing all the roles, even the police. Turn around."

"Find the links. It's all linked. The war protesters, the garbage thieves, the rock bands, the promiscuity, the drugs, the hair."

"There's some dandruff on your jacket," Clyde said.

Men entered and left, carrying a single sullen murmur in and out of the tiled room. They unzipped and peed. They urinated into mounds of crushed ice garnished with lemon wedges. They unzipped and zipped. They peed, they waggled and they zipped.

Edgar stood before the mirrors, still masked, and the sight of him prompted Clyde to think of the secret garden behind the Director's house, a sector fenced away from neighbors and never shown to guests, where statues of nude young men rose from fountains or stood draped in fall-flaming vines. Less titillating than inspirational, Clyde believed. This was the male form as Edgar's idealized double. A role livingly filled by Clyde. At least it used to be that way in the days when Edgar would stealthily tilt a mirror so he could lie in bed and watch Junior doing push-ups in the adjoining room.

That was 1939 in Miami Beach. This was 1966 in New York and we are living in muddle and shock.

He'd let that girl charm and tempt him, and he'd liked it, and he'd been disappointed when she slipped away before the kiss, and he'd been played for a fool in the oldest way—that radical enravishing self-possessed heartless come-hither bitch.

Back in the ballroom half the guests were gone. The rest measured out the time so their departure would not seem influenced by the spectacle, the protest, whatever it was—the mockery of their sleek and precious evening.

The society band played some danceable numbers but nobody wanted to dance anymore. Edgar and Clyde sat drinking with a putty-colored man in smoked glasses and his overmasked wife—satin wings, coq feathers and embedded diamonds.

Possibly Mafia, Clyde surmised.

Edgar would not speak to anyone. He sat, drank and hated. He had the sheen of Last Things in his eye. Clyde knew this look. It meant the Director was meditating on his coffin. It gave him dark solace, planning the details of his interment. A lead-lined coffin of one thousand pounds plus. To protect his body from worms, germs, moles, voles and vandals. They were planning to steal his garbage, so why not his corpse? Lead-lined, yes, to keep him safe from nuclear war, from the Ravage and Decay of radiation fallout.

And when he died, whatever the circumstances, they would suddenly, all those elements that despised his unchecked power—they would invert their distrust and begin to float rumors that the Director himself was the victim of a wry homicide planned and carried out by unknown parties in the vast and layered webwork of the state.

This is how the Boss would finally draw some sympathy, an old man put to sleep in a complex scheme so expedient and deceitful as to be widely admired even as it was only half believed. And Clyde himself was already prepared to half believe it.

Edgar dead, pray God, not for ten, fifteen, twenty years yet.

Maybe the sixties would be over by then.

The woman in the gaudy mask said, "You think they'll be waiting outside, those creeps, to make me miserable all over again?"

The husband said, "It's nearly four a.m. Hey. They gotta sleep sometime."

At four a.m. they were waiting outside. Clyde and Edgar watched from the lobby. The last partygoers straggled out and the protesters rasped and chanted, wearing children's masks again.

An hour later it finally ended. Edgar and Clyde left by the main entrance and went down to the Cadillac as the spent trash of a day and a night in a great coastal city went wind-skidding through the streets.

The armored limousine rolled slowly back to the Waldorf.

Yes, the Director would finally get some sympathy from the same people who made jokes about them both. Smutty swishy jokes. But Edgar and Clyde were not a couple of old queens doddering on. They were men of sovereign authority. And Edgar did not intend to yield control anytime on this earth.

Clyde spotted the bug.

He glanced at Edgar, who sat mute and brooding in his sequined mask. He'd worn the mask steadily since dinner. Hard, cold, laconic, with all the private fury of some unassuageable pain, he wore the leather mask because it eased, if only briefly, the burden of control.

And when Clyde spotted the bug, the poky little Volkswagen with its incandescent doodles and whorls, he decided to say nothing to Edgar. The car was a hundred feet behind them, like a day-glo roach, slow and sleepless and clinging.

He said nothing to the Boss because the night had been filled with shock and distress and he wanted to absorb this final bodeful moment on his own. He was Junior after all, now and always, willingly, necessarily, however tired and befooled, the life companion and loyal second man.

5

This was Thursday. They'd first felt the full impact of the danger on Monday evening when the President addressed the nation on radio and television. On Tuesday they were told that Soviet ships were en route to Cuba with missiles and warheads to add to the number already installed on the island. Wednesday was tense. On Wednesday they found out that our naval blockade was in effect and that fourteen Soviet ships were nearing the quarantine line.

Now it was Thursday. On Thursday evening as SAC bombers carrying thermonuclear weapons circled the Med or flew Arctic routes across Greenland or hugged the western borders of North America, people rode home from work with the radio on or the newspaper up in their eyes.

And with darkness webbing down out of the broad and soaring sky over the lake, deeper into evening now, the night people were out, slipping past the bars and tonky clubs, mingling with tourists and conventioneers who were checking out the action. On the fringe streets they sidestepped taxis on the prowl and veered around the traffic of negotiated vice and they made their way to Rush Street, finally, where Mister Kelly's stood, a big-name room in Chicago's bouncing night.

Lenny Bruce came slouching down from the second-floor dressing room and walked a little bleary-eyed through the kitchen and out the swinging doors, where he did a sidle step onto the stage.

A waiter with a tray said, "It's a human zoo out there tonight."

Fifteen minutes into his act Lenny took a condom out of his pocket and tried to fit it over his furrowed tongue. Then he tried to talk through it, or out of it. Finally he dangled the item between his thumb and index finger, holding it away from his body, specimenlike—it's a dead jellyfish that has the reflex power to deliver one last spasmic sting.

"I can be arrested in twenty-three states for waving this thing in public. You're thinking, Sure in the Bible belt. Actually I'm safe in the Bible belt because they don't know what this is. They put Saran Wrap on their dicks."

He shook his hands hallelujah and took a stagger step back.

"I swear I saw it in Time magazine. You get a box of Saran Wrap and you tear off as much as you need for your particular endowment."

The word endowment got a bigger response than Saran Wrap or Time magazine.

"Leftover meatloaf."

He did his hipster crack-up laugh, bending from the waist like some Hassid at serious prayer. There were a few people in the audience, two, three, four people going small and tight in their seats.

"Saran Wrap. It sounds interplanetary. Picture it. A little town somewhere in America. A housewife pins laundry on a line. White and Negro children play peacefully in a schoolyard. Apple pies are cooling on kitchen windowsills. Suddenly a deathly stillness. People pause in midmotion. A dog named Skipper hides under the porch steps. Then a blinding flash. It's a visit from outer space. Creatures from the planet Saran. They're very thin and sort of filmy looking. They say to the leaders of Earth, Take this new material we've just invented and test it on yourselves, because frankly we're afraid to."

Lenny's heavy lids began to lower slowly as he changed the scene.

"It's a documented thing, farm boys and ranch hands taking strips of Saran Wrap with them when they go on dates. There are teams of sociologists doing fieldwork on this matter. Not to mention admen on the Dow Chemical account, which is the company that makes the stuff, and they're looking to position their product as a food wrap *and* a scumbag, if only they could devise a diplomatic language. Ad biggies on Madison Avenue. Let's do a nice old country doctor in a lab coat. Sitting in his rustic office pulling Saran Wrap off the chicken sandwich his wife packed for his lunch and he drapes the wrap absentmindedly around his finger. Talking about freshness and protection. Maybe sneaking in a word about overpopulation. And the admen get excited by the idea. Let's run it up the flagpole blah blah blah. It's nearly subliminal, dig?"

Lenny whirls and points at some phantom confederate in the wings. In fact there are no wings—just walls and doors.

He tried to fit the condom over his tongue again.

"Never underestimate the power of language. I carry a rubber with me at all times because I don't want to inseminate someone by schmoozing with her. Some innocent teenage girl asks for directions to State Street. *Zap*. A virgin birth."

A small commotion in the middle of the room—could be some walkouts or maybe just a waiter and some noisy plates. The waiters are supposed to work quietly during performances but this was a hungry bunch of trenchermen who made a racket when they ate, gorging on sirloins, barbecued ribs, lobster tails, spaghetti and chicken livers, and more or less thrashing their way through a Mister Kelly specialty, the green goddess salad.

Lenny said, "Love me unconditionally or I die. These are the terms of our engagement."

Kelly's was jam-packed tonight, well over the legal limit of a hundred and sixty, and they were sitting, standing and stacked ten deep at the fire exit. And they were loud, they bawled and lowed like beef on the hoof, men on business trips with dilated veins throbbing at their temples, a group of touring usherettes from the Far West, half expecting to encounter themselves in one of Lenny's bits, and look at the heavyset men in big suits with star sapphires on their pinky fingers, in from the mobster suburbs with lapels so wide they do semaphores when the wind blows. And a table filled with developers chewing on Cuban cigars—a bachelor night on the town. And sophisticated women digging the weird insides of one man's psyche. And a couple of butterball college professors looking for some belly laughs, idea men from the humanistic enclave. And Hugh Hefner and a cluster of Playboy models, aspiring centerfolds on leave from the Mansion, tall, young, fair and so flawlessly complexioned they seem to be airbrushed. And Hef with his dirty paternal smile steel-seamed around a briar pipe.

Walkouts in progress—an old story of course on the Lenny Bruce circuit. Two women and a man offended by the sight of a guy sticking his tongue in a Trojan.

Lenny spotted them and fixed on the woman bringing up the rear. Big-boned, let's say, and able-bodied.

"Look who's splitting the scene. You know who that is, don't you? You can recognize her from the wanted posters. Josef Mengele's head nurse. Up from Argentina on a budget tour." Pause a beat. "She's doing the stockyards, the prisons and the morgue." Pause a beat. "When she was still active, they called her Attila the Huness."

Who else was in the room? Second City comics here to idolize the super sicko. Jazz writers and theater people. Some porko politicos and their rosary-bead wives—they're here under the impression that Lenny's an Italian crooner whose real name runs to eleven syllables and carries a serious curse.

Who else? A number of Cook County vice cops scattered through the room with notebooks and tape machines, sucking up every arraignable word.

Lenny was still hectoring the walkouts.

"Make room, make room. They got a flight to Buenos Aires in ten minutes. Eichmann Air. The stews wear striped pajamas."

Those were the terms of Lenny's act. If you didn't like the bits he did, you were a mass murderer. Or you were the Polio Mother of the Year 1952 or the subject of a brief improvised bit, which he now performed, on the flashing light in airliner toilets, a recent obsession of his.

Return to seat Return to seat Return to seat.

Lenny once had a sixty-party walkout in New York. An entire Grey

Line bus tour just upped and fled. Angelo the maitre d' looked at Lenny and said, You gotta talk dirty? Who's gonna make up the tips, you fuck?

Lenny licked and rubbed the condom. He fingered it, twirled it, snapped it.

"I just realized. This is what the twentieth century feels like."

Then he paused thoughtfully, appearing to remember something. He stuck the rubber in his pocket, absently—he was wearing the same Nehru jacket he'd sported in San Francisco, his Hindu statesman number, and the thing was rutted and crushed by now, resembling some wadded discard plucked from the gutter. He also wore a large medal on a chain, an accessory to the Nehru. You got the medal for wearing the jacket.

Yes, he was remembering something heavy and dense. Despite his weeklong anxiety over the missile crisis, the blackout at Basin Street West, the endless bulletins issuing from every surface in the land-scape, a network ranging from TV monitors in airport boarding areas to blind newsies selling tabloids on street corners, yes, whatever the level of Lenny's unease—*the nuclear showdown had slipped his mind.*

Better believe it. Their ships are approaching our blockade.

Lenny nodded, he stroked the mole on his cheek, he waggled his fingers and looked out over the massed heads humming autonomically in the low smoke.

"We're all gonna die!"

He said it four times total, passionately high-pitched, arms flung up.

"And you're beginning to take it personally," he said. "How can they justify the inconvenience of a war that's gonna break out over the weekend? You had it all planned. Friday night. Movie with your high-brow art-film friends. Serious Swedish flick at the little theater near the university. Ursula Andress naked to the waist with a slain calf slung over her shoulder. Saturday morning. Let's see. Dry cleaner, post office, grocery store, pick up shoes, put cat to sleep, call mom back home in French Lick—yeah, I'm fine, how're you, yatta yatta yatta, got a big date tonight with a real nice girl, Raytheon, she's a Mormon, they don't drink tap water or play the saxophone."

Lenny broke off unexpectedly and leaned into the face of one of

584

the real-estate barons sitting ringside, a guy with the bloated cheeks of a trumpet player doing a cardiac solo.

"Mick spic hunky junkie boogie."

There was no context for the line except the one that Lenny took with him everywhere. The culture and its loaded words. He looked around some more. He seemed to need a particular kind of face into which to deliver his scripture.

One of the college profs smiled invitingly and Lenny obliged with, "Fuck suck fag hag gimme a nickel bag."

In fact the words were thrilling. Many people had never heard these words spoken before an audience—by a guy in a Hindu tunic yet—and there was an odd turn of truth, a sense of unleashing perhaps, or disembarrassment.

Lenny followed this flurry with an erudite riff on the German word *Sprachgefühl*, a feel for language, for what is idiomatically hip—he reads up on things like this in hotels and on planes and back home in the smoky dawn of L.A. while he's waiting for a woman or a pusher.

A fight broke out in the middle of his commentary. Back near the fire exit. Five burly men in a fur ball of pummel and shove. Lenny egged them on, insulting their mothers, until they more or less rolled out the door.

He remembered the crisis again.

"Yeah so you pick up your date at the pad she shares with six other Mormon chicks. Wow what a shiksoid circus. They have strange shiny eyes and a superhuman blondness. They're the next stage of evolution after Olympic swimmers. They're right at the edge of science fiction, man. Human look-alikes from space waiting for a signal to take over the planet. They think tap water's a government plot. Their water's trucked in from a well in Utah. Raytheon's kinda cute but she's dressed so primly you feel your balls contract. You look at these girls and you mourn the lost glamour of women's undergarments. The whole nazified system of straps and harnesses. It's a legal outlet for your secret fascist longings. But chicks don't buy into it anymore. All that slithery hardware that makes wars worth fighting. You take her to a funky down-home place near the women's house of detention. She orders the knuckle sandwich. Hey, the chick digs soul food. Your spirits soar. You think of the setup at your place. Bottle of Vat 69. Zig Zag cigarette paper. Little baggy of dope from the high Andes. The mood lighting. The cool jazz on the turntable. We'll do Miles, yeah, from his blue period. If Miles can't soften her up she's probably a diesel dyke. You're thinking all the universal things men have always thought about and said to each other. Get in her pants. Did you get in? Did you get some? Did you make it? How far'd you get? How far'd she go? Is she an easy lay? Is she a good hump? Is she a piece? Did you get a piece? It's like the language of yard goods. It's like piece goods. You can make her. She can be made. It's like a garment factory. It's like work that's paid for according to the number of units turned out. He's a make-out artist. She's a piece. Knock off a piece. It's a knockoff. You can't tell the woman from the fabric she's wearing."

This is Lenny in his primitive Christian mode, doing offbeat sermons to desert rabble.

"You hail a cab and the radio's on. Khrushchev wrote a letter to Kennedy. He wants a summit. Who is this Khrushchev anyway? He's a shtarker in a bad suit. You're worried about your summit, not his. The whole point of the missile crisis is the sexual opportunity it offers. You get Raytheon to your place and convince her the whole world's about to go zippo and astonishingly it works and within minutes she's standing naked in your living room and she is all ovals and loops, like the Palmer handwriting method, and so blond she could be radioactive."

Lenny switched abruptly to ad lib bits. Whatever zoomed across his brainpan. He did bits he got bored with five seconds in. He did psychoanalysis, personal reminiscence, he did voices and accents, grandmotherly groans, scenes from prison movies, and he finally closed the show with a monologue that had a kind of abridged syntax, a thing without connectives, he was cooking free-form, closer to music than speech, doing a spoken jazz in which a slang term generates a matching argot, like musicians trading fours, the road band, the sideman's inner riff, and when the crowd dispersed they took this rap mosaic with them into the strip joints and bars and late-night diners, the places where the nighthawks congregate, and it was Lenny's own hard bop, his speeches to the people that rode the broad Chicago night.

We stopped the car half a block before the bridge and switched to a taxi. I gave the guy the address and he looked at me, looked at her, then nodded briefly. I'd been told it was better to take a taxi across the border because if you drove your car you became subject to major delays owing to inspections by customs agents on your return to the U.S. side, for guns and drugs.

The town had a strange electric brightness in the stormlight. Blue and green stucco shops with pottery on display—pottery, copper, blankets, glass.

"I think I'm having second thoughts," I said.

"Please, okay?"

"Maybe they're first thoughts. I never really thought hard enough until now."

Amy could carry a fair amount of reproach in her clear brown eyes.

"I took it for granted that this was the only thing to do," I said. "We should have talked about it some more."

Her look was the kind of look you get when someone wants you to know she is taking great pains not to pity you. When we cleared the town and drove into the brown hills the rain came hard. About six minutes later the driver pulled up in front of a fairly sizable house behind some trees and the sun was hot and bright and the ground was smoking.

The woman who let us in looked at Amy and said, "Please, your name," more or less managerially.

"Amy Brookhiser."

"Yes, you'll come with me."

And that's what happened. Amy went with the woman, who was either the nurse, the wife, the office manager or some combination of these. I thought we might have some reassuring words for each other, Amy and I, or I might say something even if she didn't, although I didn't know what I might say, but they were down the hall and making a left turn and I still had our overnight bags in my hands.

All right. I set the bags down and went into the living room, or waiting room, and sat on the sofa. There were no magazines to read. All the reading was on the walls, painted sayings and occult symbols, and this was unexpected. Circles, chevrons, arrows, birds, mucho mystical drivel, and I was trying to absorb it all. A number of shaped sayings, words that formed triangles and tall palms, trees of life perhaps—sayings in English about the passage of the soul and the eye of God, and there were mystical eyes and admonitory hands on all four walls and the ceiling.

I tried to absorb this surprise, wondering what it meant and why I hadn't been warned, and that's when the doctor walked in. A man I worked with in Palo Alto had given me his name and address, and I'd called and made arrangements, and there were assurances about safety from two other people I'd talked to, safe, clean, professional, but no one had said anything about the walls.

He didn't seem to be looking at me.

He said, "Yes."

I said, "Dr. Swearingen?"

He wasn't looking at me.

He said, "Everything seems to be in order."

I said, "Do I pay now?"

We seemed to be having a conversation that went backwards.

He thought about the question of payment, his mouth scrunched up, my hand at my wallet, waiting.

He was a tall man in a white smock, tall and stooped, with an odd pallor, and deeply introspective, I thought, six feet seven or eight, an American who did abortions, according to the people I'd talked to, out of a sense of duty and compassion, and he hadn't shaved today.

I paid him two hundred dollars cash and he said, "Expect some bleeding," maybe as a way of veiling the transaction, and then he went down the hall.

I sat there with the pictures and the words. I didn't know how to think about any of this. I didn't know what to call it. Maybe Amy knew but she wasn't saying much. All she wanted to do was get it over with.

I was willing to make sacrifices and be responsible. This is what I told myself. I wanted to fix myself to something strong, to a wife, I thought, and child.

But it wasn't strong at all. It was hopeless, worthless and weak.

We wouldn't last a month together. We were restless and grasping, we were a fling that had run intermittently for two years only because we lived in different cities, and we were religious in our attachment to risk, and she was the last thing I needed in this world.

And you felt a strange shaded grief, didn't you, sitting in the room, a sadness shaded by distance, and you tried to think yourself into the middle of the child's unlived life.

Someone was cooking a meal a couple of rooms away and this disturbed me. The savor of the food and the faint sounds of activity, someone opening cabinet doors—this disturbed and confused me and made me a little angry.

Amy was twenty-six years old, a couple of weeks shy of twenty-seven, and she lived and worked in Wichita. I was twenty-four, roughly half a continent away, and I knew she half hated both of us for what had happened.

When Amy came out I realized I hadn't told the cabdriver to pick us up and we waited a while until the woman made the call and someone showed.

They'd given her a local, only, because that's what they were equipped to do, and she wasn't groggy on the ride to the border but sat forward and gripped the edges of the front seat and didn't want to talk.

The customs men checked the cab for contraband and breezed through our bags and we were in our rented car in a matter of minutes.

I drove out of Del Rio headed east on 90. Amy slept a while and woke up and was thirsty. Up ahead of us a pickup went into a spin, just like that, the only other vehicle on the road, skidding and whipping when it came off a sandy ramp, and I slowed down so we could watch objectively.

"Swapped ends," Amy said quietly. "That's what my old granddad Parker would say. Truck swapped ends for sure."

She spoke in a tired and quiet voice and I drove slowly past the pickup, which was facing the way it wanted to face again, with two teenage boys in the cab, collecting themselves in a flurry of stupid grins, and I looked for a place where Amy could get a cool and healthy drink somewhere between here and the airport.

589

The hotel was called the Waves, and why not? This was Ocean Drive, wasn't it, in the municipality of Miami Beach.

Small rich angry men got out of rented convertibles with their dolled-up wives, women so cultishly tanned they resembled tobacco leaf.

Spoiled savvy with-it kids from northern cities flashed fake I.D.s at the bar. They were enrolled at the resort colleges in the area and were eager to catch the act in the big room.

A contingent of Cubans fell by, headed for the hotel lounge, shod, clad, tropically smart—the women in wraparound white and born to dance and the men sunglassed and wary. They looked like bodyguards for some *jefe* about to topple.

There was a Latin band in the lounge doing mambos and cha-chas and a number of Long Island sexpots were here, looking for second husbands. They traveled in pairs or with a sister, even, like a hunter and her gun bearer, one divorced, one single—dating an orthodontist here and an iffy sort of businessman there. Says he's an executive in the hotel linen supply business? But when I call him on the phone? I have to ask for Marty? And his name is Fred?

Eyelinered, tweezered, mascara'd, flashing acrylic nails, coral, with matching lipstick and blush. These were women who'd always been part of the in-group and some of them preferred the nightclub to the lounge because they wanted to get a taste of Lenny Bruce.

First you laugh, then you dance.

The room was called El Patio and the mambo music from the lounge kept seeping in. Lenny was surprised to spot some old people in the crowd, a few canes propped against the chairs, but he decided not to do any cripple bits. Not because he was getting cautious and soft. No, there was only one subject tonight and it was central to his existence.

"We're less than two hundred miles from Cuba. I know you know this. And I know this. But I still have to say it. Those missiles are just over my right shoulder, dig. A range of one thousand kilometers, which is redundant from our viewpoint but which disturbs me anyway

590

because we haven't even lost the war yet and we're already on the metric system."

And he stood nodding his head, looking semi-jetlagged, a little paranoid, a little overmedicated, his voice subdued and his eyes murky with lunar gloom.

"And we won't get killed for being Jewish. That's the tricky part. They'll kill us for being American. How do we feel about that?"

What a way to begin a night of entertainment. There was a long lugubrious silence. Then Lenny did a standing left turn, posed a moment like some discus Greek and finally shot his upper body forward and pounded the floor with his fist.

A college kid laughed.

"What I love are the names of our protectors. Check it out, Jim."

And he took a clutch of newsclips from the side pocket of the ratty car coat he was wearing. Mumbled some lines of text, made a few Mort Sahlish comments, dropped a clipping and kicked it, speaking briefly in his Transylvanian voice.

"All right, these men are deciding our fate. They're going in and out of solemn meetings all day and night. White shirts, cuff links, striped ties. But their names are where it's at. Adlai Stevenson. *Adlai*. Gases you right down to your Capezios, right? It's so exclusive it has no gender. This little boy is so special we don't want anyone to know he's a boy. Because, ultimately, dig, being a boy or a girl is so fucking common. And if anyone else uses this name within a five thousand mile radius of our Adlai, we'll pay to have him killed. And all his progeny. Completely extinguish the line. Because this is our family thing. That's it, you see. *La cosa nostra*. Only they don't have to do it with extortion and murder. They do it with names that no one else could ever think up."

The divorced women laughed. There were lowlifes from the dog track in attendance. Musicians on their night off. Pool boys and out-of-work dancers. There were two tables of travel agents on a junket from Toronto—they thought Lenny was a Scottish comic who did impressions of the royal family.

"All right, dig. Dean Rusk. *Dean*. Born to lead, to advise and instruct. Born to be bald. No, yes, wise but also tough and shrewd.

591

Look out for men with one syllable in each name. Unyielding mother-fuckers. But here's my favorite, okay. You know what I'm gonna say, don't you?"

An old lady laughed.

"That's right. McGeorge Bundy. *McGeorge.* How do you survive childhood with a name like that? Was his name reversed at birth? A mistake at the hospital? Of course not. They did it. They marked him for greatness. Besides, he had a grandmother named McMary."

The old lady loved it.

Lenny took a while to riffle through the strips of newsprint, mumbling something.

"Yes, no, here's one. Roswell Gilpatric. *Roswell.* It's not a put-on. It's real. Look, shown here in the cabinet room. Captured on film. The secretaries, the assistant secretaries, the undersecretaries, the deputy undersecretaries, the advisors on Russian affairs. Alexis Johnson. *Alexis.* Bromley Smith. *Bromley.* Llewellyn Thompson. *Llewellyn.* Four *l*'s in Llewellyn. Takes balls, baby. Secretly, see, I have to admire them. Because they understand the logic of how to conduct yourself unsentimentally in the world. W. Averell Harriman. *Averell.* This is a man who has his own exit on the New York State Thruway. And here's us, a stone's throw from Cuba. They're not drawn here but we are. Because the atomic bomb is Old Testament. It's the Jewish bible in spades. We feel at home with this judgment, this punishment hanging over us. Illness and misfortune. Speak to us, sweetheart."

But Lenny's paranoia and sense of tragedy may have had a more immediate source. He'd been tipped off at the airport that the Dade County police had planted Jewish detectives in the audience. Yes, Yiddish-speaking fuzz who were prepared to glom onto every vile syllable he uttered in the mother-in-law tongue.

"You want names, I'll give you names. My name is Leonard Alfred Schneider. What was I doing when I took the name Lenny Bruce? I was moving toward the invisible middle. I'm just like you, mister. Don't bug me, man, or insult my ancestors. I'm just another Lenny. Just another Bruce. But that's not what the *ordained* people do. McGeorge, Roswell, Adlai. They remove themselves from any taint of the big middle. And that's a genius thing. Doesn't matter where they go to church. Their name is their church. They're not only not like Leonard Alfred Schneider. They're not like Lenny Bruce. And I don't blame them, frankly."

He'd spoken quietly, conversationally, in his nasal slant, and didn't expect the large laugh. He put away the papers he'd been waving. The Latin music began to pound the walls and a heckler started talking to Lenny, a drunk with a rolled-up racing form, but Lenny only lifted the mike off the stand and blessed the man.

Then he did an impression of the Queen of England ordering Chinese takeout over the phone.

The travel agents loved it.

"If your name is Roswell or Bromley, you have a real father. Only the most responsible parents give their kids that kind of name. If you're a Roswell, you don't have a father who comes around twice a year and gives you a novelty toy when he leaves. Here, kid, a little something to deepen our relationship. You study the item. It's a rubber vomit blob. Here, kid, put it on your mother's bed." Lenny snapped his fingers and did a shoulder curl. "So happens the Office of Civil Defense is stockpiling rubber vomit in fallout shelters all over the country. They're in a frenzy right now, man. Get those shelters built and stocked. Sanitation kits, medical kits. Phenobarbital, to sedate you. Penicillin, I don't know, for bomb rash. When the radiation makes you too sick to vomit, they hand out rubber vomit, for morale. After the mass destruction of a nuclear exchange"—he looked at his watch—"they're gonna wanna rebuild. And all this cold war junk is gonna be worth plenty, as quaint memorabilia. Those yellow and black signs you've been seeing everywhere but never really noticed until six days ago—Fallout Shelter. Collector's items. All the stuff that's stashed in the storage rooms and laundry rooms that are designated shelters. Drums of drinking water. Saltines. Chapstick, for the flash. Cardboard toilets that double as salad bowls. Incidentally," he said.

A waiter dropped a tray of drinks.

"The Navy boarded a ship yesterday at the quarantine line. First ship boarded. Armed boarding party. Bet your ass it was tense, baby. Turns out the ship's not carrying missiles. Carrying truck parts and toilet paper. See, there it is, ordinary life trying to reassert itself. That's the secret meaning of this week. The secret history that never appears in the written accounts of the time or in the public statements of the men in power. Those beautiful bombs and missiles. Those planes and submarines. Ever see anything so gorgeous? The weapons get the best engineering and the most poetic names. Meanwhile some old grubby farmer in Cuba is waiting for a carburetor for his beat-up tractor. And he's been wiping his ass with the lettuce crop. They're reminding him he has to be patient, yeah, while they work out their big-power relationships." Lenny did a dip and swivel. "You remember the way your mother talked to you when you were on the potty. Make, sweetheart. Make for mommy." He did a pivot and spin. "And you cops on special duty. The linguists in the crowd. There's something you oughta know. The word smack, or heroin? Comes from the Yiddish *shmek*. You know this, experts? A sniff, a smell, like a pinch of snuff. Dig it, he's got a two hundred dollar *shmek* habit. Next time you bust a junkie who's a coreligionist"—the word gets a little barking laugh from the college kids—"and you stick your rubber glove up his ass to check what kind of stash he's got in there, that smell you smell is *shmek*, my friend. Which is just another name for ordinary life."

The detectives did not laugh.

A sea breeze blew through the room and the band was playing cha-chas now. A woman sitting down missed her chair. Dancers appeared at the far end of the bar, they were spilling out of the lounge, one-two cha-cha-cha, and Lenny rolled his shoulders and dipped his hips. The travel agents took a vote and decided to order another round. The music drilled the wall like tamale farts and a couple of college girls got up and danced in place among the crowded tables. The original dancers moved in a boxer's crouch, advancing down the bar in pastel skirts and white guayaberas while test missiles in California were reprogrammed with Soviet targets.

Lenny seized the mike and cried, *"We're all gonna die!"*

They laughed and half wept. He led them in a chorus of the chant. The cha-cha music poured into the room and the dancers followed in beautifully balanced twos and the men and women at the tables got up and danced in place, making pugilistic motions with their hands. One-two cha-cha-cha. They kicked off their shoes and spilled their drinks.

Lenny did a monologue in Spanglish and they loved it and laughed and half wept and a young man majoring in Wardrobe Management chugalugged a glass of straight scotch, a stone's throw from Cuba.

It's fabulous, it's marvelous, it's Miami.

6

Marian Bowman was talking to her mother. They were in the living room of her mother's house, her mother and father's house, where she'd grown up, and there were sprays of baby's breath in most of the rooms and in bud vases on hall tables, small white flowers in branched clusters, a plant her mother liked to display in its starkness, free of the customary larger arrangement, for whatever reason a mother might have, with the elms going yellow and the red oaks blazing on a fine fall day in Madison, Wisconsin, and students running wild in the streets.

"So you've been keeping secrets."

"He's not a secret," Marian said.

"You've known him all this time and I'm only now hearing. That's a secret."

"I've known him technically all this time."

"And now you know him how?"

The mother smiled first, then the daughter.

"Untechnically," Marian said. "And he's not a secret. There hasn't been much to say, that's all."

"There's always something to say. What do I sense about this relationship? I think you're very uncertain. You have a tendency. You always did. To act against your misgivings. Because—well, I don't know why you do it exactly."

They heard the voices more clearly now, ripping from stereo speakers set in the windows of A-frames along Mifflin Street.

"I wasn't aware. Have I expressed misgivings."

"Yes. And it's clear I'm meant to notice. And it's clear you want me to argue against the man."

"This is totally. No no no no," Marian said mildly.

"You can't bring yourself to argue against him. You want me to do it."

"And you sense all this, sort of."

"Not sort of. Hard and clear."

"And what happens when you argue against him? Do I say thank-you mother you've saved me from a fate worse."

"Of course not. You defend him. You stand up for him."

"She stands up for her man. And you what, you infer all this from a little bitty talk in which I said practically nothing about him."

"Tell me I'm wrong," her mother said, "and I'll make every effort to believe you."

Her mother turned toward the window showing a faint annoyance. They were running in the streets. They were probably throwing bricks and starting fires. There was a bullhorn voice mixed in with the music that ripped from the speakers.

"They have what they call the riot season."

"Did it ever occur to me," Marian said, "that Chicago would seem peaceful and decent?"

"I don't know if this is the riot season or not. Maybe it's just a block party that the police are trying to contain. Although, no, that can't be right. They have block parties in the spring."

"I'll come back for Thanksgiving if you'll make them stop that noise."

Her mother said, "Is he married?"

And instantly regretted it. Marian saw the self-reproach in the tilt of her mother's mouth. Yes, a rare lapse. It diminished the authority of her earlier remarks and was totally unthought-out, a lapse, a tactical mistake, and the color in her mother's face went flat. Because if he were married, one, why would Marian talk about him without saying so; and, two, why would she talk about him at all?

"No, of course not."

"Of course not. I know that," her mother said.

Marian went upstairs feeling better. She loved her old room. She loved coming back because the quiet streets were here, in theory, and the houses with screened sunporches, and the elmed esplanades and university buildings, and because her room was here, kept safe for her, spare, unspecial, unfussed over, but a place no one could see as she did, containing a sizable measure of what is meant by home.

She started packing for the trip back, taking some winter things out of the closet, and then stopped just long enough to turn on the radio. She found WIBA, Up Against the Wall FM, because she wanted to know what was going on out there, just as a point of exasperated interest, and because the noise was getting louder.

It was too soon to pack but she did it anyway. Home is the place where they have to take you in, said the poet, or said Marian's father paraphrasing the poet, and home is also the place you can't wait to get the hell out of.

She had a job in Chicago she hated. Only she didn't really hate it— she'd acquired gestures of discontent because this seemed to be a thing you were supposed to do. She was twenty-five and saw no future doing backroom work in a brokerage house. But the job was okay in a way because it forced her to be disciplined and involved and unsloppy, and anyway there was nothing else she wanted to try just now.

The radio said, DowDay DowDay DowDay DowDay.

She rummaged through the dresser, finding a couple of old sweaters that might be passable, still, and a number of bright stocking caps that were funny and dumb.

The dresser was the one object in the room worth a second look, outside the text of personal reference—an oak piece fitted with a tall scuffed mirror that was hinged to swivels in a graceful trefoil frame.

The radio said, PigPigPigPigPigPigPig.

She began to understand that some of the noise in the streets, the music and voices ripping from speakers that students had placed in their windows, was coming from the station she was tuned to.

She packed and listened.

The radio said, Faculty Document 122 authorizes force against students. Faculty Document 122 authorizes force against students.

She began to understand that this was Vietnam Week on campuses across the country. And this was Dow Day here in Madison, a protest against Dow Chemical, whose recruiters were active on campus and whose products included a new and improved form of napalm with a polystyrene additive that made jellied matter cling more firmly to human flesh.

Faculty Document 122 authorizes force against students.

She thought, Small wonder. Because it sounded as if the students were tearing up the campus and it looked as if, earlier in the day, with Vietcong flags on Linden Street and mimes in whiteface tussling with police on Bascom Hill—it looked as if what?

The station was reporting Dow Day and seemingly taking part.

The radio said, PigPigPigPigPigPigPig.

It looked as if something had happened in the night to change the rules of what is thinkable.

She began to understand that the riot out there, if that's what it was, was being augmented and improved by a simulated riot on the radio, an audio montage of gunfire, screams, sirens, klaxons and intermittent bulletins real and possibly not.

She found the old coat she thought she'd lost—how do you lose a coat, everybody said—five years ago at the lake.

The radio said, Take your belt and wrap it around your fist.

When her mother served pork loin last night her father muttered, "Off the pig," and somehow it wasn't meant to be funny although when Marian laughed he did too, a little bitterly.

The radio said, There's an ANFO bulletin coming up.

She was supposed to go to school at night but wasn't, to learn stocks, bonds, debentures and other instruments of material wealth available for the production of more wealth, but wasn't because she

599

just wasn't, but would, and soon, knowing what she knew, that she needed outside forces to counteract her tendencies.

She wanted to call Nick but knew he wouldn't be there.

The radio played recorded gunfire, car crashes, lines of gritty dialogue from old war movies.

Her mother called her remiss and indifferent. She suffered from disambition, said her mother.

Faculty Document 122 authorizes force against students. Faculty Document 122 authorizes force against students.

She listened to this because it was happening here but she also tuned out intermittently, let her attention wander, as a form of self-defense. There was a kind of tiredness to it all. It had that wearying insistence that made her want to tune out.

She packed and thought of calling, even though he wasn't there, to leave a message with someone in the school office, clever and sexy, and he wouldn't like that at all but she thought she might do it anyway.

ANFO seemed to be an acronym for ammonium nitrate and fuel oil.

She put the sweaters back in the dresser. She'd pick them up at Thanksgiving if she thought she needed them and if she didn't change her mind about their passability, which she was in the process of doing.

The radio said, Kafka without the *f* is kaka. Yes, we are talking about waste, we are talking about fertilizer, we are talking about waste and weapons, we are talking about ANFO, the bomb that begins in the asshole of a barnyard pig.

PigPigPigPigPigPigPig.

She dug a pack of cigarettes out of a pocket in the suitcase. Then she opened a window and lit one up. The noise came blowing in, bullhorn cops, news bulletins, rock music, and she turned off the radio and sat by the window smoking.

She'd seen a multicolored Volkswagen beetle with painted faces in the windows, earlier in the day, on Babcock Drive.

She sat there blowing smoke out the window because her mother was supposedly allergic and would have preferred, in any case, that Marian did not smoke, and they were taking off their belts and wrapping them around their fists.

And a Dow recruiter was trapped in Commerce Hall, listening to firecrackers, if that's what they were, going off outside the door to room 104, where he talked across the desk to a potential recruit.

There were trash fires on lower State Street.

There were rumors about Terminal Theater, a group that did not concede its own existence, and a student on a second-story porch on Mifflin Street turned up the volume when she saw police in riot gear moving in a double column down the street.

And over by the Library Mall members of the San Francisco Mime Troupe, if that's who they were, kept turning up among the police, more or less suicidally, wearing whiteface and carrying panpipes and dressed in busker costume, quaint and ill-fitting mid-Victorian drag, with cricket caps, a dozen young men and women on the police side of the skirmish line, mimicking the gestures of the cops and getting dragged to a van and beaten.

People everywhere listened to the radio, to the dialogue between what was real and what was spliced and mixed and processed and played, and the speakers dealt out heavy metal and a woman on the air read the copy on package inserts of Dow products, speaking in a hushed and sexy voice.

The police began firing tear gas and students started running toward the gas out of a sort of rompish curiosity or because the gas carried a fragrance of apple blossoms, believe it or not, a fast-acting agent now being used in Vietnam.

Common Sense, Uncommon Chemistry. This was Dow's catchy ad slogan and the woman read it on the air repeatedly in a soft and sexy voice.

There were Dow interviews scheduled in three buildings but the sit-in was taking place at Commerce and that's where the recruiter sat trapped, with a hamburger going cold in a white bag.

Two squads of police formed a wedge.

He said to the potential recruit, "So tell me about what happens between now and graduation day."

The kid said, "Someone had a live rat out there."

"Let's, I think, stick to the issue," the recruiter said, "for our own, really, peace of mind."

Or they ran toward the gas because they thought the moral force of their argument would neutralize the effect of the chemicals.

The San Francisco Mime Troupe was not supposed to be on the Library Mall. This was the interesting thing.

And affinity groups started fires here and there, or broke windows, small bands with names like the Mudville Nine, the members masked in bandannas soaked in baking soda and egg white, a folk remedy against the gas.

And smoke in white streamers rose from projectiles that came flopping down on the broad lawn in front of Bascom Hall. Students were running the other way now, moving in an agitated mass, some with dixie cups over their mouths or hankies out, and others strolled casually on the sidewalk between the squads of helmeted police and the thickening gas, which was beginning to roll in banks toward the columned hall, and a guy resting a guitar lengthwise on his head stood watching from the streetlight.

And the sexy voice on the radio repeated the Du Pont slogan now. Better Things for Better Living . . . Through Chemistry. The woman enjoyed the pause. She prolonged the pause. She moaned through the pause. She spoke urgently and excitedly up to the pause and then she paused and moaned slowly and then she finished reciting the slogan, finally, all sated and limp and moaned out, and then she started from the beginning again.

The San Francisco Mime Troupe was supposed to be in front of Old Chemistry. This was the interesting thing. They were supposed to be passing out copies of Faculty Document 122, in front of Old Chemistry, which is exactly where they were, chanting Faculty Document 122 authorizes force against students. This was interesting because it meant that the people in whiteface on the Library Mall must be members of Terminal Theater, the legendary factoidal group whose name, even, was subject to conjecture, or was an aspect, perhaps, of the group's borderline existence.

Rock-and-roll everywhere, serpentine twangs of feedback rolling from window speakers all over the campus and on nearby streets.

The police were coming down hard now, clubs out, cops acting without orders or against orders, inevitably, riding their own rampant highs.

The recruiter and the student waited to be rescued and they talked in the meantime about courses and professors as an affinity group entered the building with cherry bombs, lengths of pipe and size D flashlight batteries, the homemade makings of a mortar attack.

The radio reported that Lyndon Johnson was being dangled upside down from a towline on a helicopter, swinging in the breeze over the Primate Lab, right here in Madison, in the outright nude, after being kidnapped by parties unknown.

The radio reported that you could make your own napalm by mixing one part liquid detergent Joy with two parts benzene or one part gasoline. Shake vigorously.

The day-glo VW moved through the streets and Marian shut the window and turned on the radio and then went and flushed the cigarette down the toilet.

She began to understand that someone or some group had taken over the radio and as the day waned a man recited instructions for the manufacture of a fertilizer bomb. How to buy the nitrate, cheap, it comes bagged or bulk, from a farm-supply store, and how to add the fuel oil and what to do to ignite the mix.

There was an interval of static and a brief silence. Then the radio returned to its normal broadcast mode.

What was this?

Three voices chanting liturgically, a priest reciting the same line over and over and two altar boys delivering fixed responses.

Better things for better living.

Through chemistry.

Better things for better living.

Through chemistry.

Better things for better living.

Through chemistry.

She turned off the radio.

Then her father came home and was filled in by her mother and they all sat down to dinner with the poached bass and the baby's breath and her father said, "What is he?"

Marian thought this was funny and maybe her father did too, a little. What could she say? She could say what he wasn't. This would take a fair amount of time. But concerning what he was, well, she could say he was an English teacher in a secondary school in Arizona. But she couldn't say a whole lot more because there wasn't much he'd told her.

Her mother talked about the broken bones of the demonstrators, the students with head wounds, clubbed, gassed, bleeding.

Her father said, "Do you know what this means to me, the injuries of the students? What can I compare it with? Because I want to be fair to them. It's like the life and death of a fly, on a wall, in a village, somewhere in China. That's how much I care."

He had a drained smile that no one liked to see.

"I guess that means you can't be a Buddhist. Because the Buddhists if I understand them correctly," her mother said, and then let the thought drift toward the ceiling.

Marian sat in her room that night and dialed Nick's number. She told him about her day. There wasn't much to tell him because she left out the demonstration. She was feeling needy, moody and lunar and she didn't want distractions.

Then she told him she wanted to get married. She wanted to marry him and live with him, anywhere, wherever he wanted, and not have kids and not have friends and never go to dinner with her parents.

There was a silence at the other end that she could not read. A telephone silence can be hard to read, grim and deep and sometimes unsettling. You don't have the softening aspect of the eyes or even the lookaway glance while he ponders. There's nothing in the silence but the deep distance between you.

They finished the conversation in a halting and awkward manner and she was damn mad, angry at him and at herself, mostly herself, she decided, and she was determined to get back to the grind, to the work of hygiened perfection, shaping herself, willing herself into tighter being.

She opened the window and lit a cigarette and sat there blowing streams of smoke into the cool night air.

His mother didn't want him playing cards on the corner, even with Catholic school boys, and she waited until he came upstairs and told him.

He played a game called *sett' e mezz'*, for pennies, sitting on the one-step terrace outside the grocery store, freezing on the stone, and he memorized the cards coming out of the dealer's hand and won very regular, expecting a picture card and it would come, worth half a point, but she told him not to play anymore.

But before she told him this he sat there in the cold memorizing the cards and making his bets. When he got seven and a half, which was the best score you could get, he turned over his hole card and said, "*Sett' e mezz'*."

But when the dark seeped down around the players he had to quit the game and go to the butcher to pick up the meat his mother had bought earlier in the day.

The butcher was nicer to him now, with Nick upstate. The butcher asked him if he was old enough to get it up and Matty said thirteen, almost, and the butcher said *salut'*.

The butcher said he needed someone to tell him what it was like to get it up because he couldn't remember anymore and this was the same thing the butcher used to say to Nick, more or less, when Nick was the one who went for the meat, and Matty felt good about this, smelling sawdust and blood.

When he was walking home with the meat a woman came out of the bread store and gave Matty a tweak with her fingers, a twist of the flesh on his cheek, affectionate, like turning a key, and she told him to give regards to his mother.

He reached his street and the kids were still playing cards in front of the grocery, in the dark, some of the same kids who used to taunt him for his chess when he played chess, or because he had no father, and he sat in for a couple of hands, figuring the meat could not go bad in the freezing cold, and he memorized the cards as they fell.

Then he went upstairs and she told him she didn't want him gambling. She told him even if it was only pennies. She said it didn't look good and led to other things and other kinds of company and she told him she didn't want to say anything in front of the other boys, whether they were Catholic school boys or not, and he stood there with the meat in his arms.

They were the two of them alone and he wanted to obey. He felt the solemn weight of the situation, the size of Nicky's going, but there were always kids playing cards on the stoops and corners and he wasn't sure, when they dealt him in, that he'd say no. And not because he could memorize the cards. It wasn't so sneaky as that. It was another kind of thing completely. He was a little bit of a hero with his brother upstate, doing what he'd done, and boys from blocks around wanted to know him.

This is why he thought it might be hard to obey her, with the lamb chops knobby in his arms.

DECEMBER 1, 1969

You can't fight a war without acronyms. This is a fact of modern combat, according to Louis T. Bakey.

And where do these compressed words come from?

They come from remote levels of development, from technicians and bombheads in their computer universe—storky bespectacled men who deal with systems so layered and many-connected that the ensuing arrays of words must be atomized and redesigned, made spare and letter-sleek.

But acronyms also come from the ranks, don't they, at least occasionally? Look at old Louis strapped and cramped in his aft-facing ejection seat in the lower deck of the forward fuselage, going through the checklist. And the crews in alert barracks worldwide waiting for the klaxons to sound. And the guys on the line who load the ordnance and juice the engines. These are men who feel an armpit intimacy with the weapons systems they maintain and fly. This gives their acronyms a certain funky something.

And this is why the high-altitude bomber sitting on the ramp out there, crew of six including Louis, a great, massive, swept-winged and soon-to-soar B-52—this aircraft is known as a BUFF to tens of thousands of men throughout the command, for Big Ugly Fat Fuck.

In the cockpit the pilot and copilot hacked their watches for the second time. The crewmen at their separate stations went through the standard hundred-headed procedure, the gunner floating alone in the tail turret at the end of a crawlway, the EW officer shoehorned into a cubicle at the rear of the upper deck, and down in the squat black hole Louis Bakey let a yawn come rolling out and looked at the panels, switches and monitors that encased him in a more or less total monopoly of avionic jargon and he half nudged the navigator pressed in next to him.

"Chuckman, I find myself in a very pussy-minded mood today."

"Hell of a time to be thinking such thoughts."

"I don't think no thoughts. They just come."

"Being we're strapped in this tube for the next."

"That's the fucked-up beauty of the thing. How thoughts just come. Of and by themselves."

"Not counting debrief. Twelve hours, Louisman."

"In other words you're saying."

"Hold that thought."

"Hold that thought," Louis said. "Put it on the back burner."

"Exactly."

"First we bomb them."

"Then we fuck them," said the navigator.

Whatever the bluntness of the acronym, there was nothing ugly about the nose art that adorned the area of the fuselage just aft of the cockpit windows. A tall young leggy blond, a cheerleader type in a skimpy skirt and halter with hands on hips and feet apart and a dare-me look on her face, she wants to be sexy but isn't sure she knows how, very girl-next-doorish. And her name painted in script just above the line of mission symbols that numbered thirty-eight.

Long Tall Sally.

The pilot taxied to the runway and the tower cleared the plane for takeoff.

The copilot said, "Five, four, three."

The pilot had the throttles gang-barred to full-on position.

The copilot said, "One, zero, rolling."

When the plane rumbled past marker 7, for seven thousand feet of runway, the copilot said, speaking with a sense of enormous buffeted mass that caused his teeth to feel uprooted because this is nearly half a million pounds of Big Ugly Fat Fuckness laboring to lift itself over the marsh grass—the copilot said, "*Committed.*"

And then the dark body began to loom like some apparition of the mists, long wings bending and flaps extended and wheels breaking contact and then the gear coming up and the smoky spews of trailing black alcohol and the storm-roar shaking the flats.

In the hole the navigator, Charles Wainwright Jr., called Chuckie, continued to scan the skaty-eight meters and switches and disconnects, a whole lifetime of indicators clustered in front of him and above him and to one side—the side not occupied by Louis Bakey, the radar-bombardier.

Chuckie scanned the switches and harassed his buddy, encouraging marriage to a decent woman with church affiliations.

"Don't start in with me," Louis said. "I don't need a wife. I don't need a church. You're the one who needs these things."

"I already, Louis, have had a wife."

"Who you didn't appreciate mentally."

"I had to go through my awkward phase. I was finishing out some things," Chuckie said.

The two men had been crewmates since Greenland, flying through arctic mirages and fifty-knot gales. Their current bombing runs were strangely uneventful by comparison, or a different level of reality at any rate, easier to project as a movie.

"I know what you need," Louis said. "A woman who'll be willing to accept your history of screwups. You need to unload this stuff on someone who's innocent. You want a sweet young female who was born to understand you. Like the sweet thing on the nose of this aircraft."

Louis said sweet thing in a scornful black voice. Since Louis was a scornful black, this was not surprising. Swee' thang. Not that he didn't have a spiritual side that Chuckie responded to. You only had to listen to his stories of the early A-tests over Nevada—stories he'd told dozens of times through the years in lonely barracks in Greenland, Goose Bay and a number of remote SAC bases in the continental U.S.

"I don't think you ought to deride."

"Deride. That's nice," Louis said. "I rather deride her than ride her, tell you the truth. I believe she's too skinny for my taste. Plus she's been misnamed."

"What's that supposed to mean?"

"I get so tired. Educating these boys."

"What's it mean, Louis? Misnamed."

"Long Tall Sally."

"From the song of the same title."

"At least he knows that much. Heavens above."

"You think I don't know Little Richard and his Ow-ow-ow-ow?"

"This boy worth saving," Louis said. "But the point being."

"Used to hide his records from my parents. Oh baby woo baby. I was thirteen years old."

"This old Negro is touched, Chuckman. But the point I'm making is that the Long Tall Sally in the song and the Long Tall Sally they painted on our nose are not one and the same female of the species."

"Why not? Check her out. She's long, she's tall, she's got great legs and she looks to me like her name could be Sally. Woo. We're gonna have some fun tonight."

"Gonna have some fun tonight. That's exactly right," Louis said. "Only the Sally in Little Richard's number ain't gonna be seen in no car in no drive-in movie doing a little necking with a youth like yourself."

"Why not?" Chuckie said.

"Because she black and she bad."

Chuckie studied his radar scope and recomputed the aircraft's path over a couple of thousand miles of sea curve and mango atoll.

"What do you mean she black?"

"Because the song has a plot that somehow got lost in the wooing and wheeing."

"This song's been around thirteen, fourteen, fifteen years maybe?"

"More or less," Louis said.

"And in all these years I'm not aware of anybody coming forth with a correction to the skin color of the title character, okay?"

On the intercom the pilot said conversationally, "I wonder if that's Manila down there. Sure looks pretty, Nav."

This was an unfunny dig at the windowless pair in the lower deck, who not only lacked a skyscape but sat facing backwards and not only sat facing backwards but would be forced to eject downwards if nicked by an enemy SAM.

Another sinister acronym designed to kill.

"Pilot, this is Nav," Chuckie said.

And he fine-tuned his scope and requested a minimal turn, aligning the plane's actual path with the track he'd plotted earlier.

Then he said, "Louis, this girl out there is good luck for us. Nearly forty missions without a major incident. Don't abuse her goodwill. She's Long Tall Sally. The one and only."

When Louis became agitated he used a staccato patter, a kind of hyperdrawl with elements of falsetto pique that he strung throughout at a master pitch.

"Song say. You have any idea what the song say? This woman in an alley. Old uncle John in the alley with her. She built for speed. She got everything he need. Yes baby woo baby. Gonna have some fun tonight."

They were fifty thousand feet above the South China Sea, flying in a three-bomber formation called a cell, and there were fifteen cells in the air today, and each cell carried over three hundred bombs, and the resulting zone of destruction was known as a sandbox, and Chuckie was bizarro'd in one part of his brain by the crazy conversation he was having with old Louis even as he felt sad and hurt, in another and nearer part, by his buddy's attitude toward the girl on the nose of their aircraft.

"This song written by a black woman from Apaloosa, Mississippi. Richard add the little touches. I guarantee, brother, this Sally we're talking about ain't no skinny blond playing kissy-face in no backseat. She's an advance class of entertainment."

Sad and hurt. Chuckie's mind began to wander to Greenland, his previous posting, not a bad place to survive the breakup of a marriage. His human discontents were muted in the icy mists and the whole blowing otherworld of whiteouts and radio disruptions and unrelenting winds and total cold and objects that did not cast shadows and numerous freak readings on compasses and radar scopes and the BUFF that crashed on

610

an ice sheet with live nukes aboard, anomalies of the eye, the mind, the systems themselves, and the experience made him sense the ghost-spume of some higher hippie consciousness. Or maybe Greenland was just a delicate piece of war-gaming played in a well-heated room in some defense institute, with hazelnut coffee and croissants.

Louis was conversing with the pilot in bombspeak, which must mean it was time for Chuckie to pay attention.

Once divorced, twice expelled from school, once fled from same, many times estranged from parents, thrice charged with petty larceny, once emergency-roomed for barbiturate overdose, once experimentally wrist-slashed, many times avomit on the pavement outside a bar—the shoplifting charges expunged from the record thanks to influential friends of dad.

"Little Richard's mostly for white people anyway," he muttered to Louis.

"But Long Tall Sally's black. Just so you don't forget it."

His late great dad. Not really such a bad guy in death. But so tensely parental in life, all empty command and false authority, that Chuckie suspected the man's heart just wasn't in it. No, he didn't blame his parents for everything that had gone wrong. Chuckie was misery enough on his own recognizance. But he couldn't think of his father without regretting the loss of the one thing he'd wanted to maintain between them. That was the baseball his dad had given him as a trust, a gift, a peace offering, a form of desperate love and a spiritual hand-me-down.

The ball he'd more or less lost. Or his wife had snatched when they split. Or he'd accidentally dumped with the household trash.

One of those distracted events that seemed to mark the inner nature of the age.

Next to him Louis sat in his station with his bomb release mode and his master bomb-control panel and his bombing data indicator and his urinal and his hot cup. Everything you'd want for a fulfilling life in the sky.

Louis said, "Pilot, this is Mad Bomber. Will release in rapid sequence. One hundred twenty seconds to drop."

Bobby Thomson and Ralph Branca meant nothing to Chuckie.

611

Vague names from his unstable childhood. The memory of the base-ball itself, the night of the baseball—vague and unstable and dim.

Louis spoke through a teary-eyed yawn.

"Pilot, come right three degrees. Hold. Bomb doors open. Check. Sixty seconds to drop."

So many missions, all those indistinguishable bombs. Chuckie used to love these bomb runs but not anymore. He used to feel a bitter and sado-sort of grudge pleasure, getting even for his life, taking it out on the landscape and the indigenous population. He'd been a proud part of a bomb wing that was dropping millions of tons of ordnance off the racks and out of the bays. The bombs fluttered down on the NVA and the ARVN alike, because if the troops on both sides pretty much resemble each other and if their acronyms contain pretty much the same letters, you have to bomb both sides to get satisfactory results. The bombs also fell on the Vietcong, the Viet Minh, the French, the Laotians, the Cam-bodians, the Pathet Lao, the Khmer Rouge, the Montagnards, the Hmong, the Maoists, the Taoists, the Buddhists, the monks, the nuns, the rice farmers, the pig farmers, the student protesters and war resisters and flower people, the Chicago 7, the Chicago 8, the Catonsville 9—they were all, pretty much, the enemy.

Louis droned on.

"Steady, steady, steady. On auto now. Tone audible. Ten seconds, nine, eight, seven."

Five hundred pounders on this run, sleek and effete, one hundred and eight of them at Louis' drowsy touch, aimed at the Ho Chi Minh trail, a mission based on the bullshit readings of image interpreters who spend their days and nights scrutinizing the itty-bitty blurs on nearly identical frames of recon film that unfurl endlessly across their eyeballs more or less, Chuckie thought, the way the bombs drop end-lessly from the B-52s.

Louis droned on.

"Six, five, four."

And Chuckie thought of the Ballad of Louis Bakey, a tale the bom-bardier never tired of telling and the navigator never wanted to come to an end because it was like a great Negro spiritual that makes your whole face tingle with reverence and awe.

How Louis comes strutting out of bombardier school and finds himself crewing on a B-52 at twenty-six thousand feet over the Nevada Test Site, simulating the release of a fifty-kiloton nuclear bomb.

Simulating, mind you, while an actual device of this exact magnitude is meanwhile being detonated from the shot tower directly beneath the aircraft.

The idea being, Let's see how the aircraft and crew react, metalwise and bodywise, to the flash, the blast, the shock, the spectacle and so on.

And if they come through it more or less intact, maybe we'll let them drop their own bomb someday.

Whole plane's blacked out. Windows shielded by curtain pads covered with Reynolds Wrap. Crew holding pillows over eyes. Little nylon pillows that smell to Louis intriguingly like a woman's underthings.

A volunteer medic sits in a spare seat with five inches of string hanging out of his mouth and a tea-bag tag at the end of it. He has swallowed the rest of the string, which holds an x-ray plate coated with aluminum jelly, dangling somewhere below the esophagus, to measure the radiation passing through his body.

Louis does his phony countdown and waits for the flash. A strong and immortal young man on a noble mission.

"Three, two, one."

Then the world lights up. A glow enters the body that's like the touch of God. And Louis can see the bones in his hands through his closed eyes, through the thick pillow he's got jammed in his face.

I move my head, there's whole skeletons dancing in the flash. The navigator, the instructor-navigator, the sad-ass gunner. We are dead men flying.

I thought Lord God Jesus. I swear to Jesus I thought this was heaven. Sweat is rolling down my face and there's smoke coming off the circuit breakers and the detonation's blowing us thousands of feet up, against our best intentions.

I thought I was flying right through Judgment Day with some woman's nylon breasts plumped up in my face.

And when the shock wave hit, we got pummeled up another two thousand feet, this big tonnage aircraft acting like a leaf on a blowy night.

And I kept seeing the flying dead through closed eyes, skeleton men with knee bone connected to the thigh bone, I hear the word of the Lord.

And I thought, because, being a black man, I would be harder to see through. But I saw right through my skin to my bones. This flash too bright to make racial niceties.

All the same in God's eyes, so let that be a lesson.

And the medic with the string hanging out of his mouth and his hand on the tea-bag tag so he won't swallow it, and I can see the x-ray plate through skin, bones, ribs and whatnot, and it's glowing like a sunrise on the desert.

When it is safe to withdraw the pillow and open his eyes, Louis opens his eyes and puts down the pillow and makes his way to the cockpit and helps the copilot remove the thermal curtains and there it is, alive and white above them, the mushroom cloud, and it is boiling and talking and crackling like some almighty piss-all vision.

My eyes went big and stayed that way and ain't ever really closed. Because I seen what I seen. That thing so big and wide and high above us. And it was popping and heaving like nothing on this earth. And we flew right past the stem and it's rushing and whooshing and talking, it's pushing the cloud right up into the stratosphere.

Thigh bone connected to the hip bone.

In a few years I lost my handwriting skills. Can't write my name without wobbles and skips. I pee in slow motion now. And my left eye sees things that belong to my right.

And that was the Ballad of Louis Bakey told to a thousand airmen on wind-howling bases through the short days and long years of constant alert in the dark and stoic heart of cold war winters.

"Bombs away," said Louis blandly.

But the mean and cutting fun had gone out of it for Chuckie. He didn't want to kill any more VC. And he was developing a curious concern for the local landscape. Tired of killing the forest, the trees of the forest, the birds that inhabit the trees, the insects that live their whole karmic lives nestled in the wing feathers of the birds.

The aircraft racked into a tight turn.

"Louisman, don't you ever wake up in the middle of the night?"

"Don't start in with me."

614

"Thinking there's got to be a more productive way to spend your time."

"That's what they're thinking down there."

"Than dropping bombs on people who never said a cross word to you."

"Living in tunnels. I'll tell you what they're thinking. They're living in tunnels they dig in the ground and we're in a Big Ugly Fat Fuck pounding the shit out of them. And they're thinking there's got to be a more productive way."

A number of times lately on these routine missions Chuckie has had ejection fantasies. Check the leg guards and ankle restraints and then pull the trigger ring and *boom*. He'd be fired down and out and into the smoky sky. To come floating over Golden Gate Park, in the playful movie version, where a miniskirted blond named Sally raises her head from a copy of Frantz Fanon maybe or Herbert Marcuse, two authors Chuckie has had a tough time finding in the PX at the base, to see a polka-dot parachute dropping toward the treetops.

No, he'd never been a fan but the baseball had been sweet to have around—yes, sweet, beaten, seamed, virile and old, a piece of personal history that meant far more to him than the mobbed chronicles of the game itself.

The aircraft headed back to Guam, which rhymes with bomb, but he was thinking of Greenland now, the shadowless white maw, the tricks of light, vistas without horizons at the end of them. A place that never became more than a rumor, even to those who were based there, most of all to those—the kind of unverified information that resembled his life.

Down out of the sky finally. When they landed he heard the hot screech of the wheels and felt the drag chute pop and hold. He knew the Follow Me truck was out there on the taxiway but he couldn't see it of course, still stuck, for a few minutes longer, in the dimlit hole, surrounded by his acronyms.

Louis said, "I want pussy, Chuckman, and I want it now. But she's got to respect me and what I do."

"And what you stand for."

"What I stand for. Very good, son. I see I'm getting through to you."

The truck said Follow Me and the ground crew was already moving toward the aircraft, dragging hoses, pipes, lines of test gear, the men prepared to go through a checklist the size of eleven lengthy novels on the subject of war and peace.

"Because if she don't respect me," Louis said, "I feel empty when it's over."

"I know the feeling."

"The feeling never changes."

"First we fuck them."

"Then we bomb them," Louis said.

And it wouldn't be long at all before the massive aircraft lumbered down the runway again, fatted with ordnance, every rivet straining at the takeoff, up, out, over—a mortal power in the sky.

7

It was a place you might wander into if you didn't know the neighborhood, a graveyard bar under a bridge approach, and you might mistake the place at a glance for one of those Eighth Avenue bars that never seem to close, the Red Rose or the White Rose or the Blarney Stone, where the pipe fitters and garment workers go, or the railbirds back from the track, or the insomniacs back from nowhere, a sandwich and a beer, or a shot and a beer, but this was another category altogether, a place practically outside time, called Frankie's Tropical Bar, on the Lower East Side, and who do I see when I walk in the door but Jeremiah Sullivan, speaking of graveyards, because he didn't look too good.

"Am I seeing right?"

I said, "Hello, Jerry."

"Nick Shay? Where the hell did you come from?"

I said, "Hello, Jerry. Where are we?"

"I know where I am. Where the hell are you? I hear things every so often. California, Arizona. I saw your mother three, four years ago. It's been what? Fifteen years?"

I said, "I'm in town for a week. Doing a research project for some outfit in the Midwest. What about you?"

"Don't be so calm. Fifteen, almost, fucking years. What are you drinking?"

"What are you drinking?"

"Don't ask," he said.

"That's what I'll have."

He looked around for the bartender but the guy was gone. A man with a bandaged head sat at the far end of the bar trying to bounce a coin into a shot glass. And there were two women on stools not far from where Jerry was standing, a couple of local biddies you might assume, only they weren't cozy or talky or interested in other people's talk—just ancient and wasted regulars of the art.

We traded the pure facts of whereabouts and job and then Jerry supplied elaborate reports on people we'd grown up with, news he'd probably been storing for an occasion such as this, his suit pants sagging under his paunch and his tie knotted halfway down his shirt-front.

"You married, Nick?"

"No."

"You seeing someone special?"

"No. I met a woman recently in Chicago. But no's the answer. I'm not the marrying type. I don't see myself married. I don't feel marriage bound. I don't even think about it."

"In your wildest dreams. Me, I'm married. Two kids. I'd show you pictures but you don't want to see pictures."

The bartender showed up and I got a stinger that overflowed the glass. It was late afternoon, in fading light, and there was a palm tree mural, unfinished, behind the bar, and a live sombrero dangling from a beam. Jerry said this used to be a jazz club that failed almost immediately and after they dropped the music and after the clientele changed he found he kept coming back. He needed an hour between the office and the family to be alone, he said, and think.

He was right. I didn't want to see pictures.

618

"I'm thirty," he said. "When my father was thirty-five he looked like an old man."

"Only to you. You were in first grade. They all looked like old men."

"No, he was old. He was worn down. It's good to see you, Nick. I think about you. I go back there. The place was so crowded once. Now it's empty."

We'd gone to grammar school together, with the nuns, and then Jerry had gone to a Catholic high school and I switched to public and we saw each other only rarely, in a movie lobby maybe buying a Coke, he's with his friends, I'm with mine, and there was a curious sense of separation, not unfriendly but deep, and it was the school difference partly, the veering of habits and practices, but also something irreconcilable, the style, the friends, the future.

"You've been away a hell of a long time. A hell of a long time. Maybe you want to think about coming back," he said.

"Live here? Forget it. No. I like it out there."

"Out there. What's out there?"

"Everything you've never heard of."

"If I never heard of it, how terrific can it be?" he said.

We used to call him Jumpy Jerry because he twitched and squinted and still did, I noticed, wearing glasses now and a school ring.

I didn't tell him about the Jesuits. Too interesting. He'd keep me here for hours. I told him about the project I was working on, to alter traditional methods of school instruction, and how I'd been visiting schools in ghettos and marginal parts of town, here and in Philadelphia, as a free-lance associate in a behavorial research firm in Evanston, Illinois.

"And you teach."

"I've taught, I've taught. And I'll go back to it probably," I said, "sooner or later. Secondary schools. Civics and English. But I want to teach Latin."

This was also too interesting. He should have been royally amused but it was too interesting for that. Jerry had seemed for a time to be priestward bound, that was the word on him, or the Irish Christian Brothers maybe, and it put a look of total dislocation on his face, thinking of the Nicky he used to know and the one he'd hear about later, doing Latin in a classroom.

"You go see your mother?"

"Went up there yesterday," I said.

"She still in 611?"

"Still there."

"I like to go back," he said. "I go eat on Arthur Avenue. I walk all over. I take my kids to the zoo."

"See it now. It's disappearing."

"It used to be so crowded. Or is that just in my mind? The summer nights. Fantastic. It's great to see you, Nick. I'm having one more. Have one more."

I wanted to finish the first one and leave, or not finish it and leave. A chance meeting like this, if you run it five minutes longer than it's worth, you ruin the night and the following day.

He kept adjusting his glasses.

A man alone at a table was moaning a bummed-out monologue that involved being followed wherever he went, and they were recording his private thoughts, and they were sending the seeing-eye blind to spy on him with their dogs and their pencils and their cups, and they were doing this on buses and subways both.

"Jerry, you ought to go home and play with your kids. When you're fifty or sixty, you can come here and think about the past."

But he didn't want to go home. He wanted to recite the destinies of a hundred linked souls, the street swarm that roared in his head. The dead, the married, the moved-to-Jersey, the kid with five sisters who became a safecracker, the handball ace who's a chiropractor, the stuck-up blond in the fifth grade who married a Puerto Rican prizefighter.

"We ought to go up there, Nick. Serious. Take the subway, we'll be there in forty-five minutes. We can get dinner at Mario's. I'll make some calls. Get some of the guys. They'll love it. They'll meet us. Serious, man. Come on, drink, we'll go."

His voice carried an urgent logic. He was defensive and a little angry and about halfway drunk, gripped by the plan and a little angry in advance, wary of the thought that I might not see the beauty and inevitability of a trip to the Bronx, that I might be unswayed by the power of old-times'-sake, and he was already sensing the edges of a bitter affront.

620

"Come on, serious, we'll take the subway. We'll go see Lofaro. Some of the old faces. They'd love to see you, Nick."

I didn't want to put him off, to seem outside this or above it. Jerry knew I'd been in correction and then more or less lost to news and rumor and now here I was turned out in a tweed jacket and doing a job I liked and looking okay, stopped smoking, didn't overdo the drinking, knew a woman with a sexy cello voice and was probably, regularly banging her, and then look at him, nice Catholic boy gone baggy and stale, hates going home, a wife in Jackson Heights and two small kids, and he's lighting one cigarette with the butt of another, and drinks so much he blacks out, and sells commercial time for a radio station at the end of the dial, and all because he's never killed a man.

"This is a thing we have to do," Jerry said. "We'll grab a cab—on me."

A man named Jorge started a conversation with the bartender. Jorge wore a headband and looked sexually deranged. I didn't think of these people as regulars exactly. They were denizens. That was the word somehow, from the Late Latin, deep within, and that's what they were like, trapped souls trying to emerge, and I began to understand that Jerry came here so he could put aside self-pity and the gnaws of practical worry and be with people who would talk to him in a kind of delusional plainsong, a run-on voice without ordinary sense or strict meter but coming from deeper inside than he could bear to hear in his own locution.

The lights dimmed and flickered.

Jerry was talking to me and there was a woman with Jorge who was saying something to the bartender about the optimum temperature of beer and that's when the lights dimmed and flickered and then went out.

Jerry was saying, "Spur of the moment. I'll make some calls. I'll get some guys. I'll get what's-his-name, Allie. This is a thing, my friend, where you don't have the right to refuse."

Then the lights went out.

The man at the far end of the bar stopped trying to bounce quarters into his shot glass.

Someone said, "Is that the lights?"

We sipped our stingers, Jerry and I.

The bartender said, "You know what?"

Someone started talking in the men's room, loud enough for us to hear.

The bartender said, "Looks like from here the whole block's out."

The first voice said, "Is that the lights?"

"They must be working on something that caused a short," the bartender said. "And me without candles."

The voice from the toilet grew louder and agitated.

One of the old women said something to the other, the first words out of either of them.

Jerry and I sipped our stingers.

"But you know what?" the bartender said.

Jorge was speaking Spanish now.

The bartender came up with a flashlight from the bottom of the bar and he wedged it between two bottles on the shelf beneath the mural.

The woman with Jorge was also speaking Spanish, but badly, talking to the man in the toilet.

The bartender went over to the doorway.

"I thought Allie was killed in Korea."

"That was Viggiano. Korea."

"Stepped on a mine, I thought."

"That was Mike. Stepped on a mine. Viggiano."

The two old women were silent again, adjusted to the dark, sitting there drinking.

"So all these years, you're telling me."

"You've been carrying around the wrong war casualty."

"Or the right war but the wrong guy."

"Let's go outside," he said. "I want to see what's happening."

"I don't have to feel sorry for Allie anymore."

"I think the whole block's out. Allie's selling fish at his father's stall in the market. We'll find him. I'll call him."

We took our drinks out to the sidewalk. The block was out and the area was out. It was after five, dark now, and the traffic lights were also out and we could hear the pulse of car horns at the entrance to the bridge above us and to the west.

People were coming out of shops and apartments, the locksmith and grocery and check-cashing place, and they stood around and talked. We could look down a tenement street to the east and see the river, a narrow strip of shimmer that formed a kind of softness, a visual whisper behind the dark bulk contours in the foreground.

"Is Brooklyn out? I think Brooklyn's out."

"Brooklyn's definitely out."

People talked to each other and looked up periodically. They looked toward the midtown sky or tried to look toward the tip of the island, blocked off of course by clustered buildings, but always up, skywatching, and they pointed and talked.

I went back inside and put my drink on the bar. I left some money near the glass. Someone was still in the toilet, agitated in Spanish, saying something about his mother, or someone's mother, and I figured he couldn't find the toilet paper or he couldn't find the bolt on the door and it was a matter the denizens would have to deal with.

Then I stood in the doorway and watched Jerry talking to the bartender and three or four others, twenty yards up the street, and they were lighted intermittently by passing cars and they were animated, they were roused by the vastness of the circumstance, by the forces involved, and they were talking and pointing.

I went down the street in the other direction. After half a block I crossed to the opposite side and walked through an archway under the bridge and into an area filled with household garbage and smashed cars and mounds of rubble dumped by construction crews and at the north end of the passage I could see the silhouetted towers of midtown, exact and flat against the streaked sky, and I heard the sound of car horns building, the dinosaur death of stalled traffic at rush hour, calling and answering everywhere, and I made my way out the other end, where the headlights of barely moving cars, cars stopped dead, where rivers of barium light marked my progress through the streets.

OCTOBER 29, 1962

He was back in New York, the womb of consciousness, a midnight show at Carnegie Hall, nearly three thousand people, and he stood on the enormous stage looking out across the orchestra and up past two tiers of boxes to the gallery levels, where they stood in the aisles and crowded the exits.

Lenny Bruce in concert.

"New York, New York. We say it twice. Once to entice them to leave Kansas. And once more over their grave."

They heaved in their seats.

"New York, New York. Like a priest doing his Latin gig. Mumbo jumbo, mumbo jumbo. He says it twice because he's talking about shit, piss and corruption and he wants to be sure you understand."

His people were here, the A&R guys from the Brill Building, the fellow comics who worked toilets all over Jersey, the actors and would-be actors and actor-waiters and cabdrivers with equity cards. The balding men from the Upper West Side were here, with shaggy sidelocks and intimations of suffering, and the women were with them—frizzy, lippy, opinionated, with full bodies and big rich real faces and a brassy way of laughing.

Lenny wore a white slim-line suit, well-pressed, and a puce pimp shirt with a roll collar, like a man trying to remind himself he is indestructible.

It was midnight in a driving rain but they were all here, musicians and folkies, writers for the high-dome journals, a selection of people with wasted chalk faces and needle lesions under their clothes and there were a fair number of disembodied others just finished smoking some DMT, the quick-acting chemical superhigh devised by NASA to get us to the moon and back whether we want to go or not.

He looked up and down and around.

"What a crazy nerve-wracked morbid week. We're all drained. We were minutes from being fireballed. But now, but now, but now."

He looked past the slender columns into the depths of the third tier and then up at the faces hanging over the balustrade at the top of the house, young people glowing slightly in the overspill from spotlights placed high on the side walls.

"We're not gonna die!"

He did a minstrel dance step, mouth wide, hand high, fingers spread, and stood there laughing a while.

"Yes, they saved us. All the Ivy League men in those striped suits and ribbed black socks that go all the way to the knee so when they cross their legs on TV we don't see a patch of spooky white flesh between the sock and the pants cuff. It's so vulnerable, dig, that strip of pale skin. The legs of powerful men tend to be hairless, which makes them feel secretly weak and effeminate, so they make sure they're wearing high enough socks. Garters are a tricky business for exactly this reason. No, yes, they saved us. They did it. Russians agree to remove missiles and end construction of missile bases in Cuba. Khrushchev is retching in his latkes. He's taking hot baths to relax. Like a plastic pouch of corn coming to a boil."

Lenny's teenage fanatics were here, kids from Brooklyn and Queens who did his bits word for word, memorizing off his albums but more religiously from the rare tapes slyly recorded by traffickers in contraband goods. And Bronx boys who lope along the Grand Concourse to catch every foreign flick at the Ascot, hoping for a glimpse of titty— Lenny was their diamond cutter, their cool doomed master of uncommon truth.

"They saved us in their horn-rimmed glasses and commonsense haircuts. They got their training for the missile crisis at a thousand dinner parties. Where it's at, man. This is the summit of Western civilization. Not the art in the shlocky museums or the books in the libraries where bums off the street infest the men's rooms. Forget all that. Forget the playing fields of Eton. It's the seating plan at dinner. That's where we won. Because they toughed it out. Because they were tested in the cruelest setting of all. Where tremendous forces come into play and crucial events unfold. Dinner parties, dig it, in the Northeast corridor. Your mother used to say, Mix, sweetheart. There was anxiety, a little hidden terror in her voice. Because she knew. Mix or die. And that's why we won. Because these men were named and raised for this moment. Yes, tested at a thousand formative dinners. It started in adolescence. Seated next to adults, total strangers, and forced to make conversation. What a sadistic thing to tell a kid. *Make conversation.* Some could not do it. Some broke down and were sent to forestry school. They smoked roots and leaves and grew facial hair. They developed involved relationships with animals. But others. The others. The others masturbated to marching songs and married their second cousins and grew strong and dominant. You know they're powerful men when their wives play bridge with the curtains drawn. The sunlight gives them migraines. They twist their handkerchiefs when they talk. Remember how your aunt Tovah would sit twisting her hanky. Stand up straight, she'd say. Talk to people, she'd say. Try. For me, sweetheart."

Through the long night, too long, three solid hours nonstop, too long because it has to be too long, they've just survived a crisis and need to be intemperate, and too long because Lenny just can't stop, he looks up from under the proscenium arch and sees the ornamented ceiling and the gilded rows of boxes and he knows this is the temple of Casals and Heifetz and Toscanini and it gives him a mainline jolt, and too long because he's been running on scared fumes all week and he feels revived, alive, ready to wail the night away.

The disc jockeys were here, guys who did late-night jazz in voices of smoky innuendo. Celebrities were spaced through the orchestra, called the Parquet with a capital P. Mixed-race couples were here, displaying a honed nonchalance. People bored with ordinary comedy. People who wanted to be challenged and attacked, who wanted to hear their well-meaning sentiments exposed as so much liberal dinner prattle.

Lenny screwed the mike off the stand and blessed them all.

"Lemme tell you the untold story of the week. The President called the Pope." A stir of anticipation. But it puts him off—he's not in the mood for popes tonight. "Yeah, they were in secret communication all week long. Never mind all that separation of church and state crap. They stick together, these crossbacks." Popes are automatically funny—they don't need Lenny to dignify their shtick. "The Pope's got submarines, you know. Justa say the word, Johnny, I send. We nihilate them sonna ma bitches. Your Holiness, I'm astonished, man. You have your own fleet of subs?"

Lenny lost interest. He swerved into sermons and admonitions, streams of rumination on patriotism, communism, the income tax and women who insert cigarettes in their pussies and blow perfect smoke rings. And when he said something funny or produced an occa-

sional zing of insight, and they applauded, he said, No, don't, please—
lemme fly on my own.

"I've always known. I've known since childhood. I'm as corrupt as
they are. I grew up here. The police are crooked and so am I. The
politicians lie and I lie worse. I wanna kill myself on television so people can go to sleep with the face of a dead sinner on the rim of their
eyeballs."

They saw the lounge lizard with bedroom eyes. They saw and heard
the frisky kid with the adenoidal voice, the boy who wants to make his
mother laugh. They heard the frantic talker who chases after his own
discontinuous ideas. They saw the zonked layabout, all lassitude and
spent attention span. They heard the crusader for dirty words, the
social philosopher, the self-styled lawyer, the self-critical Jew, the
Christian moralizer and the commentator on race.

"I flew in from Miami last night and took a taxi direct to the Apollo
Theater, where I met up with some friends for the late show because I
love that scene, and we came out after the show and I've got a suitcase
and a garment bag and it's late and it's cold and we can't find a cab
because cabs don't go to Harlem and so we start wandering, dig, and
we come across an old man on a corner doing a rap for three people.
He's about a hundred years old and he's preaching to three sorry souls
and it's like Hyde Park Corner only in blackface."

Lenny did a fair approximation of a street preacher's voice, which
was surprising, which was very unhip in fact because even if he'd
started in the business as a mimic, doing Cagney and Bogart with German accents, and even if he updated frequently, doing contemporary
types of every persuasion, it was not a white comic's option these days
to do a black man's voice, was it?

"The old man holds a dollar bill by its edges. It's older than he is.
He peers over the top and says, Legal tender. He says, Which is a
name, I have to admit, I would not think to call it myself. He says, We
all seen the machines print the money in the newsreels nonstop like
bottles of pop getting capped, only lightning fast, and they print, they
print, they print, but where's it all go is my question. I ain't seen any.
You seen any?"

Lenny did the voice, standing slightly hunched beneath the vast draped curtain in his white Italianate suit and campy black boots, the ones with little fruity loops in back.

"He says, Nobody knows the day or the hour. He's standing there in a dark shrunken suit with bicycle clips around the ankles. Understand me when I say I wanted to give him everything I own. Not out of pity or charity or some vintage Christian shit. Out of appreciation. Out of gratitude for the sight and sound of him at that hour and in that place. Because this is New York, New York and we say it twice because it's half Us and half Them, all hours, dig it, in bicycle clips. The man's an actor and this is his gig that he's perfected over decades and I stand there listening and in some funny way I hear myself, all right, or I see myself— I imagine myself at the age of ten or twelve listening to a voice like this old man's. It's his voice and his week. The day and the hour. And he holds the dollar bill. When the hour comes, he says, the world be separated into those that can read the message and those that can't."

A long pause. A hush in the hall. Lenny seemed half lost in reverie, in conjure, and maybe people began to feel uncomfortable because he could not seem to stop doing the voice. It was as if the voice had been crossed with his own. It was as if cross-voices were unavoidable, whether you knew it or not, whether you liked it or not, and maybe this old black man spoke in Lenny's voice at times, alone, unknowing, in his room, on some level, hearing the bandy scales in his head, the push and shove of Lenny's own fluted music, and Lenny did the old man's, spoke in the old man's, unavoidably.

"Then he looked at us, over on the side where we're standing. We're a black guy, a white guy and two white women, except one of the women has been in the street all this time looking for a cab. He looked at us briefly. Took brief notice. Seemed to know us in this brief look. Then he turned back to the original audience, these three lost people of the streets, these wastelings of the lost world, the lost country that exists right here in America. And he resumed his rap and they stood there listening."

Lenny did the voice a little longer and when he finished he had to pause again to return to the stage, the hall and the audience.

"I wanted to give him my garment bag full of suits, my suitcase full of drugs, my house in the Hollywood Hills. We listened only eight, nine minutes. Less. A cab pulled up and we left and I won't go back because—I don't know why, I just won't. Bugged out by the whole scene. His life, his rap. I ought to tell Polish lightbulb jokes."

A laugh, finally.

"I ought to stand here doing Chinese waiter jokes."

He did a Chinese waiter joke. Got a big laugh. He went through a medley of movie bits and they loved it. He did routines he used to do when he wore a polo coat, suede shoes and a muffdiver's tickly mustache. They laughed, he moped. He did the old bits with suitable stinging irony but this only made them funnier and got him more depressed. They laughed, he bled. Lenny felt awful. He was supposed to be happy and revitalized but he wasn't. They'd all survived a hellish week and he'd gone dragging through four club dates coast to coast in a state of graduated disarray and now it was over and he was safe and he was appearing in concert and he should have been standing here chanting *We're not gonna die We're not gonna die We're not gonna die*, leading them in a chant, a mantra that was joyful and mock joyful at the same time because this is New York, New York and we want it both ways.

When he thought they were gonna die, he'd chanted the die line repeatedly.

But that was over now. He'd forgotten all that. There were other, deeper, vaguer matters. Everything, nothing, him.

"I came here tonight to be loved like no one was ever loved. Love me like you've never loved anyone before. Come rain or come shine."

There was an unguarded plea in Lenny's eyes.

"Parent, child or lover. I want to be washed in rivers of love."

Return to seat Return to seat Return to seat.

The old material was making him feel bad. And the laughs were worse than the jokes. The laughs dashed and disheartened him. He switched more or less in midsentence to a bit he'd been thinking about before all this missile shit, sitting on the can in L.A. because that's where his best ideas tended to drift into range.

In fact he'd made a casual reference to the subject earlier in the evening. Got a response that seemed to indicate they were interested and unnerved.

He decided to develop the bit on the spot.

Okay. An illiterate sad-eyed virgin lives in a whorehouse in a slum district of San Juan. She has a special talent that has nothing to do with sex per se. It's a kind of parlor trick, okay. Men pay half a week's wages to crowd into a bare room in the basement where the girl, smooth-skinned and innocent, lifts her dress, drops her panties, takes a lit cigarette from the madam and inserts it filter-first in her snatch. The men go wide-eyed. It's a king-size Kent with a micronite filter. Then she contracts her labial muscles, or whatever, and sort of inhales vaginally, and removes the cigarette, and proceeds to blow a series of gorgeous smoke rings. A gasp from the men. Perfect round rings wafting up from her fleecy bush, still somewhat fine and sparse.

Lenny's audience didn't exactly gasp, as the men in the whorehouse had, but there was a certain disquiet in the hall, underscored by a smatter of nervous laughter.

Some people interpret the girl's gift in a religious manner. They think it's an omen, a sign from heaven that the world is about to end. God has selected a poor illiterate undernourished orphan girl to convey a profound message to the world. Because isn't it possible that all these O's coming out of her womb refer to the Greek letter that means The End? Others say, journalists, scientists, priests—these men have come to the bordello to witness the event and they say the rings she is blowing are not representations of the Greek letter omega. They're just ordinary alphabet-soup O's, however beautifully formed. These people say that when the girl is able to blow actual Greek omegas, with the horseshoe effect, dig, the little dipsy-doo at each end of the opening, then they'll start believing in miracles.

This is Lenny Bruce material. This is what they came for, isn't it? Who else does this material? If it's disgusting, so much the better. If it's insulting to you as an individual, get up and leave and take your crossword-puzzle husband with you.

So a rich American widower shows up one night, slumming with friends, and the girl stares proudly, *con dignidad*, right into his face. Then she inserts the tip of the filter in her snatch and blows a ring inside another ring and then a third tiny ring inside that. The millionaire is shocked at the tawdry spectacle but also secretly intrigued and he finds himself going back there night after night, alone, and it isn't long before he falls in love with the girl, yes, her limpid eyes and dimpled knees and her sweet and fleecy pubes. He resolves to save her from this squalid life and more or less buys her from the madam for an enormous sum of money and takes her to his hilltop mansion overlooking the Hudson River, where he brings in teams of doctors, tutors, psychologists and nutritionists and where he watches the girl develop intellectually and grow into a healthy young woman who speaks four languages and shows a talent for the oboe.

Lenny paused here, pointing out that the end, the punch line, would have to involve some reversion to type, something the girl does that demonstrates the power of a single old and shocking habit over any number of civilizing influences.

Then he said, "No, yes, wait. We've got it backwards. It's not the girl who reverts. It's the man. Dig it. He's the kind of cat who questions everything he does. Begins to ask himself. Was she a twisted child or an artist? Was she jailbait or saint? In other words did he make a terrible mistake bringing her here and educating her and banning cigarettes from her life? He begins to recall those delirious nights in San Juan." Lenny gave the name of the city an authentic guttural rumble. "Yes, those nights in the basement of the stinking bordello where she performed. Admit it, fool. You've destroyed a strange, crude, beautiful and eerie perversion and replaced it with a boring oboe. Which she plays incessantly by the way. And which is anyway just a displaced version of the king-size Kent, normalized and concertized."

Lenny stood sideways, mike in hand, stroking his jaw.

"He longs to see smoke rings come out of her puss, her nook. First the cigarette between her spindly legs. Then the rising rings. When he bought her from the madam, she was on the verge of intertwining the rings, which is either a symbol of the Blessed Trinity, Father, Son and Holy Ghost, or it's the Ballantine beer logo—Purity, Body and Flavor. Either way, imagine the rush he would have gotten."

He looked into the wings, thinking.

"They marry in a smoke-free ceremony on the rolling lawn. On their wedding night, still a virgin, she stands in a negligee by the window facing west. He enters, in pajamas and smoking jacket, holding a cigarette in a cigarette holder, an unlit king-size Kent."

But he wasn't sure how to end it.

"He takes the cigarette out of the holder and extends it in her direction, glancing at the shadowy mound under her negligee. She steps back, horrified. She says, You must be mad. She says it in four languages. She says almost everything in four languages, a habit that's beginning to piss him off."

Then Lenny got a better idea, deeper, more challenging.

"Wait, listen, no. The millionaire is a myth, isn't he? We stuck him in the story because we needed a rich weak do-gooder, what, a respectable self-deluding jerk who shows his corruption in the end. We made him up. Let's tell the truth this time."

He sensed a disappointment out there. They wanted the wedding night, the negligee, the boudoir, the casually cruel ending like the bit he used to do about the boy raised by wolves, found in the wild, fed, developed, educated, who graduates with honors from MIT and is killed a week later chasing a car down the street.

"Let's tell the truth," he said. "Nobody saved the girl from a life of perversion. She fled the whorehouse on her own initiative. She saved all the meager cash handouts the customers had been giving her and she took a plane to New York, the roach coach, in order to find her mother, who wasn't dead at all—another easy myth."

Shit, he was ruining their fun. He could feel the cooling all the way up to the cheap seats, where his teenage fans craved a final grossness, draped over the rails—some epic sicko finish.

"She never worked in a whorehouse at all," Lenny said. "She never dropped her drawers or blew smoke rings from her pussy. Fact of the matter, she never lived in San Juan, baby."

He loved to say San Juan. And yes, he was disassembling the whole structure. He felt their puzzlement and couldn't blame them.

"Let's make her human. She's real like us. You take the subway to the South Bronx, where she lives with her junkie mother who can't kick. She's just barely old enough so that men are beginning to notice. Her mother comes and goes. Disappears, comes back. Phone company shuts off the phone. Landlord's been coming around. Or putting dispossesses under the door because you never actually see him. He's a corporation called XYZ Realty with a post office box in Greenland.

The girl's hiding in the empty lots, down the maze of back alleys, because her mother's gone again and she thinks the landlord will have her arrested. Let's make her human. Let's give her a name."

But he didn't give her a name. He couldn't think of a name. Not a real name. He went back to old jokes instead. He told a mother-in-law joke and they laughed because in fact it was funny. He told a Jewish mother joke, even better, and they loved it, they laughed, and he worked his way back to form, doing race, sex, religion, and it was funny and offensive Lenny and the night ended finally in booming waves of laughter and applause, in spirited shouts from the kids in the top tiers, and he stood on the great stage in his stupid white suit, small and remorseful, and then he turned and walked toward the wings.

NOVEMBER 9, 1965

Hours later I was still walking. I walked right past my hotel and kept on going, a nondescript building near Times Square, where they'd give me a candle and show me the door that led to the stairwell, but I wanted to keep on walking, and where I'd only have to climb five flights, but I wanted to walk into the night and see this thing.

I saw taxis with off-duty signs lit up but people took them anyway, just opened the doors and got in because the cabs were captive to the traffic and could not shy off and speed away and I raised the collar of my jacket and walked east a while and went past a huge crowd near the main library and finally realized it was a bus stop, six or seven hundred people at a bus stop, easily that many, massed and more or less orderly, packed along the sidewalk and up on the library steps, and the wind whipping down Fifth, and they were waiting for a bus.

I didn't have a coat. My coat was in Evanston, Illinois. I hunched in my jacket and saw people walking across the Queensboro Bridge and they were taking over the bridge, they were walking eight or nine abreast, maybe fifty deep, followed by a sequence of crawling cars, then another band of pedestrians, and they were walking home to Queens.

That's when I got the idea and felt the twinge of regret.

I stopped for dinner in a candlelit restaurant in the 70s, where they seated me with three others because it was shared tables tonight. There was only one subject, of course, at least for a while, and we wondered how widespread the blackout might be, and whether it was sabotage, and someone said, a book editor with a bow tie, that this was the title of an early Hitchcock film, with Sylvia Sidney, and he named the rest of the cast compulsively—a film that starts with the lights going out. We skipped dessert and coffee for the sake of those waiting on line and I had a drink in a bar nearby and thought Jerry was right, Jerry Sullivan, this was the twinge, the pinch of guilt—we ought to be going to the Bronx tonight, Jerry and I, not trying to commandeer a taxi but walking all the way, something crazy and emotional, a trek through a city gone dark and cold.

But then I thought stupid, no, forget it—we'd lose interest on the way or get in a fight with looters and muggers or just get tired, or Jerry would, and what happens after that?

A man directed traffic with a rolled-up magazine, a man of some girth but quick on his feet, dipping and gliding, addressing the major mess at 86th Street, a man who shrugged off beeping horns and did a hundred semaphores, extravagant of gesture, in a topcoat with a velvet collar, his glossy baton flashing and people pausing to watch, and there was a great and fervent feeling that attended his performance, which was conscientious and deft however befrilled by theater, and it spread among the people in the street.

But it would have been tremendous somehow too, a beautiful thing, I thought, walking up Manhattan and into the Bronx, as a gesture, a remembrance, and all the way to the old neighborhood, tonight of all nights, with the world coming down, but what would we do when we got there, at two in the morning?

People walked along listening to transistor radios because there were stations with auxiliary power and there were men wrapped in headscarves who sold flashlights and candles and there were candles in thousands of apartment windows and people on line for candles outside the five-and-ten and long lines at phone booths on every second corner.

The power grid gone. What did it mean? The whole linked system down. Or not linked sufficiently perhaps. Sylvia Sidney in the dark.

From certain vantages the city was all haunted silhouette, secret and recessed, its neon ego shut down. There was a sky tonight. The towers across the park were planed down to a kind of night velvet that was etched and deathly and lacking the static that makes the high nights throb.

I heard the sound of drums, drumbeats, not staccato shots but hand drums maybe, dull and soft-skinned, coming out of the park.

I was a stranger here. I knew Manhattan only at street level, fitfully, and felt a little isolated, and the place scared me with its knowingness, its offhand vaunt, a style of mind and guise that can be harder to learn than some dialect of the Transvaal. Everybody knew the same seven things. But it could take you years to work through the list and by that time the number would be different, or the whole list.

They came out of the park at 90th Street, a band of hippies on a candlelight march, with flutes, drums and tambourines, about fifty chanting people, and a man with a needle stuck in his protruding tongue, and a woman with a snake around her neck, and a haze of pungent smoke that had the whiff of some congenial misdemeanor, and there were kids walking along and babies in backpacks and slings, and the marchers chanted a sort of hummed syllable, a thing with a twang, it sounded to me like *Bomb*, a vibe with the gravid tone of prayer, repeated, repeated, but they wouldn't be chanting an ominous word, would they, with infants strapped to their chests and backs.

And maybe Jerry had been correct. I didn't have the right to refuse him. This tremendous thing of his, this trip to the Bronx—I felt guilty about slipping away and betraying a sweet idea.

I watched the marchers go south along the park edge. The streets began to darken, drained of traffic and headlights, and an odd calm set in, edged with apprehension. How many thousands, hundreds of thousands trapped in subways or aloft in packed elevators waiting. The always seeping suspicion, paralysis, the thing implicit in the push-button city, that it will stop cold, leaving us helpless in the rat-eye dark, and then we begin to wonder, as I did, how the whole thing works anyway.

I walked east on 96th Street. Going empty and dead, stores closed, bus stops deserted, phone booths unoccupied. Ego gone and vertigo too, a city without its merengue spin, and a car pulled up at the center stripe, anonymous sedan going the other way, and the driver stuck his head into the gusty wind and called across to me.

I said, "What?"

"Where you go? I take you. Cheap."

I looked at him. I was glad I'd walked away from Jerry. It would have been deadly. It would have been crap. I wouldn't have been able to listen to that crap. I got in the car and told the guy where my hotel was. I wanted to call Marian from my room, if the phones were working, Marian Bowman, and tell her what was happening here and ask what they knew about it there.

There was a hole in the dashboard where the radio should have been located. But I asked the guy if he'd heard any news.

"All out. State of Maine out. Boston, Massachusetts. Pennsylvania, my sister lives. Ontario, Canada. Very big, this thing."

I sat back and watched the streets roll by and saw what I could see in the moonlight.

We'd be married three years later. Our daughter would be born in 1970, the year a small group of radicals bombed the Army Math Research Center at the University of Wisconsin in Marian's Big Ten town by igniting a carload of agricultural fertilizer and fuel oil. Killed one man, injured five others.

We'd have a son two years later. Children. This was remote to me sitting in the Romanian's car, or the Greek's. Marriage remote. Fatherhood a vague regret somewhere in the kitchen smell of another country. The decades not exactly unpromising but remote, and maybe unpromising too, in this phantom Manhattan, with only a few stragglers astir and the darkness so dense it had physical mass.

I looked out the Greek's dusty window and could see the past and never stop seeing it but could not summon the future, even in cartoon strokes, the strong bright Sunday of the world.

We rode without talking the rest of the way.

And the enormity of the night. You could feel the night expanding, standing on the sidewalk near Times Square, a siren sounding half a mile away.

I looked at the candles lined up on the desk in the lobby. The lobby was empty and the candles threw light high on the walls. The clerk came out of a room somewhere.

"I could take you up but frankly."

"Not necessary."

"I took up people I lost count."

"I'll just take a candle."

The clerk held a flashlight. He gestured when he spoke and the beam swung across the small lobby.

"I did something to my back with the climbing," he said. "But I lit these candles you can take, in case some people come in they don't have a match."

I took a candle and climbed the stairs to the fifth floor. When I entered the room I went right to the window to see how the night looked from up here.

I didn't call Marian. I felt a loneliness, for lack of a better word, but that's the word in fact, a thing I tried never to admit to and knew how to step outside of, but sometimes even this was not means enough, and I didn't call her because I would not give in, watching the night come down.

MANX MARTIN 3

He walks along the curving base of the stadium wall, under the blue and white bunting, and he is trying to spot an easy mark.

He is in the crowd, a large and moving swarm, elbows and shoulders, faces suddenly jutting, eye to eye, and they're still coming down from the elevated train station, men and boys, talking and whooping, and the line is forming for bleacher seats even though the gates won't open until nine in the morning, hours from now, and they're coming up from the subway and streaming out of the local streets and he walks some more, caught up in the rush of sensation, flags flying and emblems bejeweling the high wall and a second long line, this one for standing room tickets, men eating and drinking, some sitting in beach chairs covered with blankets, and Manx goes walking through clouds of cigar smoke and sees whiskey flasks showing here and there, with caps on chains.

Now what does he do? Does he look for some highjiver from Harlem, a Giant fan all flush with victory and ready to drop some dollars on a genuine all-time souvenir?

Won't work, Manx thinks. Black man's not gonna believe anything he says. Think I'm some fool running a penny hustle. Black man's gonna look him down with that saucy eye he's got for outrageous plots against his person.

No. Got to go white. Only way to go. Besides, the numbers mostly white, so it's the percentage play.

A happy rumble. The street is one big buzz and rumble, a steady roar of talk and song and people calling to each other, filled with good feeling.

Manx walks over to two men. He does this on an impulse, in the spirit of why not, and because he doesn't want to stand around all night studying faces and calculating odds, even though that's exactly what he ought to be doing, and he knows it, and he'd planned to do it, but the best-laid plans, like the man says, have a habit of collapse.

His hand grips the baseball. He keeps his hand outside the jacket pocket and he grips the ball through the cloth.

And in the spirit of good feeling. In the swelling presence of two groups of fans, Giants and Yankees, both winners this year—a happy steady join-in roar that brings him up and gives him heart.

He walks over to two men standing on line in front of one of the booths. Excuse me. Something here you might be interested in. He talks to them. He tells them about the baseball, this is the baseball that the guy hit into the stands, the home run that won the game, and the longer he talks the more unbelievable he sounds to himself. He can't even believe this is him talking. His voice sounds like something released from an air mattress when you pull out the nipple.

The two men seem to step back although it's probably not actual physical motion so much as a wishful maneuver he sees in their eyes.

"I'm talking what is a fact. Whatever it sounds," he says, "this is the thing that happened at the ballpark across the river," and he knows he is working now at restoring a certain self-respect—never mind making a sale.

One guy says, "I don't think so, no. Not interested. You interested?"

Other guy says, "Not interested."

Manx takes the ball out of his pocket. He's not sure why he's doing this since it proves nothing except the fact that he has a ball, at least he has a ball, and he holds it much the way his son Cotter had held it earlier in the evening, gripping it in one hand, spinning it with the other, hard-eyed and defiant.

Then he turns and walks away, feeling their looks, seeing smirks so clear he could draw them with a pencil, and going small, bristling a little at the back of the neck, and going smaller with every step.

He walks a little ways.

He always thought he'd like to get himself a flask, flat enough to pocket conveniently, with a cap on a chain.

He puts the ball back in his pocket and walks out past the wooden barricades near gate 4.

You got these guys come out here think they own the earth.

He remembers he's supposed to write a letter excusing his son from school because he's got a fever of a hundred and two, which is a secret they are keeping from the boy's mother. Not the fever but the letter. The fever is a made-up deal.

He stands and watches a while. Then he gets an idea. He watches, thinking there's crowds of people and I'm holding something every last one of them would like to own, but who's gonna believe a story that comes out of nowhere. Then he realizes what he ought to be doing. He gets an idea. He gets it from the crowd. He ought to be looking for fathers and sons.

Get the man to do it for the boy.

Appeal to the man's whatever, his rank as a father, his soft spot, his willingness to show off a little, impress the boy, make the night extra special.

And yes there are men who have brought their sons here tonight, as an adventure, you know, a fair number of sons on the scene, as a thing you want the boy to experience, staying up all night to buy World Series tickets.

See, even if the man doesn't believe it, the boy will. And Manx can imagine a little conspiracy in the making, the father and the hustler working as a team to make the boy believe the baseball's real.

It takes these turns of mind to work a deal.

He begins to prowl the lines, to scout the prospects standing on line along the high wall, he checks out faces and attitudes, he doesn't want to rush, he follows the wall in a westerly direction and sees what he thinks he might be looking for, finally, the kid's maybe eleven, the man's pulling a sandwich from a gym bag and they're standing there in total innocence of his approach.

He does his intro, which he takes to be the toughest part, making the details clear, and he looks from man to boy and back, trying to get them both involved, and it seems to be going well, and the man tears the sandwich and gives half to the kid, and they look at Manx and eat.

They are listening and chewing and he tries to read their looks. He is stymied, though, by the names involved, the players at the climax, he doesn't know their names, faces, numbers, all the things the fans know from childhood to the day they die, and this slows his narrative and muddies it up and he tries to compensate by taking out the baseball.

Now the man is talking, through a mouthful of food.

"So what you're saying is. You're telling me. In other words."

White meat and lettuce are showing behind his teeth.

"That's right. You got it," Manx says, hearing himself adopt a high pitch that's meant to be cheerful and optimistic.

But the man's not looking at the baseball. He's looking at Manx.

"And I'm supposed to stand here."

Manx begins to understand, close range, that this guy's a bus driver or sewer worker or bricklayer.

"And listen to this bullcrap."

The man is chewing and talking.

"I think you better haul ass out of here, buddy, before I call a cop."

Manx puts the ball back in his pocket.

"They put son of a bitches like you behind bars is where you belong."

Talking like that in front of his own kid.

The kid is hungry, he's going through the lettuce like a lawn mower.

They're standing there eating, both of them, looking at Manx, and the son resembles the father to such a degree, stocky and full-faced, that Manx wants to warn him against growing up.

Think they own the earth.

It takes him an hour, scouting the lines, doing three circuits of the stadium, talking to this and that person, getting a feel for the individ-

644

ual, seeing how it goes, and it's not going well, giving himself another five minutes by the clock on the wall at the southwest end, and then five more minutes, telling himself if he doesn't spot someone in five minutes, with a wholesome kid in tow, he will give up and go home, and then one more minute, and then one more, prowling the lines, making approaches that don't pan out, and about an hour later he is talking to a man and his son who are squatted down outside the bleacher section near the end of a very long line, camped out with a sleeping bag for the kid and a duffle coat for the man, and Manx is working his way into the names.

"Which I'm saying, in all honesty."

"Wait a minute. You're saying this baseball you claim to have in your possession."

"Right right right. But I don't know the player's name, y'understand, which I'm being honest with you."

"You mean Bobby Thomson?"

"That's the one. All right. I feel better now."

See, Manx believes he can be straight-up with this man. Expose his own shortcomings. He's not a fan and shouldn't pretend to be. And at the same time, only deeper, he thinks this is a strategy that can work, it's a scheme, a plot—show the man your weakness and he will swallow your story whole.

"I'm of the attitude where if you're doing a little business, you put all your cards on the table. And I'll tell you what I think. That tomorrow a wholesale rabble show themselves at the clubhouse entrance. Carrying a baseball, every one of them, and saying I got the ace."

"When in fact, according to your claim," the man says.

"When in fact the ace is in the hole," Manx says, and he reaches into his pocket and takes out the ball.

The man smiles. The man is on his haunches against the wall and Manx is in a squat himself, holding the ball slightly atremble for comic effect, staring hard at the man, showing the man a fake intensity, which they both know is fake, just for effect, and the man holds out his hand for the ball, amused but skeptical, meaning in other words that he'll play along for now.

But Manx doesn't give him the ball.

The boy is sitting up in the sleeping bag, trying to stay awake.

"Now see this tar spot," Manx says. And he shows the man and he shows the boy. "I think I ought to rub it off, being it has no business here."

And he wets his thumb with a flourish and tries to remove a scant trace of tar, because Cotter must have bounced the ball in the street, but he only succeeds in smudging the area and has to wonder why he is doctoring the ball at all.

"By the way," the fellow says, maybe to distract Manx from his embarrassment. "My name's Charlie."

"You call me Manx. And the boy. What's your name, son?"

"Tell him."

"No," the kid says.

"We got us a rascal here," Manx says. "How old's this rascally son of a gun?"

"Eight," the man says.

"Eight. Imagine being eight. Imagine going to the first game of the World Series and seeing all these famous players. Something he'll remember for the rest of his life."

"His name's Chuckie."

Manx looks at Chuckie. Kid rather be home sleeping in a soft warm bed with dog drawings on the wall. That's okay. What we're talking about here is not the present but the future. Pop's looking to build a memory for the boy.

"Being eight. Yankee Stadium. The most famous ballpark in the country."

Manx puts the ball in the man's hand.

"But if a dozen people show up with baseballs at the clubhouse entrance," Charlie says, "how do I convince anyone? How do I convince myself this is the Bobby Thomson ball? Or anyone else?"

Manx is in his crapshooter's squat.

"Let me put it this way," he says, and he does not shy from the question because he's been waiting for it ever since he walked across the bridge from Harlem. "Do they believe you or me? Who do they believe? Put yourself in their place, friends of yours, people in the office. Then look at me and look at you. Who they gonna believe?"

Manx knows the logic in this argument is about six times removed from the question of the ball's actual history. But he thinks he can count on this fellow to see the underlying subject, the turn of mind.

"And I can believe it, personally, myself," he says, "because my own boy give me the goods on this baseball. And no way on earth he's gonna lie to the old man about a thing like this. He lie all right. Lie about school. Miss school, tell a lie. Miss a visit to the dentist."

"But this is baseball," Charlie says helpfully.

"Exactly right. But I have to admit I wasn't convinced at first. Like you. Like anyone. I was first gave over to doubt. But then I heard the boy."

"And you felt you knew."

"I felt exactly. I knew. Because I heard it in his voice."

"And saw it as well."

"Saw it right there. Wouldn't lie about this. Good boy when it counts."

"And baseball. This counts."

Manx takes heart from the man's cooperation because he doesn't want to suffer another bringdown. But at the same time he doesn't want to think of Charlie as a sucker, a rube in a duffle coat, falling for an easy line. The line is true in this case but what's the difference? Manx has told amazing lies that were a lot easier falling from his lips than anything he could say about this little spheroid fact.

The man is studying the ball.

Manx decides to shut his mouth for fifteen seconds. Let the occasion take a solemn turn. Give the customer a chance to fall in love with the product.

"Well, I see there's a green, a little sort of green paint smudge near the seam here, between the seam and the trademark," Charlie says, "and I know for a fact because someone said so on the radio that the ball struck a pillar when it went in the stands. And the pillars are green, I also know for a fact, at the Polo Grounds."

Manx does a little squat-jump. He is elated to hear this. It's as though he himself has to be convinced, as though the man's remark is the confirmation he needs to see Cotter as an honest boy, transformed from a back-talking kid who jumps turnstiles into an honest upright dutiful boy, at last.

647

The man raises his eyes from the ball and looks at Manx. It's a look that says, I want to believe. And Manx can't think of a thing to say, for the life of him, the actual life, that would bring the man across the line and clinch the deal completely.

Charlie takes up the task himself, says some fairly convincing things, this time to his son, about the company that makes the ball and the name of the league president that's stamped on the ball and other matters and details, all of them checking out okay, it seems, and the boy is sleepy and cold and unimpressed and Manx looks around for a vendor with hot chocolate because it never hurts to be considerate.

"Vendors scarce tonight."

"He had some soup."

"I was a vendor I be out here in force. Put the wife and kids to work."

"He had hot soup in a thermos. He's all right."

But Chuckie says, "I don't think I'm so all right."

"Just stay awake. I want you awake for this."

Manx understands this is for his benefit more than the kid's. The man and the kid just going through the motions. Kid's not even doing that. Kid stopped listening to the man somewhere around the diaper stage.

Chuckie slithers into the bag with that mutinous look kids get once they understand they're not property.

"I want you to remember everything that happens here tonight," Charlie says.

But the boy is already down under, even his head vanished in the flannel.

"You're a father, you must know," Charlie says.

"I wrote the book."

"What a danger-laden thing it is, in all respects, trying to raise a child."

"Take forever to grow up on the one hand. But it goes so fast on the other."

"I've only got the one."

"You're looking at four."

"Four," Charlie says, and in his look there is admiration, sympathy

648

and some wonder as well, and something else Manx can't quite identify—maybe just the sense of different lives, a thing that has nothing directly to do with the number of kids.

There's a fire going in an oil drum and Manx goes to the curb, grabs the rusty can and drags it over to the line of waiting fans, fire and all. He feels the metal burn his hand as an afterthought, burn like hell in a picture book, but the fans are impressed by the gesture, big smiles abounding, it is the kind of thing that rightly marks a night like this, and Charlie seems delighted.

But not just different lives. Completely other ways of thinking and doing. And Manx isn't sure if they're supposed to be sad about this. He's ready to do whatever's called for.

"What kind of seats you expecting you get?"

"Bleachers. Love to get reserved seats but they're long gone. Everything's gone but bleachers and standing room and I know Chuckie'll never forgive me if I force him to watch a ball game standing up."

"After he spends a night sleeping on the sidewalk? Who can blame him?"

Charlie smiles again, throwing a wayward slap at Manx's kneecap. Then he hands Manx the ball but only because he's reaching into his coat for something. Turns out to be a flask, sweet little silvery thing with a cap on a chain like those army canteens, only flat, small, expensive, that you can pocket easy, a pick-me-up on a down day.

"Now what have we here?" says Manx.

"Give you one guess."

"Could say orange juice."

"Too soon for breakfast."

"Could say spicy tea from old India."

"Too late for teatime," Charlie says.

They're having a pretty good time, the one on his haunches against the wall, the other in his crapshooter's squat, with the lump in the flannel bag gone totally still, either pouty-stiff or sleep-stiff.

Charlie says, "Do the honors," and he hands the flask to Manx, who tosses the ball back to Charlie, and this small blurry exchange has an odd depth, it's a sign of some kind, a deal that's completely outside the transaction in progress, and it brings Manx up a little higher.

He unscrews the cap and lets it dangle and he takes a connoisseur's sniff of the action in the jug.

"Do believe this is what they call spirits."

"Irish whiskey," Charlie says.

"Do love the Irish, don't we?"

"Many lasting contributions," Charlie says.

"Well said, my man."

They share a complicit grin. And Manx raises the flask and tilts his head and knocks back a not too sizable shot, for courtesy sake, and gives the thing back to Charles.

He calls him Charles now, for the social aspect, gentlemen drinkers at the club.

And he waits for Charles to drink. A moment of stinging truth. Manx has put his mouth to the rim of the flask and now he waits for Charles to do the same.

A brief, deep and knowledgeable suspense.

Doesn't even wipe off the rim. Just tips the flask and drinks, too deep, and comes up teary-eyed and gasping but happy too. Both men happy, having a princely time.

"Went down the wrong pipe," says Charlie, forcing out the words.

"Happens to the best."

"Occupational hazard," says the gasping man.

Hands over the flask. Manx takes a klondike swig and keenly feels the effect, oh yes, as the Irish aerates a number of crucial passages in his head and chest.

They pass the flask a while.

"One of mine's a girl," Manx says. "Rosie. Best ever daughter you could find."

"How old?"

"How old," he says.

He feels a drifty look come into his eyes.

"Maybe twice yours. Yours eight, right? Imagine being eight."

They pass the flask.

"I'll be honest," Charlie says. "You were honest with me. Least I can do is tell you what I'm thinking."

All up and down the line there are people crouched in sleep or in drowsy bundled waiting, out of conversation now, heads slumped, some cigarettes going, most people asleep in blankets or thick parkas or just nodding off, squinch-eyed, and a cough and a moan and a radio playing Latin music but not too loud, and shaking awake and nodding off and a cop on a horse over by the barricade, and Manx shifts position slightly to observe the stillness of the tall brown animal, a dead-still quality that is not like men when they are motionless, or dogs for that matter, or fish in a bowl, and not peaceful or unperturbed but immobile in its own way, great and strong, shining at the flanks.

"I'll be honest," Charlie says, "because what's the point of all this if we're not honest?"

"Go, man."

"I don't know if you're telling me the truth. But the ball looks like a ball they'd be using in a National League game in the year 1951. That's one mark in your favor, relatively minor, because there's balls and there's balls."

"And there's ball breakers."

They pass the flask.

"And the other mark is, the major mark, I look at you and I don't think I see a con man or a liar."

A brief pause.

"Then you the first," Manx says.

They laugh and stop and laugh again. It's one of those jokes that reverberates for ten or twenty seconds, bouncing around the premises, one meaning echoing into another, and it's only a matter now of signing on the line.

"How much?" says Charlie.

Manx looks away. He hasn't come this far in his tactics and plans and he doesn't know how much. But he feels himself get tense. The horse makes a snuffling sound behind him.

"It's entirely up to yourself," he says, and feels immediately, unspecifically cheated.

Charlie holds the ball in both hands now, pressed up under his chin.

"See, I don't know what I'm buying," he says. "This is a consideration we have to keep in mind. Sure, buyer beware and all that. But we're talking about an object that belongs properly to the heart."

You don't want to squeeze the eagle on me, do you, boss?

"Entirely up to yourself. Because I trust you to do right. You know your baseball. A fan. I want a fan to own this thing," Manx says.

He feels his gaze sliding away, drifting inward, and notes a certain tightness in his chest.

Charles. Charles is suddenly all-decisive. A little lull, you see, with the mention of money. But suddenly Charles is sliding up the wall to dig into his pockets and he's all bustle and rush.

Manx tips the flask and drinks.

Pulling bills out of two or three pockets and uncrumpling a five and smoothing out a single. Manx looks down the line at the nodding heads, men breathing steam in the chill air, sleepers and dreamers deep in the night.

The sum arrived at looks like this. A ten, two fives, another ten, two singles, a quarter, two nickels and a tiddlywink dime.

Plus the kid pops out of the camp bag.

Charlie says, "I want you to take it all because it's all I've got. Even the change. I want you to even have the change. Because I've got the ticket money here." And he pounds his chest. "And the car keys here." And he slaps his thigh. "And I want you to have every nickel in my pocket above and beyond."

Manx thinks all right. He tries to keep his eyes from fluttering while they count. He thinks this is more than he could have gotten for those snow shovels he boosted from the utility room in his building. Plenty more. A hell of a lot, actually, more.

The small angry head is jutting from the bag.

"I want to go home now," Chuckie says.

Manx takes the money. He licks his thumb to count it for the benefit of the kid. Says some things to the kid, feeling good, trying to draw half a laugh.

Says to Charlie, "Bought yourself a souvenir of the great game. Calls for a drink, old boy."

They pass the flask and this is the only thing in the course of the long night and early morning that seems to engage Chuckie, the sight of two men guzzling booze right out of the bottle.

Half sigh, half pain in the sound they make when they open their mouths to exhale the fumes, eyes tight and pink.

Charles arches his fleecy brows.

"Now that the ball is mine, what do I do with it?"

Manx retakes the flask.

"Show it around. Tell your friends and neighbors. Then put it in a glass case with the fancy dishes. You saw those crowds go crazy in the street. This is bigger than some wars I seen."

Manx has no idea what he means by this. The Irish is beginning to talk. He sees that Charlie is feeling slightly down at the moment. Charlie is probably passing from the stage of half belief to the stage of disbelief. Feeling rooked and beetle-brained. Slyed out of his honest wages by some rogue off the street with a tale so staggering Charlie's embarrassed to tell his friends.

Let the buyer, like they say, beware.

He tries to think of the word that means a thing will increase in value over the years. But the Irish is not only talking, it is thinking, and anyway it is probably not a good idea at this point to say encouraging things to Charles. Only sound phony, won't it?

They look at each other. Charles has the baseball and the flask and Manx has the money. Okay. It is one of those happenstances where the mood downshifts once the deal is made. Only normal. The boy is asleep now, his face partly visible over the flap, and Manx wonders if he'll recall any of this, ever, or if it's already sunk in the dreaming part of his mind, the vague shape of a crouched man who is part of the night.

Charles looks at Manx and smiles, complicatedly, with an element of drowned affection in the mix.

Then they shake hands wordlessly and Manx is on his feet and out of there, feeling a slight ache in his calves and a hard tight serious-minded pain in his left hand from dragging the fire drum across the sidewalk. Put some butter on it when he gets home.

He walks past the humped and bundled bodies and the smoky grills where some of them cooked their meals and he walks past the cop on the tall horse and goes back across the bridge and up to

Broadway and maybe there's the faintest line of light low in the eastern sky.

It occurs to him. A lot of things occur to him, all dulled by drink, but it occurs to him that he doesn't want to stand on an empty platform under the street waiting for a train.

He walks down Broadway and begins to wonder why the man gave him the change in his pockets. There wasn't any need for coins to be changing hands. Maybe it was just what the fellow said, the heartfelt thing of wanting to give whatever's on your person, giving the shirt off your back, or maybe it's an honest deal that two men make and one of them turns it into a handout.

He walks, he wants to walk but he doesn't want to reach home, ever, necessarily. He has to think this out, how he has the right to enter into money matters concerning any object that belongs to his family, which he is still the head of, regardless.

Being broke makes him feel guilty. Get a little cash and you're guiltier still.

He pees in an alley unashamed.

It occurs to him further that he could take a Greyhound bus out of here, ride that skinny dog into the sweet distance. The way his own sons raise up to him sometimes, all that wrangle in their eyes.

He will write the letter for Cotter. To excuse his absence from school. As he had a fever of a hundred and two.

Make the boy feel better about things.

It also occurs to him that he's approaching the corner where the street preacher spoke earlier in the evening, or last night, and then he realizes no, he's confused, he's still ten blocks north of there. Then he forgets this and looks around for the man. The man's gone of course, to wherever he goes, and this isn't his corner anyway, and there's nothing moving but a car or two, cars with mystery drivers coming out of the gloom, alive like insects all hours of the night.

Thirty-two dollars and change.

He feels the familiar stab of betrayal. Be messing with his head. Tricked him every whichway. The baseball's bound to appreciate is the word. And the cash be worth less by the minute.

He looks in doorways for the preacher because he wants to give him the money. Get it off his hands. He wants to push the money in the old man's clothes just to be done with it. Give it to someone with a scientific interest in the stuff.

Booshit, man.

Money's his and he'll keep it. Take a bus somewhere. Or a room in some shambly street only a mile from home. Find a woman who'll look at him when her eyes sweep the room.

He forgets where he is again. He walks, he wants to walk, he's writing the letter in his head.

Please excuse my son from school yesterday.

He hears the rumble and grind of a garbage truck around a corner somewhere. Cars moving, trains running under the street, he's the only walking soul.

Old Charles be laughing up his sleeve for tricking old Manx. Tell his kid we gulled that fool.

Flat enough to pocket conveniently, with a cap on a chain.

He comes into his street and goes past the shoe repair and the beauty school.

His hand hurts where it touched hot metal.

It's beginning to get light when he reaches his building. He goes inside and climbs the stairs, each step taking basically a year, this is how it seems to Manx, until he is age eighty when he reaches his floor. He goes in the door, shadow soft, a silence with a set of eyes, and he moves slowly across the kitchen.

The alarm clock goes off in the bedroom.

He sits at the kitchen table and waits. She comes out in her nightdress and slippers, Ivie, the wife, and sees he hasn't been to bed and looks him over slowly.

She says, "What's this?"

"Need to put some butter on it."

"It's all blistered up. I don't like the looks of this."

"Just a surface burn."

"This election night? I thought election night was bonfires. I don't like the looks of this at all."

"You go on, get dressed. I take care of it."

"Not with butter you won't. That's old folks' nonsense," she says. "Do you more harm than good."

She takes the fruit out of the fruit bowl and fills the bowl with cold water and gets an ice tray out of the freezer.

"This doesn't help, we're taking you to emergency."

"I don't require no emergency."

She drops ten or twelve ice cubes into the water and sits next to him, holding his hand in the bowl of ice water and looking him over slowly. She keeps her questions, if she has them, for later.

Maybe the pain is subsiding slightly, maybe it's not. The water is so cold he only feels the cold. He tries to take his hand out of the bowl but Ivie keeps it there, her own hand pressing firmly on his, and Manx looks away, too tired to make a struggle of it.

"This only helps if the burn is recent," she says. "If the burn's not recent we have to see what they can do for you in emergency."

"And I'm telling you. I don't require no emergency."

They sit like this a while, her hand pressing his into the melting ice, and then she has to dress and go to work. Manx remains at the table, staring at his hand in the water and waiting for his son to wake up.

PART 6

ARRANGEMENT IN GREY AND BLACK

Fall 1951– Summer 1952

1

Bronzini thought that walking was an art. He was out nearly every day after school, letting the route produce a medley of sounds and forms and movements, letting the voices fall and the aromas deploy in ways that varied, but not too much, from day to day. He stopped to talk to card-players in a social club and watched a woman buy a flounder in the market. He peeled a tangerine and wondered how a flatfish lying glassy on flaked ice, a thing scraped with a net from the dim sea, could seem so eloquent a fellow creature. Its deadness was a force in those bulging eyes. Such intense emptiness. He thought of the old device of double take, how it comically embodies the lapsed moment where a life used to be.

He watched an aproned boy wrap the fish in a major headline.

Even in this compact neighborhood there were streets to revisit and men doing interesting jobs, day labor, painters in drip coveralls or men with sledgehammers he might pass the time with, Sicilians busting up a sidewalk, faces grained with stone dust. The less a job pays, Bronzini thought, the harder the work, the more impressive the spectacle. Or a waiter having a smoke during a lull, one of those fast-aging men who are tired all the time. The waiters had tired lives, three jobs, backaches and bad feet. They were more tired than the men in red neckerchiefs who swung the heavy hammers. They smoked and coughed and told him how tired they were and looked for a place on the sidewalk where they might situate the phlegm they were always spitting up.

He ate the last wedge of tangerine and left the market holding the spiral rind in his hand. He walked slowly north glancing in shop windows. There were silver points of hair in his brush mustache, still so few they were countable, and he wore rimless spectacles with wire temples because at thirty-eight, or so said his wife, he wanted to convince himself he was older, settled in his contentments, all the roilsome things finally buttoned and done.

He heard voices and looked down a side street filled with children playing. A traffic stanchion carried a sign marking the area a play street and blocking the way to cars and delivery trucks. With cars, more cars, with the status hunger, the hot horsepower, the silver smash of chrome, Bronzini saw that the pressure to free the streets of children would make even these designated areas extinct.

He imagined a fragment of chalked pavement cut clean and lifted out and elaborately packed—shipped to some museum in California where it would share the hushed sunlight with marble carvings from antiquity. *Street drawing, hopscotch, chalk on paved asphalt, Bronx, 1951.* But they don't call it hopscotch, do they? It's patsy or potsy here. It's buck-buck, not johnny-on-the-pony. It's hango seek—you count to a hundred by fives and set out into alleyways, shinnying up laundry poles and over back fences, sticking your head into coal bins to find the hiding players.

Bronzini stood and watched.

Girls playing jacks and jumping double dutch. Boys at boxball, marbles and ringolievio. Five boys each with a foot in a segmented circle that had names of countries marked in the wedges. China, Russia, Africa, France and Mexico. The kid who is *it* stands at the center of the circle with a ball in his hand and slowly chants the warning words: *I de-clare a-war u-pon.*

Bronzini didn't own a car, didn't drive a car, didn't want one, didn't need one, wouldn't take one if somebody gave it to him. Stop walking, he thought, and you die.

662

George the Waiter stood smoking near the service entrance of the restaurant where he worked. He was a face on a pole, a man not yet out of his thirties who carried something stale and unspontaneous, an inward tension that kept him apart. Over the spare body a white shirt with black vest and black trousers and above the uniform his jut features looking a little bloodsucked.

Bronzini walked over and took up a position next to George and they stood without speaking for a long moment in the odd solidarity two strangers might share watching a house burn down.

Three boys and a girl played down-the-river against the side of a building, each kid occupying a box formed by separations in the sidewalk. One of them slap-bounced a ball diagonally off the pavement so that it hit up against the wall and veered off into another player's box.

He was George the Waiter in a second sense, that his life seemed suspended in some dire expectation. What is George waiting for? Bronzini couldn't help seeing a challenge here. He liked to educe comment from the untalkative man, draw him forth, make him understand that his wish to be friendless was not readily respected here.

Then the second player bounced the ball into someone else's box, hitting it hard or lightly, slicing at the lower half of the ball to give it english, and so on up and down the river.

"The thing about these games," Bronzini said. "They mean so much while you're playing. All your inventive skills. All your energies. But when you get a little older and stop playing, the games escape the mind completely."

In fact he'd played only sporadically as a child, being bedridden at times, that awful word, and treated for asthma, for recurring colds and sore throats and whooping cough.

"How we used to scavenge. We turned junk into games. Gouging cork out of bottle caps. I don't even remember what we used it for. Cork, rubber bands, tin cans, half a skate, old linoleum that we cut up and used in carpet guns. Carpet guns were dangerous."

He checked his watch as he spoke.

"You talk about the cork," George said.

"What was the cork for?"

"We used the cork to make cages for flies. Two flat pieces of cork. Then we got straight pins from the dressmaker which were all over the floor of the shop."

"My god you're right," Bronzini said.

"We stuck the pins between the cork discs. One disc is the floor, one is the ceiling. The pins are the bars."

"Then we waited for a fly to land somewhere."

"A horsefly on a wall. You cup your hand and move it slowly along the wall and come up behind the fly."

"Then we put the fly in the cage."

"We put the fly in the cage. Then we put in extra pins," George said, "sealing the fly."

"Then what? I don't remember."

"We watched it buzz."

"We watched it buzz. Very educational."

"It buzzed until it died. If it took too long to die, somebody lit a match. Then we put the match in the cage."

"My god what terror," Bronzini said.

But he was delighted. He was getting George to talk. How children adapt to available surfaces, using curbstones, stoops and manhole covers. How they take the pockmarked world and turn a delicate inversion, making something brainy and rule-bound and smooth, and then spend the rest of their lives trying to repeat the process.

Directly across the street George the Barber was sweeping the floor of his shop. Voices from Italian radio drifting faintly out the open door. Bronzini watched a man walk in, a custodian from the high school, and George put away the broom and took a fresh linen sheet out of a drawer and had it unfolded and sail-billowing, timed just right, as the man settled into the chair.

"Maybe you heard, Albert. The hunchback died, that used to carve things out of soap."

"We're going back a few years."

"He carved naked women out of soap. Like anatomical. The hunchback that used to sit outside the grocery."

"Attilio. You'd give him a bar of soap, he'd carve something."

"What's-his-name died, the softball player, the pitcher that threw

664

windmill. He had shrapnel from the war. He had shrapnel actually in his heart from in the war. That only now killed him."

"Jackie somebody. You and he."

"We used to work together at the beach. But I barely knew him."

George used to sell ice cream at the beach. Bronzini saw him many times deep-stepping through the sand with a heavy metal cooler slung over his shoulder and a pith helmet rocking on his head. And white shirt and white ducks and the day somebody got a cramp while George sold popsicles in section 10.

"Remember the drowned man?" Bronzini said.

They were playing salugi in the street. Two boys snatched a school-book belonging to one of the girls, a Catholic school girl in a blue pinafore and white blouse. They tossed the book back and forth and she ran from one boy to the other and they threw the book over her head and behind her back. The book had a thick brown kraft cover that Bronzini was sure the girl had made herself, folding and tucking the grainy paper, printing her name in blue ink on the front—name and grade and subject. *Salugi*, they cried, that strange word, maybe some corruption of the Italian *saluto*, maybe a mock salutation— hello, we've got your hat, now try and get it back. Another boy joined the game and the girl ran from one to the other, scatterhanded, after the flying book.

Or Hindi or Persian or some Northumbrian nonce word sifting down the centuries. There was so much to know that he would die not knowing.

"What about the kid?" George said. "I'm hearing things that I don't know if it's good or what."

"He's coming along. I'm pleased one day, exasperated the next."

"I have respect for people that can play that game. When I think to myself this kid is how old."

"I try not to lose sight of that very thing, George."

"I hear he beats experienced players. This could be good or bad. Not that I'm the expert here. But I'm thinking maybe he should be in the street with these other kids."

"The street is not ready for Matty."

"You should impress into him there's other things."

"He does other things besides playing chess. He cries and screams."

George didn't smile. He was standing off, faded into old brooding, and he sucked the last bland fumes from his cigarette. One drag too many. Then he dropped the butt and stepped on it with the tap toe of his way-weary shoe, the border of uniformed George, rutted and cut across the instep.

"Time I showed my face inside. Be good, Albert."

"We'll talk again," Bronzini said.

He walked across the street so he could wave to George the Barber. How children adapt, using brick walls and lampposts and fire hydrants. He watched a girl tying one end of her jump rope to a window grille and getting her little brother to turn the other end. Then she stood in the middle and jumped. No history, no future. He watched a boy playing handball against himself, hitting Chinese killers. The hi-bounce rubber ball, the pink spaldeen, rapping back from the brick facade. And the fullness of a moment in the play street. Unable to imagine you will ever advance past the pencil line on the kitchen wall your mother has drawn to mark your height.

The barber waving back. Bronzini went to the corner past a man unloading jerry cans of Bulgarian sheep cheese from the trunk of a beat-up car. He walked north again, the savor of sweet peel in his hand. He realized he was still holding the fruit rind. It made him think of Morocco. He'd never been there or much of anywhere and wondered why the frailest breath of tangerine might bring to mind a reddish sandscape flashing to infinity.

Buck buck how many horns are up?

The clear cry reached him as he tossed the skin toward some cartons stacked at a cellar entrance. They are jumping on the backs of their playpals. It is usually the fattest boy who serves as cushion, standing against a wall or pole while the boys on one team stoop head to end and their rivals run and jump one by one and come yowing down. With the stooped boys swaying under the weight, the leader of the mounted team holds fingers aloft and calls out the question. How many horns are up? Bronzini tried to recall whether the padded boy, the slapped and prodded roly-poly, the one who dribbles egg cream down his chin—is he officially called the pillow or the pillar? Bronx boys don't know from pillars, he decided. Make him the mothery casing stuffed with down.

Twenty past four. The appointment was ten minutes hence and he knew that even if he arrived after the specified time he would not be late because Father Paulus was certain to be later. Bronzini envied the blithe arrivals of life's late people. How do they manage the courage to be late, enact the rude dare repeatedly in our waiting faces? A goat and four rabbits were hung upside down in a window, trussed at the hind legs, less affectingly dead than the flounder in the market—dumb scuzzy fur with nothing to impart. Envy and admiration both. He took it that these people refuse to be mastered by the pettier claims of time and conscience.

The butcher appeared at the door of his shop, flushed and hoarse, loud, foul, happy in his unwashed apron, a man who lived urgently, something inside him pushing outward, surging against his chest wall.

"Albert, I don't see you no more."

"You're seeing me now. You see me all the time. I bought a roast last week."

"Don't tell me last week. What's last week?"

The butcher called to people walking by. He called across the street to insult a man or engage a particular woman with knowing references. The rasping spitty sandblast voice. Other women twisted their mouths, amused and disgusted.

"What are you feeding that genius of yours?"

"He's not mine," Bronzini said.

"Be thankful. That was my kid I drive him out to the country and leave him on a hillside. But I wait for the dead of winter."

"We let him chew on a crayon once a week."

"Feed the little jerk some capozella. It makes him ballsy."

The butcher gestured at the whole lamb hanging in the window. Bronzini imagined the broiled head hot from the oven and sitting on a plate in front of Matty. Two cooked heads regarding each other. And Albert is telling the boy he has to eat the brain and eyes and principal ganglia. Or no more chess.

"It puts some lead in his pencil."

The butcher stood at the corner of the window looking well-placed

667

among the dangled animals, his arms crossed and feet spread. Bronzini saw an aptness and balance here. The butcher's burly grace, watch him trim a chop, see how he belongs to the cutting block, to the wallow of trembling muscle and mess—his aptitude and ease, the sense that he was born to the task restored a certain meaning to these eviscerated beasts.

Bronzini thought the butcher's own heart and lungs ought to hang outside his body, stationed like a saint's, to demonstrate his intimate link to the suffering world.

"Be good, Albert."

"I'll be in tomorrow."

"Give my best to the woman," the butcher said.

Bronzini checked his watch again, then stopped at a candy store to buy a newspaper. He was trying to be late but knew he could not manage it. Some force compelled him to walk into the pastry shop not only on time but about two and a half minutes early, which translated to a wait of roughly twenty minutes for the priest. He took a table in the dim interior and unfolded the Times across the scarred enamel.

A girl brought coffee and a glass of water.

The front page astonished him, a pair of three-column headlines dominating. To his left the Giants capture the pennant, beating the Dodgers on a dramatic home run in the ninth inning. And to the right, symmetrically mated, same typeface, same-size type, same number of lines, the USSR explodes an atomic bomb—*kaboom*—details kept secret.

He didn't understand why the Times would take a ball game off the sports page and juxtapose it with news of such ominous consequence. He began to read the account of the Soviet test. He could not keep the image from entering his mind, the cloud that was not a cloud, the mushroom that was not a mushroom—the sense of reaching feebly for a language that might correspond to the visible mass in the air. Suddenly there the priest was, coming in a flurry, Andrew Paulus S.J., built low and cozy, his head poked forward and that glisten of spittle in his smile.

He had books and folders slipping down his hip but managed to extend a cluster of scrubbed fingers, which Albert gripped in both hands, pressing and shaking, half rising from his chair. It took a moment of clumsy ceremony with overlapping salutations and unheeded questions and a dropped book and a race to retrieve it before the two men were settled at the table and all the objects put away. The priest heaved, as they say, a sigh. He wore a roman collar fitted to a biblike cloth called a rabat and over this a dark jacket with pocket square and he could have been George the Waiter's tailored master in black and white.

"How late am I?"

"You're not late at all."

"I'm doing a seminar on knowledge. Wonderful fun but I lose track."

"No, you're early," Bronzini said.

"How we know what we know."

You had to look hard at Andrew Paulus to find a trace of aging. Unfurrowed and oddly aglow, with a faint baked glaze keeping his skin pink and fresh. Hair pale brown and fringed unevenly across the forehead in boyish bangs. Bronzini wondered if this is what happens to men who forswear a woman's tangling touch and love. They stay a child, preserved in clean and chilly light. But there were parish priests everywhere about, leaky-eyed and halting, their old monotones falling whispery from the pulpit. He decided this man was not youthful so much as ageless. He must be thirty years senior to Albert and not an eyelid ever trembles or a bristly whit of gray shows at the jawline.

"Did you see the paper, Father?"

"Please, we know each other too well. You're required to call me Andy now. Yes, I stole a long look at someone's Daily News. They're calling it the Shot Heard Round the World."

"How did we detect evidence of the blast, I wonder. We must have aircraft flying near their borders with instruments that measure radiation. Or well-placed agents perhaps."

"No no no no. We're speaking about the home run. Bobby Thomson's heroic shot. The tabloids have dubbed it for posterity."

Bronzini had to pause to take this in.

"The Shot Heard Round the World? Is the rest of the world all that interested? This is baseball. I was barely aware. I myself barely knew that something was going on. Heard round the world? I almost missed it completely."

"We may take it that the term applies to the suddenness of the struck blow and the corresponding speed at which news is transmitted these days. Our servicemen in Greenland and Japan surely heard the home-run call as it was made on Armed Forces Radio. You're right, of course. They're not talking about this in the coffeehouses of Budapest. Although in fact poor Ralph Branca happens to be half Hungarian. Sons of immigrants. Branca and Thomson both. Bobby himself born in Scotland, I believe. You see why our wins and losses tend to have impact well beyond our borders."

"You follow baseball then."

"Only in distant memory. But I did devour today's reports. It's all over the radio. Something propelled this event full force into the public imagination. All day a steady sort of ripple in the air."

"I don't follow the game at all," Bronzini said.

He fell into remorseful thought. The girl appeared again, sullen in a limp blouse and shuffling loafers. Only four tables, theirs the only one occupied. The plain decor, the time-locked thickness in the air, the trace of family smell, even the daughter discontented—all argued a theme, a nonpicturesqueness that Albert thought the priest might note and approve.

"But baseball isn't the game we're here to discuss," Paulus said.

In other shops the priest had made an appreciative show of selecting a pastry from the display case, with moans and exclamations, but was subdued today, gesturing toward the almond biscotti and asking the girl to bring some coffee. Then he squared in his chair and set his elbows firmly on the table, a little visual joke, and framed his head with cupped hands—the player taut above his board.

"I've been taking him to chess clubs," Bronzini said, "as we discussed last time. He needs this to develop properly. Stronger opponents in an organized setting. But he hasn't done as well as I'd expected. He's been stung a number of times."

"And when he's not playing?"

"We spend time studying, practicing."

"How much time?"

670

"Three days a week usually. A couple of hours each visit."

"This is completely ridiculous. Go on."

"I don't want to force-feed the boy."

"Go on," Paulus said.

"I'm just a neighbor after all. I can push only so hard. There's no deep tradition here. He just appeared one day. Shazam. A boy from another planet, you know?"

"He wasn't born knowing the moves, was he?"

"His father taught him the game. A bookmaker. Evidently kept all the figures in his head. The bets, the odds, the teams, the horses. He could memorize a scratch sheet. This is the story people told. He could look at a racing form with the day's entries, the morning line, the jockeys and so on. And he could memorize the data of numerous races in a matter of minutes."

"And he disappeared."

"Disappeared. About five years ago."

"And the boy is eleven, which means daddy barely got him started."

"Adequate or not, on and off, I have been the mentor ever since."

The priest made a gesture of appeasement, a raised hand that precluded any need for further explanation. The girl brought strong black coffee and a glass of water and some biscuits on a plate.

"The mother is Irish Catholic. And there's another son. One of my former students. One semester only. Bright, I think, but lazy and unmotivated. He's sixteen and can quit school any time he likes. And I'm speaking on behalf of the mother now. She wondered if you'd be willing to spend an hour with him. Tell him about Fordham. What college might offer such a boy. What the Jesuits offer. Our two schools, Andy, directly across the road from each other and completely remote. My students, some of them don't know, they remain completely unaware of the fact that there's a university lurking in the trees."

"Some of my students have the same problem."

Bronzini remembered to laugh.

"But what a waste if a youngster like this were to end up in a stockroom or garage."

"You've made your plea. Consider your duty effectively discharged, Albert."

"Dip your biscotto. Don't be bashful. Dip, dip, dip. These biscuits are direct descendants of honey and almond cakes that were baked in leaves and eaten at Roman fertility rites."

"I think the task of reproducing the species will have to devolve upon others. Not that I would mind the incidental contact."

Bronzini leaning in.

"In all seriousness. Have you ever regretted?"

"What, not marrying?"

Bronzini nodding, eyes intent behind the lenses.

"I don't want to marry." And now it was the priest's turn to lean forward, shouldering down, sliding his chin near the tabletop. "I just want to screw," he whispered electrically.

Bronzini shocked and charmed.

"The verb to screw is so amazingly, subversively apt. But conjugating the word is not sufficient pastime. I would like to screw a movie star, Albert. The greatest, blondest, biggest-titted goddess Hollywood is able to produce. I want to screw her in the worst way possible and I mean that in every sense."

The small toothy head hovered above the table in defiant self-delight. Bronzini felt rewarded. On a couple of past occasions he'd taken the priest into shops and watched him taste the autumnal pink Parma ham, sliced transparently thin, and he'd offered commentaries on pig's blood pastry and sheets of salt cod. The visitor showed pleasure in the European texture of the street, things done the old slow faithful way, things carried over, suffused with rules of usage. This is the only art I've mastered, Father—walking these streets and letting the senses collect what is routinely here. And he walked the priest into the acid stink of the chicken market and pushed him toward the old scale hung from the ceiling with a lashed bird in the weighing pan, explaining how the poultryman gets twenty cents extra to kill and dress the bird—say something in Latin, Father—and he felt the priest's own shudder when the deadpan Neapolitan snapped the chicken's neck—a wiry man with feathers in his shirt.

"If I were not so dull a husband we might sit here and tell stories into the night."

"Yours real, mine phantasmal."

The priest's confession was funny and sad and assured Albert that he was a privileged companion if not yet a trusted friend. He enjoyed being a guide to the complex deposits around them, the little histories hidden in a gesture or word, but he was beginning to fear that Andy's response would never exceed the level of appreciative interest.

"And when you were young."

"Was I ever in love? Smitten at seven or eight, piercingly. The purest stuff, Albert. Before the heavy hormones. There was a girl named something or other."

"I know a walk we ought to take. There's a play street very near. I think you'd enjoy a moment among the children. It's a dying practice, kids playing in city streets. We'll finish here and go. Another half cup."

He signaled the girl.

"Do you know the famous old painting, Albert? Children playing games. Scores of children filling a market square. A painting that's about four hundred years old and what a shock it is to recognize many games we played ourselves. Games still played today."

"I'm pessimistic, you think."

"Children find a way. They sidestep time, as it were, and the ravages of progress. I think they operate in another time scheme altogether. Imagine standing in a wooded area and throwing stones at the top of a horse chestnut tree to dislodge the sturdiest nuts. Said to be in the higher elevations. Throwing stones all day if necessary and taking the best chestnut home and soaking it in salt water."

"We used vinegar."

"Vinegar then."

"We Italians," Albert said.

"Soak it to make it hard and battle-worthy. And poke a hole through the nut with a skewer and slip a tough bootlace through the hole, a lace long enough to wind around the hand two or three times. It's completely vivid in my mind. Tie a knot, of course, to keep the chestnut secured to the lace. A rawhide lace if possible."

"Then the game begins."

"Yes, you dangle your chestnut and I bash it by launching my own with a sort of dervishy twirl. But it's finding the thing, soaking the thing, taking the time. Time as we know it now had not yet come into being."

"I tramped through the zoo every year at this time to gather fallen chestnuts," Bronzini said.

"Buckeyes."

"Buckeyes."

"Time," the priest said.

Across the room the girl filled the cups from a machine. Father Paulus waited for her to slide his cup across the table so he could let the aromatic smoke drift near his face.

Then he said, "Time, Albert. Both of you must be willing, actually, to pay a much higher price. Hours and days. Whole days at chess. Days and weeks."

Bronzini had his opening, finally.

"And if I'm not willing? Are you? Or not able. If I'm not able to do it. Not equal to the job. Are you, Andy?"

The priest looked at the knot in Albert's tie.

"I thought you wanted advice."

"I do."

"Please. Do you think I'd even consider tutoring the boy? Albert, please. I have a life, such as it is."

"You're far more advanced than I, Father. You're a tournament player. You understand the psychology of the game."

Paulus sat upright in his chair, formally withdrawing, it seemed, to a more objective level of discourse.

"Theories about the psychology of the game, frankly, leave me cold. The game is location, situation and memory. And a need to win. The psychology is in the player, not the game. He must enjoy the company of danger. He must have a killer instinct. He must be prideful, arrogant, aggressive, contemptuous and dominating. Willful in the extreme. All the sins, Albert, of the noncarnal type."

Chastened and deflated. But Albert felt he had it coming. The man's remarks were directed at his own genial drift, of course, not the boy's. His complacent and easy pace.

"He shows master strength, potentially."

"Look, I'm willing to attend a match or two. Give you some guidance if I can. But I don't want to be his teacher. No no no no."

Now the grandmother appeared with an opened bottle of anisette crusted at the rim. When Bronzini asked how she was feeling she let her head rock back and forth. The liqueur was a gesture reserved for select customers and took earning over time. She poured an ashy dram into each demitasse and the priest colored slightly as he seemed to do in the close company of people who were markedly different. Their unknown lives disconcerted him, making his smile go stiff and bringing to his cheeks a formal flush of deference.

She left without a word. They watched her glide moon-slow into the dimmed inner room.

"I don't know what to tell you about the older brother," Paulus said.

"Never mind. I asked only because the mother asked. It will all straighten itself out."

"We have an idea, some of us, that's taking shape. A new sort of collegium. Closer contact, minimal structure. We may teach Latin as a spoken language. We may teach mathematics as an art form like poetry or music. We will teach subjects that people don't realize they need to know. All of this will happen somewhere in the hinterland. We'll want a special kind of boy. Special circumstances," Paulus said. "Something he is. Something he's done. But something."

When they stood to leave and the priest was gathering his books, Bronzini took his cup, the priest's, and drained it of sediment, tipping his head quickly—espresso dregs steeped in anisette.

They shook hands and made vague plans to stay in touch and Father Paulus started on the short walk back to the Fordham campus and Albert realized he'd forgotten his own suggestion about visiting the play street nearby. Too bad. They might have ended on a mellower note.

But when he walked past the street it was nearly emptied out. A few boys still playing ringolievio, haphazard and half speed, the clumsy fatboy trapped in the den, always caught, always *it*, the slightly epicene butterfat bulk, the boy who's always reaching down to lift a droopy sock and getting swift-kicked by the witlings and sadists.

Is that what being *it* means? Neutered, sexless, impersonalized.

Dark now. Another day of games all ended, or nearly all—he could hear the boys' following voices as he made his way down the avenue. And when it ends completely we find ourselves abandoned to our sodden teens. What a wound to overcome, this passage out of childhood,

675

but a beautiful injury too, he thought, pure and unrepeatable. Only the scab remains, barely seen, the exuded substance.

Ringolievio coca-cola one two three.

A faint whiff of knishes and hot dogs from the luncheonette under the bowling alley. Then Albert crossed the street to Mussolini park, as the kids called it, where a few old men still sat on benches with their folded copies of Il Progresso, the fresh-air inspectors, retired, indifferent or otherwise idle, and they smoked and talked and blew their noses in the street, leaning over the curbstone with thumb and index finger clamped to old shnozzola, discharging the stringy stuff.

Albert wanted to linger a while but didn't see anyone he knew and so he joined the small army of returning workers coming around the bend from Third Avenue, from the buses and elevated train.

Time, finally, to go home.

She sat there, Rosemary Shay, doing her beadwork. She had the frame set on two small sawhorses. She had the four bolts screwed in that held the frame together, those bolts with wing nuts at one end. She had the material pinned to the edges of the frame. She had the wood-handled needle that she used to string the beads onto the material, following the printed design—greenish beads arrayed on a flossy thread.

She heard Nick doing something at the kitchen table.

She said, "You should go get the meat."

She did her beadwork and listened to him doing whatever he was doing. Writing something, it sounded like, but not for school, she didn't think.

She said, "It's paid for. And they close soon. So you should think about going."

She did her beadwork, her piecework. Sweaters, dresses and blouses. She did whole trousseaus sometimes, working off the books just as Jimmy had.

She did her work and listened to Nick, finally, go out the door. Then she went and looked at the piece of paper he'd left on the table. Made no sense to her at all. Arrows, scrawls, numbers, circled numbers, a phone number in the Merian exchange, letters with numbers next to them, some simple additions and divisions—all scribbled frantically on the page.

She listened to the radio and did her work. She made an official salary, the money she reported, answering the phone for a local lawyer and typing wills and deeds and leases, mostly, and immigration forms, and listening to the lawyer's funny stories. He told all the new jokes and had a backlog of a thousand old ones and he liked to sing "The Darktown Strutters' Ball" in Italian, a thing he did more or less automatically, like breathing or chewing gum.

The job was good for her because it put her in contact with other people and because it had the virtue of fairly flexible hours. And the money, of course, was life and death.

Bronzini walked toward Tremont, past apartment buildings with front stoops and fire escapes, past a number of private homes, some with a rosebush or a shade tree, little frame houses beginning to show another kind of growth, spindly winged antennas.

He was wondering about being *it*. This was one of those questions that he tortured himself deliciously with. Another player tags you and you're *it*. What exactly does this mean? Beyond being neutered. You are nameless and bedeviled. *It*. The evil one whose name is too potent to be spoken. Or is the term just a cockney pronunciation of hit? When you tag someone, you hit her. You're *'it*, missy. Cockney or Scots or something.

A woman rapped a penny on the window, calling her child in to dinner.

A fearsome power in the term because it makes you separate from the others. You flee the tag, the telling touch. But once you're *it*, name-shorn, neither boy nor girl, you're the one who must be feared. You're the dark power in the street. And you feel a kind of demonry, chasing the players, trying to put your skelly-bone hand on them, to spread your taint, your curse. Speak the syllable slowly if you can. A whisper of death perhaps.

Half a block from his building, on a street where the Italians thinned out and the Jews began to appear. And approaching now to see his mother in the first-floor window, cranked up in her special bed, white hair shining in the soft light.

Baseball's oh so simple. You tag a man, he's out. How different from being *it*. What spectral genius in the term, that curious part of childhood that sees through the rhymes and nonsense words, past the hidings and seekings and pretendings to something old and dank, some medieval awe, he thought, or earlier, even, that crawls beneath the midnight skin.

The young man struck the match with one hand. He'd learned this when he first started smoking, about a year ago, although it seemed to him that he'd been smoking forever, Old Golds, isolating the match by closing the cover behind it and then bending the match back against the striking surface below and driving the head with his thumb. Then he brought the flared match up to his cigarette, his hand cupping the whole book with the match still secured. He lit up, shook out the flame and conceded use of the other hand to pluck the spent match from the book and send it to match hell.

You need these useless skills to make an impression on the street.

The science teacher fading into the evening, southbound, and his former student Shay, a mopey C-plus in introductory chemistry, walking the other way on the same street, into the shopping district, taking deep drags on his cigarette, with numbers running in his head.

Ever since the game yesterday, Nick's been seeing the number thirteen. The game, the mass hurrah, the way he crouched over his radio, ready to puke his guts all over the roof. All day today, thirteens coming out of the woodwork. He had to get a pencil to list them all.

Branca wears number thirteen.

Branca won thirteen games this year.

The Giants started their pennant drive thirteen and a half games behind the Dodgers.

The month and day of yesterday's game. Ten three. Add the digits, you get thirteen.

The Giants won ninety-eight games this year and lost fifty-nine, including the play-offs. Nine eight five nine. Add the digits, reverse the result, see what you get, shitface.

The time of the home run. Three fifty-eight. Add the digits of the minutes. Thirteen.

The phone number people called for inning-by-inning scores. ME 7-1212. M is the thirteenth letter of the alphabet. Add the five digits, old thirteen.

Take the name Branca—this is where he started going crazy. Take the name Branca and assign a number to each letter based on its position in the alphabet. This is where he started thinking he was as crazy as his brother doing chess positions or probabilities or whatever the kid does. Take the name Branca. The *B* is two. The *r* is eighteen. And so on and so on. You end up with thirty-nine. What is thirty-nine? It is the number which, when you divide it by the day of the month of the game, gives you thirteen.

Thomson wears number twenty-three. Subtract the month of the year, you know what you get.

Two guys were pushing a car to get it started. Nick nearly went over to help but then didn't. He was done with baseball now, he thought, the last thin thread connecting him to another life. He saw the old man who dressed as a priest, more or less, wearing a cassock sometimes with house slippers, or one of those ridged black hats a priest wears, blessing the fucking multitudes, and ordinary shabby street clothes.

He walked into the butcher shop. The bell over the door rattled and the butcher stood above the block, Cousin Joe, hacking at a pork loin.

The other butcher said, "Hey. Look who's here."

He said it the way you say something in passing, to no one in particular.

Cousin Joe looked up.

"Look who's here," he said. "Nicky, what's the word?"

The other butcher said, "Hey. He wants to be called Nick. You don't know this?"

"Hey. I know this guy since he's four years old. A little skinny malink. How long you been coming in here, Nicky?"

Nick smiled. He knew he was only a stationary object, a surface for their carom shots.

679

"I seen him with that girl he goes with. Loretta," the second butcher said.

"You think he's getting some?"

"I know he is. Because I look at his face when they walk by."

"Nicky, tell me about it. Make me feel good," the butcher said. "Because I'm reaching the point I have to hear other people's, you know, whatever it is they're doing that I'm not doing no more."

"I think he's a cuntman. Up and coming."

"This is true, Nicky?"

Nick's mood was improving.

"I think he's getting so much there's not enough left over for the rest of us," the second butcher said, Antone, barely visible behind the display case.

"Make me feel good, Nicky. I stand here all day, I look at them go by. Big women, short women, girls from Roosevelt, girls from Aquinas. You know what I say to myself. Where's mine?"

"Nicky's got yours. He's got mines too."

"Him, I could believe it."

"And you know why, Joe?"

"He's doing something he shouldn't be doing."

"He's got that pussy smile when he walks by. Which could only mean one thing. The kid is eating box lunch at the Y."

"*Sboccato*," the butcher said happily, berating Antone, rasping the word from deep in his throat. Foulmouth.

Nick went to the door and opened it and waited for a woman to walk past and then flicked his cigarette toward the curbstone.

"Who's better than him?" Antone said.

"You going to school, Nicky?"

"He goes when he goes. Hey. Who's better than him?" Antone said. "I would give my right arm."

Antone took the bag out of the case. It held chops, chicken breasts and fresh bacon. He passed it over the top to Nick.

"Who's better than you?" he said.

"Be good," Cousin Joe said.

"My right arm I would give. Look at this kid."

A taste of blood and sawdust hung in the air.

"Regards to your mother, okay?"

"Be good, okay?"

"Be good," the butcher said.

Bronzini lay beaming in the massive bath, a cast-iron relic raised on ball-and-claw feet, only his head unsubmerged.

Salt crystals fizzed all around him.

His wife leaning against the door frame, Klara, with their two-year-old affixed to her leg, the child repeating words that daddy issued from the deeps.

"Tangerine," Albert said.

This was happiness as it was meant to evolve when first conceived in caves, in mud huts on the grassy plain. Mamelah and our beautiful bambina. And his own mother, ghastly ill but here at last, murmurous, a strong and mortal presence in the house. And Albert himself in the hot bath, back from the hunt, returned to the fundamental cluster.

He summarized the meeting with Father Paulus. A slouching Klara seemed about to speak several times, the way her body begins to drag along a surface, going restless and skeptical.

"An impressive man. I want you to come along next time. Or I'll invite him here."

"He doesn't want to come here."

"Doctorate in philosophy at Yale. Graduated magna cum laude in sacred theology from some Jesuit center in Europe. Louvain, I believe," and he formed the word as a privileged utterance. "Holds a chair in the humanities at Fordham."

"But he's not inclined to help you with the boy."

"He'll help. He'll come to a match. Tangerine," he said to the child and raised his arms out of the water.

Klara lifted the girl up over the roll-rim of the tub and Albert sat up and took her under the arms, holding her upright, feet in white socks barely touching the water so she could step along the surface, laughing, making little kick-waves. And he felt like a mother seal, yes, a mother, not some raucous coughing bull or whatever the male is called—he would have to look it up.

"Do you know the old painting," he said, "that shows dozens of children playing games in some town square?"

"Hundreds actually. Two hundred anyway. Bruegel. I find it unwholesome. Why?"

"It came up in conversation."

"I don't know what art history says about this painting. But I say it's not that different from the other famous Bruegel, armies of death marching across the landscape. The children are fat, backward, a little sinister to me. It's some kind of menace, some folly. *Kinderspielen.* They look like dwarves doing something awful."

He held the girl kicking, raising her just above the surface, then dropping her a notch so she could splash lightly, laughing when the spray hit him in the face.

"Fat and backward. Did you hear that, little girl? As a matter of fact she's getting pretty heavy, isn't she? Whoa. Aren't you, sweetheart?"

Sooner or later the daily litany of delicate questions and curt replies.

"And my mother?"

"Resting."

"And the doctor came?"

"No."

"The doctor did not come?"

"No."

"When is he coming?"

"Tomorrow."

"Tomorrow. And Mrs. Ketchel looked in?"

"Looked in, exactly."

The child stepped along the surface and he lifted her high so Klara could take her. She swung her past the end of the tub and managed to have her wet socks off about a second after she touched down. One of those thousand-a-day death struggles of mother and child. Wails and bent limbs and a certain physical insistence on the woman's part. All done in a compact blur that dazzled Albert and made him lean over the edge to espy the two dinky socks lying soggy on the tile, as confirmation.

His mother suffered from a neuromuscular condition, myasthenia gravis, and she lay helpless much of the time, eyelids sagged, arms too weak to move except in ever slower syllables of gesture, reduced to units now, and her vision evidently doubled.

He recited the word for the child one last time as she was hustled out.

He'd brought his mother here, prevailing over her own fatalism and his wife's practical misgivings. You are the son, you take care of the parents. And the illness, the drama of a failing body, the way impending death made her seem saintly, with an icon's fixedness, a stern and staring and enameled beauty. Albert, who shunned any form of organized worship and thought God was a mass delusion, sat and watched her for hours, combed her hair, soaked up her diarrhea with bunched Kleenex, talked to her in his boyhood Italian, and he felt that the house, the flat, was suffused with a reverence, old, sad, heavy and impressive—an otherworldliness, now that she was here.

The salts had stopped fizzing and he lay in silence a while. He felt the contentment begin to slip away. There was something about evening perhaps that caused a transient sadness. He heard Klara in the kitchen preparing the meal. Things there he must keep at a distance. Her moods, her doubts. He thought about his own situation. Things he must confront. His complacency, his distractedness, his position at school, his sneaky-pete drinking.

It came to him suddenly when it finally came. Tangerine. How he'd stood in the market this afternoon peeling the loose-skinned fruit and eating the sweet sections, slightly stinging as the juice washed through his mouth, and how the scent seemed to breathe some essence, but why, of Morocco. And now he knew, incontrovertibly. Tangerine, Tanger, Tangier. The port from which the fruit was first shipped to Europe.

He felt better now, thank you.

How language is webbed in the senses. Out of sand-blaze brilliance into quirky minds such as his, into touch, taste and fragrance. He thought he'd linger just a bit longer, let the bath take total hold, ease and alleviate, before he put on clothes and entered the complex boxes where people do their living.

Nothing fits the body so well as water.

2

Later they would go get the car but first they hung around a while, letting the night close in, sitting on the stoop in front of 611.

JuJu did not sit down until he spread his hanky on the steps. He was talking about the new model cars, just out, this one's got the horsepower, that one's got the handling, and he was earnest and fervent.

"You talk like you're ready to whip out your wallet," Nick said. "When you know and I know."

Scarfo stood on the corner about ten yards away eating a jelly apple, a grown man, holding it away from his body and leaning in to bite.

"There's nothing in there but a rubber."

They watched people come home from work. Nick sat haunched on the iron rail just above JuJu. It was cold and they came plugging home, clerks, bus drivers, garment workers, elevator operators.

Nick watched them and smoked.

"That's you," he said.

"What are you talking?"

"Two years tops. That's you," he said. "Could happen sooner."

"It's a job. They have jobs. What do you want them to do?"

"I'll tell you what I think."

"Save me a drag on that cigarette."

They watched Scarfo talking to the shoemaker, holding the jelly apple at arm's length now.

"Anything's better than what they're doing. That's what I think."

"They're working. Let them work."

Nick watched and smoked, secretaries, maintenance men, bank tellers, messengers, typists in the typing pool, stenographers in the steno pool.

"It's not the work. It's the regular hours," Nick said. "Going in the same time every day. Clocking in, taking the train. It's the train. Going in together. Coming home together."

"You're better than that."

"I'm better, I'm worse, what's the difference."

When Nick took the last drag on the cigarette he held the butt with his thumb and middle finger, the middle finger poised to flick so that he took the drag and flicked in one prolonged motion, sending the butt toward the curbstone.

"Thanks," JuJu said.

"For what?"

"You rather collect twenty weeks a year than have a steady job that pays decent?"

"I tell you what I rather do. I rather get my dick sucked by the one in the green coat."

"Where?"

"The one in the green coat."

"Where?"

"Across the street," Nick said.

"You like that?"

"Hey. I didn't say I want to marry her."

"You couldn't save me a drag?"

"What? Did you ask?"

"She's awful short," JuJu said.

"Good. She can blow me standing up."

"Save wear and tear on her knees."

"God makes short people for a reason."

Scarfo wore neat creased pants and good shoes and he ate with his body contorted to keep the jelly from dripping on his clothes. He was talking to the shoemaker about something and the shoemaker stood there squat-bodied and blank.

"You got gas money?" JuJu said.

"We don't need gas. For where we're going?"

"Where are we going?"

"To the poolroom," Nick said.

They watched the shoemaker think. Like watching a bulldog take a crap.

The people came home from work, thinning out over time, the merest scatter now. It was the night before Thanksgiving and there was a thing you were supposed to feel about a holiday and a day off and getting ready for the big feast with the relatives coming over but Nicky's days off had started a couple of weeks earlier when he stopped going to school and there weren't any relatives nearby, which was something, in fact, to be thankful for.

He tapped JuJu on the shoulder. They walked over to Quarry Road, a stretch of weedy landscape traveled mainly by dog walkers. This was where the '46 Chevy waited at the base of the high stone wall that surrounded the hospital for the incurable.

They were too young to have drivers' licenses but it didn't matter because the car was stolen anyway.

They'd seen it parked near the zoo about three weeks ago, key in the ignition, near nightfall, and Nick had gotten in, an impulse, a thing you don't even have time to dare yourself to do, and he started up the engine. JuJu watched for a second and got in. Vito was with them, Bats, and he got in. They drove around for much of the night and it was still a joke, an escapade, and they chipped in for gas and drove around some more and then left the car parked next to an empty lot, with Nick taking the keys, and it was still there the next day. They got a set of plates from Vito's uncle's car that was in traction, more or less, for the winter, and they exchanged these for the original plates and drove mainly at night because the brashness had given way to a responsible sense of ownership and they went only limited distances because it seemed safer and they didn't have money to spend on gas and there was nowhere to go anyway.

JuJu started the car up and they sat there listening to it throb.

"You see what you're doing to this mat," Nick said. "Only three weeks it's been. You're wearing it out. You're wearing down the ridges with your feet. You and her. Use the backseat, animal."

"The backseat's cramped."

"Animale."

"It's roomier up here."

JuJu and his girlfriend shared the front seat for hours at a time, Gloria, french-kissing into the night, the young man's hands exploratory, but it was the action of their feet that caused the trouble, it was the grinding of their feet in unavailing passion that was destroying the traction on the mat.

"Explain to her that if she puts out, Gloria, in a polite way, tell her, the damage to the car will be reduced in the long run. You won't have all this frustration that the both of you take out on the furniture."

"The furniture."

"Put out or stay out. Tell her nice-nice. Because we can't afford this girl destroying our property."

JuJu put the car in gear and drove the two blocks to the poolroom, parking away from the streetlight. They got out, examined the car and then crossed the street and went up the long flight of steel-tipped stairs and through the tall metal door into the sparse smoke of the big room, where a single dim figure was hunched over a table, cue ball spinning in the gloom.

A woman rapped a penny on the window and Klara looked up. The woman waved, missus somebody, and Klara smiled and hurried on. She had company coming and she was late.

She stopped for some things at the grocer's and then went up the front steps and there was Albert's mother in the window, cranked-up, wearing a white hospital gown and facing straight out, with a religious medal dangling, and she looked a little like a vision or someone waiting for a vision.

Klara did not want to give this striking scene a title out of some Renaissance gallery because that would be unkind. But the fact, after all, was that the woman was on display.

Mrs. Ketchel sat with Albert's mother this afternoon. The child was being minded by a girl in the building who was capable and trustworthy.

Klara tidied the place a little, not much, and then stood in the spare room looking at the sketch on the easel, a study of the room itself. She'd been sketching the room for some time now. She did studies of the door frame, the molding on the walls, she did the luggage stacked in a corner.

When Rochelle rang the bell she was standing in the kitchen smoking.

"So, Klara. Here you are."

"Don't look too closely. I didn't clean."

"You don't clean for old friends."

They sat in the living room with coffee and snacks.

"So here you are."

"Exactly, what, six blocks from where we grew up?"

"It feels strange coming back. Everybody's so ugly. I swear I never noticed."

The real Rochelle. This is what Klara wanted but wasn't sure she'd get.

"You have a new place," she said.

"Riverside Drive. How did I get so lucky I don't know."

"You're looking very Parisian or something. The hair, maybe, or the clothes. What is it?"

"Once you start, you can't stop. It's like a disease," Rochelle said. "You still have your willowy look, which is the envy of my life."

Rochelle's husband was a developer. She called him Harry the Land Man. They went to Florida and Bermuda and shopped for lingerie together on Fifth Avenue.

"So you're here, Klara. Teaching art."

"There's a community center. The children come to me, some of them kicking, some of them screaming. Others are very willing, they love to draw."

"So it's satisfying."

"At times, yes, I enjoy it."

"So you enjoy it. So it's good. And Albert. He's a teacher too. Everybody's a teacher. Half the world is teaching the other half."

"Albert's a real teacher. A professional."

"That's his mother in there?"

"A forceful woman actually, even in this condition. I admire her in a number of ways. Takes no crap from anybody."

"She's dying in there?"

"Yes."

"You'll let her die in the house?"

"Yes."

"You were always open-minded that way. You have a lover, Klara?"

"Ten minutes you're in my house. The answer is no."

"You want to ask me if I fool around?"

"I know what I'm supposed to say. You'd be crazy to fool around. Risk all that? Harry, the apartment, the underwear? But in fact."

"Once or twice only. I need something in the afternoon or I feel useless."

Rochelle wanted to see her work. There were several small canvases stacked against the wall in the spare room and they stood there a while, looking. The pressure Rochelle felt to say the right thing mashed her head into her torso.

"Harry wants to buy art."

"Tell him to get an advisor."

"I'll quote you that you said that."

Klara showed some pastels.

"So Albert's a dear sweet man, right? He likes it that you paint?"

"He thinks it relaxes me."

"So you enjoy it. You come in here and paint. I can picture you, Klara. Standing here thinking, measuring with the brush. You're trying this, you're trying that. Once I let an elevator man rub against my thigh, in Florida."

They had another cup of coffee and then went upstairs to see Klara's child. She was on the floor playing with jigsaw pieces and they stayed half an hour talking to the baby-sitter and watching the child make a world independent of the puzzle.

"Klara, say it. I should have a baby."

"You're the last person I would say it to."

"Thank you. We're friends to the end. Give me a hug, I'll go home happy."

They went down and stood on the stoop talking. Three men were pushing a car to get it started. A light snow was falling.

"So she takes no crap, Albert's mother. Take me to her deathbed before it's too late. Maybe she can tell me something I should know."

When she was gone Klara went into the spare room and restacked all the canvases and stood looking at the sketches she'd done. The door, the doorknob, the walls, the window frame.

She sent Mrs. Ketchel home and sat with Albert's mother until it got dark. Then she went into the kitchen to do something about dinner. But first she turned on the lamp near the bed so Albert would see his mother when he came up the steps.

The poolshooter was George Manza, George the Waiter, and he was playing alone at the back of the room. He was not a man who mixed with the regulars and he was a master shooter besides. It was rare that anyone came in who could play at this level.

Nick stood near a table where a gin rummy game was going but he was watching George shoot pool. Bank the six, play beautiful position for the ace, make a massé shot that Nick could barely visualize even after he saw it.

Once, nearly a year ago, George came up to Nick, unexpectedly, and asked him to go to the unemployment office with him. He needed to fill out some forms so he could collect for the next twenty weeks and he didn't say it outright but Nick understood that he required help reading the forms and filling in the information. Nick also understood that an older man might not want to ask someone his own age for this kind of help. They went to the office and filled out the forms and George didn't feel embarrassed and ever since that day he always had a word for Nick, some advice to give, regards to your mother, stay in school.

Somebody says, "What's this, fuck-your-buddy week?"

Mike the Book stood behind the counter, under the TV set, a short square-jawed man who was always about a day late shaving. The poolroom was a sideline to Mike's bookmaking operation. Sometimes he let Nick and his buddies shoot pool with the light off over the table, which meant they didn't have to pay.

He caught Nick's eye and tilted his head and when Nick walked over he said something.

"What?"

"It's called grand theft. You know this phrase?"

"What do you mean?"

Mike leaned across the counter, speaking quietly.

"You think word don't get around? What's the matter with you? I thought you were smart. That chooch over there, JuJu, I don't expect better. You, I'm surprised."

"Mike, the car is a throwaway. I honestly don't think the guy ever meant to drive it anymore. He left the keys in the car so somebody could take it. It's the kind of car you take it out in the woods and shoot it. So we saved him the aggravation."

"You're gonna think it's funny when you're booked at the precinct. I picture your mother, Nicky."

The dog came over and sniffed at Nick's shoes, a mutt, a stray that Mike the Book took in one day. Somebody named it Mike the Dog.

"All right. I'll see what we're gonna do."

"Get rid of it. That's what you're gonna do."

"I won't need it anymore. I'm getting a job. I can take taxis whenever I want."

"Wise guy. You're like your father."

Nick wasn't sure he wanted to hear this.

"Your father liked to put himself in a corner and then edge himself out. He was always at the edge. Not that I knew him that well. We were in the same business but he was downtown and I was over here and he always kept a distance, anyway, your old man. Like he's somewhere else even when he's standing next to you."

"I'll do something."

"See what you're gonna do."

"I'm this close to getting a job. My life of crime is over, Mike."

They were shooting pool at two other tables now and when JuJu started racking balls at a third table Nick went over to shoot a game.

He said, "Mike knows."

"What? He knows?"

"I think everybody knows. How could they not know? The fucking dog knows."

"Then we're shit out of luck," JuJu said. "We put the key back in the ignition and just walk away."

"Good idea. Give me the key. I'll do it," Nick said.

In the middle of the game he went to the phone on the far wall and called Loretta. George the Waiter saw him and raised his stick and Nick tipped an imaginary hat.

"Loretta. What are you doing?"

"Trying on those shoes I bought."

"Those shoes."

"I bought. You were with me."

"That was three days ago."

"So I'm still trying them on. So what?"

"You're alone?"

"My mother's here."

"You're not alone?"

"My mother's here."

"She's there now?"

"She lives here. It's her house. She has a right."

"I just thought if you were alone."

"My mother's here."

"I could come over."

"She's still here. She was here when you first asked and she's still here."

"So meet me at the car. I'm parked across from Mike's."

"Meet you at the car? *Now* you want me to meet you?"

"We'll drive somewhere."

"What am I supposed to say? Ma, I'm going out for a bottle of milk."

"Tomorrow's off. You don't have to get up for school."

"I have to get up for the turkey. We have twenty-two people. I'm up at six-thirty. Maybe when they all leave. Tomorrow night."

"Wear your shoes," he said.

He went over and watched George run the table. George had a

692

floury face and hollow eyes and he talked to Nick with his nose compassed on the cue ball.

"What's this about you're not going to school no more?"

"No more, no more. Waste of time, don't you think?"

"Stay in school."

"Stay in school. Okay, George."

"You're working?"

"I got something I'll be doing part-time."

"What?"

"In an ice-cream freezer. Packing and unpacking."

"This is union?"

"What union? The union wants ice-cream packers to do twenty minutes in the freezer, twenty minutes out. So they don't freeze their peckers off. So the company's hiring fools like me."

George slammed in the four ball with a flourish, nearly driving the stick up into the ceiling. It was interesting to see a clammed-up guy like George become a showman at the table.

"You want some money in your pocket."

"That's right."

"And you're not thinking about the right or wrong of the situation or your own danger to your health."

"That's right."

"But they're gonna pay you shit-ass wages. What are they paying you?"

"Shit-ass wages."

"And they're gonna keep you in the freezer for unsafe periods. Let me talk to a guy I know. Maybe I can get you something better. You'll work like a beast of burden but at least you don't wear no mittens."

Vito Bats had taken Nick's place at the other table. Nick went over and watched, smoking, pointing out errors in their game.

"Everybody knows," he said.

"We just have to leave it," Vito said. "We don't go near it anymore. I'll take my uncle's plates off, late tonight. They'll see a car with no plates, they'll tow it away. Goodbye, good riddance."

"You'll never get laid, Vito. Both of you guys. That car is your only hope."

"I rather die a saint in my coffin than go to jail with ten thousand tizzoons."

"Give me the keys. I told JuJu. Give me the keys, I take care of everything."

"Give me my uncle Tommy's plates, maybe I'll give you the keys."

"Take the fucking plates. I'm taking the keys."

"You're taking *u'gazz'*. That's what you're taking."

"Hard-on. Give me the keys."

"*U'gazz'*. All right?"

"See that stick? The stick you're holding. The stick you're holding."

"Alls I'm saying, Nicky."

"Cuntlap. Give me the keys."

He was talking to Vito even though he knew JuJu had the keys. He didn't want to put JuJu in a position where he would lose pride or standing. But Vito with those thick glasses and big lips, fish lips—he had those wet lips he was always licking.

"I don't get the keys, you know what happens to that stick? The stick you're holding. I give you one guess where it goes."

George the Waiter paid and left and soon the cardplayers came in, blinking in the smoke, the high-stakes poker players, they played till four, five in the morning, chips massed in the pot and a guy named Walls sitting by the door.

Walls carried a .38, this was the story, somewhere on his hip.

Four of the players were here and they stood at the counter talking to Mike and after a while two more players arrived and the lights over the pool tables began to go off and the poolshooters drifted out.

Somebody croons in a clear tenor, "Bluer than velvet was the night."

Walls was sitting by the door, different from the others, a narrow face and long jaw, hair cut short, and Nick watched him from the counter and Walls caught the look and raised his eyebrows slightly. In other words there's something you want to say to me?

Nick smiled and shrugged, taking his change.

"Be good," Mike said.

Vito borrowed a small folding knife off Mike's key chain and the three thieves went down to effectuate removal of the plates.

Mike the Dog went with them.

Nick watched them work and pointed out flaws in their method. He pissed against the hospital wall, drawing the dog's attention, and then went back to the car, where they were still disengaging the plates, and he commented freely.

Vito said, "Hey. Don't be such a *scucciament'*. All right?"

"Give me the keys," Nick said.

"We're not finished."

"You'll never be finished. Because you're a scumbag in the shape of a human. You're a scumbag that's gonna marry a dooshbag when you're twenty-one, Vito. God bless you. I'm serious. You and your lovely children."

When they got the plates off, JuJu handed the keys to Nicky. It was his car now, a green heap, naked of documentation, gas tank close to empty.

Nick said he'd take the dog back up to Mike's and the two guys went their separate ways and Nick crossed the street with the dog alongside.

He started up the stairs talking to the dog and when he was three-quarters of the way up the tall door creaked open and the man named Walls stood there with his hand in his jacket.

Nick smiled at him.

"Walking the dog," he said.

Walls stepped back so the dog could get in. Then he stood in the opening again.

"I thought that was a thing you do with a yo-yo."

"That's right," Nick said. "Walking the dog. But I think my yo-yo days are over."

Walls showed a slight smile. Nick approached and looked through the opening, hoping that Mike might see him and invite him in to watch the game a while.

Walls shook his head, still smiling, and Nick nodded once and went back down the stairs. He got in the car, started it up and drove it to the original parking spot, two blocks away. Then he got out, walked around the car, inspecting it for this and that, and went back to the stoop in front of his building, where he sat haunched on the iron rail smoking one last cigarette before he went upstairs.

3

The knife grinder came and went. Matty was supposed to listen for the knife grinder's bell and then go downstairs with the knives that she'd set out on the kitchen table—knives to be sharpened and money to pay, all set out.

On her way home she saw the fresh-air inspectors standing on the corner, elderly men mostly, they were out even in cold weather provided the sun was shining and they stood there breathing steam, changing their position inchingly with the arc of the sun, and when she went upstairs the knives were on the table, dull-edged, and there was the money in bills and coins, thirty-five cents a blade, untouched and unspent, and Matt was at his board in the parlor, waiting for Mr. Bronzini.

Rosemary took off her hat and coat and said nothing. She went into the bedroom, where the frame was set between the sawhorses, and she turned on the radio and began to do her beadwork.

What she knew about the knife grinder was that he came from the same region as Jimmy's people, near a town called Campobasso, in the mountains, where boys were raised to sharpen knives.

It took two hours to bead a sweater. She listened to the radio but not really, you know, letting the voice drift in and out. She guided the needle through the fabric and thought of Jimmy's stories. She used to fight to keep him out of her thoughts but it wasn't possible, was it? He replaced the radio in her mind.

She said, "What happened to the knives?"

There was a long pause in the next room.

He said, "He never came. I never heard the bell."

She said, "He always comes on Tuesday. He never misses a Tuesday. Since we've been here, except if it's Christmas Day, he will be here on a Tuesday."

She waited for a response. She could sense the boy's surrender and resentment, the small crouched shape squeezed in utter stillness.

"Am I wrong or is this a Tuesday?" she said in a final little dig.

She saw the pigeons erupt from the roof across the street, bursting like fireworks, fifty or sixty birds, and then the long pole swaying above the ledge—so long and reedy it bent of its own dimensions.

Mr. Bronzini knocked on the door and Matty let him in.

The Italian women in the building, which almost all of them were, called her Rose. They thought this was her name, or one of them did and the others picked it up, and she never corrected them because— she just didn't.

Never mind hello. They started right in talking about a move, a maneuver from a couple of days before. Mr. Bronzini sometimes forgot to take off his coat before he sat down at the board.

Jimmy used to say carte blank.

The boy who kept the pigeons stood invisible behind the ledge, waving the pole to guide the birds in their flight.

They lapsed into a long pondering silence at the board, then started talking at once, yackety-yak together.

She strung the beads onto the fabric.

She didn't want to be a sob story where people feel sorry for you and you go through life dragging a burden the size of a house.

Jimmy used to say, Here's some money. You have carte blank how you spend it. I don't even want to know, he'd say.

She heard a woman in the hall yelling down to her kid. Her head out the door yelling to the kid who's galloping down the steps.

"I'm making gravy," the woman yelled.

How is it we did so much laughing? How is it people came over with their empty pockets and bad backs and not so good marriages and twenty minutes later we're all laughing?

They started a legend that he memorized every bet. But he didn't. They still tell stories about his memory, how he moved through the loft buildings taking bets from cutters, sweepers and salesmen and recording every figure mentally. But he didn't. He had pieces of paper all over his clothes with bets scribbled down.

She heard the women talk about making gravy, speaking to a husband or child, and Rosemary understood the significance of this. It meant, Don't you dare come home late. It meant, This is serious so pay attention. It was a special summons, a call to family duty. The pleasure, yes, of familiar food, the whole history of food, the history of eating, the garlicky smack and tang. But there was also a duty, a requirement. The family requires the presence of every member tonight. Because the family was an art to these people and the dinner table was the place it found expression.

They said, I'm making gravy.

They said, Who's better than me?

It did not happen violent. This was a thing she would never believe, that they took him away in a car. The man went out for cigarettes and just kept walking.

She didn't want her children to see her dragging, slumping, thinking too much, brooding, angry, empty.

Conceal, conceal. But it was hard.

They told her to change her hair. The women in the building. They told her she had a Mother Hubbard hairdo.

No, she wasn't empty. Just tense much of the time, hearing a voice inside that she'd never heard before, her own voice, only edgy and angry and one-track.

She listened to Mr. Bronzini in the living room. He spoke about the truth of a position. The radio was doing a serial drama called "Bright Horizons" or "Bright Tomorrows" or "Brighter Days" and every position has a truth, he told Matty. A deep truth is what you want, not a shallow truth. You want a position worth defending to the death.

This food, this family meal, this meat sauce simmering in a big pot with sausage and spareribs and onions and garlic, this was their loyalty and bond and well-being, and the aroma was in the halls for Rosemary to smell when she climbed the flights, rolled beef, meatballs, basil, and the savor had an irony that was painful.

He used to come home and get undressed, Jimmy, and pieces of paper would fall out of his clothes, scraps of paper, bets in code, his own scrawled cipher of people's names, horses' names, teams and odds and sums of money.

They said, See what you're gonna do.

How is it she could laugh all night at his stories about a day in the garment district, or a day when he went to Toots Shor's famous restaurant, out of the district, the famous Toots Shor, out of his jurisdiction completely, but Toots Shor met him and liked him and wanted to give him some action and he was a heavy bettor, very, and Jimmy made occasional trips to West 51st Street to take limited bets from Toots Shor, a big lumbering man with a face like a traffic accident, and he told her stories about the well-heeled bums around the big bar drinking until four in the morning.

I'm making gravy, they said.

The wife of Mr. Imperato, the lawyer she worked for in her regular job, called a couple of times a week and said, Tell him I'm making gravy.

She did her beadwork off the books. The pigeons climbed and wheeled and the long pole swayed above the ledge.

Some women have one man in their life and he was the one, that bastard, in hers.

Mr. Imperato liked to joke about our famous forefathers. Abraham Linguin' and George Washingmachine.

In warmer weather Matty sat at the board in his beeveedees, how little he looked, so thin and pale, but his eyes were fixed on the pieces so hard and hot she could easily think there was someone else in there, sent to possess the boy.

The trick was, the thing was he was not the center of the family when he was here. She was the center, the still center, the strength. Now that he was gone, she could no longer make herself feel still, or especially central. Jimmy was central now. That was the trick, the strange thing. Jimmy was the heartbeat, the missing heartbeat.

It was a promise that was also a call to duty. Tell him I'm making gravy.

They said, See what you're gonna do.

This was a threat to a son or daughter who was not behaving. Straighten out. Change your attitude. See what you're gonna do.

They said, Who's better than me?

This was a statement of the importance of small pleasures. A meal, a coat with a fake-fur collar, a chair in front of a fan on a hot day.

It did not happen violent. It was the small thing of a weak man walking out the door. It was not big. It was not men with guns who tie paving stones to someone's ankles and put a bullet in his head. It was small and weak.

If you could feel the soul of an experience, then you earned the right to say, Who's better than me?

Jimmy knew some dialect. *Abruzzese*. He used to take the knives down and talk to the knife grinder and he found it satisfying to use the dialect. They talked while the man sharpened the knives and it was something Jimmy did not do with men he saw more often who came from the same region, or their people did. He talked to the knife grinder because he saw him only rarely and this was an arrangement he preferred.

They called her Rose. They had assurance and force, most of them, they had nerve and personality and loud voices, not all but most.

She did her beadwork, her piecework, working off the books just like Jimmy.

He slept continuous. Never got up in the night. Drank coffee and slept right through. Didn't seem to feel the cold. Walked barefoot on the cold floors, slept in his shorts on those winter nights when she'd finally hear the heat whistling in the pipes, her signal to get up for mass.

Somebody put serious money on a horse called Terra Firma and he began to worry when it finished first.

She listened to Matty analyze a position. They stopped the game occasionally and talked out the moves.

He was not a braggadocio. He told sly quiet stories late at night.

Conceal, conceal. But it was hard.

The baseball man Charlie Dressen was a horseplayer. Jimmy took his bets. He took bets from Toots Shor. He left seven hundred dollars in a coat that she took to the dry cleaner. The coat was his private bank, only he never told her, and she took it to the dry cleaner and went back when she found out about the money and they said, What money, lady? There was an inside pocket she didn't know was there. What money, lady?

She applied the beads with a wood-handled needle, following the design printed on the fabric.

But how is it we did so much laughing? How is it we went dancing the night of the seven hundred dollars and we laughed and drank?

He was not a harum-scarum guy who took crazy chances but the long shot came in and he began to feel the pressure to pay off.

Who's better than me, they said.

This was a statement she couldn't make, partly out of personality but also because she could not feel the ordinary contentment of things the way she used to. She could not feel favored or charmed.

He'd replaced her life with his leaving. The voice running through her head was not the voice she used to hear before he left.

But how is it we ate a German meal on 86th Street and went dancing at the Corso down the block, seven hundred dollars poorer?

There was less of her now and more of other people. She was becoming other people. Maybe that's why they called her Rose.

Nick was walking the halls at school. This close to Christmas the Catholic school kids were already off, Matty was off, the shopping area was decorated with lights and wreaths, the merchants were putting out trees at five in the morning, which you could smell from a distance, and there were eels on sale for Christmas Eve and spruce and balsam fir stacked against the walls, from upstate, and kids unloading crates of grapes from California for customers who made their own wine.

Nick wandered the halls smoking and Remo came out of a classroom wearing tight pegged pants and the Eisenhower jacket he never took off.

701

"What are you doing here?"

"Taking a walk," Nick said.

"You take walks indoors?"

"You been out? Fucking freezing. What are you doing here?"

"Hey. I go to school here. What are you doing here?"

"Talking a walk," Nick said.

"I got a pass to see the doctor."

"The nurse. That's who you want to see."

"Save me a drag," Remo said.

"Where's home economics?"

"I don't know. The end of that hall maybe. I hear you're working."

"Ice-cream plant."

"Pays decent?"

"Forget about it."

"It's steady then?"

"You have to shape up. Like the docks," Nick said, and he felt like a man, saying this. "A guy says, You, you, you, you. Everybody else goes home."

Remo seemed impressed.

"You get to eat the merchandise?"

"Actually, you want to know the truth."

"What?"

"We steal it and sell it. But we have to work fast."

Remo didn't know whether to believe this. He reached for the butt-end of Nick's cigarette and Nick gave it to him and he took two hungry drags and then dropped it, stomped it, exhaled and went into the doctor's office.

After the bell rang and the classrooms emptied out Nick spotted Loretta and Gloria and they walked out onto Fordham Road together.

"Allie's father hit a number," Gloria said.

"I know. I heard."

"He had five dollars on it if you can believe that."

"It's true. I know it for a fact," Nick said.

An older guy named Jasper, a noted cuntman, sat in a Ford convertible, with the top down yet, in this weather, motor running, listening to the radio. The two girls were quiet walking by, quiet together, by mutual consent, exchanging unspoken thoughts about Jasper.

"Who puts five dollars?" Loretta said. "They put fifty cents. They put a dollar if they're feeling very, very lucky."

"He had a dream," Nick said.

"He had a dream. What kind of dream?"

"What kind of dream. He dreamed the number. What else would he dream?"

"For five dollars," she said, "it must have been very convincing."

"It was in technicolor," Gloria said.

"If I dream a number I think I'm gonna die on that date," Loretta said. "This man gives five dollars to a gangster."

"Gangster. What kind of gangster? He gave the money to Annette Esposito."

"Who's that?"

"She's a Catholic school girl. She goes to my brother's school," Nick said. "She runs numbers for her father. Every day she makes the rounds."

"In her school uniform," Gloria said.

"The customers like a runner they can trust."

They walked past White Castle, where kids were eating sawdust hamburgers, and then Gloria crossed the street and went into her building.

"Where's your radio? You used to carry your radio all the time," Loretta said.

"I had a radio in my car. That's the only radio I needed."

"It's for the best," she said.

"You think it's for the best."

"I'm relieved," she said. "That car, my god. What wasn't wrong with it? Not to mention it was stolen property."

"We didn't have nice times in that car?"

"The drive-in was nice. Not the parking on dark streets. Like criminals."

"That's what we were," he said.

She laughed. She had two teeth that didn't exactly match, on either side of the incisors, and he thought it gave her a sexy smile.

They turned east and he saw a garbage truck and saw JuJu's father, who was a garbageman, jump down off the truck and stride across the

703

sidewalk and flip the lid off a can and muscle the can over to the truck and then upend it into the grinder.

"See that guy? That's JuJu's father," he said with an edge of pride in his voice.

He admired the graceful action, the long continuous body motion from the cellar entrance to the truck, the way the man wrestled the can across the sidewalk, all forearm action, and the freedom to make noise, skidding the can and running the grinder, and then the hoist and dump, a shoulder motion mainly, and the original pitch of the lid, a gesture of half contempt but also graceful, which he earned by the nature of the work he did.

And flinging the can back toward the wrought iron fence that guarded the basement steps. Also a privilege of the job, Nicky thought.

They reached her building and went inside.

Loretta stood in the hallway and turned to be kissed and he kissed her, moving her up against the mailboxes with her books between their bodies sliding back and forth.

"Who's home?" he said.

"They're all home."

He pressed her into the mailboxes and could hear the friction of her skirt when she moved against the slits in the metal where you could see if you had mail.

"You still think it's for the best I don't have my car?"

"It's broad daylight, car or no car."

"We could park in the parking lot at Orchard Beach. Just the seagulls and us."

She kissed him.

"So steal another car," she said slurringly.

He opened his eyes while he was kissing her and she was looking at him with wide brown eyes that seemed to be thinking seven things at once. She knew he'd had sex with other girls, handjobs, blowjobs, whatever else, putting it in taking it out, putting it in keeping it in, bareback, rubber, whatnot, and she knew who the girls were, from Washington Avenue, from Valentine Avenue, one from Kingsbridge Road, because somebody told somebody who made sure it got back to her, and he knew that she knew, from Gloria passing a remark to

704

JuJu, like one of the radio serials his mother listened to, doing her beadwork.

"You'll meet me tomorrow?" she said.

"I work tomorrow."

"They're all home. What can I say?"

"I have to work. What can I say?"

"When's the last time you washed your hair?" she said.

He walked a while and ended up going into the zoo, on an impulse, entering by the big bronze gate, and he went up past the sea lions in a cold stiff wind with the place just about empty of visible humans. He missed his shit-heap Chevy, no plates, no insurance, no license to drive it, transmission shot to hell, the door on the passenger side opening up unannounced every time he made a left turn, driving only at night in a skulking and shadowy manner, mostly alone, smoking, the radio frequently fading out.

He was angry about something but it was something else, not the car or the girlfriend—the thing that ran through his mind even in his sleep.

He walked for half an hour and then stood by the wildfowl pond. When he was in grade school he'd come to the zoo with a kid named Martin Mannion, and Martin Mannion had climbed a fence, it was a day like this, wintry and empty, and Martin Mannion climbed into the buffalo enclosure and stood there waving his jacket at the buffalo, the bison, and the huge nappy animal from off a five-cent piece just looked at him indifferent and Martin Mannion got so mad he took out his dick and peed.

It was beginning to get dark now. He stood at the edge of the pond and lit another cigarette, turning his back to the wind.

"Call me Alan, he says."

"Call me Alan."

"I says, What's Alan? He says to me, That's my name."

"That's my name."

"I look at him. I says to him, How could that be your name? You already got a name."

"What happened to Alfonse?"

"I says, What happened to Alfonse? You were Alfonse for sixteen years. Your grandfather was Alfonse."

"The both of them."

"Two grandfathers Alfonse. What happened? He says, I'm not them."

"Miserable little cross-eyed."

"I'm not them, he says."

"He's king shit, that's who he is."

"Call me Alan, he says."

"I'm not them."

"I could break his back."

"I'm not them."

"I says, Who are you?"

"He's king shit, that's who he is."

"I says, Who are you, *stunat'*, if you're not them?"

Giulio Belisario, JuJu, had never seen a dead body, including at a wake, and he was interested in the experience.

"Who's gonna die," Nicky said, "just so you can satisfy your curiosity?"

"I missed my grandmother when I had the measles."

"I'm looking around. I don't see any volunteers. You hear about Allie's father?"

"What?"

"You don't know this?"

"What? He died?"

"He hit a number."

"I was gonna say."

"He's buying a Buick. One day he's a fishmonger. The next day."

"I was gonna say. I just saw him yesterday in the market. How could he be dead?"

"How long does it take?" Nicky said.

"I'm only saying."

"One day he's selling scungilli. The next day, hey, kiss my ass."

"Who's better than him?" JuJu said.

"I'm driving a big-ass Buick. Stand clear, you peasants."

They were in the grocery that occupied a storefront in Nicky's building at 611. The grocer's wife, Donato's wife, the only name they knew her by, tolerated their presence because she liked Nicky's mother. Outside five older guys were gathered and one of them, Scarfo, was doing broad jumps at the instigation of the other four. Scarfo wanted to take the sanitation test and they'd convinced him he needed to broad-jump six feet from a standing start and he was out there in his good coat and creased pants jumping cracks in the sidewalk, to see if he could do it.

The two young men stood inside the store smoking and watching.

"I saw your father," Nicky said.

"He's picking up in the neighborhood, temporary."

"He ever find anything in the garbage?"

"What could he find? That he brings home? Forget about it."

"He could find something valuable."

"My mother would have a conniption fit. Forget about it."

Donato's wife gave them each a piece of sliced salami and they watched Scarfo work on his jump.

Matty bit his shirt cuff, a slink of a kid with lively eyes, and he looked across the board at Mr. Bronzini, who was smiling twistedly.

"You killed me," Albert said.

"I saw everything."

"You came, you saw and so on. And you killed me."

He knew that Matty loved hearing this. He loved winning at chess and he loved hearing the loser declare himself dead. Because that's what he was, kaput, and it was Matty who'd crushed him.

The boy's mother stood in the doorway watching.

"How many moves did it take? No, don't tell me," Albert said. "I want to preserve some self-respect."

Matty and his mother were delighted.

"He's beginning to think in systems," Albert said to her. "I think this is a sign that good things will begin happening again."

The adults had a cup of tea and Matt stayed at the board, a small float-

707

ing godhead above the pawns and rooks. The boy had taken some more losses lately, including a rout at the Manhattan Chess Club, and this was deeply disappointing all around because Father Paulus had appeared.

Came, saw, said little and left.

After a while Albert went over to Arthur Avenue, where he saw the chestnut man pushing his oven on wheels, a cartoon contraption, smoke coming out of the bent metal chimney. There was a peach basket appended to one end of the oven to hold the unroasted chestnuts and sweet potatoes.

He bought some chestnuts, which he more or less juggled in a piece of wrapping paper because they were damn hot, and he carried them down the side street into the barbershop.

George the Barber led him into the back room, where they sat at a small table eating the chestnuts and washing them down with wincing sips of Old Mr. Boston, a rye whiskey unknown to the Cabots and the Lodges.

Albert knew that George had a wife in a little house somewhere, and a married daughter somewhere else, but the man was otherwise unimaginable outside his barbership. Stout, bald, unblessed with excess personality, he belonged completely to the massive porcelain chairs, two of them, to the hot-towel steamer, the stamped tin ceiling, the marble shelf beneath the mirror, the tinted glass cabinets, the bone-handled razor and leather strop, the horn combs, the scissors and clippers, the cup, the brush, the shaving soap, the fragrance of witch hazels and brilliantines and talcums.

George the Barber knew who he was.

"Biaggio hit a number," he said.

"Who, Biaggio?"

"He hit a number. Six hundred to one."

"From the fish market Biaggio?"

"He hit a number," George said.

When the chestnuts were gone he refilled their glasses and they sat there sipping quietly, thinking about someone hitting a number.

"And how is the woman?" he said to Albert.

"The woman."

"Yes, how is the marriage?" he said.

708

The radio was tuned to the Italian station and an announcer was signing off with repeated cries of *baci a tutti*, which was fine with Albert, absolutely, the way he felt in the bracing wake of the whiskey.

"This is a subject so immense."

"Of course. What else?"

"Big, big, big, big."

"Too much, too much," the barber said.

"I can only say one thing."

"There's only one thing to say."

"Every marriage, every marriage. Not just mine or yours."

"Exactly."

"How can I put it, George? *Un po' complicato.*"

"Of course. What else can we say?"

"What else is new?"

"What else is new?" the barber said.

Albert licked at a dusting of chestnut on his fingers. A woman and child came in and George moved into the front of the shop and Albert drained his glass and followed because he did not want to presume on the man's hospitality.

He spoke to the woman while George arranged the boy's special seat. Then he put on his hat and coat and left. He stopped in Mussolini park and spent a few minutes talking with the old men. The fake priest went past, Benedetti, wearing a lumber jacket and a black biretta and carrying a breviary. He moved his lips as if in prayer but held the book unopened to his chest.

Albert had to sit. He realized he was slightly woozy, Umbriago the mayor of New York or of Chicago, and he sat on a bench and waited for the feeling to pass.

The other men drifted off. The sun was edging behind the extended mass of the hospital for the incurable and it was colder now, with flurries in the air, and the men drifted off to a storefront social club, or a candy store, or home.

A tow truck went by at a crazy speed, rushing to get to the wreck before the competition.

Albert sat on the bench and waited for his head to clear. The important thing is to sit and wait, to be patient. The other important thing is not to vomit. You see a man every so often standing over a curbstone vomiting. He did not want to think of himself as that kind of man.

He sat there feeling all right, feeling slightly less dizzy now and generally all right. *Baci a tutti*, he thought. To everyone on the street, yes, kisses, and the faces went muddling through his mind, the bread makers, grandmothers, street sweepers, to the priests who are and those who aren't.

The kids called it heave. I think I'm gonna heave, Johnny.

A car pulled up and he heard the hoarse voice of the butcher calling across to him.

"Albert, *che succese?*"

"Hello, Joe. Merry Christmas."

"It's snowing. Go home."

"I'm fine, I'm fine, I'm fine."

"You want a ride?"

"Go, go, go, go. Merry Christmas, I'm fine, goodbye."

He heard the train pull into the station about a block away. He heard it shriek around the bend and rumble into the station and he sat in the wind's high howl waiting for his head to clear completely.

4

There were a thousand sameshit nights when he played knock rummy with a guy named Fontana in Fontana's father's plumbing supply store, a nominal nickel a point, or shot a game of pool and had a slice of pizza at Half Moon with JuJu and Patsy, nights that always ended down, disappointed someway, and once he phoned Loretta from the candy store and told her he had his dick in his hand and studied the pause at the other end, knowing she was in a room with her mother, her brothers, her grandfather and who knows who else, and he went downstairs sometimes and stood smoking alone, late, in the doorway of Donato's grocery, spitting occasional grains of tobacco into the wind.

He had a little money now. He gave most of what he earned to his mother but at least he had something in his pocket, approaching age seventeen, and he went to the show and sat in the balcony with Allie and Ray, two guys who talked back to the screen, but after a while what could you say to a movie that wasn't the sameshit thing you'd said a thousand times before?

·   ·   ·

Klara was in the room, the spare room, the room she was painting inch by inch, and she stood at the easel working.

Yes, Albert thought painting relaxed her. It was a break, he thought, from the other things she did.

She stopped when it was time to pick up the child. For a moment she forgot where she'd parked the child. Upstairs with the regular girl or across the street with the woman whose husband made coats for rabbis.

Painters are supposed to have a line. Klara thought she had a scribble.

She went upstairs and got the child and came down saying something like, Naptime for little girls. But Teresa wasn't ready for her nap. Sleepy creepy time. But Teresa let her mother know this was not going to happen right now. She did not soften her yeses and noes. She was an open wound of need and want and powerful refusal.

Klara sat by the bed talking to her. After a while she went into the spare room and stood by the easel and looked at what she'd done. What had she done? She decided she didn't want to know.

She looked in on the child, who was sleeping now. Then she looked in on Albert's mother. Mrs. Ketchel, the woman who sat with her, was putting on her coat. Mrs. Ketchel seemed to be putting on her coat a little earlier every day. The days were getting longer now, technically, so maybe Mrs. Ketchel had so many other things to do, to fill the longer days, that she couldn't sit with Albert's mother for extended periods anymore.

Klara thought the child resembled her grandmother. A mournfulness about the eyes, she thought. But that can't be true, can it, in a child so young? A darkness, a brooding sense of misfortune. But she was making it up, wasn't she, looking for signs and omens.

She sat in the room with Albert's mother. The woman was awake and turned her head to look at Klara, an incomplete movement that brought her to the point of exhaustion, but then exhaustion was all that remained, although that's not true either. Her gestures had force, still. They were halting but strong. They showed a willful woman who could dismiss entire populations with a singsong waggle of the hand.

The gestures did not refer to practical things. They had a range that

712

extended to another level. The hand that sweeps under the chin. The pushed-out mouth. The way the eyes close and the head tilts up.

To Albert. When it's time to die, I'll die.

To friends who sat with her. God doesn't know everything. Only the things he has to know.

To Albert. Why do you want to talk about your father when all I see when I hear his name is lost opportunity?

To Albert. Be careful. That's all I'm saying.

To Klara. Go live your life. I'm not worth your time or attention.

This last is a gesture of hand and eye that both women know to be insincere.

Klara did not tell Albert that she found it an odd comfort, at times, to sit with his mother. They had one parent left between them, dying. She played Perry Como records for the woman. She brought the child in so the grandmother could touch her hands and face. The woman did not see well, or saw two things where one occurred, and her hand on the child's face seemed to work a marvel of retrospection.

Her skin was getting browner, her hair whiter, hands spotted and blotched, but there was still something strong about her, something Albert seemed to fear, a judgment, a withering conviction of some kind.

She had a gesture that seemed to mark a state of hopelessness too deep to be approached with words.

Klara sat there and talked to her a little. She kept the window open slightly to let the mustiness escape, the slow waste. She heard fire engines some distance off and watched the light fade.

Albert's sister came to visit sometimes, Laura, unable to accept the impending death, scared, dependent, betrayed, and Klara could imagine she'd try to climb into the gravehole when the time came.

How strange it was to find herself here, listening to Perry Como with a woman she didn't know, who was dying, and with everything else as well, this chair, that lamp, this house and street, and to wonder how it happened.

When Albert came home she was in the kitchen.

"How is she?"

"Sleeping."

"Did she eat anything?"

"I made a little soup."

"Did she eat it?"

"Ate some, spilled some. Your daughter caught a cold from the baby-sitter."

"I'll make it go away," he said.

She heard him telling stories to Teresa, nonsense tales he'd been told as a boy, characters with funny rhyming names, and he overpronounced certain words for effect, his voice rounded and melodic, but she shut the kitchen door because she didn't want to hear it anymore.

The story voice, the play voice was all too Albertlike, rippling with incidental music and fanciful plot. She put the dinner on the table and spoke his name.

They talked through dinner, inconsequentially. She smoked her last cigarette of the day in the spare room, looking at the wall. She put out the cigarette by grinding it into the bathroom mirror and then she flushed it down the toilet and went to bed.

The first one ran into the playground, the one with the dark cap. Nick was punching the other one, both of them skidding on the icy surface.

He'd never seen the guy before and this is why he was punching him. He punched the guy to his knees, or the guy skidded to his knees, and then Nick looked into the playground. JuJu was chasing the first one but skidded and fell, a leg flying up. JuJu sat there a moment watching the guy run toward the steps that went down to the lower level. The playground was white and still, swings hanging empty, an inch of snow on the seats.

The other one was on his knees, looking embarrassed to be there. Nick crouched and set himself and threw a punch. He knew it was not necessary to throw this punch but he'd hit the guy only glancing blows to the face and he wanted to hit him solid. It was a chance to hit someone solid that he didn't want to miss. He punched him under the eye, a short-stroke blow, and the guy rocked back on his haunches, hands to his face, and Nick felt better now.

JuJu came out of the playground and took some frozen dog shit out of the snow. He wasn't wearing gloves. He picked it up and mashed it into the guy's head, into his hair and ears.

He said, "Here, stroonz, this is for you."

Then he washed his hands in the snow and they walked over to Mike's to shoot a game.

Matty knotted the blue tie. The Catholic school boys wore white shirts and blue ties. For a long time his mother had to knot his tie for him. And he couldn't figure out how to put his jacket on, how to hold it so that a certain arm goes in a certain sleeve hole, and sometimes he had to place the jacket flat on the ground, sit down in front of it and then match an arm to a hole, sort of lying down backwards into the jacket.

Imagine what Nicky said, watching this spectacle.

But he was over that now. He was over the tantrums, pretty much, and the silent treatment he used to give his mother when he was mad at her, and the times he locked the bathroom door and tried to suffocate himself with the shower curtain.

He was over the tantrums because he wasn't playing chess. Mr. Bronzini called it a sabbatical. One of those words of his, to be spelled, explained and acted out. Matty had his own word. Sick.

He could not take the losing. It was too awful. It made him physically weak and massively angry. It sent him reeling through the flat, arms windmilling. His brother bopped him on the head and that made him madder. He did not have enough height and weight to contain all his rage. He was past the point of crying. Losing made his limbs shake. He gasped for air. He did not understand why someone so small, young and unprepared should have to squat in the path of this juggernaut called losing.

He put on his tie and went to school. First he slipped the new dog tag over his neck, for atomic attack, with his name and school inscribed on the disk, and then he put on his blue tie and walked the five blocks to school.

Matty sat in the row next to the cloakroom and was one of three pupils who opened and closed the sliding doors of the cloakroom at designated times. They worked in unison, with a whoosh and bang. This was their assignment.

It was Catherine Conway's assignment to clap the erasers every Friday, out the back door above the schoolyard, her eyes smarting in the chalk dust.

Richard Stasiak was assigned to open and close the windows. He took the window pole with the hook at one end and he fitted the hook into the loop at the top of the window and then pushed or pulled. Richard Stasiak was big and tall and this was the logical job for him.

They sat at their desks, forty boys and girls, sixth-graders, this drab gray day, backs erect, feet together, watching Sister Edgar.

Sister prowled the space between her desk and the blackboard, moving in a rustle of monochrome cotton, scrubbed hands flashing. She recited questions from the Baltimore Catechism and her students responded in a single crystal voice.

Matty believed in the Baltimore Catechism. It had all the questions and all the answers and it had love, hate, damnation and washing other people's feet, it had whips, thorns and resurrections, it had angels, shepherds, thieves and Jews, it had hosanna in the highest.

He didn't know what that meant, hosanna in the highest, and was afraid to ask. They were all afraid. They'd been afraid for a week, ever since Sister had banged Michael Kalenka's head against the blackboard when he gave a snippy answer to an easy question. They were studying the Creation and the Fall of Man, lesson five in the Baltimore Catechism, and Sister pointed to a picture in the book of a man and woman standing more or less undressed beneath an apple tree with a serpent coiled on a limb and she called on Michael Kalenka and asked him to identify the man and woman, the easiest question she'd ever asked, and Michael Kalenka stood up and looked at the picture, and he thought and looked and thought, and Sister said, "The original parents of us all," and Michael Kalenka thought and grinned and said, "Tarzan and Jane."

Sister flew at Michael Kalenka and collected the boy in the wing-folds of her habit. He was practically out of sight until she suddenly propelled him toward the blackboard headfirst. The impact was strong and true. There was a sound so real, a thud and a subsequent hum, the whole panel vibrating, that the boys and girls went slack in their seats, wide-eyed and semiliquid. Blown out of their rigid posture. And Michael Kalenka stood stunned and rag-dollish, sheepish, guilty, grinning but mostly just stunned and rag-armed and sagging.

Sister asked questions from the catechism and they responded in unison. Matty liked doing this. To hear the assigned questions and to recite the right answers was the best part of the school day.

Sister knew the catechism by heart and Matty knew each day's lesson by heart, with more time for homework now and with a secret respect for Sister Edgar, who was known throughout the school as Sister Skelly Bone for the acute contours of her face and the whiteness of her complexion and the way her lean hands seemed ever ready to administer some grave touch, a cold and bony tag that makes you *it* forever.

He liked the way the response to each question repeated the question before delivering the answer.

Sister said, "What do we mean when we say that Christ will come from thence to judge the living and the dead?"

The class replied in unison, "When we say that Christ will come from thence to judge the living and the dead, we mean that on the last day Our Lord will come to judge everyone who has ever lived in this world."

Then Sister told them to place their dog tags out above their shirts and blouses so she could see them. She wanted to make sure they were wearing their tags. The tags were designed to help rescue workers identify children who were lost, missing, injured, maimed, mutilated, unconscious or dead in the hours following the onset of atomic war.

Sister went up and down the aisles, bending to read each tag. At approach distance she smelled laundered and starched, steam-ironed, and her nails were buffed to a glassy lava finish, and the rosary beads that hung from her belt like a zoot-suiter's key chain were blinky bright, and when she rustled low and near she smelled more intimately of tooth powder and cleansing agents and the penance of scoured skin.

She said, "Woe betide the child who is not wearing a tag or who is wearing someone else's tag."

717

It had been known to happen, in other classes, that a boy and girl switched tags to signify a kind of atomic fondling.

When Sister was finished with her inspection she said nothing, which surprised the class. They were expecting a drill, the duck-and-cover drill, which they'd rehearsed before the tags arrived. Now that they had the tags, their names inscribed on wispy tin, the drill was not a remote exercise but was all about them, and so was atomic war.

Instead she went back to the catechism, to questions and answers, until Annette Esposito, an eighth-grader, came in with a note from the principal. Sister read the note and looked at Annette Esposito and said, "What are these?"

At first nobody knew what she meant. Then the class realized she was looking at Annette Esposito's chest, her breasts, which caused bulges under her blue jumper.

"What's all this? Get rid of this. I don't want to see this next time you come in here."

The boys and girls went low in their seats, tingling a little at the exposure of Annette Esposito as a freak of nature. Their eyes went shifty and bright. They bit their knuckles and made small damp throat noises. When Annette Esposito walked out the door, not unproud, flouncing slightly, shoulders thrown back, every eyeball in the room clicked in her direction, fastened on her breasts of course, not a common object of contemplation in the life of the sixth grade.

Sister did not call the drill. She did penmanship instead, demonstrating on the blackboard the cursive flair of her own hand. She showed the slant, the loop, she stressed the need to stay between the ruled lines, she told them to take their fountain pens and follow the motions she made in the air, and they did, working the wrists, looping in unison, and they shaped a tempestuous capital T that resembled a rowboat in a rainstorm.

Matty sat there nearly spellbound, writing in the air with his brother's old Parker vacumatic, a streaked green model with an arrow clip, but his mood went flat when the bell rang for lunch and Sister crook'd a forefinger in his direction.

"Matthew Shay."

718

His own name stunned him, coming from her lips.

"See me before you leave the room."

With his two assigned mates he slid open the cloakroom doors and got his coat and waited for the room to empty and then presented himself at Sister's desk.

She had tight blue eyes and thin lips and a nose that was slightly bumpy up near the bridge.

"In the schoolyard yesterday. You were huddled with several others. Looking at a magazine."

The terror of being alone with Sister Edgar.

"I would like to know. Firstly. The name of the magazine."

She leaned on a corner of the desk lightly twirling her beads, the big crucifix moving in a wobbly spin with Christ's body bowed out from the cross.

"Secondly. A summary of the contents."

The answers passed through his mind.

1. Movieland magazine.

2. Full-page faces of Rita Hayworth and Lana Turner. Also, Mario Lanza's Heart Stood Still. There were articles about stars he'd never heard of. There were ads for French nighties and dance panties.

What if she asked him about these things?

Sister peered closely, waiting. He kept his hands behind his back to conceal his gnawed fingernails and the shreds of dead skin at the edges.

Would he have to explain that a dance panty is when they embroider a fox-trotting couple on the leg of a lady's underwear?

And what if the magazine was banned by the Legion of Decency and she asked him who it belonged to? Although she would never end a sentence with a preposition.

"Matthew. Yes?"

If he had a choice between lying to Sister Edgar and snitching on a classmate, he'd have to snitch, instantly and remorselessly. And what about the ads all over the back of the magazine for bust creams and better bust contours?

Matthew-yes was not a question. It was a summons to urgency and truth. And he told her the name of the magazine and who was on the

719

cover and what was inside, sticking to the romances and heartbreaks of the stars, and Sister seemed interested and pleased.

He was surprised and encouraged and became less tentative, describing the Hollywood homes of certain stars, and Sister asked little leading questions, trying to obscure her interest by looking out the window, and he grew confident and expansive, speaking rapidly and more or less uncontrollably, making things up when he couldn't recall the details of a story or a photograph, feeling a sense of desperate elation, and Sister was eating it up.

She knew a lot about the stars. Their favorite flavors and worst insect bites and their wallflower nights in high school. Their basic everydayness inside the cosmetic surgeries and tragic marriages. She looked out the window and asked him sly testing questions and dropped little comments here and there.

He was able to stand outside the scene, hearing his own voice, watching the babbling boy at ease in the company of the hooded nun. But he wasn't completely unwary. It was her after all, habit and hood. The cloth was daunting. She was all cloth. She was a wall of laundered cloth. A woman of the cloth.

In the schoolyard after lunch Richard Stasiak did an amazing thing. Matty saw it without knowing for a moment quite what he'd seen. Richard Stasiak wore underwear so shabby and itchy and threadbare that he unbuttoned his fly and stuck his hand in there and pulled the underwear right off his body, yanking the ratty thing out of his fly and throwing it at Mary Feeley, who skipped away backwards, hands to her mouth as if she'd seen something it was best to keep unspoken.

Then they all went into class again.

Nick grabbed a ride every morning with another packer in the plant, waiting on a cold corner in the dark and then driving down to the ass-end of the Bronx where one river does a curl into the other and the ice-cream plant sits in the weeds like a pygmy prison on the Zambezi and this was better than taking the train in the lockstep drudge of the rush.

After work he got dropped near the zoo and walked west past his brother's school, where he saw a guy in one car giving a push to six guys in another. He came to the building where they lived and turned at Donato's grocery and went thirty yards down the narrow street and swung into an opening that led down a set of concrete steps into the network of alleyways that ran between five or six buildings clustered here.

Down the yards, this was called.

Close-set buildings, laundry lines, slant light, patches of weeds, a few would-be gardens and bare ailanthus trees and the fire escapes that fixed fretwork patterns of light and shade on the walls and paved surfaces.

Nick ducked under overhangs and passed through narrow openings. There were padlocked doors and doors ajar. There were basement passages connecting utility rooms and alcoves for trash cans and the old coal bins that housed furnaces now and the storage rooms where merchants on the street kept their inventory—a smell that was part garbage and part dank stone, a mildew creep and a thick chill, a sense that everything that ever happened here was retained in the air, soaked and cross-scented with fungus and wetness and coffee grounds and mops in big sinks.

He'd spent his childhood half in the streets and half down the yards with a little extra squeezed in for the rooftops and fire escapes.

He went past a furnace room and opened a door at the end of the passage. George the Waiter was sitting in a small storage room he used as a home, he said, away from home. He saw Nick in the doorway and nodded him in. George had an arrangement with the super. The room had a cot, a table, a rat trap, a couple of chairs, a couple of dangling lightbulbs and an array of paint cans and plumbing equipment, and Nick was pretty sure the arrangement involved a woman who came here to visit George, a woman he paid for sex, and the super let him use the room in exchange for some of the same, periodically, the woman taking care of the super and getting paid by George.

"I figured you'd be here."

"I'm here," George said.

"I have a sixth sense about these things."

"You see through walls."

George pushed a deck of cards to the middle of the table and Nick sat down.

"Just a sixth sense. I'm still working on walls."

"Did it tell you, this sense of yours, what happened in the poolroom in the middle of the night?"

He was a bachelor for life, George, and he had two jobs and lived with his eighty-year-old grandmother and shot pool for whole days sometimes when he wasn't working. And when he wasn't doing any of these things Nick would find him here and they'd play a card game called *briscola*, pronounced breeshk in dialect, a game the old men played, and they played just to pass the time, which there were worse ways of doing because there was something about George the Waiter that Nick found interesting.

"When, last night?"

"Last night. The place got robbed."

"The poolroom got robbed?"

"Three men with pistols," George said and he made a sound like movie music.

"Three men with pistols. You were there?"

"I went to work in the restaurant six o'clock, went back at eleven and shot a game and then went home. Happened much later. They robbed the poker game."

"They robbed the poker game?"

"You gonna repeat everything I say?"

"I'm amazed by what I'm hearing."

"And stocking masks."

"And stocking masks. What's that?"

"A woman's stocking, a nylon stocking."

"On their face?" Nick said.

"No, on their legs. Madonn', I thought this kid was smart."

"I'm amazed by what I'm hearing. On their face."

"On their face. So their features don't show."

"Stocking masks. Three men. Where was what's-his-name? The guy at the door who's supposed to be armed and dangerous. Where was this Walls?"

"He didn't show."

"Walls didn't show. That's interesting."

"They cleaned out the table nice-nice. Then they cleaned out the players one by one, turning out their pockets. Then they cleaned out Mike the Book, who's holding whatever he's holding that's a full day's take. Pool receipts and bets."

"How much?"

"Total. Over twelve thousand I hear. This is I hear. Who knows how much?"

"Twelve thousand."

"Three men with pistols. Pistolas."

And George made twirling moves with his hands at belt level like a Mexican bandit showing off his guns and it was rare for him to be so breezy.

Nick shuffled and dealt.

"I meant to get some beer," he said.

"Who sells beer to a minor?"

"I told Donato's wife I'm nineteen. She says, What do you think I'm *stunat'*?"

"But she sells you the beer."

"She sells me the beer."

"She does it out of spite."

"For who?"

"The world," George said.

"Stocking masks. I'm amazed by this."

They played cards a while and then George leaned over and opened the drawer at the end of the table and felt around for cigarettes without taking his eyes off his cards.

"You keep your rubbers in there?"

"Never mind what I keep in there."

"Who is she? Trust me. Who'm I gonna tell? Is she the one I saw you rowing a boat in the park one day?"

"If you saw me with a woman in public, then she's not the woman who comes here. And you didn't see me in no boat, wise guy."

"George, I'm being serious."

"What?"

"You fix up your friends?"

George gave him a level look from out of those deep emptyish eyes.

"This is not a girl. This is a woman. And it's not for you. I'm pushing forty, Nicky. You can get what you need without paying for it."

Maybe this is what interested Nick. The fact that George was the loneliest man he'd ever known. George was lonely in his walk, his voice, his posture and in the way a whole room, the poolroom with its clash of noises and flung insults and ragged laughs—the way George's corner of the room was different even if he was shooting a game with someone else. George carried the condition everywhere he went and it seemed to be okay with him. That was the interesting thing. Maybe it was his choice to live this way and maybe it wasn't but either way he made it seem all right.

"Talk about buying beer."

"Yeah, what?" Nick said.

"This shit-ass job of yours, which you should of stayed in school in my opinion."

"This shit-ass job, what?"

"I been talking to somebody. You can make more money on a truck. Not beer but soda. Delivering to stores and supermarkets. 7-Up."

"It makes me wince when I drink it."

"You'll wince all right. You unload the crates of full bottles and then you load up on empties. Make you a man."

"Make me a man how?"

"Brute labor, that's how. In summer you just about die. I did it one summer. I cun't fucking believe it. Lost twenty pounds my first two days."

Nick didn't think it was necessary to have one job for life and start a family and live in a house with dinner on the table at six every night and he thought about George, an older guy who'd survived the loss of these things—not the loss but the never-having. Played cards, played pool, got laid, a few dollars in his pocket, not a whole lot of time to think. Fuck you, I'll die alone. That's what George was saying in his heart.

"Pays decent?"

"Better than you're making. Steadier. Safer except you'll get four hernias your first week. And a stroke come summer. Make you a man, Nicky."

"I appreciate."

"You don't have to say nothing. Maybe they'll hire you, maybe they won't."

"I want you to know. I appreciate."

"They'll take one look at you. This is a guy all he thinks about is getting laid. We better find a polack somewhere."

Nick liked that. They played cards a while longer and he realized George was giving him an odd look, measuring him somehow.

"You think I keep rubbers in this drawer here?"

"I don't know."

"You want to see what I keep in here?"

"I don't know, George. Sure, why not?"

"No. I don't think you want to see what I keep in here."

"Sure, why not?"

"No. Big mistake. You'll talk."

"I won't talk. Who'm I gonna tell?"

All right. George was having a little fun with him, not that he changed expression. Raw, drawn, tired, with receding hair and long fingers stained with cigarette tar.

"Because I trust you, Nicky."

He reached into the drawer and came out with a box of kitchen matches and a spoon.

"We used to call these lucifers, these wood matches."

The utensil was an ordinary spoon clouded on the bottom of the bowl, stained like George's fingers, only darker and marbled.

"I'm watching," Nick said.

"You interested?"

"I'm interested," he said.

George reached into the drawer and came out with a length of elastic, medical-looking, a strapping device of some kind. He tossed it next to the matches and looked at Nick.

"I'm still watching."

"You watching?"

"I'm watching."

George reached in and came out with a hypodermic needle, a needle and dusty syringe, and he held it in front of Nicky's face.

725

"You watching? Watch."

It took Nick a minute to understand all this. This was new to him. Drugs. Who used drugs around here? He felt dumb and confused and very young suddenly.

"You use this stuff?"

George lifted a fold-over pouch out of his breast pocket. He wagged it several times and dropped it back in.

"*Eroina*," he said.

Nick felt dumb all right. He felt like someone had just sandbagged him in an alley. Wham. He almost put a hand to the back of his neck.

"Let me see it," he said.

George took out the pouch and handed it to him. Nick lifted the flap and tried to sniff the powder.

"What are you smelling? It don't smell."

He handed it back.

"How come?"

"How come what?"

"You use this stuff."

George rolled up the sleeve on his left arm. There were stippled marks and scars and in the crook of the elbow a dark mass, a fester of busted blood vessels and general wreckage.

Then he brandished the needle, enjoying himself.

"You asked me do I fix up my friends? What kind of fix?"

"Hey. Get away."

"We'll start you slow. Skin-pop. You don't hit a vein."

"I skeeve needles, George. Get that thing away from me."

"You hit the plunger, see."

"This I don't need."

"Come on. We'll tie you off."

George brandished the elastic belt and Nick felt he had to get up and stand across the room. The older man enjoyed that.

"How come?" he said.

"How come how come. You want to get laid. How come," George said.

For years kids played hango seek down the yards and there were nickel-and-dime dice games and older guys who might tap a keg on a hot day and drink a few brews standing up in the shade and women who hung out the windows to get some air and complain about the cursing.

"You could put that needle in your arm? Man, I skeeve that like death."

George smiled. He was happy. He swept his works back in the drawer and lit up a cigarette and sat there with his face in the smoke.

They talked about the robbery and after a while the tone went back to normal.

"Gotta go," Nick said.

"Be good."

"See you at Mike's."

"Be good," George said.

Nick made a turn in the dim passage and went out into a small courtyard where trash cans stood against the wall and he walked up the back stairs and through the heavy metal door into his building.

George had cut him down to size all right. George had taught him a lesson in serious things.

It happened near the end of the day when no one expected it. This was her intention of course. It happened fast and hard and unexpected.

Sister turned from the blackboard where she'd been diagramming a compound sentence, the chalked structure so complex and self-appending it began to resemble the fire-escaped facade of the kind of building most of the boys and girls lived in.

She paused just long enough to let them know that something was coming but not so long that they might guess what it was.

Then she said, "Duck and cover! Duck and cover! Duck and cover!"

For a long moment they were too shocked to think straight. Slow, shocked, klutzy and dumb. They began to tumble out of their seats, knocking over books and bumping each other, all scuttling to the three designated walls as they'd been trained to do, squat-hopping like people in potato sacks.

The fourth wall was the window wall, which they'd been told to avoid.

Matty saw Francis X. Cavanaugh blunder nuts-first into a desk edge. He felt a sympathetic quiver in his loins.

And Sister's voice keening across the room, drop and duck, duck and cover, and the kids jostling for position and then going into deep genuflections, heads to the floor, eyes shut, hands guarding the face from bomb-flash.

It was a long time before they were positioned and settled and still.

Matty had his head at the base of the cloakroom door nearest his desk. He liked to duck and cover. There was a sense of acting in unison that he found satisfying. It was not so different really from opening and shutting the cloakroom doors with two of his classmates or reciting mass answers to Sister's questions from the catechism. He felt the comfort of numbers. He felt snug and safe here on the floor, positioned more or less identically with the others. After the first moments of surprise and confusion, they were all calm now. This was the first rule of atomic attack. Keep calm. Do not get excited or excite others. Another rule, Do not touch things.

He felt an odd belonging in the duck-and-cover. It was a community of look-alikes and do-alikes, heads down, elbows tucked, fannies in the air. The overbrained boy of the thirty-two pieces and the million trillion combinations liked to nestle in his designated slot, listening to Sister's voice repeat all the cautions and commands like a siren lifting and dipping in the dopplered haze of another nondescript day.

Keep calm.

Do not touch things.

Do not answer a ringing phone.

Unplug your toaster.

Do not drive a motor vehicle.

Carry a handkerchief to place over your mouth.

In their prayer posture they could have been anyone from anywhere. The faithful of old Samarkand bending to their hojatollah. The only thing that mattered was the abject entreaty, the adoration of the cloud of all-power—forty softly throbbing bodies arrayed along the walls.

She ordered them back to their normal places. They got up, retrieved their fallen books and slid a little hangdog into their seats, watching Sister Edgar so they might ascertain how totally foolish they ought to feel.

Never end a sentence with a preposition and never begin a sentence with an And.

Sister was not pleased with their performance. She leaned over her desk, hands so tensed on the wood surface they could see the blood drain from her knuckles.

They waited for her to tell them to do it again.

"Hey Bobby."

"I'm busy over here."

"Hey Bobby."

"I'm busy over here."

"Hey Bobby. There's something we want to tell you."

"I told you, okay, I'm busy."

"JuJu wants to tell you. Hey Bobby. Listen."

"Go way, all right?"

"Hey Bobby."

"Fuck out of here."

"Hey Bobby."

"You see I'm working over here?"

"Hey Bobby. JuJu wants to tell you this one thing."

"What."

"Hey Bobby."

"All right. What."

"This one thing."

"All right. What."

"Shit in your fist and squeeze it," Nick said.

She didn't know what to call it, a lightness, a waft, something with change in it, treebloom or fragrant rain, and she stood on the stoop and watched a man across the street chip rust from his fire escape, up on the fourth floor.

A truck pulled up in front of the grocery two doors down. The grocer's son came out and unlocked the metal hatch in the sidewalk and lifted the two swing-back sections. The men unloaded crates of soda and took them on a handcart into the store, the older man, or carried them by the hand grips, the younger, down the hatchway into the storage cellar.

Klara lit a cigarette and thought about going across the street to get the child, who was being minded by the tailor's wife today, this was a Wednesday, because it was nearly time.

The younger man wandered over to the stoop on the way to his third or fourth trip into the cellar.

"You wouldn't think of saving me a drag, would you, on that cigarette?"

She looked at him, taking in the question.

"Hate to ask," he said.

She looked at him, taking in the damp shirt and scuffed dungarees, the way he held the crate at belly level, forearms veined beneath the rolled sleeves.

"One drag could mean the difference," he said, "between life and death."

She said, "In which direction?"

He smiled and looked away. Then he looked at her and said, "When you need a smoke, does it matter?"

She reached out and offered the cigarette but he didn't put down the soda crate and take it. Instead he climbed two steps in her direction and looked right at her and this meant she had to place the cigarette between his lips or withdraw the offer.

731

At first she didn't do either. She took a drag herself and said, "Aren't you afraid it'll stunt your growth?"

Six days later, or seven, she came out of the flat and locked the door. There was someone on the stoop looking in through the vestibule. She knew exactly who it was and what he was here for and she made a gesture that was either a shrug or a come-on. Then she put the key back in the door she'd just locked, unlocking it.

He followed her into the spare room and when she turned he was right there. He was pretty big and lifted her into the wall. She kicked out of her shoes and grabbed his hair, a fistful, and jerked his face away from hers so she could look at him.

When they were nearly naked they stood watching each other. There was no bed or sofa and they barely touched, his hand on her upper arm, which she pushed away. She kept waiting to feel crazy but didn't. He put his hand on her upper arm and she knocked it off. He shrugged and laughed, like what's going on. She put her hand to his chest. She could make him stop laughing by touching him.

She said, "Are you a boy I ought to know? Who are you? Not that I give a damn."

He was darkish and well-built and he moved her into the wall again. She pushed her hair out of her face. She thought as long as she kept him in this one room, no one could say there was something crazy going on. This was the spare room, the paint room. She wasn't supposed to be naked here but aside from that, her feet cold on the bare floor, there was nothing awfully strange happening here.

He had his hands all over her. He smelled of cigarettes and something else, some odd body must mixed with sweat. They kissed for a time that seemed to be hours. It seemed to be taking hours, long sluicy kisses that she disappeared into, distant, empty, feeling his hand brusque on her tit, but also practical all of a sudden, yes, pushing him off and going into the closet down the hall and getting the spare mattress for the child's bed, a Jewish heirloom of the generations.

She went back to the room and gave him the mattress, rolled up and tied in a length of twine. He stood it on end and pretended to hump it, his tongue hanging out.

She noticed the room. He unknotted the twine and flopped the small mattress down and lowered himself to his knees, waiting. The room was beautiful in this light, shadow-banded, all lines and gaps, claire-obscure, and she walked over to him, untrusting of course, and motioned for him to sit back on his haunches.

She didn't know what would come next, second to second, and kept resisting even as she moved into him, biting and stroking, the word stroke, the word cock, half resisting everything he did, smelling work and basement on his body, sour rooms webbed in dust.

They were everywhere on each other, noisy and damp, taking in air the way you drink down water, deep and sort of smacking, in drawn portions. He was here to be explored a little. She liked stopping and watching, or looking away actually, or guiding his hand, or going into the kitchen for a glass of water and coming back and pouring it partly on his chest, a body disproportionate to the bedding, and then handing him the glass and watching him drink and thinking there was nothing crazy going on that she could clearly locate except that she was naked in her workroom.

Then they were everywhere at once again, looped about each other, everything new for the second time, and she closed her eyes to see them together, which she could almost do, which she could do for the sheerest time, bodies turned and edged and sidled, one way and the other, this and that concurrent, here but also there, like back-fronted Picasso lovers.

When he went to find the toilet she thought she'd feel strange and crazy and out of her mind, finally, but she just sat on the mattress smoking.

"Thirteen inch we got."

"Thirteen inch."

"What-do-you-call. Admiral."

"Admiral. This is, what, better than Captain?"

"Clear. No snow."

"Thirteen inch. What kind of thirteen inch? You want thirteen inch? Bend over."

"Hey. You and what army?"

"Bend over. I'll show you no snow."

"You and what army?"

"You got an Admiral. I give you a Motorola."

"Your whole family couldn't come up with thirteen inches. Including your grandfather and his monkey."

Bronzini stood before his class, forty-four stoical souls in general science. Most sixteen years old, a few older, even eighteen, the dopier ones, the discombobulates, left back at some point in the long alpine march to knowledge.

He stood behind his platformed desk and spoke to the walls and the ceiling, to the windows at the far end of the room. He spoke to the bus-fumed air of Fordham Road and the university in the trees beyond, where seniors at the college wore bachelor robes and where the names of the alumni dead of World War I were engraved on capitals atop the stone posts that marked the south boundary of the campus.

Universitas Fordhamensis.

"We can't see the world clearly until we understand how nature is organized. We need to count, measure and test. This is the scientific method. Science. The observation and description of phenomena. Phenomena. Things perceptible to the senses. The seasons make sense. At a certain time the cold diminishes, the days grow longer. It happens at the same time every year. We spoke last class about the difference between equinox and solstice and you remember this, I trust, Miss Innocenti. The planets move in an orderly manner. We can predict their passage across the skies. And we can admire the mathematics involved. The ellipsoid passage of the planets around the sun. Ellipse. A slightly flattened circle. Here we detect form and order, we see the laws of nature in their splendid harmony. Think of the rhythm of waves. The birth of babies. When a woman is due to give birth, Applebaum, eyes front, we say she is coming to term. The precision of nature becomes evident in the birth-giving process. The woman follows stages. The fetus grows and develops. We can predict, we can say roughly this week or next week is the time when the child will be born. Coming to term, Miss Innocenti, as you chew your gum a mile a minute. Carrying the fetus to term. Nine months. Seven pounds two ounces. We need numbers to make sense of the world. We think in numbers. We think in decades. Because we need organizing principles, Alfonse Catanzaro, yes, to make us less muddled."

A voice piped up at the back of the class.

"Call him Alan."

A rush of amusement moved through the room like wind over dune grass. Bronzini did not have major problems of discipline. The students sensed his unwillingness to engage in confrontation and they read his museful mild delivery, sometimes far-wandering, as a kind of private escape, not unlike their own, from the assignment of the day.

A second voice near the window, a girl's, sissy-mimicking.

"Don't call me Alfonse. Call me Alan. I want to be an actor in the movies."

A deeper ripple of mirth this time and Bronzini was sad for the boy, skinny Alfonse, but did not rebuke them, kept talking, talked over the momentary rollick—skinny sorry Alfonse, grape-stained with tragic acne.

"We need numbers, letters, maps, graphs. We need scientific formulas to understand the structure of matter. E equals MC squared."

He wrote the equation on the blackboard.

"How is it that a few marks chalked on a blackboard, a few little squiggly signs can change the shape of human history? Energy, mass, speed of light. Protons, neutrons, electrons. How small is the atom? I will tell you. If people were the size of atoms—think about it, Gagliardi—the population of the earth would fit on the head of a pin. Never mind the vast amounts of energy stored in matter. Matter. Something that has mass—a solid, a liquid, a gas. Never mind what happens when we split the atom and release this energy. Energy. The capacity of a physical system to do work. I want to know how it is that a few marks on a slate or a piece of paper, a little black on white, or white on black, can carry so much information and contain such shattering implications. Never mind the energy packed in the atom. What about the energy contained in this equation? This is the real power. How the mind operates. How the mind identifies, analyzes and represents. What beauty and power. What marvels of imagination does it

735

require to reduce the complex forces of nature, all those unseeable magical actions inside the atom—to express all this with a bing and a bang on a blackboard. The atom. The unit of matter regarded as the source of nuclear energy. The Greeks of the fifth century B.C. proposed the idea of the atom. B.C., Miss Innocenti. Before Chewing Gum. Small, small, small. Something inside something else inside something else. Down, down, down. Under, under, under. Next time, chapter seven. Be prepared for an oral quiz."

Barely an audible groan.

"Maximum public embarrassment," Bronzini said.

They bundled out of the room and into the long halls, where four thousand others were beginning to mass in the vast hormonal clamor that marked the condition of release.

It was still winter but there was something soft in the air today, that rhythmic fiction of early spring, so sweet to be deceived by, and Albert took his usual route into the shopping streets, poking into stores and social clubs.

Here he ate a pignoli cookie and asked after the woman's son, an artilleryman in Korea. There he thumbed his mustache and stood amused in the company of an eager complainant, a man loud with the measliest grievance, pink-eyed and spitting.

In the pork store he talked to a couple of newcomers, Calabrian, a woman and her trail-along daughter, and it made him think of his mother and sister, down that memory tunnel, and how the girl fairly clung to her mother.

Now the mother lay in a plot in Queens, in a great wide meadow of stones and crosses, thousands of souls outside the ordinary sprawl, a sovereign people uncomplaining.

He bought meat here, fish there, and headed home. He thought about the saint's day every summer when members of the church band walked through the streets playing heart-heavy pieces that brought women's faces to the open windows of the tenements. It was the custom of the musicians to slow-step along a certain residential street and stop at a particular private house, a frame structure with a front porch and rose trellis, the home of the olive oil importer. When they stopped playing the family invited them in and they entered in their band uniforms of black pants and white shirt, carrying their instruments. Such an old and dignified custom, the elderly men, the obese trombonist, the young man hollowed out by the bass drum strapped to his torso, each shuffling into the shady house for a glass of red wine.

JuJu didn't want to follow him in but he had to. Once Nick went in, JuJu had to go in too.

He'd wanted to see a person dead and Nick was going to show him. They stood in the anteroom of the funeral home near Third Avenue, where twenty or thirty men were smoking and talking.

"Maybe this is not a good idea," JuJu said.

"Just be sure you don't laugh."

"What am I gonna laugh?"

"Show some respect," Nick said. "We want them to think we're family."

Nick shoved him and they went into the viewing room. Women sat in folding chairs saying their beads and there were sofas against the walls, younger women looking strange in black, sealed away from knowing, with several small girls placed among them, grave and pale.

They went up to the casket and looked in. It was an old man with nostrils gaped wide and the hands of a carpenter or mason, copper fingers rough and notched.

"Here's your body. Soak it up."

They knelt at the casket.

"He doesn't look that bad," JuJu said.

"I think they plucked his eyebrows."

"I thought it would be different," JuJu said.

"Different how?"

"I don't know. White," JuJu said. "The whole face chalk white."

"They put makeup and grooming."

"White and stiff, I thought."

"He's not stiff, this man?"

"He could almost be asleep. If he slept in a suit."

"So you're disappointed then."

"I'm a little, yeah, disappointed."

"Why don't you say it louder," Nick said, "so they can drag us out to the street and beat us to death."

"This was a bad idea of yours."

"We're supposed to have an envelope," Nick said.

"This was a bad idea. What kind of envelope?"

"If we're family," Nick said. "A mass card or money."

"I thought an envelope is when you get married. Not when you die."

"An envelope is when you do anything. They're always doing envelopes."

"This was a bad idea. I'm ready to leave."

"Too soon. Say a prayer. Show them you're praying. Show them respect," Nick said. "Women in black dresses. We don't show respect, they tear us apart."

In a corner of the poolroom a guy named Stevie hawked up a wad of pearly phlegm, called an oyster, and spat it down the neck of his Coke bottle.

JuJu said, "I ask you for a slug of soda, you do this?"

"Hey. I didn't say no."

"But you do this? You spit in it?"

"You asked for a slug. I'm saying. Take two slugs."

Stevie cleared another oyster out of his throat and spat it into the bottle and handed the bottle to JuJu.

"But you do this? You hack up this big thing, which you think nobody in his right mind's gonna drink from a bottle that has this big thing floating in there."

"You want a slug. Hey. Take a slug. Take whatever."

"So you're giving me your whole soda, you're saying. Take whatever. If I'm crazy enough to drink it."

"What's mines is yours," Stevie said.

JuJu smiled falsely, a look with a mocking quality. Then he drank the whole thing down in one long slug. He followed with a small gassy belch and tossed the bottle back to Stevie.

Nick watched in admiration.

Later that night he took Mike the Dog out for a walk. He walked along the hospital wall and then went east through the empty streets. He stood across the street from the building where the woman lived. There was a bed in the front room, stripped of sheets, an empty bed cranked up, easy enough to see just to the right of the stoop, the curtains half drawn, a lamp lit nearby, and he stood there a while smoking.

When he got back with the dog, two men were coming down the poolroom steps. He thought he recognized one of them from the poker game and they came down the steps in a kind of rumble, making the dog back off.

Mike was alone, at the counter, doing his tally.

"Where'd you take him, to the men's room at Grand Central?"

Nick wagged a thumb at the men who'd just left.

"I know those guys?"

"I don't know. You know those guys?"

"Serious business, right?"

"I might as well tell you," Mike said. "You'll hear about it anyway."

"What?"

"You remember the guy who sat by the door when we ran the games?"

"Sure. Walls."

"Walls was not here the night of the holdup."

"I thought that was interesting."

"A number of people did. And a number of people who were here that night thought that one of the three holdup men."

"Wait. They wore masks, right?"

"Could have been Walls. Mask or no mask. And of course Walls has not been seen since. So you can imagine the interest being shown in his whereabouts. Not to mention two of the players are very close," Mike said, "to the organization."

"The organization. And now?"

"Walls has been seen."

"Walls has been seen. They found him."

"And he's shit out of luck. In a Puerto Rican grocery about a mile from here."

"What's he doing in a Puerto Rican grocery?"

739

"Buying a green banana. Hey. How the hell do I know?"

Nick laughed. The news excited him. He found it satisfying even though he liked Walls, he admired Walls, based on the few words they'd exchanged that one time. They'd found him and killed him. He told himself to remember to get a paper first thing in the morning. It was bound to be in the papers, this kind of thing.

"He took your money too," Nick said. "Not just the cash on the table."

Mike stood on a chair to turn off the TV, which was running without the sound.

"I'm not looking to celebrate," he said. "This is a thing it brings the wrong kind of attention. I have the precinct I have to keep greased so they don't close me down. The robbery was bad enough. This thing brings homicide detectives and reporters coming around."

"How'd they do it?"

"How'd they do it. They shot him. Bang bang."

"I know. But how? How many guys? What kind of weapons?"

Photograph of blood-streaked body with towel covering head for decency sake.

"They shoot anyone else? They get away in one car, two cars?"

"I don't know. I didn't ask."

"He was armed, this Walls, when they shot him?"

"I don't know," Mike said.

"They shot him in the head or what?"

"Nicky. I say all right. Go home and get some sleep."

They went to the show downtown and walked around Times Square looking at people, all kinds, and they felt superior and dumb at the same time.

They took the el back home late at night with JuJu and Ray sitting next to each other and Nick stretched out on the long wicker seat across the aisle.

"You know, I'm thinking," JuJu said. "We never should of gone in there. It's not right. Fool around, fool around, fool around. I say all right. But this is not a thing we should of done."

"You're guilty," Nick said.

"The man's laid out. Leave him alone. If he was some jerk sat on his ass all his life, be different maybe. This is a working man. The man's laid out."

Nick assumed the position of a prepared body.

"You're guilty. Go to church and confess. You'll feel better," he said.

Ray Lofaro had no idea what they were talking about. JuJu wouldn't tell him as a matter of principle and Nick wouldn't tell him because he didn't want to be bothered.

The train was a local and took forever.

They rode past the dark tenements of the lower Bronx, past the sleeping thousands in their beds, and Nick got up and tried to rip the wicker apart, first with his hands, which was hard to do, and then by kicking it in and using his hands again to pick apart the weaved strands.

A man at the other end of the car got up and went into the next car and Nick watched him, deciding whether this was an insult or not.

Then he kicked some more, standing back and using the heel edge of his shoe to stave in the back of the seat. He poked with both hands, peeling off strips of wicker in a series of long dry snapping sounds.

His buddies had nothing to say.

He got off one stop before their regular stop and they watched him go out the door. He walked over to the building where she lived. He stood across the street smoking, watching the building. The lamp was lit in the front room but the bed was gone now.

He knew that Mr. Bronzini's mother had died recently. His own mother telling him. And over a day or two he began to make the connection that the bed was the old woman's bed, that the apartment was Mr. Bronzini's apartment, that the woman he'd fucked in the apartment was Mr. Bronzini's wife.

He found it didn't matter much. He'd walked past the building a number of times, in daylight, and never saw her. He'd stood on the stoop once or twice, smoking, and she hadn't come out. Lately he'd been standing in the dark and watching the building, after midnight mostly, those sameshit nights, passing the time before he was ready to go to bed.

He was seventeen years and some months. He'd get drafted soon and that was probably not a bad thing to happen. His friend Allie was in uniform now, finished basic, and he was headed to Korea, where he'd fuck the best-looking women, he said, and leave sloppy seconds for Nick and the others.

He stood there smoking. He watched her building and he thought about a thousand things, sane, crazy, dumb, and he thought about the woman.

6

The empty lot was less than a block from the school entrance, a rambling waste with a higher and lower level, boulders, weeds and ruined walls, signs of old exploded garbage here and there, brown bags tossed from adjacent buildings, and this is where young kids had rock fights and older kids roasted sweet mickeys in the evening chill and where a kid named Skeezer ate a grasshopper live, which was a legend of many a neighborhood, the kid with grasshopper juices running down his chin, but in this case there were reliable older men who'd witnessed, and where other and darker stories were set, a man who slept in a ditch every night and the guys from the other poolroom, Major's, taking a girl into the ruins, late, a summer night, and lining up for sex, and who was the girl, and was she willing, and other stories of the lots.

It was a single expanse of land that was called the lots the way a back alley was called the yards and this is where Matty got his hand busted up in a card game called shots on knucks.

He walked in the apartment and went into his mother's bedroom, where she was doing her beadwork, and he stuck the hand in her face.

"What's this?"

"What does it look like?" he said.

"Blood."

"Then that's what it is."

"Then you should go and clean it."

"Don't you want to know what happened?"

"What happened?"

"Never mind," he said.

He sat in the living room and examined the marks and scrapes, the mudlet streaks of dried blood. He felt a self-pitying pleasure, doing this, even a fascination, an animal attachment just short of licking, but then his brother walked in the door, earlier than usual, and he tried to conceal the hand.

"What's that?"

"Nothing."

"Show me, jerk."

"I just need to clean it."

"You need to put iodine on that. Let me see."

"I don't need iodine," he said with a soft insistence.

He extended the hand and looked away at the same time, sort of tactfully.

"He needs iodine," Nick said to their mother.

"Is that the 7-Up man?"

"Eye-oh-dine, eye-oh-dine."

Matty went small in his chair as his brother looked at the hand. Nick's own hands were dirty and bruised and so much bigger, five, six years bigger—a man's hands, almost, blistered on the palms and cut by broken glass.

"How'd it happen? You punched a little girl in the mouth?"

"Card game in the lots."

"You go in the lots?"

"Just at the edge."

"Does she know you go in the lots?"

"I don't go way in."

"You think it's a good idea, going in there?"

"What do you think?"

"I think go in. But watch yourself. There's kids in there from all over. They don't know you're my brother."

Nick held his hand and looked at it.

"It doesn't hurt the way it did."

"You played shots on knucks."

"That's right."

"And you ended up holding some cards and the winner whacked you how many times."

"I had a choice."

"I remember this choice."

"Either he gives me nine scraping shots with the edge of the deck or he gives me four scraping shots and then one killer shot with the deck held up and down."

"Blunt end. Where he hits you square on your knuckles, full force."

"That's right," Matty said.

"Let me ask. How could you lose a kid's card game, a brain like you, supposedly, playing with a bunch of little pisspots?"

"They weren't so little," Matty said.

Nick held his hand. Many times through the years Nick had bopped him on the head, a flick of the middle finger that carried slingshot force. Many times Nick had lifted him off a chair and sat himself down. Nick had held him out the window once for rubbing snot on a door edge. Many times Nick had booted him in the ass for no reason except he was passing through a room that had Matty in it.

"I think we're talking about iodine here."

"I don't need iodine," he whispered.

He looked at his hand in Nick's. His brother had an odor of work and heat and sharp salami, the spicy bright salami he ate on the job.

Their mother came in and looked at the hand.

She said, "Mercurochrome."

Nick took the hand away from her.

"Iodine," he said.

"First he washes the hand with soap and cool water, Matthew, are you listening? Then he dries the hand."

"Then he puts iodine on it."

"I don't want the iodine," Matty said. "I want the mercurochrome."

745

"Iodine. It's stronger, it's better, it's hotter, it burns."

"Mercurochrome," Matty said.

"It eats right into the wound, cleaning and burning."

"Mercurochrome," Matty said.

But he didn't want his brother to drop the hand, to let go of the hand just yet.

Klara stood on the roof watching stormclouds build bluish and hard-edged, like weather on some remote coast, a sky that seemed too lush and wild to pass this way.

The child played with a neighbor's child on a blanket nearby.

She'd taken down the laundry and put it in the basket but wasn't ready to go inside just yet. The wind was gaining force and she could see women on rooftops all up and down the block unpinning clothes from swaying lines, ducking under bedsheets walloped up, and she could hear other women pulling on the lines that criss-crossed alleyways between windows and laundry poles, the screech-song of old ropes passing through the grooved rims of all those rusty wheels.

She missed Albert's mother. It was strange to walk into the front room now, an awkward empty place, first the empty bed and now not even the bed, just floor space that needed filling.

It was also strange how they hadn't wanted to get rid of the bed, either one of them. They'd kept it around for weeks, cranked to her daylight angle, the hours when she liked to close her eyes and feel the sun on her face.

The white of her nightgown and hair and the white sheets and the sheets billowing on the rooftops and the women fisting them down to gatherable size.

The first drops hit thick and splatting.

She'd been up here once, not long ago, more or less hiding from her life, and she saw the young man standing across the street, standing smoking by a lamppost.

Most of the time when she thought of him at all she thought of him in motion, she thought of notched hands moving on her body and dirt grained deep in his fingers, she thought of the turn of his shoulder and the way he looked at her over his clenched fist.

She'd liked it when she saw him by the lamppost looking at the building. Then she thought about it and didn't like it so much. But that was the only time she saw him there.

The two children did not want to go inside but the rain was getting close.

He'd been easy in a way, natural in a way, not distant or totally unknown. At first she thought it might be nice to think of him as the Young Man, like a character in a coming-of-age novel, but she only thought of him in motion, and nameless, and nonfictional, a sort of rotary blur that hovered just off her right shoulder somewhere, the thing her brain condensed from all that pleasure and wet.

She looked over the ledge and saw three girls playing jacks on a stoop across the street, seated on different steps, the girl with the ball still-bodied and hunched, only her hand working among the strewn jacks, frantically, and Klara could hear them calling threesies and kissies and interference, an argument breaking out, steely and clear.

She didn't want more, she wanted less. This was the thing her husband could not understand. Solitude, distance, time, work. Something out there she needed to breathe.

She took the laundry basket to the door and left it just inside. The surrounding rooftops were just about empty now and the yowl of the alley lines had stopped. Even from this height she could hear the rapping sound. A woman rapped a penny on the window, calling her child in from play.

Then the rain came hard. Klara picked up her daughter and scooped the blanket under her arm and took the other child by the hand and they ran laughing across the roof under racing skies.

At dinner she told him she'd been selfish.

"I don't think that's true," he said.

He tore a length of crusty bread in two, a thing he did ritually and with such depth of dependable habit that she could not imagine him

747

getting through a full meal, all the switches and intervals and hand movements, without this crucial flourish.

"The painting's a waste. I'm not getting anywhere. We'll put Teresa in that room."

"Give it time," he said. "And anyway where do you expect to get with it? Do it for the day-to-day satisfaction. For the way it fills out the day."

She had a small print of a Whistler, the famous Mother, and she hung it in a corner of the spare room because she thought it was generally unlooked at and because she liked the formal balances and truthful muted colors and because the picture was so clashingly modern, the seated woman in mobcap and commodious dark dress, a figure lifted out of her time into the abstract arrangements of the twentieth century, long before she was ready, it seemed, but Klara also liked looking right through the tonal components, the high theory of color, the theory of paint itself, perhaps—looking into the depths of the picture, at the mother, the woman, the mother herself, the anecdotal aspect of a woman in a chair, thinking, and immensely interesting she was, so Quaker-prim and still, faraway-seeming but only because she was lost, Klara thought, in memory, caught in the midst of a memory trance, a strong and elegiac presence despite the painter's, the son's, doctrinal priorities.

"No, we'll do something with the room. That's what I ought to be doing. Getting this place in some kind of livable shape."

"We have the front room to do," he said.

"We have the front room, which is still a kind of no-man's-land. I'll do the front room. Then I'll do the spare room."

"And I'll step up my own efforts. Head of the science department. I'll make this my goal. And we'll travel this summer. To Spain or Italy. Wherever you like," he said.

She liked to watch him eat because he did it so deeply, handling and savoring things, handling utensils, chewing food thoroughly, the way he paused unpretentiously with the wineglass an inch from his lips, waiting, savoring, a sense of earth and our connection to it, that was Albert over a dish of inky squid—earth and sea and the way he looked at food in the plate, breathing it all in before he even touched a fork.

"To Spain," she said. "Madrid. The Prado." And she laughed a little coldly, with the hollow tone she used when she was punishing herself. "I want to look at pictures till I drop."

Then she saw him on the street with a friend, veering toward an army-navy store, and she stopped and stood right there, stationed in his path, and he nearly walked into her before he saw who it was, and he stopped and showed only the thinnest surprise, and his friend stopped, and then she went around them and crossed the street.

The next day he was standing by the lamppost when she looked out the window. She was putting up new curtains in the front room and he was standing there smoking. A Railway Express truck passed between them. Then he looked up and saw her. He flicked the cigarette and walked across the street.

She threw down the mattress. Nick watched her and pulled his shirt over his head. Then he watched her again. She stood there with her head down, like she was trying to remember something, and then she undid a button at the side of her skirt.

She didn't finish her kisses. This was interesting and a little puzzling, unlike last time when they kissed nearly into old age. The way she broke off now and looked away just when he thought a kiss was getting her warm and soft, and the way she looked when she did this, ripping away hurt, almost, and he was surprised at how different she looked, not what he remembered from last time but paler maybe, hands weightless and drained, these white things floating past, and eyes that bugged out a little and seemed to see things he didn't know were there.

But the eyes also looked away and that was the same and the twisty smile, the little turn at the end of the mouth. Some things the same. The tits the same, the ass and tits and bush, and the slub of folded tongue when he kissed her.

Looks that he couldn't figure out what they were supposed to mean.

And the other smile, where she smiled privately at the two of them together, or whatever she was smiling at, smiling to herself like it was three days later, after the fact, and she was walking down an aisle at the A&P thinking what they'd done, but it wasn't three days after the fact, it was still the fact, and she had his balls in her hand, squeezing slightly.

A naked woman was amazing.

He'd never seen it this way, in full light, without half-off clothes or a beach blanket across the lap or sex in a dark car. This was her whole body naked in light, standing and lying and front and back and open and showing and then different when she walked across the room, all these ways and walking toward him too and different when she walked, surer than he was, unclunky and smooth-moving, with parts that didn't bounce. She knew how to be naked. She looked like she'd been raised naked in this room, a skinny girl when she was a girl, probably, and skinny in a certain way, with a little bulgy belly and ashamed of her feet, but grown out of shyness and wrong proportions now, and being married of course, used to being seen, and she didn't have curves and swerves but was good-looking naked and stuck to him when they fucked like a thing fighting for light, a great wet papery moth.

He took her stocking off the floor and fitted it over his head. She smiled and looked away and seemed to want to say something and then changed her mind. He jammed it down so he was looking out at her more or less through the heel of the stocking. He pantomimed pulling a gun out of a shoulder holster and pointed it at her.

"Everything you own. Mine or die."

"It's hard to be serious about this, considering what you look like."

"Hey. Lady. This is what they do."

"Holdups, you mean?"

"That's right. But I have to say. They must need money pretty bad to wear this on their face."

"Well, it's used. They don't wear used stockings, do they?"

"I don't think these guys are finicky. They wear whatever's lying around."

"I have to admit you're a changed man."

"You think you'd recognize me if you came in the house and I was standing here in this mask?"

"No. But I wouldn't recognize you without the mask either."

He pulled off the mask and sat on the mattress. She went to get some water and he watched her walk out of the room, the way her ass barely jounced, and he held the stocking around his dick and then tossed it away.

The warm fusty sort of slightly tired smell, the nylon cling of the odor still in his face, sad, tired, day-old, hers, and close to him, and something he knew about her that made her less strange.

But she was still strange. She was something you didn't want to tell your friends about and that was strange. And she was something you didn't have to tell yourself was really happening. It just happened. It happened bang and that was it, with Whistler's fucking Mother hanging on the wall.

He watched her come into the room.

He said, "You know, my brother when he was a little kid, he was somewhere watching a girl taking a pee, a small girl that was a neighbor's kid probably, and she dropped her drawers and wiggled up onto the seat and had herself a pee, and my brother's watching this and then he goes out to a room full of grown-ups, as I later heard the story, and he waits for them to stop talking and then they finally stop talking and they look at him and he says, Mary Feeley has no birdy."

She handed him the glass. It was one of the longest speeches he'd ever made, Nick, not counting jokes he sometimes told. Then she reached for his bunched pants on the floor and felt in the pockets for a pack of cigarettes.

They sat on the mattress, knees touching, smoking and sharing the water.

"You know why I smoke Old Golds? I wouldn't tell this to just anybody."

"Bullshit. Why?" she said.

"That's the cigarette that used to sponsor the Dodgers on the radio. Old Gold. We're tobacco men, not medicine men. The Dodgers were my team. Were. Not anymore."

"This is a big privileged secret you're telling me."

"That's right. Now you have to tell me one of your secrets. Could be big, could be small."

751

"What's your name?"

"Nick."

"Nick, you can't come here anymore. It's too completely crazy. No more, okay? We did it and now we have to stop doing it."

"We can do it somewhere else," he said.

"Nowhere else. No. I don't think so."

Never mind the body. He's never looked at a woman's face so closely. How he thinks he knows who she is from her face, what she eats and how she sleeps, from the lookaway smile and the uncombed hair, the hair over the right eye, how her face becomes everything she is that he can't put into words.

"Nick Shay," he said with a little stab in it, a touch of vengeful intent, because she knew about the chess lessons of course, and would recognize Matty's last name, and would know Nick was the older brother, and would feel the close-knit danger of the thing.

But she didn't seem to give a damn. The way he didn't give a damn that she was someone he knew's wife, she didn't care that he was someone's brother.

"Then I might as well," he said.

"Yes, I think it's time."

He picked up the pants and got dressed and left her naked on the mattress, seated sort of leaning to one side, legs together and bent, blowing smoke away from her face with the hand that held the cigarette, and he didn't even think of looking back.

7

Rosemary sat in the law office over the bakery, filing documents in an old cabinet, and her boss came in, Mr. Imperato, returned from a rare morning at the criminal courts. He was a shambling man who told jokes expertly, who rose to the occasion of a joke. He was bald, flat-footed and carelessly dressed and he was forgetful in his work, sometimes, but when there was a joke to tell he heard the music of the spheres. He never botched a punch line or missed a pause. He did voices and accents, men, women, talking birds, unfalteringly, a quickness rising to his eyes.

"Smell the bread," he said.

"That's the trouble with being over a bakery. I keep buying bread. My boys can't keep up."

"What'd you buy?"

"It's for dinner."

"Show me. Is it round or long?"

"Last time, remember what you did to my bread. It's dinner bread. Get away."

Four or five years ago Mr. Imperato hired a private investigator on her behalf to try to locate Jimmy. The biggest secret of her life, a thing no one knew but the lawyer and the investigator. When nothing came of the effort Mr. Imperato paid the man himself and told her she could do some clerical work to settle her fee. She'd been working here ever since and he never deducted the fee from her salary because he needed someone, he said, to listen to his jokes.

"I'm buying us a bigger fan."

"I think we need it," she said.

"I got one for home. The kids sit in front of it sometimes. The TV is on the blink. I tell Anna. They're watching the fan."

"I don't want TV in my house."

"You have to have it," he said.

"I don't want it."

"The kids want it."

"Matty wants it. He goes upstairs to a neighbor and watches wrestling."

"I never miss the wrestling if I can help it. You have to have it. The kids have to have it. It's the one thing you have to have."

When she went home with her bread she climbed past her floor, going up the worn steps, seeing laundry hang outside the smutty stairway windows, because there was a thing she wanted to talk about with Mrs. Graziani, up on the top floor.

Carmela put out a coffee ring and made coffee and they sat in the kitchen.

"How you climb these steps every day."

"Three, four times," Carmela said. "I know every step by name. I have names for the steps."

"And Mickey's feeling better since the operation."

"If you could call it feeling better. He's the same as he always was. I don't know if that's better. Because these men, all they want to do is sit in a room playing cards for seventeen hours they can play. Cards till they drop."

"But he had a real scare. If he can play cards, more power to him. You nearly lost him."

"I don't think I could lose him if I went to China," the woman said.

Rosemary usually felt better after a visit with Carmela. The woman had a running argument with men, not just the husband and the sad son, Cosmo, but men everywhere, and even if Rosemary agreed with her only two percent of the time she still felt cleaner somehow, purged like confession, having a cup of coffee with Carmela.

"I wanted to ask. Did you hear about the woman at 607? The grand-mother?"

"There's nothing to hear," Carmela said.

And she made a gesture, the hand that sweeps under the chin, a sign that meant this is not a story we're obliged to take seriously. The nothing sign. A very dismissive gesture as Rosemary understood these things.

"So you don't think."

"If I thought there was anything to it, I'd be the first to go over there and wait for him to appear and get down on my hands and knees to thank God for this miracle."

The woman at 607, saying her rosary in the basement room of the narrow shingled house occupied by two families and two grandpar-ents, looked up from her beads and saw a saint standing in the door-way, Saint Anthony, and Rosemary needed guidance in this matter, a sense of how much acceptance she should be willing to risk.

Carmela put four spoonfuls of sugar in her coffee.

"You know what I say, Rose? *Domani mattin'*. In other words, sure, tomorrow morning, here he comes again, this time with an angel blowing a trumpet."

This reaction was a letdown. For all her endless skepticism, Carmela was a frequent figure at early morning mass and Rosemary wanted her to take the story more seriously, or to concede the grand-mother's credentials at least, long periods of prayer with a number of other old women, all in graveclothes, reciting the mysteries.

Carmela told her for the dozenth time to get out and see people.

"You're still young, Rose."

"I'm not so young."

"Don't argue with me. You need to spend less time at home and more time making friends. You give your whole life to those two boys. This Nicky, I hate to say it."

"Then don't say it."

"I hate to say it, Rose."

"Don't say it."

"This boy has got I-don't-know-what written all over him. You know exactly what I mean."

"He works hard. He hands over his money without a complaint."

"The other one. I don't know."

"If you don't know, Carmela."

"I don't know, Rose. The other one. But it's Nicky I'm watching. I watch this boy."

"That's funny because you know what? I don't watch him. He gets up at the crack of dawn. He goes to work. He gives me his money. He gives me his pay envelope. Plus I don't hear a word of complaint."

"The mother's always the last to know."

"He grew up fast, Nicky. He's a man now. He's more responsible than someone ten years older. He grew up like lightning, this boy."

"I'm sorry, Rose. But him I would watch."

Carmela's son had spent a year in the basket-weaving class and another year in remedial reading and a third year falling down a flight of stairs and recovering in bed, three meals a day in bed, and he lived with his grandparents now, upstate.

And she tells me she's worried about mine.

No, it was not the average satisfying visit with the woman on the top floor and in the days that followed, warm days and cool evenings, the water truck spraying the streets and dirt and grit running in the gutters—there were many days when Rosemary walked past the narrow house, 607, and thought about the old woman, Bettina, saying the rosary in the basement room with her friends, the five joyful mysteries, Mondays and Thursdays, the five sorrowful mysteries, Tuesdays and Fridays, the five glorious mysteries, and so on, but then again they probably didn't follow a set routine, no, they wouldn't, these women, because there were women like that who wore monks' robes on the feast of Saint Anthony, women and children both, brown robes and bare feet, the statue bobbing above them, and it was amazing and strange and impressive, Rosemary thought, and women like that would say their prayers without regard for schedules.

She was too shy to knock on the door but she liked to think of the

756

women sitting around the table, big beads the Our Father, little beads the Hail Mary.

She didn't have time, herself, to do this every day. She had her own form of beadwork. She had the frame and the material pinned to the edges of the frame and the needle with the wood handle that she used to string the beads onto the material, iridescent beads to decorate a dress, and she never really wondered who would wear it.

She was too shy to talk to the grandmother, who spoke no English anyway. Thirty-five years in this country and not three words of English. But this was a mark of her faith in a way, an indication of what truly mattered. What mattered were the mysteries, not the language in which you said them.

The fresh-air inspectors stood on the corner nearly every day, three or four or five men, and Rosemary walked past the narrow house and thought about the thing that supposedly happened there.

Sometimes faith needs a sign. There are times when you want to stop working at faith and just be washed in a blowing wind that tells you everything.

"Maybe, like, for an eighth of a second, she thought I smacked my lips. Or I clicked my tongue at her."

"Then what?"

"Then she understood I had food in my teeth and I was wedging it out. The way you wedge it out with the tongue. But she looked at me and she saw who it was and she decided she rather be insulted."

"I can understand this."

"You can understand this."

"I can understand this because even if you didn't insult her, you could have."

"I didn't. But I could have. This is what you're saying."

"I known you twenty years. And you could have."

"Just so I understand. I didn't. But I could have."

"That's right. Because you, I could believe it."

"But I didn't."

"But you could have."

"Regardless I was wedging food."

"Regardless Jesus walked on water. Because you could have."

"So this is where you're taking us."

"Where am I taking us?"

"To where I have to say something. And you know what I have to say? And I say it to you and your sister. The both of youse."

"Be careful."

"You're gonna hear this very good. To you but mostly to your sister."

"Be careful, Anthony."

"I'll fuck you in your heart, you fucker."

"Anthony. But what a mistake you're making."

"You and your sister. I'll fuck you in your heart."

"Who I know twenty years."

"And your mother for good measure."

"Who he thinks I'm gonna listen to this from a hard-on like him."

"And your mother," he said.

A kid went by with a baseball glove hooked to his belt, eating a melorol.

The longshoreman stood across the street with that massive mustachioed head of his, a whal-yo off the boat about a year ago, works the Jersey docks, strong as a Mack truck.

Two guys pushed a car that had no one in it.

Nick stood in front of the grocery eating a hero sandwich and holding a beer that Donato's wife had sold him, concealed in a paper bag.

The fresh-air inspectors.

Sammy Bones who ran on the field during a game at the Polo Grounds so he could be seen on TV, except nobody he knew was watching and he's been *arrabbiato* ever since, like mad-dog angry.

A girl in her confirmation outfit, a white dress and stockings and white shoes, and wearing red ribbons in her hair, and carrying white flowers in crinkly red cellophane.

JuJu came by and took the sandwich out of Nick's hand and looked inside.

The old man on the stoop across the street who spreads his handkerchief dainty on the top step and then sits and fills his pipe with cigarette tobacco and the shreddings of a crumbled DeNobili cigar, the perennial guinea stinker, and whatever else he can find that doesn't belong in a pipe.

"You're serious about these weights."

"I'm doing bench presses where my mother grabs the bar when I yell. Supine presses," JuJu said in a slightly snobbish tone.

"How many bites you're gonna take out of my sandwich?"

"I'm doing a whole program. You should come over."

"Hey. I work, remember. I got 7-Up I lift all day long."

"That's not a program," JuJu said.

"I rather die than lift weights."

"See, now that's an attitude where you're only showing your ignorance of the subject."

"I rather die the death of a thousand cuts."

"Show your ignorance."

"I rather be ignorant. Look over there. The one in the yellow blouse. That's a 36D."

"What, you measured?"

"What kind of measured? I have a trained eye."

"You can tell a D cup from a C cup from this distance."

"I rather eat sheep stomach than lift weights," Nick told him.

The super's wife looking peacefully out the window at 610, called Sister Katy. So when she got screaming raging drunk, about once a month, the kids chanted up to her, Sing it Sister Katy.

"She sells you beer on Sunday? Before one o'clock?"

"What kind of beer? This is root beer."

A boy in a white suit with a red tie and a red armband and his hair plastered down trying to wriggle out of the grip of his mother, who's swinging her handbag at his head.

"What's your confirmation name?"

"Never you fucking mind," JuJu said.

First the close air of the long stairway and the metallic taste of the air and the thick distant stir of men's voices on a busy night, the roil of muddy voices, and the smoke of the big room and a ball game on TV

759

and a player softly chalking his stick, looking like a soldier in some old eccentric war, and the beautiful numbered balls and green baize and dreamy prowl of a shooter on a run, and the endless caroming clack of the balls hitting, the touch sounds of the cue, the balls, the cushions, the slap of the pocket drop.

That night Nick shot a game with George the Waiter. George parked cars at the racetrack on his nights off from the restaurant and he told stories about the cars he parked, about flooring the pedal and slamming the brake, that sounded like dirty jokes, the chrome and upholstery and handling, all tits and ass.

Nick felt a little wary of George since the episode of the needle. He felt cut off in a way, less free and easy, but George never referred to the thing and didn't even seem to remember.

Still, he felt he'd lost some standing with George, showing shock and confusion that way.

Nick looked up from the shot he was lining up. There was something in George's face that made him follow the man's line of sight to the other end of the room.

"Who's that?"

"You don't know him?"

Mike stood talking to a man near the counter, heavyset, in a too-tight jacket, two-toned, over an open-collar shirt.

"Take your shot," George said.

He called seven in the side.

"That's Mario Badalato," George said.

He made the shot.

"Not bad," George said. "You know this name?"

He wasn't sure but shook his head.

"It's a name, over the years, that's been connected to that particular life."

Nick moved crouched to the far end of the table, studying his next shot.

"Understand what I'm saying? Father, uncles, cousins, brothers."

"That particular life."

"You're never gonna bank the four. You should be looking anywhere but the four," George said. "People in that life."

"That life," Nick said.

"*Malavita*. Who, once they're in, they're in for good."

Nick glanced at the man in question, forty years old, maybe, thick and packed, a thickness of body that had no rolling or sagging but was hard, packed, built on other men's lesser luck, on the way an unfortunate occurrence across town makes you stronger.

"You should be looking at the two ball meanwhile. The four is not your shot, Nicky."

"The two ball."

"Madonn', what do I have to do, send an engraved invitation?"

"That life," Nick said.

"That particular life. Under the surface of ordinary things. And organized so that it makes more sense in a way, if you understand what I mean. It makes more sense than the horseshit life the rest of us live."

Nick studied the table some more.

"So is this the man who had Walls, you know, put on ice?"

"What do I know? I don't know, I don't want to know, I don't even want to talk about it no more."

"No more, no more."

"Take your shot," George said.

Mario Badalato. Maybe he knew this name from somewhere. They shot a couple of games and George gave him hints and tips and a guy at the next table was singing to the tune of a popular song.

"Don't know why. I've got lipstick on my fly. Slop-py blow-job."

"It's almost beach weather, George."

"This makes you happy? I hate the beach. I used to work at the beach."

"Don't tell me lifeguard. I pity the drowning child."

"Wise guy. I used to sell ice cream. This was years ago. Ninety degrees with a cooler on my back that felt like a thousand pounds."

"They still have those guys."

"We had to wear sun helmets. Like Africa."

"They still wear them."

"I never want to see another beach. You want the nine ball here. Look. It's set up beautiful."

It was time for George to get back to the restaurant. There was a gin rummy game going and Nick stood and looked and got bored and called the dog and took it for a walk.

He stood in Mussolini park while the dog went scratching at patches of dirt. He watched a tow truck go by, doing sixty easy, the driver taking the traffic circle like a rodeo rider, slanted to jump. A guy named Grasso came up to him, they were in the same shop class once, and he pointed at two guys diagonally across the street, at the luncheonette, at the outside counter, standing eating something, black guys both of them with team jackets.

"They come out of the bowling alley. Then they go over to the window and order whatever they order."

"Ever seen them before?"

"Here? They never been here."

The two guys put their paper cups back on the counter and walked toward Third Avenue and Nick and Grasso followed, with the dog trailing. The guys knew there was someone behind them. Not that they turned. But Nick saw the way they stopped talking and the way their stride seemed, maybe, to tighten a little.

"What's it say on the jackets?"

"Hawks, I think."

"Ever hear of them?" Nick said.

"Never. Hawks? What fucking Hawks? Plus I don't think it's a team. I think it's a gang."

They went past the funeral home and walked a block and a half along Third Avenue through the slatted shadows of the el and then the two guys stopped and turned around.

Nick and Grasso walked up to them.

"Hawks? What's Hawks?" Grasso said.

They didn't answer. One guy ready, the other still thinking about it.

"You live here, the Hawks? Because I don't think I seen any Hawks before."

They didn't answer.

The dog caught up to them and began to go nose-twitching around the feet of one of the guys.

"It's better, you know, at night especially, if you stay where you

762

belong. In the day too," Grasso said. "But at night especially because otherwise people get the wrong idea."

The train passed over with a great staccato clatter and they all waited until it was past. But then the two guys didn't say anything.

"I still don't know what's Hawks. I aksed nice. But I don't hear no explanation."

Cars creeping around the el pillars when they made a turn. And Mike the Dog sniffing at the guy's shoe and the guy sort of flicking the shoe, doing a little foot-jerk that made the dog back off, and Nick stepped up and punched him.

A car stopped in the middle of a turn.

Nick stepped up and hit the guy once, a fair to good shot that caught him on the temple when he tried to duck under, and this car came to a sudden stop and four guys got out and left the doors hanging open of this car just stopped in the middle of the street.

They were guys from the other poolroom, Turk and his fuckface friends, and one of the black guys started running but the other one stood there and glared, six white guys and a brown dog more or less surrounding him.

Nick half smiled at Turk.

"He kicked my dog," he said.

The one still here was the one he'd hit and he was looking at Nick, glaring, and Nick shrugged and smiled and the guy turned and walked away slowly and the four other guys took a breath and hitched their pants and got back in the car. The doors closed bangedy bang and the car drove off.

Grasso said, "Fucking Turk."

"I know."

"Thinks he's king shit walking the earth."

"I know," Nick said.

"Where'd you get that animal?"

"Lives at Mike's."

"I never seen an animal so ugly."

Nick faked a punch to the guy's head and they walked back to the lighted streets with the roar of the el behind them.

. . .

About a month later the man was back in the poolroom, standing at the counter late one night, with Mike, they're eating baked ziti out of tin plates.

Mike flashed the light over the table where Nick was playing.

When Nick looked up he said, "Come over here."

Nick walked over with a self-conscious saunter like he was about to meet his future father-in-law.

"Mario here, he wants to say something you should listen to. Mario knew your father just after the war. During the war and after the war."

Badalato was standing with his back to the room and Nick went around the counter, where Mike was standing, behind the counter, so he could face the man.

They had glasses of wine, which Nick had never seen in here, and they had a canister of red pepper they passed back and forth, eating standing up, every forkful of ziti trailing long strands of mozzarell'.

"I knew your father. Jimmy. I liked Jimmy."

Nick could not fail to understand the consequence of the moment, a man of this particular life who is going to talk to him about his father.

"Mike told me. He said, Jimmy's son he comes in here. Jimmy Costanza. I said, I haven't heard this name in a while. I liked Jimmy, I said."

And the consequence of the man himself, the thick hands and dark brows and thick hair and the slightly flattened nose, like a boxer's.

"I said. What did I say? Jimmy had a talent, this guy, he's mister invisible."

Nick could not fail to understand the weight of the occasion. But he was also wary of it, he was hesitant, he wanted to say something unsolemn because anything about his father made him apprehensive.

"The way I understand it from Mike, you think your father had no choice in the matter. How he left. How he disappeared. Somebody put him in a car. This is what you think, as his son, is what happened to the man. And they drove him somewheres. But I have to tell you one thing."

Badalato took a sip of wine from the low squarish glass.

764

"Nothing could of been done to your father without me knowing about it. I have to tell you this. I would of known. And even if I don't know beforehand, which isn't about to happen, but even if it did, then I find out later. I would of heard. You understand what I'm saying? It's not possible this could happen without me knowing about it sooner or later."

The warm smell of the food was making Nick hungry and he couldn't help wondering how the food could be carried here from a restaurant still steaming hot.

"I liked your father. I don't think Jimmy had serious enemies. He owed money, so what? If somebody owes you money, you work out an arrangement. There are ways to do these things where you use simple business methods, the way Mike runs a business, the way a haberdasher runs a business. You buy a suit, you pay so much down, so much a month. You buy a car and so forth."

The man looked at Nick while he spoke. He didn't sound superior or offhand. He wanted to make an honest connection and get his point across.

"Jimmy was not in a position where he could offend somebody so bad that they would go out of their way to do something. No disrespect but he was penny-ante. He had a very small operation he was running. Made the rounds of the small bettors. Mostly very small these bets. This is what he did. Factory sweepers and so forth. You have to understand. Jimmy was not in a position to be threatened by serious people."

Nick watched him take a bite of food. He could not help feeling grateful. The man stood there and talked to him. The man took time to tell him something he thought would settle the matter in Nick's own mind.

"I appreciate," he said.

"I liked your father. And I know what it's like, myself, to lose a father at an early age. From cancer this was."

"Your taking the time. I appreciate."

"Forget about it. Go finish your game," the man said.

Nick still had the pool stick in his hand. He gestured toward the light over the table.

"Mike, tell me you're not gonna charge me for the time you guys spent eating ziti."

The men enjoyed that. He went back to the table and finished the game with Stevie and Ray. They wanted to know what he'd been talking about with the guys at the counter.

He thought of a half-ass joke but then said nothing.

He was grateful for the time, genuinely, but he didn't think he had to accept the logic of the argument. The logic, he decided, did not impress him.

They played cards down there, pinochle, and drank homemade wine, in the room under the shoemaker's shop, off the dim passageway that led out to the yards.

Bronzini looked on, sitting in when someone left but otherwise a kibitzer, unmeddlesome, content to savor the company and try the wine, sometimes good, sometimes overfermented, better used to spike a salad.

He was in a hurry to be an old man, Klara told him. Why else sit here with these elders of the streets, some of them nearly twice his age, spending whole afternoons in argument and aimless talk.

Outside in the deep slow swelter, cats were asleep in the shade and people keeping to the sides of buildings if they were out at all, moving dazed in the unexpected heat.

Down here in the basement room it was dry and quiet and stone-cool, quiet except for the voices of course, and he liked the voices, loud, crude, funny, often powerfully opinionated, all speechmakers these men, actors, declaimers, masters of insult, reaching for some moment of transcendence.

John the Super loosed a bullfrog fart.

He told them about the garbage he used to handle when he worked as a janitor downtown, temporary, in a large apartment building, elevators, doormen, dry cleaning delivered, taxis left and right.

Mannaggia l'America.

This goddamn country has garbage you can eat, garbage that's better to eat than the food on the table in other countries. They have garbage here you can furnish your house and feed your kids.

They played and bid and made sissing noises to acknowledge the bountiful folly of clothes in the garbage that are good enough to wear.

Albert told them about the ancient Mayans. These people did not bury their dead with gleaming jewelry and other valuable objects. They used old broken things. They put cracked vases in with the dead, or chipped cups and tarnished bracelets. They used the dead as a convenient means of garbage disposal.

This story satisfied the cardplayers. It was very satisfactory. Disrespect for the dead was a nice cruel satisfying joke, especially to men of a certain age. A joke on the dead was a beautiful joke. A joke with balls.

Albert felt isolated here in the safest of ways, the slap of the cards, the men making theatrical bids, the wine seeping into his system, and he knew finally why there was something familiar about these lost afternoons under the shoemaker's.

Like childhood, he thought. Those bedridden days when he was islanded in sheets and pillows, surrounded by books, by chess pieces, deliciously sick at times, a fever that sent him inward, sea-sweats and dreams with runny colors, lonely but not unhappy, the room a world, the safe place of imagination.

Liguori didn't take wine anymore, the printer, because he had a liver condition. He talked about the strolling musicians who used to come around, a fiddler and a trumpet player, and how people wrapped coins in paper and threw them from the windows.

Quanta sold'?

His wife used to say, How much is it gonna cost me to listen to this *cafone* play his fiddle? But they didn't come around anymore. They had liver conditions, or half a stomach between them, or the noise of traffic, Albert said, made music futile.

The men spoke mostly English but used the dialect when an idea needed a push or shove into a more familiar place. And odd how Albert, barely nearing forty, could feel his old-manness within him, here in particular, as the voices took him back to earliest memory, the same slurred words, the dropped vowels, the vulgate, so that English was the sound of the present and Italian took him backwards, the merest intonation, a language marked inexhaustibly by the past.

Someone was evicted, put out on the street, chairs, tables, bed, right around the corner—the bed, John said, the super. Frame, spring, mattress, pillows, out on the sidewalk.

Porca miseria.

What a wretchedness it was, what a complete humiliation of the spirit. You're like a museum of poverty. People walk by and look. The bed, the plates and glasses, the suitcase with your clothes, a pair of old shoes in a paper bag. Imagine shoes. And they walk by and look. Who says this, who says that, who sits in a chair, who points from a car. They should be ashamed to look. A man's shoes on the sidewalk.

There was always the neighborhood and who was leaving and who was moving in, showing up on the fringes. Tizzoons. A word Albert wished they wouldn't use. A southern dialect word, a corruption, a slur, an invective, from *tizzo*, he assumed, a firebrand or smoldering coal, and broadened to human dimensions in *tizzone d'inferno*, scoundrel, villain. But the word they used suggested a hellishness, a fiendishness that made it more unspeakable, in a way, than nigger. But they spoke it, of course, these men, these immigrants or sons of immigrants, the hordes who threaten society's peaceful sleep, who are always showing up and moving in. Tizzoon. They masked the word. They narrowed their eyes and barely moved their lips. But they spoke it, they half hissed the word in a way that made Albert wish he hadn't heard.

Spadafora told them about the washing machine that was automatic, where the woman sets a control and walks out the door and the machine washes, rinses, spins, dries, shuts off—everything automatic.

They shook their heads and made sissing noises and muttered casual curses, baffled at their luck in being here, amazed and confused, searching a way to train their skepticism on the wonders that unfolded daily.

The wine was not so drinkable this time. It was the shoemaker's own wine, Guido, and this was not wine weather anyway, and Albert wanted to be more responsible. He wanted to be a dry wise soul (Heraclitus), less slipshod and indecisive, more willing to see into the core of a complicated matter.

He needed to take a leak and the super told him there was a utility sink he could use and gave him directions through the maze of passages.

He went past storage rooms and empty garbage cans. Then he came out into a courtyard and saw the door the super had described and went into the next building.

For a long time he wanted to believe that she had ambitions on his behalf. But now he wasn't sure of this. He thought she wanted him to campaign for department head, for assistant principal, make the moves, play the game, buy a car, buy a house. And he thought these ambitions were going unfulfilled, which made her angry and distant at times. But now he wasn't sure.

He walked through the cellarways under rows of copper piping. He found the utility closet and peed in the sink. His childhood was back there, in the voices of his mother and father, guarded, suspicious, scared at times, and in the sissing noises they made to mark distrust of the unknown world around them.

He heard a radio playing round the next bend and decided to follow the sound, music, sweetness, strings, his head clear and his bladder empty, the ever gregarious Albert, curious to see what sort of company he might encounter here.

He turned the corner and stopped next to a discarded table with a missing leg.

George Manza, George the Waiter, sat in a chair in a shabby room. There was something about him. He was not dozing or deep-thinking but there was something. He was awake but unresponsive. And there was something that kept Albert from speaking.

He stood in the doorway watching.

The room had a certain anonymous squalor. It was a room you could probably spend some time in without registering clearly what was in there. A strew of lost and found and miscellaneous things, and anonymous faded colors, and things that were stored here not for future use but because they had to go somewhere.

George sat in profile, hunched a little and breathing through his nose, slow-breathing, drawing in and letting out at long intervals, a small life in every breath.

The door was ajar and Albert watched. There was only a three-inch space between the door and the jamb, three, four inches only, but this was enough to see whatever there was to see. He didn't know exactly what this was.

The man directed a dead stare at the facing wall. There was something so stark about him that Albert thought he had no right to look. He hadn't seen George in several months, or longer even, and George looked different, thinner, smaller, severe, sitting under a radio on a shelf, the music so foreign to the figure of the man that Albert felt a need to turn it off.

But he stayed where he was in the dim passage. He was seeing something completely concealed, an unwhisperable thing under the standoff man, the taciturn man hard to befriend. He felt guilty looking into the room and guilty again moving away, backing away, but he backed away quietly and turned toward the light of a dangling bulb.

He went down the wrong passage and into a narrower place, pipes running horizontally along the walls and a cloacal stink beginning to emerge. He walked over a grated drain where the smell was profound, a sorrowful human sewage, and it took him a while to find a door that led outside.

Mike the Book had a flourish he did with his hand. It was broad and Roman, a flat hand moving parallel to the earth as a gesture of burial or a way of writing finis to something significant.

That night Albert and Klara made love in the moonlight. It was sweet and easy and seemingly endless, a love so lost to time he felt they'd found a spirit-life that would protect them from human flaw, with a small fan buzzing in the corner and an aria drifting from a radio on a fire escape somewhere.

He wasn't sure who she was, lying next to him in the dark, but this was something they could overcome together.

8

Up on the roofs, the tar beaches, they put suntan oil on their arms and legs and sat on blankets wearing shorts, the girls did, or jeans rolled to the knees, and they oiled their faces and sat listening to a portable radio until the heat was too intense to bear and then they sat a little longer.

They sang the week's top songs along with the radio, down the list from forty, and they got the words, the pauses, the dips and swerves, every intonation point-blank perfect, but only the songs they liked of course.

The tar softened and fumed and the heat beat down and the green gnats stuck to their bodies and across the way the pigeon kid sent his birds into spiral flight with a bamboo pole, and waved a towel at times, and whistled like a traffic cop, and his flock mixed in midair with a rival flock from a roof three blocks away, a hundred-birded tumult and blur, and younger birds flew with the wrong flock and were captured and sometimes killed, dispatched within the rules by the rival flyer of the other roof, and after a while the girls had to leave because the sun was just too smoking hot, singing lyrics as they rolled their blankets up.

They took the bus out to the beach and people kept crowding on and Nick got jammed in the back with Gloria instead of Loretta. They stood hanging from the straps and every time the bus turned or stopped there was a certain amount of body contact that was unavoidable, except they could have avoided it, and Nick reacted deadpan and Gloria smiled and this was a ride that took approximately forever.

Section 13 was the pickup section at the beach but they put their blanket down at the first available space because they were here with each other and the beach was just as crowded as the bus.

Guys rode the shoulders of other guys and hand-fought, the riders, in shallow water.

Blankets with radios, food, rented umbrellas, sand bodies crammed together, cardplayers, sailor hats, suntan oil.

Loretta came out of the water and he threw her a towel, the only towel they'd brought, four people, and he watched her stand above the blanket, in a vast sand nation of blankets, the horseshoe beach stretching to a rock jetty in either direction, and he watched Loretta shake the water off her hair and finger-stick the towel in her ears.

A guy stood on his hands before toppling into a blanket he didn't belong to and there were looks and words and people brushing sand.

JuJu stood up to put oil on his body.

"Let them see you," Gloria said.

"The weight lifter," Loretta said.

"Show them your forearms, JuJu."

"It's funny what you can do on a beach," Loretta said, "which if you did it on a street corner, they'd throw stones."

"Flex for them, they're watching," Gloria said.

An ice-cream vendor made his way among the blankets, wearing all white, his face gone pink in the high sun, and if you bought a two-stick pop you'd never get to the second half before it melted in your hand.

Nick hit the water and went deep and felt the shatter-shock when

772

he emerged, lungs tight and eyes salt-burned, the bracing change of worlds.

Women removed the wet bathing suits of their children with the kids wrapped in towels and then dressed the kids, underwear and all, still in towels, like writhing magic acts in the desert.

Loretta was facedown on the blanket, asleep, sand sticking to her back, and he rested on an elbow next to her, blowing softly on her shoulder.

They had the rear seat of the bus to themselves on the ride back, the motor right below them, heat beating up, and they dozed on each other's shoulders, faces sun-tight and eyes stinging slightly, tired, hungry, happy, the bus belching heat beneath them.

He stood in the dark hallway and watched her.

"Gloria, you're so bad."

"I'm not bad. You're bad."

"You're so bad."

"If I'm bad, what are you?"

"Gloria, come here, Gloria."

"What do you want?"

"Come here a minute."

"What for come here? Come here for what?"

"You're a cunt, Gloria."

"What do you want?"

"You're a cunt, Gloria."

"Say something nice, Nicky."

She was smiling, he wasn't.

"You're so bad. You're really bad."

"I'm bad? Who's bad?"

She was rolling her hips under his hands and smiling.

"You're a cunt in and out and up and down. You're an all-over cunt through and through."

"Try and say something nice for a change," she told him.

· · ·

Nick carried the last crate of empties up through the hatchway and slid it into the side of the truck. Then he sat in the truck with Muzz the driver, who had sweat running through his shirt and eating up the colors, turning the whole shirt gray.

"I say all right."

"Let's move."

"I say all right. But this is ridiculous," Muzz said.

"Let's go, let's go."

"I got up this morning. I cun't believe it. I said to myself."

"Drive, drive, I'm dying."

"You take your salt pills? Take your salt pills."

When they were stopped for a light a car nudged them from behind.

Muzz looked into the side mirror.

"You hit my bumpah you fuck."

The guy in the car said something.

"You hit my bumpah you fuck."

The guy said something.

"You trying to do?" Muzz said.

The guy spoke into his windshield.

"Tell him," Nick said. "Where'd you get your license?"

Muzz put his head out the window but did not turn toward the car behind them.

"Where'd you get your license to drive that piece of shit?"

The guy said something into the windshield.

"Tell him Sears Roebuck or what?" Nick said.

Muzz looked into the mirror, his face an inch from the glass.

"Sears Roebuck you fuck?"

The light changed and people began to blow their horns.

"Get mad," Nick told him. "Tell him you'll ram your tire iron up his ass."

Muzz had his face an inch from the mirror, enunciating slowly into the glass. Sweat was running along the crease in his lower back, down into his pants. They were blowing their horns back there.

• • •

The school was empty now and Sister walked the halls sometimes, looking into classrooms. Others were gone, they were spending the summer at the motherhouse or visiting relatives somewhere or doing doctoral studies on some campus, sharing pathways under the shade trees with atheists and pinks.

Sometimes it was hard, with the silent classrooms and the halls so lifeless, for Sister Edgar to know who she was. There were a couple of other nuns, they came and went, and there was the Filipino janitor, Miguel, who scrubbed the hall floors even when they were untrod upon for days, a practice Sister admired of course, because you could never clean a thing so infinitesimally that it didn't need to be cleaned again the instant you were done.

Alone in her room she wore a plain shift and read "The Raven." She read it many times, memorizing the lines. She wanted to recite the poem to her class when school reopened. Her namesake poet, yes, and the dark croaking poem that made her feel Edgarish again, contoured, shaped, bevoiced, in the absence of her boys and girls.

Her fan mags were stacked in the closet. There was a picture of Jesus propped on the candlestand. A small mirror used to hang above the washbasin but she took it down because it disconcerted Sister to see herself unveiled. Hair, neck, shoulders, full face—these were things she'd left behind to enter sisterhood. The shock of the body, revealed. The subsistence individual, with cropped hair and bony shoulders. This was a sight to guard against, starker, even, than the empty classrooms of summer.

She memorized the lines and worked the rhythms and repetitions. She paced the floor, organizing a system of gesture and inflection. The sixth grade was hers and she wanted to scare the kids a little. She was their nun for the year, drilling them in eight subjects. A drawing teacher came every two weeks and a music teacher likewise, with a pitch pipe and a fruity perfume. All the rest was Sister.

She even gave them marks in Health, based on days absent and late, and times requesting trips to the lavatory, and amount of dirt and grime stuck under their fingernails and squeezed into the creases of their palms.

And she wanted to teach them fear. This was the secret heart of her curriculum and it would begin with the poem, with omen, loneliness and death, and she would make them shake in their back-to-school shoes.

She paced the floor and walked the empty halls and memorized the lines. Soon they'd come back, uniforms blue and white, notebooks crisp, fountain pens filled, schoolbags swinging from their soft fists, and she would arrange them along the walls in size places and she would seat them in alphabetical order and she would inspect their hands and nails and crack their palms with a ruler when it was called for.

They would know who she was and so would she.

And she would recite the poem to them, crooking her finger at their hearts. She would become the poem and the raven both, the roman-nosed bird, gliding out of the timeless sky and diving down upon them.

These summer nights the women on the upper floors could not wash the dishes because the johnny pump was on, kids dancing under the fanned spray, and there wasn't enough pressure to move water through the building.

All movement toward the air, the night, heads sticking out windows, women eating peaches in darkened windows, laughing in the dark up there, women waiting to feel a breeze and men in undershirts down on the stoops with radios going, a ball game from breezy Cleveland.

Kids running, sweating, shirtless, a kid with a boxful of bared ribs down the front of his body. Other kids on line at the rear of the Bungalow Bar truck, fudgsicles and orange pops, and there is the kid with ink on his tongue, there is always a kid with an inky tongue. Waterman's blue-black. What does he do, drink the stuff?

Women on the porch of a private house, sitting in the dark talking.

Older kids on rented bikes, ten cents an hour, and girls riding with some of the boys, sitting sidewise on the crossbar, and the boys riding into the gushing water, making everybody happy, the stoop sitters, the window heads, the shrieking girls on the bikes and the smaller kids who separate to let the bikes pass, all happy together, and finally the kid in his brother's bathing suit who holds a coffee can at the nozzle to flare the stream of water, geyser it high and wide.

Later the young men will stand on corners smoking as the lights go out, bullshitting the night away, and people will sleep on fire escapes, here and there, because there's a breath of air outside. *Finalmente.* A little bitty breeze that changes everything.

Nick sat reading a magazine with the hollow knocks volleying back from the far wall, across eight lanes.

"Nicky, what's the word?"

"Hey Jack. You're a married man, I hear."

"Went and did it. No regrets."

"She lets you out to bowl?"

"Only to bowl," Jack said.

Lonzo was crouched down there at the end of the alley, about the only black person you could see, regular, in a radius of five or six blocks. He was an ageless man, hard to tell if he was twenty-five or forty-five, and he worked setting up pins, just about every night, soft-footed, fine-featured and slightly out of tune. A little *stunat'*, Lonzo, and they were careful not to treat him badly, the regulars at the alley, because he wore the same clothes for many days and nights and seemed to have no regular place to sleep and carried a whiskey-stink sometimes, soft-footing past the counter on his way to the lanes.

JuJu came in and sat next to Nick.

"What's the word?"

"Your turn's coming," Nick said. "I see you married with three kids. Getting paunchy and going bald."

"Come on, we bowl a few lines."

"Forget about it. Not my sport. She'll let you out to bowl once a week."

"People get married and have kids. This is not normal?"

"Bowling, to me, it's like lifting weights."

"Do me a favor."

"It's something I rather be bad at it than good at it."

"But do me this one little favor."

"Because being good at it means there's something wrong with you."

"Forget I mentioned it, all right?"

"I rather die the death of a thousand cuts."

"Everytime you see a Charlie Chan movie. Which, come to think of it, don't you owe me five bucks from the last time we bowled?"

"It's a brouch," Nick told him.

"How come?"

"Because I'm not trying to win. Because winning insults my dignity. Beat me in pool I'll pay you the five dollars. Otherwise *u'gazz'*. I'm pulling a brouch."

The regulars taunted each other constantly and said things to the girls who showed up now and then and they always looked a little narrow at strangers walking in. But they were careful to be patient with ageless Lonzo even when he was slow or clumsy setting up the pins, a birdlike figure hunched aloft down there at the end of the lanes, white-eyed in the spatter of flying wood.

JuJu found someone to bowl with and after a while Nick put down the magazine and left.

"Hey. Be good okay?"

"Be good, Jack."

"Be good."

"Be good," Nick said.

It was dark and quiet now and he went up the narrow street toward his building but then swung into a gateway on an impulse and went down the steps and into the yards.

There was no light in the outer passage and he felt along the walls for the door that led inside. He smelled wet stone where the super had hosed the floors. He went inside and walked past the furnace room to the door at the end of the passage.

He still felt uneasy about the basement room, about the needle and strap and spoon, but it was passing little by little into faded time, half lost in the weave of a thousand things.

George was in the room all right, playing solitaire.

"I thought you might be here."

"Cool down here."

"That's what I thought," Nick said.

George gathered and stacked the cards and shuffled them. Nick sat across the table and George dealt out three to a man and turned over a club trump and they started playing a game.

"The trouble with cards, when you play for money," George said, "and you concentrate on all those numbers and colors for hours and hours, a poker game into the morning, you can't fucking sleep when you go home."

"Your mind's too active."

"You can't fucking no-way sleep."

"Your brain is racing."

"But we play a little friendly game of *briscola*. Maybe I can sleep in an hour or two."

"You have trouble, normally, sleeping?"

"I have trouble sleeping. I also have trouble staying awake."

They laughed and played. They played for an hour and talked about nothing much and smoked a couple of cigarettes each and dropped the butts in an old beer bottle.

"This thing I want to show you. Found it a couple of days ago," George said, "in a car I was parking at the track. Slid out from under the seat when I made a quick turn."

"The turns you make."

"I'm cautious. Hey. Compared to most guys."

"You respect the automobiles you park."

"Not so much the owners. The cars, definitely."

They laughed. George reached behind him and came up with an object from the bottom shelf, down behind paint cans and rolled linoleum.

It was a shotgun, sawed-off, the barrel extending only a couple of inches from the forearm part and the stock cut down to a pistol grip arrangement.

"What? You found it?"

"I didn't want to leave it in the car where somebody who's not responsible."

779

"Let me see," Nick said.

He reached across the table for the weapon. He sort of bounced it in his hands and then stood up to hold it more naturally.

"I know one thing about shotguns," George said. "You shoot with both eyes open."

"Sawed-off is illegal, right?"

"That's the other thing I know. Once you cut the thing down it's a concealed weapon."

"Looks old to me."

"It's old, rusty, wore out," George said. "Piece of, basically, junk."

He posed with it, Nick did, a pirate's pistol or an old Kentucky flintlock if that's the word. It was more natural two hands than one, the left hand under the forepart to steady and point.

He hefted it and pointed it. He saw an interested smile fall across George's face. He had the weapon pointed at George. He was standing a couple of yards from George and George was in the chair and he held the weapon midbody, slightly above the hip, which meant it was pointed at George's head.

A little brightness entered George's eye. Rare in George. This brightness in the eye. And an interested look moved across his mouth. It was the slyest kind of shit-eating grin.

"Is it loaded?"

"No," George said.

This made him smile a little wider. They were having a good time. And he had a look on his face that was more alive and bright than George had ever looked. Because he was interested in what they were doing.

Nick pulled the trigger.

In the extended interval of the trigger pull, the long quarter second, with the action of the trigger sluggish and rough, Nick saw into the smile on the other man's face.

Then the thing went off and the noise busted through the room and even with the chair and body flying he had the thumbmark of George's face furrowed in his mind.

The way the man said no when he asked if it was loaded.

He asked if the gun was loaded and the man said no and the smile was all about the risk, of course, the spirit of the dare of what they were doing.

He felt the trigger pull and then the gun went off and he was left there thinking weakly he didn't do it.

But first he pointed the gun at the man's head and asked if it was loaded.

Then he felt the trigger pull and heard the gun go off and the man and chair went different ways.

And the way the man said no when he asked if it was loaded.

He asked if the thing was loaded and the man said no and now he has a weapon in his hands that has just apparently been fired.

He force-squeezed the trigger and looked into the smile on the other man's face.

But first he posed with the gun and pointed it at the man and asked if it was loaded.

Then the noise busted through the room and he stood there thinking weakly he didn't do it.

But first he force-squeezed the trigger and saw into the smile and it seemed to have the spirit of a dare.

Why would the man say no if it was loaded?

But first why would he point the gun at the man's head?

He pointed the gun at the man's head and asked if it was loaded.

Then he felt the action of the trigger and saw into the slyness of the smile.

He stood above the spraddled body in the blood muck of the room, not that he clearly saw the room, and he thought he heard a sucking sound come out of the man's face, the afterbirth of face, the facial remains of what was once a head.

But first he went through the sequence and it played out the same.

When they took him out to the cop car there were people on the stoops, in robes, some of them, and heads in many windows, hanging pale and hushed, and a number of young men stood near the car, some he knew well and some in passing, and they watched him closely and gravely, thinking this was a kind of history taking place, here in their own remote and common streets.

DAS KAPITAL

Capital burns off the nuance in a culture. Foreign investment, global markets, corporate acquisitions, the flow of information through transnational media, the attenuating influence of money that's electronic and sex that's cyberspaced, untouched money and computer-safe sex, the convergence of consumer desire—not that people want the same things, necessarily, but that they want the same range of choices.

We're sitting in a pub called the Football Hooligan. There's a man at the next table and I've been waiting for him to turn this way so I can confirm the uncanny resemblance.

I'm talking to Brian Glassic, old buddy Brian, and he seems to listen intently below the music. This is a thing called cult rock, loud, yes, but mostly piercing and repetitive, on an icy kind of wavelength, and Brian sits with his head low, nodding now and then, in agreement or fatigue—it's hard to tell.

Some things fade and wane, states disintegrate, assembly lines shorten their runs and interact with lines in other countries. This is what desire seems to demand. A method of production that will custom-cater to cultural and personal needs, not to cold war ideologies of massive uniformity. And the system pretends to go along, to become more supple and resourceful, less dependent on rigid categories. But even as desire tends to specialize, going silky and intimate, the force of converging markets produces an instantaneous capital that shoots across horizons at the speed of light, making for a certain furtive sameness, a planing away of particulars that affects everything from architecture to leisure time to the way people eat and sleep and dream.

Here the people are eating ethnic fast food and drinking five-star cognac and they are crowding the dance floor and falling down, some of them, and being dragged half senseless to the sidelines.

I have to lower my head to speak to Brian, who seems to be sinking into his drink, but I resist the urge to nod along with him. True, I am mostly quoting remarks made to me earlier in the day by Viktor Maltsev, a trading company executive, but they are remarks worth repeating because Viktor has thought about these matters in the very ruck of every kind of changeover a society can bear.

Brian mutters that he finds this place frightening. I look at the kids on the bandstand, five or six gawks with fuzz heads and fatigue pants and bomb packs strapped to their bare chests—college boys probably who've appropriated a surface of suicide terror.

But it's not the music, he says, or the band and its trappings. And I think I know what he means. It's the sense of displacement and redefinition. Because what kind of random arrangement puts a club such as this up on the forty-second floor of a new office tower filled with brokerage houses, software firms, import companies and foreign banks, where private guards hired by various firms to patrol the corridors sometimes shoot at each other and where the man at the next table, with a bald dome, slit eyes and a jut beard, turning this way at last, is clearly a professional Lenin look-alike.

We take the elevator down and go out to the street, carrying our luggage. We can't find a taxi but after a while an ambulance comes along and the driver sticks his head out the window.

"You go airport?" he says.

We get in the back and Brian goes to sleep on a collapsible gurney.

About twenty minutes later, out the glass panel on the rear door, I see a huge billboard advertising a strip club.

INTERACTIVE SONYA
Nude Dancing on the Information Highway

We get to Sheremetyevo and the driver wants dollars of course. I wake up Brian and we go into the terminal and manage to find the man from the trading company. He tells us there's no particular hurry because we're at the wrong airport anyway.

"Where should we be, Viktor?"

"No problem. I have arranged. You went to club?"

"The club was very interesting," I tell him. "Lenin was there."

"There is Marx and Trotsky too," he says. "Very crazy thing."

This is what I thought after we arrived at the military airfield and boarded a converted cargo plane that went bucking down the runway and lifted swayingly into the mist. And after the plane reached cruising altitude and I got up and found a window slit in an emergency exit behind the port wing and pressed my face to the glass to gather a sense of the great eastern reaches, endless belts of longitude, the map-projection arcs beyond the Urals and across the Siberian Lowland—a sense mainly of my own imagining, of course, a glimpse through falling dusk of whatever landmass was visible in the limited window space.

And this is what I thought after I sat down again.

I thought leaders of nations used to dream of vast land empires—expansion, annexation, troop movements, armored units driving in dusty juggernauts over the plains, the forced march of language and appetite, the digging of mass graves. They wanted to extend their shadows across the territories.

Now they want—

I explain my thinking to Brian Glassic, who sits on the opposite side of the aircraft facing me. We're on parallel benches like paratroops waiting to reach the drop zone.

787

Brian says, "Now they want computer chips."

"Exactly. Thank you."

And Viktor Maltsev says, "Yes, it's true that geography has moved inward and smallward. But we still have mass graves, I think."

Viktor sits near Brian, a slim figure in a leather coat. We have to shout at each other to converse above the noise that drones and rattles through the hollowed-out interior of the massive transport. He tells us the plane was originally designed for mixed loads of cargo and troops. There are dangling wires, fixtures jutting from the bulkhead. The aircraft is all cylinder, all ribs and slats and shaking parts.

"It's a company plane, Viktor?"

"I buy it this morning," he says.

"And you will use it to ship material."

"We fix it up good."

His trading company is called Tchaika and they want to invite our participation in a business scheme. We are flying to a remote site in Kazakhstan to witness an underground nuclear explosion. This is the commodity that Tchaika trades in. They sell nuclear explosions for ready cash. They want us to supply the most dangerous waste we can find and they will destroy it for us. Depending on degree of danger, they will charge their customers—the corporation or government or municipality—between three hundred dollars and twelve hundred dollars per kilo. Tchaika is connected to the commonwealth arms complex, to bomb-design laboratories and the shipping industry. They will pick up waste anywhere in the world, ship it to Kazakhstan, put it in the ground and vaporize it. We will get a broker's fee.

The plane comes into heavy weather.

"There's some concern in Phoenix," I tell him, "about the extent of your operating capital. The kind of safety equipment we're talking about to move highly sensitive material can result, Viktor, in expenditures that are quite dizzying."

"Yes yes yes yes. We have the expertise." He unzippers this word with a certain defensive zest as if it sums up all the insufficiencies that have mocked him until this point. "And we have the stacks of rubles that are also quite, I may say, dizzying. You didn't read Financial Times? I will send you."

Brian is lying on his side wearing his coat and gloves.

"I forget," he says. "Where are we going exactly?"

I call across the heaving body of the plane. "The Kazakh Test Site."

"Yeah but where's that?"

I shout. "Where are we going, Viktor?"

"Very important place that's not on the map. Near Semipalatinsk. White space on map. No problem. They will meet us."

"No problem," I call across to Brian.

"Thank you both. Wake me when we land," he says.

I look at him carefully. It's cold and we're dead tired and I look at Brian. The knowledge of what he's been doing, the calculated breach of trust—I want to stay awake while he sleeps so I can watch him and fine-edge my feelings and wait for my moment.

Viktor takes a bottle of Chivas Regal out of his overnight bag. I do a mime of polite applause. He goes to the flight deck to get some glasses but they don't have any or won't share them. I go through my bag and come up with a bottle of mouthwash and take off the cap and lurch across the aircraft shaking out the grooved plastic piece as I go. Viktor pours some scotch into the cap and I return to my seat.

We have no seat belts and the passage is growing rougher. I have the bottle of mouthwash wedged upright in my bag so the stuff won't spill. We are the three of us alone except for the person or persons flying the aircraft and I think we feel a little forlorn in the huge tubed space, more like people in a shabby terminal late at night than lucky travelers aboard their plane. I sip my Chivas from the cap, listening to the shaking structure around us, the minimum ribbing, a sort of endoskeletal arch that makes every groaning noise in the hymnal of manned flight. The scotch tastes faintly of gargled mint.

"What did you do before you joined Tchaika?"

"I teach history twenty years. Then no more. I look for a new life."

"There are men like you in many American cities now. Russians, Ukrainians. Do you know what they do?"

"Drive taxi," he says.

I notice the way his eyes leap to catch mine, slyly, a brief merged moment that allows him to mark my awareness of his superior status.

He is drinking from the bottle.

I see the plane as if from some protected position in the sky. It is a swift shape hurtling through the dark—I felt sure it was dark by now. It is a mass of dark metal racing through the rain and wind as if in a swift scene from an old black-and-white movie, scored with urgent music.

Viktor asks me if I've ever witnessed a nuclear explosion. No. It is interesting, he says, how weapons reflect the soul of the maker. The Soviets always wanted bigger yield, bigger stockpiles. They had to convince themselves they were a superpower. Throw-weight. What is throw-weight? We don't know exactly but we agree it sounds like hurled bulk, the hurled will of the collective. Soviet long-range missiles had greater throw-weight. They had to convince themselves with numbers and bulk and mass.

"And the U.S.?" I say.

Eyes flicking my way, happy as carnival lights. It was the U.S., Viktor says, that designed the neutron bomb. Many buzzing neutrons, very little blast. The perfect capitalist tool. Kill people, spare property.

I watch Brian sleep.

"You have your own capitalist tools now. Don't you, Viktor?"

"You mean my company?"

"A small private army, I hear."

"Also intelligence unit. To protect our assets."

"And scare the hell out of the competition."

He tells me that the name of the company was his idea. Tchaika means seagull and refers poetically to the fact that the company's basic business is waste. He likes the way seagulls swoop down on garbage mounds and trail after ships waiting for the glint of jettison at the bow. It is a nicer name, besides, than Rat or Pig.

I look at Brian. It's better than sleeping. I don't want to sleep until I'm finished looking. Traveling with the man from Arizona to Russia, side by side through all those time zones, sharing magazines and trading food items from the little peel-off receptacles, my dessert for his radishes because I'm fit and he's not, Sky Harbor to Sheremetyevo, all those hours and oceans and pales of plotted land, the houses and lives below—maybe it was just the seating arrangement that made me want to wait before I confronted him. It's much too clumsy to accuse a man who's sitting next to you. I wanted a quiet face-to-face in a cozy room somewhere.

I see us hurtling through the dark.

I tell Viktor there is a curious connection between weapons and waste. I don't know exactly what. He smiles and puts his feet up on the bench, something of a gargoyle squat. He says maybe one is the mystical twin of the other. He likes this idea. He says waste is the devil twin. Because waste is the secret history, the underhistory, the way archaeologists dig out the history of early cultures, every sort of bone heap and broken tool, literally from under the ground.

All those decades, he says, when we thought about weapons all the time and never thought about the dark multiplying byproduct.

"And in this case," I say. "In our case, in our age. What we excrete comes back to consume us."

We don't dig it up, he says. We try to bury it. But maybe this is not enough. That's why we have this idea. Kill the devil. And he smiles from his steeple perch. The fusion of two streams of history, weapons and waste. We destroy contaminated nuclear waste by means of nuclear explosions.

I cross the body of the aircraft to get my cap refilled.

"It is only obvious," he says.

I see that Brian's eyes are opened.

I return to my seat, an arm out for balance, and I sit carefully and pause and then knock back the scotch and blink a bit.

I look at Brian.

I say, "The early bomb, Brian, they had to do the core material in a certain way as I understand it. They had to mate this part to that part. So they could get the chain reaction that's crucial to the whole operation. One design had a male element fitted into a female element. The cylinder goes into an opening in the sphere. They shoot it right in. Very suggestive. There's really sort of no escape. Cocks and cunts everywhere."

I see our plane racing through the wind and rain.

Because I knew unmistakably now, I was completely certain that Brian and Marian, whose names sound so nice together, a good friend now and again, that he and my wife were partners in a deep betrayal.

791

In my jet-crazed way I could almost enjoy the situation we'd found ourselves in. I was so time-zoned, dazed by fatigue and revelation, so deep in the stink of a friend's falseheartedness that I started talking nonstop, manic and jaggy, babble-mouthing into the plane noise, hinting—I hinted insidiously, made clever references. Because I knew it all now, and here we both were, and there was no place he could go to escape our homey chat.

At the gate we are given badges to wear, gauzy strips that register the amount of radiation absorbed by the body in a given period. Maybe this is what makes the landscape seem so strange. These little metered tags put an element of threat into the dull scrub that rolls to the over-whelming sky.

Brian says the gate resembles the entrance to a national park.

Viktor says don't be surprised there will be tourists here someday.

The car is driven by a Russian, not a Kazakh. He wears pressed fatigues and carries a radiation meter to go with the two badges clipped to his shirt. Far from the road we see men in white masks and floppy boots bulldozing the earth and when we come to a rise we are able to see the vast cratered plain of recent underground tests, depressions of various diameter but all seemingly well-figured—pale-rimmed holes formed when dirt displaced by the blasts slid back into the gouged earth.

The driver tells us that the test site is known as the Polygon. He tells us a few more things, some translated by Viktor, some not.

Farther on we see signs of the old tests, aboveground, and there is a strangeness here, an uneasiness I try to locate. We see the remnant span of a railroad trestle, a sculptured length of charred brown metal resting on concrete piers. A graveness, a spirit of old secrets gone bad, turned unworthy. We see the squat gray base of a shot tower, most of it blown away decades earlier, leaving this block of seamed concrete that rises only seven feet above the stubble surface, still looking oddly stunned, with metal beams ajut. Guilt in every dosed object, the weathered posts and I-beams left to the wind, things made and shaped by men, old schemes gone wrong.

We ride in silence.

There are mounds of bulldozed earth around a camera bunker daubed with yellow paint—yellow for contaminated. The place is strange, frozen away, a specimen of our forgetfulness even as we note the details. We see signs of houses in the distance, test dwellings blown off their foundations with people still inside, mannequins, and products on the shelves where they'd been placed maybe forty years ago—American brands, the driver says.

And Viktor says this was a point of pride with the KGB, to assemble a faithful domestic setting.

And how strange it is, strange again, more strangeness, to feel a kind of homesickness for the things on the shelves in the houses that still stand, Old Dutch Cleanser and Rinso White, all those half-lost icons of the old life, Ipana and Oxydol and Chase & Sanborn, still intact out here in this nowhere near Mongolia, and does anyone remember why we were doing all this?

I say, "Viktor, does anyone remember why we were doing all this?"

"Yes, for contest. You won, we lost. You have to tell me how it feels. Big winner."

Brian sits next to me, sleeping now.

We see a rusted tank with yellow brushwork marking the turret. There are roads that end abruptly, weeds pushing through the asphalt.

The car reaches the site of the test, our test. It is a slightly elevated tract of land cleared of brush and graded nearly flat. I wasn't going to be the first one out of the car and for a moment nobody moved. Drill towers stand in the middle distance. There are a dozen trailers arrayed on the flat, all packed with equipment that will analyze the blast.

The driver opens his door and we all get out.

The wind comes with a labored drone. Several technicians and military men stand talking nearby. Viktor lights a cigarette and approaches them. He looks misplaced in his long leather coat. Out beyond the road we see bluffs scarred white by earlier detonations. I keep glancing at the driver for signs and portents.

Viktor comes back and points to a corner of the cleared area where thick cables snake away from several pieces of equipment set in a pale square of earth. He says this is ground zero. We stand there nodding in the wind.

He says the shot will be fired in granite about one kilometer down. Reactor waste and cores from retired warheads are packed around a low-yield nuclear device. He says the hole drilled from the surface to the firing point has been tamped and plugged to keep radiation from venting.

The driver puts a finger to his tongue and rubs some dirt off his sleeve. I check my sleeve for dirt. Then the driver heads back to the car and we all go with him.

He drives us to a bunker complex some distance away. About four dozen people are assembled here. Generals with braided caps, uranium speculators, a man and woman from the Bundesbank. We are introduced around. Many chesty bureaucrats with interchangeable heads. There are industrialists, bomb designers, official observers here to monitor the test. And every one of us wears a badge that measures off the rads. I follow Viktor into a briefing room where tureens and serving plates are spread across a table, heaped with smoking food. I meet executives from Tchaika and high officials of several commonwealth ministries. There is a palpable wave of expectation. Dark young men in round caps serve glasses of peppered vodka cradled in porringers of crushed ice. I talk to a veteran of the Polygon, a weapons scientist looking for work. A Russian tells a joke to a huddle of burly men and I stand on the edge, startled to hear the name Speedy Gonzalez mixed into the rolling narration. I look around for Brian. I want Brian to be in on this. The joke teller is in uniform, his middle finger extended skyward, his face going ruddy as the plot winds down. He does the punch line very well, speaking the words to his lifted finger, and the line comes back to me as he does it in Russian—back in English, of course, after so many years. The huddled men nod and rock, sending plosive noises from their moon jowls.

Caviar pulsing in chilled bowls. There are geologists and game theorists and energy experts and a journalist with a book contract. I see waste traders and venture capitalists, piroshki and skewered lamb. There are arms dealers looking to make bids, Viktor says, on the idle inventory of weapons-grade plutonium floating at the fringes of the industry.

"And this explosion," I say. "Not banned by international accord?"

"Banned, not banned. We are exception. Test site was closed by local decree. But we are exception. It is necessary to do a trial demonstration. Plutonium waste is getting to a point that's very crazy. Worldwide, who is counting? Maybe twelve hundred metric tons."

"More."

"More. Okay. Has to disappear somehow."

The food makes me happy for a time. I eat everything I can reach. Meat, fish, eggs, my appetite is enormous. The vodka looks beautiful, with a lucent ruby softness that belies its spice and bite. I fill myself to near capacity, feeling rebuilt, fundamentally sound and content, proteinized, and I watch Viktor mingle with the nuclear brass. He looks a little lost among those mainframe bodies. He needs to get adjusted to an environment in which fixing and hustling have come out of the shadows of black-market speculation to create a wholly open economy of plunder and corruption. I'm not sure he can forget all the things he has to forget before he can become a man who flourishes here.

I talk to a woman with a pastry flake fixed to a corner of her mouth. Eating saves us from the fatedness of the landscape, from the dosage meters we wear on our bodies. We talk about this. How nice that the unprinted record of some stray pleasure might rebuke the exclusion out there, the forces that make it chancy for us to take a simple breath of air.

I go looking for Brian Glassic. The bunker complex is set on several levels with one large section clearly off-limits to guests—sealed and guarded. I go looking in and out of map rooms, sleeping quarters, a medical setup, down concrete passageways, often ducking my head under low openings. An economist from the U.N. is searching for a toilet. I ease myself down a hatchway that has an iron rail and hobnail steps and there he is in a small room, asleep again.

A chair, a cot and a sink. I'm carrying a plate of food. Not for him—food for me. I sit and watch him sleep and I eat my food. He is wearing his loden coat, one of those hooded Tyrolean things of coarse cloth with wooden toggles for buttons. How right for his old-fashioned face, narrow and boyish, that I could probably crush with five earnest blows. I imagine this with some satisfaction. Dealing a serious blow. But we don't do that anymore, do we? This is a thing we've left behind. Five dealt blows to the pinkish face with the paling hair. But I sit there and watch him, you know, and I'm not sure I want to hit him.

Brian thought I was the soul of self-completion. Maybe so. But I was also living in a state of quiet separation from all the things he might cite as the solid stuff of home and work and responsible reality. When I found out about him and Marian I felt some element of stoic surrender. Their names were nice together and they were the same age and I was hereby relieved of my phony role as husband and father, high corporate officer. Because even the job is an artificial limb. Did I feel free for just a moment, myself again, hearing the story of their affair? I watch him sleep, thinking how satisfying it would be, ten serious smashes to his prep-school face. But it was also satisfying, for just a moment, to think of giving it all up, letting them have it all, the children of both marriages, the grandchild, they could keep the two houses, all the cars, he could have both wives if he wanted them. None of it ever belonged to me except in the sense that I filled out the forms.

I don't have to get out of the chair to kick the side of the cot. I just extend my leg and kick.

Then I watch him come awake.

"So. The fastest lover *een Mayheeko.*"

"What's that?"

"Old joke. You don't know this joke?"

"Jesus, I was dreaming. What was I dreaming?"

"A guy's worried about his wife because there's a famous lover on the prowl. What, you don't know this joke? The Speedy Gonzalez joke. Goes way back. Took decades, this joke, to get from there to here."

"From where to here?"

"Fuck you. That's from where."

I kick the bed again.

He says, "What?"

"How long, Brian?"

"How long what?"

"You and Marian."

"What do you mean?"

"What do I mean?"

796

I kick the bed. He sits up and puts his hands over his face and begins to laugh miserably.

"We used to talk more or less. That's all."

"Don't contradict me."

"We used to exchange, all right, a confidence now and then. We were close that way but it didn't last long."

"I'm smoking a cigar and drinking a brandy. Don't contradict me."

He looks at me. I don't have a cigar and I'm drinking vodka.

"I mean now? Is this the time we want to discuss the matter? Here? Can't we think about finding a more suitable?"

"She told me everything."

He looks away.

"I'm prepared to be very open about this but I think we need to reconsider the timing," he says.

I lean over, the plate in my left hand, and I cuff him with the right. I throw a right, openhanded because we're being open about this, hitting him with the heel of the hand on the side of the head—a token blow that improves my mood. It is even better than eating. It is better than the meat, the fish, the eggs, the fish eggs and the vodka. I feel good about it. I think we both feel better.

Once he adjusts to the knowledge that he has just been hit, he looks at me again. I know what he sees when he looks at me. Someone bigger than he is, readier to act, sitting between him and the door. This is the message that hums in the air. Not the words, the personal histories, the moral advantage or disadvantage, whatever maneuvers of bluff and counterbluff might ornament the moment. It's the force of the body. It's which body crushes the other. Not that he has anything, really, to worry about. But maybe he does.

"When you say she told you everything."

"She told me everything. We talked for a long time. The talk we had lasted a couple of days, on and off. She said a lot. She told me everything. Then I got in the company car and went to the airport and there you were."

He grins at me.

"Fucking women. Can't trust them for shit."

I hit him with the flat of my hand across an ear. His head jerks

797

impressively. It is not a hard blow. It is a token blow and the head-jerk is overdone.

"Watch what you say about her, Brian."

He lowers his eyes, looking for a fetch of sympathy. Here he is, hungry, thirsty, jet-lagged, unkempt, being held prisoner, sort of, cuffed around in a basement cell. But I don't think he has serious reason to worry.

"She told you about the heroin?"

"She told me everything."

"Only once, I swear. Scared the shit out of me."

He reaches over and takes some food out of my plate and begins to eat it. I watch him. He keeps his head down, reaching into my plate, eating and reaching, and I let him do it.

"I'm sorry, Nick. Kill me. I want you to. But I have to tell you it didn't last long. And I have to tell you I was not always—how do I want to put this if I don't want to get hit again?"

"She told me."

"I was not always willing."

I watch him eat.

"I'm the one who was reluctant and I'm the one who was scared you'd find out. And when you didn't find out, she told you."

He reaches and eats, head down. I let him go to the sink and splash water on his face. Bomb or no bomb, he says, that's a boring bunch of people out there. We head back to the room with the food. The guests are spread through several areas, drinking coffee or tea or brandy, some of them, or holding dessert plates up to their chins, those who are standing.

We feel a ground motion, a rumble underfoot. There is a guncotton thud, some far-off shift or heave that is also a local sensation, a hollow body sound. Someone says, "Da" or "Ja." Then people begin to head for the exit, one by one, leaning under the low portals, room to room, trying not to be overeager, a chain of rustling sighs, and we gather outside the complex and look toward ground zero although there is nothing to see, really, but the sweep of the Kazakh plain.

We stand and look for some time, a few of us speaking briefly, soft-voiced, and there is a sense of anticipation left dangling in the wind.

No ascending cloudmass, of course, or rolling waves of sound. Maybe some dust rises from the site and maybe it is only afternoon haze and several people point and comment briefly and there is a flatness in the group, an unspoken dejection, and after a while we go back inside.

We spend the night in the city of Semipalatinsk drinking warm beer and eating horsemeat paté and in the morning, instead of flying back to Moscow first thing, Viktor Maltsev decides we ought to see something.

He takes us to a place he calls the Museum of Misshapens. It is part of the Medical Institute and I note how Brian begins to shy away, to fall back a bit even before we enter the museum proper, a long low room of display cases filled with fetuses. Viktor is a man who evidently likes to deepen the texture of an experience. The fetuses, some of them, are preserved in Heinz pickle jars. There is the two-headed specimen. There is the single head that is twice the size of the body. There is the normal head that is located in the wrong place, perched on the right shoulder.

We look into the jars in silence. We go slowly from one display case to the next because the occasion seems to demand a solemn pace and we say nothing and look only at the jars and never at the walls or windows or each other. Then Viktor says something but not about the jars. He talks about the years of testing. We look into the jars and listen to Viktor and move slowly from one display to the next. Five hundred nuclear explosions at the test site, which is southwest of the city, and even when they stopped testing in the atmosphere, the mine shafts they dug for underground detonations were not deep enough to preclude the venting of dangerous levels of radiation.

He looks at me when he says this.

Then there is the cyclops. The eye centered, the ears below the chin, the mouth completely missing. Brian is also missing. We find him outside, standing by the taxi and looking through factory smoke at the low mountains that run across the steppe. But we don't take the taxi to our hotel to pick up our luggage and go to the airport. Viktor gives directions to a radiation clinic on the outskirts of the city and we

799

drive out there in a mood of some disgruntlement (Brian and I) even if we are unresisting, too stilled by the pickle jars to make an open complaint.

He is taking us, basically, downwind. Not that the clinic was downwind of the testing in the years of frequent detonations. The clinic was probably not even here at the time. No, it is the people who were downwind, the villagers who are patients now, and their children and grandchildren, and Viktor takes us inside and we're not in a museum this time.

Viktor has been here four times, he says. He says this in a way that's hard to read. Every time he has gone to the Polygon he has also come here. This is a man who is trying to merchandise nuclear explosions—using safer methods, no doubt—and he comes here to challenge himself perhaps, to prove to himself he is not blind to the consequences. It is the victims who are blind. It is the boy with skin where his eyes ought to be, a bolus of spongy flesh, oddly like a mushroom cap, springing from each brow. It is the bald-headed children standing along a wall in their underwear, waiting to be examined. It is the man with the growth beneath his chin, a thing with a life of its own, embryonic and pulsing. It is the dwarf girl who wears a T-shirt advertising a Gay and Lesbian Festival in Hamburg, Germany, bottom edge dragging on the floor. It is the cheerful cretin who walks the halls with his arms folded. It is the woman with features intact but only half a face somehow, everything fitted into a tilted arc that floats above her shoulders like the crescent moon.

She is wearing a T-shirt like the dwarf's and Viktor says this is the result of an importing ploy gone awry. A local businessman bought ten thousand T-shirts without knowing they were leftovers from a gay celebration in Europe. Very crazy thing, Viktor says, bringing these shirts into a place where Islam is stronger every day.

But this is part of the same surreal, isn't it, that started on the forty-second floor of that Moscow tower.

The clinic has disfigurations, leukemias, thyroid cancers, immune systems that do not function. The doctors know Viktor and let us wander here and there. He talks to patients and nurses. He says there are unknown diseases here. And words that are also unknown, or used

800

to be. For many years the word radiation was banned. You could not say this word in the hospitals around the test site. Doctors said this word only at home, to their wives or husbands or friends, and maybe not even there. And the villagers did not say this word because they didn't know it existed.

Some of the rooms have rugs on the walls. Old men wear skullcaps, sitting motionless in shabby halls.

We stand in the cafeteria doorway watching a group of young people eat lunch. Their hair, nails and teeth have fallen out and they are here to be studied. I look around for Brian.

"Sickness everywhere around. And I tell you something," Viktor says. "They are blaming us. They are saying this is calculation. The Kazakhs believe this."

"Blaming who?"

"The Russians. They are saying we tried to murder the whole population. Red Army did not always evacuate villages before a test. People see the flash and then a great cloud climbing the sky. They don't know what this is. Red Army exploded hydrogen bomb, very big yield, you know, and they left behind a hundred villagers to see what effect on people."

"Do you believe this?"

"I believe everything."

"Do you believe it was intentional?"

"Believe everything. Everything is true. Every time they did a test, hundreds of towns and villages exposed to radiation. Ministry of Health says, Okay we raise limit again. When limit is passed, Okay we raise again."

Viktor is talking mostly to himself, I gather. But he is also talking to me. These faces and bodies have enormous power. I begin to feel something drain out of me. Some old opposition, a capacity to resist. I look around for Brian. But Brian does not want to see toothless people eating lunch. He is outside somewhere.

We walk the halls, Viktor and I.

He says, "Once they imagine the bomb, write down equations, they see it's possible to build, they build, they test in the American desert, they drop on the Japanese, but once they imagine in the beginning, it makes everything true," he says. "Nothing you can believe is not coming true."

I begin to see him as a very improbable man, lean and dark with the gray dyed out of his hair and a seeming need to look half gangsterish in that long slick coat. At a glance he belongs to these wild privatized times, to the marathon of danced-out plots. The get-rich-quick plot. The plot of members-only and crush-the-weak. Raw capital spewing out. The extortion-and-murder plot. But there are ironies and hesitations in Viktor's address to the moment. Too many years of slowly growing skepticism. He is in a fix, I think.

He says, "An interesting thing. There is a woman in Ukraine who says she is second Christ. She is going to be crucified by followers and then rise from the dead. Very serious person. Fifteen thousand followers. You can believe this? Educated people, look very normal. I don't know. After communism, this?"

"After Chernobyl maybe."

"I don't know," he says.

He didn't know and neither did I. We walked out into a patchy courtyard that opened at the far end onto the great wide plain running treeless to the mountains. Children played a game in the dirt, six boys and girls with missing arms, left arms in every case, knotted below the elbow. The eyeless boy was also here, squatted on his haunches, facing the players as if in careful observation of their efforts. Copper-skinned, wearing clothes that were probably Chinese-made, a hole above the welt in each shoe, his big toes poking, a fourteen-year-old, according to Viktor, who looked to be nine or ten, but unretarded, his head slightly oversized, face and forehead marked by tumors, and the spongy caps over the place where his eyes should have been.

The kids are playing follow the leader. A boy falls down, gets up. They all fall down, get up.

Something about the juxtaposition deepened the moment, faces against the landscape, the enormous openness, the breadth of sheepland and divided sky that contains everything outside us, unbearably. I watched the boy in his bundled squat, arms folded above his knees. All the banned words, the secrets kept in whitewashed vaults, the half-forgotten plots—they're all out here now, seeping invisibly into the land and air, into the marrowed folds of the bone.

He crouched under the great split sky, ears set low and his head sloped. The sky was divided, split diagonally, a flat blue, a soft slatey blue, like the head of a crested jay, and a yellow that wasn't even yellow, an enormous heartbreak yellow sweeping to the east, a smoky goldshot stain, and the kids with the knotted arms fell down in a row.

Most of our longings go unfulfilled. This is the word's wistful implication—a desire for something lost or fled or otherwise out of reach.

In Phoenix now, with the years blowing by, I take a drive sometimes out past the regimented typeface on the map and down through the streets named for Indian tribes and past the roofing supply and sandblasting and the condom outlet, painted now in ice-cream flavors, and finally I see the impressive open-steel truss of the waste facility down off Lower Buckeye Road, with grackles sparking across the landfill and the planes in a long line coming out of the hazy mountains to drop into approach patterns.

Marian and I are closer now, more intimate than we've ever been. The serrate edges have dulled away. We go to Tucson to see our daughter and granddaughter. We redecorate our house, building new bookshelves all the time, buying new carpets to set on top of the old ones, and we walk along the drainage canal in the twilight and tell each other stories of the past.

In the bronze tower I stand by the window and look at the hills and ridges and it's a hundred and ten degrees out on the street and I always wear a suit even if I'm only here to check the mail and I listen to the microtonal hum of the systems and feel a quiet kind of power because I've done it and come out okay, done it and won, gone in weak and come out strong, and I do my imitation gangster for the elevator guy.

We separate our household waste according to the guidelines. We rinse out the used cans and empty bottles and put them in their respective bins. We do tin versus aluminum. We use a paper bag for the paper bags, pressing the smaller bags flat and fitting them into the large bag that we've set aside for the purpose. We bundle the newspapers but do not tie them in twine.

The long ghosts are walking the halls. When my mother died I felt expanded, slowly, durably, over time. I felt suffused with her truth, spread through, as with water, color or light. I thought she'd entered the deepest place I could provide, the animating entity, the thing, if anything, that will survive my own last breath, and she makes me larger, she amplifies my sense of what it is to be human. She is part of me now, total and consoling. And it is not a sadness to acknowledge that she had to die before I could know her fully. It is only a statement of the power of what comes after.

They are trading garbage in the commodity pits in Chicago. They are making synthetic feces in Dallas. You can sell your testicles to a firm in Russia that will give you four thousand dollars and then remove the items surgically and mash them up and extract the vital substances and market the resulting syrupy stuff as rejuvenating beauty cream, for a profit that is awesome.

We take the TV set out of the cool room at the back of the house, Lainie's old room, our daughter, which is my mother's old room now, the room with the humidifier and the resilvered mirror and the good hard healthy bed, and we build bookshelves there.

At Waste Containment I've become a sort of executive emeritus. I go to the office now and then but mostly travel and speak. I visit colleges and research facilities, where I'm introduced as a waste analyst. I talk to them about the vacated military bases being converted to landfill use, about the bunker system under a mountain in Nevada that will or will not accommodate thousands of steel canisters of radioactive waste for ten thousand years. Then we eat lunch. The waste may or may not explode, seventy thousand tons of spent fuel, and I fly to London and Zurich to attend conferences in the rain and sleet.

I rearrange books on the old shelves and match and mix for the new shelves and then I stand there looking. I stand in the living room and look. Or I walk through the house and look at the things we own and feel the odd mortality that clings to every object. The finer and rarer the object, the more lonely it makes me feel, and I don't know how to account for this.

Marian midfifties is lean and tanned and not so edgy now, it's clear, and a little more measured in her approach to the moment. The moment, suddenly, no longer matters. We take drives in the desert and sometimes I tell her things she didn't know, or knew at an unlearned level, the way you know you're sleepy or sad.

When I come across his name on a document it always makes me pause, it gives me pause, the name in jumpy type on some stamped document, James Nicholas Costanza, the raised stamp that marks a thing official, the document in the dusty bottom drawer, the sense of slight confusion until I realize who he is.

I drive out there sometimes and see grackles sparking across the landfill, down past the Indian tribe streets, and sometimes I take our granddaughter along when she is here on a visit and we see the sage gray truss of the waste facility and the planes in their landing patterns and the showy desert plants spilling over the pastel walls above the parking area.

I fly to Zurich and Lisbon to exchange ideas and make proposals and it is the kind of desperate crisis, the intractability of waste, that doesn't really seem to be taking place except in the conference reports and the newspapers. It is not otherwise touchable somehow, for all the menacing heft and breadth of the material, the actual pulsing thing.

Everybody is everywhere at once. Jeff likes to say this, our son, who still lives at home and still says things with the smirky sort of shyness he has brought with him out of adolescence, a quality that turns nearly everything he says into a lubricious hint about some secret he is keeping.

They are making synthetic feces in Dallas. They have perfected a form of simulated human waste in order to test diapers and other protective garments. The compound comes in a dry mix made of starches, fibers, resins, gelatins and polyvinyls. You add water for desired consistency. The color is usually brown.

Nostra aetate, as the popes like to say. In our time.

He went out to get a pack of cigarettes and never came back. He smoked Lucky Strikes. He smoked the brand where they said, Light up a Lucky—it's light-up time. Be happy—go Lucky. That was another thing they said.

Jeff has jobs on and off, waits on tables in a food court somewhere, and spends tremendous amounts of time with his computer. He visits a website devoted to miracles. There are many reports, he tells us, of people flocking to uranium mines in order to cure themselves. They come from Europe, Canada and Australia, on crutches and in wheelchairs, and they sit in tunnels under rangeland in Montana, where the radon emissions are many hundreds of times higher than the federal safety level. They are trying to cure themselves of arthritis, diabetes, blindness and cancer. There are reports that crippled dogs have risen and walked. Jeff tells us this and smirks shyly, either because he thinks it's funny or because he thinks it's funny and believes it.

We have bookshelves built in the cool room at the back of the house, my mother's old room, and you know how time slips by when you are doing books, arranging and rearranging, the way time goes by untouched, matching and mixing inventively, and then you stand in the room and look.

I'll tell you what I long for, the days of disarray, when I didn't give a damn or a fuck or a farthing.

Matt came out for the funeral, he flew out the night before with two of his kids and then broke down at the gravesite and they saw this and were astonished. They were shocked to see this because they thought of him as a father, not a son, and they looked away and then sneaked a glance and then looked away again when he fell against me and wept, and they saw me put an arm around him and had to adjust to this, the shock of seeing him as a brother and a son.

I still respond to that thing you feel in an office, wearing a crisp suit and sensing the linked grids lap around you. It is all about the enfolding drone of the computers and fax machines. It is about the cell phones slotted in the desk chargers, the voice mail and e-mail—a sense of order and command reinforced by the office itself and the bronze tower that encases the office and by all the contact points that shimmer in the air somewhere.

We remove the wax paper from cereal boxes before we put the boxes out for collection. The streets are dark and empty. We do clear glass versus colored glass and it is remarkable really how quiet it is, a stillness that feels old and settled, with landmark status, the yard waste, the paper bags pressed flat, the hour after sunset when a pause obtains in the world and you forget for a second where you are.

They sit on wooden benches in the mines and breathe radon air and soak their feet in deadly radon water and they pray and chant and sing soaring hymns or maybe just ordinary songs, dinky sing-alongs, the kind of songs that people have always sung, doing things in groups.

When we go for long drives—we go for long drives out past the retirement compounds and onto the long straight interstate where kestrels sit spaced on the power lines and sometimes I apply suntan lotion to my arms and face and there's a smell of beach, a sense of heat and beach, the haze of slick stuff across the hair on my forearm and the way the tube pops and sucks when it goes empty—I get reminded of something way back when.

No one talks about the Texas Highway Killer anymore. You never hear the name. The name used to be in the air, always on the verge of being spoken, of reentering the broadcast band and causing a brief excitation along the lined highways, but the shootings have evidently ended and the name is gone now. But sometimes I think of him and wonder if he is still out there, driving and looking, not done with this thing at all but only waiting.

When I tell her things she listens with a high clear alertness, so vigilant and still, and she seems to know what I'm going to say before I say it. I tell her about the time I spent in correction and why they put me there and she seems to know it, at some level, already. She looks at me as if I were seventeen. She sees me at seventeen. We take long walks along the drainage canal. All the hints and intimations, all the things she spied in me at the beginning of our time together—come to some completion now. If not for me, then for her. Because I don't know what happened, do I?

We bundle the newspapers but do not tie them in twine, which is always the temptation.

He enters seventeen characters and then *dot com miraculum*. And the miracles come scrolling down. At dinner one night he tells us about a miracle in the Bronx. Jeff is shy about the Bronx, shy and guilty. He thinks it is part of the American gulag, a place so distant from his experience that those who've emerged can't possibly be willing to spend a moment in a room with someone like him. But here we are at the table, sharing a meal, and he tells us about a miracle that took place earlier in the decade and is still a matter of some debate, at least on the web, the net. A young girl was the victim of a terrible crime. Body found in a vacant lot amid dense debris. Identified and buried. The girl memorialized on a graffiti wall nearby. And then the miracle of the images and the subsequent crush of people and the belief and disbelief. Mostly belief, it seems. We ask him questions but he is tentative with this kind of material. He is shy. He feels he doesn't have the credentials to relate a tale of such intensity, all that suffering and faith and openness of emotion, transpiring in the Bronx. I tell him what better place for the study of wonders.

It is a hundred and eight degrees out on the street, a hundred and ten, a hundred and twelve, and I go to the airport and fly to Lisbon and Madrid, or I stand in the living room and look at the books.

Jeff is a lurker. He visits sites but does not post. He gathers the waves and rays. He adds components and functions and sits before a spreading mass of compatible hardware. The real miracle is the web, the net, where everybody is everywhere at once, and he is there among them, unseen.

The intimacies we've come to share, the belated exchange of childhoods and other ferocious times, and something else, a firm grip of another kind, a different direction, not back but forward—the grasp of objects that bind us to some betokening. I think I sense Marian missing in the objects on the walls and shelves. There is something somber about the things we've collected and own, the household effects, there is something about the word itself, *effects*, the lacquered chest in the alcove, that breathes a kind of sadness—the wall hangings and artifacts and valuables—and I feel a loneliness, a loss, all the greater and stranger when the object is relatively rare and it's the hour after sunset in a stillness that feels unceasing.

We walk along the drainage canal past tree trunks limed white— white against the sun.

The earth opened up and he stepped inside. I think it felt that way not only to us but to Jimmy as well. I think he went under. I don't think he wanted a fresh start or a new life or even an escape. I think he wanted to go under. He lived day-to-day and step-to-step and did not wonder what would become of us or how she would manage or how tall we grew or how smart we became. I don't think he spent a minute thinking about these things. I think he just went under. The failure it brought down on us does not diminish.

This is how I came across the baseball, rearranging books on the shelves. I look at it and squeeze it hard and put it back on the shelf, wedged between a slanted book and a straight-up book, an expensive and beautiful object that I keep half hidden, maybe because I tend to forget why I bought it. Sometimes I know exactly why I bought it and other times I don't, a beautiful thing smudged green near the Spalding trademark and bronzed with nearly half a century of earth and sweat and chemical change, and I put it back and forget it until next time.

They said, L.S./M.F.T.—Lucky Strike Means Fine Tobacco. Lucky Strike, in quotes, they said—"It's toasted."

The planes come sparking out of the mountains to the south, glinting in the haze as they approach in a long line to make their landings, and I see the open-steel truss of the waste facility at the end of the road. I park beneath terraced gardens that send bougainvillea spilling over the pastel walls. My granddaughter is with me, Sunny, she is nearly six now, and inside the vast recycling shed we stand on a catwalk and watch the operations in progress. The tin, the paper, the plastics, the styrofoam. It all flies down the conveyor belts, four hundred tons a day, assembly lines of garbage, sorted, compressed and baled, transformed in the end to square-edged units, products again, wire-bound and smartly stacked and ready to be marketed. Sunny loves this place and so do the other kids who come with their parents or teachers to stand on the catwalk and visit the exhibits. Brightness streams from skylights down to the floor of the shed, falling on the tall machines with a numinous glow. Maybe we feel a reverence for waste, for the redemptive qualities of the things we use and discard. Look how they come back to us, alight with a kind of brave aging. The windows yield a strong broad desert and enormous sky. The landfill across the road is closed now, jammed to capacity, but gas keeps rising from the great earthen berm, methane, and it produces a wavering across the land and sky that deepens the aura of sacred work. It is like a fable in the writhing air of some ghost civilization, a shimmer of desert ruin. The kids love the machines, the balers and hoppers and long conveyors, and the parents look out the windows through the methane mist and the planes come out of the mountains and align for their approach and the trucks are arrayed in two columns outside the shed, bringing in the unsorted slop, the gut squalor of our lives, and taking the baled and bound units out into the world again, the chunky product blocks, pristine, newsprint for newsprint, tin for tin, and we all feel better when we leave.

I drink aged grappa and listen to jazz. I do the books on the new shelves and stand in the living room and look at the carpets and wall hangings and I know the ghosts are walking the halls. But not these halls and not this house. They're all back there in those railroad rooms at the narrow end of the night and I stand helpless in this desert place looking at the books.

I long for the days of disorder. I want them back, the days when I was alive on the earth, rippling in the quick of my skin, heedless and real. I was dumb-muscled and angry and real. This is what I long for, the breach of peace, the days of disarray when I walked real streets and did things slap-bang and felt angry and ready all the time, a danger to others and a distant mystery to myself.

http://blk.www/dd.com/miraculum

Her name is Esmeralda. She lives wild in the inner ghetto, a slice of the South Bronx called the Wall—a girl who forages in empty lots for discarded clothes, plucks spoiled fruit from garbage bags behind bodegas, who is sometimes seen running through the trees and weeds, a shadow on the rubbled walls of demolished structures, unstumbling, a tactful runner with the sweet and easy stride of some creature of sylvan myth.

The nuns have been trying to find her.

Sister Grace, the younger of the two, determined to track and catch the girl and get her to a relief agency or to their convent in the middle

Bronx, somewhere safe—examine her, feed her properly, get her enrolled in school.

Sister Edgar, seeing a radiant grace in the girl, a reprieve from the Wall's endless distress, even a source of personal hope, a goad to the old rugged faith. All heaven trembles when a soul swings in the wind—save her from danger, bring her to candles and ashes and palms, to belief in the mystical body.

The nuns deliver food to people living in the Wall and nearby, the asthmatic children and sickle-cell adults, the cases of AIDS and the cocaine babies, and every day, twice a day, three or four times a day, they drive their van past the memorial wall. This is the six-story flank of a squatters' tenement on which graffiti writers spray-paint an angel every time a local child dies of illness or mistreatment.

Gracie talks and drives and yells out the window at dogs doing doody in the street. She wears a skirt and a windbreaker, she carries a can of Chemical Mace. Old spindle-shanked Edgar sits next to her and feels the aura of the streets and thinks herself back into another century. She is cinctured and veiled and would not know how to dress otherwise and would not be here at all if the children were healthy and the dogs middle-class.

Gracie says, "Sometimes I wonder."

"What do you wonder?"

"Never mind, Sister. Forget it."

"You wonder if we make a difference. You can't understand how the last decade of the century looks worse than the first in some respects. Looks like another century in another country."

"I'm a positive person," Gracie says.

Edgar has a high-frequency laugh that travels through time and space, a sort of cackle frankly, shrill and dank—she thinks the dogs can probably hear it.

"I know there's a laborious procedure you have to follow," she says, "in order to attain a positive state of mind. It's a wonder you have strength left over to steer the car."

This pisses Gracie off and she rails a bit, respectfully, as the van approaches the salvage operation of Ismael Muñoz.

A mass of junked cars, a pack jam, cars smash-heaped and jackknifed, seventy or eighty cars, shamefaced. The nuns look instinctively for a sign of Esmeralda, who probably spends her nights sleeping in one of these cars. Then they park the van and enter the derelict tenement, climbing three flights of crumbling stairs to Ismael's headquarters.

Edgar expects him to look wan and drawn, visibly fragile. She thinks he has AIDS. It is a thing she senses. She senses dire things. She stands at a distance, studying him. An affable sort of human shambles in a tropical shirt and slapdash beard—he's in a lively mood today because he has managed to rig a system in the building that produces enough power to run a TV set.

"Sisters, look," he says.

They see a little kid, Juano, seated on a stationary bike pedaling frantically. The bike is linked to a World War II generator that Ismael got cheap at an armory liquidation. The generator is throbbing in the basement and there are cables running from the unit up to the TV set and there is a wheezing drive belt connecting the TV set to the bicycle. When the kid fast-pedals the bike, the generator ekes out a flow of electricity to the television set—a brave beat-up model that two of the other kids dug out of the garbage pits, where it was layered in the geological age of leisure-time appliances.

Gracie is delighted and sits with the graffiti crew, eight or nine kids, watching the stock market channel.

Ismael says, "What do you think? I did okay? This is just a start-up. I got things I'm planning big-time."

Edgar disapproves of course. This is her mission, to disapprove. One of the stern mercies of the Wall, a place unlinked to the usual services, is that TV has not been available. Now here it is, suddenly. You touch a button and all the things concealed from you for centuries come flying into the remotest room. It's an epidemic of seeing. No conceivable recess goes unscanned. In the uterus, under the ocean, to the lost halls of the human brain. And if you can see it, you can catch it. There's a pathogenic element in a passing glance.

Ismael says, "I'm planning to go on-line real soon, Sisters. Advertise my junk cars. Go, like, global. Scrap metal for these trodden countries looking to build a military."

On the screen an image flicks and jumps. It is a man's discoid head, a fellow in a white shirt with blue collar, or blue shirt with white collar—there is a fairly frequent color shift. He is talking about the big board composite while numbers and letters flow in two bands across the bottom of the screen, a blue band and a white band, and the crew sits watching and the kid on the bike is bent and pedaling, a furious pumping boy, and the names and prices flow in two different directions with active issues blinking.

Ismael says, "Some people have a personal god, okay. I'm looking to get a personal computer. What's the difference, right?"

Ismael likes to tease the nuns. Edgar watches him carefully. She admires the graffiti wall, the angels arrayed row after row, blue for boys, pink for girls, but she is wary of the man who runs the project and she tries to understand the disappointment she feels, seeing Ismael in good spirits and evidently healthy.

Does Sister want him to be deathly ill? Does she think he ought to be punished for being homosexual?

Everybody's watching TV except for her. She's watching Ismael. No pallor or weight loss or lesions or other visible symptoms. The only thing he shows is a snaggle smile from out of his history of dental neglect.

Why does she want to see him suffer? Isn't he one of the affirmative forces in the Wall, earning money with his salvage business, using it more or less altruistically, teaching his crew of stray kids, abandoned some of them, pregnant one or two, runaways, throwaways—giving them a sense of responsibility and self-worth? And doesn't he help the nuns feed the hungry?

She studies him for marks, for early signs of incapacity. Then she steals a look out the window, hoping to glimpse the elusive girl. Sister has seen her a number of times from this window, almost always running. Run is what she does. It is her beauty and her safety both, her melodious hope, a thing of special merit, a cleansing, the fleet leaf-fall of something godly blowing through the world.

Two of the charismatics come in to watch TV. These are people from the top floor, operating the only church in the Wall, a congregation of pentecostals seeking to receive the gift of the Spirit, laying on hands, shouting out words, prophesying—the whole rocking socking package that makes Edgar want to run and hide.

Of course they look at her a little sideways too.

Ismael appoints four members of the crew to go with the nuns and distribute food in the area. But the crew is rooted right now. They urge Juano to pedal faster because this is the only way to change channels and they want to watch cartoons or movies, something with visuals better than a head.

They're saying, "Go, man, fasta, fasta."

The bicycle boy bends and pumps and the picture wavers briefly but then springs back to the round announcer's face and the moving lines of prices. Ismael stands there laughing. He loves the language of buying and selling and the sight of those clustered sets of letters that represent enormous corporate entities with their jets and stretches and tanker fleets. He starts pulling kids off the cushionless sofa and stone-slinging them toward the door while the other kids and the jivey charismatics keep urging Juano on.

They're saying, "Fasta, fasta, you the man."

The boy cranks and strains, bouncing on the seat, but the numbers keep flowing across the screen. Electronics slightly up, transports down, industrials more or less unchanged.

Three weeks later Edgar sits in the van and watches her partner emerge from the red brick convent—rolling gait, short legs and squarish body. Gracie's face is averted as she edges around the front of the vehicle and opens the door on the driver's side.

She gets in and grips the wheel, looking straight ahead.

"I got a call from the precinct near the Wall."

Then she reaches for the door and shuts it. She grips the wheel again.

"Somebody raped Esmeralda and threw her off a roof."

She starts the engine.

"I'm sitting here thinking, Who do I kill?"

She looks at Edgar briefly, then puts the van in gear.

"Because this is the only question I can ask myself without giving in to despair."

They drive south through local streets, the tenement brick smoked mellow in morning light. Did Edgar know this would happen? Lately, yes, a knowing in her bones. She feels the weather of Gracie's rage and pain. In recent days she'd approached the girl, Gracie had, and talked to her from a distance, and thrown a bag of food and clothing into the pokeweed where Esmeralda stood. They ride all the way in silence with the older nun mind-reciting questions and answers from the Baltimore Catechism. The strength of these exercises, which are a form of perdurable prayer, rests in the voices that accompany hers, children responding through the decades, syllable-crisp, a panpipe reply that is the lucid music of her life. Question and answer. What deeper dialogue might right minds devise? She reaches her hand across to Gracie's on the wheel and keeps it there for a digital tick on the dashboard clock. Who made us? God made us. Those clear-eyed faces so believing. Who is God? God is the Supreme Being who made all things. She feels tired in her arms. Her arms are heavy and dead and she gets all the way to Lesson 12 when the projects appear at the rim of the sky, upper windows white with sunplay against the broad dark face of beaten stone.

When Gracie finally speaks she says, "It's still there."

"What's still there?"

"That knocking in the engine. Hear it? Hear it?"

"I don't hear a thing."

"Ku-ku. Ku-ku."

Then she drives the van down past the projects toward the painted wall.

When they get there the angel is already sprayed in place. A winged figure in a pink sweatshirt and pink and aqua pants and a pair of white Nike Air Jordans with the logo prominent—she was a running girl so they gave her running shoes. And little Juano still dangles from a rope, winched down from the roof by the old hand-powered hoist the crew uses to grapple cars onto the deck of their flatbed truck. Ismael and others bend over the ledge attempting to shout correct spellings down to him as he drifts to and from the wall, leaning in to spray the interlaced letters that mark the great gone era of wildstyle graffiti.

The nuns stand outside the van watching the kid finish the last scanted word and then see him yanked skyward in the cutting wind.

When they get to the third floor Ismael is smoking a cigar, arms folded on his chest. Gracie paces the room. She doesn't seem to know where to begin, how to address the nameless thing that someone has done to this child they'd so hoped to save. She paces, she clenches her fists. They hear the gassy moan of a city bus some blocks away.

"Ismael. You have to find out who this guy is that did this thing."

"You think I'm running here? El Lay Pee Dee?"

"You have contacts in the neighborhood that no one else has."

"What neighborhood? The neighborhood's over there. This here's the Wall. It's all I can do to get these kids so they spell a word correct when they spray their paint. When I was writing we did subway cars in the dark without a letter misspell."

"Who cares about spelling?" Gracie says.

Edgar used to care but not today and maybe never again. She feels weak and lost. The great Terror gone, the great thrown shadow dismantled—the launched object in the sky named for a Greek goddess on a bell krater in 500 B.C. All terror is local now. Some noise on the pavement very near, the stammer of casual rounds from a passing car, someone who carries off your child. Ancient fears revived, they will steal my child, they will come into my house when I'm asleep and cut out my heart because they have a dialogue with Satan.

She says a desperate prayer.

Pour forth we beseech thee, O Lord, thy grace into our hearts.

Ten years' indulgence, a blockbuster number, if the prayer is recited at dawn, noon and eventide, or as soon thereafter as possible.

One of the girls is pedaling the bike, Willie for short, and she calls out to them, *hey, here, look,* and they gather at the TV set and stand astonished. There is a news report of the murder, their murder, and it is freaking network coverage, CNN—tragic life and death of homeless child. The crew is stunned to see footage of the Wall, two and a half seconds of film that shows the building they're in, the facade of spray-painted angels, the overgrown lots with their bat caverns and owl roosts. They gawk and buzz, charged with a kind of second sight, the things they know so well seen inside out, made new and nationwide. They stand there smeared in other people's seeing. Then the anchorwoman comes on. They tell Willamette to pedal faster man because the picture is beginning to fade and the anchorwoman's electric red hair is color-running from her head in a luminous ring, which makes her all the more amazing, and she describes their lives to them in a bell-tone virgin voice, a woman so striking of feature she makes the news her own, and Willie pedals for all she's worth and they urge her firmly on.

Sister does not watch. She sees nothing for the rest of that day and the day after and the two or three weeks after that. She sees the human heart exposed like a pig's muscle on a slab. That's the only thing she sees. She believes she is falling into crisis, beginning to think it is possible that all creation is a spurt of blank matter that chances to make an emerald planet here, a dead star there, with random waste between. The serenity of immense design is missing from her life, authorship and moral form, and when Gracie and the crew take food into the projects Edgar waits in the van, she is the nun in the van, and when Gracie maces a rat at the curbstone Edgar does not blink.

It is not a question of disbelief. There is another kind of belief, a second force, insecure, untrusting, a faith that is spring-fed by the things we fear in the night, and she thinks she is succumbing.

Keystroke 1

She sleeps on the roof when it's not too cold and this is where he sees her, on the roof of a boarded four-story building with fire escape intact. He's up there wandering, thinking his thoughts, a man who drifts in and out of the Wall, a sidler type, doesn't like to be looked at, and when you enter a name-search the screen reads *Searching*. He comes across the sleeping girl and feels a familiar anger rising and knows he will need to do something to make her pay. He's on her like that. She tries to fight but does not cry out. He beats her with the end of his fist, sending hammerblows to the head. Struggle bitch get hit. He wants to turn her over on her face and put it up inside her. She fights and whisper-cries in a voice that makes him angrier, like who the fuck she think she is, and the screen

817

reads *Searching*. Either way he's gonna hit her, she struggle or not, and he looks away when he does it, sidle-type. No eye contact, cunt. Last woman he looked at was his mother. After he does it, driving it in and spilling it out, he hits her one last time, hard, whore, and drags her up on the ledge and leans her over and lets her go. You dead, bitch. Then he goes back to thinking his nighttime thoughts. Screen reads *Searching*.

Then the stories begin, word passing block to block, moving through churches and superettes, maybe garbled slightly, mistranslated here and there, but not deeply distorted—it is clear enough that people are talking about the same uncanny occurrence. And some of them go and look and tell others, stirring the hope that grows when things surpass their limits.

They gather after dusk at a windy place between bridge approaches, seven or eight people drawn by the word of one or two, then thirty people drawn by the seven, then a tight silent crowd that grows bigger but no less respectful, two hundred people wedged onto a traffic island in the bottommost Bronx where the expressway arches down from the terminal market and the train yards stretch toward the narrows, all that old industrial muscle with its fretful desolation—the ramps that shoot tall weeds and the waste burner coughing toxic fumes and the old railroad bridge spanning the Harlem River, an openwork tower at either end, maybe swaying slightly in persistent wind.

They come and park their cars if they have cars, six or seven to a car, parking tilted on a high shoulder or in the factory side streets, and they wedge themselves onto the concrete island between the expressway and the pocked boulevard, feeling the wind come chilling in and gazing above the wash of standard rip-roar traffic to a billboard floating in the gloom—an advertising sign scaffolded high above the riverbank and meant to attract the doped-over glances of commuters on the trains that run incessantly down from the northern suburbs into the thick of Manhattan money and glut.

Edgar sits across from Gracie in the refectory. She eats her food without tasting it because she decided years ago that taste is not the point. The point is to clean the plate.

Gracie says, "No, please, you can't."

"Just to see."

"No, no, no, no."

"I want to see for myself."

"This is tabloid. This is the worst kind of tabloid superstition. It's horrible. A complete, what is it? A complete abdication, you know? Be sensible. Don't abdicate your good sense."

"It could be her they're seeing."

"You know what this is? It's the nightly news. It's the local news at eleven with all the grotesque items neatly spaced to keep you watching the whole half hour."

"I think I have to go," Edgar says.

"This is something for poor people to confront and judge and understand and we have to see it in that framework. The poor need visions, okay?"

"I believe you are patronizing the people you love," Edgar says softly.

"That's not fair."

"You say the poor. But who else would saints appear to? Do saints and angels appear to bank presidents? Eat your carrots."

"It's the nightly news. It's gross exploitation of a child's horrible murder."

"But who is exploiting? No one's exploiting," Edgar says. "People go there to weep, to believe."

"It's how the news becomes so powerful it doesn't need TV or newspapers. It exists in people's perceptions. It's something they invent, strong enough to seem real. It's the news without the media."

Edgar eats her bread.

"I'm older than the Pope. I never thought I would live long enough to be older than a pope and I think I need to see this thing."

"Pictures lie," Gracie says.

"I think I need to be there."

"Don't pray to pictures, pray to saints."

"I think I need to go."

"But you can't. It's crazy. Don't go, Sister."

But Edgar goes. She puts on her latex gloves and winter cape and heads for the door, planning to take the bus and subway, and Gracie can't let her go alone. She rushes out to the van, wearing her retainer for spacy teeth, a thing she never wears in public, and they drive down past the Wall and into dark and empty streets and the van stalls out, doing a murmurous swoon, and they walk the last eleven blocks with Gracie carrying Mace and a cellular phone.

A madder orange moon hangs over the city.

People in the glare of passing cars, hundreds clustered on the island, their own cars parked cockeyed and biaswise, dangerously near the speeding traffic. The nuns dash across the boulevard and squeeze onto the island and people make room for them, pressed bodies part to let them stand at ease.

They follow the crowd's stoked gaze. They stand and look. The billboard is unevenly lighted, dim in spots, several bulbs blown and unreplaced, but the central elements are clear, a vast cascade of orange juice pouring diagonally from top right into a goblet that is handheld at lower left—the perfectly formed hand of a female caucasian of the middle suburbs. Distant willows and a vaguish lake view set the social locus. But it is the juice that commands the eye, thick and pulpy with a ruddled flush that matches the madder moon. And the first detailed drops splashing at the bottom of the goblet with a scatter of spindrift, each fleck embellished with the finicky rigor of some precisionist painting. What a lavishment of effort and technique, no refinement spared—the equivalent, Edgar thinks, of medieval church architecture. And the six-ounce cans of Minute Maid arrayed across the bottom of the board, a hundred identical cans so familiar in design and color and typeface that they have personality, the convivial cuteness of little orange-and-black people.

Edgar doesn't know how long they're supposed to wait or exactly what is supposed to happen. Produce trucks pass in the rumbling dusk. She lets her eyes wander to the crowd. Working people, shopkeepers, maybe some drifters and squatters but not many, and then she notices a group near the front, fitted snug to the prowed shape of the island—they're the charismatics from the top floor of the tenement in the Wall, dressed mainly in floppy white, tublike women, reedy men in dreadlocks. The crowd is patient, she is not, finding herself taut with misgiving, absorbing Gracie's take on the whole business. Planes drop out of the darkness toward the airport across the water, splitting the air with throttled booms. The nuns see Ismael Muñoz standing thirty yards away, surrounded by his crew—Ismael looking a little ghostly in the beams of swinging light—and Edgar presses a knowing look on Gracie. They stand and watch the billboard. They stare stupidly at the juice. After twenty minutes there is a rustle, a sort of perceptual wind, and people look north, children point north, and Edgar strains to catch what they are seeing.

The train.

She feels the words before she sees the object. She feels the words although no one has spoken them. This is how a crowd brings things to single consciousness. Then she sees it, an ordinary commuter train, silver and blue, ungraffiti'd, moving smoothly toward the drawbridge. The headlights sweep the billboard and she hears a sound from the crowd, a gasp that shoots into sobs and moans and the cry of some unnameable painful elation. A blurted sort of whoop, the holler of unstoppered belief. Because when the train lights hit the dimmest part of the billboard a face appears above the misty lake and it belongs to the murdered girl. A dozen women clutch their heads, they whoop and sob, a spirit, a godsbreath passing through the crowd.

Esmeralda.

Esmeralda.

Sister is in body shock. She has seen it but so fleetingly, too fast to absorb—she wants the girl to reappear. Women holding babies up to the sign, to the flowing juice, let it bathe them in baptismal balsam and oil. And Gracie talking into Edgar's face, into the jangle of voices and noise.

"Did it look like her?"

"Yes."

"Are you sure?"

"I think so," Edgar says.

"But you've never seen her up close. I've seen her up close," Gracie says, "and I think it was just a trick of light. Not a person at all. Not a face but a stab of light."

When Gracie wears her retainer she speaks with a kind of fizzy lisp.

"It's just the undersheet," she says. "A technical flaw that causes the image underneath, the image from the papered-over ad to show through the current ad."

Is she right?

"When sufficient light shines on the current ad, it causes the image beneath to show through," she says.

Sibilants echo wetly off Gracie's teeth.

But is she right? Has the news shed its dependence on the agencies that report it? Is the news inventing itself on the eyeballs of walking talking people?

Edgar studies the billboard. What if there is no papered-over ad? Why should there be an ad under the orange juice ad? Surely they remove one ad before installing another.

Gracie says, "What now?"

They stand and wait. They wait only eight or nine minutes this time before another train approaches. Edgar moves, she tries to edge and gently elbow forward, and people make way, they see her—a nun in a veil and full habit and dark cape followed by a sheepish helpmeet in a rummage coat and headscarf, holding aloft a portable phone.

They see her and embrace her and she lets them. Her presence is a verifying force—a figure from a universal church with sacraments and secret bank accounts and a fabulous art collection. All this and she elects to follow a course of poverty, chastity and obedience. They embrace her and let her pass and she is among the charismatic band, the gospellers rocking in place, when the train lamps swing their beams onto the billboard. She sees Esmeralda's face take shape under the rainbow of bounteous juice and above the little suburban lake and there is a sense of someone living in the image, an animating spirit—less than a tender second of life, less than half a second and the spot is dark again.

She feels something break upon her. An angelus of clearest joy. She embraces Sister Grace. She yanks off her gloves and shakes hands, pumps hands with the great-bodied women who roll their eyes to heaven. The women do great two-handed pump shakes, fabricated words jumping out of their mouths, trance utterance—they're singing of things outside the known deliriums. Edgar thumps a man's chest with her fists. She finds Ismael and embraces him. She looks into his face and breathes the air he breathes and enfolds him in her laundered cloth. Everything feels near at hand, breaking upon her, sadness and loss and glory and an old mother's bleak pity and a force at some deep level of lament that makes her feel inseparable from the shakers and mourners, the awestruck who stand in tidal traffic—she is nameless for a moment, lost to the details of personal history, a disembodied fact in liquid form, pouring into the crowd.

Gracie says, "I don't know."

"Of course you know. You know. You saw her."

"I don't know. It was a shadow."

"Esmeralda on the lake."

"I don't know what I saw."

"You know. Of course you know. You saw her."

They wait for two more trains. Landing lights appear in the sky and the planes keep dropping toward the runway across the water, another flight every minute and a half, the backwashed roars overlapping so everything is seamless noise and the air has a stink of smoky fuel.

They wait for one more train.

How do things end, finally, things such as this—peter out to some forgotten core of weary faithful huddled in the rain?

The next night a thousand people fill the area. They park their cars on the boulevard and try to butt and pry their way onto the traffic island but most of them have to stand in the slow lane of the expressway, skittish and watchful. A woman is struck by a motorcycle, sent swirling into the asphalt. A boy is dragged a hundred yards, it is always a hundred yards, by a car that keeps on going. Vendors move along the lines of stalled traffic selling flowers, soft drinks and live kittens. They sell laminated images of Esmeralda printed on prayer cards. They sell pinwheels that never stop spinning.

The night after that the mother shows up, Esmeralda's lost junkie mother, and she collapses with flung arms when the girl's face appears on the billboard. They take her away in an ambulance that is followed by a number of TV trucks. Two men fight with tire irons, blocking traffic on a ramp. Helicopter cameras record the scene and the police trail orange caution tape through the area—the very orange of the living juice.

The next evening the sign is blank. What a hole it makes in space. People come and don't know what to say or think, where to look or what to believe. The sign is a white sheet with two lonely words, *Space Available*, followed by a phone number in tasteful type.

When the first train comes, at dusk, the lights show nothing.

And what do you remember, finally, when everyone has gone home and the streets are empty of devotion and hope, swept by river wind? Is the memory thin and bitter and does it shame you with its fundamental untruth—all nuance and wishful silhouette? Or does the power of transcendence linger, the sense of an event that violates natural forces, something holy that throbs on the hot horizon, the vision you crave because you need a sign to stand against your doubt?

Edgar feels the pain in her joints, the old body deep in routine pain, pain at the points of articulation, prods of sharp sensation in the links between bones.

But she holds the image tight in her mind, the fleeting face on the lighted board, her virgin twin who is also her daughter. And she recalls the smell of jet fuel. This is the incense of her experience, the burnt cedar and gum, a retaining medium that keeps the moment whole, all the moments, the swaying soulclap raptures and the unspoken closeness, a fellowship of deep belief.

There is nothing left to do but die and this is precisely what she does, Sister Alma Edgar, bride of Christ, passing peacefully in her sleep, the first faint snow of another dim winter falling softly on the unknown streets, flurries, crystals, shaped flakes, a pale slant snow disappearing as it falls.

Keystroke 2

In her veil and habit she was basically a face, or a face and scrubbed hands. Here in cyberspace she has shed all that steam-ironed fabric. She is not naked exactly but she is open—exposed to every connection you can make on the world wide web.

There is no space or time out here, or in here, or wherever she is. There are only connections. Everything is connected. All human knowledge gathered and linked, hyperlinked, this site leading to that, this fact referenced to that, a keystroke, a mouse-click, a password—world without end, amen.

But she is in cyberspace, not heaven, and she feels the grip of systems. This is why she's so uneasy. There is a presence here, a thing implied, something vast and bright. She senses the paranoia of the web, the net. There's the perennial threat of virus of course. Sister knows all about contaminations and the protective measures they require. This is different—it's a glow, a lustrous rushing force that seems to flow from a billion distant net nodes.

When you decide on a whim to visit the H-bomb home page, she begins to understand. Everything in your computer, the plastic, silicon and mylar, every logical operation and processing function, the memory, the hardware, the software, the ones and zeroes, the triads inside the pixels that form the on-screen image—it all culminates here.

First a dawnlight, a great aurora glory massing on the color monitor. Every thermonuclear bomb ever tested, all the data gathered from each shot, code name, yield, test site, Eniwetok, Lop Nor, Novaya Zemlya, the foreignness, the otherness of remote populations implied in the place names, Mururoa, Kazakhstan, Siberia, and the wreathwork of extraordinary detail, firing systems and delivery systems, equations and graphs and schematic cross sections, shot after shot summoned at a click, a hit, Bravo, Romeo, Greenhouse Dog—and Sister is basically in it.

She sees the flash, the thermal pulse. She hears the rumble building, the great gathering force rolling off the 16-bit soundboard. She stands in the flash and feels the power. She sees the spray plume. She sees the fireball climbing, the superheated sphere of burning gas that can blind a person with its beauty, its dripping christblood colors, solar golds and reds. She sees the shock wave and hears the high winds and feels the power of false faith, the faith of paranoia, and then the mushroom cloud spreads around her, the pulverized mass of radioactive debris, eight miles high, ten miles, twenty, with skirted stem and smoking platinum cap.

The jewels roll out of her eyes and she sees God.

No, wait, sorry. It is a Soviet bomb she sees, the largest yield in history, a device exploded above the Arctic Ocean in 1961, preserved in the computer that helped to build it, fifty-eight megatons—add the digits and you get thirteen.

Whole populations potentially skelly-boned in the massive flash—dem bones, dem bones, sing the washtub women. And Sister begins to sense the byshadows that stretch from the awe of a central event. How the intersecting systems help pull us apart, leaving us vague, drained, docile, soft in our inner discourse, willing to be shaped, to be overwhelmed—easy retreats, half beliefs.

Shot after shot, bomb after bomb, and they are fusion bombs, remember, atoms forcibly combined, and even as they detonate across the screen, again and again, there is another fusion taking place. No physical contact, please, but a coupling all the same. A click, a hit and Sister joins the other Edgar. A fellow celibate and more or less kindred spirit but her biological opposite, her male half, dead these many years. Has he been waiting for this to happen? The bulldog fed, J. Edgar Hoover, the Law's debased saint, hyperlinked at last to Sister Edgar—a single fluctuating impulse now, a piece of coded information.

Everything is connected in the end.

Sister and Brother. A fantasy in cyberspace and a way of seeing the other side and a settling of differences that have less to do with gender than with difference itself, all argument, all conflict programmed out.

Is cyberspace a thing within the world or is it the other way around? Which contains the other, and how can you tell for sure?

A word appears in the lunar milk of the data stream. You see it on your monitor, replacing the tower shots and airbursts, the detonations of high-yield devices set on barges or dangled from balloons, replacing the comprehensive text displays that accompany the bombs. A single seraphic word. You can examine the word with a click, tracing its origins, development, earliest known use, its passage between languages, and you can summon the word in Sanskrit, Greek, Latin and Arabic, in a thousand languages and dialects living and dead, and locate literary citations, and follow the word through the tunneled underworld of its ancestral roots.

Fasten, fit closely, bind together.

And you can glance out the window for a moment, distracted by the sound of small kids playing a made-up game in a neighbor's yard, some kind of kickball maybe, and they speak in your voice, or piggy-back races on the weedy lawn, and it's your voice you hear, essentially, under the glimmerglass sky, and you look at the things in the room, offscreen, unwebbed, the tissued grain of the deskwood alive in light, the thick lived tenor of things, the argument of things to be seen and eaten, the apple core going sepia in the lunch tray, and the dense measures of experience in a random glance, the monk's candle reflected in the slope of the phone, hours marked in Roman numerals, and the glaze of the wax, and the curl of the braided wick, and the chipped rim of the mug that holds your yellow pencils, skewed all crazy, and the plied lives of the simplest surface, the slabbed butter melting on the crumbled bun, and the yellow of the yellow of the pencils, and you try to imagine the word on the screen becoming a thing in the world, taking all its meanings, its sense of serenities and contentments out into the streets somehow, its whisper of reconciliation, a word extending itself ever outward, the tone of agreement or treaty, the tone of repose, the sense of mollifying silence, the tone of hail and farewell, a word that carries the sunlit ardor of an object deep in drenching noon, the argument of binding touch, but it's only a sequence of pulses on a dullish screen and all it can do is make you pensive—a word that spreads a longing through the raw sprawl of the city and out across the dreaming bourns and orchards to the solitary hills.

Peace.

AFTERWORD
STARING AT THE WALL

One dictionary definition of the word "inspire" cites divine guidance. An archaic meaning of the word is rendered this way: *breathes life into*.

The prologue to *Underworld* is set in New York City on a day in October in the year 1951. When I finished this extended segment, I began to work without delay on the first chapter. The narrative moved smoothly forward both in novel time—same city, following day—and in desk time, hour by routine hour.

It went this way for three or four weeks. No hesitation or interruption, no hovering cloud of doubt. Then something, somehow, happened. It occurred to me that the sensible approach I was taking, post-prologue, was uninspired. Whatever the quality of the writing, the novel needed something more dynamic at this crucial early stage, a departure, a breakaway point, and I found myself staring at the wall.

What is the wall?

It is the upright structure of building material located just beyond the typewriter, the manuscript pages, the jutting pens and pencils in the marmalade jar. It is also what a writer stares at during the dead times.

There were a few photographs and small paintings on the wall but there was also enough blank space for me to stare at. And the wall seemed to bounce something back at me, not a curse or a moan but a distinct idea of what was needed to animate the book and the writer. First, most immediate, a leap forward in time and a radical change of place. Eventually a first-person narration would develop as well as a flipped switch from present tense to past tense.

And so the novel proceeds from 1951 in a ballpark in New York to the 1990s in a desert waste in Arizona. Then the narrative scheme drives the action in reverse chronology gradually back to the 1950s.

And the passages that I'd intended to locate directly after the pro-logue are reborn, in the new format, as the first chapter in Part 6, roughly six hundred pages beyond their original placement and four years of work after their inception.

But this account may not be completely accurate. Was I in fact aware at a conscious level that the novel needed serious reconsider-ation? And did I act on this feeling in direct response? It may be that the call for a new structure, for a vault forward in time, simply came to me out of a subchamber in the mind, the novelist's mind, forever asprawl with scraps, schemes, needs, greeds and the hope of living long enough to finish writing thåe book that's killing him.

I did not respond to a need. I simply saw an opening to an arresting narrative path. What else can I call it but a revelation, an inspiration? And how pale are the words that one must use to describe the oddly three-dimensional depth of the insight.

(Am I revisiting this essay the way I altered the novel? And do writers ever refer to inspiration? Didn't the word get stranded in the middle decades of the last century?)

I don't remember what time of year it was, or what the weather was like, or what happened to the bamboo chair I used to sit in when I was working. But I did stare at the wall. And I clearly recall the sensation I felt, the breath of life in the lapsed meaning of the word "inspire." This was the moment that made the novel.

Don DeLillo
2015